TWO LIVES CROSSING

TWO LIVES CROSSING

— ROBERT MacBAIN —

ROBERT MacBAIN BOOKS
2024

CHAPTER

- 1 -

The cold, biting, wind of the last week of November, 1933, chilled twenty-two-year-old Tom MacArthur to the bone. He'd been at sea for four days and was now halfway across the Atlantic on his way to a new life in Canada.

"My God, Bill," he said to his older brother as the stern of the small cargo ship dropped down into a deep trough, "just look at that. You'd expect it to wash over us at any moment now."

Bill looked up at the green water towering around them. "Aye, it is quite a sight," he replied. "Never been in anything like this."

Bill was quite tall, a couple of inches over six feet, with a bushy, reddish-brown, moustache and beard and grey-blue eyes. His face was angular with high cheek bones. Tom was two years younger, about an inch shorter, and clean-shaven. They were both quite good looking and they'd had no trouble at all getting one of the lassies to dance with them on Saturday nights at the community hall near their father's small hill farm in the north of Scotland.

When the stern came up out of the trough, Tom looked across the vast choppy ocean surface again –- for about a minute. And then they dropped back down again. He was glad the ship wasn't rolling from side to side as it had done the day before. His bacon and eggs stayed down that morning.

He turned to his brother, standing beside him holding on to the rail at the stern of the small cargo ship. "I hope we're doing the right thing, Bill."

"I think we are. Had to find something better than living in that loft and shitting behind the horses."

They'd spent the last two years living in a loft above a stable on a farm in the north of Scotland. They had no heat in winter other than the little bit that made its way up through the floorboards from the animals down below. When they had to shit, they squatted beside one of the big Clydesdale work horses and wiped their bums with straw. At night, they could hear the rats scratching away at the corners of the roof. In the winter mornings, icicles hung suspended from the nails on the inside of the roof as they kneaded the frost out of their work shirts.

"Well, it's a bit late now," Tom said with a chuckle. "We're in the middle of the Atlantic. Can't swim back. We'd be as well to make the best of it."

On the afternoon of their seventh day at sea, they were sailing through the Cabot Strait that runs between Newfoundland and Cape Breton Island. "If you look over there on the left you'll see Cape Breton," a crewman who had joined them at the bow said. "That's the northern tip of Nova Scotia. A lot of Highlanders moved there. Still speak Gaelic, they do, right down to this very day. Even got the Scottish coat of arms on their flag."

"So, that's Canada," Bill said as he looked at the Cape Breton highlands from the left side of the ship. "Shouldn't be long now."

"Actually," the crewman said, "we've got about another two days to go before we dock at Montreal."

"Two days?" Bill exclaimed. "How big is Canada?"

"She's real big," the crewman said rather proudly. "Like I said, it's about another two days to Montreal and you and your brother 'll be on a train for about four days after that before you get to Calgary. And, if you want to go all the way to the west coast, to Vancouver, that'd be a little less than another two days on the train."

"My God," Tom said. "Eight days between here and the west coast, you say. That's an awful long distance. And to think that Hadrian built a wall all the way across Britain."

"Who's Hadrian?" the crewman asked with a puzzled look on his face.

"Emperor of Rome he was. Built a wall all across the narrowest part of Britain around 120 A.D. about seventy miles of it, to keep my blood-thirsty ancestors from coming down into the territory the Romans occupied."

"Blood-thirsty, eh?" the crewman said with an amused smile on his face.

"They certainly were that," Tom replied. "Picts, they called them. Painted their faces blue and ran around in animal skins. Pretty fierce bunch of savages they were. The Romans were awful fearful of them. Some parts of the stone wall Hadrian built across the whole width of the country were nine feet thick and about twenty feet high."

"Well, he'd have one helluva time building a wall across Canada," the crewman said with a chuckle. "Canada's almost three thousand miles wide. From Victoria to Halifax, that is. I'd like to see him try and build a wall across all that."

Their ship sailed on between Anticosti Island and the northeastern tip of the Gaspe Peninsula and entered the broad mouth of the St. Lawrence River. They passed Sainte-Anne-des-Monts on the south shore and then Bai-Comeau on the north. The river started to narrow a bit at Riviere-du-Loup and they sailed on past La Pocatiere and Montmagny and down the south side of the Ile d'Orleans.

"A French fella called Jacques Cartier named that the Island of Bacchus," the crewman said, "because there was lots of wild vines growing all over it. But then, later, he changed it to Ile d'Orleans after the son of the King of France who went by the name Duke of Orleans. He was an explorer, Cartier was. First came over here in 1535, I think it was. Back when the French first started to settle here."

"The French?" Tom asked with a puzzled look on his face. "I thought Canada was a colony of Britain."

"Lot of people think wrong like that," the crewman said. "But, no, the French were here first. New France they called it. Ruled it right up until just after1759 when they lost the big battle at the Plains of Abraham. Been British ever since."

Tom was standing at the bow of the ship with the sun low in the sky dead ahead in the west. It created a marvellous sheen on the water for hundreds of yards in front of him. As the ship turned left into the big bay at Quebec City, he could see the huge grain terminal straight ahead with the Chateau Frontenac Hotel dominating the steep cliff on the left above the lower town.

"Isn't that a sight, Bill?" he said pointing toward the Chateau with the turrets of the outside floors at its base and the seventeen-floor main tower with its green, sharply-slanted, copper roof rising tall in the middle.

"It is that," Bill replied. "Must have a thousand rooms in there. Never seen anything quite that big, quite that beautiful."

The passenger ferry from Levis crossed their bow and docked at the terminal directly below the Chateau Frontenac.

"Look up there, to the left of the hotel," the crewman said, pointing to a Union Jack flag higher up on the snow-covered cliff. "That's the Citadel of Quebec. There's a whole bunch of cannons on the walls up there. That was the biggest British fortress in all of North America. That fella Dickens, the one who wrote the books, once called it 'The Gibraltar of North America'."

"Those walls look pretty big, pretty thick," Tom said looking up at the Union Jack flying proudly in the wind. "And you've got to climb that cliff to get at them."

"They're thick all right," the crewman said. "Built strong. Real strong. Up at the corner there, that's where the big cannon is. See how it's pointing at an angle? It's aimed right at the point where the ships turn left after Isle of Orleans. Soon as they get their bow well out past that point, the cannon goes off. Bam, bam, bam. Three shots and they're done for. Quebec was Canada's main port back then and the British put the big cannons up there to deal with anyone sailing up the St. Lawrence from the Atlantic."

"I guess they figured the French might try to take the country back," Bill said.

"Actually, no," the crewman said. "The French really didn't have that much interest in Canada. In fact, when they lost the big battle right here at Quebec, back in 1759, the mistress of the French King, Louis the Fifteenth he was, said now the king would be able to sleep better at night."

"You're kidding," Tom said.

"No. She said the only thing Canada was good for was keeping her in fine furs. 'We can be happy without Canada,' she said. And then she said, 'Now that Montcalm is dead, the King will have some peace.'

"That's why the British worried more about the Americans than they did about the French. The Americans have always had their eye on Canada. They were here, right here, back in 1775. It was George Washington himself who sent the Continental Army up here. If they could take control of Quebec, he figured, they could prevent the British from getting their ships and troops up the St. Lawrence and into the Great Lakes. That was just at the beginning of the American Revolutionary War. The one where they won their independence."

"Did the Americans take Quebec?" Tom asked.

"Nope. Tried hard but failed. And then, about thirty-six years after that, the Americans launched the War of 1812 and, once again, Quebec, with its control of the St. Lawrence River, was what they had their eye on. The British put big cannons at the west end, too. That's in case anyone mounted an attack by land from the Plains of Abraham. Those cannons, by the way, were on wheels on a circular base so they could fire east, west, north or south."

"You're a pretty well-informed fellow," Tom said with a genuine tone of admiration.

"I reads the books," the crewman said. "It's all in the books. All you've gotta do is take the time to read 'em. It's all there. Didn't know about that Hadrian fella and his wall though. Didn't know a thing about that."

As they sailed on past the Citadel of Quebec, Tom's thoughts turned back to the hill farm in the north of Scotland where he'd been born and raised. The farm was owned by Lord Hanover, an English stockbroker who inherited five of the small farms in the valley. In exchange for the use of the land and the buildings, their father paid Lord Hanover a fixed share of the profits from the sale of the crops and livestock.

Because the farm was too small to support them all, Tom and Bill had spent the last two years working at the large estate southeast of Inverness where Lord Hanover raised Aberdeen Angus cattle. Several of his bulls and cows had placed first or second at some of the top shows in Britain. Lord Hanover lived in the huge stone manor on the edge of the river. Tom and Bill slept with four other men in the loft above the stable.

Lord Hanover had sold two champion Aberdeen Angus bulls and six prize cows to a rancher in Alberta. Part of the sales agreement called for them to be shipped by sea and rail to western Canada under the best circumstances possible. He asked the MacArthur brothers to look after them during the long journey. He also offered to get them both a job in Canada.

Tom and Bill had heard stories of Scots who'd made a good life for themselves in Canada. They were convinced that Canada offered them the chance of a better life than was available to them in Scotland. They wanted a fresh start.

Their mother had died of pneumonia just three years earlier. She was only forty-one. Father was still grieving for her when Tom told him they wanted to go to Canada.

"We'd like you to come with us, Father," Tom said. "With Mother gone, you're going to be very lonely here. Come with us to Canada."

"It's tempting," Father said. "I almost went to Australia with your Uncle Harry. Like you, he wanted something better than what we have here. Did quite well, too, your Uncle Harry did. I got a letter from him just two months back saying he's got four hundred sheep at his place. And he owns it all. Paid the mortgage off last year. Doing very well over there, your Uncle Harry is."

"Why didn't you go with him, Father?"

"I was tempted. Dearly so. But, as you might have been too young to recall, your grandfather wasn't too well at that time. Had a bad bout of the pneumonia. If both of us left, Harry and me, he couldn't have carried on. I felt I owed it to him to stay here."

"But Grandfather is gone now. If we go, and we are going, Father, you'll be all alone. Come with us, please."

"I can't do that, my son. This is where I belong. My father worked this farm and his father before him. This has always been MacArthur land and that's the way it should remain."

"I mean no disrespect, Father, but this is not MacArthur land. This is Lord Hanover's land. Just like it was his father's before him. This land belongs to the English, not to us."

"That might well be so, but this is still where we belong. Where you and your brother belong."

"But, what is there for us here?" Tom asked. "The farm's just not big enough. That's why we've been sleeping in Lord Hanover's stable these past two years. This place just isn't big enough to support us all."

Father took a couple of puffs on his pipe, looked up at the cattle grazing on the hill, and then down at the sheep in the lower meadow. "It is a bit small. I'll grant you that."

He paused again. Took another puff on his pipe. "I take it your mind is made up, both you and your brother?"

"It is that, Father. We are going to Canada. Lord Hanover has made all the arrangements. He's even lined up a job for us when we get to Alberta. We are going."

Father could see from the look in Tom's eyes that his mind was fully made up. And, as Tom was the dominant personality of the two, that probably meant Bill's mind was made up as well. While he regretted their decision, he could understand why they would want a fresh start in life.

"I understand how you feel, Son. If it hadn't been for your grandfather being so sickly, I would have left myself, along with your Uncle Harry. I can understand why you'd want to find something better than what we have here. But, I can't go with you. I belong here. This is my home and I'm a bit on in years to be starting something new with you in Canada. I've still got my health. I'm going to be all right. You'll have to go without me – but – with my blessing. I wish both you and your brother all the very best that life can bring."

"Oh, Father. I do wish you'd come with us. You've still got so much life left in you. You'd like Canada. I'm sure you would."

"You're probably right about that, my son. But, no, I won't be going with you. I was born here, just like my father and his father before him, and this is where they're going to bury me. Down there by the burn alongside your mother."

~

Tom remembered the feel of his father's grizzled cheek pressed against his as they hugged each other goodbye. He really did wish that Father had come with them. But, that was not to be.

He wondered if he'd made the right decision. *What's going to happen to Father? All alone there. Maybe we should have gone to Australia like Uncle Harry. Father would've liked that. Being with his brother and his nephews and nieces. He'd probably have come with us if we'd gone there. Gone to Australia. What's it going to be like in Canada? Don't know a soul here. Not a soul.*

Early in the morning of their tenth day at sea, the MacArthur's ship docked at the big port in Montreal. After clearing customs and immigration, they transferred the cattle to a freight train and continued their journey to western Canada by rail. The animals were in three pens on the floor of the boxcar, bulls in the middle pen and the cows at either end. Planks were laid across the width of the boxcar, about six feet from the floor, extending back from both sides of the sliding door. Hay, grain, straw, molasses and other stuff for the animals was stored on this plank platform. There was also room for two steel army cots so Tom and Bill could sleep, or at least attempt to sleep, during the bumpy, terribly cold, train ride to Alberta. The boxcar was made of steel but the insides had been lined with wood.

Three large water barrels in the centre pen by the door were refilled whenever the train stopped to take on water and coal. As they were travelling in the first week of December, the boxcar door was open no more than was necessary to let in air for the MacArthurs and the cattle. The door was on the left side of the train and they were able to see the United States on the other side of the St. Lawrence River just past Prescott, about three hours after the train left Montreal.

"That must be America," Bill said, pointing to a building in Ogdensburg, New York, with a big American flag on the other side of the wide river. "Over there like the crewman said it would be. Good thing we're not going to America. We don't know a soul there."

"We don't know a soul over here either," Tom replied with a chuckle as he mixed some oats and molasses for the animals.

They didn't see much of the St. Lawrence from that point on. Then, just before Cobourg, they got their first full view of Lake Ontario. "My God, but it's big," Bill said. "It's like being back on the Atlantic. I can't see the other side."

"Neither can I," Tom said. "We don't have any lochs like that one."

The train pulled into Toronto about eight hours after leaving Montreal and their boxcar was hooked up to a freight train that was going all the way to Vancouver. It only took a couple of hours to make the switch and they were on their way again just before sundown.

They got their first real feel of the biting cold of the Canadian winter as the train rolled its way through northwestern Ontario. By the time they got to Sioux Lookout – where Ojibway scouts used to keep a lookout for Sioux war parties – thick ice, like candle wax on a bottle of wine, covered the sides of the water barrels.

"Lord, Bill, but it's a big country," Tom said, as he stuck his head out the door, the rattling of the wheels on the steel rails below ringing in his ears. "It just goes on and on."

"Aye, it does do that," Bill replied as he rolled himself a cigarette. "Not much you could do with it though. Mostly scrub and rock out there. Desolate looking, it is."

Once past Winnipeg, they started to fully appreciate the majestic expanse of the Canadian prairies. "My goodness," Bill said, "I've never seen this far across land."

"It is big," Tom said as the train angled its way northwest from Brandon towards Regina, through wheat fields a mile wide. "Must be a thousand miles from here to the sunset and there doesn't seem to be a thing in between. These must be the prairies. Where they grow the wheat they ship to that big grain terminal beside the Chateau Frontenac."

By the time the freight train pulled into the railway yards at Calgary, they'd been in that boxcar for four days and three nights. Dust from the hay and the grain chop encrusted their faces and matted their hair.

"You really are a paleface, Tom," Bill said. "The Indians 'll have no trouble at all picking you out."

"Aye. We'd best find somewheres to wash this stuff off. I'll be damned if I'm going to use that icy stuff," Tom said, pointing to the ice-crusted water barrels.

Donald Morgan, the Alberta rancher who had purchased the prize cattle from Lord Hanover, was waiting for them when the train stopped. He'd had the number of their boxcar telegraphed ahead so he'd know exactly where to park his stake truck.

"And how was it, boys?" Morgan asked as the MacArthur brothers peered into view covered from head to toe in grain dust and straw.

"You'd be as well to ask the beasts," Tom replied. "At least they had the straw to lie down on. I'm telling you, sir, our cots didn't lie still for more than two miles at a stretch. And it was cold. Even though we had the thick army blankets, we almost froze in there. I much preferred the boat and the ocean."

They got the bulls and the cows out of the boxcar and into the truck without any problem. Morgan inspected them carefully and told the MacArthur brothers they'd done an excellent job of looking after them during the almost six thousand miles they'd travelled since leaving Lord Hanover's estate in the north of Scotland.

"And what do you boys plan to do now?" he asked.

"We have an arrangement with a Mr. Stafford," Tom said. "Perhaps you know of him. He has a big dairy in Calgary and we agreed to work on his farm for one year. That's how long the Canadian immigration people said we'd have to have work guaranteed for. Then, as I understand it, we'll be free to do whatever we want. Is that not how it is, Bill?"

"Aye. That is my understanding," Bill replied. "That is the agreement."

Morgan offered to drive them out to the Stafford dairy ranch but they said they wanted to spend the night in Calgary and get a good night's sleep. He thanked them again for the splendid job they'd done of looking after his cattle. Then he suggested they should look him up when their year with Stafford was over.

The MacArthurs checked into a rundown hotel alongside the railway yards. Their room had a badly-sprung brass bed covered by a green spread with cigarette-burn patterns. A stained, yellow, armchair occupied the limited space not taken up by the bed, the dresser with the cracked mirror, and the leaking radiator. They got out of their grimy clothes and sat naked on the bed waiting for the bathtub to fill up.

"Lord God!" Bill exclaimed enthusiastically. "We're in the new land."

Tom got out his tobacco pouch and cigarette papers and started to roll himself a cigarette. "Aye, that it is," he murmured. "A new land. A new life for us."

The dismal, tacky, surroundings of that new-land flophouse were quite depressing but the MacArthur brothers were in an optimistic mood. "I think we did the right thing," Tom said after he got his cigarette lit. "There wasn't much for us at home. Here at least we'll have a chance to get a place of our own. If we work at it hard enough."

"We'll see," Bill said as he got up from the bed. "We'll see what the future brings us. Although, I really didn't like leaving Father like that. You should have persuaded him to come with us, Tom."

Tom felt guilty about that. He'd tried. Tried hard to get Father to come with them. But Father was adamant that he was going to be buried alongside Mother down by the burn. *Would he have felt so strongly about it if we were going to Australia? I don't really know.*

There were about three hundred and fifty cows at the Stafford dairy ranch and they had to milk them three times a day – at six in the morning, at noon and at six at night. They had to be up at five every morning and seldom finished before seven-thirty at night.

After supper, they went back to their cramped, poorly-lit, quarters over the milking barn for a game of poker or cribbage with some of their mates before crawling back into their cots again at ten. That went on seven days a week for every week of the year they worked for Jack Stafford. They seldom got away from the place.

They went to work at Don Morgan's ranch after that. He had an enormous operation just north of Cochrane – eight thousand acres and twenty-five hundred head of beef cattle. Morgan had only one-quarter the men Stafford employed and it was a much better situation for the MacArthurs. No milking three times a day. No cows' tails to wash. Hardly any time at all caged up in the barn. They were much more satisfied with their life at the Morgan ranch.

But it wasn't enough for Tom. He left Scotland because he wanted more out of life than toiling and sweating over another man's soil. And now he realized they didn't stand much of a chance of getting a place of their own in Alberta. Because the soil wasn't nearly as rich as the soil at Lord Hanover's estate, they'd need so much more land to run a successful operation there – two or three times what they would have needed in Scotland. And that meant a great deal more money than the amount they were able to set aside from their wages.

That's why Tom decided to take a course on selling real estate. While Bill and the other men were in Calgary on Saturday night drinking beer at the Noble Hotel or partying it up with some of the off-duty waitresses from the Old Mansion House, Tom was alone in the bunkhouse learning all he could about selling real estate by the light of a coal oil lamp.

About two months before Tom was due to write the real estate exam, he met Howard Foster, the only son of a successful Toronto real estate broker, at a seminar sponsored by one of Calgary's biggest real estate firms. They struck up an immediate friendship. Foster had been in Calgary for about two years trying, somewhat unsuccessfully, to make a living selling real estate. He had decided to return to Toronto, Canada's second largest city, and work with his father who, despite the fact Canada was still in the grip of the Depression, was doing rather well with commissions on bank foreclosures and power of sales. Foster invited Tom to come with him after he completed the course.

"When we get out of this depression, the big boom in real estate is going to be in Toronto and southwestern Ontario," Foster said one evening when they were having supper at a local restaurant in Calgary. "There's nothing here. I've proved that over the last two years. If I hadn't had a falling out with my dad, I wouldn't have been here in the first place. Toronto's where the action is going to be. Come with me and get your slice of it."

"But, what about your dad?" Tom asked. "How are things between you and him now?"

"We're okay. Everything's settled between us and he wants me back. Dad wants to open an office in the west end and change the firm's name to Foster & Son. I could use your gift of the gab in the new office."

Tom thought about Foster's offer as he drove back to the ranch that night in the old Model A Ford he and Bill bought shortly after they started working at Don Morgan's place. It was an attractive offer. The more deeply he got involved in the real estate course, the more convinced he became that selling real estate was what he wanted to do. He didn't have the same attachment to the land and the animals that

Bill had and was looking forward to carving out a comfortable living for himself in Toronto.

"Come with me," he said to Bill after he got back to the ranch. "You can get a job in Toronto and we can still be together."

"Live in Toronto? I wouldn't give it so much as a second thought. That'd be even worse than living in Calgary. Too crowded. Too many people. No room to breathe. No, this is the life I want. Right here. I need to breathe fresh air, Tom. Drink water drawn from the river. Ride the horses. Break them. Can't do that in Toronto or Calgary."

Tom tried, two or three times over the next few weeks, but he couldn't persuade Bill to move with him to Toronto. He made one last try on their way to Calgary to hook up with Howard Foster. It was a bitterly cold morning in February, 1936, and they had trouble with some patches of deep snow on the road. At one point, Tom had to get out and give the car a push.

"It must have come down hard overnight," he said as he got back into the front seat of the Model A. "Not sure you're going to make it back to the ranch without me here to give you a shove every now and then."

"Nice try," Bill chuckled as he eased the car over an icy patch near the bridge. "I'll be okay."

"You'd be more okay if you came with me to Toronto. Really don't like leaving you out here all by yourself."

"Then don't go," Bill said with a grin. "Give up fame and fortune in Toronto and stay with me on the ranch."

"You know I'm not going to do that."

"And you know I'm not moving to Toronto. Like I said, wouldn't give it a second thought. This is where I belong now."

When they got to the rooming house on 17th Avenue SW where Howard Foster had been staying, Tom introduced Bill to Foster and put his suitcase in the trunk of Foster's 1934 Ford coupe.

He turned to Bill and gave him a big hug. "You take care of yourself. You hear? I'll come back for a visit once I get on my feet out there. This isn't the final goodbye."

"I know it isn't," Bill said, as he kissed his brother on the cheek. "We'll be together again. Aye, we will do that."

~

Bill stayed on at the ranch. Farming was the only life he knew. And he enjoyed it. He liked riding the range, breaking the horses, herding the cattle and bringing the near-frozen newborn calves into the cookhouse in the very early spring so they could thaw out by the pot-bellied stove. Sometimes there'd be as many as four of them spread out on the kitchen floor.

About a month after Tom left for Toronto, a new cook arrived at the ranch. Helen Dodginghorse was a beautiful young Blackfoot with soft, peach-like, skin and long, jet-black, hair that she tied in braids. She had been raised as a Methodist and sang in the choir at the Methodist church at the Big Thunder Indian Reserve, southwest of Calgary. She was quite slim, about five foot six, and she was a terrific cook. Bill took an instant liking to her. He'd never seen anyone quite like Helen. She had an exotic quality that drew him to her. The attraction was mutual and immediate.

Pretty soon, they were taking walks together down by the river in the early hours of the evening. She invited him over to the Big Thunder reserve one Sunday afternoon to meet her parents who lived in a two-storey log house snuggled against the shoulder of the foothills on the eastern slopes of the Rocky Mountains. There was a huge black bearskin on the wall of the living room and two pictures of Helen. The picture on the left showed her as a teenager in a traditional jingle dance dress holding an eagle feather above her head as she danced at a pow wow. The other showed her in a burgundy gown singing in the choir at the Methodist church. There was also a painting of a representative of Queen Victoria in a blue uniform shaking hands with a Blackfoot chief in full headdress at the signing of the Blackfoot Treaty in September, 1877.

It had been a long time since Bill had eaten a meal in a family atmosphere and the experience brought back warm memories of his early days at home in Scotland when his mother was still alive. The warmth of the household enveloped him and made him feel human again – after so many years of living in stable lofts and crowded bunkhouses. Squatting to shit at the heels of the horses. Enduring the farting noise and smell of his mates in the bunkhouse. Putting up with weird Harry who used to sneak into the barn at night and screw the calves. It had been such a long, long time since he had enjoyed as warm and welcoming an atmosphere as that of the home of Gordon and Vera Dodginghorse.

"Helen tells us you're from Scotland," her dad said. "What brought you to Canada?"

"There wasn't much for us back home," Bill replied. "Me and my brother were living in a stable loft on another farm for the last couple of winters. My dad's farm was too small to support us all. So, me and Tom decided to head over here and see if we could make a better life for ourselves."

"And your dad?" Gordon Dodginghorse asked. "He's still there with your mother?"

"Mum died about two years before me and Tom left. She had pneumonia. Took her away pretty quick. Only forty-one. That's what my mum was when she died. Forty-one."

"I'm so sorry to hear that," Helen's father said.

"Thanks. Anyway, we tried to get Father to come with us to Canada but he's really tied to that place. Wants to die there."

"I feel the same way. I'm going to be buried here. Right here in the land of my ancestors."

He poured Bill some tea. "Helen says your brother's in Toronto. Selling real estate."

"Aye. He's got a lot of ambition my brother has. He's had enough of stable lofts and bunkhouses. Wanted more out of life than that, my brother did. And he'll find it. If anyone's going to succeed, it's my brother Tom."

Bill found it a bit odd that he didn't feel strange eating supper there with a Blackfoot family. It really wasn't all that much different than having supper with Tom and his dad back in Scotland. *These are good people. Proud. Obviously making a good living. I thought things would be different. A lot different.*

After that first visit, Bill and Helen got into the habit of driving over to Big Thunder just about every Sunday to visit her parents. The reserve was about an hour away from the Morgan ranch. Helen's sister Sarah lived close by her parents' house and she and her husband Richard often joined them for supper.

Richard Eagletail was a lot different than Helen's parents. He had an air about him. More proud than arrogant and there was an edge there. Bill could feel it. Richard's father had been the chief at Big Thunder, as was his father before him. However, one evening when he was driving Richard's mother and two younger sisters home from a shopping trip in Calgary, a white cowboy driving a five-ton stake truck rammed them head-on. They were killed instantly, along with the cowboy who, an autopsy later determined, had a high level of alcohol in his system.

Richard, who was twenty-two at the time, was competing at a rodeo in High River that weekend and didn't learn about the fatal accident until after he got back to Big Thunder. The Band Council appointed Fred Littlelight to replace Richard's father as chief and he won the next election. The Littlelight family controlled the band's affairs from that point on. After the funeral, Richard continued to work the Eagletail ranch. He married Sarah, his high school sweetheart, in the spring of the following year.

Richard resented the destructive impact the white settlers had on his people. He believed their lands had been stolen and their way of life destroyed. The Blackfoot used to have the free run of the prairies and now they were boxed in at Big Thunder. The huge herds of buffalo they had depended on for their food, clothing and shelter were gone. Gone forever. An entire way of life had been wiped off the map.

As far as he was concerned, it would have been better if the whites had stayed on their side of the Atlantic. Mind you, after a while, he didn't act that way toward Bill. It was clear to him that Helen loved Bill very, very, much, and, on that basis, he accepted Bill as part of their family.

When Helen and Bill got married in October of that year, Bill moved from the bunkhouse to the cookhouse. It had a large kitchen, big enough to feed a dozen men, a small sitting room and two bedrooms. Bill found it to be a welcome change from the crowded, smelly, bunkhouse.

They named their first child William, after Bill and his father. Bill usually got up early to feed little William and dress him while Helen got breakfast ready for the other men. He also kept an eye on the boy while she served the men lunch or dinner. In the evenings, after a hard day's work in the fields, Bill would rock the baby to sleep in his arms. Helen got a chuckle out of that because, during harvest time, Bill would be so exhausted from forking wheat into the threshing machine all day long that he would rock himself to sleep as well and she'd have to put both of them to bed.

About a year after William was born, Helen got pregnant again. Bill's life with Helen was all he could ask for. He loved little William. And he was looking forward to that first glimpse of his second child's face. Things had worked out well for him in this new land called Canada.

It had been a difficult pregnancy, especially during the last stage. But, even at that, they had not felt it necessary to take Helen to the hospital in Calgary. They should have. The midwife from Big Thunder who came to assist in the delivery realized that soon after she got to Helen's bedside. She did everything she knew how. But it was too late.

The baby was all right. The midwife cut the umbilical cord, wiped the baby off, and wrapped it in a big towel. It was hollering away like crazy. Bill kissed it gently on the forehead and then he knelt by the bed and held onto Helen's hand as the life slipped out of her. He simply couldn't bear the thought of losing her. She had made such a wonderful difference in his life and it just simply wouldn't be the same without her. He hoped against hope that they would be able to continue their life together. But, that was not to be. Helen gave him a quiet, sad, smile, and then she was gone.

They took her body to the Methodist church at Big Thunder and buried her in the cemetery behind the church four days later. Her sister took care of little William and the newborn baby. Sarah had a four-month old baby which she was breastfeeding and she had enough milk to take care of the other little fellow as well.

On the night after they laid Helen to rest at the Methodist cemetery, Bill took little William in his arms and sat on the rocker on Sarah's front porch. The newborn was asleep in a cot in Sarah's bedroom. He wondered what the future held for them now that Helen was gone. He rocked gently with little William's head resting on his neck and thought the whole thing through. Now, he had two little boys and no mother to look after them. What, he wondered, could he, a common ranch hand, do? He couldn't be out in the fields all day and feeding and changing his sons at the same time. They needed a mother's love and care.

He clasped little William to his chest and rocked back and forth in the dark night air. The little fellow felt so soft and warm and lovable and – and vulnerable. What was he going to do now? How was he going to be able to hold on to this cuddly little bundle, this little son of his? "Oh, God," he whispered. "Why? Why, Lord? Why?"

The tears trickled down his cheeks as he thought about his Helen and their walks together down by the river. That first supper with her family. And the picnics. The picnics they used to have with little William on Sundays. All of that – all of that that would never – ever – be the same again.

CHAPTER

- 2 -

About a week after Helen's funeral, Bill drove back to the Morgan ranch and had a talk with Don Morgan. Morgan told him how deeply sorry he was for his loss. However, there were certain realities that had to be faced.

"Now you know, Bill, that I have nine men to feed. Mary Logan who, you'll remember, was my cook before we got Helen, has agreed to come back. She'll be getting here on the weekend and, of course, she'll be needing the cookhouse. She's a widow lady, you know, and she's got three young boys to take care of. So, Bill, that means you're going to have to go back to the bunkhouse with the other men. I'm sorry, but there's nothing else I can do."

"I understand," Bill said. "I know that's what you've got to do."

"What about your boys?" Morgan asked. "What are you going to do about them?"

"I'm not too sure about that," Bill replied. "They're with Helen's sister at the Indian reserve for now and they're all right with her. But, it's a bit of a burden on her. She's got a little four-month-old laddie of her own and he has a bad case of the asthma. Keeps her up all night. But she's more than willing, Helen's sister is, to look after my boys, for now anyway. I certainly can't keep them here. Not with me moving back to the bunkhouse."

"I'm sorry about that," Morgan said. "But I really don't have any other choice and, you do know, with you working in the fields all day and being in the bunkhouse with the other men at night, this really isn't a good place for you to raise two little boys."

"You're right about that," Bill said. "I'm going to have to make some other arrangements."

As he drove back to Big Thunder, the reality sunk in that he really didn't have much in the way of options. Morgan was right in saying he couldn't have William and his baby brother living in the bunkhouse with him and the other men. Widow Logan and her three sons would have the cookhouse now. There was nowhere at the ranch for Bill and his two boys.

When he explained the situation to Sarah and Richard, they said they'd be more than willing to have the boys stay with them until he was able to work something out.

"Your boys are more than welcome here," Richard said. "It's a bit of a burden for Sarah, with little Hughie having the asthma as bad as he has, but she's willing to give it a try."

"Are you sure, Sarah?" Bill asked.

"Yes, Bill. I'm sure. I am."

"Well, that takes a bit of a load off my mind, for now anyway. I'm sure I'll be able to work something out."

He had supper with Sarah and Richard, gave his two sons a hug goodbye, and headed back to the Morgan ranch.

Sarah did the best she could. But it did get trying at times, especially having three babies to care for at the same time. And, with her sleep constantly interrupted because of her own little fellow wheezing and coughing with the asthma, there were times when she found it a bit too much, much too much.

Her mother was crippled up with arthritis and wasn't in any condition to help relieve the stress on Sarah. Her sister Doreen lived at the Blood Tribe Reserve, about a hundred miles south down near the American border. Richard didn't have any relatives at Big Thunder.

Bill wrote a letter to Tom in Toronto telling him how Helen had died all of a sudden and that his young sons were being taken care of by Sarah at Big Thunder. He also told him that, with the asthma and all that, taking care of the three little boys was a bit too much of a burden on Sarah.

Tom discussed Bill's letter with Martha, his wife of a little over two years. He met her just a few months after he arrived in Toronto. Martha had been born in Aberdeen and left Scotland for Toronto with her parents when she was seven. She was a waitress at the restaurant where Tom had his lunch and he took an immediate shine to her. She was just a tiny wee bit of a thing. A little short of five feet. With a nicely-rounded figure. He thought she looked absolutely gorgeous. They got married in December, 1936, surrounded by tropical plants and flowers in the Palm House conservatory at Allan Gardens.

Tom was stunned, heartbroken, when the doctor told him he was sterile. He could never father a child. A son of his own. "Oh, lass, it hurts. It hurts so much," he said as he lay close to Martha in their bed that night and went over what the doctor told him. "He says that – that I can't. The stuff just isn't in me to get you pregnant."

"Oh, my dear Tom," she said. "And I do so much want a laddie with your eyes and your nose and your – your everything. I want a wee laddie just like you."

And then she cried. They both cried. Long into that cold winter night.

It was just a few months after that that they got Bill's letter about Helen. They had never met Helen. Not so much as seen a picture of her. But Bill had written to them soon after Helen agreed to marry him and described her in a way only a portrait of an angel could match. His love for her shone through every paragraph of his badly-scribbled letter.

"Maybe we should do something to help," Martha said after Tom finished reading her Bill's letter. "Apart from Helen's parents, he has no one out there to help him."

"He does say Helen has another sister," Tom said, "but she's quite a distance away, at the Blood Tribe Reserve down at the American border."

"Yes, that probably wouldn't work out," Martha said, "and, with Helen's mother being crippled up with the arthritis like Bill says, there's not an awful lot she could be expected to do either. Mind you, I'm surprised she has arthritis at her age. She's probably not much older than my mum."

"Well, Bill says she does have it and it seems to be pretty bad. It would be a lot better if he wasn't working at the ranch. There's nowhere else for him but the bunkhouse and I can understand why he can't have the boys living with him there. There's eight other men in that place."

He thought things through for a minute. If her own baby didn't keep Sarah up all night with its coughing and wheezing, things would probably work out quite well. But the wee thing did have the asthma and Sarah simply couldn't be expected to look after all three of them by herself.

"If he had a job in the city, that might work out better," Tom said. "But, even at that, he'd still have the problem of how to look after the boys when he was at work."

"It is a problem," Martha said. "Apart from Helen's family, he doesn't know a soul out there."

Tom made more than enough money selling real estate to keep them both quite comfortably well off without Martha having to work outside of the home. Unlike the other women she knew, however, she didn't have children and that left her with a lot of time on her hands. Perhaps, she thought, having Bill's sons come and live with them would make up for the loss of not being able to have a son of her own, the son she so desperately wanted but couldn't have. *Even if it is just for a little while, until Bill comes up with a permanent solution,* she thought.

"I'd have no trouble at all looking after the little fellows," she said. "And it would be good to have two wee baby boys in our home."

Tom thought about it for a moment. He knew how very much Martha wanted to have a son and how bitterly disappointed she was when the doctor told him he was sterile.

"Perhaps," he said. "It probably would be a help to Sarah, losing all that sleep most nights with her baby having the asthma. Yes, perhaps it would be a good idea for us to help out like that. What a burden this must be on Bill. Losing Helen so suddenly like that and, now, having nowhere to keep the boys on his own."

"It would," Martha said. "It would be better all around." By now, her heart was set on getting the boys into their home. She wanted a son so badly and this might be the only opportunity she would have to make her dream come true.

"If I had my way, I'd ask him to come and live with us and bring his boys with him," Tom said. "But, out there is where he wants to be. I tried. Really tried hard I did to get him to come with me when I came out here to Toronto. He was dead set against it. Really likes it out there on the ranch, Bill does. Don't see him coming east to Toronto. He's where he wants to be. Where he wants to stay."

"I understand that," Martha said, "but, for now, I think we should offer to have his boys come and stay with us. At least until he can make a more permanent arrangement."

Tom thought for a moment. "Maybe he wouldn't want to give both the boys up. There's two thousand miles between us and Calgary. He'd never be able to see them."

"I hadn't thought about that," Martha said. "You're right. That's an awful distance for him to be away from his boys."

"Maybe," Tom said, "we should see if he would be open to us having one of the boys. That way, he'd still have one of them out there with him. And, who knows, this whole thing might be resolved in a matter of months. He might get a job in Calgary or find a ranch to work on a lot closer to Big Thunder. He says it's two hours round trip every time he goes there to see his boys."

"All right then," Martha said, anxious to have at least one of the boys come and live with them, "let's suggest that we take one of them off his hands. Until things work out for him out there."

"But, are you sure you could handle it, lass? It could turn out to be quite a burden. And then, when the wee fellow went back to live with Bill, it would break your heart. You'd have become so attached to him."

"Oh, no, Tom. No burden at all. I'd love to do it. Even if it is just for a little while. Besides, with you being away all day, and sometimes in the evenings, it does get a bit lonely around here at times. I'd love to have one of the boys come and live with us."

Tom wrote to Bill telling him, for the first time, they couldn't have a child of their own and, if it would be a help to him and Sarah, they would be more than willing to have one of the boys come and live with them for a short while.

Bill discussed Tom's letter with Helen's parents. They said it would certainly make things easier on Sarah if one of the boys went to live with Tom in Toronto. Besides, as Tom and Martha had their hearts set on having a child of their own, they would be sure to give the boy a warm and loving home.

They then had to decide which son should stay at Big Thunder and which one should go to Toronto. Little William was used to Sarah and Richard. He had been to their place often and felt secure and familiar around them. Sending him off to Toronto would be a disruptive, alienating, experience. It would be better for him to stay with them and his grandparents. They all agreed that little William would stay with Helen's sister on the Big Thunder Indian reserve and his newborn baby brother would go to live with Tom and Martha in a middle-class neighborhood in Toronto.

Bill didn't like the idea of separating his boys or of having his youngest son living so far away in Toronto. *Even if it is for just a little while.* Toronto was two thousand miles away. But, there was no doubt the strain of looking after the three of them was taking quite a toll on Sarah and Tom and Martha would be good to his youngest little fellow. *Perhaps, at least for now, this is the best thing to do.* There didn't seem to be any other option on the table, at least not until he was able to get a good job in the city. Or, maybe, find a ranch closer to Big Thunder. And, with Canada still caught in the grip of the Depression, jobs were scarce and far between. He reluctantly agreed that this was the best option, at least for the short term.

When Martha took the train out to Calgary to bring the youngest boy home to Toronto, Bill picked her up at the Canadian Pacific Railway station and drove her out to the reserve in one of the pickup trucks from the Morgan ranch.

Bill took an instant liking to Martha. He felt right away what it was about her Tom had found so attractive. Her eyes were a soft pale blue and her wavy blonde hair came right down to her shoulders.

As the truck bounced its way south along the washboard gravel road, Martha caught her first glimpse of the magnificence of the Rocky Mountains forming a jagged line across the bottom of the pastel-blue western sky. Their snow caps glistened in the midday sun.

"What a beautiful sight it is," she said to Bill with a note of genuine awe in her voice.

"Aye, it is that, Martha. And it's not just the size of them – that they're bigger than the ones at home. But that they're almost – they almost seem alive. Asleep, but alive. I've never been up in them myself but I'm going to. I'll be taking the boys up there when they're older. Some summer when they're not in school. Aye, we will do that."

"I'm sure that you will, Bill," she said gently. "You and the boys will find all sorts of good things to do together."

"Aye, we will do that, Martha. But it would be so much better if my darling Helen could make the trip with us. So much better."

Martha noted the stiffening of his mouth and how hard he was struggling to hold in the hurt, the pain, the sense of loss. Although almost two months had passed since he laid Helen to rest in the Methodist cemetery at Big Thunder, his pain was as fresh as yesterday.

"I'm so sorry, Bill. So terribly, terribly sorry."

Bill reached over and placed his hard, calloused, hand over hers and gave her fingers a gentle squeeze. "Bless you, Martha. God bless you and Tom both."

As he squeezed her hand, it suddenly dawned on her that this was the first time she had ever been with him. She had heard a great deal about him from Tom. About their times together on their father's farm near Inverness, on the ship crossing the ocean, in the boxcar on their way to western Canada and at the Morgan ranch. Perhaps it was the warm, caring, way Tom talked about Bill that made her feel so – so unstrange – as the truck sped past the shotgun-riddled mail boxes on the road to Big Thunder. It was as if they had known each other for a long, long, time.

If you weren't looking for it, you'd probably miss the entrance to Big Thunder. There wasn't even a sign on the main road advising you to turn right onto the dirt road leading up over the shoulder of the hill. About a hundred yards down the rough road, Martha noticed a faded sign nailed to a crooked fence post.

THIS IS AN INDIAN RESERVE
TRESPASSERS WILL BE PROSECUTED

Her stomach muscles tightened as the truck passed the sign. It was as if she had crossed the border into an alien, hostile, land. The road dipped through the heavy bush and then there were fields on both sides dotted with horses and cattle grazing on the lush pasture. Bill continued past fields of growing wheat, corn and hay. As she looked west, Martha could see how the fields blended into the foothills at the bottom of the eastern slopes of the Rockies.

As they approached the bridge crossing the Big Thunder River, Martha looked across at the huddle of buildings on the other side. There was a general store with a gas pump out front, a feed mill, a lumber yard, the Methodist church where Helen was buried, a school and several other buildings.

Bill drove over the bridge and waved to the Blackfoot men sitting on the steps outside the store. They look ordinary enough, Martha thought. *They certainly don't look anything like those Indians scalping white settlers in the movies.* In fact, apart from the jet blackness of their hair, there was little that would distinguish them as being Blackfoot. Most of them wore denim jeans and jackets, cowboy boots and hats with bright, checkered, scarves around their necks. Martha had seen many Scots with the same dark complexion as the Big Thunder people. They certainly weren't anything like what she had been conditioned to expect from watching the movies.

Bill drove on up the other side of the river. About two miles past the huddle of buildings, he turned left and took the narrow path of a road up the hill to the Eagletail ranch. Like most people at Big Thunder, the Eagletails were hard workers and made a good living raising cattle and horses. This ability to pay their own way was reflected in the proud way they carried themselves – even among other native people – at the rodeos, the pow wows and other social gatherings. The Big Thunder people were self-sufficient and didn't look to the white man's government for anything. Except, of course, for the school. And, as the school was the white man's idea in the first place, it seemed only reasonable that the white man's government should pay for the teachers and keep the place operating.

Bill pulled up in front of the big log house Richard's father had built just before he was killed on the way home from Calgary and got out of the truck to open the door on Martha's side. As Martha stepped down from the truck, the barn door opened and Helen's sister Sarah walked over to greet them. As she came closer to them, Martha noted how tall Sarah was and how broad she was in the shoulders and chest. She was a big woman. But firm. Very well built. Strong. She was more handsome than pretty and had a very regal air about her. She was dressed in a plaid work shirt, jeans, black cowboy hat and a light denim jacket. She had a baby cradled under her left arm.

It wasn't until Sarah held out her hand in welcome that Martha saw the other baby strapped to her back. As the two women exchanged greetings, Bill eased the infant out of the cradle board and clasped him to his chest. He kissed the babe gently on the forehead and tickled him under the chin. Then he held him close to him again as the little fellow nuzzled contentedly against his neck.

"Will you look at this little man, Martha?" Bill said holding the boy towards her. "This little MacArthur."

Martha took the baby carefully in her arms and looked at him. Looked at him with instant love. "He's beautiful," she said in a whisper. "Just simply beautiful."

The grey-blue eyes looked up at her without a glimmer of recognition and then the boy cried out for the familiar feel and smell of his father.

"He'll get used to you," Bill assured her as he took the baby back in his arms. "Give the boy time."

Bill looked around the barnyard. "Where's my little William?" he asked Sarah.

"He's out on the tractor with Richard," she replied. "Spreading hay for the cattle. He just loves being on that machine. They'll be in for lunch soon. Come on into the house."

At supper that night, Bill told Martha they had named the little fellow Gordon, after Helen and Sarah's father. "They've been so good – so kind and gentle to me, Martha. If it had been a lassie, I'd have wanted to call her Vera. But, him being a boy, I decided to call him Gordon."

Gordon and Vera Dodginghorse had driven over in a buggy from their ranch around mid-afternoon that day. They were a delightful couple and, just as Bill had said in his letter, Vera was quite crippled up with arthritis and could barely move her fingers. Martha could see she wouldn't be much help to Sarah in taking care of Bill's boys.

She took an instant liking to little William. He was just a little under two and was a very bright, playful little fellow. It was clear that Bill loved him very much and she enjoyed watching him tickling his son.

Martha got along very well with Sarah during the week she was at Big Thunder. They were both in their early twenties and developed a bond between them because of the role they were each going to play in helping Bill take care of his two motherless boys.

"I really appreciate what you and Tom are doing, helping me out this way," Bill said as Martha got ready for the return trip to Toronto. Sarah had bought some baby formula for Gordon and put it in a bag along with the cloth diapers and other things they would need for the long train ride back to Toronto.

"It'll be our pleasure," Martha replied. "We're more than happy to help out and, Bill, we'll give the wee lamb all of the love we have in our hearts."

"I'm sure you will, Martha, sure that you will. Now, I honestly don't know how long this is going to be for. I clearly can't have the boys with me as long as I'm at the ranch. And, even if I was to get a job in Calgary and get a flat somewheres, I'd still have no one to look after them during the day. Oh God. Why, why did this have to happen? Why did it have to happen like this?"

Martha reached over and placed her hand on Bill's elbow. "I know. I know, Bill. I know how hard this is for you. But things will work out. We'll find a way for you to get back together with your boys. We'll find a way."

"I hope so, Martha. I really do. And I hope we're doing the right thing by splitting them up like this. I really do. But, right now, there doesn't seem to be any other choice."

"Mind you, Bill, there's no reason why you couldn't be staying with us too. Tom's done well in Toronto and I've no doubt, not doubt at all, that you'd also do well there."

"Aye, Martha, but what about little William? He feels safe, loved, and comfortable with Sarah and Richard. He's tied to them like bark to a tree. Moving him to Toronto would be hard on him – and on them."

"Well, as Tom always says, let's take it one day at a time. But, if you change your mind, we'd love to have you and little William too. Besides, Bill, this will only be for a short time. Things will work out for the best."

Bill drove over to Big Thunder every Sunday to spend time with little William. He wanted to visit more often but it was a two-hour round trip from the ranch to the reserve. He'd usually pick the little fellow up in his arms and walk about the reserve with him. You could often find him down by the banks of the river tossing pebbles into the stream with little William on his knee. Sometimes he'd place a pebble in William's hand and let him toss it as far as he could. About three feet.

Sarah and Richard always insisted that Bill stay to have supper and he gladly took advantage of the opportunity to share the warmth of their companionship. On the drive back from the Eagletail's place each Sunday night, little William's presence and talcum smell stayed with him all the way to the Morgan ranch. He so loved to hold that little bundle in his arms. To look at his son's face and see the happy gleam of recognition in his grey-blue eyes.

When he walked past the cookhouse after getting back from Sarah and Richard's, the light in Widow Logan's window always served as a painful, bittersweet, reminder of the happier days when Helen was alive.

Bill often lay listlessly on his bunk at night staring vacantly at the smoke-blackened ceiling and counting his losses. It got to be that the more he was with little William on Sunday afternoons, the more he missed him during the week. Being away from his son was ripping him apart. And then he'd think about Gordon with Tom and Martha two thousand miles away in Toronto. He really did appreciate the offer from Tom to have them all living together with him in Toronto. It wasn't just that he didn't want to live in the big city, there was also the fact that he would prefer not to be a burden on Tom and Martha.

Still, that might turn out to be the best way. At least until I got a job there and find a place for me and the boys to live together. Maybe a nice flat somewhere. There must be a way.

~

Bill was in the cookhouse finishing his supper with the other men on September 1, 1939, when he heard on the radio that Hitler's armies had swept into western Poland. Two days later, Great Britain and France declared war on Germany. The Second World War was under way.

The Parliament of Canada met in special session in Ottawa on September 7, 1939, and, three days later, King George VI announced at Buckingham Palace that Canada had entered the war in support of Britain and her allies. By the end of the month, more than fifty-eight thousand Canadian men and women had joined up.

Bill had been pretty restless lately. He was still mourning Helen's death and didn't like the idea of his boys not being able to live with him – especially with little Gordon being two thousand miles away in Toronto. Don Morgan had noticed quite a change in Bill. He had always been a warm, outgoing, sort of fellow. But, lately, he was becoming more and more withdrawn within himself and was just simply not the Bill he used to be. It was obvious that Bill had quite a lot on his mind and was not particularly pleased with the limited range of options he had been given to choose from.

Tom had invited him again to come and live with them in Toronto. That would have meant he would have both his boys living with him. But, he doubted very much that he would be able to get a good job in Toronto, especially with the high rate of unemployment that existed at that time.

Besides that, he had grown deeply attached to life on the Morgan ranch. He loved the feel of the horse between his legs as he rounded up strays in the early spring. The way it would move from a trot to a canter to a full gallop. The outline of the Rockies against the blue western sky. The sound of the water rushing over the rocks in the river when he took the stone boat down there to fill the water barrels.

City life didn't hold much of an appeal for Bill. Too crowded. Too smelly. And then there was little William. He was doing well with Richard and Sarah and seemed to be enjoying his stay at the reserve. Moving him to Toronto, at this stage, mightn't be such a good idea. *Damn,* he thought. *If Sarah's sister lived at Big Thunder instead of down there near the American border, she could help out with the boys. And Gordon would be here with us. But, she doesn't. And there's no one else to help us. Damn.*

Maybe, he thought, if he joined the Army, he'd be able to learn a trade, like mechanics or carpentry or something like that, and that would enable him to get a job in Calgary and have the boys living with him. He wasn't looking forward to life in the city but, at least, he would have both of his sons with him. His decision to join the Army was also motivated, to a certain extent, by the fact that it was widely believed the Germans were going to invade Britain. If they were going to attack his homeland, he wanted to be there to stop them.

When Bill went to sign up at the Calgary Highlanders' recruitment office, he was asked if he would consider serving with the Winnipeg Grenadiers. As all he wanted to do was fight the Germans, it didn't make all that much difference to him which regiment he served with. He had only one day to get his things packed and catch the train that would be leaving for Winnipeg Friday afternoon.

He packed his few belongings at the ranch, got his final pay cheque from Don Morgan, and drove over to Big Thunder to say goodbye to little William and the Eagletails. They had a big supper that night. Helen's mother and father joined them.

"How do you feel about going to war, Bill?" Helen's father asked. "I expect it could get a bit rough over there."

"I'm not afraid, if that's what you mean," Bill replied, "but there are other things I'd rather be doing. Lots of other things."

"Well, I hope you'll come back safe and sound," Gordon Dodginghorse said. "We don't want to lose you – not lose you like we did our Helen."

They were all silent for a moment, drinking their tea and thinking about Helen.

"What about you, Richard?" Bill asked Sarah's husband. "When will you be signing up?"

"It's not my war," Richard replied with a bit of an edge in his voice. "It's white men fighting white men. When we signed the treaties with the Queen of England, we made it clear we would never fight in the white man's wars. This war has nothing to do with us. Nothing at all."

Bill decided not to press the point. He'd lost more than one argument with Richard and saw no point in losing another one.

As he stirred from his sleep the next morning, he felt a tiny hand stroking his face. It was little William.

"And how's my boy today?" Bill asked as he lifted little William up and sat him on his chest. "How's my little laddie?"

The boy giggled as Bill tickled him on the belly and then he wrapped his arms around his dad and gave him a big kiss on the cheek.

"That's my good boy," Bill said. "That's my Highland laddie."

When they finished breakfast, they walked out to Bill's old Ford. His stuff was already in the trunk. He was going to leave the car at the Eagletail ranch until he got back from the war. Richard was going to drive him to the C.P.R. station in Calgary.

He said goodbye to Sarah and gave her a big hug. Then he picked little William up and held him close to his face. As he held his son, his thoughts turned back to Helen and the good life they'd looked forward to with little William and Gordon. But, she was gone. And, now, he was leaving, too.

"You be a good wee boy," he said, holding back a tear. "I won't be gone for long and then we'll do all sorts of grand things together. You be good, my son."

Little William ran his finger down Bill's grizzled cheek and gave him a kiss. Bill hugged him hard and then passed him over to Sarah.

"Let's go," he said to Richard. "I've got a war to win."

About three weeks after Bill arrived in Winnipeg, he was sent with a detail to Camp Borden, just north of Toronto, to pick up some special equipment. He was only there for two days and arranged to meet Tom and Martha at Union Station before he boarded the train for the return trip to Winnipeg. They sat around a table at the cafeteria at the York Street side of the station while Bill had a roast beef sandwich and they all drank tea.

"And how have you been?" Tom asked. "How have things been going for you?"

"As good as can be expected," Bill replied, "under the circumstances. I thought I'd be based at the Currie Barracks with the Calgary Highlanders but, for some reason or other, they sent me over to Winnipeg. But it's okay. I'm doing fine with the Grenadiers. Mind you, it's clear they weren't expecting this war. This uniform I'm wearing is from the First World War and, believe it or not, my underwear is also First World War issue. More than twenty years old!"

"My God," Tom said. "Then they really were caught by surprise."

"All of us were," Bill said, "Peace in our time didn't last very long and, as one of the regulars told me, there's a great many more surprises lying ahead of us. You can count on that."

It had been more than three years since Tom and Bill had been together at the Morgan ranch. Tom had meant to go back for a visit but he never did find the time. He'd been quite busy establishing himself in the real estate business. Bill looked different. He was a lot thinner, almost gaunt. Haggard. Dark rings around his eyes. He just wasn't the same.

"Are you sure you're okay?" Tom asked. "You've lost a lot of weight."

"It's been a rough year," Bill replied. "With Helen dying like that, so suddenly. And then, having to split the boys up. I'm still not sure that was the right thing to do. I miss them both, I really, really do."

"But you've still got little William with you out there," Tom said.

"Aye, I do that. But, it takes me two hours return every time I go to see him. It's not the same as having him with me every day. Before this damned war broke out, I had a job lined up at a ranch only half an hour away from Big Thunder. But, damn it all, the war changed all that."

"He will be with you, Bill," Martha said. "We'll find a way for you to be with your wee boys, all the time."

"Thanks, Martha. That would be good. As soon as I'm back from the war, some changes are going to be made. Aye, I am going to be with my boys."

Gordon was curled up on Martha's lap. He was five months old now and he didn't have a clue who Bill was. As he looked at his baby son, Bill thought of the time they'd been apart, months of not being able to hold him.

"And how's my little fella doing?" Bill asked. "Is he okay?"

"Yes, Bill, he's fine. Absolutely fine," Martha replied. "And he's brought so much joy into our lives."

"I'm sure he does that," Bill said with a touch of sadness in his voice. "I'm sure he has. Can I hold him?"

Martha handed Gordon across the table and Bill took him in his arms. Gordon cried right away. He wanted to be back with his mother. And then he really started to holler.

"It's all right. I understand," Bill said as he handed the bawling baby back across the table to Martha's outstretched arms. "It's been a while. I can't expect him to remember me."

"Well, when you get back from the war, you'll have more than enough time for him to get to know you again," Tom said. "In fact, you might want to come and stay with us for a while. We've got lots of room at the house. You can bring little William with you."

"That would be nice," Bill said. "I'd like that. But, I'm not so sure it would work. William's getting nicely settled with Sarah and Richard and he's got Helen's mum and dad out there. I'm not sure moving him to Toronto would be a good idea."

"Well, if you change your mind, just let us know," Tom said. "We'd love to have you – and little William, too. I'm sure we could find you a good job. I've already contacted a few of the people I know and they say there'd be no problem at all."

"Thanks, Tom, I'll keep that in mind. I do appreciate your support. What about you, are you going to sign up?"

"Yes, I probably will," Tom replied. "I've got a few things to finish up first but, yes, I will be signing up, probably early next month."

Martha didn't like hearing that. War was a horrible thing and she didn't want to lose her Tom, or Bill either for that matter. "Well, let's hope this war is over and done with as quickly as possible," she said. "The sooner the better."

"I'm with you on that," Bill said. "The sooner the better."

"And what about little William?" Martha asked, in an effort to change the subject. "How is he doing at Big Thunder?"

"Oh, he's doing just fine," Bill replied. "I haven't been able to get back to see him since they moved me to Winnipeg but I understand he's doing just fine. He'll be fine with Sarah and Richard."

"Where did Richard sign up?" Tom asked.

"He didn't."

"But he's going to, right?" Tom asked with a puzzled look on his face.

"No, Tom, he's not. He's not going to sign up. He says that, under the treaties the Blackfoot signed with Queen Victoria, they don't have to serve. They don't have to fight."

"Won't fight Hitler?" Tom exclaimed. "Won't fight for Canada?"

"Under the treaties they signed, they don't have to serve in the Canadian military," Bill explained.

"The treaties were a long time ago. Things have changed since then. This is 1939."

"I know that, Tom," Bill said. "But Richard's quite definite about it. He says it's a white man's war. 'White men fighting white men' was the way he put it to me and he doesn't want any part of it."

"Well, to hell with him," Tom said. "To hell with him. If he won't fight Hitler, then to hell with him. We certainly don't want to have anything to do with him. What a disgrace he is."

With that, they finished their tea, walked to the train, and said their goodbyes. Bill and Tom exchanged a long, slow, hug. And then he was gone.

As they drove home after seeing Bill off, it was obvious that Tom was quite upset with what Bill had said about Richard not being willing to join the Army.

"It's not as if he was a pacifist – a conscientious objector as they call them. That's not why he won't fight Hitler," Tom said. "I could accept him not fighting if it was a matter of conscience. But it's not that. He's just, at least the way Bill puts it, not prepared to fight for Canada. Says he doesn't have to under the treaties they made with the Queen. That's unacceptable, Martha. Totally unacceptable. If you live in Canada, enjoy all the benefits of living in this great country, then you should be prepared to fight for it. It's as simple as that."

"But, Tom, you might be right about Richard. I'll grant you that. I don't like it any more than you do. But what about baby Gordon? He's got a brother out there. A brother he has a right to know about. We can't just have nothing whatsoever to do with them."

Tom thought about that for a moment. "You might have a point there, lass. But, right now, the wee babe's not even six months old yet. He doesn't need to know about them this very moment. There's lots of time for that. We'll see when Bill gets back from the war. Maybe he'll take us up on the offer to come and live with us here in Toronto. And bring little William with him. Gordie will know he has a brother soon enough."

CHAPTER

- 3 -

Tom was sent to the Christie Street Veteran's Hospital, just north of Dupont, for a medical check-up when he enlisted in the 48th Highlanders of Canada. He passed with flying colours and started his basic training.

The Highlanders were billeted at the Horse Palace on the grounds of the Canadian National Exhibition. They slept in box stalls – four men to a stall on two sets of bunks. The smell of the stalls reminded Tom of his days at his father's hill farm and of the time that he spent with Bill at the Morgan ranch out in Alberta. There was dust everywhere and Tom and his comrades soon developed deep, hacking, coughs.

When the weather was okay, they paraded on the Exhibition grounds. When it was raining, they used the dirt floor of the centre show ring which had been covered over with planks.

As he marched across the Exhibition grounds one morning, Tom remembered being on the midway with Martha the year before. He could still recall the smell of the onions from the busy hamburger stands. The popcorn and candy floss. People strolling by with stuffed pandas they'd won at the various games. A special feature that year was an experiment with sound and pictures where local radio broadcaster Gordon Sinclair interviewed boxing great Jack Dempsey at the Horticulture Building. The interview was carried live by wire to the Automotive Building where Tom and Martha along with hundreds of other visitors were able to watch as it was happening.

"How on earth can that be?" Tom gasped. "They're all the way over there in the Horticulture Building and we're seeing it just like we were there. It's amazing."

"It is that," Martha said in wonder. "How can that possibly be?"

At that point, an announcer came on live and told them what they'd just seen was a relatively new technology called television. A new way of carrying sounds and pictures that would one day become available in homes throughout Canada.

After the special demonstration, Martha and Tom took a ride on the ferris wheel where they got a great view of the islands and Lake Ontario and the lit-up skyline of Toronto at night. The thought that Canada might be plunged into war a year later had not crossed their minds.

At the big farewell dance at Maple Leaf Gardens on December 13, 1939, Martha broke down and cried, convinced she would never feel Tom's strong arms around her again. "You must come back," she said. "I couldn't bear to live without you."

"I'll be back, lass," he said as he held her close. "I'll be back. You can count on that."

Tom left by train for Halifax four days later along with just under eight hundred of his comrades and, when they got there, they boarded the *Reina del Pacifico* (Queen of the Pacific), the largest and fastest liner of her time, which had been pressed into service as a troop ship.

Martha received her first letter from Tom on January 28, 1940.

My dearest darling Martha,

I miss you oh so terribly much. To hold you in my arms again for just a minute would be heaven on earth. We'll be together soon, my darling, and for now we're just going to have to make the best of it.

We're at the Corunna Barracks at the British military base at Aldershot. It's about 40 miles southwest of London. Really damp and cold it is. All we have is a coal stove and the coal is rationed because of the war and there's never enough of it to last the night. We solved that problem by raiding the coal pile outside the cookhouse. No one's caught us yet so we're reasonably warm throughout the night.

The voyage from Halifax was dreadful. Our ship kept rolling from side to side and never did lie still. There were way too many of us for the size of it and we had to sleep and train in shifts. Everyone was sea sick. Some parts of the ship you wouldn't want to go near because of the smell.

They put together a fancy Christmas dinner for us, complete with lights and decorations. Can't tell you what the turkey was like because half of us were too sick to eat anything. It was a horrible nine days. When we arrived at Glasgow we were welcomed by the Pipes and Drums of the Toronto Scottish Regiment. That's when we learned they'd used dynamite for ballast on the ship. It's a good thing we didn't take a torpedo from a German U-boat on the way over. We'd have been blasted to smithereens.

I'm not at all sure what's going to happen next. They say we'll be doing a lot of training and helping out civilians trapped in buildings after the Germans bomb the place to bits. We're also going to spend time guarding the coast against a possible German invasion. We'll just have to take it one day at a time.

I hope you are well, my darling girl, and that little Gordie is coming along well. I'd so like to give him a big hug and a kiss. You, too, my beauty.

Can't help but wonder how Bill is doing. One of my mates has an uncle in the Winnipeg Grenadiers and he says they're still in Winnipeg. I'd like to know if that is true but Bill isn't much about writing letters.

Sorry we didn't have Christmas together. It would have been our first with Gordie. Instead, it's our first without each other.

Well, I've got to go now. We're running low on coal. Time to raid the cookhouse pile.

Take care, love of my life.

We'll be together soon.

Your loving husband,

Tom

Martha poured herself another cup of tea and read Tom's letter again. And again. She was glad he wasn't fighting on the front line. There was a lot less chance of him getting shot at the military base outside of London.

She went through to the bedroom and checked in on Gordon. He was fast asleep. As she tucked the blanket around him, she was glad she had him to help fill the big hole in her heart that had been created by Tom being away in the war. *You're all I've got now. Sleep well, my son.*

Tom was right. Bill didn't write much. Didn't write well either. His letters, when he did write them, were pretty hard to read. Scribbled more than written. He sent a couple of short letters from Winnipeg and then, at the end of June, he sent this one.

Dear Sarah

I thought we'd be going to Europe to fight the Germans but I've wound up on the sunny island of Jamaica down here in the Caribbean. We arrived at the end of May and they say we're going to be here for quite a while.

It's nice enough, palm trees green hills and all that stuff you see in the films. But it's really boring. We're in short pants and those pith helmets the British soldiers wear in India and Egypt, and Africa and places like that.

We're in an old British garrison with big walls and slit holes to fire cannons and rifles from and we check the manifests and crews of foreign cargo and passenger ships. I've heard there's some German and Italian prisoners of war on their way here and we'll have to keep an eye on them.

Most of the time we eat out in the open and the food's all right but I've had nothing like those delicious apple pies my dear Helen used to bake with those flaky crusts. Nothing at all like that. Oh I do miss her, Sarah. She was the whole world to me.

I hope you're all right and that wee Hughie's coping all right with the asthma. Please give Richard my very best wishes and say hello to Mum and Dad Dodginghorse for me. I know you're taking good care of little William and thank you and Richard from the bottom of my heart for opening your home to him. I'd love to hug him and hold him close again.

I'm starting a course in automobile mechanics and should be able to get my licence when I get home from the war. With a little bit of luck, I might even get a small garage of my own. I could call it MacArthur and Sons, General Repairs. That would be a good name for it. Then, when my boys are older, they could work with me at the garage. And then they'd run it between them when I settle down to enjoy my old age. Aye, MacArthur and Sons. That's what we'll call it.

I do wish I hadn't had to split them up like that especially with Tom and Martha living so far away in Toronto. It's a long way. Too far away. But that will all change when I get

*back from this damned war. My boys will be with me again
and we're going to do great things together. Lots of great things.*

*I really miss the animals and the smells of the ranch. I'd
love to be back on my horse rounding up the cattle in the
fall. Taking the near-frozen calves into Helen's cookhouse
so they could thaw out by the stove. But, that life's gone now.
Everything's changed.*

*Quite a few of my mates have come down with what they
call Dengue fever. They all of a sudden get pain behind their
eyes and in their muscles and joints. And then they break out
in a rash like the one you get with the measles. Some of them've
had mild bleeding from their mouth and nose. The high fever
goes away for a couple of days and then it's back like blazes.
Some passed out. Others had seizures.*

*I didn't get any of that or what they call fungus infections
some of my mates came down with.*

*Well that's it for now, Sarah dear. I've got sentry duty in 15
minutes and better be getting ready.*

Your friend and dear brother-in-law,

Bill MacArthur

Sarah sat down at the kitchen table the next morning and wrote a
reply to Bill's letter.

Dear Bill

*Richard and I thank you very much for your letter. It's
good to know no one's shooting at you down there in Jamaica.*

*Little William's doing quite well. He spends a lot of time
with Richard on the tractor and all that and Dad takes him*

*for lots of rides on his buggy. Mom's arthritis has been a lot
worse lately so she hasn't been able to do much with little
William or Hughie. But she loves them both to pieces.*

*We're sorry too that you've had to split the boys up but it
won't be for long. The war can't go on forever. You'll have the
boys with you again when you get home. Maybe you can get
a job at the ranch you were going to before the war started.
That would make it easier for you to get over here and see little
William. They might even let you stay over here at night.*

*Richard says to tell you hello and he hopes you understand
why this war is really none of his business. The way the treaties
were written we Indians don't have to fight in the white
men's wars.*

*But you're white Bill and we understand why you feel you
need to fight those Germans.*

Take good care of yourself and come home soon.

Your sister-in-law,

Sarah Eagletail

Not much happened during the year and four months Bill was in
Jamaica. In fact, like he told Sarah, he found garrison duty on a trop-
ical island that was never going to be attacked rather boring. He told
Martha the same thing in the couple of letters that he wrote to her to
see how she was doing and how Gordon was coming along.
Here's the letter Bill sent to Sarah at the end of November, 1941.

Dear Sarah

*I was within spitting distance of you in the middle of
October but, because of security and all that, I wasn't allowed
to get in touch with you.*

When we got back from Jamaica, I thought I'd have some time off so I could slip down to Toronto to see how my Gordie is doing and then come and see you and Richard and give little William the biggest hug of his life.

But all leave was cancelled and they packed us onto a train with no word about where we were going. As the train headed west, I was pretty sure we weren't going to the war in Europe.

We crossed the prairies just like me and Tom did in the boxcar with Lord Hanover's bulls and cows eight years ago. I've no idea where he is now. Probably fighting the Germans somewhere in Europe. I miss him, Sarah. I truly do.

And I was thinking about you and Richard, my wee William and your little Hughie as our train rolled through Calgary late one night. The sooner this war is over the better it'll be for all of us. Especially for me and my boys.

When we got to Vancouver they marched us onto a big passenger ship. There was just under 2,000 of us including the Royal Rifles of Canada, French boys from Quebec City who speak pretty good English. They still didn't give us so much as a hint about where we were going though. We were on a luxury liner from New Zealand called the Awatea. She's been fitted out with 20 mm Oerlikon cannons and there's a 4-inch naval gun on her stern. That's not much in the way of protection but we're being escorted by HMCS Prince Robert. She's the biggest and most heavily-armed ship in the whole Royal Canadian Navy.

After we got to Honolulu to take on water and supplies we headed back out to sea and it was only then they told us we were on our way to the British Crown colony of Hong Kong. The higher ups figure the Japanese Imperial Army is going to attack Hong Kong. It's our job to stop them. I never thought I'd be going to a place like Hong Kong. It's all Chinese.

We've just arrived here, after a brief stop in Manila down in the Philippines and now I'm getting ready to get off this ship and go fight the Japs. This will be our first time in battle. They say the Japs are a pretty tough bunch. We'll see.

Anyway, I'm off now Sarah. Someone's going to mail this letter for me after I'm on my way to wherever it is they're sending us to now.

Please give Richard my very best wishes and say hello to Mum and Dad Dodginghorse for me. And give my little fellow a great big bearhug and a kiss.

We'll all be together again when this damned war is finally over.

I've finished the course in mechanics and they say I'm pretty good at it. MacArthur and Sons, General Repairs here we come.

Your friend and dear brother-in-law,

Bill MacArthur

The Winnipeg Grenadiers were poorly equipped. Instead of the standard twenty-one armoured personnel carriers, they only had six. Twelve carrier trucks instead of the standard thirty-seven. A full supply of mortars but no shells. On top of that, they were a hundred and twenty men short of full operational strength. And, they had never been in combat.

Bill and his underequipped and undermanned comrades put themselves in position to defend the island of Hong Kong. The Royal Air Force base there had only five planes – two seaplanes and three torpedo bombers. The nearest fully-operational RAF base was in Kota Bharu, Malaya, more than twelve hundred miles away.

On December 8, 1941, Hong Kong local time, the Japanese attacked Pearl Harbor, Northern Malaya, the Philippines, Guam, Wake Island, and Hong Kong. Bill's unit was protecting the southwest and west side of the island, along with the 14th Punjab Regiment and the Royal Scots.

There was precious little in the way of naval support. With the exception of one British destroyer, several gunboats and a flotilla of torpedo boats, all other naval vessels, including two destroyers, had headed out to Singapore immediately after the Japanese attacked the United States' naval base at Pearl Harbor.

Artillery and air strikes from mainland China damaged or destroyed all of the planes at the RAF base in Hong Kong. The Japanese had the skies all to themselves and used it to rain down upon the Grenadiers and other Allied troops with bombs and machine guns.

To make matters even worse, none of their vehicles made it to Hong Kong. As there was not enough room on the *Awatea,* more than two hundred of their vehicles were loaded onto the freighter *Don Jose* and didn't leave Vancouver until eight days after the *Awatea.* However, after the Japanese attacked Pearl Harbor and the Philippines, arrangements were made for the Canadian vehicles to be used by the Americans to defend the Philippines.

On December 13th, a demand from the Japanese for the surrender of Hong Kong was categorically rejected. Japanese shelling and air strikes continued. Pillboxes along the north shore of the island were systematically bombed.

The Japanese repeated their demand for complete surrender on December 17th. It was refused despite the fact the situation for the Canadians and their allies was becoming increasingly hopeless. The Japanese, who outnumbered the Allies by a ratio of three to one, launched a major land offensive the following morning. Bill and his comrades were about to become the first Canadian soldiers in the Second World War to engage in combat – much of it hand-to-hand against the battle-hardened Japanese 38th Division. By this time, the Canadians and their allies on the island had run out of food and water and were almost out of ammunition.

On the evening of the 18th, more than five thousand Japanese soldiers attacked the northeast coast of Hong Kong Island. Bill was on the other side of the mountains. All he could see was the clouds lit up by the burning oil refinery.

On the morning of the next day, Bill followed Company Sergeant-Major John Robert Osborn on a bayonet charge up Mount Butler. He hadn't had a hot meal in several days and spent most nights without sleep.

Half-way up the hill, a young Japanese soldier lunged at him from behind a pile of sandbags. Bill's reflexes kicked in and he plunged his bayonet deep into the young soldier's belly. With an unforgettable look of disbelief on his face, the youngster clutched his bleeding belly and fell to the ground. That was Bill's first kill.

While the Canadians held the hill for three hours, their position became untenable because of the superior numbers of Japanese and heavy artillery fire from an unprotected flank. Bill and his comrades started a hasty retreat down the hill and made it to relative safety, with Sergeant-Major Osborn and a handful of men providing cover for them from higher up the mountain.

When it came time for the other soldiers to fall back, Osborn took on the enemy single-handedly while the remaining soldiers successfully rejoined Bill's company. And then, while running a gauntlet of heavy rifle and machine gun fire, Osborn assisted and directed stragglers to the new company position.

That afternoon, Bill's company was cut off from the rest of the battalion and was surrounded by the Japanese who were now close enough to the depression they were taking cover in to throw grenades at them. Osborn picked the grenades up, one by one, and threw them back at the Japanese. However, one grenade landed in a position where it was impossible for him to pick up and return in time. Osborn didn't hesitate. He shouted a warning to his comrades and threw himself on top of the grenade. The explosion killed him on the spot.

The sight of Osborn's bloody, blown-up, body, triggered something deep inside Bill and he broke from his position and ran towards the Japanese firing blindly with his blood-stained bayonet fixed on his rifle. He was shot in the chest and fell to his knees. The Japanese fired again and he slumped dead to the ground.

The Japanese rushed his comrades' position and took all of those who had survived prisoner. Later that day, the first of many atrocities perpetrated by the Japanese took place at Sai Wan Battery where they murdered twenty Allied gunners who had surrendered.

Bill was but one of approximately two hundred and ninety Canadian soldiers who were killed defending Hong Kong. Five hundred were wounded. He was buried along with his fallen comrades a long, long distance away from his father's little hill farm in the north of Scotland. And from William and Gordon.

As Tom had been listed as Bill's next of kin, the notice of his death was sent to their home in Toronto and Martha passed it on to Tom in one of her frequent letters. She had also sent a letter to Big Thunder informing Sarah of Bill's death. Tom was totally devastated when he got the news. He loved Bill very much and had looked forward to getting back together with him again when they were both home from the war. He'd been hoping Bill and his two boys would be living with him in Toronto.

Tom had some leave coming to him so he travelled north to Scotland by train to tell Father about Bill's death. Father was very saddened when Tom told him Bill had been killed by the Japanese. They were in the kitchen, having a cup of tea.

"Oh, dear me," his father sighed, "I didn't want your brother to end up in a place like that. They're all Chinese over there."

"They are that, Father. According to the notice from the Army, they've buried Bill there. I've heard, from some of my mates, that it was a fierce fight and the Allies didn't stand a chance. There were three times more Japanese and our boys had run out of food and water and had hardly any ammunition left. Some of my mates say they shouldn't have been there in the first place. It was a suicide mission. That's what they say."

Father looked out the window and said not a word for a full minute. Then he got up and gave Tom a hug. "Take care, my son," he whispered. "I don't want to lose you. You're all I've got now."

~

About a month after receiving the notice informing them that Bill had been killed during the defence of Hong Kong, Sarah wrote a letter to Martha.

Dear Martha

Richard and I were very sorry to hear about Bill being killed way over there in China. Helen loved him a great deal and they were so happy together. Richard and I are going to adopt little William and put him on the Band registry as William Eagletail. With his dad being killed and buried like that, we don't see any good in him keeping the name MacArthur. It would just raise eyebrows around here. Folks would be thinking he's not really ours. We think it would be better to make a clean break like they say and hope that you and Tom agree. We want to raise William as an Eagletail. Like a Blackfoot. One of our own.

You and Tom might feel like doing the same thing with little Gordon. Raise him like he was all white. The boys haven't even spent two months together since they were born. We don't see any point now, with Helen and Bill both dead and buried, for them to know about each other. We think it would be best to make a clean break of things. Not let them know they're brothers. Not now anyway. Not now when they're both too young to understand it all. About their parents being dead and all that. Maybe later, later when they're both old enough to understand. That's when, perhaps, we should let them know. But, right now, we don't see any good reason to let them know. They're both too young, William and Gordon are.

God bless you, Martha, and hold you in His loving arms.

Your friend,

Sarah Eagletail

Richard and Sarah treated young William as if he was their own son. As he wasn't even two when Bill went off to the war, William had no clear recollection of his father. He developed a strong bond with his adoptive parents, his grandfather and other relatives at Big Thunder.

Gordon and Vera Dodginghorse spent a lot of time with William. They could see Helen in his face and missed her terribly. At first, they didn't agree with Richard and Sarah about not telling William he had a brother who was being raised white in Toronto.

"He has a right to know," Gordon said to Richard at the supper table one night. "Little Gordon is his brother."

"But, Dad, they weren't even together for two months. If Gordon had stayed here longer – say for three or four years – I'd agree with you. They'd have become close and attached to one another. But that's not how it happened. Gordon was taken away to Toronto before he was even two months old. He has no connection to here."

"He's Helen's son," Gordon said. "My grandson. Named after me, he is. He has a right to know who we are."

"Oh, Dad, I don't want to get into an argument with you on this. I know how you feel. Exactly how you feel. I sometimes wonder myself if we're making the right decision by not letting the boys know they're brothers. But, then, I think about it and ask myself what possible good could come of it. I mean, the other little fellow is two thousand miles away. They're not going to be able to visit one another. Become part of one another's lives. I think it best that we leave things as they are. Not tell them."

Gordon struggled with the question but decided, in the end, that Richard was probably right. It might be better to leave things as they were.

Martha got a job at the Lakeview Small Arms Munitions factory out in Long Branch, where, along with hundreds of other women, she helped make thousands of guns, rifles, sniper rifles, pistols and machine guns. They worked as welders, tool and die makers, riveters and carpenters, toiling up to twelve hours a day for between twenty-five and fifty cents an hour. They wore full-length, short-sleeved, navy-blue coveralls with zippers down the front.

Martha and Sarah kept in touch for a while. Exchanging information on how William and Gordon were doing. But then, Martha was so tired and exhausted from being on her feet all day at the munitions factory that she simply hadn't the energy when she got home at night to answer Sarah's letters. Eventually, the letters stopped coming.

She usually dropped Gordon off at her parents' place for the day. They were only two blocks away. Often, when she would be working the night shift, he would stay overnight with his grandparents.

When Gordon was about three, his grandfather started taking him on imaginary journeys up the Congo River. He'd sit between Grandfather's stretched out legs on the couch and they would pretend it was a big canoe. They used big wooden soup spoons from Grandma's kitchen as paddles.

"There's one," Grandfather shouted excitedly. "There's a big croc. Shoot it, Gordie. Shoot it."

Gordon took careful aim with the old wooden yardstick he was using as a rifle and shot the crocodile right between the eyes.

"Watch out for the hippo, Gordie," Grandfather shouted. "Coming up on the right side."

Gordon finished the hippo off with three shots. It was quite a dangerous trip and they encountered all sorts of hazards along the way. Big snakes lunging down at them from overhanging branches. Hippos trying to overturn their canoe. Fortunately, for them, they always made it back home safe and sound.

When Gordon started school, Grandfather walked him there in the morning, picked him up at lunch time, and walked him home again in the afternoon. They became very close.

Grandma was different. She was not nearly as warm towards him as Grandfather was. It was almost as if she wished he wasn't there. She never, ever, hugged him. Or kissed him. He often wondered why that was so.

What Gordon didn't know was that his grandmother resented the amount of time Grandfather was spending on him. Taking him back and forth to the school. Taking him over to the Toronto Islands on the ferry. Playing with him in the backyard. As far as she was concerned, it would have been better if they had left him at the Blackfoot reserve out near Calgary. He was, after all, half Blackfoot.

"Who knows what sort of naked savages he's descended from?" she said to her husband one morning. "Martha should have left well enough alone. Especially with her being away at that factory all the time. I really don't see why they couldn't have left him out there with his own kind."

"You can't mean that," Angus replied. "He's just a wee boy. None of that stuff has anything to do with Gordie today. Come, lass, don't talk like that."

"I can't help it," Susan replied. "You spend more time with him than you do with me. You're with him all the time. And why? He's Tom's brother's child. What's he to us?"

"He's a wee boy whose dad was killed by the Japanese. Fighting for Canada, he was. He's a wee boy who needs all our love and support. That's what he is to us – to me, anyway."

"Speak for yourself," Susan said bitterly. "I still think they should have left him out there – out there with those Indians."

"He's half Scottish, for God's sake. Don't talk about him like that. And, now that Martha and Tom have adopted him as their own, he's one of ours. He's our grandson, Susan. That's the way it is. And that's the way it's going to stay."

When Martha got home from work late on the night of September 2, 1943, there was a letter from Tom with some mail on the floor inside the door.

My dearest darling Martha,

> *Please forgive me for the delay in writing to you. Since landing on the beach at Pachino on the southern tip of Sicily*

on July ninth, it's been a month of sheer hell. If I could've written sooner, my love, I would have.

About 700 of us from the 48th left Scotland at the end of June along with about 2,000 soldiers from other regiments. We were on a troop ship called HMT Derbyshire and had no idea where they were taking us. German U-boats patrol the seas all the time and three of the freighters in our big convoy were sunk by torpedoes just off the coast of Algeria. I thank God the Germans didn't sink the Derbyshire. Let's hope He stays by my side until I get home to your loving arms.

When we got to Sicily the sea was just awful. Rough like you wouldn't believe. That worked in our favour because the Germans believed, and rightly so if I may say so, that no one in their right mind would attempt a landing in that kind of weather. There was no resistance when we hit the beach. According to our company commander, there were more than 160,000 Allied troops involved in the landing at Sicily and about 3,000 ships and landing craft. We got stuck on a sandbar about 200 yards from shore and the ship with our kit bags got chased away by German planes. I've had no toothbrush or change of clothing for more than a month now. Ugh.

We're fighting our way north across Sicily along roads laid with mines through the scorching heat of the Sicilian summer. Darling, I've never in my life been in heat anything like this. They say it's 114 degrees in the shade. But there's no shade! Not a damned tree anywhere to be found. It's so hot, my dearest, you could fry eggs on my helmet. The sun hits you like a welder's torch. Its glare on my eyeballs is so painful I'm marching with my head down and my eyes shut. I count six paces and open them again for a moment. Some of my mates have collapsed from heat exhaustion. I could sure use a slab of Lake Simcoe ice right about now.

The dust here is something fierce. It's everywhere. All over us. It's awfully fine powdery stuff and comes up in clouds off the roads when we're marching. I've tried putting a hanky over my mouth but it doesn't help all that much. Me and my mates are choking and coughing all the time. Covered in dust and grime we are. And there's nowhere to wash it off. Water is as scarce as hen's teeth. We're always short of water to drink and don't even have enough to make tea let alone wash our filthy clothes. Our padre, bless his soul, is forever picking up melons along the road and giving us a slice now and then to help quench our thirst. From time to time, perhaps in answer to Padre East's prayers, we come across a donkey trough and splash ourselves to our hearts' content. But that doesn't happen often enough. Most of the time, my darling, we're thirsty and dirty.

We're plagued with malarial mosquitoes, fleas and scorpions all along the way. On top of that, dearest Martha, there's the non-stop din of the shelling and the bombing and the bloody sight of comrades lying dead and wounded at my side. The Italian soldiers are no threat at all. Their hearts aren't in this war and most of them wish that Benito Mussolini, who calls himself First Marshall of the Empire, had never gotten them involved in it in the first place. Most of them surrender without putting up a fight. Now the Germans are a different proposition altogether. Our company commander has been told Hitler stocked Sicily with two crack divisions – the 15th Panzer Grenadiers and the Hermann Goering Panzer – and he says there's about 60,000 of them. They're tough as nails, believe me. Wicked fighters they are. But, my darling, whatever they throw at us we hurl back twice as hard.

Because the Germans were here long before us they've had months to plan and work things to their advantage. Their artillery, mortar and machine guns are sighted on the narrowest sections of the roads. That lets them fire at will from a distance. And the mountainous terrain and winding roads here give Jerry an even bigger advantage. The odds are in his favour but we will beat him. The 48ᵗʰ will do that. We've got the Dileas spirit. I didn't know what the English words for the regiment's Gaelic motto "Dileas gu brath" were but I've been told it means Faithful Forever. That's our regiment's heart, lungs and guts. Faithful forever. That's our motto. That's what makes the 48ᵗʰ tick. That's how we act and think. That's why we fight as well as we do. If Jerry wanted to pick a fight he'd have been better off to pick it with someone other than the 48ᵗʰ Highlanders of Canada.

We've had to climb mountain cliffs and rock-faced terraces the Germans thought we'd never scale. We get up them clinging hands-on to the rock and often standing on the other mate's shoulders. But we do get up them, always at night, and then when dawn breaks we hit the surprised Germans with everything we've got.

Who'd have thought I'd wind up here in a mess like this? I could be shot dead any day now or crushed to smithereens by a German tank. And then I'd be dead and buried – buried like Bill all the way over there in China. Gosh, Martha, but I miss him. It's not right for him to be dead like that. He was too young, way too young. But, then again, if he was still with us, I wouldn't have my Gordie, my wee Highland laddie. I wonder what he's doing right about now. You're six hours behind us. He's probably out shopping with you. God but I miss you so. I'd love to hold you in my arms right now. To feel you close to me.

Pray for me darling. It's a rough spot I'm in over here in the land of Caesar.

Love you to bits.

Your loving husband,

Tom

CHAPTER
- 4 -

When Martha opened the letter, she saw that it was dated October 17, 1943.

My dearest darling Martha,

We got across the Strait of Messina and over to mainland Italy on the morning of September third. That's the very day Italy formally surrendered. Hitler has pulled back his defences to a winter line that stretches east from the west coast just north of Naples through the Appenines and the high, rugged, centre of Italy to the deep-water port of Ortona on the Adriatic. At least that's what our commanding officer told us.

We're fighting our way north toward Naples. Believe me, Martha darling, it isn't easy. Right now, we've got no mortars or anti-tank weapons. If the Germans have tanks, they'll have no trouble at all pushing us back. Although I'm not too worried about that. Jerry prefers to fire at us from the safety of caves in the hills. Too scared to come out in the open and fight us like men.

I've met a really interesting chap by the name of Alex Montour. He's a Mohawk from the Six Nations reserve just south of Brantford. I told him Bill had married a Blackfoot girl out in Alberta and that he was killed by the Japanese in

Hong Kong. I also told him Richard wouldn't fight Hitler because the treaties they signed with the Queen said Indians don't have to fight in the Canadian army.

Alex said that's nonsense. The Mohawks have always fought alongside the British. They've even got what they call Her Majesty's Chapel of the Mohawks at his reserve, complete with a bible given to his people by Queen Anne herself when they were still living in the Mohawk Valley down in New York. It's the oldest Protestant church in Ontario. Alex says the chapel's got a silver communion service and some prayer books the Queen gave them.

He says it sounds to him that Richard is just too scared to sign up. I think he's right about that. Alex's dad was killed at Vimy Ridge back in the First World War and his Uncle Clarence lost both his legs below the knee at Amiens. He says lots of his people have bled and died for Canada and he hopes he's not going to be one of them. According to Alex, there's monuments to Indians who died in the First World War at reserves all across Canada.

So, Martha, it looks to me like Bill's brother-in-law is the exception that proves the rule. He's just too damned scared to fight Hitler. Back when the Mohawks were living in the Mohawk Valley down in New York, Alex says, they fought on the British side when the Americans started their War of Independence. They were under the command of a Captain Joseph Brant who, Alex says, was a famous Mohawk chief at that time.

Alex says Brant had a big farm of about 80 acres near a Mohawk town on the south shore of the Mohawk River. He also owned the best house in town and had a small store. Alex says there was nothing savage about him. Nothing savage at all. In fact, he wore nicely-tailored English suits. On top of that, he was a Mason and King George the Third himself gave him his ritual apron. What do you think of that, Martha?

It sounds like the Mohawks got the short end of the stick after the war ended. Their rights were completely ignored and all of the sovereign territory of the Six Nations in the United States was handed over to the Americans. All of the promises the British made in order to get them to fight on their side went up in smoke. Alex says they, sort of, made up for it by agreeing to give them land in Ontario. They got a tract six miles deep on both sides of the Grand River. That's where Brant had a good-sized farm with mixed crops, cattle, sheep, hogs, and stuff like that. He built a fancy two-storey house and staffed it with about twenty-two white and negro servants and slaves. Yes, Martha, the Mohawk chief actually had slaves.

Later, Alex told me, in 1812, when the Americans crossed the Niagara River and attacked the British at Queenston Heights, the Mohawks fought alongside Sir Isaac Brock. He was killed there. There was more than a hundred Mohawk warriors fighting on his side under the command of a Mohawk chief by the name of Captain John Norton. Alex says the British really appreciated the role the Mohawks played in that battle. When the American reinforcements heard the battle cries of the Mohawk warriors, they refused to cross to the Canadian side of the river. They scared the daylights out of them. I suppose they didn't like the idea of being scalped alive.

Alex says if it hadn't been for the Mohawks, the British would have lost that battle. Lost the whole War of 1812. So it isn't true that the Indians won't fight for Canada. Richard is hiding behind a lie. Hearing what Alex had to say about the Mohawks fighting alongside the British makes me even more convinced that we should have nothing at all to do with him and those people out there at that Indian reservation. And I don't want Gordon to have anything to do with them either.

He may be half Blackfoot but we're going to raise him white just like his father. Just like my Bill.

That's it for now, lass. I'm going to try and get some sleep tonight.

Love you to pieces.

Your loving husband,

Tom

Here's the letter Tom wrote on January 1, 1944.

My dearest darling Martha,

I'm writing this from Ortona on the edge of the Adriatic. Like most of the towns we've been to in Italy it's quite medieval. The castle is built of stone and has a great view of the deep-water port that makes Ortona a strategic location.

On the night of December 23, we were sneaking single file through the German lines just west of here. It was our job to threaten the German's rear position and block their only exit road from Ortona.

We were on a goat path in the dark and rain, each of us holding the hand of the next. We managed to get about 1,300 yards behind the German lines without being detected and dug in an all around defence. But then, my darling girl, on the morning of the next day, the Germans discovered where we were. They closed the ring and made our lives miserable for the next two days with sniping, shelling and the firing of machine guns and self-propelled guns. It was hell on earth.

Huddled with my mates in a muddy slit trench, I wished desperately that the pounding din of the guns would stop.

My ears felt like they were about to split. The cold, non-stop, winter rains had drenched me to the skin and turned the ground at my feet into a messy quagmire. And then I tensed up in anticipation of the fierce German paratroopers who were about to descend upon us in full force.

Thank God for this, the radio link with the artillery at the rear held and our gunners managed to keep the paratroopers at bay.

Our commanding officer's batman is a Private John Crockford. He decided that, despite having German troops all around us, we should celebrate Christmas with a cake made from cornmeal, powdered milk and chocolate. He used his finger to trace the words "Merry Christmas" in the icing. I must say that added a cheerful note to a day of rain and shelling.

As I munched on the cake, I remembered the wonderful trifle puddings my Mum used to make at Christmas with layers of custard, sponge cake, tinned fruit cocktail, and a wonderful topping of whipped cream with red maraschino cherries to set if all off. There was always a hint, just a hint, mind you, of sherry or port which added to the delightful taste of Mum's trifle.

And then I realized this was my fifth Christmas away from you and I've never celebrated so much as one Christmas with Gordon. Oh, Lassie, I miss you so. What I'd give to be with you now. With you and wee Gordie. But, my darling, this war surely can't go on forever. There has to be an end to it somewhere. There just has to be.

On Boxing Day, we found ourselves isolated and alone. Because of the muddy conditions brought on by the unrelenting rain, tanks couldn't get through to provide us with cover and support. The German attack began at 10 a.m. sharp.

Shelling and machine-gun fire, which was designed to keep us in the slit trenches, was followed by an attempt to rush our defences with two strong groups linked by skirmishers. After 3 days in place, we knew every inch of ground and had sited our Bren guns to cover all approaches.

With our supplies partially replenished, we got into fierce hand-to-hand fighting. The Germans attacked from all sides but we succeeded in beating off their first three attacks.

Though Jerry suffered heavily, he kept coming, infiltrating between the positions and forcing hand-to-hand clashes. Our artillery forward observation officer used a single gun to ensure accuracy and brought its fire down within yards of our position. The enemy withdrew, regrouped and tried again, but we Highlanders held our ground.

Funny how your head works when you're in battle. Right after machine gun bullets riddled the boards above my head, my thoughts turned to Bill, buried with fellow soldiers from the Winnipeg Grenadiers at the cemetery in Hong Kong. I'm going to wind up just like Bill, I thought. Dead. Dead and buried. Him in Hong Kong and me over here in the land of Caesar.

And then I thought about the first time I saw you behind the lunch counter at Murray's Restaurant. When will I see you again, my darling? When will I hold you in my arms? At this rate, that might be never. Never again. And what about wee Gordie? Am I going to get a chance to watch the wee fellow grow up? Grow up to be a man? Or, God help me, is this all there is? Is this my last day? All that went through my mind.

A gradual drop in temperature throughout the day began to solve the mud problem and our battalion intelligence officer volunteered to sneak back through the enemy lines to get tank support and lead them forward. Three of the four tanks made it through just in time to help overwhelm a company of enemy paratroopers forming up for yet another attack. We used the tanks to keep Jerry off balance. They'd charge into his lines and shoot them up. We'd race in right behind them and create all sorts of hell. Then we'd withdraw and do it all over again to another German position.

And then, on the night of December 27, it was all over. All of a sudden the enemy just simply disappeared. Cleared out. We'd won. It was a long and bloody battle but, my darling girl, the Highlanders won.

I don't know where we're off to now. But I do know that the soldiers of the 48th are the best of the best and I'm truly proud to serve with them.

And now darling I'm going to try and get some sleep. I haven't had a continuous hour of sleep in the last four days. I'm so sleepy I just want to curl up in your arms and get some rest.

Happy New Year, love of my life.

Your loving husband,

Tom

❧

The next letter was from Rome and it was dated June 4, 1944.

My dearest darling Martha,

You're not going to believe this. We're sitting on our butts on the outskirts of Rome so the Americans can march victorious into the eternal city and hog all the glory. It's their pictures you'll see in the newspapers and on the newsreels. According to my dear friend Alex Montour, the American general who's the Allied Commander in Italy has threatened to shoot any Canadian who dares show his face in Rome.

That's pretty insulting considering that they wouldn't have had a hope in hell of marching into Rome if the Highlanders hadn't broken through the Hitler Line. You might have read something about the Hitler Line in one of the newspapers. It stretched west from Monte Cassino and blocked access to the Liri Valley. I've heard there was more than 8,000 Germans protecting it. They had steel and concrete strong points, pillboxes, sunken gun emplacements, mine fields, a tank ditch and wide lines of barbed wire. There was undetectable camouflage concealing 75 mm anti-tank guns. It was really something. Something fearful.

Anyway, one afternoon when we were camped near the Liri River our commanding officer was told that the 48th, and the 48th alone, was to break through the Hitler Line at a point just west of Monte Cassino. I've been told our CO thought that was one of the most ridiculous suggestions of all time. On top of that, he was given only four hours to prepare his battle plan and pass orders to his troops. He was convinced it was a suicide mission. In fact, he was so opposed to placing us in such a foolhardy position that he asked to be relieved of his command. The higher ups turned a deaf ear to that and said the order was final – the 48th would have to go it alone. That's what I've been told, dearest Martha.

To show you how poorly planned this mission was, Martha, we had no forward observation officers to tell the artillery where to fire. And the engineers hadn't had time to do a reconnaissance and identify safe paths for us to get through the minefields. Our CO decided that, under the circumstances, surprise was to be the order of the day. He ordered the artillery not to fire while the 48th advanced – even though that meant *there would be no artillery shelling to soften up the enemy in advance of our attack.*

And so, in we went. Into the valley of death. While the Germans couldn't see us advancing through gullies and the high grain of the spring crops, they did see the tanks bringing up the rear and opened fire on them. Not one tank survived. But, we got through. Pushed through into the Hitler Line. Just the 48th. Did it on our own.

We still weren't in the clear, though. Not by a long shot. The bridgehead we'd created on the German side of the line was so narrow and cramped it left us exposed to counterfire from three Nebelwerfers which were shelling us. But, not for long. One of our officers got on the line to the artillery in the rear and, under his direction, the 5.5s took them all out.

Even at that, we were still surrounded on three sides by Germans and had no tank support. On the other side of the line from the other Allied troops, we dug in for the night further up the slope.

At dawn the next morning, a squadron of tanks arrived to give us support as we charged up the slope under fierce enemy fire. A well-dug-in German anti-tank gun wreaked havoc on the tanks. But, once again, the Allied artillery in the rear took it out.

When we got to the ridge near the village of Pontecorvo in the middle of the Hitler Line, we moved forward yard by yard, house by house. The 48th was the first battalion to break Hitler's strongest position. We beat him. Beat him bad. We have Jerry on the run. There's dead Germans lying all over the place. The stench of death is just awful. We're determined to kill them capture them or kick them into the sea so they'll all drown.

*After a march of about four days, we were within forty
miles of Rome. Any day now, we were going to honour our
months of blood sweat and death by marching victorious
into Rome with fellow soldiers from Britain, Australia, New
Zealand and the United States. However, that was not to be.*

*The American general ordered us to stand in our place
so he could lead his troops into Rome without us. We sure
didn't like that. Not after us being the ones who broke Hitler's
famous line of defence. Must say I like the British a lot better
than the Americans. General Monty Montgomery would
never have pulled off a dishonourable stunt like that.
We learned later that the main reason the higher ups
decided we should be the ones to breach the Hitler Line was
because they thought we were the only ones who could do it.
I've heard, Martha, that we've built up quite a reputation
with the Germans. We've completed every objective on time
and have given Jerry a real run for his money. No one wants
to see the 48th coming at them with guns blazing.*

Your loving husband,

Tom

Martha received a letter from a military hospital in Amsterdam. It
was dated June 5, 1945.

My dearest darling Martha,

*I'm writing from a military hospital in Amsterdam where
they tried unsuccessfully to save my left eye. Next time you see
me I'll be wearing a black patch over the empty socket. I thank
God that's all I lost. Some of my mates have lost arms, legs and,
for all too many, their very lives. So, in that way, I'm a pretty
lucky bloke – especially with a wonderful wife like you to go
home to.*

*They say I'll be here for another few days and then they'll
transfer me to a hospital in London. The doctor says that will
only be for a short while and then I'll be on my way home to
you and wee Gordie. I can't believe he's actually six now. It's
been a long time my darling. Too long.*

*We got to Holland by way of a ship from Italy to Marseilles
and they took us by truck through France and Belgium. That's
where we passed cemeteries where 48th Highlanders and other
Canadian soldiers killed in German gas attacks during the
First World War are buried.*

*We crossed the Ijssel River in amphibious tanks that they
call Buffaloes. We really appreciated the fact that we were
going to have support from the 1st Hussars of London, not
England but Ontario, with their battle-tested Shermans.*

*The thunder of our twenty-five-pounders and rocket
projectors started almost exactly at 10:00 a.m. The ground
beneath me shook and trembled in front of us as the Allied
guns spewed their deadly missiles.*

*Funny, in the middle of all that, I thought about the fun I
used to have with Bill playing marbles outside Father's house.
I liked the way the different colours reflected the sun and how
smooth and round they felt. We'd draw circles in the dirt and
take turns knocking each other's marbles out of the ring. I
really miss Bill, Martha. Miss him terribly. Marbles was a lot
more fun than this.*

*Our company was under the command of Major George
Beal, a great soldier and fine leader. We got pinned down
under heavy fire from 6 machine guns and three 72 ton
self-propelled 75 mm assault guns. Despite the intensity of
the enemy fire, Major Beal crawled forward about 200 yards
to assess the situation. He radioed directions so our artillery*

could destroy the big German guns and lay down smoke to enable the 48ᵗʰ to outflank the machine guns.

A couple of days after that, we ran into more nests of machine guns firing at us from our flank. This time Major Beal told us to "Fix bayonets" and led two platoons of us on a charge over 160 yards straight toward the enemy machine gun nests. We killed 7 and captured 18 at a loss of 3 of our own, including Alex Montour, who was shot between the eyes. Alex was a good friend, probably my best friend, and I will miss him dearly. I suppose he's off to what his people call the happy hunting ground.

And then it happened. Just as we were approaching the outskirts of Apeldoorn, shrapnel from a German mortar slammed into my face and forced me to the ground. After the field medics checked me over, I was transferred to a military hospital in Amsterdam. They tried surgery but they couldn't save my left eye.

A fine Dutch military liaison officer by the name of Captain Jack Dykstra has kept me up to date on the developments at the front.

After I was wounded at Apeldoorn, he told me during one of his early visits, our regiment swept through the north and west sections of the city ready to demolish any Germans in their path. But, my darling girl, the Germans had fled the city. Cleared out completely.

Captain Dykstra says doors of houses and apartment buildings burst open and thousands of his fellow citizens embraced their liberators with great joy. There was much weeping and cheering as they celebrated the end of the German occupation of Holland. Five years of grief and misery under the heel of the Nazi boot was finally over. I played a small part in that and I'm damned proud of it and grateful to be alive.

Not everyone was in a cheerful mood. Captain Dykstra says some citizens attacked fellow Dutchmen because they were suspected of collaborating with the Germans and hauled them off to jail. They also attacked women who were believed to have slept with the enemy, held them down and shaved their heads.

According to Captain Dykstra, the 48th Highlanders pushed on, ready to chase Jerry all the way back to his own country. However, it would appear, the Germans had had enough of us. The German commander called for a truce and said he would allow the Allies to take supplies of food and other essentials to the starving Dutch citizens – but, on one condition. The condition was that they would only allow the relief supplies to get through if the Canadians would back off and stop hunting them down. We must have made quite an impression on Jerry.

So that's it my darling. The war's over and I'm coming home as soon as I get out of the hospital in London. Shouldn't be too long. We'll be together again soon.

Love you to pieces.

Your loving husband,

Tom

          ~

When Tom boarded the passenger ship at Southampton for the voyage back to Canada, the empty socket of his left eye was covered with a black patch. Rolling a cigarette at the rail on the stern of the ship halfway across the Atlantic, he thought back to the time, twelve years earlier, when he crossed the ocean for the first time with Bill and Lord Hanover's prize cattle. Things had changed. Dramatically.

He thought about their time together at Stafford's dairy ranch, washing the cows' tails and hanging them up on the hooks so they wouldn't touch the piss and shit in the concrete gutter. Studying for the real estate course in the bunkhouse at the Morgan ranch while Bill and the other men were out partying it up at the Noble Hotel in Calgary. And then there was that first time Martha took his order at the lunch counter at Murray's Restaurant. *God but I need to see her. To hold my sweet, bonnie, lassie in my arms again. It's going to be so good to be home.*

Martha and Gordon were at Union Station waiting for Tom's train to arrive from Montreal. Gordon, who was now six, wasn't too sure what to expect. He'd seen the pictures Tom mailed to Martha: eating a melon at the side of a dusty road near Assoro; looking down the sights on the barrel of his rifle from behind the wall of a bombed out church in Regalbuto; marching past a tulip field in Holland alongside a British tank. He'd seen the pictures but hadn't connected with them. He was only seven months old when Tom left for the war. They had never bonded.

Tears welled up in Martha's eyes when she saw Tom striding down the railway platform towards them. He was in full battledress. The distinctive 48th Highlanders' Glengarry cap with the red and white checkerboard band and regimental badge was cocked to the right side of his head. He caught her in his arms and kissed her on the mouth. It was so good to feel her body up against his for the first time in six long years.

Gordon looked up at this strange man with the black patch over his left eye kissing his mum and wasn't too sure what to make of it. He'd never seen his mum kiss anyone like that before.

"This is your dad," Martha said, as Tom kneeled down and held his arms open towards Gordon.

Gordon stepped forward uncertainly and then he felt Tom's big arms circling around him. Tom gave him a big hug and kissed him affectionately on the forehead. He was a big man. Even with Tom kneeling down, Gordon felt tiny as a mouse crouching before an elephant. Tom sensed the tentativeness of the hug Gordon gave him. They had a lot of catching up to do.

With the war in Europe coming to an end, Tom received an honourable discharge, got back into the real estate business and quickly picked up where he left off. Martha quit her job at the munitions factory and became a stay-at-home wife and mother.

On October 1, 1945, Tom took Martha and Gordon down to Union Station where they joined thousands of Torontonians in the rain and welcomed the 48th Highlanders home. They were lined, five-people deep, in front of the station and across the road at the Royal York Hotel on the north side of Front Street.

The Pipes and Drums of the 48th, with the white tassels swinging from their black sporrans, marched proudly down the middle of the streetcar tracks with Lieutenant-Colonel J.R.O. Counsell leading his troops three abreast.

Tom had mixed feelings as he watched his comrades marching in the rain. He would like to have been with them to celebrate the victorious end in Holland, but a one-eyed soldier wasn't much use on the front line. Still, it had been so good to get back to Martha and Gordon.

The Highlanders marched east along Front and then up Yonge to Queen Street with crowds cheering and hundreds of Union Jacks hanging from stores and buildings along the route. They went west on Queen and then up University Avenue to the Armouries.

After Mayor Robert Hood Saunders and the other dignitaries gave their speeches praising the manner in which the 48th had done Canada proud, Lieutenant-Colonel Counsell said a few words in response. Then he looked out at the hundreds of brave soldiers lined up before him in the rain and barked "Dis-miss" for the last time. They saluted him, broke rank, and went home to their families. It had been a long and costly six years.

Tom did quite well selling real estate but did not go as far as some of his associates felt he could have. Two or three times in the course of his career, he was offered positions that paid a lot more than he was getting. But that would have cut into the time he wanted to spend with Martha and Gordon. He was not prepared to make that sacrifice. With Tom, their time together as a family always came first. When other real estate agents were out closing deals on the weekends, he was with Martha and Gordon visiting the Riverdale Zoo, the Royal Ontario Museum, or the Islands.

They never missed the Highland Games at Fergus in the fall or the other gatherings where people celebrated their Scottish heritage. Their attendance was always as a family. The sight of the burly Scots in their kilts tossing the cabers, as big as telephone poles, impressed Gordon greatly. The skirl of the bagpipes sent shivers up and down his spine.

Gordon's parents took him for a visit to Scotland in the summer of his twelfth year. He felt truly at home when they arrived at his grandfather's small farm southeast of Inverness. As his father's rented car made its way slowly up the winding dirt road to the main buildings, Gordon looked down at the sheep and the cattle grazing in the meadows on the east side of the river and thought about how great it would be to be down there walking among them.

Two days after they arrived at the farm, Gordon was walking by his grandfather's side with sacks of grain for the sheep up on the mountain piled on the cart behind the horse. His nose twitched at the smell of the sheep's wool and the clear, heather-scented, Highland air.

They came across a young ewe who refused to accept her newborn lamb. Every time the little thing tried to suck on her teat, she kicked it away. It followed her around, baa baa baaing away like crazy. But she wouldn't let it near her.

"She doesn't recognize it as her own," Grandfather said. "This is her first lamb. She doesn't know what to do with it."

Grandfather whistled to the Border Collie and got it to position itself between the ewe and her lamb. The ewe looked at the Collie and then at the lamb. Right away, like she had been struck by lightning, something clicked inside her head and she realized, instinctively, that this was her lamb and it was in danger. She lowered her head and charged at the dog.

"Now she knows. Now she knows what to do," Grandfather said as he whistled for the dog to give way and come back to his side. In a matter of seconds, the lamb was contentedly sucking away on its mother's teat.

Gordon enjoyed being with his grandfather. Kneeling beside him as he set the snares on the rabbit runs in the bottom pasture. Feeling the cow's warm flank as he pressed his forehead against it, bucket between his knees, as Grandfather patiently showed him how to pull on her teats and make the milk flow. Hearing the bawling sound of the young calves as they licked his hand in search of the salt on the surface of his skin.

As they stretched out on the heather beside a mountain stream on a warm summer afternoon, Grandfather shared his thermos flask of tea and jam sandwiches with Gordon. The bread had a delightful, fresh-baked, taste to it and the jam was made from fresh blueberries.

Gordon sensed, in that summer of his twelfth year, that his grandfather had never been fully reconciled to his sons' decision to go to Canada. He could see in his eyes and in the hard set of his mouth on his deeply-lined face that the years without their support had been a burden. If they had stayed, his tough, stocky, body would not have been as tired and bent. And he wouldn't have been so lonely.

Gordon wished that the MacArthur chain had not been broken. He'd like to have grown up on his grandfather's back-breaking hill farm instead of in a middle-class neighborhood in Toronto. The big city couldn't match the smell and the feel of the animals and all of the other wonderful things at his grandfather's place. He wanted to stay in Scotland with his grandfather.

He felt as if he had been born there centuries earlier. He felt a peculiar kinship with the rough, pungent, smell of the peat bog, the sweet purple heather on the hillsides and the early-morning mist on the moor. Something about the land and the people told him – deep down in his soul – that this one place of all the places on earth was his place. His Scottish homeland.

Early one evening, as he reluctantly packed his things for the long journey back to Canada, he listened to a piper alone in the valley facing the furnace glow of the sunset and piping in the night with *The Skye Boat Song*. The plaintive skirl of the bagpipes stirred Gordon's young soul and made him terribly, terribly, proud of his Scottish heritage.

CHAPTER
- 5 -

Richard took little William to the rodeos and pow wows that were held across southern Alberta every summer. He was one of the best bronco riders in the area. He was also an accomplished bear dancer. William got quite a thrill the first time he saw his dad ride a wild bronco at the rodeo in Cochrane. It did everything it could to get Richard off its back but he held on for the full eight seconds.

In November of the year William turned fourteen, his father took him hunting whitetail deer. William was riding the Pinto his father gave him for his thirteenth birthday and his dad had the big Appaloosa. Their tent, sleeping bags and other stuff were on the back of the old Clydesdale. They had followed a wide right-of-way that had been cut between the trees for the power lines running up the side of Thunder Mountain and could see for miles to the east. It was pretty cold. They were wearing wolfskin jackets and Kodiak boots.

"All of that belonged to us," Richard said as they sat beside the campfire eating their lunch of soup and ham sandwiches. William followed his father's hand as he traced a line in the clear blue sky. "The Blackfoot owned everything as far as the eye could see. You should have been here back then, Willie. We were the richest and most powerful tribe on the prairies. No one dared set foot on our territory, not the Crees, not the Assiniboine, not anyone. This was all Blackfoot territory and most people respected that. Those who didn't, didn't live long enough to get into an argument with us about it.

"I did a lot of reading about those times. The Minister for the Interior back then, Mills his name was, David Mills, wrote a report once in which he described us as 'the most warlike and intelligent but intractable bands of the North-West.' Now, at that time, Willie, we were friendly with the whites. There was more than enough land for everyone and we had no reason to pick a quarrel with them. But, that doesn't mean this wasn't Blackfoot territory. The Crees and the other tribes kept trying to come in from over there in Saskatchewan and we drove them back every time. Every damned time. This was good land and everyone wanted a piece of our territory."

He paused for a moment, put some tobacco in his corncob pipe, and lit it up. "You should have seen the buffalo in those days. Sometimes, the herds were three miles wide and two miles deep. They just simply blanketed the prairies. Big brown clouds of them. And that's why we lived so well. The buffalo provided everything we needed. The meat we ate, the clothes we wore, the covering for our lodges. The Creator put the buffalo here for our use and they provided us with everything we needed."

He stopped for a moment, dumped some of the ash from his pipe, took another swallow of tea and then looked down at the flat, tree-bare, prairie spread out before them. A hawk was circling in the sky over to their right, looking for rabbits in the clearings on the side of the mountain. Horses and cattle were grazing on both sides of the Big Thunder River. Cars and trucks were toing and froing on the main highway. They could see Calgary in the distance, spreading out from both sides of the Bow River.

"When I say we lived well, I really mean it. Your great-great-grand-father had four wives and one hundred horses. He was a Blackfoot chief. My grandfather was a chief and so was my dad. He was killed by a drunk driver just a few years before we had you, Willie. You would have liked my dad. Anyway, they were all chiefs and, before the white men came, we lived a good life. A very good life. But then everything changed. Changed overnight. In no time at all, our buffalo herds were reduced to about half of what they had been and then, by the late 1800s, they were gone altogether. Wiped out completely."

He puffed on his pipe and put another branch on the fire. "Not only did they wipe out the buffalo, they pretty near wiped us out as well. I've heard there was more than ten thousand Blackfoot on the Canadian side of the border back around 1860 and then our population was cut in half by the white man's diseases – the smallpox and the tuberculosis. We were pretty near killed off. All of us.

"And then there was the firewater the American traders brought up from the south. They brought it across the Montana border by the wagon load. Now, Willie, some people believe firewater was just whisky. Just whisky and that we Indians couldn't hold our liquor. But it was more than that, Son, a lot more than that. That stuff they call firewater was actually a highly addictive brew made with alcohol, chewing tobacco, pain killer, molasses, and, believe this, red ink. It sure as hell wasn't whisky. And, I regret to say, our people couldn't get enough of the damned stuff. It was as addictive as sin.

"At first it wasn't too bad. Our people traded their buffalo hides and their horses for the stuff. But then they became hooked on it and, before you knew it, they were practically giving away their horses and hides by the hundreds in order to get it. And, I regret this also, all too many of them wound up drunk as skunks for days at a time. They just couldn't get enough of that devil's brew. You'd find our people frozen to death at the side of the trail. Others were shot dead, women and children, too, by the American traders when they got into an argument about the stuff. It was awful, Willie. Just simply awful."

He put a fresh load of tobacco in his pipe, lit it, and carried on. "The social order broke down completely. People started killing one another and, before you knew it, they were separated into different little camps, afraid to come together like they used to. I remember reading a letter once from a Catholic priest, Father Scollen his name was. The letter was in an old book we had at the school library. He said it was really painful for him to watch what had once been the richest tribe of all the Indians on the prairies running around in rags and not having any horses or guns. That firewater, as they called it, ruined us. Just simply ruined us …"

Richard stopped speaking and pointed down the mountain. "Down there, Willie, down there on the left side. See that young buck down there?"

William looked down the mountain and saw the whitetail buck with a good set of antlers grazing in a clearing that was covered with light snow about four hundred yards farther down.

"Let's get him, Willie. Let's bring that young buck home to your mother. She'll make quite a few meals out of that one."

They grabbed their 30-30 Winchester rifles, slipped into the woods, and headed slowly down the mountain toward the unsuspecting deer. William followed his father through the trees and they got to within a hundred yards. As the wind was coming from the east, the young buck hadn't picked up their scent.

"Do you want to take him, Willie?" his father whispered.

"I've never shot one before."

"There's always a first time, Son. Try and get him in the chest, right in the left side."

William steadied his rifle on a low branch and trained the telescopic lens on the buck. It was still nibbling away at the snow-covered grass. Didn't have a care in the world. And then it snapped to attention and looked his way, white tail twitching nervously in the sun. William could see it through the lens like it was close up and face to face. It had beautiful brown eyes and seemed to be looking straight at him, questioning what he was doing there. William closed his eyes for a moment, in an effort to get the young buck's innocent face out of his mind. He really didn't want to kill it.

"This is as good a time as any, Willie," his father whispered. "Let him have it, Son. Get him in on the left side of the chest."

William opened his eyes again, took another look through the telescopic lens on the barrel of his gun and pulled the trigger. The buck dropped to its knees, antlers swinging wildly from side to side, and then it was down, lying sideways on the grass. The blood oozing out of its nose and chest quickly turned the snow red.

"Good boy, Willie," his dad said as they ran towards the buck. It was still alive. His dad fired a bullet between its eyes to finish it off. "That was a great shot, Willie. You did well, Son."

William didn't feel particularly well. The sight of that beautiful young animal lying there with its blood all over the snow left him feeling quite sad. It was not the feeling of exhiliration he had expected to experience on making his first kill. In fact, he thought he was going to throw up.

William went back up the mountain to get the old Clydesdale while his dad slit the buck's belly open and removed the guts. As it was a fairly young buck, it wasn't too heavy and they were able, between them, to get it on the horse's back.

"Well, we won't be staying here tonight after all," his father said. "If the wolves get a smell of the blood, they'll be all over us. We'd be best to get home before it gets dark."

"Does that mean we're finished?" William asked, still a bit shaken up from having shot his first deer.

"Oh, no. If there's one, there's bound to be others. We'll wait for another couple of hours and see if we spot another one. Your mother will be expecting us to bring her two."

When they got back up to the campsite, they removed the buck from the old Clydesdale and laid it on the grass beside their campfire. Then his father checked on the Appaloosa and the Pinto, tethered in the shade at the left side of the right-of-way, put another branch on the fire and boiled some water for their tea. They sat together looking down at the prairie stretched out before them. Richard had caught on to the fact that William was quite upset about having made his first kill.

"Kind of shakes you up, doesn't it?" he said. "I felt the same way when I shot my first moose. Took me a couple of weeks to get over that feeling."

"You mean it goes away?" William asked.

"Yes, Son. It does go away. This time next month, you won't give it another thought."

"I hope so. I can still see the look in its eyes."

They drank their tea in silence, keeping a lookout for deer in the clearings farther down the mountain on the right and left of the right-of-way. It was very quiet up there. Not so much as a sound of a crow anywhere. As his father looked out across the prairie, his thoughts turned back to the early days he had been telling William about before they killed the young buck.

"The kind of guns you have are real important," he said. "Back in the earlier days, when the American traders first came up to trade for the buffalo hides, we were able to hold them in check because we had rifles from the Hudson's Bay Company. We were pretty evenly matched. But then they got the Henry rifles and we didn't stand a chance against them. The Henry was a .44 calibre repeater that could fire twenty-eight rounds a minute. There was no way we could compete with firepower like that."

He reached over for William's Winchester and started to clean the barrel. "Yes, Willie, guns make the difference. You know, a lot has been made about the Iroquois coming up from New York State and wiping out the Hurons in Ontario. Back in the seventeenth century it was. That wasn't because the Iroquois were better fighters – better warriors. It was because, pure and simple, the Dutch and the English traders gave them guns and the French wouldn't let their allies, the Hurons, have any guns. Not a one. It was bows and arrows against muskets. That's what it was."

He paused for another puff on his pipe. "When we were negotiating the Blackfoot Treaty, back in September, 1877, the British had cannons, field guns, and battle-trained soldiers who had fought in India, in Africa, the Crimean and everywhere else in the world the British Empire needed young men to die in its name. We were completely outgunned and outmanoeuvred. Our people didn't stand a chance. That's how they were able to steal our land the way they did.

"The year before we signed the treaty, the Sioux were fighting the U.S. Army less than three hundred miles from here, down there in Montana and over in Dakota." He pointed to the south. "They sent a messenger asking us to form an alliance with them and help drive the Americans off their land. And it wasn't just down there they wanted us to fight. They wanted us to take on the white settlers up here as well. There weren't too many of them back then and we could have made life pretty miserable for them. We had guns, Willie, lots of guns.

"The Sioux were great fighters, great warriors. And it wasn't just about the land they were fighting over down there. The famous battle of the Little Bighorn was about gold. About fifteen thousand white men were trekking all over the Black Hills of the Lakota Sioux in Dakota wanting to make their fortunes with the gold that had recently been discovered. Only problem was, the Black Hills, which the Indians held to be sacred land, had been reserved to the Sioux under the treaty they signed with the American government. That gold was on Indian land. Sacred land.

"When the Sioux refused to surrender their title to the Black Hills for a pretty substantial payment, the U.S. president at the time sent

General George Armstrong Custer and the 7th Cavalry Regiment out there to drive them off the land."

"I heard about Custer," William said. "Lots of stories have been written about him. Haven't read them – but I've heard about them."

"Lots of stories with lots of lies," Richard said with a pronounced bitterness in his voice. "They don't tell the real story. The real story about Custer being a coward who preferred killing Indian men, women and children, sleeping in their tents rather than fighting out in the open. He was a hero of the U.S. civil war and, by the time he had his fatal run in with Sitting Bull, there were all sorts of stories in the eastern newspapers with pictures of him all dressed up in buckskin killing bears and other creatures of the plains. He was a folk hero. Billed himself as an Indian fighter. 'Indian killer' is more like it. Used to circle Indian villages at night and then swoop in with his mounted cavalry at dawn and kill them all off while they were still sleeping in their tents."

Richard paused for a moment, put some fresh tobacco in his pipe, lit it and then took a couple of puffs. "That's what he was planning on doing at the Little Bighorn. Sneak in under the cover of night and slaughter them all at dawn. Women and children, too. Every last one of them. Didn't happen though. Sitting Bull outsmarted him. He was twice as good a military tactician as Custer was. Caught him out in the open and killed him and all of his men. Not one of them survived."

"None?" William asked.

"None." Richard spat contemptuously into the campfire. "Killed every last one of them. There was mass hysteria in the east. The newspapers billed it as a 'massacre'. Claimed that Sitting Bull and his warriors ambushed Custer and his men. That's because there was no way in their feeble white minds that an Indian chief could outsmart their war hero. Sitting Bull outsmarted him all right. Killed him and all of his men. Killed them in an open fight. The American newspapers called for revenge – for vengeance. 'Those savages have to be dealt with once and for all.' The government sent thousands of troops west and Sitting Bull and his band had to make a run for it over the Canadian border and into Saskatchewan."

He paused for a moment and took a couple of puffs on his pipe. "It's just as well we didn't go down there to fight the Americans. They had artillery, the Gatling machine gun which had just recently been invented, the whole shooting shebang, and ten times the men Sitting Bull had. We wouldn't have stood a chance down there."

Young William was quite fascinated with what his dad was telling him about the relationship between the Blackfoot and the white settlers. The bitterness in his father's voice made it clear there was no doubt in his mind that the white people stole their land.

"But how could they just move in here and take over?" he asked.

"With guns, firewater and a barrel full of deceit," his dad replied. "Not only that, Son, by the time we signed the treaties, we were a totally devastated people. We were right down on our knees. The buffalo were pretty well gone by the time we signed the Blackfoot Treaty in 1877. The whites slaughtered them by the millions. And that meant we had no buffalo for food, clothing, and covering for our lodges. The loss was devastating.

"I can't imagine what our people went through back then. With no food and no buffalo to hunt. They used to pitch their tents around the forts and the trading posts in the vain hope someone would take pity on them and give them something to eat. Where we used to ride proudly across the prairies, living a good life, we were now reduced to the role of beggars. We were in no position to bargain with the representatives of the English Queen all dressed up in their fancy blue uniforms with soldiers, rifles and cannons, to back up the authority they claimed they had over us. We didn't stand a chance.

"Then, after we signed the treaties, they banned our sacred ceremonies, wouldn't let us speak our own language in school, stripped us of our culture and traditions. Tried to turn us into brown white men. Got us dependent on store-bought food and clothes. Made a real mess of us they did."

They both sat silent beside the campfire drinking their tea. And then his father spotted a doe entering one of the clearings. "Down there, Willie, on the left side, just below the clearing where we got that young buck."

William looked down and saw that the doe was now well into the clearing foraging in the snow-covered grass.

"Damn!" his father exclaimed as a young fawn came out of the woods on the left side of the clearing and joined its mother. "Can't kill her now. Not with that youngster depending on her like that. Damn."

They watched the doe and her fawn foraging around the clearing. His dad looked at them through the lens of William's gun just for the hell of it. And that's when a young buck came into view, walking out of the woods on the left side of the clearing.

"That's more like it," Richard said. "That's our Number Two. Let's get him."

He handed William his gun, picked up his own, and they made their way down through the woods to within a hundred yards of the clearing. The wind was still coming from the east and none of the animals had picked up their scent.

"Do you want to take this one, Willie?"

"No, Dad. I still haven't got over the other one."

"Okay, Son. Just leave it to me."

When Richard shot the young buck in the chest, it kicked its hind legs up high and then stumbled about twenty yards across the clearing before falling on the snow-covered grass. It was still alive and gasping when they got there, staring up at them with a startled look in its eyes. Richard finished it off with a shot in the head.

"Go get the horse, Willie," his dad said as he started to gut the young buck with his big hunting knife.

When William got back, they loaded the buck onto the Clydesdale and headed back up the mountain to their camp. They were about a hundred yards away when the horses tied up at the camp started neighing nervously the way horses do when they sense danger. About a minute after that, Richard spotted the lone grey wolf coming out of the woods and heading for the first buck they had killed which was laid out beside the fire. He got the wolf with the first shot.

They put the buck beside the other one and William started to pack up their things as his father skinned the wolf. After he was done, he rolled the skin and tied it with string. "Your mom will make some nice gloves out of this Willie. I could do with a new pair right about now."

They tied the two young bucks on the back of the old Clydesdale along with some of their other gear and then they loaded the rest of the stuff on their horses.

"Let's go home, Willie," his dad said as he pressed the reins against the big Appaloosa's neck and headed her down the mountain. "Let's go home to your mom. It's been a good day."

Every time Tom took Gordon to the annual Santa Claus parade put on by the big Eaton's department store in downtown Toronto, he was very proud of the fact that the parade was led by the Pipes and Drums of the 48th Highlanders of Canada.

"You know, Gordie," he once said, "when we were fighting over there in Italy, we would often march through towns and villages with a piper in front of us. Just the sound of the pipes gave you added courage – courage you badly needed during those dark days of war. There`s nothing like the skirl of the pipes."

The decorated floats and horsedrawn carriages came right after the Pipes and Drums and then, a bit later on, you heard the sound of the 48th Highlanders' Military Band in the place of honour directly in front of Santa's sleigh. When you heard the sound of the pipes and drums, you knew the jolly old boy himself would soon be right there before you.

Tom had read quite a lot about Scottish history and would often tell Gordon stories about Scottish heroes like King Robert the Bruce, William Wallace and some of the others. The first time he told him about Robert the Bruce was when they were over on Ward's Island one summer eating their sandwiches under a big tree beside the beach.

"If I'd been around in those days, back in the fourteenth century it was, I'd have fought alongside King Robert. Fought just like I did with the 48th when we chased Hitler and his goons out of Italy and Holland. Aye, I would have fought – fought hard – back then."

He reached for the thermos flask and poured them both another cup of tea. "Those were dark days for Scotland, Gordie. We'd been crushed under the heel of the English for a lot longer than we cared to remember. Anyway, King Robert and his men were fighting a guerrilla war in southwest Scotland against the English oppressors. He beat the English at the Battle of Glen Trool and again at the Battle of Loudoun Hill. Then he travelled north and captured Inverlochy and Urquhart castles and burned the castles at Inverness and Nairn to the ground. You'll remember I showed you Inverness Castle when I took you to visit your granddad. That's not the one Bruce burned down. That one wasn't built until more than five hundred years later. 1836."

Gordon remembered being at Inverness Castle and looking down at the River Ness flowing through the town. He'd sat on the seat of one of the big black artillery guns in front of the castle.

"The deciding battle," Tom continued, "was the Battle of Bannockburn. That's the one that won us our independence. Final battle of the Scottish War of Independence it was. King Edward of England was marching north into Scotland with about two thousand men on horseback and about sixteen thousand soldiers marching. That'd have been in June, 1314. Edward was commanding an army about three times the size of the force King Robert had at his disposal.

"One of the English knights, fitted out in heavy armour and riding a big black stallion, spotted King Robert out in the open and charged at him with his shield in place and lance lowered. King Robert was riding a wee highland pony and wasn't wearing any armour. All he had to defend himself with was a big battle axe. He rode towards the knight and then, just at the last moment, he turned the pony aside, stood in his stirrups and split the knight's helmet and head in two with his battle axe. They say King Robert's only regret was that he'd broken the shaft of his axe in the process of slicing the knight's head in two.

"His men were really impressed with that act of courage. They surged forward out of the woods swinging their swords and axes roaring at the top of their lungs and forced the English to retreat. On the second day, the English king foolishly ordered his army to cross the Bannock Burn.

"To their great surprise, King Robert's spearmen emerged from the cover of the woods and set upon them. And then Bruce ordered his entire army out of the woods and they made a bloody push into the disorganized English troops. This was followed up by five hundred members of the Scottish light cavalry.

"As the English formations started to break up, the Scots shouted 'Lay on! Lay on! Lay on! They fail!' This loud cry was heard by the Scottish camp followers – people who did the cooking, laundry and stuff like that – back in the woods who promptly picked up every weapon and banner they could find and charged out onto the battle-field. The exhausted English mistook them for fresh reinforcements and gave up all hope and ran for their lives.

"I'd like to have been there to see that, Gordie. What a sight that must have been. King Edward himself fled with his personal body-guards and panic spread throughout what was left of his army. They got Edward to a ship and sailed him back to England. Meanwhile, the Scots chased the fleeing English soldiers all the way to the English border. About ninety miles south of Bannockburn, it was.

"Our clan, the MacArthurs, fought with King Robert at the Battle of Bannockburn. Fought right alongside him. And, my son, he was very grateful to us for siding with him. Gave us huge tracts of land in Argyllshire. That's on the west coast, north of Glasgow. Huge tracts that had belonged to the MacDougalls who made the costly mistake of fighting on the side of the English at Bannockburn. They picked the wrong king in that one."

One day, after his dad told him another story about Scotland and the long-standing feud between the Scots and the English, Gordon wondered why his dad spoke English instead of Scottish.

"I was wondering, Dad, why it is that you roll your R's but you don't speak Scottish? Like, why do the Scots speak English instead of Scottish?"

"There's a reason for that. A reason that goes back a long way, back to the Jacobite uprising of 1746, I believe it was. The Jacobites weren't just interested in taking back the Scottish throne. They wanted the English throne as well. To rule all of Britain. The battle that settled it all once and for all, and brought about the end of our language, our Gaelic, was fought on Culloden Moor, just about five miles northeast of Inverness. You'll remember going to the castle in Inverness when we were over in Scotland visiting your grandfather. It was just a bit northeast of there that they fought the bloody battle of Culloden Moor.

"Bonnie Prince Charlie, whose grandfather had been the King of Scotland, had been living in France for some time. Protected by the King of France he was. Then, after he arrived by boat on the west coast of Scotland to prepare for war against the English, the King of France sent him troops and supplies.

"His day of reckoning came at the Battle of Culloden Moor. Didn't last long. Not even two hours. Prince Charlie and his Highlanders – armed only with a few pistols, muskets, broadswords, battle axes, pitchforks and scythes – were vastly outnumbered by the English. They were also very tired, cold and hungry. Most of them had been sent on an aborted raid that had them marching all night. They desperately wanted to lie down and sleep. And, besides that, none of them had had any breakfast. It was all over in about an hour. And that, my son, was the last battle ever to be fought between the Scots and the English.

"The English scoured the Scottish Highlands after that battle hunting down and killing Jacobites, pillaging and burning villages and raping Scottish women. All guns, swords and other weapons were banned. The English made it against the law to wear the tartans that distinguished one clan from the other. Every clan had its own distinctive tartan. That's how you told them apart on the battlefield. They also banned the kilts. If they caught you wearing a kilt, you'd be sent to prison for six months. Catch you a second time, they'd ship you off to seven years of hard labour in their sugar plantations in the West Indies.

"We weren't allowed to speak Gaelic, the language we had used for centuries. Everyone had to learn English. They also banned the playing of the bagpipes. The English were determined to eradicate all of our Highland customs and traditions. And that, my son, is why hardly anyone at all speaks Gaelic in Scotland. The language died at Culloden. I might roll my R's, but it's the King's English that I speak today."

William enjoyed the stories his father told him about Sitting Bull, Geronimo, Pontiac, Tecumseh and the other war chiefs who fought, unsuccessfully, to drive the white men off their land. He really liked the story about how Sitting Bull and his Sioux warriors wiped out George Custer and his 7th Cavalry Regiment at the battle of the Little Bighorn.

About a year after their first hunting trip together, Richard took him to the sweat lodge he had built in a clearing in the bush about half a mile away from their home. Richard made the frame for the dome-shaped structure from pine saplings and covered it with cowhide.

Ron Onespot, a boyhood friend of Richard's, was tending the fire outside the lodge. He had about five rocks on the fire and took them into the lodge with a shovel. He poured water on the rocks and the steam quickly filled the lodge.

William followed his father as he crawled through the small entrance into the darkness. They were wearing loincloths made from rabbit skin. Once inside, they settled themselves around the fire pit.

Richard reached into his medicine bag, took out a handful of tobacco, and spread it around the hot rocks as a tribute to the spirits. "Your sweat will help you remember things, Willie," he said. "As it cleans your body, it cleans your soul. Just sit back and feel it. Let the sweat teach you. Give you wisdom."

William felt his body get hotter and hotter and then the sweat started to trickle down his neck and over his bare chest. It was dark and hot in there. He'd never had a feeling quite like it.

About ten minutes later, Ron Onespot lifted the flap at the front of the lodge. "Better change those rocks," he growled as he pushed the shovel toward the fire pit. "I've got more for you."

Richard placed the shovel under three of the rocks and pushed it outside. Then he got the other two. Onespot placed newly-heated rocks on the shovel and passed them inside to Richard.

"If you want to say something, Willie, you can. Sometimes, there's about four or five of us in a sweat and we usually take turns speaking. Getting things off our chests. Talking to the spirits. This is as much for your soul as it is for your body. You don't just come in here to get clean."

"Can't think of anything right now, Dad. I'm just going to sweat for a while."

When William got to the high school in Calgary, he was only one of about thirty Indian students there. Thirty Indian kids out of about five hundred. Some, like William, were Blackfoot. Some Cree, Assiniboine Stoney and Sarcee. They stuck together most of the time. Pretty well had to because some of the white kids really didn't like Indians and roughed them up pretty bad when they found one of them alone.

William was beaten several times. They used to call him Sitting Bull. "Hey, Sitting Bull, how many girls did your daddy scalp today?"

At other times, they would circle around him and chant: "Hey, Sitting Bull, what you having for lunch today? Got any for us?" It got pretty bad at times. By the start of the second year, most of the Indian students had dropped out. By the time he graduated, he was the only Indian student left in his class.

When he turned sixteen, his dad took him to a Sun Dance. About seventy teepees had been erected in a wide circle in the middle of which there was a birch tree which had been stripped of its branches to make a sun pole. The head of a freshly killed buffalo was placed on top of it. Long leather thongs hung from the pole – the Tree of Life. There were about a hundred people seated in a circle around the pole.

At the foot of the pole, four elders sat around a sacred drum. One of them hit the drum and the others followed, pounding and singing the songs of their ancestors. Richard joined three other men and they made an inner circle around the pole. One on the north, the east, the south and the west. The medicine man pierced Richard's chest and inserted two sharp wooden dowels that were attached to the thongs reaching down from the Tree of Life. William saw his father wince in pain as the medicine man cut his flesh. Once the dowels were in place, Richard leaned back slowly until the thongs formed a straight line to the bloodied buffalo head at the top of the Tree of Life.

The drumming continued. Dum dum. Dum dum. Dum dum. Dum dum. Like the beating heart of Mother Earth. Richard shuffle stepped in time with the drums, eyes fixed on the buffalo head at the top of the sun pole. Then he closed his eyes, threw his head back, and started to chant an eagle song.

The image of his dad chanting at the end of those long thongs hanging down from the Tree of Life stayed with William for the rest of his life. He shuddered at times when he recalled the sight of the medicine man cutting into his dad's flesh. He appreciated the fact that the Sun Dance formed an important part of the Blackfoot tradition. But, he still considered it a bit gruesome. He never did take part in a Sun Dance.

Several times, as Gordon was growing up, Martha felt they should tell him about Bill and Helen and Big Thunder and that he had a brother who was being raised as a Blackfoot.

But, even when Tom would agree that was probably the best thing to do, he would change his mind at the last moment and suggest that they wait until Gordon "is a wee bit older."

He had seemed even more determined just after he got back from the war that they should have nothing to do with the Eagletails and Big Thunder. He'd remind Martha that Alex Montour had told him most native people did fight for Canada. Richard was an exception that proved the rule.

"It should have been him that died over there in Hong Kong. Not Bill. Not my brother," Tom said with a bitterness Martha had never before heard in his voice less than a month after he got home. "Sits out there on his reservation, probably drawing a welfare cheque, and he's not prepared to fight for our country."

"Oh, no. No, Tom. The Eagletails aren't on welfare. They're doing quite well out there. At least they were when I went out to get Gordon. They raise horses and cattle and sell hay and other crops. They do all right. No welfare cheques."

"Then that's even more reason why he should have joined up. He doesn't sell those horses and cattle to Indians. It's the white people he sells them to. Without us – without the white people to buy his stuff, he'd be starving in the bush."

Martha knew from past experience that she wouldn't be able to change Tom's opinion of Richard. That door was closed.

"Still, Tom, while I agree with you about Richard, that doesn't change the fact that Gordon has a brother out there who's being raised as an Indian, as a Blackfoot. He does have a right to know he has a brother."

"For what purpose? You remember the letter you got from them – saying they wanted to raise William as a Blackfoot and that it would be better not to let the boys know they were brothers. They were right about that, Martha. What good purpose would be served by telling Gordie that now? His brother's two thousand miles away. It's like someone in Inverness having a brother in Sicily. Two thousand miles apart. It's not like he was living here in Ontario. In Hamilton, London or Kingston. Here where they could visit one another. Do things together. Calgary's two thousand miles away. Took me and Bill four days to get out there in the boxcar. They'd never be able to see each other anyway."

"But still, Tom. Even if they couldn't visit like you say – be part of one another's lives – shouldn't they at least know that they're brothers? That they were both born out there at the Morgan ranch?"

Tom started to roll himself another cigarette and thought about what Martha had said for a moment. *Gordie's twelve now. That'd make his brother about fourteen. Maybe it is time. Maybe Martha's right. Maybe they should be told. Both of them. But, then again, just as Sarah said in her letter, it's clear his brother hasn't been told. If they'd told him, he'd have gotten in touch with us by now. Would've wanted to meet his brother. They probably haven't told him. Maybe, like they said just after Bill was killed, they don't want to tell him. We're worlds apart. Not just in distance. But in the way we live. We've really got nothing in common with those people out there on that reservation.*

Mind you, if William had been raised at Alex Montour's reserve – at Six Nations of the Grand River – that'd be different. Alex said the Mohawks were Christians. Loyal to the Crown. Had a Bible, prayer book and a silver communion service from Queen Anne herself. Oldest Protestant church in Ontario. Her Majesty's Chapel of the Mohawks. That's what Alex said. That'd be different. No telling what religion they practice out there at the Blackfoot reservation. Might still be pagan, for all I know. Probably are.

"You might be right, Martha. But, then again, I don't think Richard and his wife want William to know he has a brother. A brother that's being raised white. That his father was white. There's been no attempt on their part to get in touch with us and set up a meeting so the brothers can meet one another. Maybe they still don't want William to know about Gordie. Have you thought of that?"

"You might be right. Maybe they prefer things the way they are. Maybe they would prefer that we don't tell Gordon. I really don't know. Don't know what's the best thing to do."

"Then let's just let it be for now. Let's let it be until Gordie's a bit older. That might be the best time to let him know. When he's older and can understand these things."

Tom lit his cigarette and took a couple of puffs. "Strange, isn't it? Who'd ever have thought when me and Bill set sail from Scotland that he'd wind up in a soldier's grave in Hong Kong and we'd be raising his son here in Toronto? Even stranger yet that he'd have a son being raised as a Blackfoot out there in Alberta. Strange twist of fate it is."

"It is that," Martha said. "No one would ever have expected things to work out like this."

～

Tom's sterility hung heavily on his mind. If it was God's will that man should multiply and replenish the earth, he asked himself, then what good is a man who can't do his part in propagating the species? What good was he if he couldn't reproduce? *If I'm not here to ensure the continuation of the species, then what am I here for?*

As much as Tom agonized over that question, he never found an answer that satisfied him. He held himself responsible for the fact that Martha hadn't had the experience of giving birth to a child.

"But I've got a son," she said. "I've got Gordon."

"Aye, aye, lass. I know that. Know it well. But, what I'm talking about is – is –having life growing inside of you. Kicking, moving, breathing, living. And then having it come out of you and – and – having it throw back its head and holler a bawling hello to the whole wide world. Having it as your own flesh and blood. An extension of your own self. Another part of you."

Martha didn't feel any sense of loss. She appreciated Tom's concern for, what he considered to be, her barrenness. But she felt no loss. In Gordon, she had everything she wanted in a son. Having had him come out of her belly couldn't have added one ounce to the deep love she had for him. The growing love that developed day by day, year by year, as Gordon grew into manhood.

She didn't think it was her "barrenness" that got Tom so upset. She thought it was more likely that his feeling of being castrated plagued him. Tom never said anything about those feelings to Martha, but she sensed that was how he felt. She was convinced the unresolved question in the back of his mind about being sterile was one of the reasons he couldn't bring himself to tell Gordon about Bill and Helen. Or that he had a brother who was being raised as a Blackfoot at Big Thunder.

~

The doorbell rang at 10:30 a.m. one morning in June, 1953. When Martha opened the door, two police officers were standing on the porch. They asked if they could step inside for a few minutes.

They told her there had been an explosion at her parents' home earlier that morning and they were both dead. A neighbor had given them her name and address. Apparently, a construction crew working on a neighbor's property had ruptured a gas line just after 7:00 a.m. and the spark from the bulldozer's blade had set off an immediate explosion. Her parents' home had been reduced to rubble. As had the house next door.

"I'm so sorry to have to be the one to deliver this news," Sergeant George Carroll said as he sat in the big armchair beside the fireplace. "The only good thing was that your parents' death would have been immediate. The explosion was at the front of the house where, as our preliminary investigation has confirmed, they were both probably asleep in their bed."

"Is your husband at home?" the female officer asked.

Tom? An explosion? Oh, my God, this cannot be happening.

"No," Martha replied in a faltering voice. "He's at the office."

"It's probably better that he be with you at this time. Would you like me to call him?"

Yes, that would be better. I need Tom here. Need him with me now. Right now. Can't do this alone.

"That would be very nice of you," Martha said. "I'm not sure I could do that myself right now. I just can't believe they're both gone."

Tears welled up in her eyes as she reached into her purse and took out one of Tom's business cards and handed it to Constable Eileen Hunter. *This surely can't be happening. Mum and Dad can't both be gone. Not like that. Not in an explosion.*

As Constable Hunter placed the call to Tom's office, Sergeant Carroll asked Martha if there were any children at home.

"No, Gordon's all we've got. He'll be at school now. Won't be home until lunch time."

"I think we should bring him home now," Sergeant Carroll said. "The reporters will be all over this and that's not the way for your son to hear about it. How old is he?"

"Just turned fourteen last month. He's in grade eight." *What's wee Gordie going to say when he learns Mum and Dad are gone? Gone like that? In an explosion of all things.*

Constable Hunter took down the name and address of Gordon's school and then left to pick him up and bring him home.

Gordon was sitting at his desk watching the teacher writing on the blackboard when the principal's secretary came into the room and whispered in the teacher's ear. The teacher then walked to his desk and told him he was wanted in the principal's office.

Wonder what this is all about? he thought as he was escorted to the office. *Never been in the principal's office before. Never even met him.*

A female police officer was standing in the reception area. She thanked the principal's secretary and then turned to Gordon.

"Hi, Gordon, I'm Constable Hunter. Your mom asked me to pick you up and take you home. She needs to see you about something."

"Is Mum all right? Is she hurt or something?"

"Your mom's fine, Gordon. It's just that she needs to talk to you about something."

"Police business?"

"Yes, you could put it that way."

Maybe someone broke into the house, he thought. *Still, why would they need me there?*

When he got to the house, his dad was on the couch in the living room with his arms around his mum. She was crying her eyes out. A police officer was having a coffee at the table in the kitchen.

"Come, sit with me, Gordie," his dad said.

He told Gordon about the explosion and that his Grandparents were both dead.

"Both of them?" Gordon asked. "Grandfather and Grandma?"

"Yes, Son. They're both gone."

The first viewing at the funeral home was two days later. Both caskets were closed. Their faces had been crushed beyond recognition.

As he sat there looking at his Grandfather's coffin surrounded with flowers and wreaths, Gordon thought back to the many times he'd sat between his legs on the couch keeping an eye out for crocodiles and hippos as they paddled their way up the Congo River. And then there was their trips on the ferry to the Islands and how Grandfather was always waiting for him the moment he got out of school.

He wondered where Grandfather was. *Is there somewhere else to go to like Mum says there is? Heaven? Maybe Grandfather's in Heaven. Wherever, he should be here. He should not have been taken away. Not this soon.*

A little more than a year later, Gordon was at the Royal Ontario Museum with his dad on one of their regular visits. Instead of walking east on Bloor Street as they usually did, Tom headed south on Queen's Park to the 48th Highlanders of Canada Regimental Memorial at the top of the park. They walked around to the south side of the huge stone monument and looked up at the places the 48th Highlanders had fought in the Second World War engraved in stone.

"That first one at the top is the landing in Sicily," Tom said. "We took the Germans by complete surprise. They didn't expect anyone would be foolhardy enough to land in rough seas like that. Rough like you wouldn't believe, those seas were."

"The Germans, Dad?" Gordon asked. "What about the Italians?"

"Their hearts weren't in that war. Most of them waved white hankies and surrendered without putting up any fight at all. It's the Germans we had to worry about. Tough as nails, they were. Fierce fighters."

Tom paused to light another cigarette. And then he looked around the park. Playful squirrels chasing one another through the fallen leaves. Cars going about their business on both sides of Queen's Park. People walking their dogs. A couple smooching on a park bench. A rather tranquil setting.

"We fought our way right through Sicily. It was hot, Gordie. Hot as hell. I once told your mum I could have fried eggs on my helmet. They say it was 114 degrees in the shade. But we didn't have any shade. Not a damned tree in sight. Most of the time we were thirsty and dirty. But, we made it. Chased those German bastards all the way across the strait to Calabria – to mainland Italy."

He paused for a moment and took a puff on his cigarette. "It was costly, though. Left almost six hundred Canadian soldiers dead over there. Over there in Sicily, we did. And there was about two thousand wounded."

Tom pointed to the top of the monument. "Just below where it says Campobasso, you can see Ortona. That was as fierce a battle as ever I've been in. And, believe me, Son, those Germans knew how to fight. It was mostly paratroopers we were up against. Hand to hand. House to house, it was. But, we beat them."

As his father recounted the events of that time, Gordon looked up at the regimental crest of the 48th Highlanders of Canada just below the battle honours. It had a falcon's head with an open beak at the top. There was a belt and buckle around the edge of the crest with the regiment's Gaelic motto, *Dileas gu brath,* faithful forever, inscribed on it. The number 48 was featured prominently in the middle of the crest, with the word "Highlanders" right below it.

Tom paused for a moment and took a couple of slow drags on his cigarette. "And down there, at the bottom of the list, is Apeldoorn – right in the heart of Holland. That's where I lost my eye. Things have never looked the same," he said with a chuckle.

"I don't know how you do it, Dad. Sometimes, I keep my left eye closed and try getting around with just my right eye. It changes every-thing. I just don't know how you do it."

"I thank God that's all I lost. Way too many of my mates lost their arms, their legs and their lives. I was lucky to get out of there alive – to get home to you and your mum. You know, Gordie, I've heard that forty-seven thousand Canadians gave their lives in World War Two. They say another fifty-five thousand were wounded. Some of them pretty bad. It's only by the grace of God that I'm here with you today.

"My brother, your Uncle Bill, was killed by the Japs during the defence of Hong Kong. Didn't have a chance over there. The Japs had three times the men we had and our boys had run out of food and were down to their last rounds of ammunition. They buried him over there, your Uncle Bill they did. Never did get a chance to visit his grave and pay my respects."

"How old was he?" Gordon asked.

"He'd just turned thirty-two. That's way too young. And he didn't deserve to die, certainly not like that."

They sat on the bench beside the monument for about ten minutes without exchanging a word. It was obvious to Gordon that his dad was thinking back on some very painful memories, of comrades killed and wounded, of the horrors of the battlefield. Of his dead brother in Hong Kong.

"War's an awful thing, Gordie. The winter rains drenched us to the skin. Turned the ground to mud. Always short of equipment and never did have enough men for the job. I hope God spares you from ever having to go through anything like what it was like for me over there in Italy. It was hell. Sheer, unforgiving, hell."

Tom took another look up at the monument, tapped Gordon on the knee and said, "Okay, Son. Let's go home to your mum."

Martha was a born-again Christian and went to the Bethany Gospel Chapel about six blocks away from their house. She spent a lot of time reading her Bible and sending gospel tracts to the French Catholics in Chicoutimi and other towns in Quebec.

"They need to know the Lord Jesus Christ as their own personal saviour," she told Gordon one morning as she was stuffing gospel tracts into envelopes. "The Pope can't get them to heaven."

"Not so sure about that, Mum," Gordon said. "I'm pretty sure when the Catholics pray God listens to what they have to say."

"Not really, Gordon. Unless a man be born again he cannot enter the Kingdom of God. That is what the Bible says. The Catholics must be born again. They have to take Jesus into their hearts."

That didn't seem fair to Gordon. But, he respected his mother's faith and saw no point in getting into an argument about whether or not all of the Catholics were going straight to hell.

Tom didn't share Martha's belief in a caring God. He simply couldn't believe in a God that allowed so much that was bad to happen in the world. Famines. Floods. Disease. Leprosy. The horrors of the battlefield.

"I can't believe in God the way your dear mother does," he said one day as they were fixing the back fence. "Not after all I saw in the war. Mates crushed under the tracks of the Nazi tanks. Still breathing but dying. Dying in agony. A merciful God would not let so horrible a thing as that happen. Some with their arms or legs blown off. Blood and screaming everywhere. And the children over there in Italy. Bombed to bits in their houses. Limbs torn apart by the blast. Blood everywhere. Not quite dead but suffering horrible pain. And there was nothing I could do about one little girlie but just hold her in my arms as the life slipped out of her. She must've been around four or, perhaps, five. A merciful God would not just stand idly by and let such suffering happen in front of his own eyes. He'd have done something to prevent it.

"I did believe. Before the war. Went to church with your mum every Sunday. But, not now. Not after all I saw in the war. Now, your mum and the people at her church – not the one I used to go to but the gospel hall she goes to now – say there's not a sparrow that falls without God knowing about it. They say God keeps his eye on the sparrows and watches over them. His eye is on the sparrow, they say, and they believe he's watching over them, too. That's what they say. Can't possibly be true. No merciful God would stand by and let Hitler slaughter six million Jews. Burn them in the ovens at Dachau and Auschwitz. Doesn't make any sense to me. Any sense at all.

"But, your mum does believe. Means a lot to her to believe that there's a god in Heaven watching over her. Listening to her prayers. Keeping a place for her in the mansion in the sky."

"Do you believe in Heaven, Dad?"

"Nope. Don't believe in Hell either. Having a place like Hell for people to burn in for all eternity doesn't make any sense to me. No more sense than having a place like Heaven where you can live with the angels for millennia after millennia and never grow old. Don't believe in either one. When I'm gone, I'm gone. Fini. No more Tom MacArthur."

"What if there really is something after?"

"Don't know. I really don't know, Son. Don't think there is. When you're gone, you're gone. Does that make sense? No, it doesn't. But, that's not the only thing that doesn't make sense in this crazy, mixed up world of ours. A lot of things don't make sense. I really don't know. There may be something. Then, again, there might not. Guess we'll just have to wait to find out."

Gordon thought about his Grandfather. *If Mum's right, he's in heaven with the angels. If Dad's right, he's probably still in that coffin. Hope Mum's the one that's right. Grandfather really should be in heaven.*

Gordon didn't go to church with his mum on Sunday mornings. Instead, he went walking with his dad. During one of their long walks, Gordon and his dad were sitting on a bench at Sherwood Park.

"Never forget that you're a MacArthur, my son. It's a proud family name. We can trace our roots a long ways back. Some claim we're descended from King Arthur himself who defended Britain against the Saxons back in the sixth century. That same Arthur who had the Knights of the Round Table. Can't say that for sure but it's a definite possibility."

Gordon was very impressed to hear that he might be descended from the legendary King Arthur. He'd seen MGM's *Knights of the Round Table* when it came out in 1954 with Robert Taylor playing Sir Lancelot and Ava Gardner playing Lady Guinevere. He was enthralled with the sight of King Arthur's men mounted on their warhorses charging toward the enemy, some drawing their swords and others lowering their lances. The clashing of steel against steel as swordsmen exchanged blows. He wondered what it would have been like to sit as a knight at the round table. *With King Arthur, Sir Lancelot and Lady Guinevere and all the lords and ladies. To live in Camelot. Dance in the king's court. Fight his battles.*

When William arrived in Edmonton to study sociology at the University of Alberta, he found a room over a grocery store a short bus ride away from the university campus which was on the south bank of the North Saskatchewan River. He was the only Indian at the university.

While no one came right out and said it, he was aware that there was a significant number among the student body who didn't think he should have been admitted in the first place. But, then again, considering that he was now a couple of inches over six feet and weighed more than two hundred pounds, no one was prepared to make a point of it. Still, William knew what they thought. He could feel it.

Given his size and the excellent shape he kept himself in, the coach invited him to try out for the football team. William quickly made a name for himself as a defensive tackle with the Golden Bears. Running backs from the other teams used to wince when they saw William coming their way. He hit them hard. Pretty soon, the sportswriters at the *Edmonton Journal* gave him the nickname "Bull Bill". He was a really ferocious player and became a minor celebrity around the campus. This earned him shy, inviting, glances from some of the white girls at the university. But he didn't have much time for girls.

Every afternoon after class, he would hop on a bus that took him to the service station where he did lube and oils on big trucks from five until ten on weeknights and on Saturday to help defray the costs of going to school. That workload meant he had to do most of the studying for his B.A. in sociology on Sunday.

When he headed home for summer after that first year, his dad met him at the railway station in Calgary.

"Bull Bill, eh?" Richard said as he gave him a big hug. "Your mom showed me that picture you sent her from the *Edmonton Journal*. Bull Bill Eagletail. That's quite a moniker."

"Yup," Bill, as he now called himself, said a bit sheepishly. "That's what they call me up there. Bull Bill Eagletail. But, if it's okay with you, Bill will do just fine. Just call me Bill."

"No problem," Richard said. "Bill it will be. But, my son, I'll bet you dollars to donuts you won't get your mom to call you that. To her, you'll always be William."

Richard didn't tell him the reason for that was because his birth father's name was Bill and Sarah liked to keep the two names separate.

"So, William," Sarah said as they sat around the kitchen table having their afternoon tea, "how is it at the university? Made any friends? Girl friends, that is."

"No time for girls, Mom. I'm at the university all day, greasing trucks at night and on Saturday and studying all day Sunday. On top of that, there's the football practice and games away from home. No girls. Not one."

"Bet you could get one if you wanted one," his younger sister Janet said. "You looked really cool in the newspaper crashing into that guy with the ball under his arm. The look on his face was awesome. Knocked the ball right out of his hand."

"Yeah," Hughie piped in. "You don't want to mess with Bull Bill. Big Bull Bill. Bet the girls would like to mess with him, though."

"Okay, you guys," Bill said as he cuffed his younger brother affectionately on the back of the head. "Enough of this already. No girls. Period. End of story."

"Sounds like you have your work cut out for you up there – at the university," Sarah said. "Strikes me as a pretty heavy load."

"It's heavy okay," Bill replied. "But, it's going to be worth it. Going to take a while – almost eleven years between now and the time I get my doctorate. It'll be worth it though."

"Why eleven years?" Hughie asked. "Why do you have to be in school for that long?"

"I want to be a professor. A professor of sociology," Bill said. "For that, I need to have a PhD. And that, Hughie, will take about another eleven years at the grindstone."

"You'll be able to teach here by then," Janet said. "By the time you get your doctorate, the University of Calgary will be really well established."

"Don't think so," Bill replied. "I want to teach at the University of Toronto."

Sarah hadn't been expecting that. She understood why he would prefer teaching at the university to working at the ranch. He had a fine mind. Everyone commented on it. On more than one occasion, the Band Council had asked for his advice in preparing presentations for the Department of Indian Affairs. Bill was good with words and ideas and all that.

"Why Toronto?" she asked. "I'd hoped you'd be staying here with us. Teaching at the university during the week and being here with us on the weekends and in the summer. Why Toronto?"

Bill picked up on the fact that his mom was not too happy with this news. He'd have to be careful not to get her upset. *I should've let her know about it earlier. Shouldn't be springing this on her as a surprise like this.*

"I guess you could say Edmonton's one of the main reasons," he said. "I really don't like the place. Wouldn't want to live there. It's just – just nowhere. Not much to do there. And, I've seen some real sorry sights. Indians from the northern reserves passed out drunk on the sidewalks. Puking their guts out in the gutters. They get their welfare cheques, head for the bars in Edmonton and drink it all away."

"I've been to some of those reserves," Richard said. "Nothing at all like here at Big Thunder. Most of them used to live pretty good – twenty or thirty years ago. Hunting, trapping and fishing. Not anymore. The game's all gone now. Left when all the trees were cut down. They've got some good farmland but it's all rented out to white people. They don't work any of it. Just pick up their government cheques and go drinking. Living in tar-papered shacks, most of them are. Filth and squalor like you wouldn't believe. Bill's right. Edmonton's a pretty horrible place."

"Never been there myself," Sarah said, "but, if it's like you say it is, William would be a lot better off in Calgary. You'd probably like that a lot better, my son. You could teach there when you finish all your studies."

"Don't think so, Mom. It's going to take a great many years for the University of Calgary to establish anything comparable to the international reputation Toronto enjoys right now. Toronto, to me, is the centre of the universe as far as Canadian universities go. That's where I want to be."

And that's where Tom and Martha and his brother are, too, Sarah thought to herself. *We should have kept in touch. Should have known what happened to his brother. How things turned out for him. I don't even have Martha's address anymore.*

Richard was thinking along the same lines. *His brother's most likely still out there. Out there in Toronto. What if they run into each other? What would they say if they knew they were brothers? Both born at the Morgan ranch.*

"What you say about the university out there in Toronto might very well be just the way you say it is," Sarah said. "But I'd still like to have you close to home. Here with your family. Give Calgary a good second thought. It is a lovely city. With the river running through it like that. And, so close to home."

"I will, Mom. There's lots of time between now and when I get my doctorate. I'll give it lots of second thought."

Because he didn't want to get her upset, he didn't tell her that there was absolutely no doubt in his mind that Toronto was where he wanted to be.

After breakfast the next morning, Bill rode over to the Dodginghorse ranch to visit his grandparents. They were both glad to see him. He told them how things were going at the university.

"You have a pretty busy time of it up there?" Gordon asked.

"That's for sure, Granddad. I'm at the university all day and then, every night and Saturday, I'm at a service station doing lube and oils on big trucks. Sunday's the only chance I get to do some studying."

"That sounds like quite a load," Vera said. "How're you bearing up?"

"I'm doing okay, Grandma. Tired but doing okay."

"That's good William. Getting your education is a real good thing. You're gonna do well. I just know you will."

"Thanks, Grandma. I'm giving it my best shot."

"Well," Gordon said, "you keep at it. You've got a good mind, William. We're expecting great things for you. Real proud of you, we are."

CHAPTER

- 7 -

The Conservative candidate for the Toronto riding of Eglinton in the federal election scheduled for Monday, June 18, 1956, had a storefront campaign office quite close to Gordon's high school. One afternoon as he was walking home from school he stopped outside the office. There was a big blue banner across the top of the window that said: "Build a better Canada. Vote Conservative." Below the banner was a huge picture of Toronto lawyer Pat O'Brien.

Gordon decided to go in and have a look around. There was a very attractive young woman at the front desk wrapping rubber bands around bundles of campaign brochures. No one else was in the room.

"Can I help you?" she asked, looking up with a welcoming smile.

"Just looking around," Gordon said. "Never been in a campaign office before."

"Just looking won't get you anywhere in life," she said good-naturedly as she handed him one of the brochures. "Please. Take a moment and read this brochure. You can sit over there by the coffee pot."

"Thanks," he said as he took the brochure from her hand. "Maybe I'll do just that."

"Are you a Conservative?" she asked.

"Nope. I'm only seventeen. Not old enough to vote yet."

"You don't have to vote to be a Conservative. There's a lot more to democracy than voting."

"I'll keep that in mind," he said as he headed to one of the chairs beside the table with the big coffee pot.

"Have a coffee while you're at it. The milk's in the fridge. Help yourself to the cookies."

The brochure with Pat O'Brien's smiling face plastered on the cover was quite impressive. Well-known criminal defence lawyer. City Alderman for eight years. Chairman of the Parking Authority of Toronto. On the board of directors of Toronto General Hospital, Art Gallery of Toronto, Law Society of Upper Canada, March of Dimes and the Children's Aid Society of Toronto.

"He's quite the guy," Gordon said. "Very impressive."

"Mr. O'Brien's got what it takes all right. He's going to win," she said in a very confident tone.

"You sound pretty sure of that."

"Oh, I am. Our canvass is going really well and the response at the doors has been amazingly positive. People really like Mr. O'Brien. He's been the alderman here for eight years. Very popular. Lot's of support. By the way, my name's Jennifer. Jennifer Holden."

"Then I wish you luck, Jennifer," Gordon said as he held out his hand. "I'm Gordon MacArthur."

She shook his hand. "We need more than luck, Gordon. Luck's never enough. Why don't you lend us a hand? We can use all the help we can get."

"But you said you were sure he was going to win."

"Win, yes. But it's going to be close. The Liberal MP has been here for seven years and he's pretty popular, too. The main thing we've got going for us is that the Liberals are doing very poorly in the national polls. Down twelve points in the last two weeks alone. We think they're on the way out at the national level and that's going to make it possible for Mr. O'Brien to become the MP here. So, how about it? Are you going to help us? Can I count on your support?"

Gordon took another sip of his coffee. Being involved in an election campaign could be quite interesting. What would be even more interesting would be a chance to get to know Jennifer better. He found her very attractive. Her auburn hair was tied back in a ponytail that stretched down past her shoulder blades. Her blouse was opened slightly at the neck and showed a glimpse of two nicely-rounded breasts. She had a very inviting smile.

"Wouldn't know what to do," he said. "Never been involved in anything like this."

"There's always a first time," she said. "Join us tonight. We're going canvassing at six thirty and you'll enjoy it once you get into the swing of things. Come by around six fifteen and I'll introduce you to the candidate. Mr. O'Brien's even more impressive in person than he is in that brochure."

When Gordon got back to the office just after six fifteen it was abuzz with activity. About ten people working the telephones. Four elderly people bundling brochures at a long table. Two people entering information about the polls that had been canvassed on the chart covering the back wall. People coming in to pick up their poll kits or literature to drop off at the doors. Jennifer was with Pat O'Brien showing him the area they were going to canvass that evening.

"Oh, Gordon," she called out as he came through the door. "Over here. I want you to meet our candidate."

She introduced him to Pat O'Brien who thanked him very much for offering to help. "We need all the help we can get, Gordon," he said. "I am so glad that you're going to join us."

"Jennifer said you need all the help you can get, Mr. O'Brien. But, I warn you, I've never done anything like this before."

"No problem," O'Brien said. "Jennifer's a pro. She'll show you the ropes. Stick to her and you'll do fine."

Gordon found the thought of sticking to Jennifer quite appealing. He'd never seen her standing before. Figured she must be about five foot eight. Her long slender legs were wrapped in tight jeans that hugged her bum.

Jennifer found herself quite attracted to Gordon, despite the fact he was seven years younger than her. She was going to graduate in political science at the end of the month and had recently broken up with her boyfriend of two years. He'd dumped her for the lead cheerleader for the Varsity Blues football team. She was deeply hurt and badly in need of some comforting.

They were canvassing houses and apartments in the area around Mount Pleasant and Eglinton. Gordon held the bag of brochures as Jennifer knocked on the doors and made the pitch. After about an hour, she told him it was time for him to do the talking.

"Good evening," he said to the lady in the smartly-tailored pantsuit who opened the door, "I'm here on behalf of Pat O'Brien, the Conservative candidate for Eglinton. He …."

"Oh, you don't need to tell me about Pat," she said with a big smile. "He's the best alderman we've ever had. He's got my vote. No doubt about it."

"Then I'll mark you down as Conservative," Gordon said as he started writing on the poll sheet.

"Absolutely," she replied. "Conservative is what I am. We simply must get rid of those Liberals in Ottawa. They've made a real mess of things."

"Will you take a sign then?" Gordon asked.

"Of course I will. Give me one of those big ones and stick it beside the tree there. I always had one of Pat's signs when he was running for alderman. Yes, make sure it's one of those big ones."

"Mr. O'Brien's canvassing on the other side of the street," Jennifer said. "Would you like to meet him?"

"No, that's okay. I've met Pat many a time. Let him keep working the doors that need a bit of convincing."

Not everyone who came to the door was as positive as that first lady. But, overall, the response was very good. A lot of voters had soured on the Liberals and were in the mood for a change of government.

"You did well," Jennifer said as they headed back to the campaign office. "You're a good canvasser. A natural."

Gordon appreciated the compliment. *She's right. I am good. Convinced at least six people who were going to vote Liberal to switch to the Conservatives. All they needed was for me to hold up the brochure and point out some of Mr. O'Brien's accomplishments and what the Conservatives plan to do after they're elected. The Liberals really are in big trouble.*

For the next week, which was the last week of the election campaign, Gordon headed over to the campaign office every afternoon after school. He helped Jennifer with some of the things that needed to get done in the office and then went canvassing with her after six thirty.

Right after school on election day, he was out in the riding with poll sheets listing all the people who had indicated, either at the door or over the phone, that they were going to vote Conservative. His job was to make sure that they did. He was pleased to find that most of them who were at home when he knocked on their door had either voted or were going to do so before the polls closed.

After handing in his poll kits at the campaign office after the polls closed, he headed over to Ostrander's Bingo Hall where the victory party was going to be held. There were only about thirty people there. There was a bar set up on one side of the room with a counter heaped with sandwiches and cookies. Two big TV sets on the wall above the bar were tuned to the CBC. The wall on the other side of the room was covered with huge sheets of paper where all the polls and candidates were listed. As results were phoned in from the campaign office, they were marked on the sheets.

The Liberal incumbent was ahead by a hundred and twenty votes.

"Doesn't look too good," Gordon said to one of the volunteers.

"Pat's okay. We're going to win this thing," the volunteer replied. "The polls in the north end won't come in for another half hour. We always poll good up there. Strong Conservative territory."

"Hope you're right," Gordon said.

"Count on it. Pat's going to take it."

The results did change after the polls in the north end of the riding started to come in. In no time at all, O'Brien was leading by two hundred votes. About fifteen minutes later, he was ahead by four hundred and held the lead for the rest of the night.

The bingo hall was quite crowded now. Must have been more than three hundred people there. Munching on the sandwiches and drinking beer and soft drinks. Cheers went up every time O'Brien's lead increased. By the time the final poll reported, he'd won by nine hundred and forty-eight votes.

"We did it, Gordon," Jennifer said excitedly as she threw her arms around him and gave him a big kiss on the cheek. "We won. Won big."

"You won," he said as he put his arms around her and returned the kiss. "You did a fantastic job."

"Thanks," she said. "But it's Pat's victory. Not every Conservative in Toronto did as well as he did. We've lost three seats. But we're looking good in western Canada and, when those results come in, we will be forming a Conservative government. We did really well in Nova Scotia and New Brunswick tonight. A lot better than last time. It's been a good night. Let's get a drink. I could use one."

O'Brien was on the stage with his wife and three teen-aged daughters thanking them all for their support. "Couldn't have done it without you. You're the best campaign team there is. No one could have asked for a more enthusiastic bunch of supporters. You're just absolutely marvellous. Each and every one of you."

He went on to thank the key members of his campaign team, including Jennifer, and then spoke about some of the things he hoped to get accomplished for Eglinton as their new Member of Parliament. After he finished speaking, he left the stage to mingle with his happy crowd of supporters.

When the music started, Jennifer took Gordon's hand and led him onto the section of the floor that had been cleared for dancing. "Let's dance, Gordon. I'm in the mood to celebrate."

She pressed her body tight against his as they danced to the sound of Al Hibbler singing *Unchained Melody.* As Hibbler sang *"I've hungered for your touch a long lonely time,"* Gordon sniffed Jennifer's perfume and kissed her on the nape of her neck. *"I need your love,"* Hibbler sang in his rich baritone voice. *"I need your love. God speed your love to me."*

By the time the song ended, Gordon was sexually aroused. He'd never been with anyone like Jennifer before. She was a totally-sensuous young woman.

They danced some more. Nat King Cole's *A Blossom Fell,* the Four Lads' *Moments to Remember,* the McGuire Sisters' *Sincerely,* The Platters' *Only You,* and Perez Prado's *Cherry Pink and Apple Blossom White.*

The more they danced, the more Jennifer pressed against him and nibbled his earlobe. "Let's go to my place," she said. "I'm in the mood for some real celebrating."

That took him by surprise. He hadn't expected an invitation to her apartment.

"It's getting late," he said. "I really should be getting home. School tomorrow."

She reached her hand down and stroked the inside of his thigh. "I'm only two blocks away from here. We've got lots of time."

Wow. She really means it. And, God, I would like to get inside her. First election. First ejaculation. A big night of firsts.

When they got to Jennifer's apartment, which was above a flower shop on Mount Pleasant, she immediately took all her clothes off and started unbuttoning his shirt. The only time he'd ever seen a naked woman before was in *Playboy* magazine. Her legs were really long. Flat belly and nice rounded breasts. Hair out of the ponytail and streaming down her back.

As they lay on her bed after making love, Gordon reflected on what a terrific experience it had been. He'd never had an orgasm before. Hadn't even masturbated. This was his first time. And it felt great.

Jennifer turned on the radio to get the final results from British Columbia. The Conservatives won most of the seats there to give them an overall total of one hundred and forty-nine. Enough to give them a comfortable majority of the two hundred and sixty-five seats in the House of Commons.

Jennifer wrapped her arms around Gordon and gave him another kiss. "Isn't this wonderful? We're going to form a government. And Pat's probably going to be a cabinet minister. The Prime Minister likes him. They went to U of T together. Isn't this great, Gordon?"

"It is," he said. "And I'm glad I had a small part in it. I'm really starting to like politics. And you. You're just simply incredible."

"You're kind of incredible yourself," she said. "I really like having you with me like this."

"Me too. But I really must get going. My parents will be wondering where in the Devil I am."

"I understand," she said as she ran her fingers across his chest. "Let's do this again. Sometime when you have more time on your hands."

"You serious?"

"Of course I'm serious. I really like you, Gordon. Wouldn't have you in my bed if I didn't like you. Like you a lot."

~

Gordon helped clean out the campaign office after school the next afternoon. They moved the furniture to a garage behind a house on

Merton Street. He also went out with the truck picking up lawn signs which also went to Merton Street.

He started seeing Jennifer a couple of times a week. They usually had take-out Chinese food at her apartment along with a bottle of Chianti. Their times together in bed were something he looked forward to all day long.

Jennifer was right. Pat O'Brien was appointed to cabinet. Minister of National Revenue. It wasn't as high up the ladder as O'Brien had been hoping for but it was a cabinet position. Big office, staff, limo, the works. Two days after being sworn in by the Governor General at Rideau Hall, he phoned Jennifer and offered her a job in his Ottawa office. She was in bed with Gordon when she got the call.

"I'd really like to have you with me, Jennifer. You did an excellent job in the campaign and I just know that you would do well with me here. Howard Rosen is going to be my chief of staff and he's more than comfortable with you being my special assistant for policy. What do you say?"

"I say yes. Of course I want to be part of your team. When would you want me to start?"

"How about yesterday? We've got a lot of work to do up here. Thank God the House won't be sitting until October. I'd hate having to take questions in the House before having a chance to get to know my ministry. Even without the House being in session, there's a tremendous amount of work to get done. I guess what I'm saying is the sooner the better."

"The university closes down at the end of the week and I'll need a couple of days to get a few things done but, after that, I would be free. I could fly up Monday night or Tuesday morning if that works for you."

"Tuesday morning will be just fine. We'll book you a seat and you can pick the ticket up at the airport. Kathy Jordan, my legislative assistant, says you can stay at her apartment until you find a place of your own. I'll leave it to Howard to take care of all of these arrangements. He is my chief of staff and you do understand that, despite how highly I think of you, it's best that you report directly to Howard. Got to keep the pecking order intact."

"No problem. I understand completely. I like Howard and I'm sure we'll get on well together. So, again, thank you for expressing confidence in me and, on that note, I'll say goodbye and look forward to seeing you in Ottawa."

O'Brien said how much he was looking forward to having her on his team and ended the call.

"That was Pat," Jennifer said as she hung up the phone and turned her naked body towards Gordon. "He wants me to work in his office in Ottawa. Special assistant, policy."

"From what I could hear, you're already hired," Gordon said as he drew her body toward his.

"Yup. Start Tuesday."

"No need to think it over?"

"Nope. When it looked like the Conservatives were going to form a government and that Pat would probably make it to Cabinet, I decided right there and then that that's where I want to be. They've got a four-year mandate – and – a clear majority. They can do just about anything they want. And yes, Gordon, I do want to be part of that. My heart has always been in politics. I'll probably pick up French while I'm at it."

"Sounds like a great opportunity. I wish you well."

"Thanks. And now, let's get back to business. Love business."

They made love again and then Gordon got dressed and headed home.

Gordon didn't see much of Jennifer that summer. She got romantically involved with a lawyer in the Department of Health and they spent a lot of time at his cottage on Big Rideau Lake. Gordon had been looking forward to seeing her again, and getting back into her bed. *That's life, I guess. Still, it would have been great to spend more time with her.*

Pat O'Brien spent most weekends in Toronto meeting with constituents Saturday morning and attending events throughout the riding in the afternoon. Gordon often drove him to the various events.

"What do you plan on doing with your life, Gordon?" O'Brien asked one afternoon as they were on their way to a picnic organized by the Eglinton Boys and Girls Club.

"Not too sure about that," Gordon replied. "I'll be going to U of T next year and figure I've got lots of time to decide what happens after that."

"What will you be taking?"

"Political science. Working on your campaign really got me interested in the whole political process. Talking to people at the doors gave me a different perspective on things. One door they're one hundred per cent Liberal. Next door they can't wait to kick the Liberals out of office. They're just all over the place."

"I'll vouch for that. Right up until the last week, I was convinced I was going to lose. Everything changed in the last five days. I took political science when I was at U of T. Not sure they should be calling it a science, like genetics or chemistry. There's nothing scientific about it. Like you found at the doors, the voters are all over the map."

"That's for sure. Anyway, Political Science is what I'm going to take."

"They've got some good professors there. I can vouch for that," O'Brien said. "One of the best departments in all of North America. You'll do well there."

About two months before Bill completed the third year of his B.A. at the University of Alberta, Dr. Robert Johnston, Chairman of the Department of Sociology at the Berkeley campus of the University of California, came to Edmonton as a guest lecturer. He was a very close friend of Dr. Hector Spencer, his counterpart at the University of Alberta, whom he had first met when they were both students at the U of A.

Bill was one of Spencer's most promising students and he invited him to dinner at his home so he could meet Johnston who had taught at the University of Alberta before being hired away as Chairman of Sociology at the University of California.

"So, Bill?" Johnston asked as they started in on their glazed Virginia ham with the pineapple and maraschino cherries on top, "where are you going to take your master's?"

"Right here," Bill replied. "It's a bit of a struggle financially, but this is where I'll be taking my M.A."

"It would be less of a struggle if you joined us at Berkeley," Johnston continued. "We could offer you a scholarship that would cover your fees and books, not just for your master's but all the way through until you get your PhD."

Spencer waved his knife good-naturedly at Johnston. "Now, Robert, don't you go poaching one of my best students. Bill's at the top of his class and we want to keep him here – right here on the banks of the North Saskatchewan."

He considered Bill to be one of his brightest students and had taken a particular interest in him right from the start.

"There's more to education than this beautiful campus you have on the banks of the Saskatchewan," Johnston replied. "I'll bet you can't match a scholarship that will take him all the way through his master's and the doctorate."

Bill decided to just listen and hear them both out. *Kinda nice to be fought over – from both sides of the border.*

"How can it possibly cover the master's and the doctorate?" Spencer asked with puzzlement. "I've never heard of anything that generous."

"It's a new scholarship program from the R.W. Dempster Foundation," Johnston said. "R.W. graduated from Berkeley in 1912 and made a tremendous amount of money in real estate. The foundation is now awarding one scholarship a year to exceptional Canadian students and, as I just said, it covers the books and the fees. All Bill will have to pay for is food and rent. And, yes, it will take him all the way through his doctoral studies."

"But, that's Berkeley," Spencer said. "How would a student from Canada qualify for something as generous as that?"

"You don't remember R.W.? R.W. Dempster? Originally from Calgary? One of our best success stories?"

"Oh, that Dempster," Spencer said. "Yes. Yes. I remember that story now. His father ran a small shoe store in Calgary as I recall."

"That's right. R.W. is a genuine rags-to-riches American success story," Johnston said as he reached for the bottle of white Zinfandel. "A Horatio Alger success from Cowtown. Dropped dead at sixty-two about three years ago. Heart attack."

"Well, I'll tell you right now," Spencer said emphatically. "I'm going to do everything I can to keep Bill right here in Edmonton. I've got a lot of time and energy invested in that fine young mind of his. What say you, young Bill?"

"Nice to be fought over," Bill chuckled. "The interest on both sides of the border is very much appreciated. However, I must say, the scholarship does sound very attractive. With a scholarship like that, I'd be able to cut back considerably on working evenings and Saturdays just to keep my head above water. It does sound good. Very good indeed."

There were very few native people living in Berkeley. All of the people Bill socialized with after he settled in there were white. There was, however, one native person that he met. At a meeting of the Berkeley Social Planning Council.

Josephine Honanie was in her mid-forties and was originally from the Hopi Reservation in northeastern Arizona. She was a registered nurse and worked at a local long-term care facility.

Josephine told Bill she felt embarrassed when she saw native people on the television or in the movies dancing at pow wows. She said she experienced real shame and hoped to God nobody watching would find out she was native.

"I don't want people to think I'm one of them," she said. "Dancing around in feathers and buckskin, for God's sake."

"But how can you be embarrassed watching your own people?" Bill asked with a perplexed look on his face. "That's who we are. Indian. There's nothing to be ashamed of in that. What in the world would make you feel like that? To be ashamed of your own kind. Embarrassed about who you are."

"Try a lifetime being treated as second-class. Indians in the movies screaming their heads off scalping white women and children. Tonto playing second fiddle to the Lone Ranger. Wasn't it like that for you?"

"I've felt discriminated against. Lots of times. But never ashamed of who I am. We live well at my home reserve. Don't owe anything to anyone. I'm not embarrassed to be who I am. I'm a Blackfoot and damned proud of it."

"Well I'm a Hopi and damned well ashamed of it. Got off that reservation first chance I got and haven't been back since. Not going to neither. No one knows I'm Indian. Not going to neither. I'm only speaking to you 'cause I saw the article about you in the *Chronicle* being the first Indian ever to attend Berkeley. Pretty flattering piece if I do say so myself. Not going to write something about me like that they're not. Not someone who changes old folks' smelly diapers and empties bedpans for a living. Not someone like me."

"But I don't see why ..."

She cut him off. "Really don't want to talk no more. Just wanted to say hello and shake your hand. Congratulate you on making something of yourself. Got to go now. You take care. Keep doin' good stuff. You're gonna make it. Real big I bet."

And then she shook his hand and left.

As he reflected later on what Josephine had said, Bill thought again about the enormous amount of damage the white man's religion and culture had done to native people. So many of his people were ashamed of their past. Of their heritage. Like those lying drunk on the sidewalk in downtown Edmonton. It made him angry. Very angry.

He remembered being up on Thunder Mountain hunting deer with his father when he was fourteen and the stories his father told him about the Blackfoot and the white settlers. He imagined what it would have been like living with his great-great-grandfather and his four wives and one hundred horses. *Dad says the minister for the interior back then called us the most warlike and intelligent of all the bands in the northwest. "Intractable." That's what he said we were. Hard to control. Hard to deal with. They got us under control all right. Exterminated the buffalo. Left us with no food, no clothes, no hides to cover our lodges. Infected us with their smallpox and TB. Got us drunk with that goddamned firewater. Pretty near killed us all off. Made us sign treaties surrendering our lands with the Red Coats pointing their field cannons straight at us. Cheated us out of our lands with guns, firewater and a barrel full of deceit. That's what Dad said. Turned us into beggars. Forced us right down on our knees. We didn't have a chance. Didn't have a chance.*

Bill first saw Jean Weasel Fat at a pow wow down at the Blood Tribe Reserve just north of the American border. He had just finished the first year of the PhD program at Berkeley and was spending the summer at Big Thunder.

About two hundred Blackfoot were circling, shuffling, around the floor of the school gymnasium – they had moved inside because of the rain – keeping time to the beat of the drums. Round and round they went in traditional costumes with a multitude of colours. The jingles on the women's dresses went jing jing, jing jing. Jing jing, jing jing.

Jean was a very attractive nineteen-year-old with long black hair that streamed down to the small of her back. She was wearing a purple jingle dance dress. Her feet barely touched the floor. Just sort of kissed it as she circled the gym with an eagle feather fan clasped in her hand. She was dancing to the drums. Feeling the dance. Getting power from it. Feeling who she really was. Where she belonged. In a safe place. Feeling at one with the other dancers. At one with Mother Earth.

Bill went up to her after the dance and told her Doreen Many Fingers was his aunt and he had come down from Big Thunder to visit her and dance at the pow wow. Bill was an accomplished bear dancer. Jean had known the Many Fingers family since she was a child. She felt quite comfortable with this handsome dancer from the Big Thunder reserve up near Calgary. They got hot dogs, fries and pop, from one of the stands and sat down at a picnic table under the branches of a huge tree.

Bill told her he would be leaving for California at the end of August to start work on the second year of his doctorate. Jean had never met a Blackfoot who had gone to university before. Most Blackfoot kids never made it to high school and most of those that did, like her, dropped out before the end of the first year.

"Doesn't that cost a bit?" she asked. "Going to university in California?"

"Actually, it costs a lot. But I have a scholarship that covers all my fees and books. Right through until I get my PhD. All I pay for is rent and food and stuff like that."

Jean was quite attracted to Bill. She'd seen him dancing earlier that day and was impressed with the way he moved. Really stood out from the other dancers. Looked like someone who was going to make something of himself.

"I'm really missing Big Thunder," Bill said. "Haven't seen enough of it over the last several years. Really like it there. It's a lot like down here. Lots of room. Big river. Mountains to look at when you're out riding. Do you ride?"

"Yes. I ride. Sometimes."

"Want to come riding with me?"

"Don't see why not," she answered rather coyly.

"Okay. Where do you live?"

"My folks have a trailer behind Fred Tail Feathers' store. It's just…"

"I know where it is. I've been there a couple of times. Does your dad work at the store?"

"No. Dad works at the school. Janitor stuff."

"Okay. How about if I pick you up at ten tomorrow morning?"

"Sounds okay to me."

"Good. I'll bring lunch. We can go for a long ride."

They went riding the next day and had lunch in the shade of a big tree by the Belly River. Bill was very attracted to Jean. He'd had a couple of girlfriends but no one like Jean. There was a wild, untamed, quality about her. She got him really hot and bothered.

The attraction was mutual. But, for different reasons. Jean was totally bored with life on the reserve and desperately wanted a way out. She thought that Bill, with his university degrees and all that, might be just the right ticket.

When they got back to her family's trailer later that afternoon, Bill told her he had to go up to Big Thunder the next morning but he'd be back on Tuesday.

"I'd like that," she said. "Like that a lot."

Bill got down to the Blood Tribe Reserve several times that summer. They rode together a lot and, one weekend when he was riding broncs at a rodeo in Fort Macleod, Bill took Jean with him.

"My dad told me this was where the Mounties built their first fort, back in 1874," Bill said when they took time out for hot dogs, fries and pop. "They were called the North-West Mounted Police back then. They named the fort after their first commander, a Scotsman by the name of Colonel James Farquharson Macleod. That's who he was. A Scotsman. Led his troops all the way from Ontario about ninety years ago. Crossed the prairies when they were almost completely free of the white settlers. Back when things were the way they were supposed to be. Teeming with buffalo. The way the Creator gave this land to the Blackfoot."

"Why'd they build their fort here?"

"It was a crossroads. Wagon trains from different directions used to stop here. Indians from all over – they called Macleod's troops 'Red Coats' – used to camp here. It was a grazing ground for the buffalo. Always lots to eat. You know that buffalo head that's on the Mounties' badge?"

"Yes. I've seen it."

"That was Macleod's idea. The buffalo were a huge factor back then. Back before the white people wiped them all out. Ruined everything. My dad says we never stood a chance against them. Not a hope in hell. They outnumbered us. Outgunned us. We didn't have a chance."

He munched on his hot dog and took another sip of Coke. "The big treaty, Blackfoot Treaty they called it, was signed over at the Blackfoot Crossing on the Bow River. Took Macleod's soldiers three days to march there. Back in 1877. There was about four thousand Indian men, women and children there. Squatting on the grass in a semi-circle around their chiefs and the white negotiators during the day and sleeping in tents beside the river. It was quite the occasion. Blackfoot, Blood, Piegan, Stony, and Sarcee. Chief Red Crow from your reserve was there, too. Made a lot of problems for the white negotiators, he did. When it was all over, Macleod's soldiers fired off their big field cannons. Scared the hell out of everyone. Could have wiped them all out on the spot. If they'd felt so inclined."

"How'd you know all this?"

"My dad told me. My grandfather – he's dead now – killed in a car crash about three years before I was born – was there when they signed the treaty. His dad was chief at the time, just like my granddad was before he was killed. Anyway, my granddad told my dad all about it and Dad wrote it down in a book he kept at our house. That's how I know about it. The book's still there."

"I didn't know any of that," Jean said. "They didn't tell us anything about it at school."

"Good reason why not," Bill said with a sharp edge to his voice. "They've got nothing to be proud of. Swindled us out of our land. Pretty near wiped out the entire Blackfoot nation. Like my dad says, they had the guns, the firewater, and a bad habit of lying."

Jean took the bus to Calgary in early August and Bill picked her up at the bus terminal and took her to Big Thunder to meet his family. He had met the Weasel Fats a couple of times and didn't think much of them. Jean's dad drank too much and her older brother was in jail at Lethbridge. Armed robbery. The mother worked in the laundry at the hospital. She didn't get drunk like the father. Just the same, Bill didn't have much use for her. Seldom said much. Looked totally worn down by the cares of living. Cigarette hanging out of her mouth all the time.

It was around six when they got to Big Thunder. Sarah had laid out a big supper of roast moose, boiled potatoes and peas. Sarah's sister Doreen had already filled her in a bit on the Weasel Fat family and she had reservations about Bill getting involved with Jean.

"What do you do down there?" Sarah asked in an effort to strike up a conversation.

"I'm working with my mom in the laundry at the hospital," Jean replied. "There's not much else available on the reserve."

"I don't suppose there is," Sarah said as she passed Jean the bowl of peas. "I don't suppose there is."

"I've told Jean she should get out of there," Bill said. "Get some training as a cashier or something and get a job in Calgary. There's nothing down there. Absolutely nothing."

"How'd you feel about living in Calgary?" Sarah asked.

"That'd be okay. Anything would be better than down there."

Richard hadn't said anything. Just sat there eating his moose meat and potatoes. Listening to them talk. Sizing Jean up. He could see why Bill had taken a shine to her. She was a sexy little thing. Had a real nice figure. And she knew it. And used it. Apart from that, there really wasn't all that much to her. Dropped out of high school before finishing her first year. Works at the laundry in the hospital. *Bill could do a lot better than her. Maybe, when he gets back to California, he'll find someone more suitable. Let's hope so.*

Sarah was thinking somewhat along the same lines. She couldn't put her finger on it. But, there was something about Jean Weasel Fat that set off the warning bells. *Good thing William's leaving for California at the end of the month. This is not the best girl for him.*

That feeling was shared by Bill's younger sister. Janet had met a lot of Jeans in her young life. Always using their sex to get what they wanted. Rubbing up against guys' legs and turning them on. *Don't like her. Don't like her at all.*

Hughie, who was two years younger than Bill, knew exactly what his brother saw in Jean. *Great tits. And that ass – that ass that's something to die for. And that long, black, shiny hair. Love to bury my head in it. Her pussy's probably black and shiny too. Bet Bill knows all about that by now.*

"You'd like Calgary," Hughie said to Jean as he offered her some more meat. "It's a great place. You'd like it there."

"Thanks, Hughie," Jean said, letting her fingers rub against his as she took the big china platter from him. "If you say it's good, I'm sure Calgary would be a great place. Couldn't tell much from the bus terminal. But, if you say it's good, I'll take your word for it."

"Take his word for it," Bill said with a smile. "There's lots more for you in Calgary than you'll ever find down by the border. Not knocking it, mind you. It is a beautiful place to live. But there's nothing there. Lots of landscape but nothing to do."

"That's not quite so, William," Sarah said. "There's good ranching land down there. Your Aunt Doreen and Uncle Mike make a good living down there. A very good living."

"Maybe so. But Jean's folks don't. Her dad's a janitor at the school and her mom works in the laundry at the hospital – like Jean does. They don't make much. That's why they're living in a trailer. Jean needs to get out of there. There's nothing there for her. Nothing at all."

"No argument from me on that score," Jean said. "I can't wait to get out."

CHAPTER
- 8 -

During his second year in political science at the University of Toronto, Gordon attended classes taught by Dr. Donald Henderson, Chairman of the Department of History. Henderson, whose great-grandfather had been a blacksmith in Liverpool and moved his family to London, Ontario, in 1872, held a deeply-entrenched belief that every major advance in western civilization was spearheaded by the English-speaking peoples of the world.

Gordon was a very bright student and Henderson liked some of the interventions he made in class. After a while, he invited Gordon to have tea with him in his office.

"You know, Gordon," he said during one of their many teas together, "when I was growing up, the British Empire stood for something in the world. I used to look at all that pink spread across the face of the world map and feel that I was part of something magnificent. All of India, Burma, and Malaya was pink. Pink was also used for Egypt and almost one-half of the African continent.

"And, of course, Canada, Australia and the United Kingdom herself were also painted pink. It was a sight to behold. On the flag-poles in those days, the Union Jack waved proudly in the Canadian breeze just as it did in Great Britain and Africa and Australia, India, the West Indies and every other part of the British Empire. We were part of a worldwide enterprise. Part of something truly magnificent.

"The Empire is nothing like it used to be in the old days. India's a republic now. So are all too many of the others. It's just not the same without them. Now, of course they're still part of the commonwealth, the British Commonwealth, but you can't compare a commonwealth to an empire. Certainly not to the British Empire."

He paused for a moment and puffed on his pipe. "And, here in Canada, things are now altogether different than they were when I was growing up. It wasn't until after the end of the Second World War that we had this mass movement of non-British immigrant people into Canada. More than a million and a quarter of them came in through Pier 21 at Halifax. Before their arrival, we enjoyed more than two centuries of white, Western European, civilization under the British flag. It's not like that now. Not like that at all."

Gordon got a lot of inspiration from his times with Professor Henderson. He always spoke highly of the man and there was no doubting the fact that Henderson had a profound influence on his way of thinking.

Gordon was quite smitten the first time he saw Carol Winston in the University of Toronto's Davidson Hall. She was a very beautiful twenty-four-year-old. About five foot seven with a gorgeously-curved body which she kept in great shape. Her eyes were olive green and her long black hair cascaded over her shoulders.

He was studying for his master's degree and working evenings four days a week and on the weekends as an assistant manager at the Chicken Hut, a popular family restaurant at Yonge and St. Clair. He was still living with his parents. He was the president of the Young Conservatives Club at the university and vice-president of the Conservative Party of Canada's Youth Commission.

He made some inquiries and learned that Carol was in her final year in law. Her father, Granville Winston, was a very successful real estate developer and owned properties stretching from Halifax to Victoria. He also learned that, while Carol had no particular interest in politics, she was interested in national unity and in building bridges between the English and the French.

He asked her to help him with a seminar on *"Confederation. Today and Tomorrow"* he was organizing for mid-January. It would be very much appreciated, he said, if she could identify two speakers to partic-ipate in a debate on the distribution of powers in a modern federation.

The seminar went very well and, as people were leaving the room, Gordon asked her if she would like to have a coffee with him at the restaurant on College Street, across the road from the university. She would.

"Thanks for helping me out," he said as he stirred his first cup of coffee. "I really did appreciate it."

"You're more than welcome. I'm not into politics like you but I really am interested in finding ways to resolve the differences between the English and the French."

Gordon was quite handsome, just a little under six feet, and Carol rather liked the way he parted his hair on the right side. In fact, she'd gotten a bit of a crush on him the first time she saw him playing with the Varsity Blues. He cut quite a figure carrying that football across the goal line. She really liked him.

"You're right, Carol. We can't possibly reach our full potential as a nation until we resolve this long-standing feud about Quebec's proper place in Confederation. It's gone on for altogether too long. Not only that, as that professor you brought in from Laval clearly demonstrated, there's altogether too much misinformation being bandied about."

Carol smiled for a moment. "Well, you did say you wanted the issue to be argued from both sides. Professor Lesage certainly did a fine job of presenting the French nationalists' side of the issue."

"He did that. I'm surprised that he didn't insist on delivering his arguments in French."

"Why not?" Carol asked. "We are a bilingual country. Why shouldn't he be able to speak in his first language?

"If we were to adopt a policy of official bilingualism, that would mean being able to speak English or French, your choice, in dealing with federal institutions – Parliament, passport office, civil service – stuff like that. It would not mean that he could speak French in Davidson Hall.

"So, if you were to speak at Laval, or some other French univer-sity, it's okay for you to speak English. Right? But, not the other way around. When they speak at our universities, they must speak English?"

"Touche," Gordon conceded. "Good point. Let's save this argument for another day."

He was glad she'd agreed to have coffee with him. She was so alive. So animated. So absolutely sexy.

Three days after their discussion over coffee, Gordon asked Carol to have dinner with him at the Old Spaghetti Factory. They got on well. The conversation was animated. Carol didn't pull back when Gordon reached across the table and held her hand.

"I'm glad you're here," he said.

"Me, too."

They had lunch together a couple of times after that. And then, on the one night a week Gordon wasn't working at the Chicken Hut, they started having supper together and taking in a movie.

As much as Gordon wanted to, they didn't make love. Carol was a virgin. They did get into some heavy petting and she enjoyed that. Enjoyed it a lot. But, for now, that was as far as she wanted to go. At least, she thought it was. She did get quite aroused when they were petting and sometimes wondered if it was time to find out what sex was really all about.

One day, during the spring break, Carol invited Gordon to come to her home and have dinner with her on his night off from the Chicken Hut. Her parents were at their condominium in Florida and Carol had the house all to herself.

"Welcome to my home," she said as she gave him a kiss on the cheek.

"And quite a home it is," Gordon said, as he returned the kiss and handed her the red roses.

He'd never been in Carol's house before. The foyer was large and tiled with Italian marble. Oak bannisters followed the circular stairway to the second floor. A fire was crackling in the living room. The mahogany table in the dining room was set for dinner.

"Come with me to the kitchen," she said. "I'm just finishing the salad."

Carol poured them drinks. Scotch and soda for her. Vodka and orange for Gordon. It was a large kitchen. Table for six. Tiffany lamp hanging from the ceiling. Granite countertops. The big picture window looked out on a huge garden at the back.

"You can see the river from back there," Carol said. "We get down from the steps at the end of the garden."

She put the striploin steaks on the plates, along with the baked potatoes and vegetables. "Bring the salad, will you, Gord? The wine's already on the table."

The steak was tasty and juicy. Medium rare. Just the way Gordon liked it.

"It's good," he said. "Real juicy."

"Cooked too much?"

"Nope. Just right."

After they finished their lemon meringue pie, Gordon stood up and reached for the plates.

"Don't worry about them," Carol said. "I'll put them in the washer after."

She picked up the half-empty bottle of Bordeaux and said: "Let's finish this in front of the fire."

They moved through to the living room and sat on the chocolate brown leather sofa in front of the fireplace. Carol snuggled up against Gordon and held up her glass. "To us and all that comes to us."

"To us," he said, as he clinked her crystal wine glass and put his arm around her shoulders.

They sat there, not saying a word, just watching as the flames licked the logs and cast a warm glow around the room. Carol snuggled up even closer. They kissed. A long, deep, kiss.

"I'm ready," Carol whispered in his ear. "Let's do it."

"You mean – make out?" he asked with pleased surprise.

"Make out. Make love. Whatever. I'm ready, but, be gentle. This'll be my first time."

"I want to," Gordon said. "But we can't. I don't have a condom."

She wrinkled her nose mischievously. "I thought football stars carried condoms with them all the time."

"Haven't played football for more than a year now. Besides, I wasn't a star."

"To me you were. You looked great in the blue and white. When you carried that ball across the goal line, the first time I saw you, I got a rush."

Gordon took another sip of wine and thought for a moment. "I could pull out – before I come. That way, you'd be safe."

"Done that before? Pulled out?"

"Couple of times."

"So, there have been other times. Other girls."

"Never said there wasn't. Not born yesterday. Anyway, getting back to the priority of the day, if I pull out, you'll be okay. I'll go slow so you can come first. Then, just before I'm ready to pop, I'll pull out."

"You sure it will be okay?"

"Absolutely. There's not a thing to worry about. Promise."

It felt good having him inside her. She'd masturbated a couple of times. But, it never felt this good. Never felt like this. Just as she felt she was about to have her orgasm, Gordon started pumping faster, let out a moan, and flopped on top of her.

"What? What happened?" she asked in a startled voice.

"Oh, shit! I'm so sorry. I – I went off inside you. I just got so excited. It felt so good in there and then – all of a sudden – I just went pop. Couldn't hold the stuff back. Didn't have time to pull out."

"Goddammit, Gordon!" Carol said angrily. "You weren't supposed to do that. You said you would pull out. You promised you'd do that before you had your precious orgasm."

"Okay. Okay. I'm sorry. What else can I say? Besides, you're not going to get pregnant the first time you have sex. The odds of that happening are a billion to one."

"That may be so but it should be my decision, and my decision alone, whether or not I'm prepared to take that kind of risk. That is not your decision to make. No matter what the odds of my getting pregnant are, you had no business – absolutely no business pulling off a stunt like that."

"I'm sorry. I really am," he said as he started to get dressed. "You're right. It was absolutely wrong of me to do that. Really stupid. But, it just felt so good."

She cuffed him on the side of the head. And then she put her blouse back on. "What's done is done. You're probably right about the odds of my getting pregnant first time out. I should be okay."

They finished getting dressed and got back on the sofa in front of the fire. "Next time," she said, "make sure you wear a condom. And, just as important, make sure I get an orgasm. I didn't get a damned thing out of that. Came close. But no cigar."

He was glad there was going to be a next time. For a moment there, he thought he'd blown it with Carol and that their relationship was over. "I promise. Condom and an orgasm."

From that point forward, on the few occasions that they found time to have sex, Gordon always wore a condom.

Gordon was in the middle of organizing another seminar. This one was going to focus on the demands of French-speaking Quebeckers for special status within the Canadian confederation. They wanted increased powers for their province and more rights for people whose first language was French in the federal civil service. Carol was in charge of preparing all the background papers for the seminar. She enjoyed pulling all of the research together and boiling each subject down to a two-page background paper.

She liked working alongside Gordon. He had a sharp mind and she admired the way he was able to grasp a concept, run with it, and persuade others that it was God's honest truth. Not that she agreed with everything he expressed himself on. They had some sharp differences of opinion. There was a fair bit on which she did not agree. But, she did like the way his mind worked.

Carol expected that she would have her period towards the end of March. It didn't happen. At first, she figured it was probably coming late. Like it had done on other occasions. But, it wasn't late. It didn't happen at all. That got her worried.

He said the odds of me getting pregnant were a billion to one. There was no chance I'd get pregnant first time out. Absolutely no chance. No chance at all. What if he's wrong? What if I am pregnant? Goddammit, Gordon, why the hell didn't you pull out? Like you promised you would. Damn you.

Towards the end of April, Carol felt a slight swelling of her breasts and her nipples were very sensitive when she touched them. She was a lot more tired than usual and started taking naps in the afternoon. She also felt a bit nauseous after getting out of bed some mornings. *Oh, God, no. Don't let me be pregnant after all. This is not the right time. Not the right time at all. Maybe I'm just imagining these things. Overly hyper because of getting ready for the seminar. Exams coming up. This is most likely all in my mind. False alarms designed to drive me crazy. Which they are.*

When she didn't get her period in April, she set up an appointment with Dr. Morton Turner. He asked her a few questions, took some tests, and asked her to wait outside his office until he reviewed the results. Carol ran all sorts of permutations through her mind as she sat in the waiting room. *What if I am? Then, what do I do? Dammit. The timing is all wrong. Absolutely all wrong. Why couldn't Gordon just keep his promise? Pull out like he was supposed to. Why didn't he have a goddamned condom? Guys are supposed to have them with them. All the time. It works fine with the condom. Why did he have to be so selfish and pull out too late? Why?*

After about forty-five minutes had passed, the nurse asked her to go back into Dr. Turner's office. He was seated at his desk, reading glasses perched at the end of his nose, going over her file and the test results.

"You're pregnant, Carol. About two months along. You'll be having the baby some time toward the end of December. Sorry. But, that's the way it is."

"No mistake?" she asked, a bit shaken. "The tests couldn't be wrong?"

"No mistake, Carol. There's a little human growing inside you and, by the end of the year, it's going to be a living, breathing, crying, little baby girl or boy wanting its diaper changed. No mistake. You are pregnant."

He reached over and gave her hand a consoling squeeze. "I'm so sorry to have to tell you this, Carol. The tests don't lie. You are going to be a mother."

"But," Carol said, regaining her composure, "We've been using a condom all along. We only had sex without it – once. The very first time."

"When would that have been?" Dr. Turner asked.

"During the March break. I'd never had sex with anyone before that."

Dr. Turner leafed through her file and the medical chart. "March break? Are you sure that's when it was?"

"Yes. Definitely. We were off school that week. Mom and Dad were in Florida."

"You couldn't have picked a worst time, Carol. According to your file, you would have been in the ovulation cycle. Worst possible time to be having unprotected sex if you don't want to get pregnant."

Her mother and father were out when she got home from Dr. Turner's office later that afternoon. She went up to her room, turned on Jazz FM, and sat in the chair beside the window. She had a lot to think about.

First, there was the baby. What to do about the baby? Betty Fuller had a botched abortion when she got pregnant in her second year at high school. It almost killed her. Abortions were illegal in Canada and the unlicensed doctor who performed the abortion made quite a mess of it. Carol was with Betty when they rushed her to the emergency room at Toronto General Hospital. If they'd gotten her there half an hour later, she'd have bled to death.

When Jane Potts, Carol's best friend, got pregnant just before they were about to graduate from high school, her father sent her to a private girls' school in England for a year. In one of several letters Jane wrote to Carol at the time, it was clear that she regretted having to give the baby up for adoption. She had grown very close to it during the pregnancy. She wanted to keep it. When they took it from her arms, she wrote, she cried uncontrollably for more than an hour.

"Giving my baby away was the worst thing I've ever had to do. He looked so beautiful. And then he was gone. Gone forever. Oh, Carol, it hurts so much. So very, very, much. I should've kept him."

Carol reflected on her friends' experience – with abortion and adoption. While she would have preferred that she hadn't gotten pregnant in the first place, she didn't consider abortion to be a viable option. Not because it was illegal but because she truly did believe in the child's right to life. She just couldn't imagine flushing her baby down some toilet. *It is my child. The more I think about it, the more comfortable I feel about carrying it to term. It's part of me now and I'd kind of like things to remain that way.*

Abortion was out. What about adoption? As she considered the option of putting the baby out for adoption, she thought back on the letters she had received from Jane Potts and how heartbroken she was when they forced her to put her baby out for adoption. "Oh, Carol, it hurts so much," Jane had written. "So very, very, much. I should have kept him."

Do I want to put myself through a painful experience like that? Carol asked herself. *To have my baby ripped out of my arms and placed with strangers? Never, ever, to hug it or see it smile again? I don't think so. That would be altogether too hurtful.*

The more she thought about it, the more convinced she became that, while she would have preferred not being pregnant, she wanted to keep the baby. But, that didn't mean she wasn't angry, very angry, with Gordon. *How utterly selfish of him to go off inside me instead of pulling out – like he promised he would. Whatever was he thinking about? Not thinking at all, that's what he was. What a selfish thing to do.*

She went down to the kitchen and poured herself a glass of milk. After having some milk and cookies, she decided to take a walk down by the river. She made her way down the wooden steps at the end of the garden. Before long, she was at the side of the river skipping pebbles across the surface of the water.

It was a clear late afternoon in May. The sun was starting to set above the ridge on the other side of the valley. As she watched the sun getting closer, and closer, to the top of the ridge, Carol's thoughts turned to Gordon. *I suppose I'll have to tell him. He is the father. Never had sex with anyone else. There's nothing immaculate about this conception. Gordon is the father.*

Carol tossed another pebble. Almost skipped its way right over to the other side of the river. *Do I love him? Love is too strong a word for it. I am very attracted to him. He looked great in that football uniform. And, he does have a fantastic mind. But, no, I wouldn't say I was in love with him. Could I love him? Over time, I suppose. Especially if I was to marry him. Marry him on account of the baby? Yes, I suppose I could love him. He says he's crazy about me. Already been talking about how things will be when we get married. Seems to have big plans for us – as a married couple. Wait till he finds out I'm pregnant.*

She headed back up the steps to the house, picked up a bag of Oreos in the kitchen, and sat beside the fireplace in the living room. Her parents hadn't come home yet. As she sat there, looking at the rug where she made love for the first time only two months ago, she thought about the effect having the baby would most likely have on her career.

She had planned on graduating in June, starting the bar admission course, and becoming an articling student at Haldimand and Brock, the big Bay Street firm that handled all of her father's legal affairs. *At least, according to Dr. Turner, the baby won't be here until around Christmas. I can start studying for the bar exams and get an entry level position with Haldimand and Brock. Work there until, probably, late November and then take a couple of months off to have the baby. Become a junior associate at Haldimand and Brock by the end of next year. Yes, it could work. Work out okay. I can still make it as a top-ranked lawyer. Argue cases before the Supreme Court. Represent top 500 corporations. It could work. Even with the baby.*

❧

Carol's father arrived home about half an hour after she got back from her walk down by the river. He had to pack for a business trip he was taking to Halifax that evening. She told him what the situation was and that Gordon was the father. He was furious.

"What were you thinking? Getting yourself pregnant by someone who works at a chicken restaurant. He's not one of ours. Not one of our circle. How could you possibly make a mistake like this?"

"I didn't plan it, Dad. Gordon didn't have a condom and then he didn't pull out like he promised he would. This is not what I had in mind."

"Damn it, Carol. How's this going to affect your career? Your future? Everything I had planned for you? How could you throw it all away like that?"

"I'm sorry, Dad. Really I am. I'd never had sex before – with anyone. I should have known better."

She seemed to be on the verge of tears. *Oh my dear, Gran thought, she looks so distraught. This is tearing her apart. No point compounding matters by going on and on about how disappointed I am in her for making a terrible mistake like this. She's hurting. I can see that.*

"What do you plan on doing – about the baby?" he asked after he gave her a consoling hug.

"Well, I certainly didn't plan it," she said. "This was the last thing I was expecting."

"But you are expecting," her father said with a smile. "No pun intended."

She was glad he seemed more interested in helping her decide what to do next than he was on lecturing her about getting pregnant in the first place. "That's a good one, Dad. Who writes your material?"

"I've got some of the best speech writers in the business. But that one was my own. Seriously, what do you want to do now?"

"While I would much rather it hadn't happened in the first place, my initial inclination is to keep it. To have the baby. Abortion is not an option. Not because it's illegal but because I truly believe every child, born or as yet unborn, has a right to live. I just couldn't imagine my baby being flushed down some toilet. I do intend to keep it."

"That's good," Gran said. "You know that I share your view on abortion one hundred per cent. It is illegal and that's the way it should remain. However, you also know what this means for your legal career. You'll have to sit things out for a spell."

"Yes, Dad, but not for long. I'm still going to graduate. Dr. Turner says the baby won't be here until around the end of December. And I don't see why I couldn't start at Haldimand and Brock after I graduate. And then, when I start popping out like a pumpkin, take a couple of months off to have the baby."

"Actually, I'm looking forward to seeing you 'popping out' as you say. You're going to make a great mother."

"I'd still rather be a great lawyer. This is not what I had in mind as the highlight of my twenty-fifth year. Not at all. Anyway, that takes care of step Number One. You are going to have a grandchild."

Gran liked the sound of that. Carol was his only child and he did want to have grandchildren. Although, this one was going to be illegitimate. "What about Gordon?" he asked. "Have you told him?"

"Not yet. I wanted to talk things over with you first. Quite frankly, I'm very angry with him right now. You might not believe this, Dad, but I was a virgin. Gordon is the only man I've ever slept with."

"I have no doubt about that, Carol. What's done is done. The main thing is what do you want to do now – about Gordon?"

"I suppose I'll have to tell him. He is the father. I've never had sex with anyone else. Gordon is the father."

"You've been going out with him for how long now – about three months?"

"Yes. The *'Confederation. Today and Tomorrow'* seminar was in the middle of January and we had dinner a week after that. Actually, it's closer to four months. "

"How do you feel about him? Not about the fact that he got you pregnant. But, overall, how do you feel about him? Are you in love with him?"

"I'd have to say love is too strong a word for it. I find him very attractive. He's great to be around."

"Could you – love him?"

"Over time, I suppose. Especially if, as I get the feeling you're suggesting, I was to marry him. Marry him because I'm going to have his baby."

"I think that would probably be the wiser course, Carol. You don't want to go through the embarrassment of being a single mother. Bearing a child out of wedlock. Most people we know would not find that acceptable."

In fact, many of them will wonder how in the world I can go along with something like this. Why I don't insist on her going off to Europe like Harry Potts did when his daughter got herself pregnant and put the child up for adoption. It could be passed off as a graduation holiday.

"I could always put the baby up for adoption" Carol said, as if she had been reading her father's mind.

"Do you really mean that?"

"Not really. It is my child. And, the more I think about it, the more comfortable I feel about carrying it to term. The baby is part of me now and, I think, I'd prefer for it to remain that way."

"Then it would appear that marriage is in order. How would Gordon feel about that?"

"He says he's crazy about me. He's already been talking about how things will be when we get married. Seems to have big plans for us – as a married couple."

Why couldn't she have gotten pregnant with someone from our own circle? Someone who was going to make something of himself. In law, finance, engineering or something like that. Why an assistant manager at a chicken restaurant? Why ask why? The die is cast. There's no round trip over Niagara Falls. It's Gordon's child. Can't change that.

"Then, I suppose, the next step is for you to tell him he's going to be a father and see how he reacts. Based on what you've told me, I expect he will probably suggest that you get married. Right away. He's got a relatively good future ahead of him and, when he gets his doctorate and starts teaching at the university, he should be able to provide a rather decent life for you and the children."

"The children, Dad?"

"Well, if you're going to give me one grandchild, you might as well give me several. The more the merrier."

"That is not going to happen. I will have this first child and give it all of the loving care that only a mother can provide. But, a couple of months after it's born – maybe four at the most – I'm back at Haldimand and Brock."

"I know how much you want to be a lawyer, darling. And, while you seem to be bearing up rather well, I know how upsetting this situation you are now in must be for you. You will be a lawyer – and a damned good one at that. All I'm asking for is two or three grandchildren for me to enjoy before I go completely bald."

"You'll have grandchildren, Dad. One this year and one or two nine or ten years down the road. But, not before. I'll be arguing cases in the Supreme Court before I have another child."

"We'll see," Gran said with a warm smile. "The mother instinct might get the better of you yet. Once you've had one child, you're bound to want more."

"I will, eh? And how come I'm an only child?"

He looked quite sad for a moment. "That's because," he said rather slowly, "your mom had a very difficult time when she gave birth to you. Something went wrong and she can't have children."

"Oh dear, Dad. I had no idea. I'm so sorry. I – I just didn't know," she said as she gave him a big hug.

"We enjoyed you so much, Carol, and we wanted you to have brothers and sisters but it just wasn't meant to be. The doctor told us your mom simply could not have another child."

"I'm so sorry, Dad. So terribly, terribly sorry."

"Don't be, my darling. Just get me grandchildren. Lots of them."

"One is all you're getting right now. Let's take it one child at a time."

"Deal," he said. "Now let's focus on the present. Gordon won't be able to support you – not with him still working on his master's degree. And then, as I understand it, he'll be starting on his PhD right after that. It's going to be a long time before he'll be bringing any money into the home."

"He does work part-time at the Chicken Hut. But, you're right, it doesn't amount to a great deal. But, then again, I will be earning a salary at Haldimand and Brock. An entry level salary, grant you, but it will provide income."

Gran paused for a moment and took a sip of his Scotch and water. Then he looked at the fire and let his eyes scan the room.

"There's plenty of room in the old servants' quarters on the third floor. You and Gordon could stay there – with my first grandchild. Your mother would have no objection to that, none at all."

"You're moving right along at a fast clip, Dad. Maybe we should hold off on all this advance planning until I have an opportunity to break the news to Gordon. We're having lunch tomorrow and I'll tell him about the baby then."

"Not until tomorrow?"

"No. This is a big step. A major life-changing step. I want to be sure I'm completely comfortable with it – that I have thought it all out – before I bring Gordon into the picture. I'll let you know what he says. And now, if you don't mind, I'm going to my room to listen to some good music. My mind needs a bit of a break right now."

"All right, my darling. Your mother will be back from her bridge club in about half an hour. Should I tell her about – about your situation?"

"I'd rather do that myself, Dad. It's going to hit Mom like a ton of bricks. This is something I really should handle by myself. I'll be back down in a couple of hours and I'll break the news to her."

"You're probably right. I'll be gone by then. My flight's at eight. I'll pop my head in to say goodbye before I leave."

"Okay, Dad. Good luck with Halifax." With that, she gave him a big hug and a kiss.

Gordon and Carol were having lunch at the restaurant across the street from the university.

"I'm pregnant," she said, halfway through her grilled chicken salad.

"You're what?" Gordon said, almost choking on his home fries.

"The doctor told me yesterday afternoon. The baby should be here by late December."

"But – but how? How could that happen? I've been using a condom like – like you asked me to."

"Not that first night, you didn't. Not that first night when you promised you would pull out before having your rapturous orgasm. Not that night, you didn't."

"I'm sorry, Carol. I really am. But, you know, I just got so excited. It felt so good being inside you. And then, pop, the stuff came before I could pull out."

"Well, it's done now. We can't reverse it and, in about seven months from now, I'm the one who's going to be popping. You're going to be a father, Gordon MacArthur. What do you think of that?"

"I think it's just great. You know how crazy I am about you. December, eh?"

"Yes. Probably about a week before Christmas."

"Well, that's going to be some Christmas present."

"It's not the present I had in mind, Gordon. I expected to be at Haldimand and Brock this Christmas. This is not, most definitely not, what I had been planning on."

"Again, I'm sorry. I can't believe it could have happened on our first time. That's really weird." He paused for a moment, drank some Coke, and then asked: "What do you think we should do about it?"

"I'm glad you said we. This does involve both of us. It's something we're going to have to deal with together."

"Yes. Yes. No argument from me on that. None whatsoever. What I mean is, you've had more time to think about it than I have. What do you want to do?"

"Well, I wouldn't give a moment's consideration to abortion. I'm totally opposed to it. And, having thought about it a bit since yesterday afternoon, I don't consider adoption to be an option either. I want to have our baby."

Gordon thought about that for a moment. *Wow. This is quite an unexpected turn of events. I really hadn't expected anything like this. How selfishly stupid of me. I should have pulled out. It would have felt just as good spilling the stuff on her belly. But, like Carol says, what's done is done. She **is** pregnant.* "What about law? Haldimand and Brock and all that?"

"Well, with the baby not due until Christmas, I could go ahead and get an entry level position with them after I graduate and then take a couple of months off to have the baby. Meanwhile, I'll start the bar admission course. If everything works out as planned, I'll be back with the firm by March at the latest. It should work out. Meanwhile, if I am going to be a mother, and it looks like I am, then I want to be the best mother I can possibly be."

Gordon sipped his Coke and thought for a moment. "Are you planning on doing all that on your own? Taking care of him or her and still practising law?"

"With all you've been saying lately about how we're meant to be together – and how happy we're going to be when we get married and have kids – all of that – I thought it might be better for us to tackle this together."

"You mean us get married?"

"You've talked about it often enough," she said with a warm smile.

He reached across the table and took her hand in his. "Yeah, I have. And yeah, if you're serious, you're damned right I would want to marry you. Absolutely!"

"Is that a proposal?"

"No, that's an acceptance. You're the one who proposed. Less than two minutes ago."

"I wouldn't put it that way. But, if you're all right with it, so am I."

"Guess that means we're getting married, Carol."

"Guess it does, Gordon. Not quite the way we'd thought we'd be starting out but, yes, I'm perfectly fine with it. I do care for you. A great deal."

They both stood up, put their arms around one another, and kissed.

"We're getting married," Gordon called out excitedly to the people at the other tables in the small restaurant. "We're getting married."

They all clapped and smiled, held up their glasses, and wished them well.

Carol told Gordon about her father's offer to have them move into the house and use the servants' quarters on the third floor. "It would save us the cost of having to rent an apartment right away," she said. "At least until the baby is settled in and I'm bringing in an income from Haldimand and Brock."

Gordon didn't answer right away. The offer was generous all right but he wasn't too sure he wanted to move into another man's house. He'd prefer to have a place of his own.

"It's really good of your dad to offer," he said. "And you're right. It would save us a good chunk of money. Still, if we could afford it, I'd rather we paid our own way and had a place of our own."

"I can understand that," Carol said. "We all have our pride. But, let's look at this from another angle. If we were living with my parents and I was bringing in money from Haldimand and Brock, you could cut back on your hours at the Chicken Hut and spend more time on your studies. Maybe even cut out the Chicken Hut altogether."

He sipped his Coke and thought about that. *She does have a point. Juggling the Chicken Hut and the master's is taking its toll. I am a bit behind in my studies. So much is happening. So fast. The baby coming. Getting married. And now, maybe moving in with her parents after the wedding. Too much too fast.*

"Let's sit on it for now," he said. "We don't have to decide that today. Not on top of all the other decisions we're making. Keeping the baby. Getting married. That makes for a pretty full plate. I appreciate your dad's offer but would just like a little more time to think about it."

"Take all the time you need," Carol said. "Speaking of time, I've got to get back to class. We'll talk about this, all of this, later." She reached across the table and gave his hand an affectionate squeeze. "I think we should accept Dad's offer. That way, I won't have to pack all of my worldly belongings and move out of the house. Selfish me."

CHAPTER
- 9 -

About a week before he was leaving for California, Bill went riding with Jean down by the Belly River at the Blood Tribe Reserve.

"How'd you like to come to California with me?" he asked shortly after they'd made love under a tree beside the river.

"Could we go to Hollywood?" Jean asked as she buttoned up her blouse.

"Sure. It's a bit of a drive from Berkeley. But, yes, we could go there. Sometime."

"I'd like that," Jean said. "I'd like to go to Hollywood."

"Okay, but what about Berkeley? I'm not just talking about a visit down there. I want you to stay there. Live with me. Until I get my PhD."

"Sure. Living with you sounds great. I'd like that. Like that a lot. But, I do want to go to Hollywood. Go to one of the studios. See where they make the movies. I saw Marlon Brando in *Mutiny on the Bounty*. It was great. Down there on that island in the South Seas. I want to go to the MGM studio. One of my friends says you can see the ship there. The *Bounty*. Oh, Bill, I'd love to have been on that ship. With those big white sails taking me to all sorts of wonderful places. We can go, can't we? To MGM?"

She seemed more interested in seeing the *Bounty* than she did in living with him in Berkeley. But, that was okay with Bill. If she got a job down there, that would cover the rent and he'd be able to spend more time on his studies. On top of that, their love making was absolutely fantastic. He couldn't get enough of her. If a visit to the

MGM studio in Hollywood was part of the deal, that was okay with him. *She'll probably want to see Marlon Brando, too. If he's there when she's there.*

Sarah and Richard were both upset when Bill told them he was taking Jean with him to California. They were so proud of him. Of how well he had done at the University of Alberta. How well he was doing at Berkeley. But, now, it looked like he might be putting his academic career at risk because of this girl from the Blood Tribe reserve.

"Why take her with you?" Richard asked when they were having supper one night. "She'll just weigh you down. Keep you from your studies."

"I really like her, Dad. I just really like being with her."

Sure you do, Hughie thought to himself. *Sure you do. Here, Pussy Pussy. Black shiny pussy. Sure you do.*

"I just don't understand it," Sarah said. "You've done so well. Made us so proud of you. Why risk it all for that young girl?"

"I'm not risking anything, Mom. I just feel better when Jean's around me. She's good for me. Really good for me."

Janet decided not to weigh in on the conversation. She'd seen, more times than she cared to remember, the way young women like Jean got men hooked. Bill would just have to find out for himself what sort of woman Jean really was. Nothing she could say at that particular time had a hope in hell of stopping him.

Bill packed his bags the following Saturday and got ready to head back to California. Sarah cried as she hugged her son goodbye. "You take good care of yourself," she said as the tears trickled down her cheeks. "I don't want to lose you. You take care of yourself down there. You hear me?"

"I hear you, Mom," he said as he kissed her fondly on the cheek. "I'll take care. Promise."

Richard held back the tears as he hugged Bill goodbye. "Take care," he said rather brusquely. "Come back to us as soon as you can."

Bill felt truly blessed to have such wonderful parents. They really did love him and he loved them, very, very much. He turned to Janet, held out his arms and gave her a big hug.

"I'm going to miss you, Sis. Really will."

"Me, too," she said as she placed her cheek against his shoulder.

Hughie was at a rodeo in Cochrane. He hadn't expected his brother to leave until the middle of next week.

"Say goodbye to Hughie for me," Bill called out as he got into his car. "Give him a big hug. Squeeze the juice out of him."

"We will," Sarah said as she wiped away a tear. "A great big hug is what he's going to get."

Bill drove over to the Dodginghorse ranch to say goodbye to his Grandparents. Grandma had been quite sick lately. Her arthritis had got progressively worse, and painful, but that wasn't it. She'd picked up a virus and had developed a bad case of bronchitis. She was wheezing a lot and had a pronounced shortness of breath.

"Don't get too close to me William," she said with a big smile. "Don't want you carrying this infection all the way down to California and wiping out half the population."

"I don't care about the good folks down in California," Bill said. "It's you I'm worried about, Grandma. Don't like seeing you like this."

"Doctor says she should be out of it in a couple of weeks," Gordon Dodginghorse said. "It was a lot worse a couple of days ago. Your Grandma's going to be okay."

"That's good. She's the only Grandma I've got. Don't want to lose you, Grandma."

"No need to worry about that," Vera said. "I'll still be here when you get back. All crippled up with arthritis, but I'll be here."

He blew a kiss to his grandmother and hugged Grandfather goodbye.

When he got to the Blood Tribe Reserve, he left his luggage at his Aunt Doreen's house, borrowed the big Palomino and the Pinto and rode over to Jean's trailer. She was outside reading a magazine.

"You coming to California with me?" he asked while still in the saddle.

"What?" Jean asked in a startled, almost frightened voice. She hadn't heard him coming. "Oh, it's you. The man from Berkeley."

And then she broke into a big smile, got up from her chair and walked towards him.

"Come on," he said. "Let's go for a ride. We leave for California in the morning."

"Pretty sure of yourself, aren't you?" she said as she climbed onto the Pinto. "What makes you think I'd go to California with you?"

"Oh, I have a hunch that you will," he said as he gave the Palomino a soft kick in the ribs and headed him out toward the Belly River.

They made love under their favorite tree and then stretched out on the grass and looked up at the clouds.

"You are coming with me, aren't you?" Bill asked.

"Yes. I'm coming," she said. "I want to be with you."

"Good. And I want you with me. You do good things to my head, Jean. You really do."

"Your head?" she asked teasingly. "Is that all? What about the rest of you?"

"The rest of me is pretty happy too," he said. "Nobody has ever made me tingle all over like you do. You are fantastic. Fucking fantastic. No pun intended."

They both laughed at that.

"Let's go for a swim," he said. "The water's nice and clear here."

They took their clothes off again, jumped into the river, and splashed playfully in the water.

Next morning, they headed south and crossed the border into the United States. Pretty soon, they were in Glacier National Park. Several mountain sheep high up on a ridge caught Bill's eye. A cow moose and her calf were knee deep in the river at the side of the road. A bald eagle was circling in the sky ahead of them. He slammed on the brakes. A black bear and her two cubs had come out of the bushes and started across the road in front of them.

"That was close," he said to Jean. "Didn't see them coming."

"She's gorgeous," Jean said. "We had one just like her poking around our garbage the other day. Had a cub with her, too."

"Got to steer clear of them when their cubs are with them," Bill said. "They won't let anything come between them and their cubs."

They started up the road along the lower side of a high peak. Looking down, they could see the valley that had been carved out by glaciers millions of years ago. The water on the lake was quite iced up. But there was a clear spot near the shore where a white trumpeter swan was ushering her youngsters up the bank.

"Look, Bill," Jean said excitedly. "Up there on the ridge."

There was a pack of wolves looking down at them from the nearest ridge. Must have been about eight or more of them. They reminded Bill of the wolf his dad shot when they brought the second whitetail deer to the campsite on Thunder Mountain. The gloves his mom made for him after they got home lasted for several years.

They made it to Boise, Idaho, shortly after dark and stayed overnight. Next morning, they headed for Reno, Nevada. Jean got quite nervous after they started out across the desert.

"This is scary," she said. "There's nothing here for hundreds of miles – just sand and those funny looking things. What if we run out of gas?"

"They're cactuses," Bill said. "As for the gas, I've got four five-gallon containers in the trunk. We'll be fine."

"And water?" she asked. "What if we run out of water? What if the car boils over in this heat?"

"Got five gallons of water, too," Bill said. "Like the Boy Scouts say, 'be prepared'. I'm prepared. I've crossed this desert several times. We'll be fine."

Jean wasn't so sure about that. She couldn't see a thing anywhere. No animals. No houses. No buildings. Just sand. Hundreds of acres of it. The last gas station they passed was two hours ago.

They stayed overnight in Reno, slept in in the morning, and headed over to Harrah's Casino in the afternoon.

"Let's do the slots," Jean said excitedly when they arrived at Harrah's. "I feel lucky."

Bill was quite disturbed by the way she sat at the slot machine for the next hour, eyes fixed on the brightly-coloured fruits and numbers spinning on the reel, arm yanking the lever down about six times a minute. She lost about $6, more than half a day's wages at the hospital laundry.

"My luck's going to change. Any minute now," she said, almost desperately.

"I don't think so," Bill said in a gentle tone. "That's $6 you've lost. I think it's time to go."

"Just a few more times," she said. "My luck's going to change. I just know it will. It will."

It didn't. She lost another $5 to the one-armed bandit in less than an hour.

"Let's go," Bill said. "Let's get something to eat."

They took in a supper show featuring a dance troupe from Brazil. There was a great buffet with shrimp, oysters, salad, smoked salmon, ribs, chicken, roast beef, vegetables and dessert. The music was wild and infectious. When the show was over, Jean wanted to go back to the slots. Bill said "no". He was quite firm about it and she got very upset when he refused to give her any more money. She didn't let him make love to her that night. Just curled up there with her back to him and her face buried in the pillow, crying her eyes out.

When they got settled in at Berkeley, Bill went back to his part-time job as a salesman at a local car dealership. He was able to cut back on his hours selling cars and spend more time on his studies after Jean got a job as a waitress at the Denny's Diner.

But then, at the beginning of December, Jean found out she was two months pregnant. Bill wasn't at all sure how that had happened. He'd been wearing a condom on a regular basis. *Maybe one of them leaked,* he thought. *Damn. This is altogether the wrong time for her to get pregnant. This shouldn't be happening until after I get my doctorate. But, the doctor was pretty definite about it. She is pregnant. Just going to have to accept it as something we can't change.*

He'd planned on driving up to Big Thunder to spend Christmas with his family. *Might as well go anyway. Jeez. Just wait until Mom and Dad find out about this. There's going to be a lot of "I told you so's."*

Things didn't work out as he'd planned. The people at Denny's told Jean the holidays were their busiest time of year and they couldn't let her have any time off.

"They say if I take time off now they'll have to let me go," she said. "Maybe we should stay here and wait until next summer before going home. You'll be out of school for the summer and, by that time, the baby will only be a few weeks away from being born. I'm going to have to quit work for a while around then anyway."

"You're probably right," Bill said. "We probably should stay here. For now anyway."

"You do want the baby, don't you?" Jean asked. "You don't want me to get rid of it?"

"No. No. Hell no. I do want you to have the baby. It's just that —
just that — now's not really the best time for you to be pregnant."

"I'll get rid of it if you want," Jean said. "I'll find a doctor who'll
give me an abortion."

She'd had an abortion a year before Bill showed up at the pow
wow. In fact, she'd had two abortions. When she was still in Grade
Nine, she'd gotten involved with the son of a rich cattleman who had
a ranch about fifteen miles away from the Blood Tribe reserve. When
she got pregnant, the rancher, who was dead set against his son having
anything to do with her in the first place, arranged for an abortion. It
was done on the kitchen table in the cookhouse at the ranch by a nurse
who had just been fired by the hospital for stealing drugs. She messed
Jean up pretty bad. Almost died.

And then, about a year before Bill started dating her, she'd had
another abortion. The father this time was a white travelling salesman
from Lethbridge. He was about twenty years older than Jean and
had promised he was going to marry her and they'd be moving to
Calgary. On learning that she was pregnant, he fessed up to the fact
that he was married, had five children, one of them just about four
years younger than Jean, and had no interest whatsoever in making an
honest woman out of her. He did agree to pay for the abortion. Same
unqualified nurse as last time. Same life-threatening bloody mess. She
hadn't told Bill about either abortion. *What he don't know can't hurt
him.*

"No. Absolutely not," Bill said. "I'm dead set against abortions.
They're illegal and that's the way they should stay. No, Jean, have the
baby. Please. We can make it work."

She was glad he wanted her to keep the baby. She didn't want to go
through the near-death experience of having another abortion. It had
been a pretty stressful scene.

"I want to keep it too, Bill," she said. "I want us to be a family."

"That's what we're going to be," Bill said as he gave her a big hug.
"You, me and the bayyy-beee." And then he started to sing. "Just
Jeannie and me and the baby makes three. We'll be happy in my
blue-hoo heaven."

She laughed. A laugh of relief, actually. She had expected that he might want her to get an abortion. The very thought of going back to another back-alley butcher made her skin crawl.

"Maybe, now that we're going to have a baby, it's time for us to get married," Bill said.

"You really think so? You'd really want to marry me?"

"Wouldn't have brought you down here to California if I wasn't crazy about you. Sure I want to marry you. Right now."

"But, what about your parents? I got the feeling they really don't like me all that much. Sometimes, your mother looks at me real suspicious like."

"You're not marrying my parents. You're marrying me. They'll accept it as my decision. Mine and mine alone to make. They'll be okay with it. And you? Are you okay with it?"

"I'm more than okay with it. Yes, I do want to marry you. The sooner the better."

"Okay. We'll get married here. At the City Hall. And then I'll take you to Hollywood for our honeymoon. We'll go to MGM. See the *Bounty*. And, if he's there, we'll let Marlon Brando kiss the bride. You'd like that, wouldn't you?"

"Going to the studio or kissing Marlon Brando?"

"Who said anything about you kissing Brando?" he asked with a chuckle. "It'll be him kissing the bride on the cheek."

"No problem," she said. "It's the *Bounty* I really want to see. Can't wait to stand behind the wheel on that ship and imagine myself heading for the South Seas. Palm trees and coconuts. Beautiful white sand to walk on."

"Maybe that's where we should go for our honeymoon," Bill said. "Tahiti. Tropical splendour. Swimming in the moonlight. Munching on pineapples."

"Tahiti can come later," Jean said. "Right now, I'll settle for Hollywood and the MGM studio." She paused for a moment. "Aren't we forgetting something?"

"Forgetting? Forgetting what?"

"Denny's won't let me go. This is their busiest time. We can't go to Hollywood right now."

"We can for three days," Bill said. "Christmas is three weeks away. You're off on Mondays and we'll just tack two days on. They'll be okay with a couple of days before the big rush starts. They'll be okay with it."

They were married at Berkeley City Hall. Two of Bill's friends from the university and a salesman from Karl's Auto Sales were there along with three of Jean's waitress friends from Denny's Diner. After the civil ceremony, they all went to Carmello's for a steak dinner accompanied by a bottle of Dom Perignon and three bottles of Chianti.

Bill and Jean took off for Hollywood the next morning.

Jean returned to serving tables at Denny's Diner after their short honeymoon in Hollywood and Bill dug into his studies. Jean liked being Mrs. Bill Eagletail. Bill liked having her living with him. He was looking forward to the birth of their first child.

Sarah was extremely upset when she received the pictures Bill sent her of the wedding at Berkeley City Hall and Jean holding the wheel of the *Bounty* at the MGM studio in Hollywood with Bill's big arms wrapped around her. Not being able to attend the wedding was one thing. But, William marrying Jean Weasel Fat was something else again. *This is a mistake. A huge mistake. What'd he have to go and marry her for? He could have done so much better. And why now? Why's he married and expecting a child when he's still got two years to go on his doctorate? This is all so wrong. And, I'll bet, it was no accident she got herself pregnant. Perfect way to trap William into marrying her. Perfect way. Cunning little devil that girl is.*

Doreen, whose daughters had gone to school with Jean at the Blood Tribe Reserve, had done some digging around and told Sarah some rather disturbing things about her. She told her about Jean getting pregnant in Grade Nine and having to have the abortion. She also told her about the travelling salesman who got her pregnant the year before she met Bill and how the same nurse had performed the abortion and almost killed her.

That girl seems determined to get away from the Blood reserve, Sarah thought. *Even if it kills her. Wonder if William's told her he's got his heart set on teaching sociology at the University of Toronto after he gets his doctorate?*

～

Bill and Jean drove north from Berkeley at the end of the school year. They took a day longer than usual for the trip because Jean was only three weeks away from having the baby. They spent a couple of hours with Jean's parents at the Blood Tribe Reserve shortly after crossing the Canadian border and arrived at Sarah and Richard's big log home on Friday.

Bill had called home just before they left Jean's parents' trailer and Sarah had a good supper waiting for them.

"Welcome home, William," she said as she gave him a big hug. "It's been too long. Way too long."

"Too long for me, too, Mom. But we're here now," Bill said as he kissed her affectionately on both cheeks.

Sarah then turned to Jean with open arms and gave her a gentle hug. Had to be careful about the baby. While she still had reservations about William having gotten involved with Jean in the first place, now that they were married she considered it would be as well to make the best of it. Especially with her first grandchild expected in less than three weeks.

"Where's Dad?" Bill asked.

"Calgary," Sarah replied. "He's up there for the Stampede. Three-time champion in saddle bronc riding he is now. Made quite a name for himself, your dad did. Took Hughie with him. They'll be back after it's over."

"And Janet?"

"She'll be here just after supper. Some strays found their way up the right-of-way on Thunder Mountain and she's bringing them home. Left about an hour before you got here. Won't be long though. There's only three of them."

"So, when they hear I'm coming, they all take off," Bill said with a smile. "Dad and Hughie at the Calgary Stampede and Janet up with the strays on Thunder Mountain."

"You know that's not the way it is, William," his mom chided good-naturedly. "Dig into this chicken and you'll see your sister soon enough."

She put a leg and a breast on his plate and passed him the roast potatoes. Then she served Jean some chicken and peas.

"How're you coming along with the baby, Jean?" she asked.

"He kicks quite a bit," Jean said. "Doctor says it's going to be a boy. But, I'm okay. Bit tired after all that driving though."

"Well you can have a lie down after supper. You and William can use the room off the kitchen so you won't have to climb those stairs in the last couple of weeks before my grandson gets here. William's dad put a two-piece bathroom in here on the main floor just this spring. It's real handy. You'll be fine down here."

"Thanks, Mom, I'm sure we'll be fine," Jean said.

That was the first time she called Sarah Mom. Sarah wasn't too sure how to take it. The last thing she'd expected the first time she set eyes on Jean Weasel Fat was that she'd be calling her Mom some day. Someday soon, actually. *I didn't even know who she was this time last year. And now she's calling me "Mom"? Maybe it will work out. William seems to like her a lot. Bit crazy about her when you come right down to it. They seem happy enough. And I'm going to be a grandmother. I like that. Like that a lot. We'll see how things go.*

About four days after Bill got home from Berkeley, Sarah called him to the phone in the kitchen. "There's a Doctor McArchibald on the line for you, William. Says he's from the University of Toronto."

"Yeah," Bill replied. "I had dinner with him at Berkeley. At Dr. Johnston's house. He gave a really good lecture in April. Wonder what he's calling about?"

It turned out that McArchibald was a big rodeo fan and came to Calgary every year to see the Calgary Stampede. He'd been reading the *Calgary Herald* in the lobby of the Palliser Hotel that afternoon and there was a feature article about Richard and his prowess as a bronco rider. The article said Richard had used some of his prize money to help support his son who was taking a PhD in sociology at Berkeley.

"So, I determined that might very well have been you," McArchibald said on the phone. "Three-time champion. That's what the article said and that your father had a ranch at the Big Thunder Reserve."

"Yep, that's my dad all right," Bill said rather proudly. "Not many horses can get my dad off their back in a hurry. He's one of the best there is. Best there ever was."

"That's what it says in the paper," McArchibald said. "One of the best there is. I see they call him Glued-on Eagletail."

"Yeah, Dad gets a chuckle out of that. When he's on the bronc, it looks like he's glued onto the saddle."

Bill wasn't too sure where the conversation was going. "So, what can I do for you, Dr. McArchibald?"

"I was hoping you could join me for lunch one day this week. I'm at the Palliser until next Monday."

"Sure, that would be okay. I've got a few things to do here but I'm coming up on Friday to spend a couple of days with my dad. Want to be there for the big prize ride on Sunday. Haven't seen him since last August."

"Then let's make it Friday. Here at the Palliser," McArchibald said. "And then, if it is acceptable to your father, I'd like an opportunity to meet him at the Stampede. 'Glued-on Eagletail' sounds like quite the champion."

"No problem," Bill said. "I can get you right beside the chutes with our family pass. Dad gets them every year. You'll be able to reach through and feel the horses. Smell them, too. And, it's no problem at all. I'm sure he'd be glad to meet you. Show you around a bit when he's not riding."

McArchibald was pleased to hear that. He'd been quite impressed with what he'd read about Richard in the *Herald* and wanted to get his picture taken with him so he could show it to his friends back in Toronto.

"That sounds perfectly fine, Bill. Please join me in the dining room at one o'clock. I will reserve a table for two."

McArchibald was quite fascinated with native people and had a special interest in Tecumseh, the Shawnee war chief from Indiana who helped the British win the War of 1812. He had two paintings of Tecumseh in his study. The first showed him dressed in buckskin, eagle feather hanging from the side of his head, tomahawk tucked in his belt, shaking hands with General Isaac Brock at their first meeting at Amherstburg, Ontario. The second showed him lying wounded and dying at the foot of a tree during the Battle of the Thames on October 5, 1813, after British Major-General Henry Procter abandoned him and his warriors and fled to Burlington.

When Bill got to the imposing Palliser Hotel at 9th Avenue and 1st Street Southwest, he paused for a moment and looked up at the three fifteen-storey towers and wondered how many business deals must have been struck there since the Canadian Pacific Railway first opened the hotel in June, 1914. *Lots of money made in there,* he thought. *Lots of white money. This is the place to meet in Calgary. No other hotel quite like it. Bet Dr. McArchibald's paying an arm and a leg for his room. Our lunch won't be cheap either.*

As he watched the uniformed doorman carry two brown leather suitcases to the trunk of a red 1964 Buick, Bill wondered again why McArchibald had asked to see him. *Maybe he's going to offer me a teaching position at the U of T after I get my PhD. He did hint at it during our dinner at Dr. Johnston's house. Didn't come right out and say it, mind you. Then again, maybe he just wants a chance to meet my "Glued-on" Dad.*

He walked up the steps under the bronze and glass canopy stretching out over the sidewalk and entered the luxurious lobby with its oak panelling, candelabras, columns finished in Botticino and Sylvian marble, handmade rugs and magnificent paintings. Successful looking people were seated around the tables engaged in animated conversation.

When he got to the elegant dining room, the maitre d' directed him to a corner table where McArchibald was enjoying his first Scotch.

"Ah, Bill," McArchibald said as he stood up and reached out to shake his hand. "Join me. Please sit."

Bill shook McArchibald's hand and then sat down at the table with the white linen tablecloth almost reaching to the floor. All of the chairs were upholstered in blue and the thick carpet was rose coloured. The cutlery was sterling silver and the glasses were crystal.

A waitress in a white blouse and black cap held up her order book and asked him what he would like to drink.

"Scotch and water, please."

"Let's deal with the menu first," McArchibald suggested, "and then you can tell me more about 'Glued-on Eagletail'. No disrespect but it is a wonderful name."

"And he's a wonderful dad," Bill said as he reached for the menu in the black leather jacket. *Guess this isn't about teaching at the U of T after all.*

"I'm having poached salmon," McArchibald. "The chef does wonders with it."

"Think I'll settle for a steak," Bill said. "Not much of a fish man. We've always been meat eaters. All the way back to the days of the buffalo."

The waitress brought Bill his Scotch and took his order for a medium rare AAA Angus steak.

"Tell me about your father," McArchibald said. "The article in the *Herald* depicted him as quite a remarkable fellow."

Bill told him about how his dad got started out on the rodeo circuit and some of the famous broncos he'd ridden and beaten. He also told him he had high hopes that his dad would be champion again after the finals on Sunday.

"Well I most certainly hope that he does, too," McArchibald said. "Being four-time champion would be quite a feat. Quite a feat indeed. I truly am looking forward to meeting your father."

He lit a small Cuban cigarillo and took a couple of puffs. "Now then, Bill, what about you? What have you decided about Berkeley versus Toronto? Has my good friend Dr. Johnston invited you to take a position there after you complete your doctorate?"

"He has, actually. As you will recall, he made that quite clear when we were at his house for dinner. The position is there if I want it. It's my call."

McArchibald flicked some ash off his cigarillo. "Your call?"

"Yes. My call."

"I couldn't help but notice how impressed Dr. Johnston was with you when we were at his home. You could see in his eyes and in the way he lit up how much he thought of you. You are a good student, William. One of the best. You have the makings of a champion, just like your father. I think you should take a position with us. Build your career in your own country. In Canada."

"Actually," Bill replied with a soft smile, "I had decided that before we had dinner with Dr. Johnston. Toronto has always been my first preference. I simply didn't want to offend Dr. Johnston by making it known right there on the spot. The U of T is where I want to be."

"I had as much as surmised that," McArchibald said. "I could be teaching at Berkeley or Harvard – or Oxford or Cambridge for that matter – but Canada is where I want to be. This is my home. I want to make my contribution here."

"I feel much the same way," Bill said. "As soon as I complete my doctorate, I'm heading for Toronto." He paused for a moment and looked directly into McArchibald's eyes. "That depends of course on whether or not there would be a position there for me."

McArchibald puffed on his cigarillo and looked at the floor-to-ceiling painting on one of the walls of three cowboys riding the range. His thoughts turned to Bill's father, "Glued-on Eagletail", who was probably getting ready to ride the broncos later that afternoon. The photo in the *Herald* of him glued to the saddle as a wild bronc did its utmost to get him off its back had impressed McArchibald.

"I should be able to do something about that," he said as he took another puff. "Yes. I most certainly could arrange that. Let's keep in touch. You've still got, what, three years to go on your doctorate?"

"Only two to go after this one," Bill said.

"Then we will keep in touch. I'm here for the Stampede every year. We can get together when I'm here."

"That would be – that would be fantastic," Bill said with enthusiasm. "Toronto is where I want to be. But, are you sure? Could you really arrange that?"

"It will take a certain amount of persuasion, a word here and there in the right places, but, yes, I believe that I could arrange for you to join our department when you get your PhD."

Bill glanced around the room, which was only about one-third full, and allowed his eyes to rest on the giant stone fireplace. *That would really be something. Wonder what brought that on?*

"You could really do that?" he asked again.

"Yes. Bill, I believe that I could. I most certainly could. I am the chairman of the department."

Bill was a bit overwhelmed by it all. The last thing he'd been expecting was an invitation to teach at the University of Toronto. And that was where he wanted to be. *Good thing the* Herald *ran that feature article about Dad. Without that, I doubt that this would be happening. But, like Dad says, you take opportunity wherever it finds you.*

"Well, Dr. McArchibald, this is most certainly a surprise. I had not been expecting anything quite like this. And yes, most definitely, I most certainly do want to take you up on your most generous offer."

"Good. Then, that's settled. I'll let you know when I have everything in place. But I am confident that I can get you a teaching position in my department."

"I don't know what to say."

"Just say 'Thank you. Thank you very much.' Now, you finish up your coffee while I go upstairs to my room and change into my rodeo clothes. Please meet me in the lobby in fifteen minutes and then we'll go down to the Stampede and watch your 'Glued-on' father ride the wild horses."

McArchibald signed the bill for their lunch and left the dining room. Bill looked at the big picture of the cowboys riding the range. It reminded him of the time his great-great-grandfather rode those same prairies with his four wives and one hundred horses. *Herds of buffalo two miles wide and three miles deep. That's what Dad said. And now here's me in the dining room of the most prestigious hotel in Calgary just finished lunch with the Chairman of Sociology at the University of Toronto. And I'm going to teach there. Teach sociology at one of the top universities in the western world.*

His thoughts turned to Big Thunder and the good life the modern Blackfoot had made for themselves raising cattle and horses. *We got our pride back. We live well. Don't owe nobody nothing. Dad's one of the best bronco riders in the entire west. Three-time champion at the Stampede. We're doing okay. A lot better than our people were back when the Red Coats forced us to sign the Blackfoot Treaty. Back in 1877. Back when, like that Catholic priest said, we were killing one another and running around in rags without horses or guns. Yeah. It's a lot better now.*

CHAPTER
- 10 -

Carol's mom was shocked when she told her she was pregnant. *Wasn't she on the pill? Couldn't he afford a condom? How could she put her bright future at risk like this?*

"Whatever were you thinking about, Carol? This could ruin you."

Carol gave her mom a sheepish little smile and said: "It was my very first time, Mom. He promised to pull out in time but then he got all caught up in the thrill of it all and went off inside me."

"That's not good enough, Carol. You should have insisted that he wear a condom."

"He didn't have one, Mom. It's not like we planned it. It just, sort of, happened."

Ethel remembered the first time it "just, sort of, happened" between her and Winston.

"Well," she said in a softer tone, "I suppose what's done is done. The main thing now is to decide what's best to do next."

She agreed that abortion or adoption was not the best answer. Marrying Gordon seemed to be the best, and only, option available to them at that time. She did feel, however, that it would have been so much better if Carol was marrying someone from their own circle. Someone who was going to make a name for himself in business or one of the professions and would be able to provide the lifestyle Carol had become accustomed to.

Then again, as Gran says, Carol herself is going to do quite well as a lawyer. Going to do well, very well, in corporate law. It's not like things were when I was her age. When the man you married determined the life-

style you were going to enjoy for the rest of your life. She'll do well. Things will work out for them. I do hope so.

Ethel was actually looking forward to the birth of their first grandchild. *It'll be nice to have a baby around the house again. A grandchild.*

When Gordon told his parents he was going to marry Carol, they were happy for him. They both knew how much he loved Carol, kept her on a pedestal. They would have preferred that it had happened under different circumstances but had no doubt that things would work out well for them.

Tom had mixed feelings, though, about Gordon moving into Gran Winston's house. He had only met him twice – at a social event at Hart House and at the engagement party they threw for Gordon and Carol at Winston's big house on the edge of the river valley – and found him to be rather overbearing and inclined to take charge of things. He also felt a bit intimidated by Winston's wealth and prominent position in Toronto society. He'd read more than a few glowing articles about Winston's accomplishments in the business section of the *Globe and Mail.*

Gordon and Carol were married in Timothy Eaton Memorial Church, just a month after Carol graduated at the top of her class. Long-time friend Jane Potts was her maid of honour.

As he walked up the broad steps on the St. Clair Avenue side of the church that was built as a memorial to Irish-born department store founder Timothy Eaton, Gordon thought back to the times when his dad used to take him to the big Santa Claus parade sponsored by the Eaton's department store. He remembered how thrilled he was by the sight of the 48th Highlanders' military band with their pipes and drums marching in the place of honour directly in front of Santa's sleigh. *Should have them pipe me in today,* he thought. *This is one very special day.*

Although Carol was four months pregnant, she showed only a slight rise at the tummy on her wedding dress. Gordon fell in love with her all over again as she walked down the aisle. There was absolutely no doubt in his mind that she was the perfect match for him.

The reception was held in the Grand Ballroom of the Royal York Hotel. The cream of Toronto society was there. Lawyers, judges. Doctors, dentists, architects, engineers, accountants. The Premier of

Ontario, Mayor of Toronto. Federal and provincial Cabinet Ministers. The Chief of Police. The publisher of the *Globe and Mail.* The president of the University of Toronto. The conductor of the Toronto Symphony Orchestra. The Chairman of the Board of Governors of Toronto General Hospital. Business associates of Gran Winston's from the real estate and development industry. You name it, they were all there.

After shaking hands with the bridal party and wishing Gordon and Carol all the very best, they all sat down to a sumptuous dinner of shrimp cocktail, Scotch broth, prime rib with Yorkshire pudding, roast potatoes, carrots and peas, and topped it all off with baked Alaska. Every table had a bottle of Dom Perignon, Bordeaux and Riesling. And then they danced the night away to the swinging music of the Frank Cardile Orchestra.

When she woke up beside Gordon on the big king bed in their suite on the eleventh floor of the Royal York Hotel at around eight o'clock the next morning, Carol reflected on what had been an absolutely perfect wedding day. Nothing had gone wrong. Nothing at all. The seamstress had been able to let the wedding dress out just enough to conceal the bulge created by the baby growing inside her belly. No one would have known that she was pregnant. Not that she was worried about that, mind you. It's just that she was terribly aware of how very much her father and mother would have preferred that she hadn't been. *And, when you come right down to it, they would rather it had not been Gordon who got me pregnant in the first place. "Not one of our own circle," Dad had said. "Not one of our own kind."*

Now Dad is right about the money thing. Even when Gord's teaching at the university, he won't be making all that much. Still, when I get into my stride as a lawyer, I'll be bringing home three times as much as he'll be making. We'll be okay. More than okay. As for him not being "one of our own kind", can't think of anyone from "our own kind" that I'd want to spend my life with. Bunch of preppy jocks. That's what they are. All of them living off their father's money – his success. Not theirs. At least Gord is moving a couple of steps up the ladder from his dad. He'll be the first professor in their circle. He's making something of himself. Moving up the food chain.

She gave her tummy a gentle rub. *And then there's you. Growing away inside my belly. The timing is God-awful. But, I'm kind of glad you're on your way. Like Gord says, you're going to be a delightful Christmas present. Going to have to share me with H and B, though. Might as well get that through your head right here and now. I am going to be a career woman. I am going to argue cases – multi-million dollar cases – before the Supreme Court of Canada. You're not going to have me all to your wonderful little self. Not by a long shot. Let's put that on the record right now. We're going to have lots of time together. But, not necessarily as much as you'd like.*

⌒

Gordon and Carol checked into a third-floor corner room in the Chateau Frontenac Hotel in Quebec City two days after the wedding. It was a very large room overlooking the wide St. Lawrence River. The half-circle alcove had three windows and room enough for two armchairs and an Ottoman. There were also two huge windows on both sides of the room with fabulous views. The king bed faced a built-in fireplace which, given that it was the end of July, was more for decoration than heat at that time of year.

It was after 8:00 p.m. by the time they got to the room and Carol was quite tired from the long train journey from Toronto. Gordon called room service and ordered them both striploin steaks, medium rare, with baked potato and apple pie with ice cream. He also ordered a bottle of Bordeaux.

The waiter put the room service cart in front of one of the large windows, opened the flaps and took the steaks out of the warmer. Gordon signed the bill, with a fifteen per cent tip, and the waiter thanked him in English with a thick French accent. They had been hearing people speaking French ever since they got off the train. Even the taxi driver had difficulty understanding where it was they wanted to go.

As they started into their steaks, they could see the ferry crossing from Levis on the other side of the river and a large cargo ship heading for Montreal. As dark was approaching, the ship had its running lights on.

Carol raised her wine glass and said: "To us and all that comes to us."

Gordon smiled. "The first time you said that, I got you pregnant."

"Yes you did, you bugger. You should have known better. But, I still say, to us."

"To us," Gordon said as he clinked his glass against hers. "And to that other part of us you're hiding under your skirt."

Carol smiled back at him and sipped her wine. "Regrets?" she asked. "About us having to get married and that, as you put it, other part of us?"

"None whatsoever. The timing could have been better. But, no, no regrets. Not a single one."

"Neither have I. You're right about the timing. It is Godawful. But I do have a good feeling about us. A very good feeling. And – about that other part of us."

"Me, too," Gordon said. "We're going to do just fine. All three of us."

They slept in the next morning and had a late breakfast downstairs. Then they went for a slow walk along the Dufferin Terrace. It was a clear warm day. Sail boats were out on the river and the ferries were toing and froing between Quebec City and Levis. The CNR passenger train from Halifax was pulling into the railway station on the Levis side of the river in order to pick up passengers en route to Montreal and, from there, to Toronto.

Gordon and Carol stood at the rail on the Terrace and looked down the steep, sheer, cliff at the road running alongside the river and the Canadian Coast Guard and other ships tied up at the dock. A cruise ship was docked near the ferry terminal.

"Want to go for a cruise on the river?" Gordon asked.

"Don't think so, Gord. Not with me more than four months' pregnant. I felt a bit nauseous when we got up this morning. A cruise would not be the best idea."

"So, that's why you settled for corn flakes and toast at breakfast?"

"You got that right. The bacon and eggs you had would have hit the wrong spot. Definitely the wrong spot."

"Okay, we'll stay on shore. There's lots to do here."

"Let's just sit down for a while and look at the boats on the river," she suggested.

They sat on one of the benches near the row of ancient cannons pointing at the river.

"My dad told me this is a pretty strategic military location," Gordon said. "A crewman told him all about it when he and my Uncle Bill sailed past here on their way to Montreal. Back in 1933." He turned sideways to his right and pointed up at the cliff behind their backs. "See that Union Jack flying up there at the top of the cliff, where those big walls are?"

"Yes, I see it."

"Dad says there's a big cannon up there – at the Citadel of Quebec – pointing at an angle straight to where the ships turn left over there." He turned left and pointed to the Ile d'Orleans. "That island over there where that gap is at the other end of Levis. That's the control point. If you want to prevent hostile ships from getting into the Great Lakes, you've got to knock them off right here. There's a whole battery of cannons up there on the walls. My dad's got a picture of the Citadel, and of the Chateau Frontenac, on the wall at his office. On the other side of the Citadel is the Plains of Abraham where the British conquered the French back in 1759."

"Gord," Carol said good-naturedly, "I took all that in Grade 9. I don't need your learned self to tell me where the Plains of Abraham are."

"Sorry. Guess I got a bit carried away. My dad gets real enthusiastic when he tells me about it. Him and my uncle came all the way here on a ship from Scotland with a bunch of prize cattle. They'd have passed by right there. Down there where we're looking. Took them ten days to get from Glasgow to Montreal and they went the rest of the way in a boxcar – all the way to a ranch in Alberta."

"You mean your Dad was a cowboy?"

"Ranch hand, actually. For a couple of years. Then he moved to Toronto, got into real estate, married my mum and then they had me."

"What happened to your uncle? Your dad's brother?"

"Dad never says much about him. He stayed at the ranch and then got killed fighting the Japanese at the Battle of Hong Kong. That's all I know about him. Dad says the Army buried him over there."

"Must have been young," Carol said.

"Dad says he was thirty-two. He was two years older than my dad."

Gordon didn't say anything for a couple of minutes. Just looked at a big oil tanker headed for Montreal and thought about his dad and his Uncle Bill sailing past that very same spot on their way to Alberta thirty-two years ago.

"How'd you feel about a carriage ride?" he asked. "It would save you walking around in this heat."

"Sounds lovely," Carol said. "My stomach's quite settled now. I should be okay. It is getting a bit hot out here."

They walked back to the hotel and got into a brightly-painted carriage at the square on the city side of the Chateau Frontenac. The horse was white and looked kind of old and tired.

"Are you sure he's up to it?" Gordon asked the driver.

"Ben's only six," the driver replied. "Looks a lot older and tireder than he is hoping I'll take pity on him and leave him back at the stable. He's a wise one, Ben is."

He gave Ben a light whack on the rear with his whip and they headed down the cobbled streets of old Quebec.

Gordon and Carol moved into the former servants' quarters on the third floor of her parents' house after they got back from their short honeymoon in Quebec City. Carol started at Haldimand and Brock at the beginning of August. They were short-staffed because of the summer holidays. Gordon kept his part-time job at the Chicken Hut and concentrated on his studies.

About two weeks before the baby was due, Carol took a leave of absence from Haldimand and Brock on the understanding that she would be back at the firm on or around the middle of February. It was a very easy birth and Carol was back at her parents' home two days later.

Things went well for Gordon and Carol. Soon after she got back to Haldimand and Brock, she got involved in some very interesting cases and found working at the firm as stimulating as she had always imagined that it would be. With the money that she was making at the law firm, Gordon was able to quit his job at the Chicken Hut and concentrate full-time on the final year of his master's degree.

Carol's mom was more than happy to take care of little Charlie while Carol was at work and Gordon was at the university. While they had their own kitchen in the servants' quarters on the third floor, they took most of their meals with Carol's parents. Both Ethel and Gran were delighted to have a grandson in their home. In a certain way, little Charlie made up for the second child that Ethel was unable to have. They doted on him. Spoiled him like crazy.

Gordon had started on his PhD and was looking forward to teaching political science at the University of Toronto. Carol had moved up the ladder at Haldimand and Brock and was handling some very challenging cases. Their life together was good and neither one of them regretted having had to get married.

Gran and Ethel drove to their condominium in Florida after celebrating Charlie's third birthday at their home with Carol and Gordon, Tom and Martha. When Gran got back at the end of January, he told Carol he'd bought an apartment at Avenue Road and St. Clair and would be moving there with Ethel, who was still in Florida, at the beginning of March. He wanted Carol and Gordon to remain in the house on Kennedy Circle.

"I want you to be happy," he told Carol on the evening he got home. "You were born in this house and this is where I want you to stay – with my grandchild and all the brothers and sisters he's going to have."

"You're determined I'm going to have more," Carol said with a chuckle. "But you're just going to have to be patient, Dad. Charlie is all there is going to be for at least another five years."

"Charlie's all I need right now – but – I'm sure you're going to want more. He really should have a brother or a sister to grow up with."

"Don't use Charlie as leverage, Dad," she said with a warm smile. "This isn't another one of your business deals you're putting together. This is family. Our family. Let me take things at my own pace."

"You've got a deal," he said. "I won't say anything more about it – for at least another year." He paused for a moment and poured himself another Scotch. "Now, about the house. I'm going to transfer it to your name. Consider it a delayed wedding present."

"Why leave? Why move to an apartment?" Carol asked. "Mom and Charlie get on so well together. Why leave now?"

"It's just something your mother and I have been talking about for some time now. We believe that you and Gordon should have the house to yourselves. We've always planned on moving to an apartment after you got married."

"I've been married for three years, Dad. You still haven't answered why now?"

"That's between me and your mom," Gran said. "We've made the decision and now we want you to have the house. I'll have the papers drawn up so we can transfer the title to your name."

"I appreciate that, Dad. I really do. But the title really should be in both our names. Gordon feels a bit awkward as it is, us being here without paying any rent. If it's okay with you, I really would prefer that the house was in both our names."

Winston thought about that for a minute. He had always intended that Carol would get the house when she got married. And, now that he had a three-year-old grandson, this did seem like the right time. But he had reservations about Gordon owning fifty per cent. *What if things don't go well and they wind up getting a divorce?*

"I think I would prefer that it was in your name only. You never know how things are going to work out. Who knows? You might be divorced this time next year."

"I don't see that happening, Dad. We are really happy together. Especially having Charlie in our lives. No, I don't see a marriage breakup in the cards. And, don't take offence, I think it's more your business instinct that's at work here. Keeping the assets in the family. The Winston side of the family. I understand that. But, I also understand how Gordon would feel if the house was in my name only. He just wouldn't feel right about it. I really would prefer if the title was in both our names."

"All right, my darling, that's the way it will be. I'll put the title to the property in both your names."

Bill arrived in Toronto in August, 1968, along with Jean and their two-year-old son Albert. They rented an old, spacious, home on Sussex Avenue near St. George Street which was close enough for Bill to walk to the university. With Bill pulling in a salary as a Professor of Sociology, Jean was able to stay home and take care of Albert.

This was Bill's first teaching position and he was determined to succeed. He put virtually every waking moment into it. He always brought papers home with him at night and spent most of his time in the sunroom on the second floor which he was using as a study. Jean saw even less of him than she had at Berkeley. Albert didn't see very much of him either.

Things went well for Bill at the university. He had a solid grasp of the subjects he was teaching and a manner of speaking that kept the students interested and thirsting for more. There was no doubt in Dr. McArchibald's mind that he had made a wise decision in inviting Bill to teach at the University of Toronto.

While he was getting a good salary at the university, Bill wasn't making anything near the kind of money Jean had hoped he would be making after finishing his studies. She wanted him to be a businessman, an entrepreneur, or something else that made a lot of money.

"You're just wasting your education," she said one night after he came home from a late meeting. "You could be making ten times as much with an oil company or one of the big banks. We could be living ten times as good as this."

"Listen, Jean," Bill responded. "Ninety-nine point nine per cent of Indian people don't live as well as we do. Never will live as well as we do."

"You, listen. Ninety-nine point nine percent of Indian people don't have degrees from Berkeley. I didn't marry ninety-nine point nine per cent of Indian people. I married you. Now, when are you going to get off your ass and make us some real money?"

Jean didn't want a rented house on Sussex Avenue. She wanted a house of her own. Like the stately mansions she had seen in Rosedale, Forest Hill and up on "Millionaire's Row" east of Bayview and Lawrence.

The money Bill made teaching was not at all what she had in mind. She had thought that, when he got his doctorate, especially after her waiting on tables at Denny's Diner to support him so he could go to Berkeley, they'd have a lot more money. A pile of money. But the desire just wasn't there. High finance and all that didn't interest Bill. Not at all. He wanted to teach. He was teaching. Jean wanted something altogether different. She had too many things driving inside her to accept the life of a professor's wife.

On top of that, she felt uncomfortable on the few occasions when she was invited to afternoon tea or some other social event with the faculty wives. She found them quite patronizing. She particularly disliked the first time she met Professor Donald Henderson's wife.

Jean had a small mole in the centre of her forehead, just above her eyebrows. Henderson's wife mistook it for the red dot Hindu women put on their foreheads.

"Oh," she asked rather excitedly, "and do you have any good curry recipes I could use?"

"Actually, no," Jean replied. "I'm not from India. I'm from the Blood Tribe in southern Alberta."

"Oh, what a dreadful pity," Mrs. Henderson sniffed as she turned on her heel and headed to the other room.

Jean felt quite justifiably insulted. *If I was an Indian from India, the white bitch'd be okay with that. But, me being an Indian from the Blood Tribe, she just turns and walks away. What a rude cow. The rest of them are probably just like her underneath. Smile to my face but talk about me behind my back.*

~

About two years after Bill arrived in Toronto, he was at a pow wow up on Manitoulin Island. There was dancing there. Indian dancing and singing and ceremony. He was there with Jean and Albert, who was now four.

There was an old man there Bill had known back at Big Thunder. He was dancing and, just as they were finishing one of the dances, he spotted Bill and smiled. A beautiful warm, broken-toothed, smile of recognition. And then he shuffle-stepped towards them. Came right at them. He was wearing a full headdress. Must have been a hundred eagle feathers. His pants and shirt were made of deerskin and covered with turquoise beadwork.

The drums and the dancing stopped and the old man knelt in front of Albert. Right there on the grass before them. Then he started to undo the buttons on Albert's shirt – it had a Mickey Mouse decal on the back of it. Jean reached out to stop him. And then, before he realized what he was doing, Bill caught her arm and held her back. The old man undid all the buttons and took the shirt off.

Albert stood stripped down to his jeans and then the old woman who was with him passed him a necklace made with three bear claws hanging from a string of turquoise beads and he put it around Albert's neck. The drums and the singers started again. The old man reached out his hand. Albert took it. They walked into the circle and started to dance. To dance a dance of the Blackfoot.

Bill looked at his son and that old man and saw how quickly Albert picked up the rhythm of the dance and how joyfully his face shone in the sun. He watched his son dance the dance of his forefathers, of his people.

After the dance, they sat with the old man in his tent and drank tea. He told them about the dance – about the legends – about their Blackfoot heritage. Just before they left, he gave Bill the bear claws necklace. Bill promised the old man that he'd teach Albert all that he could about their traditions and about the customs and value system of the Blackfoot people. But first, he'd have to relearn. To relearn all he had set aside during his years at the University of Alberta and Berkeley. To recapture a glimpse of the Blackfoot past. To help build up a body of knowledge about Blackfoot people, Blackfoot culture and Blackfoot thought.

It was soon after that experience that Bill decided there had to be a North American Indian Studies program at the university. *Sure, it's important to provide our young people with the knowledge that can be learned at universities like the U of A, Berkeley and here at the U of T. But that knowledge is of no use to them if they don't have a good sense of self-esteem. A pride in their Indianness. That university knowledge is of no value to them if they've been made to feel ashamed of their own people. Like that lady I met when I was at Berkeley. The knowledge is no damned good at all if they're ashamed of our customs, of our dances, our music and our way of life. Ashamed of who they are.*

About a month after he got back to Toronto, he phoned Dr. McArchibald and asked if he could meet with him. They got together for coffee at the Davidson Lounge and Bill outlined his plans for establishing a course in Indian studies.

"But we've only got a handful of Indian students," McArchibald said. "I doubt very much that there's more than five of them."

"I understand that," Bill said. "What I'm talking about is a correspondence course that Indian kids on reserves all across Canada can get involved in. Even though they don't have the grades to be admitted to university, many of them are quite bright, quite intelligent. I'm talking about something they can take even though they haven't finished high school."

McArchibald reached for his pack of cigarillos, lit one and took a couple of puffs. "I don't want to throw cold water on a good idea," he said, "but I really don't see how this could work."

Bill explained that what he envisioned was a special course on North American Indian culture and traditions that would be taught to all students taking sociology at the university. The course would cover everything from the life the Indians lived before the whites arrived, the fur trade, the first settlers, the treaties that were entered into, the important role Indian warriors played in the initial struggles between the French and the British, the American Revolution, the War of 1812 and other historic events.

McArchibald's life-long interest in all things Indian started to come into play. He was getting quite interested. "That would be a monumental task. I'm not at all sure we would have the resources to pull it off."

"It's big all right. But, I've been doing some research on this and I'm quite confident that most of the material we would need already exists. In the museums, historical associations, books, other universities. All that we would have to do is pull it all together and work it into a curriculum."

"I've done quite a bit of work along this line on my own," McArchibald said. "I'd certainly see Tecumseh playing a major role in the historical part of it all. Without the invaluable support he and his warriors provided to the British in the War of 1812, there wouldn't be a Canada. We'd all be Americans."

They talked on, in a rather animated manner, both quite excited about the prospect of launching a new field of study within the Department of Sociology. Once the curriculum was in place, the course would be made available to young Indians so they could learn about the culture and traditions of the Indian. They'd take the course by correspondence.

"This course will show young Indians how their own culture fits into the universal scheme of things," Bill said. "We'll be able to show them how Indian values, customs and traditions, can be adapted to modern life. That way, they'll be able to keep a solid footing in both worlds – the white man's world of today and the Indian world of their forefathers. Right now, they only have one choice – both feet in the white man's system or both feet on the reserve. There's no middle ground. Now, with this correspondence program, they'll be able to develop their own individual lifestyle by picking the best of both worlds and applying it to their own lives."

"That all sounds fine and dandy," McArchibald said, "but I would have to find a way to make it economically feasible. I would have to pull this together in a manner that would have all of the considerable costs of the program covered by the fees the students – the white students taking sociology – pay. The correspondence program – which would be provided to the young Indians free of charge – will be the icing on the cake. Meanwhile, I have to come up with a way to pay for the cake."

"But, you do think the cake's worth baking? No pun intended," Bill said. "You do agree with me that this thing is doable. Don't you?"

"Doable and worthwhile," McArchibald replied. "I can see the benefit a program like this would provide. It would be a breakthrough for a whole generation of young Indian people. Something of value. I'll start working out the financial end of things. Meanwhile, you should start pulling together the information we will need. Books and papers on the early years. The Hurons backing the French. The Iroquois with the British. The Royal Proclamation of 1763, early treaties between the Dutch and the Iroquois, the Selkirk, McDougall, and Robinson treaties and the treaties Alexander Morris negotiated with the Indians living west of Thunder Bay in the 1870s. The fur trade. The Hudson's Bay Company forts and posts. Annihilation of the buffalo."

He paused to light another cigarillo. "It's a monumental task, Bill. A huge – but very worthwhile undertaking. You'll need help with this. I'm going to assign MacMillan and Donaldson to work with you on it. More resources will be added on an as-required basis. But, yes, it is something on which you will have my full support. My unreserved support. This is something we should have done a long time ago."

Bill set about the task of identifying and collecting information for the new course that they were going to establish at the Department of Sociology. Hugh MacMillan and Douglas Donaldson, the two associate professors McArchibald had assigned to the project, turned out to be very helpful indeed. Bill hoped they would have everything in place so that the course could be up and running by September of the following year.

He met with the curator of the Indian section at the Royal Ontario Museum, the Director of Archives at the Department of Indian Affairs, the President of the United Indians of Canada Association, a hereditary chief of the Six Nations of the Grand River, the person in charge of the archives at the Hudson's Bay Company, and others who might help identify and collect information that could be incorporated in the new course.

The time and effort that he put into the project put an added strain on his troubled relationship with Jean.

CHAPTER
- 11 -

Towards the end of October, 1970, Carol was feeling a lot more tired than usual and there was a noticeable amount of sensitivity in her breasts. She had missed her last two periods. When she went to see Dr. Turner, he told her she was pregnant again and the baby would be arriving around the middle of May.

Not again, she muttered to herself. *This was not supposed to happen. Not again. Here goes another big chunk of my life.*

Gordon had told her about a year before that he didn't want to use a condom anymore. He said it felt better when he didn't have one on. Carol started using a diaphragm – which didn't always work the way it was supposed to. On more than one occasion, she had to take it out in the middle of their love making and readjust it.

That must be it. The diaphragm must have slipped out of place. Why the hell won't he use a condom? It's so utterly selfish of him.

Charlie was going to be in Grade One next year and she was moving up fast at Haldimand and Brock. Having the baby would mean taking more time out of her career.

This is altogether the wrong time. We'll be finished discovery with the Gotham Gold Corp. case by the end of January and the trial is bound to take up at least several months. I can't afford to take time out now to have another baby. I'm a lawyer, for God's sake. A damned good lawyer. Going to be one of the top litigators in Canada. Damn. Why won't he use a goddamned condom? I didn't stand first in my class by accident. I've got what it takes. The royal jelly. Maybe, if I'd used some more spermicidal jelly, I wouldn't be in this mess. Damn. This was not supposed to happen. Not again!

As soon as Carol told Jonathan Hollinger, the managing partner at Haldimand and Brock, that she was pregnant, he assigned another lawyer to take her place on the multi-million dollar Gotham Gold Corp. case. Carol had been working on the file for almost a year and had been looking forward to the high-profile trial. The pregnancy couldn't have come at a worst time. She was losing her place in the Haldimand and Brock pecking order.

"Goddamn you," she said to Gordon when they were alone after supper that night. "Why won't you use a goddamned condom? Hollinger took me off the Gotham Gold Corp. case this morning. Said he needed continuity and couldn't take the chance of me being out of action while I'm having the baby. That's twice your goddamned orgasm has fucked up my life. Once with Charlie and now with – with – whatever this one is going to be. You're a totally selfish, self-centred prick."

"That's not fair. Not at all fair. Yes, I screwed up the first time. Should have pulled out like I said I would. But you can't pin this one on me. It's not my fault the diaphragm became dislodged or – or whatever. I can't be expected to control that."

"I wouldn't be using the diaphragm in the first place if you'd use the goddamned condom. You're just so utterly selfish. Two times now you've screwed me over. Disrupted my career."

With that, she stormed out of the house and went for a walk in the river valley.

Gordon was quite shaken by Carol's verbal tirade. She had never gone at him like that before. She was white-hot angry. He could understand why she was so upset about being pregnant and hoped she'd get over it in a couple of weeks. As for him, he was looking forward to having another child. He felt bad about how little time he had spent with Carol and Charlie over the last few years and really wanted to make it up to them.

Carol had taken Charlie to her parents' condominium in Florida for a month when he was two. Gordon couldn't join them because of the pressure he was under keeping up with his studies. He did join them the following summer when they went to her parents' farm up near Peterborough. But, even then, Gordon spent most of his time with his nose stuck in his books.

He spent a month with her at her parents' cottage on Lake Simcoe when Charlie was four. He had his master's now and needed a break before continuing with the heavy load of getting his PhD. Carol's mom and dad were travelling in Europe that summer and they had the cottage all to themselves. But, even then, he spent most of the time with his books.

That's not going to happen with this child, he told himself. *Now that I'm teaching, I'm going to have a lot more time on my hands. Quality time that I'm going to spend with Charlie and his little brother, or sister, whatever it may turn out to be. This time I'm going to be the father that I should have been all along.*

It was a complicated pregnancy. Dr. Turner, in consultation with his colleagues at the clinic, recommended a caesarean section. Carol didn't like the idea of having her belly sliced open. But, if her condition was as problematic as Dr. Turner said it was, that was probably the best option. *There's no point in putting both our lives at risk.*

Carol reacted quite differently toward Diane than she had to Charlie. She had actually been looking forward to having Charlie. It had meant she'd have to put her career in law off for a few months but, at the same time, she was looking forward to the experience of being a mother. And, she was only twenty-five back then. She would soon be practising law and would have her whole career ahead of her.

Diane was a different situation. Gordon noticed a marked change in Carol after Diane was born. She became quite moody. Quite withdrawn. Snapped at him a lot. And at Charlie. Didn't get enough sleep. Refused to breast feed Diane and put her on a bottle. Then she started drinking. Not a lot. But a lot more than she used to.

He had expected she would be back at work at Haldimand and Brock in a couple of months, just like she had done with Charlie. But she didn't go back. Just sat at home and brooded a lot. After some convincing from Gordon and her parents, Carol reluctantly agreed to book an appointment with Dr. Turner.

She liked Dr. Turner. He had what you would call an excellent bedside manner. She had a lot of confidence in him. He asked her to describe what changes having Diane had made to her life and what, if any, changes she'd noticed in her overall health.

"I'm tired all the time," she said. "Try as I will, I can't seem to get to sleep at night. And, I'll have admit, I've become real bitchy. Snap at Gordon and Charlie for no good reason. Can't seem to help myself."

"And what about Diane?" Dr. Turner asked. "How do you feel about her?"

"The truth?" Carol asked.

"The truth, Carol."

"I'd rather she hadn't been born. She's messed up my whole life."

"In what way?"

"In every way imaginable. A court case, a really important court case, I`d been working on for a year will soon go to trial and I won't be there. I'll be home looking after Diane when I should've been in court making a name for myself. That case would have made me. Set me apart from the herd."

"That didn't happen with Charlie," Dr. Turner said rather gently. "As I recall, you were back to work in less than three months."

"It's different this time. Maybe it was having the caesarian. Having you slice into me like that. Or, something else. It's just different. That's all."

Dr. Turner sensed that she was starting to withdraw within herself at that moment and decided not to press the issue. From what she had told him, it appeared that she had postpartum depression compounded by her sense of having lost a big break in her legal career. He prescribed an antidepressant medication and urged her to try and get more sleep.

"During the day, when Diane is napping, might be a good time," he said. "When she starts to nod off, that's a good time for you to catch forty winks. You really must get more sleep Carol. I also want you to make sure that there is sufficient nutrition in your diet and that you exercise on a daily basis."

The antidepressant medication helped and Carol followed the diet Dr. Turner had prescribed for her and started to exercise more. That didn't change the fact that, in her mind, the timing was all wrong and having Diane was a major setback in her career.

Bill and Jean went back to Big Thunder for a visit that summer. Albert had just turned five and Sarah was really pleased to see him again. She gave him a great big hug and kissed him on both cheeks.

"My but he's a fine-looking boy," she said. "Looks just like his dad when he was that age."

Albert stuck to Sarah like bark to a tree. Followed her everywhere. He was at her side when she gathered the eggs in the chicken coop and when she milked the cows. He really enjoyed being with his grandmother and the smell of things at the ranch.

While Bill was glad to be home again, he had a lot on his mind. The North American Indian Studies program was due to be launched in September and there were several loose ends that had to be tied up. He spent a lot of time on the phone with McArchibald, Donaldson and MacMillan. The pressure was such that McArchibald had even cancelled his annual visit to the Calgary Stampede.

One afternoon, about two weeks after they arrived at Big Thunder, Ian Starlight pulled up at the Eagletail's house in his 1970 powder-blue Cadillac convertible. He was wearing a white suit, blue shirt and a red tie with a diamond tie pin. Starlight's parents ran the general store in Big Thunder and he was delivering some groceries Sarah had ordered over the phone.

As Sarah was in the barn with Albert tending to a sick calf, Jean answered the door. She'd heard a lot about Starlight. How he'd built up a big construction business in Calgary and was said to be worth a couple of million dollars. She liked what she heard.

The interest was mutual. Starlight had seen Jean around the reserve and liked what he saw. She was a very attractive young woman, in a sort of slinky way. Just turned twenty-five.

When he handed her the two bags of groceries, she let her fingers rub up against his and gave him a warm, inviting, smile. "Thanks," she said. "Didn't expect you to be delivering groceries. They tell me you're a big-time contractor in Calgary."

Starlight smiled back at her. "Don't usually," he said. "But they're pretty busy today and I offered to help out. Just with this one special delivery. Besides, I was on my way to my parents' ranch. Keep my horses there."

"I know that," Jean said. "They say you've got the best Arabians in western Canada."

"In all of Canada," he stated rather proudly. He took a satisfying puff on his $5 Cuban cigar. "Mine are the best there is."

"I've no doubt at all about that," Jean said with a coy smile. "I'm sure everything Ian Starlight owns is the best that money can buy."

"You've got that right," he said with a self-satisfied smile. "I'll show them to you sometime. Even let you ride one of them. You do ride, don't you?"

"Yes. I ride."

"Good. Then we should go for a ride together sometime."

"Maybe we should," she replied. "But I've got to go in now. Sarah's coming back from the barn with Albert."

"Okay. But we are going to take that ride sometime. Sometime soon."

"We'll see," she said as she started back into the house. "We'll see about that."

Starlight stopped to say hello to Sarah.

"What on earth are you doing in a suit like that on a hot day like this?" she asked.

"Had an important lunch in Calgary," Starlight replied. "Met with some of my investors. I'll change when I get to my mom's."

"Get into something cool," Sarah said. "It's hot as the Devil's place this afternoon."

"I'll do that," Starlight said as he got back behind the wheel of his powder-blue Cadillac convertible. "I'll keep cool, Mrs. Eagletail. Don't you worry yourself about Ian Starlight. Cool's the word."

And then he was off in a cloud of dust.

"Watch out for him," Sarah said to Jean as she started to put the groceries away. "He's a real womanizer that Ian Starlight is."

"That's what Janet told me," Jean said. "Quite the ladies' man."

"He is that," Sarah said. "Broke a lot of hearts that Ian Starlight has. Him and his money and fancy suits and those cars. That Cadillac isn't the only car he has. Keeps a Rolls Royce at his big house in Calgary.

Least that's what Hughie told me. Got a lot of money that Ian Starlight has. Piles of it."

"I'm sure that he has," Jean said reflectively. "No doubt about it."

Two days later, Bill got a panic call from McArchibald. The launch of the North American Indian Studies program was in jeopardy. The lawyers had run into some last-minute snags on copyright issues regarding some of the material they were including in the course, the curator of the Indian section at the Royal Ontario Museum had changed his mind about loaning them the Huron and Algonquin exhibits and the Minister of Indian Affairs was objecting to the release of copies of some sensitive archived papers regarding the treaty-making process of 1871-1877.

"This is not something we can resolve over the phone, Bill," McArchibald said. "I need you back here at the university to help work these things out. As things stand now, we might have to delay the launch of the program until next year."

"Certainly sounds ominous," Bill said. "And things seemed to be going so well."

"They were – until these last-minute issues came up. We should be able to straighten things out. Hopefully, in time to launch the program as planned."

"I'll catch a plane out first thing tomorrow morning," Bill said. "How long will you need me?"

"As things stand now, it shouldn't take more than a week. I'm truly sorry about cutting into your holiday and your time with your family like this but I know how important the program is to you and that you will want to do all that you can to ensure a successful launch."

"I'll be there late tomorrow afternoon," Bill said. "I'll be there for as long as it takes."

"Thank you, Bill. I have already contacted Donaldson and MacMillan. They will both be here by late tomorrow night. Donaldson is at his parents' farm in the Eastern Townships and MacMillan was whale watching in Newfoundland."

Bill had been enjoying a cup of tea with Sarah and Jean when McArchibald's call came in. He filled them in on the urgency of the situation and that he would probably be back in about a week.

"But you only got here," Sarah exclaimed. "You haven't even been home for three weeks."

"I know, Mom. But, it's only for a week and it is important. Very important. I really don't have a choice in the matter."

"That's for sure, Mom," Jean said rather bitterly. "Your son's married all right, but it's not to me. He's married to the university and that damned course he's starting up. We never see him, Albert and me. He's wrapped up in that stuff twenty-four seven. Day in and day out. That's all, absolutely all, he cares about or thinks about."

"That's not at all fair," Bill objected. "I'm usually home every night."

"Yeah, holed up in that sunroom of yours all night. We never hear from you except when you want a fresh pot of tea. That's your life, Bill. Studies, studies, studies. It was that way at Berkeley and that's the way it's been in Toronto. Study, study, study."

Sarah had noticed that things weren't going very well between them. She hadn't been able to put her finger on it but, listening to Jean, she started to get the picture. *There's no happiness in their marriage. No warmth. None whatsoever.*

"Well now," she said. "I don't see much point in getting into all the details of that right now. You obviously have some issues to resolve, you two do. The important thing right now is this emergency call William got from the university. Sounds to me, William doesn't have much choice in the matter. You've said yourself, Jean, that he has a lot of time and effort tied up in this project. Time and effort that you believe he should've been putting into his marriage. That might very well be so. But, the important thing right now is that this Professor McArchibald fellow seems to feel the whole thing is in danger of falling apart."

"That is what he said," Bill said. "As things stand today we might very well have to delay the program for another year."

"Then, my son, you should be packing your things and getting ready to ride out there to the rescue. I'm not here to judge you but, it sounds to me from what Jean just said, that you decided quite some time ago that the university and that special studies program were your Number One priority. Not your family. Not Albert and Jean."

"That's for sure," Jean interjected. "Me and Albert are way down on Dr. William Eagletail's list of priorities. His whole life is centred around the university and that special studies program of his."

Bill decided it would be better not to argue the point. Jean was right. He was totally absorbed in his career. There wasn't much point in denying it.

"I don't want to get into this right now," he said. "Mom's right. The important thing is for me to fly back to Toronto tomorrow morning and help get the program ready to launch as scheduled. Things might not be quite as bad as Dr. McArchibald says they are. The lawyers should be able to work out the copyright issues and I'm pretty sure the other matters can be resolved as well. I'm certainly going to give it my best shot."

Two days after Bill left for Toronto, Jean drove down to Starlight's General Store to pick up some cloth for Sarah. She was quite pleased to see Ian's powder-blue Cadillac convertible parked outside. He was at the counter.

"Well, what brings you here?" he asked.

"Sarah ordered some cloth and your Mom called to say it's here."

"Mom's out back right now. I'll take a look in the drawer."

Ian knelt down to look in one of the drawers under the counter. "Here it is," he said as he came back up. "Two bolts of denim for Mrs. Sarah Eagletail."

He put the denim in a bag and handed it to Jean.

"Thought you were coming to see my horses," he said. "Expected you'd have been there by now."

"Expected you'd have been back in Calgary," she replied with a mischievous smile. "Back there making money."

"Going back tomorrow," he replied. "That was the plan. Could always change it if there was something worth changing it for."

"You could, could you?"

"Yep, I could do that. Can do anything I want."

"Pretty sure of yourself, aren't you?"

"Yep, that's me. Sure enough to know that you'd like to see my horses. Like, right now."

"I would, would I?"

"Yep, and let's stop playing around. Let's do it right now. I was only here to pick some things up. You are free, aren't you?"

"Could be. Albert's Grandparents took him with them to do some shopping in Calgary. Won't be back until after supper."

As she followed Ian's powder-blue Cadillac to the Starlight ranch, with Sarah's denim on the seat beside her, Jean wondered if Ian had another woman in his life right then. *Sarah says there's been lots of them. Lots of broken hearts. Still, if he was seeing someone right now, she'd probably be with him. Not staying behind at his fancy big house in Calgary. Maybe there is no one else.*

Ian saddled up two of the Arabians after they got to the stables and they went for a ride on the flats alongside the Big Thunder River. They stopped under a big tree and she let him make love to her on the grass.

This wasn't the first time Jean had spread her legs in order to get something she wanted. Starlight had money. Lots of it. She wanted everything his money could buy. This was fine with Starlight. He'd wanted to make out with her from the very first time he set eyes on her. They were made for each other.

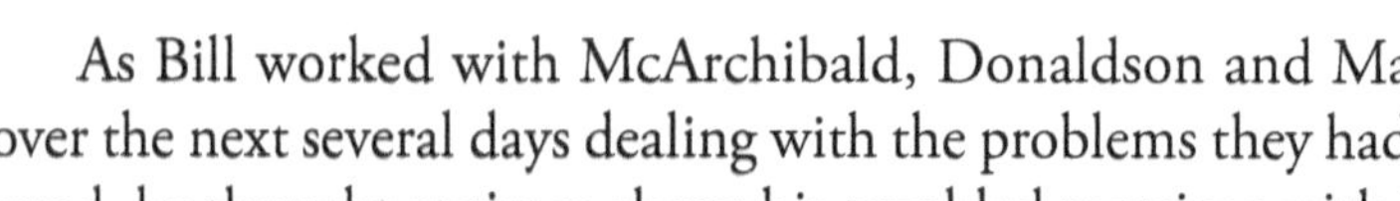

As Bill worked with McArchibald, Donaldson and MacMillan, over the next several days dealing with the problems they had encountered, he thought at times about his troubled marriage with Jean and grew more and more accepting of the fact that Jean was right. The North American Indian Studies program was his Number One priority. The most important thing in his life.

It turned out that the planned launch was in deeper trouble than McArchibald first thought. The copyright issues were more complex than had been anticipated and the lawyers needed at least another three weeks to get them resolved. The curator at the Royal Ontario Museum was proving to be quite difficult to deal with and the Minister of Indian Affairs was adamant that the treaty documents they wanted to incorporate in the program would not be released.

"Well, gentlemen," McArchibald said as he sat at the boardroom table with Bill, Donaldson and MacMillan, at the end of the second week "the problems appear to be much greater than I had at first anticipated. I don't see any option but to ask the three of you to forfeit the balance of your holidays and work with me until everything is resolved. I hate to do this to you, and to your families, but I honestly don't see any other way."

"No argument from me on that score," Bill said. "This program was my idea in the first place and I really do want to see it up and running. I'm prepared to give it whatever time it takes."

"You can count me in, too," MacMillan said, "The more we get into this, the more fascinating it all becomes. This truly is a worthwhile undertaking."

Donaldson was also onboard. They would all cut short their holidays and dedicate all of their attention to the launch of the North American Indian Studies program.

Bill flew back to Calgary the next morning to break the news to Sarah and Jean.

"There doesn't seem to be any way around this," he told them both at the kitchen table. "The problems really are quite serious and I simply must go back there until they are resolved. There's no other way."

"Well, my son, if you must go back I'm sure that you must. Still, I had so looked forward to having you with us for the summer. It's so good having you around."

"I'm sorry, Mom. That's what I wanted, too."

Jean hadn't said a word. With Bill in Toronto, she would be able to spend more time with Ian Starlight. She'd been to his fancy big house on Crescent Road and wanted to live there. He could provide her with everything Bill couldn't.

"Do you want me and Albert to go back with you?" she asked, hoping he would say no.

"Oh, no," Sarah interrupted before Bill had a chance to say anything. "Let Albert stay here for the rest of the summer. He really likes it here. Richard's been taking him riding with him on the flats and up Thunder Mountain. I've been letting him help me gather the eggs and milk the cows. Another month here will do him the world of good. The world of good."

"I think your mom's right, Bill," Jean said. "I've noticed a real change in Albert since we've been here. He really likes being on that horse with your dad and helping your mom around the barn. She's right. Taking him back to Toronto right now wouldn't be a good idea. Besides, what would Albert and me do out there? You'd be at the university all the time."

Bill thought about it for a moment. He was going to be spending a lot of time fixing the problems with the North American Indian Studies program. *And, like Mom says, Albert does seem to be having a great time here. Maybe letting him stay until the end of August wouldn't be such a bad idea after all.*

"Well, I guess you both make a lot of sense. If Albert's having that good a time of it out here then it probably is a good idea to let him stay until the end of summer. What about you, Jean? How would you feel about staying here a bit longer?"

"I'll be all right," Jean replied. "I know how important that program is to you and I'd only be getting in your way. I'll be okay here."

"Then, that settles it," Bill said. "I'll talk to Albert when he gets back from his ride with Dad, make sure he's okay with things, and then I'll head back to Toronto tomorrow afternoon."

Good idea, Jean muttered to herself. *Go back to your precious program. It's the only thing that means anything to you anyway. As for me, I'm going to work on Ian and get him to marry me. Live in that big house with the great view of the city. Take trips to Hawaii and Europe like Ian says we're going to do. Live the real life. Bye bye, Bill. You don't have what it takes to look after a woman like me.*

"Albert's going to be fine," Sarah said. "Between me and your dad, Janet and her two girls, he'll have a wonderful time here. He's got my mom and dad, too. They're over here quite a bit and Albert really likes riding in my dad's buggy. Takes him all over the place with it. You concentrate on getting that program of yours going the way it's supposed to. We'll all be okay out here at Big Thunder."

When Bill took Albert aside after supper that night, he told him that there was something he had to attend to in Toronto but that he would be back for him at the end of August and they would catch up when they were back in Toronto.

"I'm going to miss you," he said. "But it's only for another few weeks. And then you'll be back in Toronto and starting school there."

"Why can't I go to school here?" Albert asked.

That came as a surprise. *Wonder what brought that on?*

"Why would you want to go to school here?"

"I like it here. Grandfather takes me riding all the time and Grandma lets me take the eggs out from under the hens and milk the cows. She says I'm a real good milker. It's fun here, Dad. Lots of things you can't do in Toronto. No horses or cows or hens there. It's just not the same as here. And I really like being with Cousin Sandra and Debra. We do all sorts of things together. I'd like to stay here."

"Well, this is a surprise. I'd no idea you felt that way. But, still, I think you'd be better with me and your mom in Toronto. There's a lot more opportunity for you in the city and I'd like you to be there with me."

"But I hardly ever see you," Albert said. "You're never around. We never do anything together. Not like me and Grandfather or Grandma. Or Grandfather and Grandma Dodginghorse. They like spending time with me."

"I like spending time with you, Son. Of course I do."

"Then how come we never do anything? You're never around. Never take me anywhere."

Bill decided now was not the best time to deal with this unexpected situation. He'd have to give it more thought and decide what was the best thing to do. *I'd no idea he felt like that. He's almost — almost — hostile. We're going to have to talk this thing out. Not now, though. Got to get back to Toronto. Maybe, a couple of weeks from now, I'll be able to slip out here for a couple of days and straighten things out with Albert. Never expected anything like this to happen.*

Bill kept in touch with Sarah by phone as he put his heart and soul into getting the North American Indian Studies program up and running on time. While he missed not having Albert with him, he decided that it was just as well to leave him at Big Thunder for now so that he could devote every waking moment to the program.

Albert missed his dad but found all sorts of wonderful things to do at the ranch. He liked the life out there and found it much better than living in the city. His cousins were about the same age as him and treated him like a brother.

As for Jean, she wasn't around that much. Slipped into Calgary every chance she got to spend time with Ian Starlight. Living on a ranch was most definitely not the life for her. She wanted to live in the city – in Ian's five-bedroom house in Crescent Heights.

Sarah suspected that Starlight was the reason she was spending so much time in Calgary but decided not to make an issue of it. It was clear to her that Bill's marriage was in jeopardy – mainly because of him putting his career ahead of everything else – and she didn't see that situation changing any time soon. She liked having Albert with her, teaching him things, showing him how to make things, tucking him in at night. It was like having Bill at home with her all over again.

When Bill phoned to say that they had managed to get the North American Indian Studies program back on track but that he would most definitely not be able to make it back to Big Thunder right then, Sarah suggested that he give some consideration to having Albert go to the school at Big Thunder – at least until such time as the North American Indian Studies program proved to be the success that she was quite sure it was going to be.

"You've put so much effort into getting that program running," she said. "You know, William – know as well as I do – that is the most important thing in your life right now. I'm not faulting you for that, Son. But, it would appear to me, that does seem to be the reality of it all. Until that program is running the way you want it to, there just wouldn't be enough time to give Albert all the loving and care he so rightly deserves. He likes it here. Really does. Plays with Janet's kids all the time. Goes riding with your dad. Helps me out with the chores. This is a good place for him, William. Next year, after your program is going well, you can take him back to Toronto. But, for now, my son, I think Albert would be better off staying here with us."

Bill thought about it for a moment. Albert had said that he wanted to stay at Big Thunder and go to school there. The North American

Indian Studies program was taking up an awful lot of time. *Most likely take an awful lot more time over the next six months. Going to have lots of problems to sort out. Big problems. Maybe Mom's right. Jean's right, too. I really haven't given Albert the time he needs. Quality time. But, after the course is up and running, things will settle down a bit and I'll be able to spend more time with him. It's not even for a year, when you come right down to it. Then, next summer, I can spend time at Big Thunder and bring him back with me in the fall. With or without Jean. Mom's picked up on the fact that things aren't right between us. Haven't been for a long time. Long, long, time.*

"What about Jean?" he asked. "How would she feel about that? Can I talk to her?"

"She had to go to Calgary to do some shopping," Sarah replied. *Probably getting more involved with Ian Starlight*, she thought. *If I tell Bill that, he'll probably hop on a plane and take Albert and Jean back to Toronto on the next flight. And I'll lose Albert.* "Judging by what she had to say when you got the call from that Dr. McArchibald, I don't see her raising any serious objections. She's clearly not too happy with the way things are between you two. Maybe a break – a few months of separation – would be good for you both. Help clear your heads."

"Maybe you're right," Bill said. "That might be a good idea. For now, anyway. I'll come home for Christmas and we can review things when we're all together. Yes, for now, this is probably the best decision all around. Is Albert with her?"

"No. He's up on the mountain with your dad. Really likes it up there."

"Okay. I'll call him after supper your time. Talk to Jean, too. Tell her what's up."

"That sounds good. And now, my son, I've got to get back down to the barn. Got a sick heifer down there that needs my tender, loving, care."

Bill and his team got the North American Studies Program in place in time for it to be incorporated in the sociology curriculum when university classes started up again in September. They were a bit behind with setting up the correspondence courses for the young Indians out on the reserves but hoped to have it in place early in the new year.

Bill was quite pleasantly surprised by the number of Sociology students who signed up for the course and the interest they showed in the subjects. While his primary goal had been to establish a correspondence course for young Indians, he quickly realized the benefit of having the white students get a more meaningful perspective on the culture and traditions of the first peoples of Canada.

He did most of the teaching himself but brought guest lecturers in on a regular basis. Among the first to address Bill's students was Russell Means, the National Director of the headline-making American Indian movement.

The interest in the lecture Means was going to deliver was such that Bill arranged to have it held at Davidson Hall. Word that Means was coming quickly spread and, by the time he started to speak, there was standing room only in the auditorium.

Means was an Ogala Sioux and had been born on the Pine Ridge Indian Reservation in South Dakota. While he was two years younger than Bill, he seemed a lot wiser and stronger. He was certainly more deeply involved than Bill in the ongoing struggle to get out from under the oppressive yoke of colonialism.

As they sat in the Davidson lounge after the lecture drinking tea and sharing views on the oppressive conditions native people were living in, Bill became more and more fascinated with this militant leader with braided hair hanging down over his shoulders, beaded shirt and bear claws necklace.

Bill was surprised to learn that Means' parents had left the reservation when he was three and moved to the San Francisco Bay area where his father worked at the shipyard – less than an hour away from Berkeley.

Means told him one of the first things he did after becoming National Director of the American Indian Movement was to organize the seizure of a replica of the *Mayflower* in Boston Harbor on Thanksgiving Day, 1970, to protest the landing of the Pilgrims in November, 1620, and the squalid conditions under which altogether too many American Indians were now forced to live. He told Bill about how they took over Mount Rushmore in South Dakota in June of the following year and other sit-ins and demonstrations he had organized to keep the plight of native people on the front page of the nation's newspapers.

"I've never been involved in anything like that," Bill said.

"Gives me a real high," Means replied. "You should try it some time."

About two weeks after meeting Russell Means, Bill started wearing the bear claws necklace the old man from Big Thunder had given him at the pow wow on Manitoulin Island and let his hair grow long. By the time he headed back to Big Thunder to spend Christmas with his family, he was wearing his hair in braids.

"What's with you?" Hughie asked as they pulled out of the airport parking lot and headed for Big Thunder. "What's with the braids and the necklace?"

"Middle-age crazy," Bill joked. "Going through a mid-life crisis."

"No, seriously," Hughie persisted, "why this big change? You look completely different."

"I am different," Bill said. "The more I get into the material we pulled together for the North American Indian Studies program, the more I realize what an incalculable price we've paid for letting the white man live on our land. We should have dealt with them when we had the chance. Back when there was more of us than there was of them. Back before they were able to bring their soldiers to the west on the C.P.R. Back when we still had the buffalo for our food, our clothing and our lodges. Back when our great-great-grandfather had four wives and a hundred horses."

"Four wives?" Hughie exclaimed. "I didn't know anything about that."

"Dad told me one day when we were hunting whitetails up on Thunder Mountain. Lived a pretty good life our great-great-grandfather did. And, yes, he did indeed have four wives. Polygamy was quite normal back in those days. With so many warriors killing one another over territory, hunting grounds and stuff like that, there was more than enough women to go around."

"Sounds pretty good to me," Hughie said. "Don't know if I'd have the energy for it, though. That's a lot of women to keep happy."

Hughie reached for the cigarette lighter on the dashboard. "You dress like that all the time? Like when you're teaching class and all that?"

"All the time."

"Next thing they'll be calling you Chief Bull Bill," Hughie said with a chuckle.

"No one's done that yet," Bill said. "But I do get some odd, questioning, looks at times."

"What about your boss? That Dr. McArchibald guy? How's he about it?"

"Fine. I sometimes think he's a wannabe Indian. He's got pictures of Tecumseh hanging in his study and his house. I was there for dinner a couple of times. He has all sorts of Indian carvings and paintings by Norval Morrisseau, the Ojibway artist who started the Woodlands style of native art. McArchibald's fine with my new look. Big supporter of Dad, by the way. He was excited as a kid with a new toy when I took him back to the chutes at the Stampede. Dad gave him the Royal tour."

Albert was at the door waiting for them when they pulled up to the house. He ran towards his dad. "Dad, Dad," he called out. And then he jumped into Bill's open arms. Bill hugged him tightly and kissed him.

Hughie got Bill's luggage out of the pickup truck and followed them into the kitchen.

"Well, my good Lord! Look at you," Sarah exclaimed as she put her arms around him and hugged him tight. "What on earth have you done to yourself?"

"Big Chief Bull Bill," Hughie said before Bill had a chance to answer. "Came out here to get our land back from the white folk."

"Somebody should," Richard said as he got up to give his eldest son a welcoming hug. "Somebody sure as hell should."

"Where's Jean?" Bill asked as he sat down to eat.

"Hawaii," Sarah said as she put the first platter on the table.

"Hawaii?" Bill exclaimed. "What the hell's she doing in Hawaii?"

"Down there with Ian Starlight," Sarah said. "Moved in with him about a week ago."

"But – but you didn't say anything to me about that. Why am I only hearing this now?"

"Well I figured," Sarah said, "since you were going to be here for Christmas anyway, there was no point in bothering you about something like that. It was inevitable. I could tell the first moment she set eyes on him with those fancy suits and that Cadillac convertible of his that's where she'd wind up. No point in telling you. Nothing was going to change that girl's mind. Money's what she's after, William, and you plain don't have any."

"Still, she is my wife. You should have told me what was going on."

"What was going on, my son, was that you were totally wrapped up in your university stuff – just like you've been since you first married her – and she figured it was time to move on to greener pastures."

Bill looked over to Albert who was quietly eating his steak and potatoes.

"This really isn't the best time to be talking about this stuff. Not with Albert sitting here at the table."

"I'm fine, Dad. Grandma explained it all to me. Everything. Mom was hardly ever around here. She likes being in that big house in Calgary. Uncle Hughie showed me it one afternoon. It's super colossal."

"You should see it," Hughie interjected. "It's up on Crescent Heights. Jean says it has five bedrooms and marble bathrooms. You can see the city, Husky Tower and Elveden House, on the other side of the river and the Rockies over on the western skyline."

"Yeah," Albert said rather excitedly. "Uncle Hughie let me have his binoculars and I could pick out Thunder Mountain."

"Did you go in?" Bill asked Hughie.

"Nope. Jean wasn't there at the time."

"But you've been in there, haven't you?" Bill asked Albert.

"No. The boy has never set foot in the house," Sarah said. "Seems the wealthy Blackfoot isn't into kids. Got three children from his first marriage living in Calgary but never sees them. Big Bucks Starlight will never be Father of the Year."

Bill reached for the bottle of red wine and poured himself another glass. "You sure you're okay with this?" he asked Albert. "Your mom not being here?"

"You're not here either most of the time," Albert replied with a bit of an edge in his voice. "I'm fine here with Grandma and Grandfather. We do all sorts of great things together. And, when I'm a little older,

Uncle Hughie's going to teach me how to hunt whitetail deer up on Thunder Mountain."

Bill let his thoughts drift back to that day up on Thunder Mountain when his dad told him about the early contact between the Blackfoot and the white settlers. That day, right then, seemed to be a long, long, time ago. He certainly didn't have the relationship with Albert that he had enjoyed with his dad back then. *We really have grown apart. Me and Albert. I could probably have stayed in Toronto and he'd have had a great Christmas with Mom and Dad, Hughie and Janet and her kids.*

CHAPTER

- 12 -

When Diane was a little over a year old, Carol started to draw an extra $500 a month from her trust fund so she could hire on a part-time basis the housekeeper she'd had after her mom moved to the apartment and she was still working at Haldimand and Brock. After the housekeeper, Anne McAllister, had been with them for about six months, Carol started spending more and more time out of the house. Having lunch with Jane Potts, her best friend from high school, going to seminars, watching the odd movie, walking in High Park.

Gordon wasn't sure what to make of it. She became increasingly distant as the months went by. He suggested that, now that Anne was back looking after the children again, she should get back to building her career. Pick up where she had left off at Haldimand and Brock. But she said she wasn't ready for that yet.

"I feel I owe it to Diane to be here for her until she starts Grade One," she said. "She needs me."

"She needs you all right but you're hardly ever here. Anne spends more time with her than you do. And what about Charlie? How much time have you spent with him lately? I just don't understand what's got into you."

"Nothing's got into me," she snapped. "I've been here for Charlie and I let them slit my belly open so I could have Diane. I've served my time. Done my duty. Right now, I don't feel ready to go back to H and B. I need some time for me."

Gordon couldn't think of anything else to say. It was obvious that something was wrong. That she was in a real deep downer. But he didn't know what to do about it. She certainly wasn't the Carol he'd fallen in love with.

~

Tom was standing at the intersection of Queen and Sherbourne one afternoon in June, 1971, waiting to cross to the other side of the road. The light turned green and he stepped off the sidewalk. A car ran the red light and struck him down in the middle of the road. The drunk driver came from the left, his blind side, and Tom didn't see him coming. He was killed instantly. He was only sixty.

Gordon was at his office at the university when his mum called.

"Your dad's been in an accident," she said.

"Is he okay?"

"No, my son, he's not okay. Someone ran him over when he was crossing the street. He's gone."

"Gone? Like dead?"

"Yes, Gordon. Your dad is dead."

She started to cry. And then, with her voice choking, she said: "I'd like you to come home, Son. I'd like you to be with me right now."

"I'll leave right away, Mum. I'll be home in about half an hour."

As he got into his car and started driving towards his mother's house, Gordon couldn't quite believe what she'd just told him. *Dad dead? Just like that? Gone? Knocked down crossing the road?*

When he passed the 48th Highlanders' Regimental Memorial at the top of Queen's Park, he remembered sitting on the bench when he was fifteen as his dad told him about fighting his way through Italy and Holland. He started to cry.

His mother was sitting on the front verandah waiting for him. She didn't want to be alone in the house right then. Not without Tom. She fell into Gordon's arms and cried her eyes out. They both cried.

The funeral service was held at St. Andrew's Church on King Street at University Avenue. It was conducted by the padre for the 48th Highlanders of Canada. Quite a few of Tom's friends from the Royal Canadian Legion were there in their navy-blue jackets and grey flannel pants proudly wearing their ribbons and medals. The closed casket was covered by the Scottish flag with the blue background and white St. Andrew's cross.

As he sat there holding his mother's hand and giving her all the comfort he could, Gordon recalled what his dad had said about not knowing whether or not there was a heaven or a hell. "Guess we'll just have to wait to find out," his dad had said.

Gordon looked at the closed casket, the padre reading a passage from the Bible, the flag of Scotland draped over his father's dead body. *Guess Dad knows by now. He's either in heaven with Grandfather or he's nowhere. Still in that coffin.*

Young Indians spread as far apart as the Mi'kmaq of Newfoundland and the Haida of the Queen Charlotte Islands on the Pacific coast were enrolled in the correspondence program by the beginning of 1972 and learning more every day about the customs and traditions of their people.

Some of the letters Bill got were really inspiring. Young native students wrote about the positive impact the courses were having on them. How much better they felt about themselves because of the things they were learning. He was also getting positive feedback from the white students at the U of T who were taking the course. Some of the exchanges he had with several of them in class showed that they were really interested in learning about the way Canada's first inhabitants had lived. They were quite surprised by some of the things they were learning. It was vitally important to Bill that the program continue, and expand.

Yes, I'm making a difference in their lives. An enormous difference. But, Albert's my son. What difference am I making in his young life? Here I am working seven days a week to create something of value for kids on the reserves across Canada and losing contact with my only son in the process. There's something wrong here. Something really, dreadfully, wrong. Got to find some way to fix it. Fast.

Bill got involved with Sally Hurst in early October of that year. He had called her personnel agency to see if they could get him a secretary for the North American Indian Studies program. Sally Hurst Personnel was one of the agencies on the university's preferred list. About a week after she found a secretary for him, he met her at a cocktail party. They started to talk and she found herself strongly attracted to him. She thought of him as her noble savage and wanted to discover for herself how wild and primitive he would be in bed. She was more than satisfied with what she found.

They spent about an evening a week together after that. They didn't talk much. Because of that, Bill soon started asking himself what he was doing with her. He didn't like all sex and no conversation. And yet, he had become quite frustrated sexually during the lengthy separation from Jean. Sally was an excellent form of release. She was very responsive and their love making was fantastic. But he wanted to know more about her on an emotional and an intellectual level. He wanted there to be more to their relationship than their sessions in bed.

When he asked her to have dinner with him or go out to a movie, a play or a concert, she always said she had something else to do. So, for a while, he settled for their times together in her luxuriously-furnished townhouse at Bayview Avenue and York Mills Road. The furniture alone must have cost as much as a small bungalow. Sally's ex-husband was a stockbroker.

Sometimes, when they'd agree to spend the evening together in her bed, Bill would phone to let her know he was on his way over and there would be a strangeness in her voice – as if she had no idea who he was or why he was calling.

"I got the last of the papers marked," he said, one night early on in their relationship. "I'll pick up a couple of bottles of wine and be over in less than half an hour."

"Oh, well. I can't. I can't manage that tonight," she replied, stiffly.

"Have you got company?" he asked, hearing voices in the background.

"Yes. Some friends have dropped by and we're having a drink and catching up on things. So I'm not going to be able to manage that other thing."

When that happened a few times, he wondered if she didn't want him to meet her friends. *Why doesn't she just invite me over and introduce me to them?*

He thought about that one night, as she lay curled up in his arms after an exhausting session. He thought about the number of times plans for spending the evening together had been cancelled on account of visits from her friends. Could it be that she didn't want them to know about him? Was it because her divorce hadn't gone through yet? Was that it? Was it a money thing? Something that would affect her alimony? Or was it because she didn't want them to know she was sleeping with a Blackfoot? A Blackfoot with braided hair and bear claws. Was that it? Was that why she had refused his invitations to dinner, to the art galleries, to the Royal Alex? *Is she embarrassed to be seen with me in public?*

"Sally?" he said as they lay together in her bed with the glow from the flickering candles casting a warm sheen over the pink velvet-covered walls of her bedroom.

"Mmmm?" she responded, drowsily.

"Does the fact that I'm Blackfoot bother you?"

She was silent for a moment and then she said, "I'd rather not answer that question."

As far as he was concerned, she had answered it. That was their last night together.

Carol's mom was diagnosed with pancreatic cancer in March, 1972. She was only fifty-seven. It was at an advanced stage when they detected it. They started radiation and chemotherapy right away. By June, it looked like the treatment was having a positive effect. But then, about two months later, tests showed the cancer had spread to her bladder. They put her back on radiation and chemo. The treatments took quite a toll on Ethel. At times, she seemed to be in a world of her own. She didn't recognize any of them. "La la land", she called it during her more lucid moments. She lost all of her hair and often had debilitating bouts of diarrhea. Her skin turned quite yellow.

While Carol had always been closer to her dad, she loved her mother dearly and did not want to lose her. Especially not at the age of fifty-seven. Week by week, her mom lost more and more weight until, by mid-November, she was down to eighty-eight pounds. In the early morning hours of December 10, Carol was at her mother's side in a private room at Princess Margaret Hospital.

Ethel had been in a great deal of pain and the doctor had increased the dosage of morphine. It had been hours since she had uttered so much as a word. She just lay there with her eyes shut.

"Mom," Carol said as she placed her hand under her mother's right hand, "squeeze my hand if you can hear me."

There was a pause of about five seconds and then her mom squeezed her hand. Her eyes were still closed and her breathing was very irregular.

"I love you, Mom. I simply can't bear the thought of losing you," Carol said, tears welling up in her eyes. "Please don't – don't go."

At that moment, her mom clasped Carol's hand and drew it up to the left side of her face and held the back of it against her cheek. She held it there for about thirty seconds and then it fell to her side. She was gone. Carol laid her head on her mother's wasted breast and cried uncontrollably.

Oh, Mom, Mom. It's too soon. Way too soon. I need you. So much. I need you so – so – much. You can't go. Not now.

Carol was still crying convulsively, arms wrapped around her mother, when Gran entered the room. He had been in Winnipeg on business and caught the first available flight after Carol called to tell him Ethel had taken another turn for the worst. He put his arms around her and held her tight to his chest as the nurses removed the IV tubes and other equipment from Ethel's dead body.

"Daddy, Daddy," Carol sobbed, "Why? Why now? Why did Mommy have to go now?"

"It's for the best," Gran said, choking back a sob. "Your mom just couldn't take that pain any longer. It was too much. Way too much, for anyone to bear. She's at peace now, darling. At peace with the angels."

～

Carol met Derek Parkington about three months after her mother's death at a lecture the Law Society of Upper Canada sponsored on corporate takeovers. He just came right up to her after the lecture, in the room where they were serving coffee, and told her she was the most beautiful woman in the room. It was a total surprise.

"I mean it," he said with a confident, experienced, look in his eyes. "You are the most beautiful woman here."

"I'd take that as more of a compliment," she said, regaining her composure, "if there were more women here. There can't be more than five of us in the entire group."

"No matter," he said. "Even if there were five hundred, you'd still be the most beautiful. Are you married?"

She held up the gold band on the second finger of her left hand for his inspection.

"Pity," he said. "A dreadful pity."

And then he simply turned around and went to the other room. She couldn't for the life of her understand his behaviour. *What an odd person he is.* She followed him to the other room and found him sitting alone on the sofa by the big, stone, fireplace.

"Do you make a habit of that?" she asked.

"Of what?" he asked with a questioning look in his eye.

"Of telling women how beautiful they are then summarily dismissing them when you establish that they are married."

"No."

That was all he said. Just "no". She didn't know how to deal with the man. What did she want to deal with him for anyway? Why hadn't she stayed in the other room? *This is ridiculous.*

"But you are beautiful," he said, just as she was about to leave. "You are the most beautiful woman I have ever met."

She could see in his eyes that he meant it. He really did think she was beautiful.

"Come, sit with me," he almost demanded, reaching his hand up for hers. "I want to talk to you."

Derek was an unusual man. He was not at all handsome. In fact, he was almost ugly. He'd been in Vietnam with the CIA and the hotel he'd been staying at in Saigon was bombed. He'd spent eight months in a military hospital after that and the experience left him with a jagged scar running down from his left eyebrow to his jaw. It gave his face an almost lopsided look. He'd left his wife and sons just a short time before he met Carol.

They had lunch the following week. After lunch, they spent the afternoon in a room at the Windsor Arms, a quaint carriage-trade hotel in midtown Toronto with a delightful courtyard cafe. Derek was a superb lover and introduced her to some exquisite delights.

At the beginning of May, he suggested they spend a week together in Bermuda. Carol balked at the idea. Afternoons at the Windsor Arms were one thing. A whole week together in Bermuda would be an altogether different and involving proposition. Finally, after a considerable amount of persuasion, she agreed to go.

It turned out that Jane Potts wanted to spend a week with her lover and she, also, needed a cover story. They agreed that they'd tell Gordon and Jane's husband Al a week away from the children would be good for their marriages. It was too bad Gordon and Al couldn't get away. But they'd try and enjoy themselves as much as they could without them. Gordon and Al thought the Bermuda trip was a great idea.

Two weeks after their time together in Bermuda, Derek suddenly announced that he was going back to his wife and children. He told Carol his relationship with her had been beautiful, but he was finding the separation from his two young boys unbearable.

"The family thing is what I really want, Carol. I want to be with my sons again and do all the things happy families used to do together in the movies. Besides, you've got kids of your own and going through with the divorce would be such a goddamned, complicated, messy thing. For both of us. I'm sorry, Carol. I really am. But I've decided to go back to Sharon. And, when I do that, I'm going to make a commitment. I'm going to have an exclusive relationship with her and – and – well, you know. Do the whole family thing. We'll probably rent a houseboat and take the boys up the Trent canal this summer. You do understand, don't you?"

She didn't. The experience left her feeling absolutely numb. She had become quite emotionally involved with Derek. Especially after the beautiful time they spent together in Bermuda. She might even have considered leaving Gordon and the children if he had asked her to. But he didn't ask. Instead, he simply announced, in the king-size bed at the Windsor Arms Hotel, that it was all over.

About two weeks after Derek broke off his relationship with Carol, Gordon came home late from a bore of a faculty meeting. Throughout its interminable length, it didn't end until quarter-to-eleven, he thought about how much better it would be to spend the evening experiencing the warmth and excitement of Carol's gorgeous body. They hadn't made love for several months but he was hoping this night would be different.

She was in bed when he got home, reading the Warren Commission's report on the assassination of President John F. Kennedy. She looked at him in an odd manner, as if she hadn't been expecting him, as if she was questioning what he was doing there.

He said hello and asked how her day had been. He accepted her lack of response as an indication that she was thoroughly absorbed in sorting out in her mind the conflicting accounts surrounding Jack Kennedy's death. He undressed, put his clothes away and went into their bathroom to take a shower. The hot water felt good on his body and eased the tenseness from his muscles. He shaved, brushed his teeth and sprinkled on some cologne. Then he presented himself to her.

"Boy, do I need some time with you tonight. It's been a hell of a day."

"You can't sleep here tonight, Gordon," she announced, book still open on her covered breast. "I want to sleep alone."

He stood there physically and psychologically stark naked and exposed. *She can't be serious*, he thought. "Don't joke like that, Carol. You really gave me a scare."

"It isn't a joke, Gordon. I want you to move to the bedroom on the third floor. You can sleep there tonight and move your things out of here tomorrow."

"You what? What are you talking about?" *What on earth could have brought this on?*

She closed the book, eased herself up on her elbows and eyed him indifferently over her reading glasses for a moment. "Put your robe on," she commanded. "You'll catch a cold."

Obediently, he pulled his robe on and waited for what she was going to say next. She said she had thought things through and no longer wanted to sleep with him. She said it wasn't a sudden decision. It had been coming for quite some time.

"I just can't relate to you in a sexual way," she said. "And I can't put it in any other words. I just can't seem to get in the mood for sex anymore. I just find that, when we make love, I don't enjoy it. It's just – just not enough. I'd rather sleep alone. I need more time by myself."

She had been even more cold and withdrawn lately. Ever since she returned from the week's holiday in Bermuda with Jane Potts. She'd told him she expected to return home feeling rested and refreshed and the week away from the children would be good for their marriage. It wasn't. Gordon was convinced that something happened down there in the tropics because Carol was frigidly cold toward him when she got back. Rather than helping their marriage, as she said it would, the week in Bermuda widened the gap between them.

"Did something happen down there in Bermuda?" he asked. "Did you meet some guy?"

"Oh, good God, Gordon! Of course I wasn't with 'some guy' down there. It was me and Jane. That's all. And we had a wonderful time – despite the rain. Bermuda has nothing to do with it. There's reason enough for us to sleep apart without you imagining some romantic interlude in Bermuda."

"But still, isn't this sort of sudden? Why now?"

"Now? Because it's over between you and me. Now? Because I want to sleep alone. It's as simple as that."

Gordon wasn't sure what to say next. *Maybe it's a reoccurrence of the postpartum thing. Maybe it's because of the way her mother died. So young. Maybe it's – oh shit I don't know what it is. Maybe, after a week or so she'll change her mind. Who the hell knows with the way she's been behaving since Diane was born? I just don't understand her anymore. Just don't get it.*

Carol didn't change her mind. The separate room arrangement became permanent. Gordon often felt like coming home to see Charlie and Diane and spend time with them as a family, but, especially that winter, he often found good reasons not to. He'd look at the cars crawling west in the snow and figure it would take him a couple of hours to get home. The children would be in bed soon after he got there and he simply couldn't face the prospect of another frigid evening with Carol. So he'd phone home and say the traffic was awful and he was going to have dinner downtown and head home after the traffic cleared up. Then, being downtown around seven, he'd take in an early movie.

After a while, he started spending time with Ruth Applebaum, a fourth-year student who had caught his eye in the Davidson Hall Cafeteria. She was about five foot five and very full in the breast. Her straight black hair was thick and shoulder length. She always wore a silver necklace with the Star of David around her neck. Gordon was strongly attracted to her and her youth was a definite factor.

His relationship with Ruth, compared to life with Carol, was a definite ego booster. Many times, when something went wrong at the university or in some other area of his life, he'd arrange to spend time with her and their time together in bed left him feeling like a king. She was a totally giving young woman and enjoyed doing anything that gave him pleasure.

At the beginning of March, 1974, Bill got a call just before noon saying his dad was in the emergency room at the Foothills Hospital in Calgary.

"It's pretty bad," Hughie said. "You should get out here right away."

"What happened?" Bill asked.

"We're not sure. He was eating breakfast, talking away actually, and then he just passed out and slumped over. Mom took a wet cloth to him but couldn't get him to come out of it. We got him into the truck and took him here. The doctors are with him right now."

"Heart attack?" Bill asked.

"Could be. The doctors haven't told us anything yet. We've only been here for a little more than an hour.

"I'll take the next plane. How's Mom?"

"Real shaken up. She knows it's pretty bad."

Bill grabbed a taxi, went straight to the airport and bought a ticket on the next plane leaving for Calgary. But, by the time he got to the hospital, Richard was gone. The doctors said it was a heart attack brought on by a stroke.

They buried his dad four days later at the family plot at the bottom of Thunder Mountain, alongside Richard's parents and two younger sisters. Bill's great-grandfather and great-grandmother were also buried there. All of the graves had simple white wooden crosses on them. There were no names.

Gordon and Vera Dodginghorse were at the funeral. Vera, who was quite a bit smaller than Sarah, kept her arm around her throughout the ceremony. At one point, Sarah buried her face in Vera's shoulder and cried convulsively. Richard had been the whole world to her.

Bill stayed at the ranch for the rest of the week in order to provide comfort and support to his mom, sister and brother and Albert. Sarah was glad Albert was staying with her. She liked having him around, teaching him things, and just simply enjoying him.

While Bill was really broken up about losing his dad, he decided that he would have to stay strong for Albert.

"I'm really going to miss Grandfather," Albert said as they sat together on the sofa in front of the fire. "He was going to teach me to fish this year and we were going to trap martens on Thunder Mountain."

Tears welled up in Albert's eyes and Bill cradled him in his big arms and hugged him tight. They didn't say anything. Just hugged each other as Albert sobbed softly.

"You will learn how to fish this summer." he said. "I'm going to teach you. And that's not all. We're going to do all sorts of great things together, you and me."

"I hope so, Dad. I really, really, miss you. Mom's never around. Spends all her time at that big house in Calgary. Don't miss her. She shouldn't have left me like that."

"Your mom had her reasons," Bill said. "It was more a problem between your mother and I than it was anything to do with you. Grandma says Ian Starlight doesn't like having kids around. Doesn't even spend any time with his own. It wasn't because of you that she left, Son. It was because of me. Your mother and I just weren't getting along together."

"Then it wasn't because of me?"

"No, Albert. Absolutely not. It was because of things that were between me and your mom. Things that got to the point where they just couldn't be fixed. Anyway, back to fishing and good stuff like that. The university shuts down for the summer at the end of June and I'll be on the first plane back here so I can spend the summer with you. Fishing, riding, all sorts of good things."

"I hope so, Dad. I really miss you. Miss you a lot."

"Me, too. But, we are going to be together. That's a promise. I'll be here at the end of June and we'll take it from there."

As he looked down at the snow-covered prairies below the plane that was taking him back to Toronto, Bill recalled some of the things his dad had told him about the Blackfoot and all of the other Indians who had been dispossessed of their lands and their way of life as the swarms of white settlers kept pushing their way west. *That used to be ours. All of it. And what have we now? Less than nothing of the land the Indians used to have on the prairies. No room to live.* For once, he wasn't feeling particularly good about flying back to Toronto. There was a sense of having left part of himself back there. Back at Big Thunder where his dad was now buried. *Why am I going back to Toronto? What am I doing out there that I couldn't do in Calgary? At the U of C. If I was teaching there, I could have Albert living with me again. Maybe get a house near the university and spend our weekends at Big Thunder. He likes it there. That's for sure. Maybe that is where we both belong.*

Bill flew to Calgary immediately after the university closed down for the summer to be with his mother and Albert. Sarah was grieving bad. She'd been tied at the hip to Richard for more than forty years. Losing him was like having all the lights go out. She was glad Albert was living with her. It was a real comfort having him around. Teaching him things every day. Watching the smile on his face when he got on the Pinto for the very first time. Seeing how wary he was putting his hand under the hens to snatch the eggs without getting pecked.

"It's just wonderful having him here with me," she told Bill about a week after he got back to Big Thunder. "Gets so lonely at times with your dad gone and then, just like magic, Albert brightens everything up and makes life worth living again. And, William, he really likes it here, too. Not so sure he enjoyed Toronto all that much. Except being with you, that is. But he fits like a glove here. Never talks about wanting to go back to Toronto. Misses you. But he likes it here."

"I know he does, Mom. He's told me that several times. In his mind, Toronto doesn't even come close to living here with you and Hughie, Janet and her kids. I know this is where he'd rather be."

"Doing real well at the reserve school, he is," Sarah said. "Teacher says he's probably the brightest child in her class. Brings home A's all the time."

"Mom," Bill said with an amused smile, "are you trying to convince me not to take Albert back to Toronto? Not ever? Stay here with you?"

"Suppose you could put it that way," she said rather coyly. "He's been sround here for quite some time now. Getting along real well, Albert is. Certainly don't see how it'd be better for him getting lost in a big school in Toronto – with all them white children – when he could be at this nice school here at Big Thunder and learning with students of his own kind. Just a suggestion. I'm not pushing anything, mind you."

"Sure you are and, as usual, you're doing a pretty fine job of it. I'll talk to Albert about it sometime when we're out riding together. We don't have to decide right here and now. I'd like to hear from him what he really thinks about this. And, if it makes you feel any better, I am open to the idea. I want to do what's best for Albert."

Sarah liked the sound of that. She enjoyed having Albert with her and he liked being at Big Thunder. *Things are going to work out just fine for me and Albert.*

"Jean been around?" Bill asked.

"Couple of times," Sarah replied. "Seen her and Ian Starlight riding his Arabians on the flats a few times. She usually drops in to spend some time with Albert after the ride. Not for long, mind you. Maybe an hour at the most. Starlight's not got much use for kids – not even the three he's got of his own – and he's always impatient for her to get the visit over with and head back to Calgary."

"I suppose I should arrange to see her and get the divorce under way. No point leaving things in limbo like this."

"She's away. Starlight took her for a cruise. Up the B.C. coast from Vancouver to Anchorage, Hughie says. Won't be back for another two weeks."

"Then I'll see her when she gets back."

"Don't mean to pry," Sarah said. "Interfere in your affairs. But you are doing the right thing. Divorce is the right thing for you to do. No way you'll ever be able to give that girl the things Starlight can get for her. She wants to get as far away from that trailer down there on the Blood reserve as she possibly can. And Ian Starlight's money is the bus that's going to take her there. Hughie says they're going to Tahiti for Christmas."

Bill thought back to their brief, three-day, honeymoon in Hollywood and Jean holding the wheel of the *Bounty*. "Oh, Bill, I'd love to have sailed on that ship," she'd said. "With those big white sails taking me to all sorts of wonderful places. Heading for the South Seas. Palm trees and coconuts. Beautiful white sand to walk on."

Guess she's going to Tahiti after all, he thought. *Jet plane instead of the* Bounty *and its big white sails. The palm trees and the white sand will be the same, though. She's getting the life she's always wanted. No doubt about that.*

When Bill talked to Albert about the possibility of staying at Big Thunder for another year, Albert said he missed him a lot but really did like being at Big Thunder.

"Toronto's not the same," he said. "Some of the kids there don't like Indians very much. I got picked on a lot. Sometimes they really pushed me around. Beat me up. I'm the only Indian kid near our house."

"I didn't know that," Bill said. "Why didn't you tell me?"

"Knew how busy you were with things at the university. Didn't want to bother you. Besides, it wasn't all bad. Some of the kids were real nice."

"Still you should have told me. Did you tell your mom?"

"Yeah. She said life is tough and I've got to, something like, roll with the punches. Not sure if those were her exact words, but it was something like that."

"If I'd known, I'd have done something about it. You didn't deserve to be treated like that."

"No problem, Dad. It's all over now. Nobody bothers me here. I've got lots of friends at Big Thunder."

"And you'd like to stay here, right?"

"Sort of. And it'd be even better if you stayed here, too. I really miss you, Dad. Can't you stay? Come and live here with me and Grandma? You like it here, don't you?

"Yes, Son. I miss Big Thunder a lot. And, you're right, Toronto's not the same. No comparison. Life here's as good as it gets."

"So? That mean you're going to stay?"

"Can't say yes right now. But things might be different this time next year. A lot different. You stay here with Grandma and Aunt Janet and Uncle Hughie for now and let's see what I can arrange between now and next summer."

Before he left for Toronto at the end of August, Bill had lunch with Harold Chamberlain, the new Chairman of the Department of Sociology at the University of Calgary. Chamberlain's son had been at the Edmonton campus at the same time as Bill and they were both on the football team. Chamberlain had quite an interest in football and had been very impressed with Bull Bill Eagletail.

They talked about the possibility of Bill teaching sociology at the University of Calgary and, perhaps, creating a new version of the North American Indian Studies Program. With the growing number of native students that were enroling at the University of Calgary, Chamberlain, who was a very progressive individual, believed that there would be real interest among them in the program and, as had proved to be the case in Toronto, a significant number of the white students would also want to take it as a credit course. There was also the very real probability of attracting native students from British Columbia, Saskatchewan and Manitoba.

"The course would pay for itself," Chamberlain said. "No doubt about that. Indian Affairs would cover their fees and residence. Last time I talked to Dr. McArchibald, he said the correspondence part of the program was actually running in the red. However, if we have enough native students taking the course, on campus here at the university, that should balance things out as far as the financing goes. No reason why the correspondence course can't be run out of here instead of in Toronto."

"I'm sure that would work," Bill said. "And, for me, even more important is the interaction that we would have with the native students. You would be providing them with a unique learning opportunity."

They agreed to discuss it at length with McArchibald over the next couple of months. See what he thought about it. Get his views on how best to replicate the program.

"If Dr. McArchibald agrees that replicating the program is feasible, and worthwhile, and agrees to let you go, then we could get things under way at the beginning of next year. It will, as was the case in Toronto, require several months of preparation. However, I see no reason why the course could not be ready to go by this time next year."

"That sounds perfectly reasonable to me," Bill said. "I truly do believe that it would work. Especially if we can get several hundred native students taking the course right here on campus. Like you said."

"Then we'll leave it at that," Chamberlain said. "If you're serious about wanting to teach here, I must have a commitment from you by the end of November. No later than November thirtieth."

"I will know for sure by then," Bill said. "Perhaps even sooner."

Bill decided against telling his mom or Albert about the possibility of moving back to Calgary. *No point getting their hopes up until I'm absolutely sure this is the best thing to do.*

Gordon had become increasingly concerned about guest lecturers from the United States, some from the black civil rights movement and some from the militant American Indian Movement, who seemed to be taking perverse delight in making the white students feel ashamed of their race. Some of the more radical lecturers put the white students down every chance they got. Made them apologize for the sins of their forefathers. It angered Gordon to hear them baiting and embarrassing the white students.

He took particular exception to Dr. Arthur Staples, a black Professor of sociology at the University of California's Berkeley campus. Staples had developed somewhat of a national reputation for the role that he played in riots that broke out in crowded black neighborhoods in the early 1960s. According to a profile in *Time Magazine*, he helped start riots in Rochester, Philadelphia and New York in 1964 and, in August 1965, he was at the heart of the week-long riots in the black neighborhoods of South Central Los Angeles which resulted in almost $40 million worth of damage.

The article in *Time* quoted witnesses as saying that Staples was seen throwing Molotov cocktails at white-owned stores and buildings during the six-day riot in Detroit in July, 1967. According to *Time*, he had never been charged with any criminal act but it was widely suspected that he had played a key role in inciting people to riot.

The profile in *Time* also said that Staples had helped organize the seizure of the Bureau of Indian Affairs' headquarters in Washington in November, 1972. About five hundred Indians occupied the building for seven days to protest appalling living conditions on the reservations and caused $700,000 worth of damage. According to *Time*, many records, including original treaties, deeds, and water rights documents, were destroyed in the process.

When Staples showed up at the University of Toronto in June, 1974, he was wearing an afro hairstyle and a richly-embroidered traditional West African gown. Gordon remembered, vividly, Staples leaning over the podium at Davidson Hall railing against what he called a litany of sins committed against black people and describing white people as the scourge of the earth.

"White people are scum," he said contemptuously. "White people get off on dumping on black people, red people, yellow people – all people under God's bright sun who don't have that sickly-looking white parchment covering their bones. But those days are over. Over! You hear me?"

They heard him all right. Hundreds of young, white, middle-class university students filled the Davidson Hall with the roar of their applauding hands.

"That time is over," Staples declared. "White people are the minority group on this earth now. We are the majority. Black people. Red people. Brown people. Yellow people. Not whitey. Not Mr. Whitey. No, sir, people. There's a new dawn a coming. Colour us anything. But don't colour us white."

They were on their feet. Clapping and beaming and nodding their heads in approval. Listening to the sound of their applause, Gordon wondered why so many of those young university students had such an overwhelming urge to disown their whiteness. Perhaps, he thought, it was a form of release from the tremendous amount of guilt they had been forced to carry because of the way white people had treated people from other races in the past.

Not all of the students were on their feet. Or clapping. Some of them sat with strained, perturbed, expressions on their faces. They had found the black lecturer's sixty-minute tirade profoundly disturbing. He had pinched a sensitive nerve in their innermost being. Reached deep down inside and made them feel shame. Put them down in the name of those of this world's billions of coloured people who believed that every last one of their individual and collective problems was the fault of the white minority.

Gordon went up to the microphone during the question and answer session and told Professor Staples that his comments were inflammatory and completely uncalled for. He told him that whatever he was being paid for the lecture was a flagrant misuse of university funds. Then he asked him how much he was being paid.

Some of the students started to boo and yelled at Gordon to sit down. And then young Donald Frampton, the president of the Student Administrative Council, went to the other microphone and told Gordon that Staples was being paid by the students and he had no right to embarrass their guest by raising such questions.

"I'm embarrassing him?" Gordon exclaimed. "This is my university and …."

"Sit down. Sit down," some of the students started to chant.

Gordon recognized a lost cause when he saw one. He left the auditorium.

Gordon – who still didn't have so much as a clue about the fact that he was adopted and his birth mother was a full-blooded Blackfoot from Big Thunder – believed that the white race had contributed more than any other group to the overall betterment of mankind. That's why he felt that white, Western European, students coming into the university environment should be encouraged to demonstrate pride in their special racial and cultural heritage.

People from every race except the white race were being encouraged to be proud of their racial and cultural heritage and he felt that the white students were paying too high a price for this new-found pride of the non-whites. He was convinced that the special studies programs on Indian and black history and culture that had recently been established at the university had a built-in bias against white, Western European, Canadians. He believed that they were part of an orchestrated effort to undermine confidence in white values, customs and traditions.

What was needed, he felt, was for the University of Toronto to set up special studies courses for the white students. He figured that was the only way to ensure that they would have the necessary knowledge to stand up to the white-baiting blacks and Indians making the rounds of the university lecture circuit and telling white people that they were garbage.

Things had been allowed to degenerate too far. Much too far. One day, as he was sitting in one of the cubicles in the faculty washroom, he saw the writing on the wall: "Don't forget to flush. White people will eat anything." Now that got him mad. How had things gotten to the stage where he couldn't even go to the washroom without having to read that sort of crap on the cubicle walls? It had to have been one of the guest lecturers who wrote that stuff on the wall. The students were not allowed to use the faculty washroom.

That writing on the wall was the last straw. Something had to be done about the situation. Gordon was not going to lie down meekly in the soiled pasture and let the black, the Indian and all of the other rabble-rousing racists trample on his Scottish heritage. White students were being discriminated against and the only way to correct the situation was to get the university to set up special studies courses for them.

"But we already have a – a – white studies program," Barry Cooper, the young Associate Professor of English, argued during a heated lunch-hour discussion in early September. "Our entire education system is geared to the white, Western European, tradition. All that the non-white groups are asking for is an opportunity to study the contribution their own people have made to the development of the whole community."

"They have that now," Donald Henderson, the crusty old Chairman of the History Department, snorted as he sprinkled more salt on his roast beef and potatoes. "They have all the opportunity they need to consider every non-white contribution – within the context of the white majority-group whole. We form the majority in Canada. It is only right and proper that the majority perspective should have the higher priority."

Gordon, who had spent a lot of time in discussions over tea with Henderson, was in complete agreement with his position. White people might have done certain things in the past about which they should be ashamed – like taking the native peoples' land and shipping their children off to be abused in the residential schools – but he believed they had also done much, much more, of which they could be proud.

"Professor Henderson is quite right," Gordon said. "Our values, customs and traditions are second to none anywhere on this earth. There's no reason why the white perspective shouldn't be given an even higher priority. Our white students need to be inoculated against the increasing attacks from the black and the Indian and all of the other rabble rousers touring the university lecture circuit and trashing the values, customs and traditions of our race."

"Of our race?" Cooper exclaimed. "Hold it! Hold it! Gentlemen, one moment please. As I hear it now, you are proposing a pro-white studies program to counter the opinions expressed by some of the guest lecturers. You seem to be suggesting, Professor MacArthur, a white pride campaign. Something along the line of 'white is beautiful', I suppose. Don't you see that that would be fighting racism with racism? Surely you can all see my point. I couldn't possibly give my support to that – to that sort of campaign."

"Well I certainly could!" Walter Huntington, an Associate Professor of Engineering, exclaimed. "I most definitely could support that type of affirmative action. The pendulum has been allowed to swing too far. Much too far. Only yesterday, for God's sake, the police picked up two young Toronto Nazis for painting, what the *Star* called, racist slogans on the hoarding at the site of some construction project. And what were those so-called racist slogans? Two words. 'White – power.' White power, for God's sake! Those young skinheads were placed in jail, without bail I suppose, for painting the words white power on some pieces of plywood. By God, gentlemen, if we can have black power and red power and all of the other coloured powers, why on God's earth can there not be white power? I say the time has come to take a stand for our own kind. I am certainly not ashamed of being white. And yes, Professor Cooper, given a choice, I would most definitely say that white is beautiful."

Cooper couldn't believe his ears. *They can't be serious.* Surely Ross Palmer, the Chairman of the English Department, didn't agree with them. There certainly wasn't a hint of anything white supremacist about Palmer. He had always shown himself to be more than willing to give his time and financial support to such organizations as the Canadian Council of Christians and Jews, the Unitarian Service Committee and the Social Planning Council. And, during the year Cooper had taught under him in the English Department, Palmer had always appeared sympathetic toward the problems and aspirations of the minority groups.

"What about you, Ross?" he asked in a tone of voice that projected a plea for a return to sanity around the oak dining room table. "Do you not agree that what Professor MacArthur is proposing represents a dangerous course?"

Palmer tapped his pipe against the ash tray and thought for a moment before replying. "No, Barry. I don't think you could describe the course that is being suggested as being dangerous. It need not be. And, to answer your question about my position on the matter, I am rather inclined to go along with the general thrust of this proposal."

He stopped to take a couple of puffs on his pipe and then continued. "A definite imbalance has been allowed to develop and I feel that it should be corrected. It was, as you yourself know, the Marxist-Leninists who argued for the fragmentation – the setting up of the special studies programs. And they did get exactly what they wanted. We now have a program specializing in the history and culture of the North American Indians and we also have one specializing in the history of the black people ...."

"Hold on, Ross," Cooper interjected. "There's nothing Marxist-Leninist about Bill Eagletail and his North American Indian Studies program. There's no reason to use language like that. That is not at all fair."

"Maybe he isn't a Communist," Gordon cut in, "but he sure looks weird wandering around the halls in those braids and bear claws. Doesn't he know this is 1974? I hear some of the students call him Chief Pie In Sky behind his back."

"Not the students who take his class," Cooper said. "They have a great deal of respect for him. They ..."

"All right. All right," Palmer said. "Let's get the discussion back on track. Barry's right. My comment was a bit over the top. I should not have described Dr. Eagletail as a Marxist-Leninist. That was wrong of me. However, that does not, in any way, minimize the damage, the fragmentation, that is being caused by those special studies programs. As Professor MacArthur just pointed out, our white students are being denied those special educational opportunities. As a result, we must consider them to be, comparatively, disadvantaged. For that reason, I support his suggestion that we press for white studies courses to correct this unfortunate imbalance."

"And," Gordon interjected, "if we didn't have the special studies programs we wouldn't have those agitators from the States telling our students that white people are, as that Staples professor from Berkeley put it, the scum of the earth."

"Look, I'll admit, Staples was a bit over the line," Cooper said. "He has become a bit more radical over the last few years. But, I suggest that you've got to appreciate where he's coming from. He was with James Meredith when the rioting broke out at the University of Mississippi because of him becoming the first black American to attend a white university. And that was only twelve years ago. Staples was there. In Mississippi. There were two people killed and at least seventy-five injured during those riots. Even President Kennedy couldn't calm things down. Staples lived through that. He braved the rocks, the lead pipes, gas bombs, rifles and shotguns. Those white people were enraged, and he was black. He experienced all that.

"And then, in '68, he was with Dr. Martin Luther King when he was assassinated in Memphis. King was there to show support for black public works employees who were on strike for better wages and better treatment. Blacks doing repair work on the streets got only two hours' pay when they were sent home because of bad weather. If you were white, you got a whole day's pay. King was objecting to that and a multitude of other injustices. So, they shot him. Shot him dead on the balcony of that Memphis motel. That was only six years ago."

"Fine. Fine," Henderson muttered impatiently. "But, Toronto isn't Mississippi or Memphis. We don't have anything like that up here. Neither Staples nor any other of those black radicals has the right to come up here, to Toronto, and make our students squirm because of something that happened way down there in the American south."

"All that I'm saying," Cooper said, "is that there is a reason, a very sound reason, for why Staples is, sometimes, a bit more toxic than is helpful. He's a product of that system. Of that society."

"Maybe so," Henderson said. "But this is here and he has no business speaking to our students like that. I was there. Gordon is quite right. What that man said, and the way he said it, was totally uncalled for and unacceptable."

"Yes," Gordon said. "Professor Henderson is quite right. The more radical guest lecturers are, definitely, going out of their way to make our white students ashamed of their race. To, as he just said, make them squirm. That is why we have to have something to counter-balance the special courses about the Indians and the blacks. Something to, as I said earlier, inoculate our students from these unjustified, and completely unwarranted, attacks."

"But," Cooper protested. "Can't you see that what you're proposing is no different than what we've been hearing from the Black Muslims and all of the other race-based groups? If you persist on this course, you're going to increase the polarization, the alienation, the emphasis on race and nationality that's keeping the people of this world fragmented and apart. This is a dreadful thing that you're proposing. Your children certainly won't thank you for this horrible day."

That last comment got under Gordon's skin. "Leave it to us, Professor Cooper," he interjected with obvious irritation, "to determine what our children will or will not thank us for. You, obviously, on the basis of what you've just said, will be of no effective use to us in accomplishing our objectives. In fact, dealing with attitudes like yours will be one of our biggest obstacles. I suggest that you finish your coffee and leave us to get on with our business."

Cooper glanced from face to face around the dining room table, hoping against hope for a hint that one of them recognized the awfulness of what they were proposing. But it looked as if Gordon had spoken for them all – even for Ross Palmer.

"All right then," he said with a sigh of exasperation. "I will leave. I don't appear to be getting through to any of you. Draw your covered wagons in a circle if you wish. That is your prerogative. But I could never support your white-is-beautiful campaign. You'll have to ride the white horses without me."

Not one of them said a word as he reluctantly swallowed his coffee and pushed himself away from the table. On the walk back to his cubbyhole of an office, he worried about the harmful effect Gordon and his group could have on the university and on the general community. He would like to have been able to dismiss the unfortunate affair out of hand. But that wasn't possible. Henderson was, after all, Chairman of the History Department. Palmer was Chairman of the English Department and both Gordon and Huntington were respected within their departments. Among them, they exerted an impressive amount of influence.

It was almost certain that Gordon was going to be the Conservative candidate in the Toronto riding of Meadowbrook for a federal election that was expected to be called in late October, 1974.

Henry Bracken, Chairman and Chief Executive Officer of Bracken Department Stores and long-time president of the Meadowbrook Conservative Association, told Gordon he would most likely be appointed to the cabinet if he won the election. The Meadowbrook Conservatives certainly felt they had a cabinet seat coming to them.

Both through personal donations and through contributions from the major corporations they represented – many of whom had only recently moved their corporate head offices to suburban Meadowbrook from downtown Toronto – the Meadowbrook Conservatives contributed a substantial amount of money to the Conservative Party of Canada.

They would have had their seat at the cabinet table the last time the Prime Minister shuffled his cabinet if Toronto lawyer Hal Davies, the MP for Meadowbrook for the last seven years, hadn't become romantically involved with the youngest daughter of the president of the United Indians of Canada Association.

Davies met the girl, an exceptionally beautiful third-year political science student at the University of Ottawa, during a weekend conference dealing with the enormous problems faced by the increasing number of Indians leaving the reserves and moving to the cities. She enjoyed being with him and they soon started spending time together on the weekday evenings when he was in Ottawa for the sittings of the House of Commons. At one point, Davies even considered the politically unwise course of asking his wife of twenty-three years for a divorce so he could marry the young Indian beauty.

When the girl became pregnant, her father went straight to the Prime Minister about it. Now that was something Prime Minister Walter Floyd simply would not tolerate. He always drew the line, short and fast, when the messier personal problems of any of the Conservative Members of Parliament reached into his office.

Immediately after a senior member of his staff confirmed the father's story, the Prime Minister summoned Davies to his office and told him, dispassionately, that he demanded a higher level of personal conduct from those who represented the Conservative Party of Canada. It would be in the party's best interest, the Prime Minister said, if Davies didn't run in the next election. He instructed Davies to issue a press release saying he was retiring from politics in order to spend more time with his wife and family. He would serve out his term but would not be a candidate in the next election.

Davies' sudden resignation took the Meadowbrook Conservatives by surprise. They had expected he would be representing Meadowbrook in the upcoming election. But, despite the pleadings of several members of the riding executive, Davies said he was quite definite about leaving politics and they would have to find themselves another candidate.

In the midst of that confusion, Gran Winston said he would finance more than half the cost of the Meadowbrook election campaign on the condition that no one was to compete against Gordon for the nomination. He knew from several conversations that he had had with him over the years how deeply interested Gordon was in politics. He had indicated on more than one occasion that he would like to run for office some day. Based on those comments, Winston was quite certain that Gordon would jump at the chance to run in a safe Conservative riding.

Winston was a shrewd businessman. Having a member of the family in Ottawa keeping a lookout for his business interests would be a good investment. Gordon could keep his eyes open for things that could be a benefit to, or hinder, his extensive real estate operations. He could also help set up meetings with key cabinet ministers and, for that matter, the Prime Minister himself.

Some members of the riding executive would have preferred a contested nomination so they could be sure the best possible candidate represented Meadowbrook in the campaign. They also questioned whether or not they were opening themselves up to accusations of conflict of interest given that Gordon was, after all, Winston's son-in-law. However, they also recognized how poorly the party's national fundraising effort was going and the $25,000 Winston had promised for the Meadowbrook campaign was only about one-tenth the amount Winston Holdings Limited would pump into the national campaign coffers.

Besides that, with the election coming up so soon, they had to move fast. Most of them believed Gordon would be an excellent candidate. He was rather impressive. Professor of Political Science at the University of Toronto, former Chairman of the National Conservative Youth Commission, former president of the Young Conservatives Club at the U of T. Thirty-five. Married with two children.

Henry Bracken knew, from discussions he'd had with some of his friends and business associates, that there was a growing undercurrent of unease in the white, Anglo-Saxon, community. Too much of what they held to be worthwhile, of what they had enjoyed as Canadians before the huge influx of people from other countries and cultures, was being swept away. Bracken felt it was high time someone swung the pendulum back closer to where it had been when he was growing up. Things were changing altogether too rapidly.

Just that summer, while sailing on Lake Simcoe, he did a double-take on spotting a middle-aged man in a turban at the helm of a sleek, twenty-eight-foot, yacht. While Bracken quickly concluded that the yacht was most likely rented or borrowed, it did symbolize the fact that some of those middle-class East Indian merchants might eventually be buying cottages on his lake. Bracken didn't want to see a Sikh in a turban barbecuing chicken on the beach next to his. Something had to be done about the situation.

Bracken saw Gordon and his small group of professors at the University of Toronto, they had decided to call themselves the Equal Opportunities Council, as a welcome breath of fresh air. They were quite an impressive, influential, group of WASPs and he was confident that they would be able to put the brakes on what he considered to be a mad rush toward turning Canada into a multicultural society. He considered the Equal Opportunities Council to be even more reason why Gordon should have the Conservative nomination for Meadowbrook.

"We've moved too fast," he said to Gordon as they were discussing plans for the Meadowbrook election campaign over lunch at the Commonwealth Club. "Much too fast. We're moving too rapidly toward this new concept of a multicultural society. Too much that is good and worthwhile is being lost – abandoned – in the process. Just look at the way the Queen and the Royal Family have been downgraded. It's a disgrace, Gordon. An outright disgrace. Too many of our British institutions and traditions are being pushed into the background in the name of multiculturalism."

He paused for a moment to nibble on his beef tenderloin medallions. "These days, Gordon, you hardly ever see the Union Jack flying in Canada. Instead, we've got this red maple leaf monstrosity that doesn't give so much as a hint of who and what we are as a people. There's a constituency out there and there is no one around whom they can rally. I'm talking about white people, Gordon. The black people have their spokesmen. The Indians have theirs. But who in Canada speaks out on behalf of white people?

"Over in Rhodesia, Prime Minister Ian Smith is doing the best that he can against overwhelming odds. The black nationalists are disrupting the Rhodesian economy by lacing the roads with anti-tank land mines provided by the Russians. They're using Russian surface-to-air missiles against Rhodesian airplanes and they're also getting weapons from the Communist regime in China. The Rhodesian jungle is now a key battleground of the Cold War.

"The South Africans are also fighting to uphold the basic values of white society. Just this June, for God's sake, the Japanese said they would no longer grant visas for white South Africans to travel to their country. Whites are under pressure – all over the globe. But, Gordon, this is not Rhodesia or South Africa. This is Canada and, in particular, the white, middle-class, riding of Meadowbrook."

Bracken paused as the waiter placed the dishes of English plum pudding in front of them and topped-up their wine. "If you were an Indian, they would probably consider running you up on Manitoulin Island or somewhere where there is a significant number of Indian voters on the reservations. If you were Italian, they might run you in St. Clair where sixty per cent of the voters come from Italy. If you were Greek, they would sell you to the Greeks out on the Danforth as one of their own. But, Gordon, you are not Italian, Greek or Indian. You are a white, Western European Canadian. Just like most of the voters in Meadowbrook. I challenge anyone to tell me why the people of Meadowbrook should not have the right to be represented by one of their own kind. Someone who will uphold the basic values of white society. It makes sense to me, Gordon, and, on that basis, you have my full support. I want you to have the nomination."

Gordon was looking forward to becoming a Member of Parliament. To take his seat in the House of Commons and debate issues of national importance in the same chamber in which once sat Sir John A. Macdonald, Sir Wilfrid Laurier and war-time Prime Minister William Lyon Mackenzie King who was in office when his dad went to fight the Germans in Italy.

And now, after twelve years studying politics, four years teaching it, and knocking on doors during election campaigns, he wanted to run for office. To be in the cabinet, give speeches in Parliament, at the Canadian Club and the Canadian Chamber of Commerce. To be the Honourable Gordon MacArthur, P.C., M.P. All of that. That's what he had his heart set on now. And, judging by what Henry Bracken had told him, it was all about to become a living reality.

Much of what Bracken had said about the rapid pace at which Canadian society was changing as a result of the hordes of newcomers from other cultures, other worlds, had struck a chord with Gordon.

Bracken's views were very much along the lines of those Professor Henderson had expressed during their discussions in his office at the university.

Don Mitchell, the Harvard PhD in charge of Prime Minister Walter Floyd's political affairs in Ontario, was totally opposed to any thought of Gordon being a representative of the Conservative Party of Canada.

"We couldn't possibly run a – as you call it – a white candidate, Henry," Mitchell said during a heated telephone conversation a week before the nomination meeting . "It wouldn't work. Not in Meadowbrook. Not in any other riding. It's simply out of the question."

"That's where you are wrong, Donald," Bracken persisted. "It would work. I just know that it would work. The Italians, the Portuguese and the Greeks hold the balance of power in just about every one of the downtown ridings. They control the membership of most of those riding associations. No one, and I mean no one, can get a nomination to run for the party without their support. They are in complete control of the party. Are you telling me that they represent the white, Anglo-Saxon, point of view? Is that what you're trying to tell me?"

"No. But the point that you're missing is that not one of those ridings is represented by a Member of Parliament who is Greek, Italian or someone who is Portuguese. While it is true, as you say, that the ethnics control the nomination process in the inner city ridings, they usually nominate and elect someone who is white Anglo-Saxon Protestant."

"That's not the point. The point is that they control those ridings. Determine who will and who will not be a candidate. And that, Donald, is wrong. Dead wrong."

"Henry, Henry. Just step back a bit and put things in perspective. Whether you like it or not, I suggest that you've just simply got to adjust to the fact that the people you are expressing concern about this morning represent the viewpoint of the majority of the voters in their ridings. That's what democracy is all about. They represent the majority point of view in their areas. There just happens to be more of them now than there was before. They are now the majority in the inner-city ridings."

"You're forgetting one thing. One very important thing. Those ridings used to be white, Anglo-Saxon, Protestant. Those ridings used to be controlled by white, Western European, Canadians."

"Used to be, Henry. Used to be. But times change. Those ridings have changed. The white, Western European, Canadians, as you refer to them, are no longer in the majority. They are ..."

Bracken was starting to get quite worked up. "That's just what I'm getting at. Dammit. We were pushed out of those ridings. Pushed out by Italians, Greeks, and all of the others taking the neighborhoods over block by block, swarming across the entire city until hardly any properties remained in the hands of the white, Anglo-Saxon, Canadians who settled those neighborhoods in the first place."

Mitchell decided to try a more conciliatory approach. "Your point is perfectly understandable, Henry. Everyone wants to be with their own kind. That's why Greek families, Italians, and all of the others that you seem to be so upset about this morning moved to those areas in Toronto where their relatives and friends had moved before them. They, also, wanted to be with their own kind. That's human nature."

"The only thing wrong with that argument," Bracken snapped, "is that we were there first. We're the ones who first settled and developed those neighborhoods. It's only in the very few ridings like here in Meadowbrook that we still form the majority. This is still a riding primarily made up of people of British stock. And I want someone – someone like me – someone who is a white, Western European, Canadian – to represent me in Ottawa. That is why I am supporting Gordon MacArthur and that is why I want him to be our candidate in the next election."

"And I'm telling you you've bitten off more than the Prime Minister will chew, Henry. He's not going to support someone who is on the radio saying white is beautiful or some of that other stuff MacArthur has been spouting. You're going to find that he'll spit this white-pride thing right out of his mouth."

"Nonsense, Donald," Bracken said confidently. "I have known the Prime Minister a lot longer than you. You will find that his reaction is not at all reflective of your own. You are, as always, over-reacting. And, by the way, white is beautiful and it is about high time that we were not ashamed to say so. Anyway, Meadowbrook is our affair and the nomination meeting will proceed as planned. Gordon MacArthur will represent Meadowbrook in the election. Now, Donald, I have some rather pressing matters to attend to. I must go. I have listened to what you have had to say and, in my judgment, you are wrong. Completely wrong. Now I simply must go."

With that, Bracken placed the phone back on the hook. Mitchell couldn't believe the dial tone buzzing in his ear. Bracken had actually hung up on him. *The stubborn old fool is going to stick to his course and ruin any chance we have of holding Meadowbrook. I should have spoken to him earlier. When that first story about MacArthur came out in the* Globe. *Damn. I got so busy with the preparations for the First Ministers' Conference and just didn't take the time. Things have gotten out of hand. Must speak to the PM. Fast.*

Actually, Bracken didn't know the Prime Minister all that well. At least not on a personal basis. While he had campaigned with him when they were both young Conservatives at the University of Toronto, they lost touch when the future prime minister returned to Winnipeg to run his father's profitable chain of hardware stores. That was around the same time Bracken's father appointed him to a middle-management position at Bracken Department Stores.

What was needed was someone who had the Prime Minister's ear. Someone like Gordon's father-in-law. A man of Granville Winston's stature, especially considering how much the party depended on him to raise money for them, could talk to the Prime Minister man to man. Gran Winston would be able to put things in proper perspective, in the best interest of the party. Bracken was certain that a call to the Prime Minister from Winston would be just what was needed at that particular time.

It turned out that Winston was out in Calgary negotiating for the land he needed to build an airport hotel out there. Calgary was the only missing link in his national hotel chain. If he got the Calgary property, at the right price, there would be a Winston Inn out there within two years.

Bracken instructed his secretary to get him Winston in Calgary. Then he lit a cigar and waited for the call. Winston was on the line in a matter of minutes.

"This is a welcome surprise, Henry," Winston said. "I certainly didn't expect to be talking to you over breakfast this morning. What can I do for you?"

Bracken glanced at the sterling silver clock on his mahogany desk. It was 11:15 a.m. in Toronto. That would make it 9:15 a.m. two thousand miles away in Calgary. Winston always did enjoy late breakfasts in bed.

"Well, Gran, I don't want to interrupt your breakfast. I could call back ..."

"No. No. Not at all," Winston said graciously. "I've just finished. Please go right ahead. What can I do for you?"

Bracken described the telephone conversation he had with Don Mitchell and how determined Mitchell was that Gordon should be asked to withdraw from seeking the Conservative nomination.

"Withdraw?" Winston asked incredulously. "Out of the question. Who does Mitchell think he is? Damn him and all those other political-science elitists. They're always trying to do things by a book that should never have been written. No. Withdrawal is out of the question. We need someone like Gordon in this country. Need it badly."

"That is my position, exactly," Bracken said. "I agree with you one hundred per cent, Gran. What Gordon and his group are on to is dynamite. I can see this movement catching on like a prairie wildfire."

"You're damned right," Winston said. "What Gordon is doing is simply magnificent. I was so proud of what he said on the radio the other morning about the importance of our white, Anglo-Saxon, values and traditions. He's right, Henry. We do need to give our young people a better sense of pride in themselves. Self-esteem, Henry. That's the key to successful living. If you don't feel right about yourself, about who you are, who your people are, what your place in the world is, then you're no damned good to a living soul."

"You're so right, Gran. So right."

"Gordon and his people are on to something important. Something of value. And I really liked what he said about people in turbans sprouting up all over settled neighborhoods where white people were born and raised. By God, Henry, it was good to hear someone, someone with standing in the community, speak out about that one and on the problems those people create when they move into white neighborhoods. Sometimes, they have as many as three families living in one house. But, let's get back to Mitchell. If I've said this once, I've said it a hundred times, I am sick and tired of having these staff people in Ottawa calling the shots. And calling them wrong. Without us, they'd be nobodies."

"Exactly!" Bracken interjected. "Without us and the party, they'd all be out on the street looking for work. I told Mitchell that, exactly that, this morning. But I don't think he was listening."

"They never do," Winston said. "But they're going to. Goddammit! They are going to. It's only in the last few years that those people have been positioning themselves between the Prime Minister and the party. And this situation of Gordon's is as good a one as any to bring things to a head. I'll be damned if some Ontario desk secretary is going to tell me who will, or who will not, run in Meadowbrook – or in any other riding. Gordon is going to be the candidate and that's all there is to it."

"Will you call the Prime Minister then?" Bracken asked.

"I'll go one better than that, Henry. Harland Edwards is involved in this deal I'm putting together out here. He's a lot closer to the Prime Minister than I am. I'm certain Harland will call the Prime Minister on our behalf."

Harland Edwards was a very prosperous Toronto lawyer. He was also Chairman of the National Conservative Campaign Finance Committee. He and Winston had been involved in quite a few deals together – both in business and in politics. Usually with a bit of both thrown in for good measure.

"Harland is in the suite next to mine. I will speak to him right away. He will be through to Ottawa within half an hour," Winston said. "The main thing now is for us to stop this nonsense about having Gordon withdraw. I'll be back to you shortly."

And then he was gone. But that's the way Gran Winston operated. As soon as he decided on a course of action, he slipped into high gear and forged right ahead. Only a man like that could have built Winston Holdings Limited into one of the major real estate development companies in North America. He might enjoy late breakfasts in bed, but, when he was up and about, he moved right along at an astounding clip.

Harland Edwards got through to the Prime Minister before Mitchell did. In fact, Mitchell didn't get through to the Prime Minister at all that morning. The Prime Minister left for a private meeting immediately after taking Edwards' call. He'd been preparing to leave for the meeting when the call came through from Calgary.

After identifying himself to the Prime Minister's private secretary, Edwards was on the line to the Prime Minister himself. "I realize how pressed you are for time, Prime Minister. However, this is an urgent matter and I would appreciate a few minutes of your time right now."

"Certainly, Harland," the Prime Minister said in a welcoming tone. "I know that you wouldn't call me like this unless it was a matter of pressing importance. What is on your mind?"

"Well, Prime Minister, young Gordon MacArthur – Gran Winston's son-in-law – is going to be nominated as the candidate for Meadowbrook next week. The riding executive spent a considerable amount of time assessing his qualifications and they decided he was the best man to replace Hal Davies. They see an excellent future for MacArthur, for Meadowbrook and for the party. And that is despite MacArthur's lack of experience in comparison to Hal Davies."

The Prime Minister did not react positively to the reference to the MP who had recently announced that he was retiring from politics. "There are, Harland, as you well know, certain experiences of Hal Davies' that MacArthur, or any other candidate, would do well not to replicate. I'm not at all sure how things would have turned out if that young Indian girl hadn't had the miscarriage. Davies should have known better than to get himself into that sort of predicament. He didn't protect his investment. Still, I know that is not what you were referring to. But do, please, come to the point."

"Well, Prime Minister, I have been given to understand that your Don Mitchell has got it into his head that Gran Winston's son-in-law should withdraw from seeking the nomination. Mitchell, as I have been given to understand, favours another candidate."

"That doesn't sound like Don Mitchell," the Prime Minister said with a note of puzzlement in his voice. "He usually leaves such matters to the local riding association. I can't imagine him interfering with something like that. Are you sure of your facts, Harland?"

"That is what I have been given to understand, Prime Minister. Don Mitchell called Henry Bracken this morning and said he wanted young MacArthur to withdraw."

That sounded a bit unusual. "I don't understand why Mitchell would do something as arbitrary as that. There must be some other explanation for this, Harland. What is it?"

"The root of the matter, as I have been given to understand, is a couple of articles which have appeared in the Toronto newspapers about a group MacArthur is starting up at the University of Toronto. He's a professor in the Political Science Department. MacArthur's group is pressing for equal educational opportunities for the white students – equal to the special studies programs that have been established, for example, on the culture and traditions of the Indians in North America and on the role of the blacks in society.

"Some of the professors at the university believe these courses and, more importantly, the manner in which they are being taught, place white students at a disadvantage. They, as I have been given to understand, believe these programs discriminate against the white students – against white society."

"I certainly don't recall any such newspaper articles being drawn to my attention," the Prime Minister said. "Mind you, Harland, there is a great deal that never does reach my desk. Still, getting back to MacArthur's group, this strikes me as more of an internal matter for the university to determine. After all, it is their responsibility to decide what should, or what should not, be taught at the university and the manner in which it should be taught. Why would that be a matter of contention?"

"Well, actually, it goes a bit beyond the confines of the university. In responding to questions from the reporters about the special studies courses his group wants the university to establish, young MacArthur has broadened the debate a bit. He has, shall we say, expanded his comments somewhat and delved into things like the growing numbers of immigrants spreading out across Toronto and, shall we say, skewing the demographic balance away from the white, Anglo-Saxon, Canadians who created those neighborhoods in the first place."

The Prime Minister didn't like the sound of that. Not at all. "Well, Harland, if that's the case, I can see why Don Mitchell would have expressed concern. We don't want to get into anything like white power, like the trouble Enoch Powell stirred up in Britain. He cost the Conservative Party there a lot of support – a lot of votes. I do not, absolutely do not, want anything like that here in Canada."

"No. No, Prime Minister. I can assure you young MacArthur is nothing at all like Enoch Powell. Nothing at all. He is not at all extreme in his views. All he is doing is drawing attention to the concern, the rather wide-spread concern, on the part of the white, Anglo-Saxon, majority towards the increasing number of immigrants who have settled in Toronto in recent years. And it is, Prime Minister, a real concern. I've felt it myself. But, no, it is nothing at all like white power. He's not saying we should turn those people away – send them back to the countries they came from. No, he's nothing like that. Nothing at all like Enoch Powell."

"That might very well be so, Harland, but I can understand why Don Mitchell would see having young MacArthur running for us as creating a problem – a problem we don't need on the eve of an election. Even a hint of white power would create a backlash among the non-white voters. And, as you just said, we do have an increasing number of them."

"Yes, Prime Minister, indeed we do and that is precisely why there is such a high level of concern among the white, Anglo-Saxon, voters. They see their city, their society, changing dramatically and it makes them uneasy."

This wasn't news to the Prime Minister. Every day of the week, some group or another was offended by the tough decisions he often had to make. Only last month, the Polish community was upset because he appointed Alberto Verdi to the Senate instead of Ignacy Raczkiewicz. But there was only one Ontario vacancy and there were a lot more Italian voters in Toronto than there were Polish. And yet, as he realized at the time, Rackiewicz had done an enormous amount of work for the Conservative Party. It had been a difficult decision. But that was the only way it could turn out. You couldn't avoid offending one group or another.

"I can understand that," he said. "I've heard that concern expressed before. Some of the letters that have come across my desk recently certainly express that point of view. But that does not cancel out the concerns, very legitimate concerns, expressed by Don Mitchell about the potential political repercussions of a movement like MacArthur's. I think he is right in this instance."

Edwards decided to press on. "This is how the local riding executive sees it, Prime Minister. In Meadowbrook, the majority vote is white, Anglo-Saxon, Protestant. Henry Bracken and his riding executive believe, and I am inclined to agree with them, that, rather than working to the party's disadvantage as your Don Mitchell has claimed that it will, young MacArthur's position will win us votes."

"A white power candidate?" the Prime Minister asked in a disapproving tone.

"Well, no. No, Prime Minister. Young MacArthur would not be presented in that way. Not at all. But he would stand for pride in being white – white, Scottish-Canadian, Protestant. Just as Senator Tootoosis from Saskatchewan symbolizes pride in being Indian, in being Cree."

This was something that might be worth considering. "Hmm," the Prime Minister mused. "You might have a point there. I think I am starting to see what you are driving at. If it would be considered advantageous to run certain candidates because of their ethnic or racial origin, there is no reason not to, in the same way, run a white, Scottish-Canadian, candidate in a white, Anglo-Saxon, riding. Is that it, Harland? Is that your point?"

"Yes, Prime Minister. That is it. Exactly."

The Prime Minister reflected on what Edwards had been saying. "It is a rather novel idea. But I think I can follow your reasoning. I can appreciate your point of view. However, and have no doubt about this, Harland, I will pull the plug immediately if this develops into a white power campaign. There is a distinct difference between white pride and white power. A revolutionary difference. I will take Mitchell's side without a moment's hesitation if this turns out to be a white power movement. Even if it means losing the riding, I will pull the plug without a moment's notice. I mean that, Harland."

"I do understand, Prime Minister. All I can say to you is that, as a person who is white, Anglo-Saxon, Protestant, I reacted in a positive manner to what young Gordon MacArthur had to say on the radio. And I know from talking to Gran Winston and Jack Saunders and some of the others out here that a great many white voters will react in as positive a manner as we did. I think, Prime Minister, that Gordon MacArthur's candidacy will be good for the party."

The Prime Minister remained silent for a moment. "I don't think we can determine, at this early stage, that MacArthur's candidacy will be a good thing for the party as a whole. However, if Henry Bracken and his executive believe he is their best bet for Meadowbrook, then I will see to it that my office does not intervene. I must warn you, however, if his personal activities interfere – in the manner that Hal Davies' did – with his effectiveness as a representative of the Conservative Party of Canada, I will cut him off without so much as a blink of an eye. Even if it means losing Meadowbrook. And now, my friend, I must rush off to another meeting. It was good talking to you again. Do come up and have dinner with us at 24 Sussex the next time you are in Ottawa. I would enjoy having a couple of hours in conversation with you."

"Thank you, Prime Minister. I will certainly try. And thank you for backing Henry Bracken and the others on the MacArthur matter. I could ask nothing more of you."

As the Prime Minister placed the receiver on the ornate phone cradle, he reflected on Edwards' style and tact. Not one word had been mentioned about how anxiously the party was looking to Edwards to raise the rest of the $9 million they needed for the upcoming national election campaign. Not so much as a hint of the substantial contributions Edwards and Gran Winston made to the party. Just a clear-cut expression of concern about how the autonomy of a local riding association was being undermined by a senior member of the Prime Minister's staff. Put like that, there was hardly any way the Prime Minister could reasonably have refused Edwards' appeal on behalf of the Meadowbrook executive.

Of course, there was more to it than that. He knew how upset people like Gran Winston and Jack Saunders got when he appointed a Jew to the Supreme Court or an Italian to the Foreign Investment Review Agency or something like that. Some legislation was presented in a way that would appeal to the ethnic and racial groups. But that seemed to be the only way to stay in power. They could hold ridings like Meadowbrook and the other white, middle-class, areas. It was the inner-city vote that had to be courted and that meant Italian, Greek, Portuguese, Chinese and every other type of special-interest group appointments.

The Prime Minister understood the concern of men like Harland Edwards and how, as Edwards had just said on the phone, hearing from people like Gordon made them feel better about being white and less worried about the rapid changes that were taking place in Canadian society.

Perhaps, he thought, young MacArthur could serve as an escape valve for the growing concerns of the white, Anglo-Saxon, wing of the party. Something that would enable them to articulate their frustration. To get things off their chest without causing any significant amount of harm. Besides, as Edwards had just said, it was rather refreshing to hear someone say something positive about being white for a change.

Gordon was marking papers in his office when Gran Winston called to say Edwards had spoken to the Prime Minister and he agreed that Gordon should be the Conservative candidate for Meadowbrook.

"There is no way Mitchell and his people can stop you from getting the nomination now, Gordon. You have the endorsement of the Prime Minister himself."

"That's simply terrific, Gran. Just marvellous. I was not at all confident about how things would work out when Henry told me what Don Mitchell said. We would never have succeeded without your intervention. Thanks."

"It was my pleasure, Gordon. You know the personal interest that I have in your political career. It is important for me to have someone in Ottawa I can trust. Someone who is aware of my business affairs and is sympathetically disposed toward them. I'll be looking to you to keep me informed of developments which could have an adverse – or beneficial – impact on my business. I'll be expecting you to keep your ears open, Gordon."

"You can count on me, Gran. I'll keep you informed."

"Good. Good lad. I want you to succeed, Gordon. What you are on to affects every white person in Canada – perhaps in North America. You've got something that can address itself to the problems white Canadians face in every sphere. In employment, in housing, in community affairs, in business and things like – like the problems Jack Saunders is running into with this Big Thunder affair.

"I'm sure you've heard something about the opposition Jack is running into from the Indians over that gas pipeline he wants to run through the Big Thunder Indian reservation. Jack's sitting on one of the biggest sour gas discoveries in recent history. He'll have enough gas to heat every home in Ontario for years to come.

"Jack needs to get the gas from the processing plant he's building to TransCanada PipeLines' main line which runs north of Calgary. Running his pipeline through Big Thunder is the most direct route. But those damned Indians won't let him lay so much as a foot of pipeline across their land. They're determined to block him and they've been putting their case before the Energy Resources Conservation Board of Alberta.

"That hearing is turning out to be an utter disgrace, Gordon. The Indians are using it as a soapbox to air their complaints about the so-called mistreatment they received at the hands of the whites. Any alleged mistreatment they received in the past pales in comparison to the enormous difficulties we will face if we don't get ourselves out from under the thumb of the OPEC oil cartel. The Arabs jacking up the price of oil like they did last October and cutting back production inflicted enormous damage on our economy. We have to move off oil and onto natural gas in order to get their thumbs off our throat. If we don't do it – convert to domestic resources like natural gas – we run the risk of having white women and children freeze to death in the dark of winter next time the Arabs hold us to ransom because of our support of Israel.

"That's why Jack Saunders must be allowed to get his gas to market. That's why those Indians must not be allowed to win their case at the energy board hearings. I believe public opinion can play an important part in that. Now, Gordon, an organization like yours could do something to build a case for Jack's side of this issue. Your being a university professor and all that will carry a lot of weight out here – especially with all those other professors you've got backing you up.

"Jack Saunders and I've been talking and we think you could do some good out here. We'd like you to come out and speak to the Calgary branch of the Empire Club of Canada three weeks from today. They had a speaker cancel out on them because of a health problem and we'd like you to speak in his place."

Gordon wasn't expecting anything like that. "Gosh, I'm not sure I'm ready for that, Gran. I wouldn't know what to say."

"Don't worry about it. All we want you to do is outline the reasons you and the other professors had for forming your council. Like you did on the radio the other morning. That was just fine. Just expand on that theme, Gordon. That's what they will want to hear. Something good about being white for a change – a welcome change.

"You should have heard Saunders and the others talking about you. Especially about you being on the radio saying white is beautiful. Saunders said it was the first time he'd heard anyone – especially on that socialist-leaning CBC – say that white is beautiful. I'm telling you, Gordon, and I say this sincerely and from my heart, I felt really good about being white when I heard you on the radio.

"Our white values are under attack – global attack – and we need someone – someone like you – to stand up to the malcontents and say: 'Listen, dammit, white is beautiful.' That's the sort of thing the people at the Empire Club will want to hear from you. Something to cancel out all this stupidity coming out of the pipeline hearings about us stealing the Indians' land. What nonsense. And now I have to go.

So, we're covered as far as the nomination goes and you'll come out to speak to the Empire Club. It'll be right here in Calgary."

"Three weeks is cutting it a bit thin as far as time goes." Gordon said. "I'll need time to read up on the industry and on the pipeline hearings so as to be able to ...."

"Don't worry about all the technical stuff, Gordon. Just give the speech the way I outlined it. The way you did on the radio the other morning. That was just fine. Exactly what we've been waiting to hear. We'll fly you out first class and get you a suite at the Palliser. Now I must be off. Keep me posted and, Gordon, press right ahead. You're doing magnificently."

"Thanks, Gran. I only wish that – that Carol felt the same way. She feels that I'm an embarrassment and that I'm – that I'm doing just about everything wrong."

Winston was well aware of the separateness that had developed between Gordon and Carol. And he regretted it deeply. There was a bitterness there and he felt a terrible sadness for her at times.

"Don't let Carol's attitude discourage you, Gordon. She'll come around when she sees things coming together for you. And things will come together, rapidly, now. Yes – they will. As soon as Carol gets a proper perspective on what you're doing, she will come around. Believe me, Gordon, I know that daughter of mine."

"I hope you're right, Gran. I really do. God knows how much Carol's approval – and support – mean to me. It would be so good to have her truly proud of me and involved with something I was trying to accomplish. To have her at my side – like Eleanor Roosevelt or Olive Diefenbaker and – and Pat Nixon. She stuck by him right through this summer's bitter end."

"I know what you mean, Gordon. I miss Ethel so terribly much. If only she could be with me now to share everything that's coming my way. To be with me now – with me – instead of those lonely break- fasts every morning without her. At times, Gordon, the loneliness is unbearable. Well – that's my story. Give Carol time. Time to see you as you really are. It will work out. Believe me."

"Thanks, Gran. I really do hope that it does."

∼

After the call from Gran Winston telling him he now had the backing of the Prime Minister, Gordon called Ruth Applebaum and told her he wanted to spend some time with her that evening. He said he would be at her apartment around eight.

As they lay in her waterbed, he told her he had spoken to Henry Bracken that afternoon and he was now even more convinced than ever that he would be appointed to the cabinet after the election.

"Just think," she said. "The Honourable Gordon MacArthur. It's just fabulous! Oh, Gordon, I am so proud of you. And you'll make such a good cabinet minister. You'll be – you'll be in the newspapers and on the radio – and on TV. You'll be famous. Just like a movie star. Oh, I'm so thrilled for you, Gordon MacArthur!"

Whenever Ruth spoke his name, she always placed the accent on the Mac part of it. She thought it sounded so delightfully white, Anglo-Saxon, Protestant.

"Mrs. Gordon MacArthur," she would sometimes whisper to herself. "What a great-sounding name."

Gordon told her not to get her hopes about the cabinet seat up too high. There was still the nomination meeting and, after that, the election campaign. Nothing was guaranteed.

"You'll win, Gordon. You'll win. I just know that you'll win. Honourable Gordon MacArthur, P.C., M.P. Oh, I just know that you will make it!"

And then she started to cry. "I'm so terribly happy for you," she sobbed. "I just know you can be anything you want to be. You have such a terrific mind, Gordon. You're going to be great."

As she wiped the tears of joy from her cheeks, she felt an overwhelming urge to take him in her mouth and bring him to orgasm.

"Jesus," he sighed, as he lay beside her panting, heaving, and tingling all over afterwards. "It's never been like that before. You are fantastic. Fucking fantastic."

"Gordon MacArthur!" she chided teasingly. "That's no way for a future cabinet minister to talk."

"All right, my lady. Explosively fantastic. How's that?"

"That's better," she said. "Explosively fantastic is just fine."

She felt good. He had never had an orgasm quite like that with her before. She had done it, all by herself. It gave her a delicious sense of power.

He cupped her face in his hands and kissed her gently on the nose. Then he passed her the box of Kleenex so she could wipe his semen off her lips.

"Time for a bath," he announced, as he slipped out of her bed and walked naked to the bathroom.

"I'll be with you in a minute," she called after him. "Don't make it too cold."

As she lay there, listening to the sound of him running the water for their bath, she thought it would have been kinda nice if he'd taken the time to make sure she had an orgasm, too. *Maybe next time. Let's hope so.* She wondered when he was going to ask Carol for the divorce. He had mentioned the possibility of a divorce or, at least, a separation, only two weeks ago. Maybe, with this thing about the nomination meeting and being in the cabinet and all that, he just hadn't found the right time yet.

"And who's been soaping in my tub?" she asked mischievously as she settled into the scented soap suds.

He smiled at her warmly and she realized afresh how very much she adored him and wanted him.

"Gordon MacArthur has been soaping in your lovely tub, Miss Applebaum, and he is now Ivory Snow white."

Gordon swung his Pontiac into the driveway. The headlights picked out Charlie's bicycle lying halfway up the drive. He got out of the car, wheeled the bike to the side, and made a mental note to speak to his eight-year-old son about showing a greater sense of responsibility.

Carol was alone in the living room reading Arnold Toynbee's *A Study of History.* She arched her eyebrows and gave his entry an unsmiling acknowledgement. "Home early for a change," she remarked in a dry matter-of-fact voice.

He ignored her welcoming remarks and made himself a vodka and orange. "Would you like a drink?" he asked.

She would. He fixed her a Scotch and soda and joined her on the chocolate-brown leather sofa. Then he settled back into the plush comfort and put his feet up on the coffee table.

"Gordon," she said reprimandingly, "I have asked you, repeatedly, not to do that. Your heels leave marks."

He took his rubber-soled shoes off and placed his stocking feet on the coffee table.

"Gordon," she said. "Your feet smell."

He took his feet off the table and placed them under it and out of sight. "Is that better?" he asked.

"Not really. The smell is still rather irritating."

And then it dawned on him. He'd just had a bath at Ruth's apartment. "My feet can't possibly smell! I had a bath – less than an hour ago."

"You might have had a bath, Gordon, but you didn't wash your socks. They smell. Perhaps you could have your young woman rinse them for you next time. She can do your underwear, too – whenever she's ready to assume responsibility for that function."

"Let's not get into that again tonight," he said. "I'm home early, as you put it, because I have some rather exciting news to share with you."

"Have you now?" she asked indifferently.

"Yes. I have. I had a rather interesting discussion with Henry Bracken this afternoon. If I win the election, he's even more confident than ever that I'll make it into the cabinet after the election. In fact, the way Henry sees it, there's no way I won't be in the cabinet."

"I certainly hope you won't expect us to move to Ottawa, if you happen to win the election," she said. "We do have our roots here, Gordon. You simply can't expect us to pick up and move to Ottawa because you want to be a cabinet minister."

"I merely wanted you to know," he said, "that there is a distinct possibility that I will be in the cabinet."

"Well, you've not so much as won the nomination yet, let alone the election. Besides, Gordon, you should think twice before disrupting your academic career to pursue some rather unpredictable destiny in Ottawa."

"There's nothing unpredictable about it," he said. "I am going to get the nomination. I am going to win the election. And I am going to be in the cabinet."

"To do what? To save us all from those black and Indian lecturers you've been complaining about in the newspapers? To keep Canada safe for white people? Some of the things you've been quoted as saying are beyond belief. And, I'm telling you, Gordon, even as a person who is white, I am shocked by some of the things you have been quoted as saying.

"It is utter nonsense to compare the needs of white people with the special needs of the black, the Indian, and all the other minority groups. There is absolutely no valid comparison. You should know better than to compare the needs of members of a majority group with those of a minority. You're making yourself out to be a racist fool and I'm embarrassed for you. Painfully so. Humiliatingly so. I'm ashamed to be your wife."

"No," he said, "as I told you the last time we had this conversation, I'm not trying to save the world for white people. All that I am saying is that a definite imbalance has developed and I'm simply trying to do something about it. To balance things out a bit."

"Well, quite frankly, as I told you before, I think you're out of your tree."

"I can assure you that I'm not off on some crusade to keep the world safe for white people. All I am saying, tonight anyway, is that Henry thinks I will do well in politics and there is a very good chance that I'm going to be appointed to the cabinet."

"Be in the cabinet if you wish, Gordon. The children and I will remain here in Toronto. I wouldn't give the slightest consideration to spending a winter with you in Ottawa. That city is totally removed from everything, absolutely everything, I consider to be civilized and worthwhile. Ottawa is out of the question."

She seemed quite determined. And he knew his chances of changing her mind were quite slim. About zero. "All right, then," he said. "If you are that definite about it, I suppose you could remain here with the children and I could come home on the weekends."

"Whatever for?" she asked. "If we can manage without you during the week, I am sure we can get by perfectly well without you on the weekends. What possible difference could it make to us to have you spending most of your time in Ottawa instead of at the university or with that young woman of yours?"

"That is not at all fair, Carol. If we had moved closer to the university when I got my appointment, like I asked you to, I wouldn't be facing that insufferable drive in winter every time I want to come home. And I do, Carol, often, want to come home. But no, you refused to move and now, before I'm so much as nominated, you're announcing that you won't even consider moving to Ottawa with me. Why do you always insist on making it so difficult for me to spend time with you and the children?"

She set her book aside, took a sip of her Scotch, and looked directly at him. "You're talking rubbish, Gordon. Absolute rubbish. It has nothing to do with making it difficult for you to be with the children. It just so happens that our roots are here. I was born in this house. The children were born in this house. We belong here. And this is where we will stay."

He cursed the day he moved into her father's house. If only he'd had some money of his own when they got married. But he hadn't. He'd had another year to go on his master's degree and the money he made at the Chicken Hut was barely enough to cover the basic necessities. And now, he felt chained to the house Carol had been born in and wished they had been able to get a home of their own. Even a small one would have been okay – a starter home as they call them.

"Maybe it is a bit too early to decide whether or not you and the children should move to Ottawa with me after the election," he said. "Could we just, for the moment, spend a little time together enjoying a civilized drink?"

"Oh, we are civilized all right," Carol sighed. "Deadeningly so."

Her life had turned out so depressingly different from what she had looked forward to in her last year at Osgoode Hall Law School. If she had it to do over again, if she could have chosen how her life would unfold, she would have practised law and waited until she was at least thirty-five before getting married. There were so many things she had wanted to do. She had wanted to be a top litigator and represent nothing but *Fortune 500* corporations. She had wanted to go up against the best lawyers in the country and win. She had wanted that. Wanted it very much.

But, that was not how things turned out. Gordon getting her pregnant changed everything. And now, here he was, with his smelly feet under her father's coffee table, wanting her to have a "civilized" drink with him and expecting her to pack up and move to Ottawa with him.

"It would help a lot," he said, "if you would come to the nomination meeting with me next Thursday. I really would feel better if you were with me."

"What on earth for?" she asked. "To be photographed and stuck in the family section of your election literature?"

He looked hurt. "You are my wife, Carol. It won't look right if you're not identified as being with me, you know, like supporting me."

She looked mockingly at him. "Supporting you? That is a laugh. Father's house. Father's furniture. Father's $25,000 to get you the nomination. We're supporting you all right, but it's not the sort of thing that lends itself to campaign brochures and photography."

"You're not being fair," he said. "Gran's putting that money up because he needs someone in Ottawa with a feel for his business interests. I understand that. He'll get his money's worth. Now, maybe I couldn't get the nomination without his money – and I don't believe he grudges me one cent of it – but, if the party didn't think I could win, they wouldn't have me as their candidate. They aren't going to take a chance on losing the riding. I am not without qualifications, Carol. I was Chairman of the National Conservative Youth Commission."

"That was a long, long, time ago, Gordon."

"So, it was a few years ago. But I have kept my name in the right places. I am considered, by some of the key people in the party, to be an excellent choice."

She looked at him for a moment with a sense of sadness, of mutual loss, in her olive-green eyes. Things really hadn't gone well for either one of them. She wanted to be arguing high-profile cases in the Supreme Court of Canada and he, it would seem, desperately wanted to be a Member of Parliament or, even better, a cabinet minister. She knew how bored he was of teaching at the university and how enthusiastically he had responded to her father's suggestion that he go for the nomination in Meadowbrook. It was an opportunity for a new lease on life for him.

"Gordon," she said, in a gentler tone, "I don't want to take anything away from you – from your enthusiasm about politics – or anything else you care about. I know you feel I'm dragging you down – selling you short. I really don't mean to be as negative as I sometimes appear to be about your plans. Now, if you want to run in the election, that's fine by me. If you win and want to be in Walter Floyd's cabinet, that's fine by me, too. All that I ask is that you don't try to involve me in it. Especially not in this stuff about white pride and the negative attitude you have developed toward blacks and Indians and immigrants. You do whatever it is that you want to do. Just leave me to work out what is left of my own life as best I can. Okay? And now I am going to my room. What about the morning? Will you be having breakfast with us?"

"No, thanks. I want to be down at the university quite early so I can get caught up on some work that's been piling up on me. I'll grab something there. But, thanks just the same."

"All right then. I'm turning in. I'll probably see you before you leave."

With that, she picked up her book and her drink and started up the stairs to her room. As soon as he heard her bedroom door close, he put his feet back up on the coffee table and settled back to enjoy his drink. It was at times like this, he thought, like when she said she didn't want to take anything away from him, from his enthusiasm about politics or anything like that, that it appeared as if she still felt something for him. As if she still cared. *Whatever happened to us? Where did it go wrong? We were happy. Really happy. Right up until Diane came along. That changed things. Changed them a lot. And then her mum died. Died such a fast, horrible, death. And our marriage died too. Got cancer, just like her mum. Inoperable cancer. That's what we've got. Marriage is dying of terminal cancer.*

〜

Gordon was in the Davidson Lounge at the University of Toronto. The sound of piped-in soft jazz embraced the gracious surroundings.

The setting sunlight of the late fall afternoon filtered through the windows and created a twilight mood. As Gordon looked across the table at Marilyn Russell, the education reporter for the *Globe and Mail*, he concluded that she was a truly beautiful young woman.

He had wanted to ask her out for coffee ever since the first time he laid eyes on her – at that lecture where the black professor from Berkeley said all white people are scum. But something about her independent, assertive, manner intimidated him and he hadn't worked up the nerve to ask her to spend time with him. When she phoned just after lunch that day to ask him some questions about the Equal Opportunities Council he suggested that they discuss the matter over coffee in the Davidson Lounge.

"That was quite a quote the *Star* got from you," she said. "Their afternoon edition has you saying university funds are being used to downgrade white values and the entire North American way of life." She paused and opened her steno pad. "You're quoted as saying: 'Enough of all this special studies nonsense. Enough of all this red power, black power, yellow power and every other coloured power Commie fronts.' That's a pretty strong statement."

"It's happening," Gordon said. "And it certainly shouldn't be news to you. You've seen it. You've heard them. Remember? That black, racist, lecturer who was here – the one the Student Council brought in from Berkeley."

"What black racist are you talking about, Professor?"

"You were there. That was the first time I ever saw you. Back in June. In Davidson Hall. You were at the press table. You've got to remember. I'd never seen you before."

Perplexity furrowed her brow. "I can't remember a particular lecturer standing out like that. Are you sure it was me that you saw?"

"Of course it was you. You were wearing that – that red pantsuit and that navy blue scarf you sometimes wear around your neck. The one that's like a – a choker."

His intimate awareness of her dressing habits startled her. She dragged on her cigarette and looked more closely at him – trying to recall the event he was referring to. And then it started to come forward in her mind.

"Now I remember what you're talking about. When Arthur Staples, the black professor from Berkeley, was here. Yes. Yes, of course – and – and, yes, now I remember you, too. You got up, during the question period, and, yes, even then, you were raising questions about what you called the misuse of university funds. You asked Staples what he was being paid for the lecture and, before he even opened his mouth to reply, young Donald Frampton marched up to the microphone and said the lecture was being paid for by the Student Council and you had no right embarrassing their guest by raising such – such irrelevant questions."

"Yes. That's the way it was. Staples was up there on the stage saying white people are scum and their bones are covered with sickly-white parchment and I – a white person at my own university – was being told to sit down because I was embarrassing him. I just couldn't believe my ears when those young people applauded Staples the way they did. Couldn't believe it. They gave him a standing ovation. And they booed me – actually booed me. Remember?"

"Yes. I do remember. I was a bit unsettled by the whole affair myself. I do remember it."

"What Staples said was defamatory. Out and out defamation. I'm telling you, Marilyn, things have been allowed to degenerate too far, much too far. Now don't you, as a person who is white, feel something of what I felt – of what I'm feeling – like about Arthur Staples and what he told those students?"

She was silent for a moment, looking into her empty cup of coffee. "Yes. I suppose you've got a point. When I first heard some of the things you said, I thought you were a bigoted nut. Especially that time you came out on the radio saying the media discriminates against white people. I thought that was a load of crock. But then I thought about it and I realized that we do, sometimes, print disparaging things about white people and about the WASP establishment. The word WASP has, more often than not, become a term of derision. I'd never thought of it as being discrimination against white people in general. I guess I was reading it as being about some white people. Rich white people. But, you might be right. The way it comes out in the newspapers, it reflects on us all – on all white people."

"Now you're starting to understand," Gordon said. "Like, in articles about the Indian land claims disputes, the reporters are always slipping in something about the 'harmful effects' our values have had on Indian people. What harmful effects? Without the hundreds of millions we spend on them every year, they'd all be dead in the bush. I really get mad when I come across statements and comments in the media which can have no other intent than to downgrade the white, North American, way of life.

"I mean just look, like you've said, at the widespread, derogatory, use of the terms 'WASP' and 'white man' in so many of those newspaper articles. White people should enjoy the same protection against defamation as any other group. But they don't. We've just been lying back and letting it all happen and, when we all wake up freezing in the dark, it will be too late."

That caught her attention. "Freezing in the dark? Who's going to be freezing in the dark?"

"You are. And – are you going to quote me on any of this? Shouldn't you be writing some of this down?"

"No. My only interest is in what you had to say about the special studies programs being a misuse of university funds. There's ..."

"But that's only part of the overall problem. We've got to deal with a lot more than the problem at the university. We've got to deal with things like the very real possibility – I should say probability – that white people will be freezing in the dark one winter not too far away. Are you going to take this down?"

"I don't think so, Professor. My beat is education and I don't usually dabble in general news."

"But this is education. The educating of the white, Western European, majority to the manner in which their rights – and their means of survival – are being eroded. Undermined. The radio reporters will be using it."

"What radio reporters?" she asked, alert to the competitive nature of the news business.

"Oh," he replied off-handedly, "Harold O'Connor from CFRB, for one. He got a good clip off me this afternoon. He'll probably have it on their major newscast tonight."

"What did you tell him?" she prompted.

"Are you going to use what I say?"

"Maybe."

"Okay," he said. "I'll give you a statement. An exclusive statement. A statement that is relevant to the future of every white man, woman, and child in Canada. A statement of national significance."

He was getting quite carried away and she sort of liked that. While she didn't particularly like what he stood for, he did, indeed, stand for something.

"Okay, Professor. Tell me about whites freezing in the dark."

"In the form of a statement?"

"Sure, if that's the way you want it. In the form of a statement."

"Okay then. You're going to take this down?"

"Yes. I'm going to take it all down."

"Okay. Here it is. This is the statement. Are you ready?"

"Yes, I'm ready," she said in a warm, slightly-amused, tone. *You'd think he was drafting the Declaration of Independence*, she mused to herself.

"Okay then. Here it is. Quote. The rights of white, Western European, Canadians – the people who made this great country what it is today – are under attack.

"I refer, for example, to the manner in which a bunch of renegade Indians have been allowed to jeopardize the vital energy supply of all Canadians because of their stalling tactics. I'm talking about the Indian opposition to the Saunders' gas pipeline proposal in Alberta.

"Our nation needs the gas the Saunders Energy Corporation will send through that pipeline. He's got enough gas out there to heat every home in Ontario. However, those Indians are blocking that pipeline because they don't want it to cross through the Big Thunder Indian reservation.

"The fact of the matter is that white Canadians run the risk of freezing in the dark of winter if that pipeline is not allowed to go through. To yield to the demands of those Indians would be to accept the risk of having white Canadian women and children freeze in their homes because those Indians won't allow for a minimal easement across their land.

"We're facing an energy crisis such as this country Canada has never before confronted. We are altogether too dependent on Arab oil. Last year's OPEC oil crisis was a wakeup call. We've simply got to get off Arab oil and onto Alberta gas. Jack Saunders has discovered an almost unlimited supply of gas and they simply must be allowed to get it down here to the eastern market. Down here where it's so desperately needed.

"This is no time to argue over the alleged sins of the past. It's to the future that we've got to look. And the Saunders' pipeline proposal represents that future. It is our best hope for weaning ourselves from Arab oil.

"That is why we on the Equal Opportunities Council say that the energy needs of all Canadians must be given priority over any pie-in-the-sky claims of a bunch of Indians. Common sense dictates that the Saunders' pipeline should go through the Big Thunder Indian reservation. End of quote. How was that, Marilyn?"

"Well," she said in a hesitating manner. "I don't know enough about it to make an intelligent response. I don't know. It still isn't an education story. I don't know if ..."

"Of course it's an education story. I am a university professor. The Equal Opportunities Council is made up of university professors. It's just that, instead of poring over dusty old tomes on lost civilizations, we're attempting to save this civilization. That's what education is all about."

"Well, okay. Leave it with me. I will pass it on – exactly as I took it all down – to my editor. I'm sure the paper will probably do something with it."

"Okay," he said with a pleased smile on his face. "Let's leave it at that. Now I have to rush. I've got to be at CBC-TV in about half an hour for an interview. Would you like a ride down to the *Globe*?"

"No thanks. I have a few things to clear up at the press room before I go home and that will take me more than half an hour."

"But, what about the story? The whites freezing in the dark? I thought you were going to go over it with your editor."

"I will. On the phone. Right now. Don't worry about it. You'll probably be back on the front page again tomorrow."

"Hey," he said, with a grin, "I'm starting to like you even more."

CHAPTER

- 15 -

The slim young woman who met Gordon at the reception desk and led him to the television studio wore a red turtleneck sweater and jeans that hugged her bum. As they waited outside the sound-proofed door of the studio, he sniffed the fresh-washed scent of the wavy blonde hair streaming down her back. She leaned against the wall, long thin legs slightly parted, and waited for the red "ON AIR" light to go out.

As Gordon eased his body closer to hers, she turned up the volume control knob on the television monitor and he heard the host of the program announcing the next guest – Gordon.

"Our next guest," the host said in a somewhat disdainful tone, "is Professor Gordon MacArthur of the Political Science Department at the University of Toronto. Professor MacArthur has formed what he calls an Equal Opportunities Council to – his words – keep Canada safe for white people. But first, these messages."

The "ON AIR" light went out and the pleasant-smelling young woman led Gordon to the tastefully-furnished set in the centre of the studio. The host, a bland-looking bald middle-aged man in a navy blue blazer, directed him to sit down in the brown suede chair on the opposite side of the coffee table. He said his name was Fraser Deacon and he would be asking the questions. When Gordon held out his hand in greeting, Deacon simply ignored it and reached for some papers at the other side of the table. *This doesn't look good,* Gordon thought.

The floor director gave Deacon a signal and they were on the air. "Here, ladies and gentlemen," Deacon said as he pointed off-handedly at Gordon, "we have Canada's answer to Enoch Powell – the much-publicized white power leader in Great Britain. As you all know, Powell is the maverick Conservative MP who has been embarrassing his party with outlandish demands that black, Asian and other coloured immigrants be refused admission to Britain. He also insists that many of the coloured people now living there should be shipped back to the countries they came from.

"Professor MacArthur here – I should add, by the way, that he hopes the Conservatives will nominate him next week as their candidate for the Toronto riding of Meadowbrook in the upcoming federal election – says that we in Canada have too many people in turbans sprouting up all over settled neighborhoods where white people were born and raised. His words. His exact words.

"What do you propose to do about the situation, Professor MacArthur? Send the people you don't like back to the countries they came from? Is that what you propose? And, while you're at it, what are you going to do about the Indians who have lived on this land for thousands of years?"

With that, Deacon leaned forward, fixed his eyes on Gordon, and glared at him as the camera zeroed in for a close-up. "Well, Professor MacArthur, we are waiting," he said with an impatient tone in his voice. "What do you propose to do about those people?"

"Hold on. Hold on. Just hold on a minute," Gordon started. "Despite your somewhat distorted introduction, I want your audience to know that I have nothing against the blacks, the Pakistanis, the Chinese, or any of the others who are appearing in increasing numbers in our Canadian cities. They have their rights and I respect those rights. However, I feel that we have to draw the line when their presence results in black pride, Pakistani pride, Chinese pride, and every other coloured kind of pride – except white pride.

"Instead of white pride, we're seeing white shame. The non-white groups are building their pride by making white students at the University of Toronto, for example, feel ashamed of their heritage and of their race. That is altogether wrong. And it must be stopped. Now! That is why I say the time has come, not just at the university, but in the general community – in the marketplace, in politics, everywhere the interest of white, Western European, Canadians is in jeopardy – for us to take a stand for our own kind. For us to stand up and be counted. While there is still time."

"My God!" Deacon exclaimed. "You really are an out and out racist. I've never heard such – such ..."

"Now you hold on. Hold on a minute," Gordon demanded. "Don't try to pin a racist tag on me. I won't have it. Let's keep this thing in perspective, Mr. Deacon. That is what your program is all about, isn't it? Focus? *Toronto Focus*? Let's keep things in focus. If it is acceptable to have black pride and Chinese pride and every other kind of coloured pride, then it should be equally acceptable to have white pride.

"That's all that we are asking for – equal pride for whites. And we are, after all, Mr. Deacon, the majority. It's only right and reasonable that our culture and traditions should have the higher priority. That, simply put, is our position. That is what the Equal Opportunities Council is all about. Equal pride for whites."

"It still sounds unmistakably racist to me," Deacon said challengingly. "Out and out racist. And you haven't answered my question. What do you propose to do about the minority-group people? Send them back to the countries they came from? Is that what you are proposing?"

"No," Gordon replied impatiently. "That is not what I am proposing. I have already told you I have nothing against those people. I'm not saying they're inferior – or superior – to white, Western European, Canadians. All I am saying is that they are different. They look at life differently. They live differently. They even eat and cook differently. Recognizing the reality of those differences – those racial, cultural, and historical differences – does not make me a bigot or a racist.

"All I'm saying is that this world is made up of about four billion people who can be broken down into seven or eight major racial and cultural groupings. I happen to be a white, Western European, Scottish-Canadian. And, because of my racial and cultural difference, I could no more identify with a Pakistani than I could with a North American Indian or a Chinaman. We're just different. That's all."

"And because of that difference you want to ship them back to the countries they came from?"

"No. I don't want to ship them back to where they came from. That's not what I said. They're here now and they might as well stay. We can find room in our society for all of those people – but – within our society. Not as something separate and apart from it. But as an assimilated part of the white, Western European, whole. After all, they moved to our country. We didn't move to theirs. That's why things should be done our way – the white, Western European, Canadian way."

Deacon wasn't impressed. "It still sounds like a white power movement to me. Your only interest is in white people."

The floor director gave Deacon the signal to break for a commercial. "We've got to take a break right now," Deacon said, obviously relieved at having an excuse to shut Gordon up.

"But we will be right back with a different viewpoint on Professor MacArthur and his white rights council. We will be right back with Dr. William Eagletail, the Director of the North American Indian Studies program at the University of Toronto.

"Dr. Eagletail has described Professor MacArthur's views as being – quote – neanderthal nostrums which are not worthy of the University of Toronto. End quote. Dr. Eagletail says Professor MacArthur and his white-is-beautiful clique represent a leap backward into the racist thinking of the nineteenth century. But first, these messages."

This was a surprise. Gordon hadn't expected Eagletail to be on the show. He'd seen him around the university and, as far as he was concerned, Eagletail was nothing more than a professional Indian. *No wonder Eagletail is upset and coming out with all of the name calling. He knows the game is up. I'm on to him. We'll soon put a stop to the free ride he and all the other rabble rousers have been getting. The free ride they have used to undermine and ridicule just about everything I hold to be sacred and dear.*

And there Eagletail was. Hair braided and hanging down over his shoulders. Bear claws necklace hanging around his neck.

As the young woman adjusted Bill's microphone, Deacon reached across the table and shook him warmly by the hand. "Welcome to *Toronto Focus*, Dr. Eagletail. We'll be on in about thirty seconds."

Gordon and Bill eyed one another like prize fighters in a ring taking each other's measure. Neither one of them had any reason to suspect that they were brothers or that they were both born on the Morgan ranch. If it wasn't for the braided hair and the bear claws necklace, Gordon concluded, no one would be able to tell that Eagletail was an Indian. On taking a closer look, he noted that Eagletail's eyes were a grey-blue colour. *That's odd*, he thought to himself. *The white-baiting rabble rouser has the same colour of eyes I have. He's probably a half-breed. Passing himself off as a full-blooded Indian. But he's more likely the product of some drunken, one-night, stand. What a phony.*

"Hello, there," Deacon said to the camera after the floor director gave him his cue. "Welcome back to *Toronto Focus*. I'd like you to meet Dr. William Eagletail, the Director of the North American Indian Studies program at the University of Toronto. Dr. Eagletail was born on the Big Thunder Indian reservation just outside of Calgary. After receiving his early education at the reservation school, he attended high school in Calgary and was the first Indian to attend the University of Alberta. On completing his studies there, Dr. Eagletail was admitted to the University of California's Berkeley campus on a scholarship.

Dr. Eagletail holds both a master's degree and a doctorate in sociology. It was at his urging that the University of Toronto established the North American Indian Studies program to help give Indian people a better sense of themselves – of their race – a better sense of self-esteem. Dr. Eagletail, we are, indeed, honoured to have you on our show tonight."

Bullshit, Gordon muttered under his breath. *What a set-up. What a boot-sucking display of reverse prejudice. No wonder Deacon didn't shake my hand. And Berkeley, eh? Same place as that black agitator who said all white people are scum.*

"Thank you, Fraser," Bill said. "Thank you for that splendid introduction. You are, as usual, much too generous in your praise."

So that's it. The son of a bitch has been on Deacon's show before. Sure. The whole thing's rigged. They've cooked it up between them.

"Now, Dr. Eagletail," Deacon intoned almost reverently, "we understand that you are familiar with the views of our other guest and that you consider his thinking to be – ah – to be neanderthal. That was the word. Neanderthal and not worthy of the University of Toronto. What made you feel that way, Dr. Eagletail?"

"Well, Fraser, as I said the last time I was on your program, so many of our young people enter kindergarten bright and eager and willing to learn. But, something about the Western European orientation of our education system has an undermining effect on them and they start going out like light bulbs. We're still paying the price of successive waves of missionaries and teachers and self-described do-gooders who have rendered incalculable harm to the collective North American Indian psyche. An entire race of people has been psychologically crippled. Lobotomized."

He paused for a moment and took a sip of coffee from the mug with the *Toronto Focus* logo on it. "Our children have been put down for such a long time. For thinking in the ways of our forefathers. For speaking the language of our own people. For dressing in a manner contrary to the white man's way. They don't know which side is up anymore. They are drowning in a sea of prejudice, intolerance and – and what amounts to – cultural genocide.

"We Indian people are being killed. They're killing us culturally and psychologically. That's why, fighting odds like that, we're hoping that the North American Indian Studies program will help Indian people develop a better sense of themselves – of who they are. Our young people, especially, need all the help we can give them if they're going to stand any chance at all of coping with this Western European culture and all of the confusing demands that have been imposed on them."

Bill glared across the table at Gordon. "Now it really burns me up, in the face of what we are attempting to accomplish, to have someone like Professor MacArthur here publicly accuse us of trying to downgrade his white values and traditions. We aren't trying to destroy white pride. My God, all that we are trying to do is restore to our people, to our children, one-tenth of the pride that we had before the white man came to our land.

"We're trying to restore part of the vast reservoir of spiritual and cultural strength that we once shared and drew upon. The spiritual strength of our people that has been drained dry by the white man and his culture and the innate need of the white man to change everything that is different, separate or apart.

"We want to restore pride in what we are – North American Indians. We want back part of that pride which has been taken away from us. Stolen from us. To have to deal with neanderthal nostrums like Professor MacArthur's white power council is beyond comprehension. I can't believe some of the things he has been saying and the way his group is placing our entire special studies program in jeopardy."

Bill pointed the index finger of his right hand directly at Gordon. "Do you know what you are doing? Do you understand what you are destroying? Have you thought it – any of it – out? It made my heart sick to hear your comments on the radio this morning. I couldn't believe that we would be subjected to such nineteenth century, racist, nonsense in 1974."

"Well," Deacon said with a pleased beam on his face, "we will get Professor MacArthur's reaction to that right after this commercial break. We will be right back."

As the floor director gave the signal letting them know they were off the air, Gordon glared angrily at Deacon and said, "Am I going to be given an opportunity to state my case? To clarify my position? Or would a proper stating of the reasonableness of my point of view spoil the effect of your carefully-scripted show?"

"This is not a scripted show, Professor MacArthur," Deacon replied indignantly. "You are receiving equal time. And now, sir, we are about to proceed." With that, he started to make some notes on the pad beside his coffee mug.

The floor director gave the cue and Deacon turned toward Gordon. "Now, Professor MacArthur, what do you have to say about what Dr. Eagletail is attempting to do for his people? What's your reply to his charge that your white power council is threatening his program?"

"We formed the Equal Opportunities Council, Mr. Deacon, because of the undermining effect the special studies programs about the blacks and the Indians are having on the white students. The children of the parents from the majority group. The majority, Mr. Deacon. Middle Canada. The people who pay for all university funding. The people who carry on their backs the largest share of the cost of this government-financed broadcasting system that you have, obviously, been using as a platform for the minority group viewpoints. The majority community that is being milked to finance those special studies programs and those renegade Indians who are trying to block the Saunders' gas pipeline out there in Alberta. They ...."

Bill pushed back his shoulders, stuck out his jaw, and cut in. "I'm glad you brought that one up. I heard you going on about that on the radio this afternoon. And that, Professor MacArthur, is another example of you mouthing off about something you know absolutely nothing about. You have absolutely no first-hand knowledge of that matter.

"It might surprise you to know that it is through my mother's property that that pipeline is going to be rammed. Forty feet from the house in which I was born. And – and God but it's insane when you think about it – they want to run that gas pipeline between the house and the barn. Right down the middle of my mother's barnyard. Cutting the house off from the barn. And what's the white man's solution? They say they'll build her a ramp over that pipeline.

"A ramp!" Bill exclaimed. "Can you imagine my mother having to cross a ramp every time she has to go to the barn? God but it makes me angry. Especially having to listen to you – almost two thousand miles away from the situation – on the radio saying white women and children will freeze in the dark of winter if they don't run that stupid pipeline through our yard."

Deacon was puzzled. "Oh? This is new. I was not aware that Professor MacArthur had said anything along that line. Will white people actually freeze in the dark, Professor?" he asked Gordon in a different, almost deferential, tone.

Gordon quickly caught on to the fact that he had struck a sensitive chord. He decided it would be better to back off a little and play on Deacon's self-interest as a white person.

"Well, maybe saying people will actually freeze in the dark is a bit dramatic. Overstating things a bit. But we are, as you know, facing an energy crisis such as this country has never confronted before. We are totally dependent on the Arabs for our oil supply and we simply must convert to natural gas as much as we possibly can. The huge deposit of natural gas that the Saunders Energy Corporation has discovered is our best hope for the short-term.

"As I understand it, the Saunders Energy Corporation spent a considerable amount of time and money investigating alternative routes. It was their opinion, after exhaustive study of the social and environmental considerations, that the route through the Big Thunder place was the best way to bypass Calgary.

"They wanted to start construction this summer but they've been hogtied by public hearings on the pipeline proposal. No one – including the people from Dr. Eagletail's reservation – has come up with an alternative route. They simply say they don't want the pipeline running across their land and the public be damned. What can we do? We need that gas.

"If that gas does not get down to central Canada, we could eventually be facing a situation where Canadian women and children will be without heating fuel in the middle of winter. I can't say for sure, Mr. Deacon, what might happen to your wife and children if they are forced to go without that heat. I can only imagine that the consequences will be quite horrendous."

Gordon paused for a moment and took a sip of coffee from the *Toronto Focus* mug. "Faced with the possibility that our women and children will freeze in the dark, I don't think it is asking too much of Dr. Eagletail to let us run a pipeline through his mother's barnyard. His people will be compensated quite generously for their land. They always are. So, it's as simple as that. The majority community has a need that can only be met by running that pipeline through the Big Thunder place."

Deacon thought about that prospect for a moment. "I think, Professor MacArthur, that what you are suggesting is this: Sometimes, unpleasant decisions have to be acted upon in the interest of obtaining the maximum good for the maximum number of people."

"That's very close to it," Gordon said in a tone one would use to compliment a piano student on getting the scales right for the very first time.

Bill was disappointed, but not surprised, at the way Deacon's attitude had changed so markedly. One moment, he seemed appalled by Gordon's pronounced racism and the next, when Gordon raised the prospect of Deacon's wife and children freezing in the dark of winter, he seemed to be with Gordon all the way.

"Things had turned out that way so many times before. He'd feel that a white person understood his point of view, sympathized with his problems and with those of his people. They'd identify with him, empathize with him, understand with him, deplore with him. But then, the moment they felt threatened by his difference, his Indianness, they would close ranks with all of the other whites. Draw their covered wagons in a circle and glare suspiciously at all those like him who were different.

They were only with him until, as was now the case with Fraser Deacon, someone suggested that their women and children were endangered by his existence. *By my opposition to Saunders' goddamned pipeline.*

"I had no idea that pipeline was so essential in the energy scheme of things," Deacon said. "I must say the prospect of women and children freezing in the dark of winter is quite alarming. Quite alarming indeed."

"It's alarming all right," Gordon said, "and our chances of surviving the deep cold of winter without that major new source of natural gas are minimal. We might make it through next winter. There are, apparently, sufficient reserves for that. But that will depend on the extent to which we have to draw on our dwindling reserves to get through this winter. If we are still without that gas after our reserves are fully depleted, we could, quite literally, freeze in the dark."

"Come off it," Bill challenged. "No one's going to freeze in the dark if that gas doesn't get through. That's a smokescreen. Scare tactics. Saunders' discovery is a mere drop in the bucket in the overall scheme of things. Besides, that pipeline was not predestined by God to push through my mother's barnyard. There's another route. A more direct route. But that route runs through land adjacent to the border of our reserve that a big law firm in Calgary is holding in trust for some unknown developer.

"They've spelled it out loud and clear that they won't let the Saunders pipeline anywhere near their property. And, because there's a greenbelt on the north side of that property, that means Saunders can't go around the south side of Calgary. That's the only reason he's now trying to ram his pipeline through Big Thunder. Use that other route for your pipeline. It's not going across our land. Take it through the white developer's property – if he will let you."

"Why should we do that when your reserve isn't even under development?" Gordon asked. "It's just uncultivated scrub. It's not being used."

Bill had heard that expression before, altogether too many times. "That's your key word, isn't it?" he responded heatedly. "It's not being used. If you're not using something, the white man comes along and takes it from you. And they've been doing that for centuries.

"No one was using the cod off the Grand Banks of Newfoundland. So you came over in your boats and hauled them off to Europe. No one was using the trees in New Brunswick and the St. Lawrence Valley. So you cut them down and shipped them off to Europe. No one was using the beaver, the buffalo, the coal, the gold, the nickel, the oil and all the other natural resources. So you shipped them off, too. And now, dammit, because my mother isn't 'using' her barnyard, you want to chop it up and lay a gas pipeline across it. Where will it end? My wife and my son? Will you take them, too? And my life? If I am not using it in the prescribed WASP way, will you take that away from me, too? Where does it end?

"That land that you say is not being used is part of my mother's life. Of her soul. You don't come up to someone sitting under a tree and offer him $100,000 for his feet because he's not using them at that particular moment. His feet are a vital part of his existence. You don't sell your existence, your life, in order to be 'compensated quite generously'. What good's a hundred thousand dollars for your feet if you can no longer walk?"

At that point, the floor director gave Deacon the signal to wrap things up. "Gentlemen, gentlemen," he interrupted. "I wish we could explore all of this at greater length but we have run out of time. You both made some excellent points, but we don't have enough time to deal with it all tonight. Would you consider coming back on our program some other time? Would that be possible? I'd like our viewers to learn more about both sides of this truly vital, national, question."

"I don't see why not," Bill said. "We certainly didn't get much of a chance to deal with anything in a meaningful manner tonight. Yes. I could be here."

"Splendid," Deacon said. "And what about you, Professor MacArthur?"

"I'd be pleased to come back on your show, Mr. Deacon. Any time."

"Good. Good. We'll check our schedule and let you know when we have an opening," Deacon said.

"And now, ladies and gentlemen," he said looking straight into the camera, "we will be right back with a close-up look at the shattered life of a young Toronto soldier who has just returned from a tour of duty with the U.S. Army in Vietnam. He volunteered to fight with the Americans because the late President John F. Kennedy said that Vietnam was a just war. A just war for which this young Canadian soldier paid a horrible, horrible, price. We will be right back."

Gordon's mother had watched the *Toronto Focus* interview. He had phoned that afternoon to tell her he was going to be on the program. But he had been quite vague about why they wanted to interview him. Martha didn't get the *Globe and Mail* or the *Toronto Star* so she knew nothing about the stories they had written about Gordon and his Equal Opportunities Council.

She had lived alone in a small apartment on Bloor Street near High Park for the past two years. She could have stayed on in their house after Tom was run over, it was fully paid for, but she felt the apartment would be easier to look after.

She missed Tom terribly and wished he could be sitting beside her to watch Gordon being interviewed on the television. And yet, in a way, he was with her still. The walls of the apartment were sprinkled with framed photographs of their many happy times together.

There was a photograph of Tom and Martha on their wedding day in December, 1936, in the Palm House conservatory at Allan Gardens. Another picture showed them strolling through High Park with Gordon in the snow that first winter after Tom got back from the war. There was the picture of Gordon and Tom setting off on one of their long walks through the city. Martha particularly liked that picture. Gordon had been about nine at the time and there was something terribly touching about the look of trust on his face as he looked up at his dad and held on to his hand. There was also a picture of Gordon with his arm around the neck of a little Shetland pony at his grandfather's hill farm that had been taken during their holiday in Scotland when he was twelve.

As she waited for Gordon's part of the television program to begin, Martha glanced over some of the other pictures on her wall. Her eye fell on a framed faded snapshot of Tom and his brother Bill on the doorstep of the small stone farmhouse near Inverness. It had been taken a week before the MacArthur brothers left for Canada with Lord Hanover's prize Aberdeen Angus bulls and cows.

Martha felt terribly proud when she heard Fraser Deacon announce that Gordon was going to be the next guest on the television program. She was so happy for Gordon and the way his academic career had advanced. Now that he said it was pretty certain he would be running for the Conservatives in the federal election, it appeared as if all the hopes she and Tom had for their son were going to be realized.

She was a bit startled when Deacon said Gordon was going to keep Canada safe for white people. She wondered what in the world he could have meant by that. And then she saw Gordon on the television screen. She thought he was looking in extremely good health. He didn't work out or anything like that, but he did walk a great deal. His father started him out on that good habit.

Martha couldn't understand what Deacon was driving at by comparing Gordon to the white power politician in Britain. She thought there had to be some mistake. *Gordon would say no such thing as there being too many people in turbans sprouting up all over settled neighborhoods. Gordon is not like that. Not at all.*

She thought Deacon was quite disrespectful. His questions were rather harsh and it was clear he didn't like Gordon very much. If what Gordon was saying about white students being made to feel ashamed was true, then Gordon was absolutely right. *Something should be done about that.*

Martha's mind snapped to attention when she heard the name Eagletail. William Eagletail. Dr. William Eagletail. Director of the North American Indian Studies program at the University of Toronto.

The name jolted her consciousness and brought back memories of her trip to Big Thunder to bring Gordon home to Toronto. Sarah walking across the barnyard towards her with her baby under her arm and Gordon in the cradle board strapped to her back. *It surely cannot be. It can't be little William. Good Lord but it is! It is little William. Gordon's brother.*

In braided hair and what looks like bear claws. And yet – and yet – they do look alike. They both have the MacArthur nose. And the eyes. The eyes. Yes, yes. William's eyes are that same grey-blue colour as Gordon's. My good Lord, what do I do now? How could this possibly have happened?

Berkeley? A doctorate? My but little William has done well, too. And Gordon is looking at him in such an angry way. There's a tension between them. You can feel it. What would Gordon say if he knew that William is his brother? What would William say if he knew?

William is such a pleasant young man. So cultured and refined in his speech. It's obvious from the way he's talking that he knows nothing at all about his father. But then how could he? He was just two years old when Bill went off to get killed in Hong Kong.

Oh, Lord God, Martha muttered to herself. *Now they're talking about Big Thunder. And it's Sarah's place they're going to run that pipeline through. Right between her house and her barn. It is insane. Building a ramp for a woman my age to climb over in the middle of winter! Utterly ridiculous! Oh, Gordon, how did you get mixed up in this? Sarah is – is – is your mother's – your mother's? – sister. What am I saying? Calling Helen your mother?*

A shiver ran down Martha's spine as she thought about the woman who sacrificed her life so her son could live. Her son? Her son, or Helen's? Or was Gordon the son of them both?

Later that evening, as she dried her few supper dishes, Martha thought about Sarah and the pipeline they wanted to ram through her barnyard. And that silly ramp they expected her to climb over in the middle of winter. It was, indeed, as William had said on the television, totally insane. She only wished there was something she could do to help stop that pipeline from going through.

And to think that it was Gordon, her own son, saying on the television and on the radio that they should run that pipeline through Sarah's yard. But then, how was the boy to know? How was he to know something that has been kept secret from him all these years? How was he to know it was from Sarah's breast that he got his first taste of milk?

He should have been told, Martha decided, as she put the last dish back into the cupboard. He should have been told a long time ago. *Perhaps, now that he and his brother have gotten into a scrap over Sarah's barnyard, now is the time to tell him. If he gets himself more deeply involved in the matter – wait – wait. What was that he said about going out there? Yes. The Empire Club. That's what he said. He'd been invited out there and they were going to fly him out first class and put him up in a suite at the Palliser Hotel. That's what he said when he phoned to say he'd be on the television program. That means he'll be in Calgary and – and – yes, he'll probably get his impulsive self out to Big Thunder and to – and to Sarah.*

Does Sarah know? That man Deacon said on the television that there had been stories in the newspapers about that new council Gordon has started up. Would Sarah have seen any of that? Not likely. But if the CBC runs something about Gordon and the pipeline – about Big Thunder – Sarah is bound to hear that or see it. Or be told about it.

And what is she going to say when she hears the name MacArthur? And that it's that same Gordon MacArthur who was named after her own father? Her – her nephew. Oh, Gordon son, there's no doubt about it, especially if you go out there to speak to the Empire Club, somebody somewhere is going to put two and two together and – and –would they tell you? Would they tell you that Helen was born at Big Thunder and that she – your natural mother – was Indian? Was Blackfoot?

Oh, Tom, we should have told the boy ourselves. He shouldn't be hearing this from strangers. It's we who should have told him. A long time ago. And now, my darling man, wherever you are, I'm going to have to tell him myself. He has to hear it from my own lips.

But how do I tell him? What will he think of me for keeping it from him all these years? How will he accept it? Will he accept it? He does, at times, seem so disinclined to accept people who are different – who aren't white. And he didn't get that from us.

It wasn't until Gordon was at the university and spending time with Professor Henderson that all the – Martha didn't think you should call it intolerance – that all this pride in being white started working its way into his vocabulary.

All that aside, how is he going to react when he finds out that on his mother's – might as well say it – on his mother's side he is – is – savage? That's what Mum said he was, part savage. That's why she said we should have left him at Big Thunder with "his own kind". That's why she was so resentful of all the time Dad spent with the little fellow while Tom was away at the war. But, no, savage is too strong a word for it. Savage isn't the right word. And yet, when you consider the almighty status he bestows on white, Western European, society, savage or, at least, primitive, is the only way to describe Indian society. Half Indian is what he is and he's just going to have to adjust to that fact as best he can.

And then she thought about how the way she told him about Helen would influence his acceptance, or rejection, of his Indianness. Of that other part of him. She would simply have to find the right way, and time, to tell him. The sooner the better.

But then she thought about Bill. *Shouldn't William also be told? How can one be told and not the other? Maybe – and yet I doubt it – maybe William has been told. Maybe Sarah and Richard explained it all to him at the right time. But no, if he knew he was a MacArthur, he wouldn't be saying all those things about white people. He can't possibly know.*

And then she remembered the letter Sarah had sent her just after Bill was killed in Hong Kong. *That's right. They said in the letter they weren't going to tell him. Not let him know about Gordon out here in Toronto. Probably didn't tell him.*

She saw again in her mind's eye the image of Sarah walking towards her the day she went out to Big Thunder to get Gordon. Walking across that same barnyard they now wanted to ram that gas pipeline through.

She wondered what Sarah would have done if it had been her that first saw Gordon and William on the TV together. *Would she've told him? Told him right away? What would she've said? How'd she explain not having told him about Gordon all these years? Thirty-five years.*

She wasn't too sure what to do now. It would probably come as a bit of a shock to Sarah to hear that Gordon and William had been on the TV together. Fighting about the pipeline they want to run through her barnyard. *Whatever would she think if she knew it was Gordon saying all those things in support of the pipeline? Her – her nephew.*

She remembered how impressed she had been with the strength of Sarah. The way her presence permeated that home. The quiet, firm, assured manner in which she spoke. Sarah would know what they should do. She'd know the best way to tell Gordon and William that they were brothers. She'd know.

Sarah should be the one who tells William. She'll know how best to tell him the true facts of his background – of his Scottish heritage. Sarah will know how best to deal with it. She'll know. We really should have kept in touch with them. It's been such a long time. Thirty-five years. But Tom was so angry when Bill told him Richard wasn't going to fight in the war. He didn't want to have anything to do with them. I can understand why he felt that way. Especially with Bill being killed by the Japanese in Hong Kong like that.

What's Sarah going to think, hearing from me after all these years? I really should have kept in touch with her. Still, after Bill was killed like that, there really wasn't all that much left to say. And yet, there was actually. The boys should have been told. Gordon really should have been told that he had a brother. And William should have been told, too. Is it too late now? I really don't know. At least, not tonight I don't. I'll think about it some more tomorrow. Take it one day at a time. That's what my dear Tom always used to say. "One day at a time."

～

Carol had also watched Fraser Deacon interview Gordon on *Toronto Focus*. The children were watching *Sesame Street* on the television in the family room and she had taken her drink to Gordon's study to watch the interview from there.

While waiting for Gordon's part of the program to begin, she had sipped her Scotch and allowed her eyes to wander around his study. She had not been in the room for weeks. Actually, as there was so little communication between them, the only reason she had for being there was to watch something on television whenever Charlie and Diane were monopolizing the TV in the family room. And, as Carol seldom found anything in the *TV Guide* that she considered worth watching, that situation seldom arose.

She looked at the Royal Herald of Scotland Gordon had draped across the wall above the rough, stone fireplace. Red lion on a yellow background with blue tongue and claws. She thought the creature looked more like a Chinese dragon than a lion – at least from a distance. That was probably because of the way its tail went right up past the top of its head in the shape of a dragon's. Above the flag, to the right, Gordon had hung an oil painting of Robert the Bruce, the King of the Scots from 1306 until his death in 1329. King Robert was mounted on a sturdy Highland pony facing an armour-clad English knight on an enormous black stallion just before the start of the Battle of Bannockburn. The sharp point of the knight's long lance had just missed the unprotected chest of the Scottish king, providing a splendid opportunity for King Robert, standing in the stirrups, to smash his battle axe against the Englishman's helmet, splitting the head and helmet in two.

To the left of the flag, there was a painting of Dunstaffnage Castle, an ancient ruin of a building squatting on a rocky promontory on the west coast of Scotland, surrounded on three sides by the sea, at the southwest entrance to Loch Etive. The castle was given to the MacArthurs by King Robert, along with vast tracts of land that had belonged to the MacDougalls, after the Battle of Bannockburn in 1314 where Bruce and his kilted Scots defeated the English despite being outnumbered two-to-one.

Storm clouds painted on the horizon reflected the troubled times of that turbulent era. Just a few inches above the painting of the castle, there was a gory painting of the Battle of Culloden Moor where more than fifteen hundred loyalist Scottish Highlanders, supported by regulars provided by the King of France, were either killed or wounded in the spring of 1746 in a valiant effort to overthrow English rule and put Bonnie Prince Charlie on the throne.

When Gordon suggested that they name their son Charlie, after the bonnie prince, Carol thought it was probably better than naming him Granville or Thomas and thereby hurting the feelings of one of the grandfathers.

Just to the right of Culloden Moor, there was a plaque with the MacArthur Clan crest and tartan. It featured two laurel branches and the Latin words *fide et opera* – by fidelity and work. On the left side of the painting of Culloden Moor, Gordon had hung a plaque with the badge of the 48th Highlanders of Canada. It had a falcon's head with an open beak at the top which had been adapted from the crest of Clan Davidson in honour of Lieutenant-Colonel John Irvine Davidson who became the Canadian regiment's first commanding officer on November 20, 1891.

As she looked at the oil paintings of King Robert the Bruce, Dunstaffnage Castle and the blood-drenched painting of the Battle of Culloden Moor, Carol concluded that Gordon's study was somewhat of a Scottish shrine. Right down to the dagger-like brass letter opener he used with the Highland piper on its handle. Considering the fact that he had only spent one month in Scotland, back when his parents took him over there for a summer visit, she thought it was odd that he wore a tartan tie just about every other day and, on special occasions like the St. Andrew's Society Ball, insisted on wearing his dead father's kilt.

Actually, she thought, as she looked at the photograph of him striding to the speaker's lectern at last year's Robbie Burns dinner, he cut a rather odd figure with his swishing kilt, jewelled dagger handle peeping out of his right sock, white rabbit fur sporran with the black tassels over his groin, green, pleated, jacket with the brass buttons and his father's distinctive 48th Highlanders' Glengarry cap with the red-and-white checkerboard band, regimental badge and two black ribbons at the back topping it all off.

Carol thought Fraser Deacon's reference to Gordon keeping Canada safe for white people was quite appropriate. She was still having difficulty believing he was serious, or could be serious, about this white pride campaign. When Deacon compared Gordon to the white power Conservative MP in Great Britain, she was pleased to see he appeared to have a proper perspective on him and his white-pride colleagues. She only wished the program wasn't being broadcast into thousands of homes in the Metropolitan Toronto area.

Bill caught Carol's attention right away. She thought he looked somewhat like a chief. His hair, braided and hanging over his shoulders, set his face off magnificently. His eyes, set against the rich tan of his face, looked like diamonds on black velvet. He was a handsome man. And what presence he had. He looked so confident. So assured. So unpretentious.

My God but he's real. What impressive credentials he has. The advanced studies school at Berkeley has about the most exacting standards of any university in North America. To come out of there with a doctorate in sociology is a truly remarkable academic feat. That makes him one of the top academics in his field of study. His voice is so deep. So resonant. And what a firm, polished, way he has of articulating his views.

What's this about running a gas pipeline between his mother's house and her barn? And building a ramp over it. Totally ridiculous! Whites freezing in the dark? What's Gordon up to now? It's obviously news to Deacon. Gordon said nothing to me about whites freezing in the dark if that pipeline doesn't go through that poor woman's barnyard.

Then she sensed that Fraser Deacon was falling for Gordon's line. He seemed to believe all that stuff about white women and children freezing in the dark if that pipeline went anywhere other than where Jack Saunders wanted it to go. When Bill charged that Gordon was putting up a smokescreen, she almost applauded.

Right! Tell him, Dr. Eagletail. It is nothing but a smokescreen. Scare tactics. There are other routes. Right. Common sense dictates that. Someone probably wants to develop that land on the northern border of the Big Thunder community. Within spitting distance of Calgary. And they don't want a gas pipeline running through their cookie-cutter houses, office buildings and shopping centres. Better to run it through Mrs. Eagletail's barnyard.

Hah, a greenbelt! That's why he has to go through the Indians' land. There's a greenbelt between that property and the south side of Calgary. He's boxed in. Talk about self-interest! Oh, Gordon. Why are you spouting Jack Saunders' line? You have no first-hand knowledge of any of this. They are feeding you lines and you're parroting them on television. You have no idea what you're talking about.

She thought Bill was right on when he described how things were being taken away from the Indian people all the time. That was true. If the native people weren't using something according to the WASP definition of the word use, it was taken away from them. That's what happened to the fish, the beaver, the buffalo, and the trees, and the coal, the gold, the nickel, the oil. *And now it's his mother's barnyard they want. Her tiny plot of land.*

"Where does it all end, Gordon?" she asked his image on the television screen. "You're helping them steal his mother's land. And what are you going to leave her with? A hundred thousand dollars for her feet? Why not offer $200,000 for her eyes while you're at it? Saunders has the money. More than enough. You can talk her into throwing in her right thumb while you're at it."

Carol was extremely upset by the time she switched off the television set and poured herself another Scotch. A short time later, she looked out the kitchen window at the stately maple trees with their leaves transformed into the multi-coloured hues of autumn. She wondered what she would do if someone wanted to chop those trees down to make room for a gas pipeline. What would she do if she was confronted with that sort of prospect?

The tree house she played in as a child was still up in the branches of the maple beside the woodshed. Charlie had converted it into an after-school fort and covered it with army surplus camouflage. She wouldn't let anyone cut those trees down. Not one of them. She'd fight it. Just like Dr. Eagletail was fighting the pipeline they wanted to force through his mother's barnyard.

She decided there was more to this fight than the pipeline. There was the North American Indian Studies program and the awesome task of instilling in young native people a supportive sense of self-esteem. Dr. Eagletail stuck out in her mind because he represented such a proud contrast to the media-induced stereotype of drunken Indians rolling in the gutters of Kenora and other Canadian towns.

Dr. Eagletail had the presence of a Sitting Bull, a Red Cloud or a Geronimo. She imagined that he must have an enormous influence on native students participating in the special studies courses. They must take great pride in identifying with him, she thought. Using him as a role model example of what they themselves could become if they tried hard enough. He seemed truly committed to those young people and helping them discover pride in their roots.

And Gordon's white power group was like a monster serpent coiled and ready to strike at the special studies courses. Gordon would do to that Indian studies program exactly the same thing Saunders' oil pipeline was going to do to Mrs. Eagletail's barnyard – rip it apart. Gordon had to be stopped. She looked up Dr. Eagletail's number in the university directory and dialled. He was there.

"This is Bill Eagletail," he answered.

She said her name was Carol Winston and she had watched the show. She said she wanted him to know how very much she appreciated what he had to say and the way he had explained what was involved with the special studies program and with the gas pipeline.

"I had no idea, until I heard you explain it on the television just now what was involved and how important it is that you succeed in what you're attempting to do – both at the university and in your home community. I just wanted you to know that you've got – for whatever it's worth – my understanding and total support."

This is a welcome call. "Well, thank you, Miss Winston. I'm glad my message got through. That's the only justification for accepting these interview situations. It's only worth the time if we can add something to the majority group's information profile on Indian people. Something to provide them with a better understanding of the situation my people face. I really do appreciate that you cared enough to call."

"It was my pleasure, Dr. Eagletail. Common sense dictates that what you said is the only reasonable and humane way to approach the situation at the university and on the – and in your home community."

"It is a reserve, Miss Winston. I don't object to you calling it what it is."

"I know that," she said almost apologetically. "It's just that I don't particularly like the term. It's too easy to think of it as something separate and apart when you use a term like reserve. I prefer the term community."

"But we are separate and apart, Miss Winston. There's no harm in accepting that reality. No harm at all."

"Your community might be separate and apart in the physical sense of the word. But, if people are trying to ram that pipeline through your mother's barnyard and they're using the argument that they're doing it on behalf of people like me down here in the east, then it's no longer separate and apart. They've made me a part of it by using my energy needs as an excuse for taking your mother's land. Looking at it that way, I'm an integral, and completely unwilling, part of the whole sorry exercise."

"You've got a point there," Bill said. "They are using your energy needs as the main justification for what they want to do. They are suggesting that your need for the Alberta gas means that all white people must be in favour of running that pipeline through my mother's land."

"Exactly. And I'm one white woman who doesn't for one minute believe my children will freeze in the dark if Jack Saunders doesn't get to run his pipeline through your mother's community. It's all, like you said on the television program, a smokescreen. A con job. Scare tactics. It's all about money. If Saunders pays them the right price, he'll be able to run his pipeline around the edge of that other property. Money's what it's all about. And I'll bet it's a lot cheaper to run it through your mother's community instead of through the other route."

Bill said he had no doubt that was the case. Then she asked him what he was going to do next. She said the television interview was a good start, but he needed to get on with some follow-up activity.

"What's your next move?" she asked.

He liked the sound of her and the way her mind worked. She was quite business-like. And yet there was a warm, deliciously-feminine, manner about her. She had a beautiful, husky, voice and he sensed that she was quite well-bred and educated.

"We're having a meeting on that very question at the university tomorrow night," he said. "It's our regular monthly meeting and we'll be discussing that white power council and, to a lesser extent, the pipeline question."

"Why would the pipeline question be considered to a lesser extent?" she asked.

"It's more of a personal matter," he replied. "I was born there. My roots are there. If they run that pipeline through, they'll be ripping up a part of me. But that's all personal. I wouldn't expect the committee to get involved in that. It's two thousand miles removed from the situation we're dealing with here at the university."

"No it's not," she said with a slight rise in her voice. "It's not at all removed. By bringing me and several million other Canadians into the picture, they've brought it very close to home. Their main argument for going through your land is the fact that it's not being used. Now, to my way of thinking, that brings into question the centuries-old conflict between the native people and the Western Europeans about how we should all live on this planet. The Indians living in harmony with the land and the whites wanting to harness and redirect nature. It's all relevant.

"This pipeline issue you're dealing with symbolizes everything that can possibly be said about relations between the whites and the Indians. It's a perfect example of the erosive process that has been going on for centuries. The gradual diminishing of Indian culture, tradition, identity, and land. I think your committee should seize the initiative on this issue and get the Canadian public to support what you're trying to accomplish. Not just at the university but everywhere Indian people are attempting to co-exist with the intolerant white majority on this North American continent."

Bill said he appreciated what she was saying, but that it had never been their intention to muster public opinion in support of their programs.

"My committee is entirely made up of native people and we've never even thought about trying to get large numbers of the majority community to accept our point of view."

"I think that's where you're making a big mistake," Carol said. "That's why you're susceptible to attacks from people like the Equal Opportunities Council. You've never properly explained what it is you're trying to accomplish. I think you're going to have to do that – to sell your special studies program and your whole way of life to the Canadian people. If you don't, you'll never get groups like the Equal Opportunities Council and the Saunders gas company off your backs. You've got to go to the people."

"Well, you certainly seem all fired up about it. We seem to have won you over," he said. "But you're but one – one highly-intelligent and, if you will permit me to say so, refreshingly tolerant and percep-tive white woman."

"I'm not alone, Dr. Eagletail. You'd be surprised, if you gave them half a chance, at the number of Canadians who would devote their time and energy to support what you're trying to accomplish at the university and the fight for your mother's land. Just give us a chance.

Now, then, why don't you invite me to your meeting? I am a lawyer and I might be of some assistance in resolving issues involving land rights and whether or not the Energy Resources Conservation Board of Alberta has any authority over, what I am certain that you consider to be, sovereign Indian land."

Oh, so that's it, Bill thought with a pronounced feeling of disappointment, *just another white lawyer trying to cash in on our troubles. Another ambulance chaser.*

"Actually, Miss Winston, we're not in a position to afford a lawyer at this time. We are working on these issues on a strictly voluntary basis."

"As would I," Carol replied. "I wouldn't give a moment's thought to billing you. My services, if you determine that they could be of some assistance, would be offered pro bono."

Then I read the lady wrong. She's not in it for the big bucks like most white lawyers are. She really does want to help. He was quite taken aback by the forcefulness of her personality and the direct manner in which she expressed herself. He could see that there might be definite advantages in having someone like her working with them on the committee. If the others would accept her into their confidence, her support might turn out to be very worthwhile.

"Well, you're most welcome to come," he said. "We've never reached outside before but, with the way things are coming to a head, it might be worth having another opinion on some of the issues we're dealing with. So, if you still feel like it, please join us tomorrow night in meeting room 16 of Davidson Hall. We'll be starting at 7:30 p.m."

"Very good," she said with a touch of excitement in her voice. "I'll see you there."

CHAPTER
- 16 -

Marilyn Russell was right. Gordon was on the front page of the *Globe and Mail* next morning. Complete with a file picture of him speaking to a class of students.

'Kids will freeze in dark'
U of T professor warns
By Marilyn Russell

Women and children in eastern Canada could "freeze in the dark of winter" because of Indian opposition to a proposed Alberta gas pipeline, University of Toronto Professor Gordon MacArthur told *The Globe and Mail* in an exclusive interview yesterday.

MacArthur, who is expected to be nominated as the Conservative candidate for Meadowbrook next week, said the Alberta Indians are "jeopardizing the vital energy supply of all Canadians."

The Saunders Energy Corporation wants to lay the pipeline across the Big Thunder Indian reserve near Calgary.

The Energy Resources Conservation Board of Alberta started hearings on the controversial application two weeks ago. The hearing is expected to continue at least to the end of the month.

"The fact of the matter is that white Canadians run the risk of freezing in the dark of winter if that pipeline is not allowed to go through," MacArthur said in an exclusive interview with *The Globe*. "To yield to the demands of those Indians would be to accept the risk of having white Canadian women and children freeze in their homes because those Indians won't allow for a minimal easement across their land.

"We're facing an energy crisis such as this country Canada has never before confronted. We are altogether too dependent on Arab oil. Last year's OPEC oil crisis was a wakeup call. We've simply got to get off Arab oil and onto Alberta gas. The Saunders Energy Corporation has discovered an almost unlimited supply of gas and they simply must be allowed to get it down here to the eastern market. Down here where it's so desperately needed.

"This is no time to argue over the alleged sins of the past. It's to the future that we've got to look. And the Saunders' pipeline proposal represents that future. It is our best hope for weaning ourselves from Arab oil."

MacArthur, 35, is a professor of political science at the University of Toronto. He is the driving force behind the recently-formed Equal Opportunities Council – a group of university professors fighting for "equal rights" for white students.

"We on the Equal Opportunities Council say that the energy needs of all Canadians must be given priority over any pie-in-the-sky claims of a bunch of Indians," MacArthur said. "Common sense dictates that the Saunders' pipeline should run through the Big Thunder Indian reservation."

That's more like it, Gordon thought as he read the newspaper while drinking his morning coffee in the living room. *This time they've got it right. My God but they've got it right. This time, we're down to the bottom line. The energy needs of the majority community versus the obstructive tactics of those goddamned Indians. The picture's pretty good, too. My left profile is better than my right. Looks good.*

MacArthur has been dubbed the "white power Conservative" because of allegedly racist comments he has made about minority group people.

In a recent interview, he complained about the growing number of "people in turbans sprouting up" in Toronto neighborhoods.

MacArthur has also complained about what he called "clamouring, lobbying, high-pressure, special-interest minority groups" who have immigrated to Canada over the last three decades.

He is on record as saying white, Anglo-Saxon, Canadians form the majority in Canada "and it's high time that this country and its Parliament reflected that fact."

The phone rang just as Gordon finished reading the article. He took another look at his left profile as he picked up the receiver. It was Henry Bracken and he was ecstatic about the coverage.

"Things are coming together," Bracken exulted. "Now even the media understands that you are on to something good. Things will pick up smartly now, Gordon. You'll see. You're doing fine. Magnificently – hold on a minute, Gordon, my other line's going."

Gordon waited as Bracken answered his other line. He couldn't make out who Bracken was talking to.

"Gordon?" Bracken said after about three minutes.

"Yes, Henry."

"Sorry to keep you on hold like that. That was Dave Saunders – Jack's brother. He just read the story and he says it's splendid. Simply splendid. That's exactly the kind of story they want written about the pipeline deal. This story cannot help but do them good. Dave says they want us to hold on to – or even build upon – the momentum that's picking up."

"Did he have any suggestions, Henry? About building momentum?"

"No. No, he didn't. But I'm having lunch with him today. Do you want to join us? I think that you should."

"Yeah, sure. Okay."

"Meet me at the Commonwealth Club at twelve-thirty. I have a table there. Just give them my name like you did the last time. Can you make that?"

"Sure. No problem. I'll see you there, then."

"Good. Good, Gordon. Good boy. I must say things are working out very well. Splendidly."

Carol had entered the room about halfway through the telephone conversation. Charlie and Diane were having breakfast with the part-time housekeeper in the kitchen. She read the story about Gordon as he spoke to Bracken on the phone.

"Do you have any idea of what you're doing?" she demanded as he hung up the phone.

"What do you mean? Doing?"

"All this stuff about white women and children freezing in the dark. Dr. Eagletail told you that pipeline doesn't have to go through his mother's land. They can ..."

"Screw his mother," Gordon snapped. "We've got to consider the needs of the majority community. That pipeline is going through and that's all there is to it."

"Don't talk nonsense, Gordon. There's no reason to ..."

"No. You hold it," he said in a self-confident tone she had seldom heard in his voice lately. "I'm not going to be somebody. I am somebody. I'm news. Front page news."

"But – but this is just a newspaper story," she started. "It'll probably be wrapped around some fish by tonight. Around some garbage. This story is not reality. Not ..."

"You're damned right it's reality," he snapped. "Henry Bracken had a real reaction to that story. Dave Saunders had a real reaction to that story. That story will influence people's minds. Read it again, Carol. Read it and you'll realize how important what I'm saying is to every man woman and child in Canada.

"Think of your own kind, Carol. You're not Indian. It's not your mother's land they're putting that pipeline through. It's Eagletail's mother. Let him worry about that old woman. You worry about your own kind. About the energy needs of white people. Get a hold of yourself and see life for what it is. Survival of the fittest."

"For God's sake, Gordon," she said, no longer thrown off balance by the unusual fervor of his conviction. "This isn't a jungle. This is a civilized society. A society where, when the strong do eat the weak, they do so by due process of law. Don't drag Darwin into this. The only point at issue here – and you're as aware of it as I am – is that it's probably a lot cheaper for Jack Saunders to go through Dr. Eagletail's land than it is to go through the land they want to use for that new project they're developing. Don't muddy things up by pitting whites against Indians with your scare stories about whites freezing in the dark if Jack Saunders doesn't get to run his pipeline through the Big Thunder community. It's like Dr. Eagletail said on *Toronto Focus*, you have absolutely no first-hand knowledge of any of this. You're talking through your hat."

"I am, eh? And I suppose he's just simply a walking encyclopedia of verified information on this and every other subject he decides to address. Is that what you're implying?"

"He certainly knows a great deal more than you do about Big Thunder and the Saunders pipeline. After all, it's his mother's property they're cutting in half."

"Oh, come off it. They aren't cutting that old woman's property in half. They're simply asking for an easement through part of it. Nobody's cutting her land up more than necessary."

"And who decides what's necessary?"

"Need. Need decides it every time. The need, in this particular case, to ensure that gas gets down to central Canada where it's so desperately needed."

"This discussion is pointless," she said impatiently. "As Dr. Eagletail told you on *Toronto Focus*, neither need nor God dictates that that pipeline has to go through that property. And, if his mother trips crossing that ramp next winter and breaks her hip, you – with your nationally-publicized statements in support of that pipeline – will be directly responsible."

"You're talking nonsense. I haven't any responsibility toward that old woman. She's Eagletail's mother. Let him worry about her. She's nothing to me. My responsibility is to my own kind. Not to some renegade Indians who want to fight progress."

"Renegade Indians? I can't believe I'm hearing this. I am absolutely, totally, opposed to your position. So opposed, that I'll fight you to my last breath to make sure Dr. Eagletail's mother doesn't have to climb over any pipeline ramp in the middle of winter. You're dead wrong on Big Thunder, Gordon. Just as you are on a lot of things. Like, this need you seem to have developed to put down the immigrant groups. Here it is," she said as she picked up the newspaper and started to read.

"It says that you were critical of what you called 'clamouring, lobbying, high-pressure, special-interest minority groups' who had immigrated to Canada over the last three decades. And then it quotes you as saying that white, Anglo-Saxon, Canadians make up the majority in Canada and, quote, 'it's high time that this country and its Parliament reflected that fact.' What is that supposed to mean? The House of Commons is packed, wall to wall, with lily-white, male, Canadians. There are hardly any people of immigrant background in the whole bunch.

"You've no idea what it's like to live the immigrant experience, Gordon. And don't bring up your father and his brother coming here from Scotland. They spoke English and came here on British passports. That doesn't count. Just last week, the *Star* had a feature article on immigrant kids who are being streamed into technical and vocational schools because the school boards don't believe they have what it takes to become doctors or lawyers.

"Are they serious? Those kids have Galileo, da Vinci, Verdi, Puccini, and Michelangelo in their genes. They'd make great lawyers, composers, scientists. Painters, too. But, because of attitudes like yours, they're not going to get that chance."

"Oh, come off it," Gordon said. "I'm not saying those kids shouldn't get the chance to go to university. Although, I must say, I didn't know about what you refer to as 'streaming'. I really didn't know about that."

"Well, it's true. The article in the *Star* says the immigrant experience is absolute hell for most of those kids and their parents. In fact, they even quoted one teenager, who had been born here to Italian parents, as referring to the other kids in her school as 'the Canadians'. She just simply did not fit in. Despite the fact that she was born here. Right here in Toronto."

"I didn't know about that, either," Gordon said.

"Yeah, and I'll bet you don't know how Jack Saunders made his money, and it wasn't in gas."

"What do you mean 'wasn't in gas'?"

"Saunders made his first money from a big sand and gravel operation up near Caledon that was confiscated from an Italian family during the war. Not only did they round the Italian men up, people who had lived here most of their lives, and ship them off to the Army camp at Petawawa, they also had the Custodian of Alien Properties seize their properties.

"That's how Saunders got control of the gravel pit. I read about it in a case study just before I left Haldimand and Brock. And it wasn't only the gravel pit. He also got hold of a property the government had confiscated from an Italian family up near Kirkland Lake and, later, in 1955, he found gold on it. He made a fortune with that gold."

"Jeez," I didn't know about that," Gordon said.

"No, you didn't, and that's just one of all too many things about which you have an almost complete lack of knowledge or understanding. And, last night, as I watched you on television parroting Jack Saunders' line on *Toronto Focus* and recycling Don Henderson's Rule Britannia version of history, I realized that you have become someone I no longer know. Or want to know. I just don't relate to you at any level. As Dr. Eagletail said on the TV program, you are stuck in a nineteenth century time warp."

Before he had a chance to respond, she left the room and joined Anne and the children in the kitchen. She was more determined than ever that she was going to do everything within her power to help Bill fight Jack Saunders' pipeline – and Gordon.

He started to follow her but decided it would be better not to argue in front of the children. They'd seen more than enough arguments lately. He would deal with her later.

Jack Saunders' brother Dave, a Toronto lawyer and backroom Conservative powerbroker, sat across the table from Gordon and Henry Bracken in the elegant dining room of the Commonwealth Club.

"The energy issue is going to be one of the key elements in the election strategy," he told them, between sips of his Scotch and soda. "Now that the Arabs have hiked the price of oil again, we've got to re-examine the whole energy picture. The one thing that's clear in all this is that natural gas is critical to our survival as a nation. We've simply got to get more natural gas down to the eastern markets. It's imperative. And we're on a critical time frame. We could, as Gordon said in the *Globe*, run critically short of heating fuel if we don't get more gas on stream. Whether or not we'll actually freeze in the dark if that doesn't happen is neither here nor there. While that might not be true, it is plausible. The main thing is that we've got to get more gas down here. Fast. My brother says the Big Thunder route is the fastest and cheapest way to get his gas down here where it's needed."

Saunders, a disgustingly paunchy man, stopped for a moment to chew on his thick New York sirloin. Then he wiped the grease from the corners of his mouth and downed some more Scotch. "This publicity Gordon's getting could be just what we need to turn this whole thing around and get the Big Thunder business settled once and for all."

"What do you propose, Dave?" Bracken asked as he signalled the uniformed waiter to bring them another round of drinks.

"If we can bring Big Thunder to a head over the next couple of weeks, we can create the right level of public support to ensure us a favorable ruling from the Energy Resources Conservation Board out in Alberta. Some members of Premier Harrison's cabinet are leaning, a bit too strongly if you ask me, toward the Indians' side of this thing. They're starting to talk about having Jack find another route. A route that'll cost us a helluva lot more money and create even longer delays. We've got to turn that negative thinking around. Fast."

"I still don't see the connection with Gordon and what we're attempting to do in Meadowbrook," Bracken said.

"You will, Henry. You will. What we need is some way of dramatizing this issue. Politicizing it. Like Gordon's been doing with the media. We've got to create an enormous hue and cry in eastern Canada demanding that Jack's pipeline go through Big Thunder. We've got to whip up public opinion to the point where they'll go out there with picks and shovels if they have to to make sure the pipeline goes through. As proposed. With that kind of climate, the ERCB can approve our application. They'll do it with a close vote so it doesn't look like we're railroading it through. And, when it's all over, the public will be thanking us for saving their sorry asses from freezing in the cold of winter."

"But," Bracken said a bit doubtfully, "even if you can whip up that sort of public support, you can't know for sure that the Energy Resources Conservation Board will vote for Jack's proposal."

"Of course we can. They're all appointed. If Bob Harrison couldn't predict how they'd vote, he wouldn't have appointed them in the first place. Just leave that to us. We can handle that end of things."

He stopped talking long enough to butter his fourth roll. "You probably don't know this, but the fact of the matter is we wouldn't be having the goddamned hearing in the first place if that MP of yours, Hal Davies, hadn't made such a stinking fuss about us going through the Indians' land. He should have settled for having his Indian affairs in bed. Anyway, that's our end of the problem. We can handle it.

"What we want you to do, Gordon, is get the momentum building. Your father-in-law has discussed all of this with my brother. They've talked it all through. What we want you to do is get the people out on the streets demonstrating. Get them writing to their MPs. To the Prime Minister. To the newspapers. Whip them up to a fever pitch. With that kind of demonstrated public support for the pipeline, we'll be able to take care of the Energy Board panel.

"This thing's got to get off the ground fast if it's going to do Jack any good. We've got to have hundreds of people out demonstrating on the streets of Toronto by the middle of next week. What do you say, Gordon? Can we count on you?"

"But I don't know anything about that sort of thing," he protested. "I wouldn't know where to begin."

"I've taken care of that. I've lined up a lunch meeting with Steve Foreman and Dave Lawson for tomorrow. In my suite at the Harbour Castle Hotel. Steve is one of the party's best organizers. He'll get the bodies you'll need to get people out on the streets. Dave is one of my brother's people. He'll come up with the right ideas about what you should be saying to whip up the support we need for the pipeline. He's good at his job. One of the best."

"I still don't know," Gordon said. "I've never been involved in anything like that. I don't know if I could do it."

"Your father-in-law thinks that you could. He told Jack you'd do an excellent job and we could count on you to co-operate. This is what your father-in-law wants to see happen, Gordon. He's counting on you."

"Well, I suppose there's no harm in talking about it at the meeting tomorrow. It's just that I'm not sure I'm the person you need for this sort of thing. What do you think, Henry? What do you think I should do?"

"If it's what Gran wants you to do, I can't see any harm in it. The publicity you get from it might even help us with the Meadowbrook campaign. Give you a higher recognition profile. You know, fighting to make sure white women and children don't freeze in the dark. It could work out and, as Dave says, it does seem to be what Gran wants you to do."

"All right, then. I'll go to the meeting. And I will try to do all that I can for you, Dave. I'll be there. What time do you want me?"

"Drop by around twelve-thirty. Suite 2804. Harbour Castle. I'll be expecting you. And relax, Gordon, this is going to be a ball. You're going to have one helluva time."

"Will you want me at the meeting?" Bracken asked as he signed the bill for their lunch. "I had intended to go to the cottage for the weekend."

"No, thank you, Henry. Not at all. Gordon is all that we need," Saunders said. "By the way, Gordon, Henry tells me you're going to be nominated as our candidate for Meadowbrook next Thursday night. Tells me he thinks you're going to do rather well as an MP."

"He will do that," Henry said. "Gordon is an excellent fit for Meadowbrook. He's one of ours. One of our own kind."

"Well, the national polls are looking quite good for us right now, Gordon," Saunders said. "We'll have some local polling done for you in Meadowbrook so you'll be able to fine tune your message."

"Thank you, Dave. I really appreciate that," Gordon said.

"And you'll be needing space for a campaign office," Saunders continued. "We've got a mall in the middle of Meadowbrook and we'll fix you up with a couple of thousand feet with outside exposure. The phones are in already. All you'll have to do is change the numbers. The Prime Minister could be calling the election any day now and you'll want to be ready."

"I hadn't expected that," Gordon said. "That's very generous of you, Dave."

"Generosity has nothing to do with it, my boy. You help us out with the pipeline deal and we'll see to it that you're taken care of in Meadowbrook. That's how it works. Right Henry?"

"Right, Dave. That is how it works."

With that, Saunders raised what was left of his third glass of Scotch to Gordon and said, "Cheers."

Ross Palmer phoned about half an hour after Gordon got back to the university. He didn't like the way the Equal Opportunities Council was being dragged into the Big Thunder affair.

"In reading the story about you in the *Globe* this morning, I got to wondering if that is what we started out to accomplish, Gordon. It was never my intention that the Equal Opportunities Council would be dealing with things like the Saunders gas pipeline and that Indian reserve out in Alberta. We've never so much as discussed it and yet there you are in the *Globe* saying that the Council is opposed to the Indians' position on the pipeline. I don't like the way the Council is getting dragged into all this.

"It was never our intention to deal with things like that. By involving ourselves in this issue, we're diluting our effectiveness in getting the special educational opportunities established for the white students at the university. I think you're getting us way off track."

"Maybe you're right," Gordon conceded. "If it hadn't been for the fact that Gran – my father-in-law – was in Calgary when I spoke to him, I wouldn't even have known about Big Thunder. It was the farthest thing from my mind. Maybe you're right. Maybe I shouldn't have made a statement about Big Thunder in the name of the Council.

I should have checked it out with you and the others, Ross. You're right. I did shoot from the hip on that one and I regret having done so."

"Well, what's done is done," Palmer said. "Please give me your assurance that you won't make any future statements in the Council's name without checking with us first. We are in this together, Gordon."

"I will. I most definitely will. So many things were happening – and at so fast a pace. I guess I got a bit carried away by the whole thing. I'm sorry, Ross."

"Well, you certainly aren't the first to get caught up in the media mill and fashioned into some figment of their imagination. Don't be unduly harsh on yourself. The main thing now is that we cool things down. Put a damper on things. Particularly on this Indian business. While we still can."

"You're right. This Big Thunder publicity isn't the right way to go about getting the white studies course established. I should have known better. You're right. I'll ease off on the public statements. I'll cool the Big Thunder business down altogether. Does that sit better with you?"

"Yes, Gordon. It certainly does. And I think, in the longer term, you'll see that pulling back now will work out to be in the Council's longer-term best interest. You are doing the right thing. Now, I must be off."

He's right. I should have checked with them first. Not that that means I can't keep speaking out on the Big Thunder issue. I'm certainly not going to let that one go. It's just that, from now on, I'll do it as the Conservative candidate for Meadowbrook. That way, Ross and the others will have no say whatsoever about what I say. I can say what I want – when I want.

～

Gran Winston called about half an hour after Ross Palmer. He was still in Calgary.

"Dave Saunders says he had a very good meeting with you over lunch today and you're getting together with him and some of his associates tomorrow. That's good, Gordon. They certainly could use your help. That story in the *Globe* this morning is just what Jack Saunders needs. Can't help but be of benefit to him. Good work."

"Carol certainly doesn't see it that way," Gordon said. "She chewed me out about it this morning. Went on and on about the piece in the *Globe*. She was very angry."

"That's my Carol," Winston said. "Always did have a soft spot for the underdog. But, don't worry about it. You're on the right track, Gordon, and I am truly appreciative of the effort you're putting into this issue. Being a professor at the U of T gives you a lot of credibility. Keep up the good work."

"I will, Gran. You can count on me."

Harold Stewart from the *Toronto Star* called to ask Gordon about some of the things he had been quoted as saying in the *Globe and Mail*.

"Isn't it a bit of an exaggeration to say that white women and children will actually freeze in the dark of winter if that pipeline doesn't go through the Indians' land?"

"Not at all. According to the information that I have been provided, our oil reserves are at an all-time low. We are in desperate need of that Alberta gas. The Big Thunder route is the best way to bypass Calgary. All the Saunders gas people are asking for is an easement across the reservation. It's no big deal. And, as always, the Indians will get top dollar for their useless bit of land."

"I still don't see how you get to whites freezing in the dark."

"Because of the time delay. The more those Indians hold the project up at the Energy Board hearings the less chance there is of getting the pipeline up and running before our reserves hit rock bottom. If that happens, it's game over. Our women and children will, quite literally, freeze in the dark."

"Then, you're quite serious about this?"

"Absolutely. We must connect that new gas to the main Trans-Canada pipeline and get it down to the eastern markets before our reserves are totally depleted. Before we run dry."

"With all due respect, professor, that's not the main issue. Everyone agrees that we need the Alberta gas. The main issue, as I understand it, is getting it to the main Trans-Canada pipeline. We got a statement from Dr. William Eagletail of the North American Indian Studies program this morning and he says it makes more sense to take the pipeline through land running adjacent to the border of his reserve. What do you say about that?"

"I say that's what one would expect to hear from someone who has a vested interest in this matter. Of course he doesn't want it going through his mother's land. It's the standard Not In My Back Yard response. That doesn't change the fact that it makes more sense to lay the pipeline through land that's not being used rather than ramming it through an area that's slated for development. A lot more sense."

Three other reporters called that afternoon. Two radio and one TV. He told them all basically the same thing he had told Harold Stewart from the *Toronto Star*.

As Carol drove toward the university after supper that night to meet with Bill and his committee, it became even clearer in her mind that the time had come to end her relationship with Gordon. She was totally opposed to just about everything he stood for. His opposition to the increasing number of immigrants moving to Toronto. This deep need he had to promote white values, customs and traditions.

This isn't the Gordon I married. He was never like this. Not even about the Quebec separatists. Something has changed and it's most definitely not for the better. I just can't see going on like this.

Some of the things he said on the *Toronto Focus* program were, as Fraser Deacon had said, out and out racist. Whatever reason he had for saying those things, she wanted no part of it. Or of him. She was going to tell him it was over between them at the very first opportunity. She wanted a divorce. *This isn't the way I'd expected things to turn out for us but, really, I can't see any other way. The sooner we get this over with the better.*

As she had seen Bill on *Toronto Focus* the night before, she had no difficulty recognizing him among the dozen or so people huddled around the coffee pot in Meeting Room 16. She walked right up to him and, with outstretched hand, said: "Hello, Dr. Eagletail. I'm Carol Winston."

His eyes sparkled a warm welcome. "Well," he said, holding her hand in a gentle, but firm, manner. "I'm glad you were able to come. Very glad. Can I get you a coffee?"

"No thanks. I can manage," she said as she fixed herself a coffee with no sugar.

She allowed him to pour the milk. "I'm not going to introduce you right away," he said. "I don't think they'd understand."

"Understand?" she asked with raised eyebrows. "Whatever do you mean?"

"About you being Gordon MacArthur's wife," he replied with a smile. "They wouldn't ..."

"How were you able to find that out?" she asked with surprise.

"It was simple. I just looked you up in the phone book. You're the only Carol Winston there."

"But how could you determine from that that I'm Gordon's wife? I don't understand."

"By the address. It says 'Winston, Carol, 48 Kennedy Circle.' I knew from trying to get more information about your husband in the staff directory that he also lived on Kennedy Circle. Forty-eight Kennedy Circle."

"I could have been a roomer."

"I had a hunch that you weren't."

"Well," she said with an amused smile. "Congratulations. So, we've got a Sherlock Holmes in the house. But, seriously, do you mind? About me being Gordon's wife?"

"Do you?"

"Sometimes."

"What about right now?"

"Right now, this white power business makes me wish that I wasn't. But that's another story. What about you? Do you mind?"

"Not at all. Life gets curiouser and curiouser. And more interesting. But I'm still wondering. Why the separate listings?"

"That was my father's idea. Right from the time I turned fourteen, he felt I should have my own phone. Or maybe it was that he should have the full use of his phone. The separate listing is just something I've held on to. It's part of my identity. As an individual."

"I get the idea that you like being Carol Winston."

"That's who I am."

"Okay. You'll be introduced to the others as Carol Winston. Just hold on."

He pushed back his shoulders and stuck out his jaw. "Friends. Friends. Could I have your attention please? Just for one moment."

The conversation around the coffee pot subsided. He had their attention. "I'd like to introduce Carol Winston. She was watching the television interview last night and phoned me after to say she wanted to support what we're doing."

Bill noted the questioning look on some of their faces. "Now, I know. I know. We've gone through this before. The question about involving white people in our affairs. And I'll admit I'm not all that certain myself about the best way to resolve it. But I would like to have Miss Winston sit in on our meeting tonight. She could be an observer. And then when ..."

"As an observer for who?" a strikingly-handsome young Indian wearing a smartly-tailored brown corduroy suit interjected. "This is no ping pong tournament that we're into. We're fighting for our survival. The survival of an entire race of people. This isn't something you can 'observe' from the sidelines. Let's move on to the discussion of the important matters before us tonight – without the presence of this outsider."

Carol hadn't anticipated anything like this. She looked questioningly at Bill. From the look in his eyes, she realized he wasn't going to impose his will on the meeting. She was on her own. And yet – and yet she got the feeling he wanted her to state her case.

"I didn't come here as an 'observer'. I came because I believe you need help," she started carefully. "You have neither the numbers nor the resources to guarantee your cultural survival without the understanding and support of, what you call, outsiders. I came here to help."

"So did the missionaries," the young man snapped. "That's what they said. They helped us all right. Helped bring about the virtual annihilation of an entire race of people. We've had as much of that kind of help as we can use. Too much. The last thing we need right now is a twentieth century missionary trying to save our souls. You'd be better off trying to save yourself."

She glanced at Bill and the others and got the distinct impression that none of them was going to say anything. The young man in the cords seemed to be speaking for them all. He was the one she'd have to deal with.

"That's why I'm here," she said.

Her remark threw him off balance. "What do you mean by that?" he asked. "Are you saying you're here to save yourself?"

"You could say I'm here out of pure self-interest. I make no apologies for that. I'm not here like some bleeding heart trying to 'help' native people. To try and save you. I'm here to help myself. To help my country. Yes, if you'd rather put it that way, to help the white, majority, community. Let me explain."

She paused for a moment and scanned the faces around her. She wanted them to understand where she was coming from.

"This country is plagued with racial and cultural tension. Tension looking around for somewhere to explode. If we don't do something about it now, we're going to have Detroit-style riots in our cities. It could be worse than Watts. If we're going to – you can use the word save ourselves if you want – if we're going to save ourselves from outbreaks of violence and decades of smouldering hatred and distrust, we're going to have to work with the people from the minority groups and help them and their children develop a better sense of self-worth.

"I believe that the reinforcement of minority group pride is absolutely essential to the healthy social and economic development of this country. Now, Dr. Eagletail, in the television interview last night, said Indian students have been dropping out of the school system at an alarming rate. He said Indian children have been put down for so long they don't know which side is up anymore. He said he was doing something to restore their pride in being Indian. And I say you can't accomplish what you've set out to do in a vacuum. You can't do it entirely on your own. You need help. That's why I'm here.

"It's in the best self-interest of the majority community to work with you and help build a more tolerant and sensitive society. A society that respects human worth. The worth of all humans. That's what I want to talk about tonight. Maybe you'd rather hold a memorial service for the sins of the past. But I want to address my mind and energies to the realizable potential of today and tomorrow. That's why I'm here."

They all nodded their heads in approval. So did the young man in the brown cords. "Okay, okay," he said with a friendly smile. "And I am glad that you're here. I'm sorry about putting you through the third degree like that but we've been disappointed so many times before. So many times by people who meant well but turned out to be no earthly good at all to us. We had to know where your head was at."

"You mean I was set up?" she asked, turning towards Bill.

"Sort of," Bill replied with a soft smile. "But you do understand. Don't you? We need all the help we can get, but it has to be from people who want to do something with us. Not for us. There's an important difference. But I think you've made it clear you'll be working with us, Carol. Providing the essential help we need and want."

"I'm glad I passed the test," Carol said. "And I don't mean that in a flippant way. I can appreciate why you'd all feel the way that you do. But you've got to understand that all whites are not one congealed mass. There's innumerable types and attitudes and philosophies. Just as I'm sure there are a myriad number of individual Indian attitudes. Even in families, you'll often find a pronounced difference of viewpoints."

"Speaking of families," Bill said, "I think it's time, now that we know where you stand, Carol, to let the rest know who you really are."

His remark generated considerable confusion among them. There was an exchange of questioning glances. Carol decided to take the initiative. "Perhaps you're right." She paused. There was total silence. "I am Carol Winston. My husband is Gordon MacArthur."

"MacArthur?" The collective murmur rippled like a shock wave. "How?" "Why?" "What?"

"I just finished telling you not all white people think alike. Even families are often divided on important issues. My husband has his views and I have mine. And I think it would be fairer of you to base your opinion of me on what I think and say. Not on what my husband happens to be thinking or saying at any particular moment. I'm not Gordon MacArthur. I am Carol Winston."

"But you're married to him," the young man in the cords said. "You're his wife. You've got to ..."

"I don't 'got to' do anything. Just because I'm married to the man is no reason why I should have to account for his opinions and actions. I can think and say whatever I want and act as I please. The only relevant question is this: are you willing to accept me for what I am or are you going to transfer all of your negative feelings about Gordon MacArthur onto me?"

Bill liked the way Carol handled herself. She was her own woman all right. Quite an exceptional one at that. And he could see from the looks on their faces that this impression was getting through to most of the others. They accepted her. They respected her. They wanted her.

"The lady asked a question," he said. "Do we accept her for who she is or do we treat her like she's her husband's pet poodle?"

"We accept her for what she is," the young man said. "I want her at the meeting. We need her. She'll bring a perspective to the problem none of us can provide." The others nodded their heads in agreement.

"Do you mean by that that I think white?" Carol asked.

"Sort of," Bill said softly. "Nothing personal. But white is what you are. I can't think white any more than you could think Indian. We're different. We've got different brain processes. Different bodily chemistry. Different perceptions. But, when you put those different perceptions together – in harness together – the Indian and the white – you get a winning combination. We could use your perspective on things, Carol."

All of a sudden, she felt the reality of their difference. She felt something of what it's like to be a lone Indian or a black in a room filled with white people. For the first time in her life, she felt what it was like to be different. To be in the minority. Bill was right. How could she possibly hope to think or feel or see like them? The difference, the centuries-in-the-making difference, was there. She could feel it. But she could also sense something of the hope that those differences could be bridged and that they could work together for a better country, a better society. She was glad she was there. And that they wanted her there.

When the meeting got going, the discussion centred on the situation at the university. They talked about the positive manner in which many young Indians were responding to the special studies courses they were taking by correspondence. Gordon's white-pride group also got quite a going over. The way the media had seized on it. The threat it posed to the special studies program. And then they got into a discussion about Jack Saunders' gas pipeline. Some way had to be found to counteract Gordon's influence on the outcome of the pipeline hearings. He was turning it into a national story. Whites freezing in the east because of the 'selfish' Indians in the west. A power play. Cultures in conflict. The media would lap it all up and lick the dish dry. There would probably be worse to come. Gordon and his council were just getting started. Now, with him certain to be the Conservative candidate for Meadowbrook, the situation was bound to get worse.

"Tell me about your mother," Carol asked Bill after the meeting as they had a cup of coffee together in the Davidson Lounge. "About your home. What was it like being at Big Thunder? What's your mother like?"

"Oh, she's quite a lady," Bill said. "Dad died earlier this year. Got a stroke in March while he was having breakfast and, less than five hours later, he was dead."

"Just like that?" Carol asked.

"Just like that. The doctors said the damage caused by the stroke was quite severe and there was nothing that could've been done to save him. I was on my way there in the plane at the time that he died. I was too late. Didn't get a chance to say goodbye."

"I'm so sorry, Bill. So sorry. My mom died of cancer just a little less than two years ago. December, 1972. I was there. It was important for me to be there so I know how bad you must have felt about not being there for your dad."

"It was tough," Bill said. "If I'd been at home at the time, it would've been different. A lot of things would've been different if I hadn't left Big Thunder."

They were quiet for a couple of minutes. Just sat there drinking their coffee.

"About your mother," Carol said. "Tell me about her."

"Mom's never been a hundred miles away from Big Thunder in her whole life. Most of her time's been spent at the ranch or around about there. We used to go off to the pow wows in the summer and Dad always liked to get over to the rodeos at Cochrane and places like that. But Mom usually didn't go with us. She just didn't like being any great distance away from home."

"Were they happy together?"

"Definitely. I know this sounds sort of corny, but I think they were happy together because they knew what it was like to be happy when they were apart. They both had a tremendous sense of themselves. There was no doubt in their minds about who they were. This, I guess you could call it inner strength, inner resource, gave them a larger-than-life dimension few people ever achieve. Like, they were two people who were quite capable of being happy apart, but, for some good reason, they preferred being together."

"I get the impression that when you refer to them being happy apart you don't mean with someone else. Like with another man or woman."

"Hell no. No. There was a commitment there. A special place they filled in each other's lives. A space neither one of them would ever want to share with anyone else. No, that's not what I meant about them being happy apart."

"I didn't think it was. They sound like quite a remarkable couple."

"Yeah. They were that. I've often talked about them with my brother and sister. We all agree they were two of the most special people in the whole world. There was something almost charismatic – like an aura – about them. You couldn't ask for better parents than my mom and my dad. I think you'd like her, Carol. She doesn't say much. But, I guess it's something like body language. She says a lot by her physical presence. Like, if my mom leaves the room, there's an emptiness there. It becomes cold without her warmth. You know what I mean? She's a truly radiant woman. She gives off a tremendous feeling of warmth. Like she was the sun."

Carol had never heard a full-grown man talk about his mother like that before. It was delightful to hear in his voice and see in his eyes how much he loved that mother of his.

"What effect will the pipeline have on her?" she asked.

"It's as bad as I said on television. The hens and the cows are at the barn. Mom has to go over there to gather the eggs and milk the cows. She's too old to be climbing over a ramp every time she has to go back and forth to the barn carrying eggs and milk. It's insane. Can you imagine what it'll be like when she tries to cross that ramp in the winter? With the snow and the ice all over it? She's going to fall and break her hip or something. I've got to stop that crazy pipeline!"

Carol remembered him saying something about his wife and child. "When you were on the TV program, you said, 'My wife and my son? Will you take them, too?' I take it from that that you're married."

"Sort of. I've been living apart from my wife for about three years. We're getting a divorce. My son's eight and I try and get back to see him as much as I can."

"Back where?"

"Big Thunder. It's sort of complicated."

"I'd like to hear about it. If you don't mind."

"Okay. My wife never did fit the academic scene. Never did accept this sort of life. The money I make teaching is not at all what she had in mind. She wanted something altogether different. And, I guess, she's getting it."

"From someone else?"

He chuckled and swallowed some more coffee. "From Ian Starlight. He built up a pretty big construction business in Calgary. I hear he's worth a couple of million or more. Works his ass off for it, too. She's with him in Calgary now and ..."

"Your son?"

"Albert's with my mom at Big Thunder for now. I'd like to bring him down here to live with me. But it's better for him to be with her until we get this divorce thing settled. It's all a bit mixed up right now."

"But – with you teaching at the university here – how could your wife and son wind up in Calgary?"

"I told you it was complicated," he replied with the same sly smile she'd seen on his face earlier that evening. "I was working on a book and decided it would be a good idea to spend the summer back at Big Thunder. To get my boy in touch with his roots. His land and his people. Ian's folks live up the road from my mom and, one fine sunny afternoon in July, he pulled up in front of our place with his powder-blue Cadillac convertible and that was it. Jean, my wife, took one look and saw, like it was a vision from God, exactly what she'd been looking for all her life. The Cadillac, the $200 silk suit, the $5 cigar and Ian Starlight. Got to admit, he's a stylish looking son of a bitch."

"Okay, but you said your son was living at Big Thunder. With your mother. Why not with your wife in Calgary?"

"That's mainly because of the school thing. Indian Affairs covers all the costs of schooling for our kids living on the reserves. The Calgary School Board, because we don't live there and pay taxes, won't accept our kids. Neither Jean nor I pay taxes in Calgary."

"No, but I suppose this Ian Starlight does."

"Yes, he does. But he and Jean are just living together. If they got married, Albert could go to school in Calgary but, it would be over my dead body. I'll never agree to Albert living with them. Anyway, Albert's at the school on the reserve. Same one I went to. I didn't realize until I was back there for a couple of months this summer how upset he was at us living apart like this. Him at Big Thunder and me here in Toronto. My mom and I got talking and she told me that, about a year after I left him out there so I could get the North American Indian Studies program up and running, he told her that he wished I was killed by a truck."

"Killed by a truck?" Carol exclaimed.

"Yeah. They were having lunch. Just the two of them. Albert just looked down at his soup and muttered something about wishing that I was dead. Mom decided not to press him at that point. But then, about two weeks later, he said it again. 'I wish he was dead,' he said. 'I wish someone would run him over with a truck.' That time, my mom decided she should deal with it on the spot. Find out why he wanted me dead."

"Oh, my God!" Carol exclaimed. "That must have been rough. I can only imagine what it must have felt like hearing about that from your mom."

"It was rough all right. Anyway, Mom asked him why he would say something as horrible as that. 'Your dad loves you, Albert. Why would you want him to be dead?'

"And then, she says, he just started to cry. Just sat there with tears running down his cheeks and said, 'Because then I wouldn't have to worry about him all the time. If he was dead, I wouldn't have to worry about him all the way out there in Toronto. I wouldn't have to worry anymore.'

"Isn't that beautiful, Carol? He was worrying about me all the time and he figured, if I got hit by a truck, he wouldn't have to worry about me anymore. Mom just grabbed him, and hugged him, and told him how very much she loved him. And that I loved him. We all loved him. And he was okay after that."

"I'd hate to have to go through something like that with Charlie," Carol said. "To actually have him wish that I was dead."

"Tough all right. But Albert's okay with it now. He knows we're going to be together soon."

"In Toronto?"

"Not necessarily. There's a very progressive new Chairman of Sociology at the University of Calgary. He wants me to replicate the North American Indian Studies program at the U of C. Like, right now, all our Indian students take the course by correspondence. There's no meaningful interaction. However, there's a growing, although still quite small, number of Indian students enrolling at the University of Calgary. He figures that, if we replicate the program there, we can attract students from Saskatchewan, B.C. and, even, Manitoba. Indian Affairs would cover their fees and residence. We could find ourselves with more than a thousand Indian students taking our course at the U of C. I think it could work, a lot better than the situation we have now.

"Dr. McArchibald, my boss at U of T, is okay with it. North American Indian Studies would still be part of the Sociology program here. The two professors who helped me start it up would do the actual teaching but we would move the correspondence course to Calgary. That's fine with Dr. McArchibald because we actually lose a considerable amount of money with the correspondence program. Simply doesn't pay for itself.

"If I take the offer, which will pay a lot more than I'm getting now, I could live at Big Thunder and commute. But I think I'd probably wind up buying a house in Calgary. We could spend the weekends at Big Thunder. Anyway, I haven't decided about that yet. I don't have to let him know until the end of November."

"From what you're telling me, I think you'd prefer that you were both out there," Carol said. "Back at Big Thunder."

"Yes, that is what I would prefer. Albert really likes it out there. He's living with my mom for now. My sister's nearby and she's got two kids around his age and they get on really well together. My Grandma and Grandfather on my mom's side are still there and they spend a lot of time with him, too. Albert's doing real well at Big Thunder. He's settled in at the school out there and moving him here wouldn't be a good idea. I haven't told him about the offer from the University of Calgary yet. Either way, we are definitely going to be together again. I really miss him."

"Is Albert's mother from your community? From Big Thunder?"

"No. She's a Weasel Fat. From the Blood Tribe reserve down at Standoff, just south of Fort Macleod. Near the American border."

"Weasel Fat? How would she get a name like that?"

Bill smiled. "Sounds kinda weird, doesn't it? It's a common name down there. The chief right now is Harry White Quills. My Aunt Doreen's married name is Many Fingers. And there's Bull Calf, Tail Feathers, Weasel Head. All sorts of names like that. Anyway, Jean's a Weasel Fat. I met her at a pow wow down there. Just after I finished the first year of my PhD at Berkeley. She was working with her mother at the laundry in the hospital."

"And I take it that you didn't have to get married."

"I wanted to get married – wanted to very much. I was crazy about her."

Carol decided not to pursue that line of conversation.

"I was wondering," she said, "about the North American Indian Studies program. How did that get started?"

He told her about the Hopi woman in California who was so embarrassed every time she saw Indian people dancing at the pow wows on TV and about the old man from Big Thunder at the pow wow on Manitoulin Island who danced with Albert.

"That's when I decided that we needed a special program to present all that is good about the Indian experience. To provide an opportunity for our people to learn about our culture and traditions. To instill a sense of pride in being Indian."

As she listened to Bill talking about the special studies program, Carol experienced a growing awareness of how strongly attracted to him she was. He was so together. He exuded self-confidence, self-reliance, self-esteem. He was a singularly special man. And he was so committed to his work. So dedicated. Not in any starry-eyed-idealist sense. But in a pragmatic, down-to-earth, sensible – yes, sensible, manner that was having a positive influence on the lives of the young Indian students he came in contact with.

He was such a refreshing contrast to Gordon. He had a presence, an air of assurance, that Gordon would never possess. Could never possess. Bill's strength was entirely his own. It wasn't a reflected glory like Gordon's. Gordon relied so heavily on his position at the university, his connections within the Conservative Party of Canada and his tartan ties for his identity. His status was a reflection of the status of those he associated with. Bill's came entirely from within. He seemed to have so many of the characteristics that he had described his mother and father as having.

Carol was fascinated with the things he told her about the Indian people. A shiver actually ran down her spine when he told her about his son doing the prairie dance with the old man from Big Thunder. They really were people from a different world. They had an altogether different way of living from what she was accustomed to. And yet, Bill did seem comfortable in both worlds. He seemed to be a blend of the best of both of them.

Bill ordered more coffee for them both. "Enough of that. Tell me about you and the white power Conservative."

"That's as good a way as any to describe him. And, to be perfectly frank about it, I find some of the things he says to be completely unacceptable. In fact, I'm ashamed to be his wife. I'm going to get a divorce. End it all."

"Does he know that?"

"No, but he will soon enough. It's time to end things, to get on with the rest of my life. I've been thinking about it for quite some time – for a couple of years actually. This white power nonsense has accelerated things. Brought them to the point of no return."

So, Bill thought to himself, *This is interesting. She's had enough of the white power nut. Going to divorce him. She's a very, very, attractive woman. This could get interesting. Quite interesting indeed.*

"You said you're a lawyer," Bill said. "What area do you specialize in?"

"Corporate law, but, I've been out of the game for about four years now."

She told him about being with Haldimand and Brock and how things got derailed after she got pregnant with Diane.

"Four years is a long time," Bill said. "What's stopping you from going back?"

"Me, I guess. I just haven't been able to will myself back to that life. Guess I've been sitting around feeling sorry for myself."

"Strikes me that's one helluva waste of talent. You've got a good mind. Speak well. Got a lot to offer. If I were you, I'd start living again. Life's too short to waste any of it."

She sipped her coffee and reflected on what he had just said. *He's right, you know. Life is too short not to be getting the best out of each and every day. Like back when I was at H and B. I was just loving it. Every day was a new challenge. Back when I was alive.*

"You're probably right. Maybe it is time to pull myself together and get back into the fray of things. To feel alive again."

"I'll drink to that," Bill said, raising his coffee mug. "I'll drink to that."

Carol clinked her mug against his. "Yes. Let's drink to that."

"Now, my learned friend," Bill said, "let's get back to Big Thunder. You did say you'd be prepared to offer some assistance with some of the legal issues. Is that still on?"

"Absolutely. I would be delighted to provide whatever help I can in that regard. As a first step, I suggest that you let me review whatever files you have on the matter. I'll go over them and see if I can spot something that could work to your advantage at the Energy Board hearings. Something you might have missed."

"I'd really appreciate that, Carol. Two heads are better than one. And, with your legal training, you'd probably pick up on things that I have missed."

"That's settled then. Where do you keep the Big Thunder file?"

"At my house. It's not much of a file. My dad was working on it when he died and most of the material is out at Big Thunder. But I've got a few of the documents at my house."

"Then, I'll come to your house. How about Monday night? I've got a few things to do this weekend but I'll be free Monday night."

"Sounds good. After supper?" *Maybe I should offer to cook dinner for her. Then, again, maybe not. Better to keep it strictly business. For now anyway.*

"Yes. Around seven-thirty would work best for me."

"Good. I'm at 15 Sussex Avenue. That's just about five or six houses west of St. George. You've got my number in case there's any change in plans."

"There won't be. I'll be there."

They finished their coffee and headed their separate ways.

CHAPTER
- 18 -

Gordon climbed out of his bed on the third floor Saturday morning and went to the bathroom to have his shower. After the shower, he put on a pair of jeans and a sweater and went to the front porch to get the *Globe and Mail.* There was a story about Big Thunder on the front page. It said the *Globe* had obtained Xerox copies of documents showing that the Saunders gas pipeline was supposed to have gone through the land on the northern border of Big Thunder Bill had talked about on *Toronto Focus.*

> Lawyers representing the company that owns the 1,000 acre property on the northern border of the reserve are said to have refused permission to let the pipeline run though the property.
>
> At the time that the Saunders Energy Corporation made its big gas discovery, the property in question was owned by a German syndicate that planned to develop a major commercial/residential project.
>
> However, the syndicate went bankrupt and the property was purchased in trust for an unnamed developer believed to be based in Ontario.
>
> As of press time, the *Globe* investigative team was unable to identify the owner of the property.
>
> "It was because of the refusal to let the pipeline go through that property," a former employee of the Saunders Energy Corporation told *The Globe* in a sworn affi-

davit, "that we had to go through the Indians' land which lies immediately south of the property. There's no other reason to go through Big Thunder."

The Saunders Energy Corporation documents clearly establish that the route through the area that is zoned commercial/residential is the most logical way to go. They also show that the Big Thunder route will require at least another 12 miles of pipeline.

"Going through Big Thunder, from an engineering standpoint, makes no sense at all," the former employee, who is a professional engineer, said. "There's no reason to destroy the Indians' land."

The documents uncovered by a *Globe* investigative team are expected to be introduced at the Energy Resources Conservation Board of Alberta hearing on Tuesday. Lawyers representing the Indians said the new evidence will probably save their land. (See picture A10)

Gordon turned to the tenth page of the first section of the newspaper. There was a picture of Sarah forking hay to her calves. There was no story. Just a cutline about the threat Saunders' pipeline posed to her property. *So, that's Eagletail's mother. Looks to be about the same age as Mum. She's his problem. Not mine.*

Gordon's grandfather had some calves like that at his small hill farm in the north of Scotland. He let Gordon help him feed them one night and one of them spilled the bucket of milk all over Gordon's new trousers.

There seems to be more to this Big Thunder business than I first thought. Still, there's nothing in the paper to get particularly worked up about. So they don't particularly want to have a gas pipeline running through that other property. So what? It still makes more sense to go through land that's not being used — to go through Big Thunder.

He went through to the kitchen and poured himself a cup of coffee. Carol had taken Charlie to his swimming lessons and Diane went with them. He returned to the living room, picked up the copy of the *Globe* and settled back into the plush comfort of the sofa. He put his feet up on the coffee table and carried on with the enjoyment of his morning coffee and the newspaper. The business section had devoted a full half page to the text of a speech the Chairman of the Economic Council of Canada delivered to the Empire Club in Calgary that week.

They'll probably give my speech the same treatment when I go out there. Wait until Carol sees that. That'll make her think twice about who and what I am. Everything's coming up roses, like Mama Rose used to say to Gypsy.

The phone rang. It was Dave Saunders' secretary saying he had to make an unexpected trip out to Calgary. He wanted to know if Gordon could have lunch with him at the Harbour Castle Hotel on Wednesday. Same time. Same suite. Gordon told her he could make it. As he put the phone back on the hook, he had a pretty good idea what had prompted Saunders' sudden trip to Calgary. *All hell will break loose now that that former employee of theirs has decided to spill all that he knows to the newspapers. The shit's going to hit the fan. Big time. Maybe we're not going to be out demonstrating on the streets after all.*

Carol reflected on what Bill had said about pulling herself together and getting back to practising law at Haldimand and Brock as she watched Charlie swimming confidently in the deep end of the pool. It had been a long time. Four years. *Maybe I could go back. Should go back. Start living again. This Big Thunder stuff is interesting and I will give Bill all the help I can with it. But, it's nothing compared to the challenge presented by the Gothic Gold Corp. case. Nothing compared to locking horns with Jack Goodman and his team from Gerstein and Sniderman. Nothing like trading blows with a top-ranked team like that and winning. We would have won that case if I'd been able to take it all the way through to the end. Not lost it like H and B did because of the inadequate job Bruce Kelly did as lead counsel. I would have won.*

"Hey!" Diane shouted. "Stop that."

Charlie had splashed them both as he cruised by on his way to the shallow end.

"I'll get you for that," Carol called out good-naturedly as she wiped her face with the towel. "Just wait till I get my hands on you."

Charlie laughed and waved to them both. As she dried Diane's face and arms with the thick terry cloth towel, Carol's thoughts turned to Gordon. *It is time. Time to end this foolishness. Time to get on with my life without Mr. Rule Britannia. What's got into him lately is beyond me. I just can't understand how he could have become so twisted – almost hateful – in his attitude towards the immigrant groups. And this nonsense about setting up special studies courses for the white students. And now his group is supporting Jack Saunders' plans to ram that pipeline through the Indians' land. The article in the* Globe *did say that the Equal Opportunities Council was opposed to the Indians' position on the matter. Why on earth would they get themselves involved in an issue like that? What's that got to do with them?*

Charlie's lesson was over and he was heading to the change room to get back into his street clothes. "I'll meet you at the front door," he called out to Carol.

As she drove them back to the house, Carol's thoughts turned to the effect divorcing Gordon might have on Charlie and Diane. She thought about Albert wishing that Bill was dead. *Certainly don't want it to be anything like that for Charlie and Diane. Going to have to handle it in a way that will keep the trauma of it all to an absolute minimum. It will be traumatic. Divorce always is. It's always the kids who pay the highest price. Like Albert out there at Big Thunder. Missing Bill so much he wished he was dead. Got to make sure nothing like that happens to Charlie and Diane. Everything will have to be done in a way that puts their interests front and centre. Have to make sure they get through this messy business with as little trauma and emotional damage as possible.*

Her thoughts turned to the prospect of going back to work at Haldimand and Brock. *I'll have a lot of catching up to do. Four years' worth. Still, it will be good to get back into the swing of things. To have something to look forward to every morning. Maybe I should call Jonathan next week and tell him I'm ready to go back to work. I could bring Anne on full-time until Diane's ready for regular school. Just another two years at Montessori. Anne could have the apartment on the third floor. But, Gordon's up there. At least for now he is. Since we're going to get a divorce, he might as well move out now. Get it over with. That will free up the third floor for Anne. It makes sense that he should be the one to move. After all, I was born there. There's no reason why I should be the one to leave. He can visit Charlie and Diane on the weekends. Or, better still, they can spend time with him at his place. Wherever that is. That way, I won't have to put up with any more of his Rule Britannia view of the world. It's from Henderson he got all that stuff. Henderson's as bigoted as they come. Mind you, Gordon's a close second on that score. Can't believe some of that stuff he comes out with about the Indians and the immigrant communities.*

After she made lunch for Charlie and Diane, Carol read the article in the *Globe* about the engineer saying it made more sense to run Jack Saunders' gas pipeline through the property on the northern border of Big Thunder. *That figures,* she said to herself. *The only reason they're ramming that pipeline through Bill's mother's barnyard is because it's a helluva lot cheaper than using the most logical route.*

Gordon was in his study going over some papers.

"Did you read the article in the *Globe* this morning about Jack Saunders' pipeline?" she asked.

"Yeah. I read it."

"Well? Don't you see now that there is no valid reason to run that pipeline through the Indians' land?"

"Not really. Still makes a lot more sense to me to run it through land that's not being used."

"Not being used? There's people living there. That's their land. They've lived there for thousands of years."

"Oh, come off it, Carol. It makes no sense at all to run the pipeline through the new development they're planning. Not when it's a lot less disruptive to run it through the reservation. All they're asking for, for God's sake, is an easement. Probably not much wider than the length of our living room. There's more than enough room on the Indians' land for that pipeline."

"This discussion is pointless," she said in an irritated manner. "Like I said, you're on the wrong side on this one, Gordon, and you're just too full of yourself to admit it. You —oh, never mind."

She was just about to tell him she wanted a divorce. Wanted him out of her father's house. *If I tell him about it now, he'll go on about it all weekend. That's all he will be talking about. 'Why?' 'Why now?' 'Why today?' Probably better to wait until breakfast Monday morning. That way I can get it over and done with and then drive Charlie and Diane to school. Yeah. That is the best way to go about it.*

"I what?" Gordon asked.

"Forget it. There's no getting through to you. Your mind's sealed tight like a drum on Big Thunder, the immigrants, the blacks and the Indians and just about everything else that doesn't fit into your twisted view on life. There's no point in talking to you, Gordon. Absolutely no point."

"Might be if you had something useful to say," he said. "Might be if you didn't have such a Pollyanna view of the Indians. Might be if you didn't let their so-called rights blind you to the fact that Charlie and Diane might very well freeze in the dark a couple of years from now if we don't get that Alberta gas down here where it's needed."

"Good God! Now I've heard everything. Does Saunders write all of your material? Next thing you know, you'll be operating out of his PR department. Don't even try to pull the white children freezing in the dark stunt with me, Gordon. It just doesn't wash. Like Dr. Eagletail said on the TV program, that's just a smokescreen. Scare tactics. And you know it. There's another way to get the Alberta gas down to the east. It does not have to go through the Indians' land. Whites freezing in the dark, my ass."

"Doesn't change the fact that's the most logical way to go. Through the Indians' land."

"That's it. Enough. I'm not going to continue this ridiculous discussion with you. Do what you want. I don't really care either way. Screw you, Gordon, you're in a class of your own."

And then she headed back to the kitchen.

"Where you off to now?" he asked.

"We're going to Sherway Gardens. Charlie needs a new windbreaker and Diane's shoes are too small for her. We'll be back in a couple of hours."

Martha's gout was really acting up that day. Her foot was so painful she almost cried. Couldn't bear to stand on it. She'd had the gout for about two years and it was getting progressively worse.

As she sat in her chair looking out the window at the autumn leaves that had turned from green to red and gold, she wrestled with the question of what to do about Gordon and Bill. *What did he have to come to Toronto for? If he'd stayed out there at Big Thunder, we wouldn't be having this problem. And why now? Why now when everything's going so well for Gordon? He's going to be an MP. He'll be in the cabinet. Honourable Gordon MacArthur, P.C., M.P. Not if they find out he's half Indian he won't. Not if they find out his mother – his biological mother – was a Blackfoot Indian they won't. Prime Minister Floyd's not going to have a half-breed sitting at his cabinet table. Not by a long shot, he won't. Oh, Gordon Son, the timing is all so wrong. This is something you should have been told about when you were a wee boy. Not now when you're going to be a cabinet minister.*

She reached for her cane to ease the weight on her right foot and hobbled over to the kitchen to make a fresh pot of tea. When the tea was ready, she sat down at the kitchen table, put her right leg up on one of the chairs, and poured herself a cup. Then she turned her mind back to the problem of what to do about Gordon and his brother.

Martha liked Sarah. Liked her a lot. Despite the fact she'd only been at the ranch for a week, Sarah had made quite an impression on her. And Richard wasn't too bad either. She found him a bit reserved. Not as welcoming as Sarah. But there was nothing about him to dislike. Not as far as she was concerned.

Still, Tom was adamant that there was no good reason to have anything to do with the Eagletails or with Big Thunder. Especially not with Bill being killed in Hong Kong and Richard refusing to fight Hitler.

And then there was the letter Sarah sent saying they weren't going to say a word to William, Martha said to herself as she reached for the pot and poured herself another cup of tea. *That's the way we left it. Never did tell him. Never did tell Gordon he had a brother. A brother who's now living in Toronto and was on the TV with him. We should have told him. He shouldn't be learning this now. Not at this late stage. Not when he's going to be elected as an MP and sit at the cabinet table. We should've told him.*

The phone rang. It was Gordon reminding her about the nomination meeting coming up on Thursday night.

"I do so very much want you to be there, Mum. It's going to be a big night for me. We're expecting quite a turnout."

"I'd love to be there, Son. Wouldn't miss it for anything."

"Good. I won't be able to pick you up but I will arrange to have someone get you there. I'll let you know later who that'll be."

"That will be fine, Son. I'll wait for your call."

"Good. Got to run now. Just wanted to make sure you hadn't forgotten about it. I'm really looking forward to it, Mum. There's no one running against me. I will win. And, as things stand now, I'll have no problem winning the election. The Conservatives are really strong in Meadowbrook. Then, pretty soon after the election – at least as Henry Bracken sees it – I'm going to be in the cabinet. Maybe Defence, or Foreign Affairs or something big like that. I'm on my way, Mum. Fasten your seatbelt, it's going to be a great ride. Now, I've got to go. Got some things to get done. Sorry, but I'm up to my eyeballs in things and there's just not enough time to get them all done."

"All right, Son. You do what it is you have to do and I'll see you Thursday night. At your nomination meeting. Take care, Gordon. I love you, my son."

As she put the phone back on the hook, Martha reflected on how excited Gordon sounded on the phone. *He wants so much to be an MP and to be in the cabinet. So much. So very, very, much. William showing up here like this couldn't have come at a worst time. This is going to ruin everything. Finding out he has a brother who's Blackfoot. That his biological mother was Blackfoot. The timing is just so terribly wrong.*

She grabbed her cane, hobbled through to her bedroom, kneeled down beside her bed and asked Jesus what she should do. *Guide me, Lord. Show me with your divine wisdom what I should do now. Reveal unto me the path that I should follow.*

Carol got Charlie his new windbreaker and new shoes for Diane and got them both a banana split at the Dairy Queen. As they ate their splits at a table in the Food Court, she went to a pay phone from which she could keep an eye on them and phoned Bill at his apartment. She wanted to talk to him about the article in the *Globe* about the engineer saying the pipeline wasn't supposed to go through Big Thunder in the first place.

Bill wasn't home. The answering service said he was away for the weekend and there was no phone where he was. If it was an emergency, the lady on the other end of the line said, he could be reached through the local marina.

"No, it's not an emergency," Carol said. "But, thanks anyway."

As she put the phone down, she wondered where Bill might be. *She mentioned a marina. Maybe he's at some cottage for the weekend. With someone? He says he's getting a divorce from his wife. Maybe he does have someone in his life. Wonder if she's Indian, too.*

Charlie and Diane had finished their banana splits. "Okay, you two, time to go home. Let's go."

Gordon was still marking essays in his study when they got home. Charlie and Diane went to the family room to watch TV. Carol fixed herself a Scotch and soda and moved to the armchair beside the fireplace to read Nikos Kazantrakis' *Zorba the Greek*. She'd seen the movie when it first came out in 1965 with Anthony Quinn giving the performance of his life as Alexis Zorba, the middle-aged Greek peasant with an extraordinary lust for life, and Alan Bates playing the uptight English writer.

She remembered how captivated she had been watching Zorba teach the young writer how to dance the Sirtaki at the end of the film. Anthony Quinn broke into a deep throaty laugh as they danced on the sand to the sensuous music of Mikis Theodrakis with the waves kissing the shore. Bill reminded her a bit of Anthony Quinn. He had that same earthy, vibrant, quality. She imagined him dancing the Sirtaki on the beach of a sun-drenched island in the Aegian Sea.

Bill was alone at a cabin on Lake Muskoka, about half an hour west of downtown Bracebridge. It belonged to an engineer friend of his who was working on a project in Texas.

As he sat at the table writing in longhand about the Canadian government's appalling track record in honouring its obligations under the treaties the chiefs signed in the late 1800s, his thoughts turned to Carol. He liked her. Liked her a lot. Still, she was white. He didn't want to have a repeat of the sorry experience he'd had with Sally Hurst. *And yet, she's not at all like Sally. Not nearly as self-centred and empty-headed. Carol has twice the intelligence Sally has. And, when she was speaking to the folks at the meeting, she showed a pretty solid grasp of relations between the whites and the Indians. With lots of good ideas about what needs to be done to improve the situation. No, she's not like Sally. Not at all like Sally. Sally was ashamed to be seen with me in public.*

He went over to the kitchen area to make himself a fresh pot of tea. As he waited for the kettle to boil, he thought about what Carol had said about getting a divorce from Gordon. *From the sounds of it, that marriage's been dead for quite some time now. No life left in it. Just like me and Jean. Wonder when she's going to tell him it's over? Fini. Dead as a dodo.*

He was glad Carol was coming to his house Monday night to go over the Big Thunder documents. Her experience as a lawyer could come in quite useful. Like she said, she'd probably notice something in the documents and background material that would have escaped his untrained eye. On top of that, it would be nice to get to know her a bit better. *She's quite the lady.*

He hadn't seen the article in the *Globe* that morning quoting the engineer who said the pipeline was originally supposed to go through the other property. Bill made a point of avoiding the newspapers and the news on the radio and TV when he was away at the cabin.

After about another hour working on his book, he went down to the dock, got into the boat, and headed to the windward side of the island, about a quarter mile out in the bay, to catch a couple of fish for his supper.

Anne was off until Monday morning and Carol didn't feel like cooking that night. She went through to the family room and asked Charlie and Diane if they'd like to go to the Pirates' Cove for dinner.

"Can we have lobster?" Charlie asked.

"Sure you can have lobster. That's their specialty. Anything you want."

"Me, too," Diane said. "I want lobster, too, and apple pie and ice cream."

"You've got a deal," Carol said. "Lobster and apple pie and ice cream. Now, both of you, wash your hands and get your jackets on. It's pretty cold tonight."

As Charlie and Diane left to wash up and get into their jackets, Carol went to the door of Gordon's study.

"We're going to the Pirates' Cove. Want to come?"

"No, thanks. I've still got quite a bit of work to clear up here. I'll make an omelette later on."

"Your choice. See you later." With that, she pulled on her windbreaker and waited for the children.

The Pirates' Cove was quite full but they managed to get a table for four by the window. As she watched Charlie and Diane pry the meat out of the lobsters with their forks, she reflected on the fact that she hadn't been much of a mother to them. Especially over the last four years. Since she got Diane.

It's not her fault I got pregnant. But I have held it against her. I've never hugged and kissed her the way I used to Charlie. She must feel it. Feel that I don't love her. That I resent her. And yet, I do. If it wasn't for her, I wouldn't have lost the Gothic Gold Corp. case. I'd still be at H and B making a mark for myself. Arguing cases before the Supreme Court. Still, why blame Diane? Why hold her responsible for that? It's Gordon who refused to use the goddamned condom.

Diane had spilled some butter from the lobster on her white T-shirt. "Let me get that," Carol said gently as she dipped a napkin into the water in her glass and started to dab the stain.

"I'm sorry, Mommy," Diane said contritely. "Really I am. Didn't mean to do it."

"That's all right, darling. It's not your fault. Not your fault at all."

And then she caressed Diane's cheek with her hand, pulled her towards her, and gave her a great big hug.

"Not your fault at all," she said as she kissed Diane on the forehead. "These things happen. That's all. Don't you worry about it. Not at all."

Diane liked having her mom hug her and kiss her. She'd hardly ever done that before.

After they finished off the lobsters, Carol ordered apple pie and ice cream for the children and a fresh fruit salad for herself. As she watched them eat, she wondered again how the divorce was going to affect them. It was bound to be traumatic. Always is. Not having Gordon living with them anymore. Visiting him on the weekends. Maybe taking in a movie or a hockey game and then having him leave them at the door before heading home to his own place. *Must be careful about this. Can't let them go through the pain Bill's Albert had to go through. That was awful. Wishing someone would run him over with a truck. Poor kid. Must have been ripping him apart. He's going to be glad to have his dad back if Bill takes that job with the University of Calgary. Then again, Bill might very well decide to stay here. Bring Albert to Toronto. He clearly loves Albert very much and seems determined they're going to be together again. One place or the other.*

CHAPTER

- 19 -

Gordon was reading the *Sunday Star* at the kitchen table. Carol was making pancakes. There was nothing about Big Thunder or the Equal Opportunities Council in the paper.

Charlie and Diane came into the room. "Hi, Mom," Charlie said. "We having pancakes?"

"You bet we are. Be ready in about five minutes."

Diane walked up behind her mom and put her arms around her waist. "'Morning, Mommy. I like pancakes."

"I know you do, darling," Carol said as she turned around and gave Diane a hug and a kiss. "Have your bran flakes. The pancakes won't be long."

That was nice, Diane thought. *Two hugs and two kisses in two days. Maybe Mommy likes me after all.*

After breakfast, Carol asked the children if they would like to go for a walk in the valley. It was a beautiful, sunny, morning, and she felt like getting some exercise and fresh air. They would.

"You want to come with us, Gordon?" Carol asked.

"No thanks. I'm really behind on the student essays and, with the nomination meeting coming up Thursday night, I've got a lot to get out of the way."

Carol and the children walked to the back of the garden and descended the wooden steps to the valley. As she watched them tossing the beach ball back and forth, Carol thought back on the afternoon when she'd tossed pebbles across the river after Dr. Turner told her she was pregnant with Charlie. She was glad she'd decided to keep him. Not to have an abortion or put him up for adoption. She'd really enjoyed having him in her life. Up until she got pregnant with Diane.

I've been just as unloving of him as I've been with Diane. We used to have such good times together. And then, I shut him out of my life. Just like I did Diane. Wonder what he thinks of me? Probably asks himself why. Why I don't hug him or kiss him as much as I used to. Why I seem to accept him more than love him. But I do love him. Love him a lot. Just that I haven't shown it lately. Lately? It's been four years, Carol. Four years for a little boy to wonder why his Mommy doesn't love him anymore.

"Hey, you two. Let me in on this," she called out. "Throw me the ball."

Charlie threw the ball over to her and she tried to dribble on the grass. Didn't work. The grass was too soft. She tossed the ball over to Diane.

After about five minutes tossing the ball around, they sat on a big rock on the bank and tossed pebbles across the water. Diane wasn't having much luck.

"Hold it like this," Carol said as she placed the flat pebble between Diane's index finger and her thumb, "and then just aim it on the top of the water. Not into the water. Just on top of it."

Diane gave it a try and the pebble skipped three times, almost to the middle of the river.

"That's my good girl," Carol said. "Now you've got it."

Diane was quite pleased with herself. She'd never made a pebble skip before. *Mommy said I did that real good. She's proud of me.*

They went for a long walk along the riverbank, all the way down to the railway bridge. There was a freight train making its way slowly across the bridge with a large number of boxcars headed for western Canada.

As they walked back towards the house, Charlie holding her one hand and Diane the other, Carol asked them if they'd like to go out for lunch.

"We could go to China King and have the buffet," she said. "You can have Chinese, chicken, seafood, anything you want."

"And apple pie and ice cream, too," Diane said. "I really like apple pie and ice cream."

"I know you do, darling. And that's just what you're going to have."

"Can Dad come with us?" Charlie asked. "He likes Chinese food."

"Sure he can," Carol said. "I'll ask him the moment we walk in the door."

Actually, Carol did not want Gordon to come with them. She was enjoying her time with Charlie and Diane. It had been fun being with them in the valley. Tossing the ball and the pebbles. Holding their hands as they walked together along the path. If Gordon came with them, he'd probably start talking about Big Thunder or the immigrants again. *I don't need that. Not now that I'm so enjoying being with Charlie and Diane. Not now when I'm catching up on all the things I've not done with them. Being their mom for a change. A much-needed change. Gordon being there would spoil all that.*

"We're going to the China King for lunch," she told him when they got back to the house. "Want to come with us?"

"I'd love to," he said. "But Henry Bracken called. I'm having lunch with him and some of the people from the Meadowbrook executive. We're going to talk about the nomination meeting and getting the campaign office up and running."

"Oh, I see. Well, I know how important that is to you. Will you be back in time for supper?"

"Yes. I'll probably be back before six."

"The children will be pretty filled up by the time they get through the China King buffet. I'm just going to make some sandwiches for supper. And maybe heat up some soup."

"Sounds good. I'll be having a good lunch with Henry and the others so soup and a sandwich sounds just right."

Actually, Gordon wasn't going to meet with Bracken and the executive. He'd gotten quite bored marking the student essays and phoned Ruth Applebaum to see if she was home. She was. He told her he'd be at her apartment around one thirty.

Ruth seemed a bit pensive as she lay naked beside Gordon on her waterbed later that afternoon.

"Something on your mind?" he asked. "You seem different today."

She turned towards him and leaned on her left arm. "That stuff in the paper. About the Indians and the immigrants. Do you really mean all that?"

"What do you mean by 'really mean'?"

"Well, like that pipeline. I thought Dr. Eagletail made a lot of sense on the TV when he said there was no need to disrupt his mother's life like that. That there are other ways to get the gas down here. And then, in the *Globe* yesterday morning, there was that engineer saying the pipeline was supposed to go through some other way but it was too expensive to do that so they were shoving it through his mother's barnyard."

Gordon repeated what he had told Carol when they had argued about the Big Thunder issue.

"It just makes more sense to go through land that's not being used," he said. "The Indians will get paid for the tiny easement Saunders wants for the pipeline. No one's taking their land for free. They'll get paid. Market value. Maybe even better than that."

Ruth decided to drop the Big Thunder matter for now. She'd never had an argument with Gordon before and didn't want to get into one now. "Okay, but what about those things you said about the immigrants? About them sprouting up in turbans all over neighborhoods that used to have nothing but white people in them. That's what they quoted you as saying in the *Globe* Friday morning. You said there was too many of them."

"Yeah," he said rather firmly, "and there is. Altogether too many of them. That's a fact, Ruth. I'm not making this up. There's all sorts of neighborhoods that used to have nothing but British people living in them and now they're all filled with Italians, and Greeks, and Portuguese and God knows what else. They're taking over the whole city. One block at a time. One neighborhood at a time. Swarming all over the whole place. Like bees. That's what they are. Swarming like bees."

Ruth was quite taken aback. He really didn't like immigrant people. What he told the newspaper reporter was no exaggeration. He really did think there were too many of them. *Does he feel the same way about Jews? That there's too many of us?*

She decided not to raise the issue of her being Jewish. "Want a glass of wine? I've got a nice Riesling in the fridge."

"Yeah, that would be good. I'd like a glass of wine."

She went to the kitchen and brought back the chilled bottle of Riesling and a couple of wine goblets. They drank for a few minutes without saying anything. Ruth was still going over in her head the things he'd said about the Greeks, and the Italians and the Portuguese. He'd never said anything like that to her before. And then she wondered if it was because she was Jewish that he hadn't said anything lately about divorcing Carol or, at least, getting a separation agreement.

"You still want to marry me, don't you?" she asked, a bit tentatively.

Actually, he didn't. She was great in bed but he couldn't picture being married to her. She had nothing approaching Carol's intelligence or beauty. And now, with the nomination meeting coming up and it being pretty certain that he would be elected and probably make it to cabinet, she could prove to be a liability he could very well do without. *"Candidate in adulterous relationship with student." That'd make a great headline. Real vote-loser that one.*

"This really wouldn't be a good time for us to be planning a wedding. Not now with the nomination and the election coming up. I've got to factor in the political implications. You know what happened to Hal Davies when he got that Indian girl pregnant. The Prime Minister told him right away he couldn't run in the next election. He's really strict about these things. About messy divorces and affairs and things like that. Really strict. It'd be best to wait until after I win the election before making any plans."

She hadn't expected him to equivocate like that. Just three weeks ago, he seemed dead certain he was going to marry her. Divorce Carol. Marry her and live happily ever after.

"But, you were pretty sure before," she said. "Pretty sure that we were going to get married after I graduate."

"I'm not saying we're not going to get married," he said in as reassuring a tone as he could fake. "All I am saying is that we have to go slow right now. Get the nomination and the election over with. If word got out that I'm getting a divorce right now – and marrying a fourth-year student – the media would be all over it. It could really mess things up."

"Okay," she said, not at all sure she should believe a word he had just said. "After the election's okay with me. Will you want me to help out in the campaign? Canvassing and stuff like that?"

"Maybe not. We should keep our relationship as low profile as possible until after the election. Don't want any loose talk about maybe me being involved with you. Like, in a sexual way. Better to keep our relationship out of the prying eyes of the media for now. Just for a couple of months. Okay?"

"I guess. I don't want to do anything that would mess with your career. I can wait."

She was now almost totally convinced that he had no intention whatsoever of them getting married. *I'm just his little Yiddish sex toy. Should have known better than to get involved with an older guy who's married and into politics. This is the end of the line, Ruthie. Once he's an MP and making fancy speeches up there in Ottawa, you're not going to see him again. This is the short, fast, goodbye.*

As he gave her a peck on the cheek on the way out the door, she was convinced he would never be back in her apartment again. *He's off to bigger and better things. Gordon MacArthur, P.C, M.P.* She was hurt. Deeply hurt. She realized now that he'd just been leading her on. Letting her think he was going to marry her without the slightest intention of doing so.

After Charlie and Diane were off to bed, Carol curled up on the chair by the fireplace and started reading *Zorba the Greek* again. Gordon was back in his study marking essays.

Try as she could, she couldn't get her head into the book. She kept thinking about how much she'd enjoyed being with Charlie and Diane that day and all the enjoyable days with them she'd missed because of the funk she'd been in for the last four years. *I did resent them. I really did. Blamed them for the fact I'm not practising law. Blamed them for the fact I didn't make my mark. Dad used to be so proud of me. Told all his associates they'd be hearing from me. "Whatever she decides to do, you'll be hearing a lot about this Winston." He was so convinced I was going to set the world on fire.*

But the only fire I lit was one kindled by resentment. Resentment toward Charlie and Diane for needing me to mother them when I wanted to be out practising law. I see it all so clearly now. I wonder if they ever felt it. I know Gordon did. And I was glad he did. Stuck that knife of resentment deep into his gut and twisted it every chance I got. But, my God, what about Charlie and Diane? Did they feel it, too? Did they know that I — that I accepted them more than I wanted them? I've held back so much of the loving they should've had. And I did want to love them. I really did. But I just couldn't let it out. Letting it out would have been saying it was all right that I wasn't proving myself against the top lawyers in the country. I've held back so much — so very, very, much.

And then she thought about the divorce and how that was going to affect Charlie and Diane. Watching Gordon pack his things and move out of the house. Having their father living in another part of town. It was going to hit them hard. She was quite definite about telling him it was over. That she wanted him out of the house. She just wasn't so sure tomorrow morning was still the best time to do it. *Maybe I should let it sit for a couple of days. Think it out more fully. See whether or not I have the option of going back to H and B. They might think I've been out of the game too long. Not up to speed on what's going on in law. Things change all the time and I've been out of the game for four years. Four long years.*

She went to the kitchen and fixed herself another drink.

As Bill drove south on Highway 400 on his way back from the cabin Sunday night, he thought about his dad's funeral. Seeing him in his buckskin jacket in that casket, hands clasped on his chest. The four Calgary Stampede saddle bronc trophies at the side of the casket surrounded by flowers. Looking like he was asleep but really dead. Dead. Dead and gone forever. It was all so final. He wanted to say, "Hey, Dad, wake up. Wake up, Dad." But it wouldn't have been any use. His dad would never wake up again.

It had all been so sudden. One minute he was having breakfast with Sarah chatting away about how this was going to be his last year competing at the Stampede. He'd had a bad fall that winter and his knee hadn't healed properly. Next thing you know, he's passed out on the kitchen table and going into a coma from which he would never recover.

If only I'd had a chance to say goodbye. To have one last ride with him along the flats or up Thunder Mountain. To have seen his last ride at the Stampede. Although, when you come right down to it, he shouldn't have been even thinking about competing with that bad knee. Wouldn't have the strength in it to hold on tight enough.

The Saturday edition of the *Globe and Mail* was on Bill's front porch when he got back to his house on Sussex Avenue. After he put his things away, he made himself a pot of tea and then read the article about the engineer who said it made more sense to run the pipeline through the property that ran up against the northeast corner of Big Thunder.

Bill turned to the tenth page of the first section of the newspaper and saw the picture of his mom forking hay to the calves. *She shouldn't be put through all this stuff. Not when she's still all torn up about Dad's death. Anyway, this news is helpful. Real helpful. Should let her know about it.*

He went to the phone and checked with the answering service to see if there were any messages. Some lady had called Saturday afternoon but didn't leave a message. Dr. McArchibald wanted to see him first thing Monday morning and Doug Donaldson wanted to go over some problems they were having with the correspondence course. That was it.

Wonder if that was Carol who called. Too bad I missed her. Like to have talked to her. Maybe she was calling about the article in the Globe. *Probably read it and wanted to make sure I didn't miss it. Find out tomorrow night. When she comes over to review the documents.*

He poured himself a fresh cup of tea and dialled his mother's number at Big Thunder. It was a little after eight thirty Calgary time. She had just finished the supper dishes and was going over some homework with Albert. He read her the article in the *Globe*.

"That is good news, William. That will help, won't it?"

"Yes, Mom, it'll be a big help. The lawyers will be able to use it at the hearings Tuesday morning. Was there anything about it in the *Herald*? Canadian Press usually distributes articles like this all over the country."

"Can't tell you that. We stopped getting the *Herald* about a month after your Dad died. Never did spend much time reading it myself. So, no, I can't really say if there was anything in there or not."

"Don't worry about it. It's not that important. Anything new with you? About the pipeline or anything like that?"

"Can't say that there is. Pretty quiet out here. Not much happening. Just the way I like it." She paused and reflected for a moment. "There was one thing. A reporter from the *Herald* was out here last week. Asked me a couple of questions. Nothing I couldn't answer. Then he took a picture of me feeding the calves."

"I saw that," Bill said. "It was in the *Globe* yesterday morning. You're looking good. Getting back to your old self."

"I am feeling a bit better these days. Having Albert with me is doing me the world of good. Want to speak to him? I'll be sending him off to bed pretty soon."

Bill spent about ten minutes on the phone with Albert. Catching up on how he was doing at school and how he was getting along at Big Thunder.

"When're you coming out here?" Albert asked.

"I'll be home for Christmas."

"Not that. I mean really coming out here. Living with me and Grandma."

"I'm working on it. Might have something to tell you soon. Real soon."

"How soon?"

"You'll know soon enough. Now, I've got to go. It's almost eleven out here and I've got a busy day tomorrow. Got to get to bed."

After they said their goodbyes, Bill cut the picture of Sarah and her calves out of the *Globe* and pinned it on the cork bulletin board next to the fridge.

~

Dr. McArchibald was a bit of a stickler for long-range planning and he wanted an update on Bill's intentions.

"If you are going to accept the offer from the University of Calgary," he said soon after Bill got to his office Monday morning, "and I am inclined to believe that you are most definitely leaning that way, I will have to make immediate arrangements for the transition. I don't want to pressure you, Bill, but I do have to plan ahead."

"I appreciate your position," Bill said. "But it's not that easy a decision. Quite frankly, my preference would be to remain here. This university is Mecca as far as I am concerned. As you well know, I have always had my sights set on teaching here. No one can match us. That said, I have my son's needs to take into consideration. He really likes it out there. Albert had some problems with white kids in Toronto that I only found out about this summer. He doesn't have any problems at the school out there and I know that's where he'd rather be."

"I can most certainly understand that," McArchibald said. "You know how much it means to me to go to the Stampede every July. Dressing up in my cowboy hat and boots. I'll never forget when you took me back to the chutes where the broncos were and seeing your 'Glued-on' dad riding those wild horses. It is an altogether different world out there. I can see how your boy would just love being at the ranch. But, still, Bill, I hope you will understand why I would want you to stay here. You are one of my best professors and the work you've done with the North American Indian Studies program is exemplary. If you go, you will be leaving a very big hole to fill. A very big hole indeed. I've got to find a way to fill that hole."

"Dr. Chamberlain said I don't have to let him know until the end of November. He's got some planning to do, too. I could move that up a couple of weeks. Let's say November fifteenth? I'll know for sure by then. One way or the other. But, you are right, that is the way I'm leaning right now. Mostly because of Albert."

"Very well, then. November fifteenth it is. That will leave me a little more time to make arrangements to accommodate the transition. If you really are going to leave me."

McArchibald paused for a moment. "Interesting, isn't it? I poached you from Berkeley and now Dr. Chamberlain is poaching you from me."

"Actually, it's my Albert that's doing the poaching. If he didn't like it so much out there, I wouldn't be giving a single thought to leaving Toronto. Not now, anyway."

"Good, then we will leave it at that. By the way, I am glad that Dr. Chamberlain's prepared to take the correspondence program off my hands. We were losing a considerable amount of money on that, Bill. It has, quite frankly, been a bit of a drag. Financially, that is."

"I really do regret that it turned out to be such a burden. Guess that's the price of success. If we didn't have so many Indian students taking it without charge, the costs would have been significantly lower."

"Don't get me wrong," McArchibald said. "The correspondence course was a great idea. I've read some of the letters you received from the students. It truly has made a difference in their young lives and I'm proud to have been associated with it."

They wrapped things up and Bill headed off to teach a class.

~

Gordon was at the Commonwealth Club having lunch with Henry Bracken and three members of the Meadowbrook riding executive. They were going over plans for the nomination meeting and the election.

He had told Carol the truth when he said Bracken had called to set up the meeting. What he didn't tell her was the lunch was set for Monday. Not Sunday as he'd said when he needed an excuse to go over to Ruth's apartment.

James Crockford was a sales manager for Imperial Tobacco, Mark Lawrence was a senior partner at Haldimand and Brock, and Richard Oliver was a lobbyist for the New Zealand Meat Producers Board.

"I see you've been building some profile, Gordon. Getting your name in the papers," Oliver said. "That was a good piece the *Globe* had Friday. I particularly liked the part about people in turbans sprouting up all over white neighborhoods. You're right. There are too many of them."

"You're damned right about that," Bracken cut in. "And why do they have to wear those towels around their heads? When you're in Canada, you should dress like Canadians do."

"Like, when in Rome, do as the Romans," Crockford from Imperial Tobacco said.

"Damned right," Bracken said. "They're changing the whole face of Canada. Them and all those other people from across the ocean. And, if you ask me, they aren't changing it for the better."

Gordon hadn't had a chance to get a word in edgewise. He just sat back and listened to them go at it.

"Just last week," Bracken said, "one of my managers told me he'd been driving through his old neighborhood. Where he'd grown up as a boy. Said he was standing outside the movie theatre where he used to spend Saturday afternoons watching cowboy movies and Charlie Chaplin and he couldn't read the posters outside because now they're all in Italian. Do you know, do you have any idea, what that must have felt like? Not to be able to read the movie posters?"

"One of my old school chums had an experience a bit like that," Mark Lawrence from Haldimand and Brock said. "A lot of Italians started moving into his area about twenty years ago. Next thing you know, he was the only WASP living on a street full of Italians. Catholic Italians. He got out of there as fast as he could and moved to a new development at Royal York and Dixon. He didn't ask to be forced out of his own neighborhood. Didn't expect to wind up in a new subdivision and go through the aggravation of having no sidewalks for three years and trees that are only now one-quarter the size of the trees on the street where he grew up."

"Yes," Bracken said. "Altogether too many Canadians have had to go though that experience. And that's why we need someone like Gordon, one of our own, to get to Ottawa and start balancing things out. Making sure the rights of the British Canadians who built this great country of ours are respected for a change."

"What about that pipeline?" Crockford asked. "The one Jack Saunders is building out in Alberta. The *Globe* said that they have an engineer who swore an affidavit saying there's no reason to run the pipeline through the Indians' lands. That must cause Jack some concern."

"No concern whatsoever," Lawrence said. "Jack's been a client of ours from back when he opened the gold mine at Kirkland Lake. We're representing him at the Energy Resources Conservation Board hearings. What the *Globe* didn't tell you was that Jack fired that son of a bitch three months ago. Caught him drinking on the job. Third time in a row. Three strikes and you're out. He lost no time firing his sorry ass. We'll make mincemeat of him if he testifies at the hearing."

"But," Gordon said, "he signed an affidavit. The *Globe* says they have documents proving the pipeline was supposed to go through the property on the north side of the reserve."

"Still not a problem, Gordon. On a project this size, you get reams of documents. Feasibility studies. Geological surveys. Engineering studies. Environmental assessments. The documents the *Globe* got hold of are easily explained away with documents that disgruntled former employee has never set eyes on. Jack's going to be fine. We'll see to that."

They spent the rest of the lunch going over the details of the program for Thursday night's nomination meeting and making arrangements to move into the campaign office Dave Saunders had offered Gordon at the mall in the middle of Meadowbrook.

As Carol drove toward Bill's house after supper that night, she was glad she hadn't said anything to Gordon about the divorce. She still had quite a lot to sort out. How the children would react to it. Whether or not she was going to be able to go back to Haldimand and Brock. It was a big step. She wanted to be sure she was handling it right.

"Would you like a glass of wine?" Bill asked after he took her coat.

"Prefer Scotch if you've got it."

"Got lots of it. Always have Scotch around. How'd you like it. Water? Ginger ale?"

"Prefer soda if you've got it."

"Got that, too. Be back in a minute."

He went to the kitchen and came back with two glasses of Scotch. He told her about his meeting with Dr. McArchibald that morning and that he was even more certain than ever that he was going to take the job at the University of Calgary.

"If it was just me, I'd stay here. The U of T is where I've always wanted to be. But I've got Albert to think about. Turns out he was not all that happy here. Got picked on because he was the only Indian in our neighborhood. Got beaten up a couple of times."

"Oh, that's dreadful," Carol said. "Did you know about it at the time? About Albert getting beaten up?"

"No. And, I must confess, there was a lot about Albert I didn't know about while we were in Toronto. I was so totally wrapped up in my work at the university. Setting up the North American Indian Studies program and all that. I pretty well shut him out of my life. Shut him out completely. So, no, I didn't know. Didn't find out until I was at Big Thunder this summer."

"Then, what about his mother? Your ex-wife?"

"He told her about it and, get this, she told him something like life is rough and he'd have to learn to roll with the punches. No pun intended."

"Is she part of his life now? At Big Thunder?"

"No. She's living with moneybags Starlight in a big fancy house up on a hill in Calgary. Hardly ever sees Albert."

"I forgot. You told me they were living together. But, still, Albert's happy out there? Even without his mom?"

"Real happy. My mom's got a big void in her life because of my dad dying so suddenly like that and she does everything with him. Teaches him all sorts of things. Loves him to pieces and he loves her back. They get on great together. And then he has my sister and her kids and my brother Hughie. Hughie's taking him trapping martens next month. He's really excited about it. My Grandfather takes him out on his buggy lots of times. Lets him take the reins. Yes, Albert likes it out there. A lot better than he does Toronto."

"Then I suppose that's where you're going to be, too. Out there with your son, and your mom at Big Thunder."

"Guess so," he replied. "Looks more that way every day."

"Well, I hope it works out for you. For both of you."

"And what about you?" he asked. "How are things coming along between you and the Great White Hope? You still getting a divorce?"

"Yes. Absolutely no doubt about that. He doesn't know it yet but he will by the end of the week. I was going to tell him this morning but I've still got some things to work out. Especially about Charlie and Diane."

He was glad to hear that the divorce was still on. He wanted to get to know Carol better, a lot better. Things would be a lot less complicated if she was actually getting a divorce.

"I'm glad you're thinking about the children," he said. "You don't want them to have to go through anything even close to what Albert went through. Don't want them wishing someone would roll you over with a truck."

"Not quite the same, Bill. I'm not going to be living two thousand miles away from them."

"Two thousand miles, two thousand yards. To the children, there's often not all that much difference."

"Well, anyway. I will take your advice. I'm going to make sure, make damned sure that this doesn't hurt Charlie and Diane any more than it has to. I will make sure of that."

They started to talk about the pipeline Jack Saunders wanted to ram through Big Thunder.

"That article in the *Globe* Saturday morning should be helpful," she said. "About the engineer who said the pipeline was supposed to go through the proposed new development on the northern border of your community."

"Yes. That will be a big help. That property is directly east of Saunders' project and that is the route he should be taking. He's not going through our land. Not with something as dangerous as sour gas, he's not. From what I've heard, the owners of that property are adamant that they won't let Saunders run his pipeline through there. They're building high-end luxury homes facing the mountains right across the west end of the property and down the south side. There's no way their buyers will want a sour gas pipeline running through their gardens."

"Have you got a map? It would help get my head around this thing if I could see it all laid out on a map. Where the sour gas was discovered. Where the processing plant is going to be. Where that new development is. Where Big Thunder is in relation to it all. And, while we're at it, where the house you were born in is."

"Sure, I've got a map. Give me a minute to find it."

He shuffled the documents on the dining room table and came across a map of Big Thunder. He laid it out in front of Carol. The map showed the Rocky Mountains at the top. There was a pass on the right where the Trans-Canada Highway went through the mountains. The northern border of Big Thunder started at the foothills, ran east for about two miles, jogged south for another two miles and then east almost directly in line with the southern border of Calgary. Judging by the scale at the bottom of the map, it appeared to be about twenty miles wide.

"Where's Saunders' gas processing plant?" Carol asked.

"It's right there," Bill said, pointing with his pencil to a spot at the bottom of the eastern slopes about a mile south of the northern border of the reserve. "Just before the property line jogs south. And his wells are just west of there."

"But, isn't that your land? It's on the south side of the border?"

"It most certainly is. I'm really not up to speed on this but, from what my brother Hughie tells me, the band chief made a deal under the table with Saunders and arranged for him to have a ninety-nine-year lease on the property."

"The chief could do that?"

"Yes he could. Harold Littlelight controls the majority vote on the Band Council and can do pretty much anything he wants. He's got a new addition on his house and a nice new swimming pool in his back-yard to show for it. And, from what Hughie tells me, Saunders put a big chunk of dough in a bank account in Calgary for him."

"I see. And the proposed new development, where is it located?"

"Down there on the northeast corner of our land," Bill said as he ran his pencil down the northern border of Big Thunder.

"Why can't Saunders just go around that property and run his pipeline between it and the city limits?"

"Because there's a greenbelt there. He can't run his pipeline along the south side of Calgary. The city won't allow it and the owner of that property won't let him go through his land. He's stuck. That's why he's trying to run his pipeline through my mother's land."

"I see." She looked at the map of the reserve more closely. "And the owners of that property at the northeast corner of your community won't let him run his pipeline there?"

"That's what we've been told. They won't budge."

"Who owns that land?"

"We don't know. Hughie says it's owned by a numbered company from Ontario that's represented by one of the big law firms in Calgary. It's all zoned and ready to go – sewers in and everything – but the company that owned it went bankrupt. The new owner picked it up about six months ago."

"And you don't know who that new owner is?"

"I don't. Maybe Hughie does. I'll phone him and see what I can find out."

"Show me where your mother's house is."

Bill pointed to a spot which looked to be about only half a mile away from where Saunders was building his gas processing plant.

"That is close," she said. "Way too close."

"It sure as hell is. With Hughie having the asthma, fumes escaping from that plant could kill him. Smells like rotten eggs. Ranchers along the foothills from down near Pincher Creek all the way up to Olds had a real problem with sour gas. Their wire fences were actually rusting, cattle were sick, kids were sick, even the trees got sick. And all because they were downwind of the sour gas plants. There's no way we're going to accept that kind of risk.

"Just three years ago, the Queen of the Netherlands demanded that Shell Canada settle a big-figure lawsuit fifteen of the families down by Pincher Creek had launched against them. They documented about fifty serious cases of ill health among the people and dead cattle. Sour gas is serious stuff."

"Didn't you object to the plant when they started building it? When you knew about the risks it posed?"

"I wasn't involved at the time. From what Hughie tells me, Dad was going to try and get an injunction against it. Fight it in court. But then he died. And, from what I understand, no one else was prepared to take Chief Littlelight on. He's got a lot of control over everything that happens on that reserve."

Carol thought things through for a minute. "So, the gas is on your land. Saunders paid the chief off so he could get the lease. That makes the lease illegal. We have to get a copy of that lease and see what it says about mineral rights. We will also need the names of the councillors who approved that lease and the minutes of the meeting where that was done."

She paused for a minute and took another look at the map. "Looks to me like you should be able to challenge that lease in court. There's a *prima facie* case of bribery and fraud here and that shouldn't be too difficult to prove. In my opinion, you should be able to get an injunction and a stop-work order issued against Saunders until this matter is resolved to the satisfaction of the people of Big Thunder."

"You mean shut him down?"

"Yes. If we can prove that Saunders bribed the chief and some of the councillors, the court will declare the lease null and void. That will mean your people will have a clear and unfettered right to the gas that was discovered on their land."

"You're moving right along," Bill said.

"This is what I do for a living, Bill. I see all sorts of possibilities here. First we challenge the lease. I doubt very much that all of the band councillors voted in favor. We need to speak to some of those who voted against. We need to know what, if anything they know or suspect about any money Saunders paid under the table. Find out from Hughie where he got the information about Chief Littlelight's bank account in Calgary. However, no one should be approached – none of those who voted against Chief Littlelight – until everything is lined up. Not even in confidence. We must maintain the element of surprise.

"And then, when we are ready to move, we'll hit them all at once. When they understand that there's a chance that we can cancel that lease and take control of the project, they'll open up about what they know. There's an opportunity for the Big Thunder people to make hundreds of thousands, perhaps even millions, on the safe recovery of that gas. To develop it in a manner that will pose no threat to human health. They'll talk, once they realize what's in it for them and their families."

"Yes, they most likely will."

"Right. Now, first step. I need you to get me a copy of the lease. We also need the Band Council Resolution authorizing Chief Littlelight to negotiate the lease. Then we need the names of all those who voted in support."

She reviewed the map again. Drew her pencil from Sarah's house to the gas processing plant that was being built and then over to the property owned by the company represented by the law firm in Calgary.

"This will have to be done in one fell swoop," she said. "We don't want a word to get out about the fact that we're snooping around. We must have all of the background information together and then hit them all at once – within a twenty-four hour period. That's the only way it will work. Especially in a small community like Big Thunder. We've got to get all our ducks lined up and then – before Saunders knows what we're up to – off with his head."

"Sounds good to me," Bill said with a note of genuine admiration. "You do seem to know how to go about this."

"I think this is doable, Bill. I think that we can ensure that the Big Thunder people get the main financial benefit from this discovery. That they get every cent coming to them."

"Anyway, I'll be glad when it's all over," Bill said. "I really will."

"Hang in there, Bill. This is going to work out for you," Carol said. "And for your mother."

"Thanks, Carol. I'm pretty sure that it will. Especially with you on board."

"My pleasure. I haven't felt so energized and alive in years. This is just what the doctor ordered."

"Good. What're you doing Thursday night?"

"Nothing in particular. It's the night of Gordon's nomination meeting but I don't have the slightest interest in being there. Especially not now that I'm going to initiate the divorce proceedings. Why do you ask?"

"We're having a special meeting of the committee Thursday night. Same room as last time. Same time. I was thinking, now that you're our official pro bono legal adviser, you might want to join us."

"Sure. I'd like that. Maybe they won't treat me as an outsider this time."

"That was only at the beginning of the meeting, Carol. They just wanted to know where you were coming from. And you know how receptive they were after we got that out of the way. They'll want you to be there."

"Okay, you've got a deal," she said. "Room 16, Davidson Hall, seven thirty Thursday night. Meanwhile, I suggest that you get started on pulling that background information together. We need to build an airtight case in support of your community and against Saunders and his sour gas pipeline. I'd like nothing better than to sue his bloated ass off."

"I will. I'll call Hughie the moment you leave. I'll get the information you need."

CHAPTER
- 20 -

Carol placed a call to Jonathan Hollinger, the managing partner at Haldimand and Brock, Tuesday morning. Hollinger had handled all of her father's legal affairs for more than twenty years.

She told him she was interested in joining the firm again and wondered if it would be possible to meet with him. He said he would most definitely be interested in seeing her and had always thought highly of her. He'd be tied up in court for the rest of the week but could have lunch with her on the following Tuesday.

"I'll be in court all morning and then again in the afternoon. But I could have a quick lunch with you here in the office, say just after one o'clock?"

"That'd be fine, Jonathan. I really do appreciate the fact that you're prepared to see me."

"The pleasure is all mine. If we hadn't lost you, we wouldn't have lost the Gothic Gold Corp. case. You are a good lawyer, Carol. One of our best."

"Thanks. I appreciate that. Really do."

"Fine, then I'll see you just after one next Tuesday. We'll have soup and a sandwich in the conference room."

She was glad she had made the call. This was the first step. It felt good to be back in action again. *Back with the living.*

Carol's father called her just before noon Toronto time. He'd run into some problems with his hotel project and would have to stay in Calgary until a week Friday.

"That means I'm going to miss Gordon's nomination meeting. Damned sorry about that. I really had wanted to be there to show support for him. Please pass on my apologies. This really couldn't be helped. The city zoning people are making things a lot more difficult for me than they need to be."

"I'll tell him, Dad. I'm sure he'll be disappointed but I'll explain it all to him."

She decided not to mention a word about the fact that she was going to ask Gordon for a divorce. *Better to wait until the proceedings are actually under way. Dad's got enough on his plate to worry about right now.*

"I've got some rather good news," she said. "I spoke to Jonathan Hollinger this morning and told him I'd like to go back to H and B. We're having lunch next Tuesday."

"That is good news. Very good news indeed. What brought that on?"

"Nothing in particular. I was walking down by the river with Charlie and Diane and had a great time with them. We were playing with a beach ball and tossing pebbles across the water. It's been so long since I've done anything like that with them. So long since I've done much of anything, actually. Can't explain it all to you, Dad, but I do feel that it's time to get back in the swing of things. Pick up where I left off. Catch up on four years of doing not very much about anything."

"Ease off on the self-flagellation about the 'missing' four years," Winston said. "You got me a granddaughter. Wasn't supposed to have another grandchild, you said, for at least nine years. Diane is most definitely not time wasted. She's a little angel. The important thing now is the next four years. Living up to the potential I've always known you had. I just can't tell you how happy I am that you made the call. It's a great firm. I've never had anything but good work from them. Would you like me to call Jonathan? Put in a word for you?"

"I appreciate the offer, Dad. But, no, I'd like to do this on my own. Get back because they want me in my own right. Not because I'm Gran Winston's daughter."

"I understand," he said, determined that he was going to make the call anyway. "You're right. It is better that you do it on your own."

"It's not going to be all that easy, getting my stride back. I have been out of action for four years. Four lost years. But, I'm getting my life back. One step at a time. I will make it."

"I have no doubt about that, Carol. No doubt at all. You were doing well at Haldimand and Brock. Jonathan told me he believed you were going to have a great future with them. He was very impressed with how well you were doing. It won't take long. You will rise to the top. Believe me. I have absolute faith in you."

"Thanks, Dad. Your support has always meant a great deal to me."

They said their goodbyes and Carol drove to Carmen's Bistro on Yorkville Avenue to have lunch with Jane Potts.

Carol told Jane she was getting her life back together again and would probably be going back to Haldimand and Brock.

"That's wonderful news, Carol. I'm so happy for you. Frankly, I've been really concerned about you. Ever since you got Diane. I kept wondering where my Carol went. You just weren't the same. Not the strong Carol I had always known. Looked to me like you were going through some pretty rough patches."

"Patches?" Carol said. "No 'patches'. It was all one long – depressingly long – patch. I've no idea what got into me. Just couldn't bring myself to do anything."

"Now, Carol, you did have PPD. That's what Dr. Turner told you. That can really mess up your life. And then, with your mom dying so sudden like that – and so young – things were bound to go sour for you." She stopped for a minute to pick at her salad. "And yet, when we were in Bermuda, you seemed to be okay. Seemed to have snapped out of it. Having Derek Parkington in your life seemed to perk you up a bit."

"It did. But then he went back to his wife and sons and made my life even worse than it was before. Everything turned to shit."

"What about now? Got anyone in your life besides Gordon?"

"Might have," Carol replied with a little smile. "Might have."

"Well now," Jane said rather excitedly, "let's have it. Tell me all about it."

"Not much to tell, really. He's a professor at the university. I only met him last week. Seen him a couple of times since then and, yes, I am interested in him. I really like him."

"Married? Divorced?"

"Separated. He's in the process of getting a divorce from his wife. Just like I'm going to be with Gordon. I've had more than enough of him and his intolerance of people who are different and want to bring it all to an abrupt end. I'm going to tell him sometime this week and retain a lawyer."

"I'm not interested in Gordon," Jane said impatiently. "That's old stuff. You should've left him years ago. I want to hear about the new. The new professor in your life. Tell me about him. All about him."

"He's Indian."

"From Delhi by any chance? Al and I were in Delhi last year. Took the kids to see the Taj Mahal at Agra."

"Not that kind of Indian. He's a full-blooded Blackfoot from a reserve near Calgary."

"A real, genuine, Canadian Indian?"

"Yep. Wears his hair in braids and has real bear claws hanging around his neck."

"My God. That is real. Dresses like that all the time? Even at the university?"

"Yep. He's the director of the North American Indian Studies program. Dresses like that all the time."

"Well now. That's quite a switch from Derek. From Gordon, too, for that matter."

"Nothing's happened yet. Might not happen. He's probably moving to Calgary at the end of the year to teach at the University of Calgary. His son's been living at the Indian reserve and really misses his dad. And he misses his son. His name's Bill. Dr. Bill Eagletail."

"The end of the year's months away, Carol. That's more than enough time to get him out of those braids and into your bed."

"Slow down," Carol said. "I never could move as fast as you. At least not in that department."

"Strike while the iron's hot. You never know when it's going to cool down. No time like the present. Want any more clichés today?"

"No. That's more than enough for now, thank you."

Jane raised her wine glass for a toast. "To you and the new love in your life. Happy hunting, like the Indians say."

"He's not the love of my life," Carol said as she clinked her glass against Jane's. "At least, not yet he isn't."

Ross Palmer phoned Gordon a few minutes after one o'clock.

"Suggest you turn on to City-TV. There's quite a commotion outside Davidson Hall. And it's all about you. Bit of a ruckus over there."

Gordon turned the television set to City-TV. About a hundred students were parading back and forth in front of Davidson Hall carrying large picket signs. City-TV was covering it live.

The camera panned over some of the signs: "STAMP OUT HATE; FREEDOM FOR ALL; Deport MacArthur; FREE THE INDIANS, No Pipeline; OUR DADS BUILT THE SUBWAY, da Vinci's kids; CANADA FOR EVERY ONE; ALL YOU NEED IS LOVE; Dante's Infernos; WE'RE CANADIANS TOO; Michelangelo loves US."

One of the students, with dark wavy hair and olive skin, was speaking to a City-TV reporter. "We think Professor MacArthur is way over the line. He's as bigoted as they come. We're not going to take any more of his bull. Canada's our country, too."

"And may I have your name?" the reporter asked.

"Orsini. Elvio Orsini."

The reporter turned to another student carrying a big sign saying: "It's our Canada 2."

"Why are you here?" the reporter asked.

"Because some of the stuff Professor MacArthur says in the newspapers insults us. Insults our parents. They gave up everything to come over here and build a new life for us. They don't deserve the crap he's mouthing all the time."

"Could I have your name, please?"

Sure. I'm Celistino Piccininni . And I am a Canadian."

The reporter signed off and they switched back to the newsroom.

"Good God!" Gordon exclaimed. "What the hell brought that on?"

The phone rang about five minutes later. It was Henry Bracken.

"Did you see that, Gordon? The protestors in front of Davidson Hall?"

"Yes I did. Kind of disturbing."

"Disturbing? Not at all. This is just wonderful. Shows how radical and intolerant those immigrant students are. Shows their true colours. Looked to me like most of them were Italians or Greeks. Maybe a few Portuguese, too. Not at all disturbing, Gordon. This stuff is tailor made for our base. This is good stuff. The sort of stuff that will get you votes in Meadowbrook. This is good. Very good indeed."

"I'm glad you see it that way, Henry. Didn't look all that good to me. One of those signs said I should be deported."

"Yes, and that is exactly what I mean. Shows how intolerant, how radical, they really are. Those students are not at all reflective of most of the student body. Of the students who are of British heritage."

"Still, Henry, looked to me like there was about a hundred of them."

"One hundred out of a student population of twenty thousand. A hundred immigrant kids with nothing better to do on their lunch hour but cause trouble. Don't worry about it. They don't mean a thing in the overall scheme of things."

That might be so, Gordon thought as he hung up the phone. However, he was glad he didn't have any reason to go over to Davidson Hall at that particular moment. Some of the demonstrators looked pretty angry. Pretty angry at him.

A reporter from the *Globe and Mail* called Gordon just after three o'clock. He wanted Gordon's reaction to the student demonstration.

"I don't think those students are at all representative of the majority opinion on campus," Gordon said. "Not one of my students has uttered so much as a word – not a single word – about this issue to me. What we had over the lunch hour was a bunch of disaffected immigrant students with nothing better to do with their time."

"What was your reaction to them saying you should be deported?"

"If they want to send me back to Scotland, where my parents came from, that's just fine with me. Of course, I'm only jesting with you. I don't take those students or anything they have to say about me seriously. Not at all."

"Do you see this affecting your chances at the nomination meeting Thursday night?"

"As I understand it, no one else is standing for the nomination. I expect that I will be nominated as the Conservative candidate by acclamation."

"What about the election, then, Professor? Will the demonstration have any impact on your chances in the election?"

"I really don't think so. From what I saw on TV, most of the demonstrators were of immigrant background. We don't have many immigrants in Meadowbrook. The voters in my riding are mostly middle-class whites. No, I don't see today's event having any impact at all."

The reporter thanked Gordon for his time and then he was gone. There were five more calls from reporters over the next couple of hours. The *Toronto Star,* City-TV, CFTO, 1050 CHUM and CBC Radio. Gordon handled them all in pretty much the same way as he had dealt with the reporter from the *Globe.*

Henry Bracken called again just before five.

"I just got a call from Don Mitchell in the PMO. He's in quite a snit about the demonstration at the university. Says you're going to cost them votes in the inner cities."

"He did? What did you say to that?"

"I told him Meadowbrook is not in the inner city and we're going to do everything we can to make sure you win the election. What happens in the inner cities is no concern of mine. None whatsoever."

"You did? You were that blunt about it?"

"Damned right I was. Put it to him straight. Told him I'm sick and tired of the inner city voters leading our party around by the nose. It's high time we did what's best for the majority of Canadians for a change. Not for, as you called them in the newspaper, the clamouring, lobbying, high-pressure, special-interest minority groups who've immigrated to Canada over the last three decades. That was a great quote, Gordon. Really stuck in my mind, it did."

"So, Henry, did Mitchell accept that? Accept what you had to say?"

"You can bet your life he didn't. Not Mitchell. He will never see things our way. But that doesn't matter. Doesn't matter at all. Don't worry one bit about this, Gordon. Everything is going to work out splendidly."

"I hope so, Henry. I found the demonstration very unsettling. Nobody has ever suggested that I should be deported before. That was a first."

"Don't worry your head about that. They're a bunch of nobodies. They don't matter a damn. Bunch of worthless immigrant kids with nothing better to do."

⁓

Professor Henderson popped his head inside Gordon's office just after he got off the phone with Bracken. "Got a few minutes, Gordon?"

"I most certainly do, Donald. Please come in."

Henderson sat on one of the chairs in front of Gordon's desk and put some tobacco in his pipe.

"You certainly got those young immigrant students all riled up," he said. "That was a sight to behold."

"Did you see it on TV?"

No. I was there. Right in the very thick of it. They were marching in front of Davidson Hall as I was on my way in. Gave some of them a piece of my mind I did. 'Michelangelo loves us' my arse. Mussolini's more like it. They haven't had a Michelango over there for more than four hundred years. Haven't had a Dante or a da Vinci either. All those names are from a bygone era. Centuries ago."

"I got a few calls from the reporters," Gordon said. "They wanted to know what I thought about them saying I should be deported and they also asked me if I thought the demonstration might affect the election."

"It will win more votes than it will lose," Henderson said. "Votes where you need them. In Meadowbrook where there are hardly any of those kind of people. The only votes the Conservatives might lose will be in the inner city where the parents of those young people live and most of them vote Liberal anyway. Don't give it a second thought.

"As for those signs calling for you to be deported, that just shows how intolerant and impudent those young students are. If there is any deporting to be done, it should start with those people on the picket line today."

"Sounds like a good idea to me, Donald. Some of them were quite mouthy. Didn't know their place."

The conversation turned to the Equal Opportunities Council and the negative reaction they were getting from the administration to the idea of establishing a special studies course for the white students.

"President Campbell and his board are not buying into our proposal," Henderson said. "If we were to suggest a special course on Dante, da Vinci or Michelangelo, they would jump at the opportunity. Pour all sorts of money into it like they are doing with that North American Indian Studies program Bill Eagletail is running. But, when it comes to the white students, to the needs of their own kind, they're not prepared to spend one penny. Not a cent."

"Are you really that pessimistic about it? Do you really believe they're going to turn us down?"

"In my opinion, they've as much as said so. The vibrations around the table at that last meeting we had with Campbell and his special committee were quite negative. Very negative if you were to ask me. I think Saul Goldenberg is the root of the problem. He raises an awful lot of money for the university. Bags of it. Because of that, Goldenberg exerts a lot of influence on Campbell and the Board of Governors."

He paused for a moment to relight his pipe. "You know as well as I do, Gordon, that the Jews have always supported the blacks and the Indians. Goldenberg raised a lot of money for the American Indian Movement. I found out when I was doing some research on him. Compiling some background information. He also raised a considerable amount of money for the radical Black Panthers. A lot of money. Yes, Gordon, Goldenberg is the problem. He will not, most definitely not, support spending any money on the special studies program for the white students."

"I didn't know that," Gordon said. "About the Jews and the blacks and the Indians."

"It's true. Believe me, Gordon, it is true. They throw fundraising parties for the Black Panthers and other terrorist organizations in their multi-million-dollar apartments overlooking Central Park. Bunch of hypocrites, that's what they are. Rolling in dough and raising money for the poor, downtrodden masses. Passing themselves off like they were the Statue of Liberty. 'Give me your tired, your poor. Your huddled masses yearning to breathe free.' Radical Chic. That's what Tom Wolfe called them. Wrote a book exposing the double standard by which Leonard Bernstein and other world-famous Jews live. Radical Chics who support terrorists in their midst."

He let go another cloud of smoke into the air. "No, Gordon, as long as Goldenberg is on the Board of Governors, the university is not going to fund our proposal."

"Are you saying we should just give up, Donald?"

"You pick your battles, Gordon. Only fight battles you're reasonably confident you're going to win. We're not going to win this one. This one is lost."

"Then what are you suggesting that we should do? Disband the Equal Opportunities Council? Is that what you're suggesting?"

"No. Not disband. Re-focus. That's what we must do. That demonstration today gave me an idea. That's why I dropped by to see you. Rather than focus all our energies on the situation here at the university, I believe we should expand our horizon. Address some of the issues you have been raising in the newspapers. There are too many people in turbans sprouting up in white neighborhoods. Immigration levels from third-world countries should be cut back dramatically.

"We do need more legislation that is in the best interest of the white majority. We should protest the way the government is pandering to those people with all of these special programs financed by money out of our pockets. You're right, Gordon. There are a lot of things that need to be changed. And I now believe that the Equal Opportunities Council could be a credible voice for change."

"Ross Palmer won't like that. He got really cross with me when the first article came out in the *Globe*. Ross said the Equal Opportunities Council should most definitely not be getting itself involved with issues like the Saunders pipeline and that Indian reservation out near Calgary."

"Palmer is wrong about that. If, as you've been saying, white women and children will freeze in the dark of winter if that pipeline doesn't get built, then that most definitely is an issue with which we should be involved. Don't worry about Palmer. I'll deal with him. As for the pipeline, we should be supporting it in every way possible. We need that Alberta gas."

"You'll get no argument from me on that score, Donald. I really like what you're saying."

"It's not just the gas pipeline, Gordon. We've got to speak out on those other issues as well. No one else is addressing the rapid changes that are taking place in Canadian society. We have to step in and fill that void. The Equal Opportunities Council is a splendid vehicle for doing just that. Given that we are all university professors, we will have a lot of credibility. People will listen to us."

"Sounds good to me, Donald. What's our next step?"

"We should call a meeting of the other members and get ready to make a difference. We should be speaking out on current issues, issuing position papers, appearing before committees of the House of Commons. Doing our best to, as you put it so well, restore some balance. Put things back closer to where they were when I was growing up. Putting the British back into British North America. After all, Gordon, our constitution is still called the British North America Act of 1867. Our Queen is British. Parliament is based on the Westminster model. We are British, Gordon."

Henderson took another puff on his pipe. "Your parents were British, weren't they? From Scotland?"

"Yes. My dad was born on a farm near Inverness and my mum's from Aberdeen. Dad came over here with my uncle when he was twenty-two and my mum came over with her parents when she was seven. We're British, all right. And proud of it."

"That's what I thought. British we are and, as you just said, proud of it. Although you'd never believe it with the way things have changed since all those other people moved into our country. And that's an issue we must address, ASAP."

Henderson took out his appointment book. "I'm pretty tied up for the rest of the week. Let's set up a lunch meeting with the other members of the committee for a week tomorrow. You'll be the Conservative candidate for Meadowbrook by that time and I am sure we can use your position to our advantage. Would, say, one o'clock work for you, Gordon?"

"One o'clock will be fine. And you're right about the benefits arising from me being the official candidate for the Conservative Party and, after that, the MP for Meadowbrook. We'll work hand in hand and bring about the change that is so desperately needed in this country."

Just as Bill was about to leave the office and go home, he got a call from one of his students who had helped organize the demonstration in front of Davidson Hall.

"We'd really like for you to join us tomorrow," Alfred Howell said. "We're expecting to have twice as many students out demonstrating against Professor MacArthur."

Bill was inclined to say yes but, because of his growing interest in Carol, he decided it might not be such a good idea. *She's probably not too happy about people calling for her husband to be deported. Even if she is going to divorce him.*

"I don't think that would be appropriate, Alfred. I am a professor. A member of the university faculty. I think it best for these demonstrations to be restricted to the students."

Howell was quite disappointed. It was mainly because of Bill and the Big Thunder issue that he'd gotten involved in the demonstration in the first place.

"That's really too bad. I'd been hoping that you'd join us, especially with them wanting to run that pipeline through your mother's yard."

"How did you know about that?"

"I saw you on *Toronto Focus* duking it out with Professor MacArthur. You really put the boots to him. Made him look really foolish."

"Well, thank you for that, Alfred. I always try to do my best. But that doesn't change the fact that I can't join your demonstration tomorrow. I do appreciate what you and your friends are doing. The picket signs supporting our position on the pipeline controversy were very much appreciated. We're in a tough fight with the gas company and, at the very least, demonstrations like yours will be a morale booster for our people on the front line of this fight."

"We're behind you one hundred per cent, Dr. Eagletail. It makes no sense at all to ram that pipeline through your mother's property."

"Thank you again, Alfred. The publicity you're generating cannot help but increase our odds of winning this thing. In the court of public opinion if nowhere else."

"We think you'll win at the hearings, too, Dr. Eagletail. You've got a good case. Even their own engineer said the pipeline wasn't supposed to go through your land."

"Well, Alfred, we'll just have to wait and see how things turn out. Good luck with the demonstration tomorrow. And now, I must go. I've got a meeting to attend in about twenty minutes from now."

Carol was preparing supper when Gordon got home. Charlie was doing his homework at the dining room table and Diane was watching TV in the family room. He hung his coat in the closet and took his briefcase through to his study.

"Hi, Dad," Charlie said as Gordon passed by. "We saw you on TV."

"But I wasn't on TV," Gordon said. "No one with a camera interviewed me today."

"Not a real shot. They just showed a picture of your face with a report they had on the demonstration."

"You saw the demonstration?" Gordon asked.

"Just a bit of it. It was on the news a couple of minutes after six. One of the signs said they want to deport you. What's that mean? Deport? Like, kick someone out of the country?"

"Yes. It means expelling you from a country where you don't belong. But don't worry about it. There's no way anybody's going to deport me. I've been here all my life. Born right here in Toronto."

Charlie seemed a bit relieved. "That's good 'cause, if you got deported, they'd kick me and Diane out, too, right? We're your family."

"Charlie. Charlie. Don't get all tied up in knots about this. No one's going to deport me, or you, or Diane. Those kids are just making things up. Making trouble."

"That's good. I like it here. I don't want to be deported. Kicked out of Canada."

Carol called through from the kitchen. "Supper's ready in five minutes, everyone. Please wash up, children. We're having spaghetti. You hear that, Charlie?"

"Yes, Mom, I heard. Be there in a couple of minutes."

"Diane. Diane," Carol called. "Did you hear me?"

No answer. Diane had the headsets on.

"Charlie, tell your sister supper's ready."

"Okay, Mom. Will do."

It was a pretty silent supper. Carol seemed quite withdrawn. As if she had something heavy on her mind. Gordon decided not to force the issue. *She'll open up when she has something to say.*

"Daddy was on TV," Diane said. "Me and Charlie saw him on CTFO."

"It's CFTO," Charlie said. "Not CTFO."

Diane decided to ignore her brother's correction. "The picture of you was good, Daddy. You looked important. Had your name right under it. In big letters."

"I saw the demonstration when it was going on but I didn't see the later report," Gordon said. "The one you and Charlie saw."

"Why are they so mad at you?" Charlie asked. "One of them said you're a bigot."

Carol was tempted to join the conversation but decided to keep her cool. *Those students are right. He is a bigot. Out and out racist as Fraser Deacon put it on* Toronto Focus. *Maybe they should deport him. Send him back to bonnie Scotland where he can skip across the heather in his kilt playing the bagpipes.*

"Let's just forget about them, Charlie," Gordon said. "They're just a bunch of troublemakers with nothing better to do on their lunch hour. None of the other students feel the way they do. It's all political. I think the Liberals were behind the whole thing. Just stirring up trouble for me because I'm going to be a Conservative candidate. Forget about them. They're not relevant."

"Okay," Charlie said. "I'll leave it alone."

"Me, too," Diane piped in. "Not a word. Close my lips, Daddy, and not say another word."

"That's a good idea, Diane," Carol said, "and, as a reward for keeping your little lips sealed, I have a treat for you."

"You do? Something for me?"

"Yes. I went to Hunter's Home Bakery today and picked up a fresh apple pie for dessert. That's what you're going to have tonight. That and vanilla ice cream."

"Whoopee," Diane said excitedly. "I love apple pie and ice cream."

"So do I," Charlie said. "And ice cream."

"Me, too," Gordon said with a smile. "Hunter's is the best there is. You can't leave me out of this."

"Don't worry, Gordon. You're going to get apple pie, too." *Should be in his face he's getting it. With those kids out demonstrating, things are really going to escalate now. What a mess he's making of his life. And embarrassing me in the process. Everyone knows I'm his wife. For now, anyway.*

〜

After Carol got Charlie and Diane off to bed, she fixed herself a Scotch and soda and joined Gordon in the living room. He was sitting by the fireplace nursing a vodka and orange.

"Those students were absolutely right," she said as she settled into the other armchair. "You really are a bigot. I simply don't understand what has got into you over the last few years. You're in a time warp, Gordon. A nineteenth century time warp."

"You said that before. Got anything new you want to add?"

"Good God! There's just no point in talking to you. You're a lost cause, Gordon. An absolute lost cause and that's why I want a – a ..."

She almost said "divorce" but checked herself at the last second. *Not the right time yet. Still haven't determined how best to handle things with Charlie and Diane.*

"You want a what? That's the second time this week you've started to say something and then stopped. Got something you want to get off your chest?"

"No, I don't have anything I want to get off my chest. And I don't want to prolong this useless conversation with you either. It's like talking to a wall."

"My, my, aren't we just overflowing with original expressions tonight. 'Talking to a wall. Stuck in a time warp.' Nineteenth century time warp at that. Surely you can do better than that, Carol."

"Actually, Gordon, I can't. That was my best shot."

With that, she picked up her glass and headed for the family room.

After she left, Gordon just sat there looking at the fire. He wondered what it was she had almost said. Almost said and then stopped. *That's twice this week. Maybe she's going to ask me for a divorce. Use my affair with Ruth as grounds. Accuse me of adultery. Actually, she doesn't have to do that. You aren't required to prove adultery or anything like that to get a divorce these days. Then again, maybe that's not what it was. Whatever it was, it's bound to come out sooner or later. Be interesting to see what it is.*

He went through to his study and set about marking the last of the student essays.

Carol was in the family room trying to read *Zorba the Greek*. It wasn't working. She was too unsettled to get her head back into the book. She really did see the student demonstration as the start of an escalation. *They'll probably be at it again tomorrow. And there'll be more of them. A lot more of them. Wonder if Bill will be there. Some of the signs were about Big Thunder and Saunders' pipeline. It would make sense for him to be there. Maybe I should join him. Maybe not, Carol. You're still Gordon's wife and they do want to have him deported. Not seriously. But that's a good way to get their message across.*

She went through to the kitchen and fixed herself another Scotch and soda. Then she picked up the book and went upstairs to her bedroom. *Might have more luck reading it up there.*

CHAPTER

- 21 -

There was an article about Gordon on the front page of the *Globe and Mail* Wednesday morning.

About 100 students demonstrated at the University of Toronto yesterday to protest the views of a professor who is expected to be nominated by acclamation tomorrow night as the Conservative candidate for the Toronto riding of Meadowbrook.

The students, most of whom appeared to be of immigrant background, said political science professor Gordon MacArthur had "crossed over the line."

MacArthur, who is expected to be acclaimed as a Conservative candidate for the next election tomorrow night, is on record as saying there are too many people in turbans "sprouting up" in white neighborhoods.

He has also said that too much legislation is introduced to win votes from the waves of immigrants who moved to Canada over the last three decades.

"We're Canadians, too," 23-year-old Rocco Di Giorgio said as he held up a sign saying "Deport MacArthur". "What he's been saying insults our parents. They pay taxes, too, you know."

Some of the signs the students, who appeared to be mostly Italian, brandished as they marched back and forth in front of the entrance to the university's Davidson Hall around 1:00 p.m. yesterday said: "OUR DADS BUILT THE SUBWAY, da Vinci's kids, CANADA FOR EVERY ONE, Dante's Infernos, Michelangelo loves US."

"Professor MacArthur's as bigoted as they come," 20-year-old Elvio Orsini said. "We're not going to take any more of his bull. Canada's our country, too."

Loretta Delfino, 19, had a sign that read: "STRENGTH THROUGH DIVERSITY." She said it was important for the students to speak out.

"We can't just sit on our butts and do nothing," she said. "Hate mongers like MacArthur must be confronted."

There were several signs that said: "FREE THE INDIANS, No Pipeline."

MacArthur is a strong supporter of a gas pipeline the Saunders Energy Corporation wants to run through an Indian reserve southwest of Calgary.

He is also the driving force behind a small group of professors at the University of Toronto pushing for "equal rights for whites."

Reached at his office yesterday afternoon, MacArthur said: "What we had over the lunch hour was a bunch of disaffected immigrant students with nothing better to do with their time."

Asked for his reaction to some of the students saying he should be deported, MacArthur said: "I don't take those students or anything they have to say about me seriously. Not at all."

MacArthur claims that the student demonstration will not hurt his chances as a Conservative candidate in the next election.

"From what I saw on TV, most of the demonstrators were of immigrant background. We don't have many immigrants in Meadowbrook. The voters in my riding are mostly middle-class whites."

Gordon looked at the three-column picture of the students parading in front of Davidson Hall and read the article for the second time.

"Bigoted?" he muttered. "Hatemonger? That's libelous. I should sue the *Globe* for printing this shit. Why would they publish slanderous statements like that?"

He counted the number of lines in the article. Fifty-six. Then he counted the number of lines about what he had to say.

"That's short shrift. I only get fifteen lines about the demonstration. Fifteen out of fifty-six. Why'd they even bother calling me?"

He put the paper down on the kitchen table, put some ground coffee in the coffee maker, and got himself a bowl of bran flakes. He'd gotten up earlier than usual because he had to be at the university before eight-thirty.

Anne arrived just before seven-thirty and started to prepare breakfast for Carol and the children. Gordon opened the paper and read the article again. Carol came into the kitchen just as he had finished reading the article for the third time, said good morning to Anne and poured herself a cup of coffee.

"Anything new in the *Globe*, Gordon?"

"They did a piece on the student demonstration. It's on the front page."

Carol picked up the paper and started to read the article.

"That's quite a picture," she said. "They've got the 'deport MacArthur' sign front and centre."

"The *Globe* is obviously biased," Gordon said. "I only got fifteen lines. Fifteen out of fifty-six."

"You actually counted them?"

"Yes, I counted them. I had a feeling the article was biased in favor of the students and the Indians. I wanted to confirm my suspicions. And it is fifteen out of fifty-six. That article's a smear job."

"I wouldn't say that," Carol said as she read the last sentence. "You've been doing quite a bit of smearing yourself lately. If my parents were from Italy, I'd be pretty angry with you, too. Some of the things you've said were totally uncalled for. The demonstration was quite appropriate in my opinion. If my parents had come here from Italy or Greece, I'd have been out demonstrating, too. Cause and effect, Gordon. You can't expect to say the things you've been saying about the immigrant communities with immunity. Yesterday's demonstration was a predictable reaction. I'm surprised it took them so long to speak their minds."

"Might have known you'd feel that way. You just don't see what's happening in our country. The rapid changes that are taking place before your very eyes."

"Like what?"

"Like – like …"

"Got you stumped there. You can't think of anything off the top. What's happening, Gordon, is that we now have people who, like the students' signs said, come from the land of da Vinci, Michelangelo, Puccini and Dante. They're bringing a vibrancy, a life force, to Canadian culture that we didn't have before. Change, Gordon? Yes. But, change for the better. They're bringing us some of the best features of other worlds, other cultures, and making Canada an even better country to live in. The sidewalk patios we didn't have before. The great food we now have on College, St. Clair and out on the Danforth. The CHIN picnic on the Islands. Luciano Pavarotti at Massey Hall. That's what's happening. Happening for the good. You're just too steeped in all things British and beautiful to see the benefit of Canada becoming a truly vibrant multicultural society."

Gordon looked at his watch. It was five to eight. "I've got to go. I've got a meeting at eight-thirty and I'm late already. I simply don't have time to argue about this right now. That doesn't change the fact that the article in the *Globe* was a hatchet job. Pure and simple. An unadulterated smear. And I'll wager there will be worse to come. They've got it in for me. I'm sure there'll be more where that came from."

"I hope so, Gordon. I really do. You deserve some much-needed pushback. I hope this really is the tip of the iceberg. Someone needs to take you on."

Gordon decided to let that one go. He pulled on his coat and headed out the door.

There were more than twice as many students demonstrating outside Davidson Hall over the lunch hour. City-TV covered part of it live. As Bill watched on the TV set in his office, he recognized quite a few students who were taking the North American Indian Studies course. Most of them were of British background.

"University campus police estimate there are about two hundred and fifty students taking part in this demonstration," the City-TV reporter said. "So far, the police have had no trouble managing the situation."

There were a lot more signs this time about Big Thunder and the gas pipeline.

"RESPECT TREATY RIGHTS; IT'S THEIR HOME AND NATIVE LAND; STICK YOUR PIPE IN YOUR EAR; KEEP BIG THUNDER FREE; SUPPORT THE INDIANS; STOP BIG GAS; LET THEM LIVE."

The reporter was talking to a young woman with one of the DEPORT MACARTHUR signs.

"He doesn't speak for us," the student said. "We support the Indians' position. They shouldn't run that pipeline through Indian land."

"May I have your name please?"

"Jessica MacFarlane. I'm a third-year sociology student."

The reporter turned to a student with a SUPPORT TREATY RIGHTS sign.

"And what brings you here?" the reporter asked as she held up the microphone.

"Under the treaties the Indians signed with the Queen, that is their land. We should respect the treaties. The Indians have already been forced to give up too much of their land. We made a deal with them. We should stick to it."

"And your name is?"

"Parker. Margaret Parker."

"Are you in sociology, too, Miss Parker?" the reporter asked.

"Yes. I'm in my second year and I'm taking Indian studies under Dr. William Eagletail. He's a Blackfoot from a reserve near Calgary and he's got a PhD from Berkeley."

The camera panned the demonstration. It was clear that, this time, the students of British background outnumbered those from the immigrant communities.

"I'll bet Alfred Howell had a lot to do with this," Bill said to himself. "This is quite a show. Quite a show indeed."

He was quite moved to see so many white Anglo-Saxon students taking part in the demonstration. He could understand the immigrant students being there because of the statements Gordon had made about their communities. But he was pleasantly surprised, and quite touched, to see the significant show of support for the Indians at Big Thunder from the other students.

The reporter stuck her microphone in front of a blonde male student with a sign that said "IT'S THEIR HOME AND NATIVE LAND."

"May I have your name please?"

"I'm Michael Harrison and I'm in fourth-year sociology."

"Why are you here?" the reporter asked.

"Because someone has to speak up for the Indians. We've taken their culture, their language, and their sacred ceremonies away from them. All they have left is their land– the little bit of it that they've got left – and that pipeline should not be rammed through the Big Thunder reserve."

The cameraman panned the demonstration one more time, zooming in on the campus police monitoring the situation from the steps in front of Davidson Hall. The reporter signed off and they switched back to the newsroom.

Bill turned the TV off and got himself a cup of tea. As he sat at his desk, drinking his tea and looking out the window, he thought about some of the things the students had said. *I really have had an impact on them. The North American Indian Studies program definitely is changing their perspective on Indian people. Some of them were so strong in what they had to say. So passionate. They really do support us.*

The phone rang. It was Carol and she was quite excited about the coverage of the demonstration.

"Did you hear them, Bill? You couldn't have done better yourself. Those young students are with you one hundred per cent. This is going to have an impact. This is going to build up more support for your position on the pipeline. They were great. Just great."

"Yes, I saw them. Quite a few of them have been in my classes. Mostly sociology students. And, yes, they were great. I'd no idea they felt that way."

"It's because of you that they think that way. Your course has done a lot of good. They'd never have spoken out so strongly on behalf of the Indians three years ago. Your course has made a difference. It's brought about a paradigm shift. A much-needed shift in public opinion."

"I wouldn't go that far. It's certainly had an impact on my students and on our young people taking the course by correspondence. But that's a long way from bringing about a significant shift in the negative attitude most white adults have towards Indian people."

"Hope you're not including me in that category."

"No. No. Sorry. I'd never say anything like that about you. But, as I said when we first spoke on the phone, you're an exception, Carol. An exception that, unfortunately, proves the rule."

"You're probably right about the rule. But that doesn't change how wonderful it was to see those young WASPs out there demonstrating on behalf of Indian people. It was just marvellous."

They discussed the demonstration some more and then Carol asked if he had been able to get any information about the Saunders gas pipeline.

"I spoke to Hughie. He doesn't know much about it. Dad's the one who was going to take them to court. Hughie's going to ask Mom if he can see the file Dad put together on it. Meanwhile, we're making progress. We'll get the information you need."

"Good. That's good news. I'm really looking forward to nailing Saunders to the cross on this one. We're going to put things right."

"Speaking of putting things right, how are things progressing between you and the White Power Conservative?" Bill asked. "Are you still going to divorce him?"

"Yes. I put a call in to Ben Horowitz this morning. He's one of the best divorce lawyers there is. He's tied up on a case until Monday but I've got an appointment for Tuesday morning. Yes, I am going through with the divorce."

"Good for you. You seem to be in control of the agenda."

"Yes, for a change. I haven't controlled much of anything these past four years but I'm getting things back to normal. The divorce lawyer Tuesday morning and lunch with the managing partner at Haldimand and Brock. Things are coming back together again. I am getting my life back. One piece at a time, but I'm getting there."

"That's great. I'm very happy for you. Now, I've got to run. I've got a class at two."

"Okay. And I will be there tomorrow night. You can count on it."

"I'm looking forward to it. Wouldn't miss having you there for anything."

As he put the phone back on the hook, Bill wondered what, if anything, was going to happen between him and Carol. *She's serious about the divorce. Already has an appointment set up with the divorce lawyer. Can't see her changing her mind. Not after some of the things she's said about MacArthur and his white supremacist crap. So, we're both getting a divorce. Me from Jean and Carol from MacArthur. Things get more interesting all the time.*

~

Gran Winston got a call from Harland Edwards just after one o'clock Calgary time.

"What in the world is Gordon up to?" Edwards asked. "There were almost three hundred students demonstrating against him over the lunch hour at the university today and he's been saying some negative things about immigrants that are not at all helpful to the party. I got a call from the Prime Minister's chief of staff a short time ago and he's out for blood."

"Good gracious," Winston exclaimed. "I have absolutely no idea what you're talking about. I'm up to my ass in alligators on the hotel project and haven't been paying attention to anything else."

Edwards told him about the two demonstrations the students had held in front of Davidson Hall protesting Gordon's statements about the immigrants and voicing support for the Indians at Big Thunder.

"And then, in the *Globe* this morning, he made some unacceptably dismissive comments about the immigrant students. He was quoted as saying that yesterday's demonstration was orchestrated by, quote, a bunch of disaffected immigrant students with nothing better to do with their time. He compounded that by saying he didn't take anything the students said seriously and then added, quote, we don't have many immigrants in Meadowbrook. The voters in my riding are mostly middle-class whites."

"He's right on that point, Harland. There are hardly any immigrants in Meadowbrook. Thank God for that."

"That might have worked in regard to yesterday's demonstration, Gran, but not today's. I saw some of the television coverage. Most of the kids were white, Anglo-Saxon."

"Seriously?"

"Yes, I'd say more than half of the students at the demonstration today were of British heritage. Just like the majority of the voters in Meadowbrook. And that is what has got the PMO's shorts in a knot. They think Gordon is doing a significant amount of damage. They want him to withdraw from seeking the nomination."

"That's the same story we heard from Mitchell last week. You were able to fix that one, Harland. Can you not work your magic again this time?"

"I will try and do that, Gran. I will speak to the Prime Minister. However, I must warn you, it took a lot of persuasion to get him to tell Mitchell to back off the first time I called. He was quite clear, adamantly so, that if Gordon gave off so much as a whiff of white power he would, in his words, pull the plug on him – even if it meant losing the election in Meadowbrook."

"That does sound rather ominous. He was that serious about it?"

"Dead serious. Floyd has zero tolerance for anything that could cost votes in an election. And, with the strong chance that he'll be calling one within the next couple of weeks, he's even less tolerant today."

"Damn, that does put a different complexion on things. Are you saying it's hopeless? That the PM will drop Gordon?"

"What I'm saying is that this is a very serious matter. Gordon should have known better than to get himself into this predicament. However, Gran, he is your son-in-law and you're one of my best friends. I'll do my best. Can't promise anything but I will try. I'll give it my best shot."

"I appreciate that, Harland. I really do."

"Well, let's see how things turn out. I called you because I wanted you to understand the gravity of the situation. If – and it's a big if – I am able to persuade the Prime Minister to allow Gordon to have the nomination, I'll be relying on you to ride herd on him. Make sure he toes the line. Keeps his opinions about the immigrants to himself – at least for now."

About an hour later, Edwards called again.

"It was tough but the Prime Minister has agreed – reluctantly I must add – to let Gordon have one last chance. The nomination meeting will go ahead tomorrow night as planned and Gordon will be the candidate. However, and I must emphasize this, Gran, if there is one more damaging situation for the party, he'll be out on his ear quick as you can say Jack Flash."

"That's a relief," Winston said. "Thank you, Harland. I am forever grateful."

"You're more than welcome. Now, here's what's going to happen. The PMO is drafting a brief statement saying Gordon is extremely sorry for the statements he has made about the immigrant communities and sincerely regrets any hurt he might have caused."

"You're not serious. Apologize to the immigrants? What the hell for?"

"This isn't just about the immigrants, Gran. This is about winning the election. If Gordon has to grovel a little in the process, that's the way it must be. Some of the calls coming from the leadership in the immigrant communities are quite disturbing. Some of them are threatening to sit the election out. They're not going to vote for anyone."

"There we go catering to the immigrants again. We don't need them. We can win ridings like Meadowbrook without them. Screw them, I say."

"I know how you feel, Gran. I appreciate where you're coming from on this issue. However, this is going to be a tight election. We're trying for a third term and it's going to be tough. I've just been told that, according to our internal polling, there are at least nine seats we can take away from the Liberals in the inner cities. We need those seats to form a majority. That's what's different this time. Those seats are up for grabs and we can't let Gordon's views on the immigrant communities kill any chance we have of winning them. He must apologize."

"And, if he doesn't?"

"The Prime Minister won't sign his nomination papers. Even if he gets the nomination tomorrow night, he won't be allowed to run as a Conservative candidate. It's as simple as that."

"That's blackmail," Winston muttered.

"No, Gran, it's politics. This is how the game is played."

"So, the immigrants win again."

"No, Gran, Gordon lives to fight another day. Once he gets the nomination and wins the election, he will be an MP. From that point on, there's not much the Prime Minister can do to shut him up. He can keep him out of his cabinet but he can't stop him from speaking his mind. Once he's in Ottawa, Gordon will have unlimited opportunities to speak out on the issues we've been discussing with Jack Saunders and the others. He can still be a voice for the white community. For British values. He can still be our voice in Parliament."

Winston thought about it for a moment. Edwards was right. Once Gordon got to Ottawa he would be able to speak out freely on the issues. And, more importantly, he could still keep a watchful eye out for anything that would benefit, or hurt, Winston's business interests. He could still set up meetings with important cabinet ministers and, after the current crisis was put to rest, with the Prime Minister himself.

"All right, Harland, how do you want to handle this?"

"I should have the statement from the PMO in less than an hour. I will read it to you in order to make sure you are in agreement with the overall thrust. I will then fax it to you so you can read it to Gordon. If he is okay with it – actually, he doesn't have much choice in the matter – the statement will be released to the media from party headquarters. While the PMO will have drafted the statement, they want to distance themselves from it and that is why it will be released by the national office.

"Meanwhile, they want Gordon to button his lip. Say nothing that's not covered in the statement. Not another word about, what he calls, quite correctly, the clamouring, lobbying, high-pressure, special-interest minority groups. He'll have plenty of time for that after he gets elected. Right now, our job is to make sure he gets the nomination and the PM's signature on his nomination papers."

"All right, Harland, I will wait for your call."

"You're not too pleased with this, are you? I can tell from your voice."

"You've got that right but, as you yourself said, this is how the game is played. I'll go along with it and, as you said, once Gordon is elected we will have more control over the situation."

Gordon was at home when Winston called. He'd just finished supper. Winston told him about the two calls he'd received from Harland Edwards and that the situation was quite serious.

"There are those in the PMO who believe you should be dropped like a hot potato. The only thing we have going for us right now is Harland's close personal relationship with the Prime Minister. They've worked together for decades and there is also the fact that Harland raises millions for the party. No one else could have persuaded the Prime Minister to give you another chance."

"But Henry thought everything was just fine," Gordon said. "He even told Don Mitchell to keep his nose out of Meadowbrook's affairs."

"Henry's wrong on this issue, Gordon. There's more than Meadowbrook involved here. The Prime Minister has to consider, and rightly so, the impact you're having on Conservative voters in the inner city ridings. Some of the ethnic leaders are hopping mad right now. They're not going to switch to the Liberals but they are prepared to sit this election out. Not vote for anyone. And that, as Harland says, means we will forfeit the opportunity to pick up several Liberal seats we need to form a majority government. This is going to be a tough election and we need every seat we can get. Anyway, let's not prolong this discussion. You have only one option. Make the apology or forfeit the nomination."

"That's putting it rather bluntly," Gordon said.

"Gordon," Winston said with an edge to his voice, "if you weren't my son-in-law, we wouldn't be having this conversation. They would have dropped you as a potential candidate a long time ago. After the first articles came out in the newspapers. I strongly urge you to make the damned apology. You have no other option at this time."

Gordon could tell that Winston was quite cross with him. *He clearly thinks I've screwed up rather badly. Created a problem for the PMO that reflects on him because I'm his son-in-law.*

"I'm sorry, Gran. I didn't mean to cause problems for you. I really should have been more careful about what I said."

"That's water under the bridge. The main thing now is to let them issue the statement of apology. Don't take it too hard. Harland says this is only a temporary setback. Once you get the nomination and win the election, you'll be able to say and do pretty well anything you want. You can still be a strong voice for British values. You'll still have your whole career ahead of you. But, for now, let's make the apology and move on."

Gordon was glad to hear that Edwards and Winston felt this was only a temporary thing and that he'd still be an MP and, if he smoothed things over with the PM, he might still make it to cabinet.

"All right, Gran. Please read me the statement they've prepared."

"You're making the right decision, Gordon. Things will work out for you. This is the statement Harland faxed to me. Quote. University of Toronto professor Gordon MacArthur has apologized for unacceptable comments about immigrant communities that have been attributed to him in recent newspaper articles. Quote: I regret very much any hurt that might have been caused to anyone because of my negative statements. Statements which have been attributed to me in the media were intolerant and completely unacceptable. I welcome the contribution that immigrant communities have made to Canada and truly believe that Canada is a better place because of their having come to our country. End of quote…"

"But …"

"Let me finish, Gordon. Please. The statement goes on to say quote: MacArthur is expected to be acclaimed as the Conservative candidate for the Toronto riding of Meadowbrook Thursday night. No other candidate filed an intention to run prior to the deadline. MacArthur says he regrets any embarrassment his statements might have caused for the Conservative Party of Canada. Quote: I know that my statements run counter to the position of the Conservative Party of Canada with respect to immigrant communities. The Conservative Party has always welcomed and supported immigrants. End of Quote.

That's it, Gordon. I suggest that you should authorize them to release the statement,"

"I've been jotting it down as you read it, Gran, and there is one change that I would want to make. I am not prepared to say the part about welcoming the contribution of the immigrants and saying Canada is a better place because of them. At the end of the statement I say that what I said runs counter to official party policy. That should be enough. If they'll take out the part about me, personally, welcoming the immigrants, then the rest of the statement is okay. I just can't say the welcoming thing. I'd be lying if I said that. And, on top of that, I don't want to have a statement like that on the record. It would come back to haunt me later on."

"They're in no mood to make changes, Gordon. They want you to approve the statement as is."

"Would you let them put out a statement like that under your name? Welcoming the immigrants and saying Canada is a better place because they're here?"

"Probably not. Give me a minute to take another look at what Harland faxed to me."

After about a minute, Winston came back on the line and said: "You're right. Having a statement like that from you on the record would undermine anything you say about the drastic changes that are taking place and the way the government cooks up programs to keep them happy. Let me see what I can do. I'll call Harland and see what can be done."

"Thanks, Gran. I just couldn't bring myself to say anything like that in writing."

"I understand. I'll get it changed. Meanwhile, they don't want you to say anything to the reporters that isn't in the statement. They want to put a muzzle on you until after the election. You can talk about transportation, health care and things like that during the election campaign but nothing about the immigrants until you're sworn in and they assign you a seat in Parliament."

"It's a bit late for that, Gran. I did four or five interviews this afternoon. Nobody told me I wasn't supposed to say anything. The reporters asked me questions and I gave them answers."

"Damn, that does complicate things."

"But, it should be all right. Most of the questions were about the Indians and their opposition to Jack Saunders' pipeline. I didn't say anything negative about the immigrants. Nothing that would cause problems for the party or the PMO."

"Well, that is a relief," Winston said. "I wouldn't want you to be starting another fire while I'm still trying to put out the first one. By all means, keep speaking out on the pipeline issue. I don't see how the PMO could object to that. And now, with those damned white students out there demonstrating their support for the Indians, we'll need your voice more than ever. Yes, keep speaking out in support of the pipeline. Meanwhile, I'll talk to Harland and get this matter resolved. I'll get back to you within the hour."

Gordon had a sense that things were starting to unravel. The *Globe* had done a hatchet job on him that morning. Dave Saunders' secretary had called around ten to say he was unavoidably delayed in Calgary and would appreciate it very much if their meeting could be moved to Saturday. Same time. Same suite at the Harbour Castle Hotel. And now the PMO had drafted a statement in which he was supposed to apologize to the immigrants.

This isn't what I was expecting. Things seemed to be on a roll. And now this. Me having to apologize publicly to a bunch of damned immigrants.

Winston called back just before seven. The PMO had accepted the revision to the statement. They were not at all happy about it. The statement had now gone out to the media. They did not want Gordon to utter a single word to the media that was not in the statement.

"At first, they fought Harland on dropping the line about you welcoming the immigrants and saying how much better Canada is now that they're here. But, like you said, that can be implied from the part where you concede that your comments run counter to official party policy. So, on that basis, they reluctantly agreed to make the change. This thing will blow over, Gordon. You will get the nomination. You will get elected and be the Member of Parliament for Meadowbrook."

"Thanks, Gran, I really appreciate everything you've done. I couldn't have got through this without you."

"You're more than welcome, Gordon. I want you to be an MP and I have every confidence that, despite this setback, you're going to do well up there. You'll be a voice of sanity in the House of Commons. A voice for British values and traditions. Now I must go. This business with the PMO has taken up more than enough of my time today. I have to get back to something that makes me money."

CHAPTER
- 22 -

When Gordon picked up the *Globe and Mail* on the front porch Thursday morning, he saw an item on the bottom left side of the front page with a headline that said: "Conservative candidate withdraws comments about immigrant groups."

He read the article right there on the porch.

> The Conservative candidate for the Toronto riding of Meadowbrook has apologized for making "unacceptable" comments about immigrant communities.
>
> In a statement released from the national headquarters of the Conservative Party of Canada last night, University of Toronto political science professor Gordon MacArthur said: "I regret very much any hurt that might have been caused to anyone because of my negative statements."
>
> MacArthur said his statements were "intolerant and completely unacceptable."
>
> MacArthur, 35, is expected to be acclaimed as the Conservative candidate for the Toronto riding of Meadowbrook tonight. No other candidate is running.
>
> MacArthur has been dubbed the "white power Conservative" because of negative comments he has made about immigrant communities. He has claimed that there are too many people in turbans "sprouting up"

in white neighborhoods. He is also on record as saying that too much legislation is introduced to win votes from the waves of immigrants who moved to Canada over the last three decades.

However, in the statement that was released to the media by the national headquarters of the Conservative Party last night, MacArthur said: "I know that my statements run counter to the position of the Conservative Party of Canada with respect to immigrant communities. The Conservative Party has always welcomed and supported immigrants."

MacArthur said he regrets any embarrassment his statements might have caused to the Conservative Party.

A highly-placed Conservative source told *The Globe* last night that MacArthur "is on probation."

If he causes any more problems for the Conservative Party, the source said, "he will be replaced overnight."

(See story A12)

Gordon went to the kitchen, poured himself a coffee, moved through to his study and closed the door. He turned to page A12. There was a big picture of the student demonstration on top of a headline that said: "Students show support for Indians on pipeline." Several of the comments made by the students were included in the story.

This is just great, Gordon muttered sarcastically to himself. *An apology from me to the immigrant hordes and a big demonstration in support of the Indians. Things really are going downhill.*

Carol and the children were in the kitchen having breakfast. He didn't want to get into a discussion with Carol about this latest setback. She didn't know about the phone calls he'd had from her father and he was in no mood to explain the situation to her now that the damage was done. *"See, Gordon," she'll say, "I told you things would get worse. We're only seeing the tip of this iceberg." I don't need any more of her patronizing crap. Screw her. I'm getting out of here.*

He left the newspaper on his desk, popped his head in the kitchen door to say hello and goodbye to Carol and the children, and headed off to the university. As he drove east along Lake Shore Boulevard, he reflected on the events of the last few days. Everything had looked so good. He'd been on the front page of the *Globe* warning that white women and children would freeze in the dark of winter if the Indians were allowed to block Saunders' pipeline. Bracken and Winston had told him he was doing splendidly. He'd been asked to give a speech to the Empire Club in Calgary. Flying out there first class. The Prime Minister had given his personal okay for him to be the candidate for Meadowbrook. Dave Saunders was going to do some local polling in Meadowbrook and provide him with a campaign office and phones in the heart of the riding. Henderson was pleased as punch with the publicity he was getting and wanted the Equal Opportunities Council to deal with broader issues. *And now, here I am on the front page of the* Globe *apologizing to the goddamned immigrants. That should make Carol happy. She'll be pleased as hell to see me looking stupid on the front page of the* Globe.

Carol was pleased when she read the article. *Wonder what brought this on?* she asked herself. *He didn't say a thing to me about apologizing to the immigrant groups. Someone must have got to him. Forced his hand. Probably the PMO. There was bound to be a reaction to those things he's been saying about the immigrant communities. Cause and effect. That's what I told him. Cause and effect. Those student demonstrations would also have been a factor. Things really were escalating. The PMO probably laid down the law and forced him to apologize. He certainly wouldn't have done it on his own accord. Not Mr. Rule Britannia Gordon MacArthur.*

She turned to page A12 and read the story about the latest student demonstration. *This is good news for Bill and his people. Having white students demonstrating in support of the Indians cannot help but strengthen our hand. We need all the support we can get.*

Charlie and Diane were ready to leave for school. Anne had them all dressed up and ready to go. Carol dropped Diane off at Montessori and then drove Charlie to Brookdale Elementary. When she got home, she went to Gordon's study, closed the door and called Bill.

"Did you see the story about Gordon on the front page of the *Globe* this morning?" she asked. "Apologizing for the comments he made about the immigrants?"

"No. We don't get it out here in the west. Please read it to me."

Carol read the full article to him. "I doubt very much his apology was sincere," Bill said. "It was very carefully worded. He says he regrets any harm his statements might have caused but he does not withdraw them. Look at it closely, Carol, and you'll see he says the comments he made quote run counter to the position of the Conservative Party. He does not say they run counter to his own position. That he has all of a sudden seen the light and can't believe he said those things. No, all he does say is that his comments do not reflect the official line of the Conservative Party of Canada. He still thinks the same neanderthal way. Nothing has changed. He still has a hate on for immigrant people and Indians."

Carol had been rereading part of the article as Bill spoke. "You're right," she said. "There's no way Gordon would make a statement like that on his own. This whole thing's being run out of the PMO in an effort to stem some of the damage he's causing them in the immigrant communities. It's all about votes. Making sure his comments don't do any more damage to their base in the ethnic communities. But, Bill, what's even more important is the story about those white students out demonstrating again in support of Big Thunder. That was great. Your side certainly has the momentum on this one. Those students are not going to give up. They'll probably be out again today. Maybe even more of them than yesterday."

Carol was right. There were more students in front of Davidson Hall that day. More than three hundred of them. Gordon's half-hearted apology had had no impact on them at all. It was the Indians at Big Thunder that they were most interested in. They wanted to do everything within their power to help the Indians block Saunders' pipeline.

Instead of demonstrating in front of Davidson Hall as they had done the day before, they started marching – fifteen abreast – north on King's College Circle towards Hart House. The students at the front held a huge banner that said: "U of T students support Big Thunder Indians."

At the very last moment, they veered right, crossed under the bridge and got onto the road leading up onto Queen's Park Crescent. Causing traffic to back up all the way to Bloor Street. They marched south and assembled in front of the Ontario Legislative Building. Once there, they started to chant: "Respect Indian land. Respect the Treaties. Respect Indian land. Respect the treaties."

Six police cruisers and four cops on motorcycles arrived within minutes. The officer in charge told them they couldn't demonstrate in front of the Legislative Building without a permit. After a heated argument and a minor scuffle with the police, the leaders of the demonstration started them all marching back onto Queen's Park Crescent, down to College Street and west back to Davidson Hall.

They had made their point. It had all been captured by the TV stations, the radio reporters and the reporters from the *Globe and Mail,* the *Toronto Star* and the *Sun.* They'd be back on the evening newscasts in a matter of hours.

Professor Henderson came storming into Gordon's office just after two o'clock brandishing the front page of the *Globe and Mail.*

"What the hell is this?" he fumed. "Why in God's name would you be on the front page of the *Globe* apologizing to those goddamned immigrants?"

Gordon told him about the calls he'd received from Gran Winston and that the senior officials in the Prime Minister's Office were demanding that he step down as the candidate for Meadowbrook.

"There really was no other option," he said. "It was either agree to the statement of apology or be dropped as the candidate. The first statement they drafted was even worse. They had me saying I actually welcomed the contribution the immigrants have made and that they'd made Canada a better place. There was no way I was going to say anything like that. If they had insisted on it, I'd have given up the nomination. I would never say anything like that. Especially not on the front page of the *Globe.*"

Henderson lit his pipe and reflected for a moment. "Well, I'm glad you held your ground on that one," he said. "You have to draw the line somewhere. Sounds like they really had you by the balls and were squeezing hard."

Gordon told Henderson what Winston had said about this being a temporary setback. Something that had to be done to stay in the game and live to fight another day.

"But, Donald, once I'm elected, I can do and say anything I want. The PMO will have no control over me whatsoever. What needs to be said to further the goals of the Equal Opportunities Council will be said. They can't stop me,"

"The PM can keep you out of his cabinet," Henderson said. "He can control you that way."

"Gran, my father-in-law, doesn't think that will necessarily be the case. He says most of the people in senior positions in the Conservative Party see things pretty much the same way we do. Once we form a majority government, we'll have a four-year mandate that will allow us to do pretty well anything we want to do. When that happens, my father-in-law says, we won't have to worry about the ethnics until the next election.

"He believes the PMO will allow me some more slack and I'll probably still make it to the cabinet. Not so much because of me but because the Conservatives in Meadowbrook feel they are owed a cabinet seat. They raise one helluva lot of money for the party and they will be demanding that I be appointed. It will happen. Not as fast as it would have before this immigrant apology fiasco, but my father-in-law is quite confident that it will happen."

That seemed to sit well with Henderson. He'd been red-hot angry when he read the article in the *Globe*. He simply couldn't understand how Gordon could have said anything like that. But, now, he understood. It was all a subterfuge. A sop to the immigrants to keep them onside until after the election.

"I believe that I do understand now, Gordon. This is, as you say, temporary. A minor setback. Things will get back on track after the election."

"Yes, Donald. That is the way I see it. A little detour along the way. I hate like hell seeing that statement in the paper but it was the only option at this time. They really did put the screws to me."

The people at the special meeting Bill had called for Thursday night were in a great mood. They were simply ecstatic about the show of support from the students at the University of Toronto.

It turned out that the young Ojibway in the smartly-tailored corduroy suit – Fred Manitowabi from the Wikwemikong reserve on Manitoulin Island – was a close friend of one of the students who helped organize the demonstrations.

"They'll be at it again tomorrow," he said. "Only this time with a big difference. They're going to march to City Hall and occupy Nathan Phillips Square. They won't have a permit, so the cops are going to hassle them. Rough them up a bit. That's when they're going to have the sit-in. Just sit on their asses on the square and have the cops drag them one by one to the paddy wagons. It'll be great TV."

"That does sound good," Bill said. "The coverage of that will be even better than the demonstration they had yesterday."

"They're determined," Manitowabi said enthusiastically. "They'll do whatever it takes to stop that pipeline. By the way, Bill, in case you don't already know, the main organizers are from your classes. They're all taking the course on the North American Indians."

"I suspected that," Bill said. "One of my students wanted me to join the demonstration."

"Why didn't you?" Carol asked. "I think we should all join them. Show solidarity with the people at Big Thunder."

"I don't think that would be a good idea," Bill said. "We have a vested interest in the outcome of the hearings. It's Indian land they want to run that pipeline through. People expect us to be out demonstrating. They don't expect white kids to be willing to get themselves arrested in front of City Hall in order to show support for our cause. They have a lot more credibility than any one of us on this issue. Their white faces give the demonstration a lot more credibility than ours do."

"I think Bill is right, Carol," Manitowabi said. "I discussed this issue with Alfred Howell. He's my friend and one of the key organizers. He's the one who asked Bill to join them on the front line. It does look better if it's mostly white faces there. They do, like Bill said, give the demonstration a lot more credibility than we ever could."

"You might be right," Carol said. "But I'd just love to be marching with one of those signs."

At that point, Bill told them he had called the special meeting to let them know that the legal fees for the Energy Resource Conservation Board of Alberta hearings were running a lot higher than the Indians at Big Thunder had expected.

"They need some help to pay the lawyers," he said. "They'd like us to do some fundraising here in Toronto to help them out."

"I would have thought the Band Council would be able to handle those costs," Carol said.

"They could, but they won't," Bill said. "Actually, the majority of the councillors are with Jack Saunders and Chief Harold Littlelight on this one. From what I understand, Littlelight is going to testify in support of Saunders running his pipeline through Big Thunder at the hearings next week. The action before the Energy Board is being financed by a small group my dad put together before he died. And they need our help. Pronto."

"With the show of support from the students, that shouldn't prove too difficult to do," Manitowabi said. "Some of those kids would be more than willing to hit their parents up for a contribution."

"That would be good," Bill said. "Maybe you could talk to Alfred Howell and some of the other student leaders and see what they can do along that line. Meanwhile, I have a very good friend on the university's board of governors, Saul Goldenberg. Saul raised a lot of money for the American Indian Movement over the last couple of years and he's willing to raise some money for us. He's going to have a cocktail party at his house in Rosedale next Thursday at which he thinks he can pull in somewhere around $10,000. If Alfred can get the students to raise $3,000, that will take care of the lawyers for now. We can always raise more later."

"I think I know someone who will contribute a couple of thousand," Isaac Montour of the Six Nations of the Grand River said. "He's a lawyer at one of the biggest firms in Toronto. Can't let us use his name, but he will cut us a cheque."

Three other members of the committee said they could raise about $3,000 among them.

"That was a very good meeting," Bill said as he sat with Carol at a table in the Davidson Lounge having coffee later that evening. "We're on a roll."

"No doubt about that," Carol said. "Those students out there demonstrating on the streets were a much-needed shot in the arm."

"Were you serious about wanting to be out there demonstrating with the students?" Bill asked.

"Definitely. I'm with you all the way on this. You'll remember, when we first spoke on the phone after you were on *Toronto Focus* with Gordon, I said the pipeline issue brings into question the centuries-old conflict between your people and the Western Europeans. The age-old conflict about how we should all live on this planet. Indians living in harmony with the land and the whites wanting to harness and redirect nature. I said it was all relevant. And I really mean that, Bill. I'll fight to my last breath to make sure Jack Saunders doesn't run that pipeline through your mother's yard."

"I appreciate that, Carol. I really do. And I appreciate being here with you. You are a truly remarkable woman. I'm glad you made that call after I was on *Toronto Focus*."

"And I'm glad that I did, too. You're quite a remarkable person yourself," she said with a warm smile.

Perhaps it was Bill's Indianness, she thought, the part of him that was from the rodeos and pow wows and drinking tea with wise old men, that was drawing her to him so strongly. She felt an almost magnetic desire to experience more of him. To experience all of the pleasures that his mind and his body could provide. To explore his mind and body and, through that, learn more about herself. To find through Bill a way out of the life she now fully realized she no longer wanted to share with Gordon.

She had never experienced the kind of vibrations with Gordon that she was getting from sitting across the table from Bill. She imagined that the red tablecloth was a coverlet spread over their naked bodies early on a Sunday morning. A morning where they would have toast and coffee in bed and share the joys of conversation and loving until long past noon. A morning where they would have the time only weekends can provide to learn more of each other. To be together as a man and a woman.

Bill was feeling pretty much the same way. He found her very attractive, both physically and intellectually. Maybe, he thought, as she was going to divorce Gordon anyway, it might be good for them to spend some time together.

"Will you be in the city this weekend?" she asked.

Bill was not entirely surprised by her question. He had been looking deeply into her eyes and quietly suggesting with his that they make love. They were on the same wavelength.

"No. I'll be up at the cabin. I've got another three chapters to go on my book and I was figuring on working on it over the weekend."

"Oh," she said, with an unguarded trace of disappointment in her voice.

"You'd like the cabin," he said with a twinkle in his eye.

"Would I now?" she replied with a mischievous smile. "Where is it?"

"Up on Lake Muskoka."

"Lake Muskoka? That's pretty expensive real estate."

"Oh, it's not mine. The cabin belongs to an engineer friend of mine who's working on a project in Texas. It's only about three hours from here. If we left at four tomorrow, we'd be up there in time for steaks before the fireplace around eight."

"We would, would we? Are you suggesting?"

He reached across the table and took her hands in his. "Carol, you're too intelligent, too mature, to play the games of our childhood. I want you with me this weekend and I can see in your eyes that you would enjoy that too. Let your mouth say 'yes' as loudly as your eyes have already said it. It'll be good for both of us. It'll give you a chance to get your head straight."

"I can't," she said. "I'll be at the farm for the weekend. With Gordon and the children."

"Is that where you want to be?"

"No. It's not. It's just that …."

"Look, I like to get everything out front and in the open. That's the way I am. I do what I feel. I feel what I do. And, right now, I want to spend the weekend with you. Your mind is so vibrant and alive. You're a very special person, Carol Winston. And life is so short. Too short to do things we only half want to do. Right now, I only half want to work on my book. The other half of me wants to make love to your body and your mind. Come with me."

"But you said you only half want to make love to me," she said in a teasing, testing, tone.

He continued to stroke her palm sensually. "Right. But put that half together with the writing half and I'll have – we'll both have – a very whole weekend. A good weekend."

"I can't," she said reluctantly. "I have to …"

"Hey. Hey. You're on record, Carol Winston. You're on record as saying you don't *have* to do anything. Remember what you said to Fred Manitowabi at that first meeting? 'I'm a free agent,' you said. 'I can do as I please.' Remember?"

She smiled and nodded her head in pleased agreement. He was right. She didn't have to do anything. She was a free agent. Besides, the time had come to end the foolishness with Gordon. To get him out of the house so she could get on with the rest of her life – without him. *If I do go to the farm, that will mean another weekend with Gordon and his Rule Britannia view of the world. The children will be fine with Anne. They spend most of the weekends playing with the kids at the farm next door anyway.*

The evening with Bill had been so stimulating. So invigorating. So freeing. He was right. Life was too short to waste time on things she only half wanted to do. And how foolish a waste of time it would be to play coy with Bill and hard to get. To make him coax her into going. To make, as he had put it, a childhood game of it. They were two adults in the prime years of their lives. They were both too wise to engage in the stereotypical preliminaries of conventional courtship. She wanted to be with him. To experience more of him.

She realized, of course, that the weekend with Bill was going to be an altogether different experience from the time that she had spent with Jim MacMillan in the spring. Her relationship with Jim had been more of a brother and sister sort of affair. They did make love, but that was not the reason that she wanted to be with him. She really got off on his mind and she would have preferred it if he would have accepted a relationship without sex. But Jim got sexually aroused whenever they were together and this created tension between them. She discovered, early on in their relationship, that it was better to let him make love to her soon after they came together. With that out of the way, she could get on with her real interest – the enjoyment of his mind.

Jim taught English at the university and specialized in English literature of the sixteenth century. He used to read to her for hours at a time from the works of Spenser, More, Shakespeare, Dekker and the others. His strong, rich, voice had an uncanny ability to bring their works to three-dimensional life in her mind.

Sitting across the candlelit table from Bill, she thought back to the Sunday morning in the late spring when she had lain beside Jim in his big brass bed as he read to her from Edmund Spenser's letter of 1589 to Sir Walter Raleigh. Spenser described to Sir Walter what it was that he had hoped to accomplish by writing *The Faerie Queene.*

"The generall end therefore of all the booke," Spenser had written, "is to fashion a gentleman or noble person in vertuous and gentle discipline. Which for that I conceived shoulde be most plausible and pleasing, being coloured with an historicall fiction, the which the most part of men delight to read, rather for variety of matter than for profit of example."

Later in his letter, Spenser wrote: "So much more profitable and gratious is doctrine by ensample than by rule."

Spenser had been referring to the life of the legendary King Arthur of Camelot and Carol thought that the words described exactly how she was starting to feel about Bill. He was a gentle man – "a noble person in vertuous and gentle discipline." And, just like King Arthur of old, he was teaching by the example of his own unfolding life. Not by rule of law. He was, to the young Indians, what King Arthur had been to the Knights of the Round Table. To Sir Lancelot and Sir Galahad. A truly noble man. An example of what they themselves could become.

She felt more comfortable with Bill than she had felt with any man in her entire life. That was the odd part of it. Her desire to be with him was not based entirely on passion or on any compulsive urge to be with him. It was just that being with him seemed as natural as breathing. She felt a sort of oneness with him. A fusion of kindred souls.

She had been looking forward to spending time with Charlie and Diane at the farm that weekend – even if Gordon was going to be there. It had felt so good being with them in the river valley. Playing with the beach ball and tossing pebbles across the surface of the river. But, on the other hand, it seemed pretty definite that Bill was going to take the job he'd been offered at the University of Calgary. He'd probably be leaving Toronto in a couple of months to set up the North American Indian Studies program in Calgary. This might be the only chance she would have to spend time with him. To get to know him as a lover. *I can always make it up to Charlie and Diane later.*

"All right," she said. "Steaks by your fireplace tomorrow night at eight."

~

The Meadowbrook nomination meeting went very well. Henry Bracken delivered an impassioned speech about the need for white, Western European, representation at a time when the minority groups were having a disproportionate influence on national policy. Most of the people in Meadowbrook were white, Western European, Bracken said, and Gordon was the best man to speak for them in the House of Commons. Most of the assembled doctors, lawyers, dentists, accountants, managers, small businessmen and their wives seemed to agree with him. They all clapped enthusiastically as Gordon went to the podium to address them.

He got the nomination by acclamation and he could tell from the look in the eyes of those who came up to shake his hand that they were supporting him for what he stood for. Not because Gran Winston was footing the bill for more than half of the cost of the Meadowbrook campaign. They really did appreciate what he had to say and many of them said they had been anxiously waiting for someone to stand up and "tell it like it is." Many of them said he had articulated exactly what had been on their mind and it was about high time someone gave their side of the story.

Bracken was tickled pink with how well Gordon's nomination speech went over. It confirmed what he had said earlier. There was a constituency just waiting for someone like Gordon they could rally around. He had been right. Gordon was going to win them votes. Bracken was confident that he had done the right thing.

Things were working out magnificently and Gordon wanted to share the glow of his success with Carol. Now that things were getting back on track – as Gran had said they would – she was bound to see that what he was attempting to do was the right thing. She'd have a better impression of him now. Perhaps, he thought, she'd come out and have a drink with him and he could tell her how the Meadowbrook Conservatives applauded him all through his speech.

But Carol wasn't at home when he phoned. The babysitter said she'd gone out to some meeting. He decided he might as well go home anyway. After he paid the babysitter and drove her the short two blocks to her home, Gordon sat on the bed beside his sleeping daughter and ran his hands gently through her dark brown hair. Diane was a beautiful child and she was going to be a particularly attractive woman. Just like her mother. He switched off the toadstool lamp on the dresser and crossed the hall to Charlie's room. The covers were in a ball at the foot of the bed. He straightened them out and spread them over his sleeping son.

Later, as he sat in his study drinking his cup of Ovaltine before getting ready to turn in for the night, he reflected on how well the nomination meeting had gone. *Nothing can stop me now. I'm on my way. Next stop the election. Then taking my seat in the House of Commons. Then the swearing-in ceremony at Rideau Hall when the Prime Minister makes me Minister of Defence. Or, maybe, International Trade. That comes with a limo, flying across the country in a government jet. Press conferences. Major announcements. The whole works. This I'm going to like.*

He took another sip of Ovaltine and looked at the oil painting of the Battle of Culloden Moor his father had left him. The one with the kilted corpses of loyalist Scots littering the blood-drenched heather. He wondered if being Scottish was important enough to die for. He had never even thought about that before. There had never been any reason to. Not even the Scottish National Party proposed going to war and restoring the Scottish throne through a repeat of a gory debacle like Culloden Moor. Perhaps, if he had been around in 1746, he would have fought the English at Culloden. But, in the nineteen seventies, he couldn't see an awful lot to be gained by taking up arms against a sea of Englishmen and trying to win back Scottish sovereignty.

No, he was not prepared to die for the privilege of being Scottish. Life itself was more important to him than that. Being Scottish added an extra dimension to his life. An identification with something other than himself. But he wasn't prepared to be killed because of it. Faced with that sort of prospect, he'd just as soon be someone else. A Frenchman? A German? A Russian? *Yes, a Russian.*

He could identify with the land and people of Dostoyevsky, Tolstoy and Tchaikovsky. He could enjoy being a Russian. An Englishman? He wasn't so sure about that. He identified with the writings of Chaucer, Shakespeare, Milton, Dickens and the others. But, to be an Englishman? That'd be something else again. He'd have to think twice, maybe three times, about being an Englishman. Especially after everything his father had told him about the way the English kings had mistreated the Scots.

He would most definitely not want to be an Indian and run around like Bill Eagletail with braided hair and a bear claws necklace. *What sort of example is that for the young Indian people? Why emphasize the past? The things that have gone the way of the buffalo. There's no way they'll ever get back that pride Eagletail was talking about on* Toronto Focus. *Their race has been stricken from the record. So, their land's been taken from them? So what? Whose hasn't? Where in the world can you find people who have held on to their land for thousands of years? The whole history of the world is made up of people moving in on other people. That's the story of mankind. It's happened everywhere. Even in Scotland.*

If the Scots have been able to hold on to their identity despite the English conquests, the Indians should have been able to hold on to theirs. If their culture had been worthwhile, it would have survived. Even the gypsies, for God's sake, have no land of their own – no possessions other than what they haul around in those rickety carts – but they've survived.

Eagletail isn't doing those Indian kids any favour. He's pinning their hopes on a horse that was scratched centuries ago. Their culture just didn't have what it takes to survive. It was too primitive. Like Don Henderson says, they were savages. Uncivilized.

Despite everything Eagletail says about us taking the fish and the beaver and all that, the fact remains that they weren't being used. The supply of precious resources on this planet is too finite to let things go to waste. Is it better that white women and children freeze in the dark so the Indians can save their land? Of course it isn't. We've got to get that Alberta gas down to the eastern markets. Eagletail's mother is just going to have to move over a bit. She'll get a good price for the easement they want through her useless little bit of land. She'll be able to take herself for a holiday to Hawaii or something like that. She'll be compensated. Generously. That's the price we're willing to pay so my Diane and Charlie will be warm next winter. It's a fair exchange.

Where the hell did Carol go? It's not the same. Her not being here at this time of night. It's almost midnight. What kind of meeting goes on this late? A meeting, that's what the babysitter said. Carol should have been with me at the nomination meeting. I told her it wouldn't look right her not being by my side. She should have seen them applauding me. Should have been there. Maybe the babysitter meant to say she was meeting someone. A man? Could Carol actually do to some man the sort of things Ruth has done for me? Where the hell did she get to?

CHAPTER
- 23 -

There was a picture of Gordon addressing the Meadowbrook nomination meeting on the front page of the *Globe and Mail* Friday morning. The headline said:

'White power' Conservative
acclaimed in Meadowbrook.

University of Toronto professor Gordon MacArthur was acclaimed as the Conservative candidate for the Toronto riding of Meadowbrook at a well-attended nomination meeting last night.

MacArthur has been dubbed the "white power Conservative" because of recent statements he has made about immigrants.

The Conservative Party of Canada issued a statement on his behalf Wednesday night saying he had apologized for those comments.

Despite that "apology" Henry Bracken, president of the Meadowbrook Conservative Association and Chairman and CEO of Bracken Department Stores, said in his speech nominating MacArthur that there is a "pressing need for someone to represent the interests of white people in Ottawa."

Bracken got an enthusiastic round of applause from the totally white audience of lawyers, accountants, doctors, dentists, managers, and small businessmen.

MacArthur told them that he was going to "give Meadowbrook, and the majority community, a voice in the inner circles of power. A voice representing – for a change – the viewpoint of the forgotten, neglected, all too silent, majority.

"We need more legislation that is in our best interest and less of all these special programs the government is concocting on a daily basis to court the minority-group vote. To court them with money out of our pockets."

MacArthur says there is a need "to restore some balance. To even things out a bit."

MacArthur is a vocal supporter of a gas pipeline the Saunders Energy Corporation wants to run through the Big Thunder Indian reserve southwest of Calgary.

In his speech last night, he repeated his claim that white women and children "will freeze in the dark of winter" if the Indians stop the Alberta gas from getting through.

About 300 students at the University of Toronto demonstrated in front of the Ontario Legislative Building yesterday to show support for the Indians.

Carol came into the kitchen just as Gordon had finished reading the article.

"I simply can't understand why those students are out demonstrating in support of a bunch of renegade Indians," he said. "What business is it of theirs?"

"They're not renegade Indians, Carol said. "Most of them are exceptionally aware and very well informed."

"How would you know? They're all two thousand miles away, for God's sake."

"The ones at the meeting at the university last night were all – all of them – well above average in intelligence and social awareness. They ..."

"What meeting?" he asked, curiosity triggered to arousal. "What meeting are you talking about?"

"There was a meeting at the university last night to discuss your Equal Opportunities Council and the pipeline situation."

"And you – you – you were there?" he asked in a thunderstruck tone. "You mean, that's where you were last night?"

"I wanted to hear their side of the issue so I went to their meeting."

"But ...," he said as the pieces started to fall into place without forming a meaningful pattern. "How would you know about their meeting in the first place?"

"Dr. Eagletail invited me."

"Eagletail? Eagletail invited you? How – how? What the hell's going on around here?"

"Nothing is 'going on'. I simply phoned Dr. Eagletail after the two of you were on the *Toronto Focus* program last week to discuss the Big Thunder matter with him. He told me about a meeting they were having and said it would be all right for me to go. So I went. And, last night, I went to another meeting he was having."

"So you went? Just like that. I'm at the nomination meeting by myself. By myself despite the fact I specifically asked for your support. For you to be at my side at that terribly important meeting. When I needed you. Really needed you. And you, where were you? At a meeting with some goddamned Indians and that braids-framed redskin. God damn it, Carol. Where is your sense of responsibility? After all, you are my wife."

She remained silent for a moment and sipped some of her coffee before replying. "Perhaps that's the problem," she said in a tone indicating that she wanted to get something heavy off her chest.

"What?" he asked, obviously thrown off balance. "What do you mean? Perhaps that's the problem? What problem? What that's? What are you talking about?"

"I'm talking about the problem of being your wife," she said exhaling a deep sigh. "As you said yourself the other night, it creates problems when I don't support you like an Eleanor Roosevelt or a Pat Nixon. But that's a fact we should have faced up to a long time ago, Gordon. I am not Eleanor Roosevelt. And I'm not Olive Diefenbaker.

Or Pat Nixon. Or Muriel Humphrey. Or any of the others on your 'ten-women-I-most-admire' list.

"As I watched you on *Toronto Focus* last week parroting Jack Saunders' line and recycling Don Henderson's Rule Britannia version of history, something – something I have felt for some time now – was confirmed with an almost startling burst of clarity. I realized that I don't want to be your wife."

He looked at her in stunned amazement. "You – you. What are you talking about now? Don't want to be my wife?"

"It's as simple as that, Gordon. I don't want to be your wife."

He couldn't believe his ears. She couldn't be serious. "Come on, you're – you're. You're putting me on. You're not – not serious. You can't be. I mean that's – that's silly."

"Being your wife is what is silly, Gordon. We should have ended this marriage a long time ago. We have nothing in common. I'm not saying we didn't have. Somewhere back there. But we don't have it now. And, considering the way things are going – the fact that you want to be in the cabinet and live in Ottawa, this white power council you've started up, the Big Thunder issue, and all the rest of it – I think this is the best time to – to end it."

She is serious. What on earth brought this on? "But – why? Why now when everything is just starting to come together for me? Coming together in a way that I didn't dream possible. Being the MP for Meadowbrook. Getting a seat at the cabinet table. You can't do this to me now. Not now."

"I'm not doing anything to you, Gordon. I'm simply saying that I now see you in an altogether different light. I see you as – as someone I would purposefully avoid at a cocktail party. I abhor everything you represent. Your attitude toward the immigrant groups, toward Bill Eagletail, the pipeline question – everything. Everything about you repulses me."

"Wow. That's quite an assessment."

"Well, that's the way I feel. And I want it over and done with. Now."

"I still don't understand why you'd do a thing like this to me now. Just as I'm about to become an MP and go into cabinet. I mean you can't just snap your fingers and say 'fini'. It's just – just not that simple."

"Look, I don't particularly care how they deal with these things in the afternoon soap operas. They can complicate and melodramatize things all they want. Theirs is, as they say, another world. This is my world. My life. And I don't want to share it with you. I want you to go."

"Go? Go where? What are you talking about now? Be serious."

"Go to your young woman if you want. Go to Ottawa and be in the cabinet. Go wherever you wish. Just get out of my life. I want our marriage – what we call a marriage – ended."

"But you can't make a decision – a decision as important as that – on the basis of one television interview. I mean, my God, that's – that's simply unreal. You've got to – to give it more thought."

"I've had sufficient time to think about it, Gordon. We probably shouldn't have gotten married in the first place. Never should have gotten me pregnant. Never have done a lot of things. But that's over. Over and done with. Now, I want to get on with the rest of my life– without you."

She looked at her watch. "I've got to run. It's my turn to drive the children to school. They'll be finished breakfast now. I'd better go."

"You can't just – just run off to your goddamned carpool. We've got to talk this thing through. We've got to ..."

"There's nothing more to say," she said firmly.

"Of course there is. We – we will discuss this tonight. All of it. At the farm. After the children have gone to bed. We will ..."

"I won't be going to the farm."

"You what?"

"I've made other plans for the weekend. Anne will look after the children – and you. She'll take her own car."

"Other plans? What the hell's going on around here? You can't do things like this to me."

"Be adult about this, Gordon. Don't complicate matters. If you don't want to go to the farm, then don't. The children will have a super time with Anne. Spend the weekend with your young woman if you want. But try, by Monday, to resolve exactly when you'll be leaving the house. I'd like you out of here as quickly as possible."

He felt like a tenant receiving notice to vacate after being caught dropping banana peels on the stairway. "This is insane. You can't just expect me to pack up and leave."

"Why not? One of us has to go and I was, after all, born in this house. There's no reason, or sense, in my being the one to leave. It has to be you. And now, I've got to dash. Let's be, as you said the other night, civilized about this, Gordon. There's no reason to get ourselves bogged down in a lot of emotional baggage. Let's have a clean break."

"A clean break? God damn it, you're talking about my life. Not some – some." He felt suddenly overcome by a hopeless, sinking, feeling. Like a top-of-the-line ship that had just smashed its nose against an iceberg. His pride was hurt and he wanted to lash out at her in anger and frustration. "All right, then, you frigid bitch. I'll go. I've had enough of you anyway. Enough of your constant carping. Of the way you're always dragging me down. Selling me short all the time. Maybe you're right. Maybe I don't need you – you and your constant undermining slights. Your holier than thou frigidity. Screw you, Carol. I don't need you. Don't need your mocking glances. Your – your knowing sneers. The way you make me feel like dirt – like an animal – whenever I want to touch you. I don't need that. I've got better things to do with my life than trying to coax an ounce of acceptance – of – of understanding out of you. That's why I'm on the front page of the *Globe*. I'm a reality. Living history. Screw you, you goddamned virgin."

With that, he stomped out of the room, grabbed his coat from the closet and left the house.

As he drove towards the university, his thoughts were preoccupied with what had just happened between him and Carol. Maybe he shouldn't have lost his temper like that. Maybe he should have tried to reason with her. *And yet, how do you reason with someone who just sits there so goddamned cold and collected and announces that your marriage is over? Like she was saying "dinner's ready", or "the light is green" or – or – "Gordon, your heels leave marks."*

Maybe she was right. Maybe there was nothing left to say. Maybe what she was suggesting – suggesting? – demanding was the logical next step up, or down, from separate rooms. She'd told him she wanted him out of her bed. And now she wanted him out of her father's house. He thought about the negative way Carol had reacted toward his involvement with the Equal Opportunities Council. She seemed to think he was some kind of goose-stepping Nazi. It had gotten to the point where he couldn't think or say anything out loud without putting someone's nose out of joint.

The whole race thing seemed so filled with contradictions. Everyone was being encouraged to express their roots. To get things off their chests. Everyone except white people. He'd spotted a bumper sticker while driving down to the university the other morning. It said, "THANK GOD I'M JEWISH". That was considered perfectly acceptable. But there'd be hell to pay if he drove around Toronto with a bumper sticker saying "THANK GOD I'M WHITE".

And then there was that picture the *Toronto Star* ran of the winner of the "Miss Black Ontario" beauty contest. He'd wondered at the time what the Ontario Human Rights Commission would have done if anyone had sponsored a "Miss White Ontario" contest. There's no way they'd have allowed something like that to take place. That would be "racist". But Miss Black or Miss China was considered perfectly acceptable. He couldn't understand why that was so. *And what about that black son of a bitch from Berkeley who told the students all white people are scum? If I said something like that about black people in public, they'd string me up by the balls.*

Too many things were happening at too fast a pace. Dave Saunders was making plans for him to be out on the streets demonstrating like some zealous peacenik. Gran Winston and Jack Saunders were making plans for him to speak to the Empire Club and influence the outcome of the pipeline hearings. The PMO had tried to prevent him from becoming an MP. And now Carol wanted him out of the house ASAP. *A messy divorce is the last thing I need with the election coming up so soon. She'll probably drag Ruth into it and that's going to turn off a lot of voters.* "Candidate screwing student." *That'll make a great headline. Damn. Timing's all wrong.* All of the control buttons were being pushed by other people. He wasn't calling any of the shots. None of them. *And what is it all adding up to?*

The producer from *Toronto Focus* called just after lunch to ask Gordon if he could come back on the show Tuesday night.

"Dr. Eagletail has already confirmed and Mr. Deacon would really appreciate it if you could be on the show as well, especially now that you're the official Conservative candidate for Meadowbroook."

Gordon thought being on the show again would be good publicity for his election campaign. Help build some profile. It would also provide a good opportunity to nail Bill Eagletail to the cross once and for all.

"I'd be delighted," he said. "What time would you want me to be there."

"About quarter to six would work best for us," the producer said. "That will allow enough time to do the makeup and get you feeling comfortable."

"Fine," Gordon said. "Quarter to six it is."

Later that day, Gordon wondered what Carol would be doing for the weekend. If he hadn't blown up at her like that, she might have told him what "other plans" she'd made. Maybe she was going up to Beaverton to spend the weekend with Jane Potts. That's what she'd always done before when the situation between them had gotten so intolerable that she had to, as she put it, get away from it all for a couple of days. That probably was what she was going to be doing for the weekend.

Perhaps a couple of days with Jane and Al Potts would do her good. *God knows the Potts' marriage is nothing to write home about. They're at each other all the time. And those fat children of theirs are an absolute pain in the ass. A couple of days in that environment will make her realize the mistake she's making. She'll think twice, maybe three times, about asking me to pack up and leave after a weekend with the Potts.*

Damn. If only they had a phone at their place. I could phone her tomorrow night and see if she's in a better mood. Maybe I'll drive up there tomorrow and just sort of say hello and patch things up. No. That's not such a good idea. When she takes the weekend off, she wants to be left alone. She's always made that quite clear. She's got to be totally removed from our situation for the weekend to do her any good. I'll just have to wait until she gets back. And hope to God she's changed her mind about wanting me out of the house.

Maybe I should phone her now — at the house. Before she leaves. I can tell her I'm sorry for blowing up like that and calling her a frigid bitch. I shouldn't have said that. Or any of those other things. I had no right to do that. Maybe not. Maybe she's still really mad at me for saying all those things. Maybe I should let things cool down a bit. Give her time. Maybe that'll be better.

What about Charlie and Diane? Maybe I should go up there and spend the weekend with them. No – no. I can't do that either. I've got to be down at the Harbour Castle tomorrow for lunch with Dave Saunders and his people.

I can go up to the farm after the meeting with Saunders. Or, perhaps on Sunday. The children will be fine with Anne. She'll see to it that they have a great time. She'll find all sorts of good things to do with them. And I'll get up there in time for us to have a nice lunch together. Yes. That's what I'll do. Maybe, as Carol won't be there, I'll ask Mum if she'd like to spend some time at the farm with us. With Dad gone, she must get pretty lonely at times. Yes. I'll ask Mum to go up to the farm with me. In fact, I'll ask her out for dinner tonight so I'll have a chance to prepare her for the fact that Carol's not going to be there. Yes, that's what I'll do. It'll be nice to have dinner with Mum.

When Gordon phoned his mother and asked her to come out and have dinner with him, she said she'd love to, but she had a roast in the oven. It would be ready by around six-thirty and she'd be delighted to put a couple of extra potatoes in the pan for him. The moment he stepped out of the elevator, his nose twitched in response to the delicious smell of good roast beef. He'd always enjoyed the taste and smell of his mother's cooking.

She gave him a hug and a kiss as she took his coat and hung it in the closet. "I've still got your father's winter coat in here," she said. "Would you like to wear it this winter?"

She held up the herringbone coat with the seal fur collar so he could try it on. It fitted quite snugly. "I'd love to wear it, Mum. It feels good."

"I should have given it to you last winter," she said. "But, better late than never. That's what your father always said, Gordon. 'Better late than never'."

Martha kept her hair shorter now. It was still quite wavy but had gone almost completely white. She enjoyed having Gordon in her home. It was so seldom that they saw each other lately. And he was looking well. Even better than he had looked on the television with – with William.

He noticed that she was limping. "How's your foot?" he asked.

"It's not too bad right now. It's a bit better tonight. But, my Lord, it was so painful yesterday I nearly cried. And I did, so much, want to be with you at the nomination meeting. But I just couldn't, Son. I couldn't bear to walk on it."

"I understand. I was able to call off Wally Hunter – who was going to drive you to the meeting – before he left his house."

"That's good. I wouldn't 've wanted to have caused him any bother."

"No bother, Mum. You're never any bother."

"Thank you, Son. Would you like to pour yourself a drink?" she asked as she went into the kitchen to check on the roast. Martha didn't drink herself, but she always kept something in the cupboard for Gordon or for company dropping in unexpectedly.

"Love to, Mum. That would be splendid. What about you? Will you have a ginger ale?"

"That will do me just fine, Gordon."

He poured a ginger ale for his mother and fixed himself a double vodka and orange. He was still having trouble dealing with Carol's sudden demand for a divorce. *Maybe I should have seen it coming. She has been more withdrawn lately. Pretty frigid. Maybe it's that stuff in the newspapers and on the radio about the immigrants and the Indians. Who knows? She seems pretty determined about it all. About it all being over for us. That's for sure. Boy, could I use a drink right now.*

"Tell me how the nomination meeting went," his mother said as he sat down beside her on the large floppy sofa in the living room.

"Great. It was just great. The people there really liked what I had to say. They were with me one hundred per cent."

"That's good. I only wish I could have been there. This gout seems to be getting worse and worse. Sometimes, it is just unbearable. Anyway, I'm glad the meeting went well. You're going to make a fine Member of Parliament, Gordon. Your Dad would have been so proud of you."

"Did you see the article on the front page of the *Globe* this morning?" he asked. "About me?"

"No, Son. I don't get the newspapers anymore. It was your father who got the most use out of them. I don't think I miss all that much by not reading them. They're always writing about what's wrong in the world. Not about what's right. What did the *Globe* have to say about you today? Was it about the nomination meeting?"

"Mostly. They had a good write up about it. They even had my picture with it – on the front page. The *Star* had an article, too. It was in the afternoon paper."

"Oh, my. How wonderful, Gordon. You must get me a copy of both stories. I would love to have them. If only your father could have seen that."

"Yeah. He'd have gotten quite a bang out of that one. There was a pretty good picture in the *Star*. Had me looking like I was the Prime Minister."

"Don't make light of it, Gordon. If you get appointed to the cabinet after the election, like that Mr. Bracken says you will, you could very well be the Prime Minister some day. Keep your sights on the highest peak, Gordon. That's what your father always said."

"I'm still a long way from anything like that, Mum. But I really do appreciate the way you believe in me. The way you've always believed in me. You're just wonderful."

He looked fondly at her as he sipped his vodka. "There was a picture of that old woman who's blocking the Saunders gas pipeline in the *Globe and Mail* last Saturday. She was forking hay to some calves. I think they're using her to build up sympathy for the Indian side of that business. I'm telling you, Mum, from the looks of her, they'll need a bulldozer to get her out of there. She's a real tough-looking old bird."

Oh, my Lord, Martha thought. *What do I say? How do I tell him about Sarah and about – about little William? Why won't the right words come?* "It seems a shame," she said, "to disrupt her life by running that pipeline through her yard. There must be, Gordon, surely, some way of resolving things without running that pipeline between her house and her barn. It does seem to me, Son, to be quite an imposition."

"I don't think you should look at it that way, Mum. That old woman is just simply going to have to move over – like we had to move when they built the Macdonald Parkway."

"That was an altogether different matter, Gordon. And I do wish you wouldn't refer to her as 'that old woman'. She is, after all, a human being. Someone with feelings and needs and rights. Just like the rest of us."

"Maybe. But she's nothing to me. She's Eagletail's mother. Let him take care of her. I don't want to appear too rigid about these things. I really don't. But I had an argument with Carol about this very thing. Just this morning. We've got to look after our own kind. We've got to protect the energy supply of the white majority. Those Indians are jeopardizing our whole energy supply infrastructure. They've got to move over. Or we'll all freeze in the dark – including the Indians."

Not knowing how to go about telling him about his brother and his Aunt Sarah, Martha decided it was time to put the dinner on the table and get on with their meal. The roast tasted delicious – as usual. The potatoes were nice and crisp on the outside. His mother was a superb cook.

"How would you like to go up to the farm with me tomorrow?" he asked. "I have a meeting to attend at lunch time, but I'd like to get up there in time for dinner. Would you like that, Mum?"

"Why yes," she said. "That would be lovely." *What a delightful surprise*, she thought. "But – but won't that be an extra bother for Carol?"

"She won't be there."

"Oh, I see." She decided not to press the point. She'd let him take his own time to tell her anything he wanted to say about Carol. They continued to eat in silence.

"She wants a divorce," he said, as he made himself another double vodka and orange.

"She what?"

"She says she wants to end things – get me out of the house. She wants me out of there as soon as possible."

"Oh, Gordon. I'm so sorry. So terribly sorry."

"It's okay, Mum. I think it's been coming for quite some time. I think she almost came out with it a couple of times earlier this week. This morning, she finally got it off her chest."

"Is it – is it another man?"

"No. Carol's never been involved with anyone else. That's not it. It's – oh it's a lot of things. She says I'm a bigot – a racist – and that – that my attitude repulses her. She said this morning that I'm the sort of person she'd deliberately avoid at a cocktail party. She was quite definite about it."

"Well, Son, I did hear about you being on the radio saying that white people are going to freeze in the dark. The superintendent told me about it this morning. You did say some – some – well, some of the things he said he heard you say on the radio were very much along the line that Professor Henderson used to push. And you know how your father reacted to him. Some of the things you say, Gordon, are, to those who don't know you, a wee bit uncharitable – a wee bitty intolerant."

Tom heard Henderson talking about it, about the benefits the English-speaking peoples of the world had brought about over centuries, at one of the evening lectures at the university. Tom said afterwards he thought Henderson was quite extreme. Not at all tolerant of other people. Tom didn't like the drift of what Henderson was saying. Not at all.

Tom didn't know very much about history so he couldn't very well argue with a man who made his living teaching it. But he did think, and he said so to Gordon at the time, that Henderson was quite bigoted and narrow in his train of thought.

"Okay, Mum," Gordon said, "I'll admit that I've got some pronounced preferences. I lean toward that which is white, Western European – with a generous helping of Scottish thrown in for good measure. But I'm not a racist. I'm just proud of what I am – a white, Western European, Scottish-Canadian. I'm not against the Indians, or the blacks or the Pakistanis, Mum. I just prefer being with my own kind. That's all. But Carol sees me as some kind of goose-stepping Nazi trying to exterminate all things coloured and different. That is not the way I am. Not at all."

"I know that, Gordon. I know that well. But, perhaps it's the way things come across, especially in the newspapers and on the radio and the television, that give people the wrong impression of you. That, somehow, distort your true position on those things. Perhaps that's what it is."

"I think you're right, Mum. Anyway, Carol seems quite determined and I'll – I'll have to be out of there as soon as I can arrange it. It is her house. She was born there."

Martha had noticed, on the few occasions she had been to their home lately, how distant Gordon and Carol were with one another. There was a coldness there. The coldness of death. She had known that something was wrong. That things weren't right between them. But she was reluctant to appear as if she was meddling in their lives.

"You're welcome to stay here, Gordon. I'd be happy to have you with me. If it does come to that. Perhaps Carol will think better of it and things will work out between the two of you. I do hope so. Especially for Charlie and Diane. And for you, my son."

"I hope so. I hope you're right, Mum. Things are happening so terribly fast. I just don't seem to be in control of anything anymore. I feel more like a pawn than a player."

He poured himself a glass of wine. "What did you think of that redskin?"

"What?" she exclaimed, completely startled by his change of subject.

"Eagletail with his hair braided like a woman. The Indian guy who was on *Toronto Focus* with me last week. Wasn't he something? With those bear claws and his hair in braids and all that nonsense about us taking their fish and their trees and their gold and – and – and all that other nonsense he was talking about."

"I didn't think it was nonsense, Gordon," Martha said, slowly gaining back some of her composure. She hadn't wanted to talk about the TV program and William. "I felt that he put things in a way that I'd never thought of before. What he said, and the way he said it, gave me a much better understanding of the way things must be for Indian people – especially for those young students."

"Come on, Mum," Gordon said, after another swallow of wine. "Don't fall for that line. He's a professional Indian if ever there was one. It was a snow job. He was conning you. If I'd had the time, I'd have shot his story full of holes and the audience would've seen him for the phony that he is. I don't even think he's a real Indian. Did you see his eyes? They're grey-blue. Just like mine. You ever seen an Indian with blue eyes? He's a phony, Mum. I'll bet he's the product of some one-night stand in a cheap, chintzy, motel room. He's a half-breed. You can tell by the colour of his eyes. A two-bit phony half-breed passing himself off like he was a real Indian."

The truth churned around in Martha's belly screaming to get out. "He's your brother," she blurted.

"Come on, Mum. Don't give me that brotherhood of man stuff – that stuff about us all being God's children. Eagletail's a phony and he should be identified as such."

"Don't Gordon. Don't say that." She bit her lower lip and toyed with her fork. "I mean it, Gordon. In the true sense of the word. William is your brother."

The image of Bill Eagletail's braids-framed face flashed across his mind. She was serious. *What the hell is she driving at?* "Come on, Mum. Don't say things like that. Of course he's not my brother. How – how could he be? You – you're kidding. Now come on, be a good girl, and stop this nonsense."

"Oh, Son, my darling boy. It isn't nonsense. And this isn't the way I wanted you to hear about it. But I just can't sit still and let you say those things about – about your brother. William is your brother, Gordon."

He refilled his wine glass and reflected for a few moments on what she had said. "You mean – Dad? Dad had – had – had a son by someone else? By some Indian woman? When he was out west? Is that it?"

"No, Gordon, it wasn't that way. Not that way at all." She searched for the right words to tell him. But they kept running away from her.

If it wasn't his father, he thought, then it must have been – it must have been – "Then – then you? You had – no. It couldn't have been. Was it? Did you have a son by some Indian man? Is that it, Mum? Something that happened a long time ago. Before you and Dad got married. Is that it?"

"Let me try and explain it to you, Gordon. In my own way. Just listen – listen to what I have to say and I'll try and make it as clear as I can for you. Just hear me out."

Gordon sat back with a stunned, perplexed, look on his face and drank some more wine. She sipped some more of her tea until she was sure that he was prepared to hear her out.

"Remember, Son, how your dad and I told you about your Uncle Bill? How he was killed in the war. Over there in Hong Kong. We told you about that and how he and your dad first came over here with Lord Hanover's cattle. You remember, how they went out west in the boxcar and all that? What we didn't tell you – and I know now that we should've – but we simply didn't – what we didn't tell you was that your Uncle Bill got married soon after your dad came here to get into the real estate business. Your Uncle Bill married a cook at the ranch where he and your dad had worked together. She was Indian, a Blackfoot, and they had a son. Dr. Eagletail, who was on the TV with you, he was that son. About a year after that ..."

She paused for a moment and sipped some more tea. "About a year after that, they were expecting again and – and on the night that she had their second son, she died. She died giving birth to that second son. Bled to death." She looked at him with deep love and continued. "You – you were that second – that second son, my darling boy. You were that second son. Your uncle Bill was your father."

He formed his lips as if starting to interrupt. "No. No. Don't – don't say a word. Not yet, my son. Let me finish what I have to say. Your Uncle Bill had a real problem on his hands. He'd been living in the cookhouse but now he'd have to go back to the bunkhouse with the other men. And he wouldn't be able to take his sons with him. Even if he'd been able to keep them there, he wouldn't have been able to care for them during the day because he would be out working in the fields and looking after the cattle. It was a very difficult spot for him to be in.

"Anyway, Sarah, your mother's sister, agreed to take you and your brother into their home at the Big Thunder Indian reserve until he could make some other arrangements. They were the only family he had out there. And, yes, it's that same Sarah whose picture you saw in the newspaper."

She stopped for a moment, reviewed in her mind the events of that time, took another sip of tea and continued. "Sarah had a wee baby boy of her own and he had the asthma and kept her up all night. It became just too much for her to look after him along with you and your brother, little William, at the same time.

"Now, your dad and I had found that we weren't able to have – to have a son of our own – by the – the natural way. When we heard what happened, about the death of Bill's wife, and about Bill not being able to keep the two of you at the ranch, and the trouble Sarah was having looking after you both, we said we'd be more than happy to have one of you come and live with us for a while – until your uncle could make some other arrangements."

She sipped her tea and looked lovingly at Gordon for a moment. "We wanted to have you, Gordon, come and live with us – to be our son. That's how it all happened. I went all the way out there in the train and brought you home to Toronto. And I loved you, Gordon. I loved you from the very first moment I held you in my arms. And I always will love you – love you – my son. And your father loved you so very much, too. You've always been everything we could possibly have wanted in a son."

Gordon just sat there sipping his wine with a blank look on his face.

"Now, Gordon, you should know that your Uncle Bill always did want to have you living with him. He was looking forward, after the war, to getting a job in the city so he could have you and little William living with him. He didn't abandon you, Gordon, not in any sense at all. He loved you, my son. But then, with him getting killed like that in Hong Kong, everything changed. The war changed everything, and not just for your Uncle Bill. For everyone."

Gordon was quite confused by what his mother was saying and yet, at the same time, he found himself sort of detached from it all – as if what she was saying was about someone else – not at all about him. It was as if he was a spider up in a corner of the ceiling eavesdropping on this fascinating tale, but not at all personally involved with it.

"And Bill Eagletail?" he asked. "What happened to him?"

"Your brother was raised at Big Thunder by – by your mother's – your mother's sister. And yes, it's her yard they want to run that pipeline through. It's Sarah's yard. That same yard where I held you in my arms for the very first time."

"I see," he said, as if commenting on a less than brilliant observation made by some undergraduate student at one of his lectures. "Then that Indian woman is my aunt. Is that it? Is that what you're saying?"

"Yes, Gordon. Sarah is your aunt. Your mother's sister."

He tapped out a nameless tune with his dinner fork and swallowed some more wine. "Why didn't you tell me all this before? And why are you telling me about it now?" he asked, no longer feeling as detached. "Why, after keeping silent all these years – these thirty-five years – would you tell me something like this now? I don't understand."

"Oh, but I've wanted to tell you, Son. I've wanted to tell you so many times. But, it seems, every time your father would agree that we should tell you – every time – he would put it off. He felt that, what with Bill being dead and buried so far away in China like that, there was no point in telling you about it. 'What good purpose would it serve?' he'd say. 'What possible difference could it have made?'"

Gordon was silent for a full minute, sifting through all that his mother had told him. *How on earth can all of this – or even any of this be true? I can't possibly be Indian. I'm nothing at all like Eagletail – like Eagletail with that braided hair and bear claws. I'm nothing at all like him. Why couldn't she just leave well enough alone?*

"I think Dad was right. No good purpose could possibly be served by telling me something like this. I think you should have listened to him. You should have left well enough alone. You should've done what Dad said and left well enough alone."

"But, Gordon, with you and your brother fighting each other on the television like that and – and with it being Sarah's yard they're going to ram that pipeline through – I – I had to tell you. I had to let you know the truth."

"Why? Those Indians are nothing to me. That old woman means absolutely nothing to me. That Eagletail person means nothing to me. We might have come out of the same belly, like you said, but that does not make him my brother – or his mother my mother. You are my mother and I'd have preferred it if you hadn't tried to tell me differently. You should have left well enough alone. Those Indian people are – are – are totally foreign to me. I am what I am – what I've been for thirty-five years – your son. You are my mother and that's all there is to it."

"Oh, Gordon, lad. I don't know what to say to you. And I know that I've probably said all the wrong things tonight. But I did feel, and I still do feel, that – that you simply had to be told about – about your biological mother and about – about your brother. William is your brother, Son. You can't change that. He *is* your brother."

No. He's no brother of mine. Maybe what she's saying is true. Probably is true. But that doesn't make that redskin my brother. "I don't agree with that. Not at all. He's an Indian. I don't care if he's eighty per cent Scottish – or Scandinavian. Indian is what he's chosen to be – of his own free will – and Indian is what he is. He's no brother of mine."

"But he is. Oh, I know how hard this is for you – especially with the two of you going at one another on the television and in the newspapers. But, Gordon, you're just going to have to face up to it. William is your brother. There's no getting away from it."

"There would have been if you had left well enough alone, as Dad said you should've. There would have been if you hadn't decided to meddle in my life like this. And for what, Mother? What possible benefit can you see in telling me all this now? You are my mother and that's all there is to it. Now – now listen – this is the way it is. You are my mother, right?"

"Yes, Gordon. I am your mother," she said with a helpless, lost, feeling in the pit of her stomach. This wasn't the way she'd wanted it to be. Not at all.

"And you're not Bill Eagletail's mother. Right? No matter whose belly I happened to pop out of, you are not – are not Bill Eagletail's mother. Right?"

"Right."

"Then that settles it. If you're not Eagletail's mother, he can't possibly be my brother. So, let's leave it at that. You are my mother and that's all there is to it."

His mind was refusing to deal with the reality of what she had told him. Some form of mental block was preventing him from accepting the fact that he was half Indian. Martha decided it would be better not to worsen matters by prolonging the discussion. They could talk it all out at the farm – when his mind was ready to deal with it.

"All right, my son. I'll say nothing more. Whether I was right or wrong, I did mean well and I thought, in my own, imperfect, way, that I should put these facts before you."

"Facts? What are the facts, Mother?" he asked in a changed, almost strained, voice. The wine on top of the vodka was having its effect.

"What is truth? It's all relevant. Changing, shifting, evolving. Nothing is constant. Nothing is, in the true sense of the word, fact. Reality is what we conceive it to be. A perceived illusion. An intermingling of greys. Sometimes the illusion is more real than the real. Who knows? It's all relevant. Irrelevant. You are my mother and there's no vacancy. That is the fact. The only fact. Is there any more wine?"

She noticed that he'd finished the whole bottle. "Yes, but, I think, as you're going to be driving, you should settle for what you've had already. I think you've had enough."

"Not at all. This is a time for celebration. A birth should be celebrated. It's not every day you get a baby brother – no – no that's backwards. He was first. I'm the baby. What we're celebrating here tonight, folks, is the birth of a big brother. Big Brother Eagletail. Grand Chief of the underminers. Architect Supreme of the fall of the WASP Empire. Hail to the Chief. Let's hear it for my big brother. My big Indian buck of a brother."

"Let me get some coffee for you, Son. It'll clear your mind."

"Why, Mother Dear? Do I appear impaired? Under the influence? Is that it? Do you think I can't hold my liquor? They always did say Indians couldn't handle it. See, Mother Dear, if you hadn't told me about – about my dark side – I could have gone on holding my liquor with the best of them. But now, now that you've chosen to reveal the thirty-five-year-old secret of my birth – now that you've told me I came forth from the belly of some Blackfoot woman – my other half's getting the better of me already and I'm finding myself incapable of holding my liquor."

She brought the coffee through from the kitchen and filled his cup. "Here, Gordon, take the coffee. It'll do you good. Take some." *He looks quite disoriented. Probably too much wine, on top of all that vodka. Black coffee should fix him up a bit.*

"Thank you, Mother Dear. Bearer of good cheer. Bearer of – of everything except me."

"Oh, Gordon, don't. Don't talk on about it like that. Please don't say any more."

"Why not? You said – you said it was better to tell me – tell me what Dad would never have told me. And now you've told me. Told me. Too much. Told me too, too, too much. Much too much. Enough.

Enough. Enough of all this Indian brother and Indian mother nonsense. Enough. Enough. This worm has had enough."

He sat silently for a few minutes as the harsh taste of the black coffee trickled down his throat and swished through his system. *This is just great. Just fucking great. On the same day Carol tells me she wants a divorce, Mum tells me I'm a half-breed. Been one all my life. Thirty-five fucking years and counting.*

His mother sat across the table from him, truly at a loss as to what was the best thing to do. She thought of her trip back from Big Thunder and how he had curled up in her arms, lulled to sleep by the rhythmic motion of the train. *Oh, dear Tom, we should have seen this coming. We should have prepared him for this. This is not the way it should be. Not at all the way he should be hearing this for the first time.*

Gordon finished his coffee and she refilled his cup. *Might as well have some more of that. I have had a bit too much to drink. But, Jesus, this is all so confusing. It's all too much, much too much. Still, Mum isn't telling me this to hurt me. She really does care about me and, like she said, it probably did seem to her to be the right thing to do. Especially after seeing me next to him on TV.*

He drank some more coffee and then reached over and traced his mother's face gently with the tips of his fingers. "I'm sorry I spoke to you like that, Mum. I just wasn't prepared for – for anything quite like that."

"It's all right, Son. I understand. It wouldn't have happened like this if we'd told you about it when we should have. Back when you were a wee boy."

Snatches of what she had told him about his birth flashed across his mind in a nonsensical blur. And then he saw the image of Bill Eagletail, with the full headdress of a chief, painted for war and mounted on a Pinto pony.

"Does he know he's adopted?" he asked, as he raised the cup to his lips. "Does he know?"

She toyed with whether or not to tell him about the letter Sarah had sent saying they thought it better not to let the boys know they were brothers but decided that would only complicate things. "I don't believe so, Gordon. We didn't keep in touch with your mother's people. In fact, we hardly knew them. I was only there for a week. And with Bill – your father – dead like that – dead before you were even three – we didn't see any real reason – your dad and I – to be in touch with anyone from that part of the country. But, when I saw you on the television last week and – and William beside you – I knew at once that he was your brother. The eyes, the nose. You do look so very much alike. Perhaps, being your mother, I can see the resemblance in a way no one else could. You are quite alike."

"Half-breeds! Isn't that what we are?" he asked with a touch of bitterness. "Isn't that why you think we look so much alike? Isn't that it, Mother?"

Martha fiddled with her tea cup. "Your father's always said you shouldn't use that word when you're talking about people. He said it was correct to say that a cow is half Holstein and half Ayrshire or half some other breed of cattle. Because they are breeds. Breeds developed by men. But Indian people aren't a breed of animal. Scottish people are not a breed – like – like Hereford cows or Aberdeen Angus bulls. They're people. And, with the way people move around in the world these days, it's only natural that people from one group or another will meet people from other groups. And, with your Uncle Bill being out west on the ranch like that, the chances of him meeting a Scottish lass were altogether less likely than the chance of him meeting an Indian.

"The ranch is only an hour's drive from the Big Thunder place. It was only natural that they would meet and – and love – and marry. It was only natural, Gordon. It was a – a – a pairing of two individual human beings. Two people who fell in love. Not a mixing of breeds as the word half-breed suggests. It was just something that happened between – between your natural father and mother. Something that's happened thousands of times since the streams of people from the old world started coming to this country. Don't cheapen their experience – the natural coming together of two individuals from different cultures – by using a word like half-breed. You're not a half-breed, my son. You are what you are. What you've become as an individual."

She paused for a moment and took another swallow of her tea. "Oh, Gordon, this isn't the way I wanted you to learn about all this. Not the way at all. You should have been told a long time ago. A long, long, time ago. And, you should know, it wasn't just the fact that your Uncle Bill was killed at the battle of Hong Kong like that. One of the reasons we didn't keep in touch with the people at the Big Thunder place was on account of your father being so angry when he found out Sarah's husband wasn't going to fight in the war. He said something about the treaties they had with Queen Victoria saying Indians didn't have to fight in the Canadian army. That really got your Dad angry. He didn't want to have anything more to do with them.

"Perhaps, in a way, that's another reason why your father, God rest his soul, was so opposed to telling you about little William and about Big Thunder. Perhaps he felt it better that you didn't have any contact with the Big Thunder people. I know he always felt that what you are today is more important than the particular circumstances of your birth. Isn't that what you said about your brother, Gordon? That, even if he's eighty per cent Scottish or, perhaps it was Scandinavian you said, that even if he's eighty per cent something else, Indian is what he has chosen to be. And Indian is what he is. I'm not sure, but I think this is what your father always said. You are what you are, what you've been raised to be. You are Gordon MacArthur. My son."

She reached across the table and stroked his cheek with the back of her hand. "Don't react in a rash manner to what I've told you, Gordon. Think about it when you get home. Try and see it for what it is. If your mother had lived, you'd have been raised on the Morgan ranch and your life would have turned out altogether differently. But she didn't live – and you were raised here. You've been here for thirty-five years. Your whole life. Don't get yourself all upset over – over – no, I can't finish. I honestly don't know what to say to you. I truly don't have any good answers to offer you, Son. You're going to have to find those by yourself. I'm sorry. I am so – so sorry, Gordon. I just don't have the words to give to you. I'm sorry. So terribly, terribly, sorry."

Now she's getting all upset again. She shouldn't be beating up on herself like this. "Don't, Mum. You've done the best you could. You meant well and I know that. You've always done your best. And now, I think I'll just go home and think about what you told me. Think about it hard. It's all a bit confusing right now. But, I'll be okay. Don't worry about me."

He got up from the table and walked to the hall closet. As he took his coat off the hanger, he looked fondly at his father's herringbone winter coat for a moment. Then he turned to his mother, cupped her face in his hands and kissed her on the lips. "I love you, Mum. Good night."

Carol felt perfectly at peace as they drove north toward Bill's cabin. The cares of the day passed from her mind as the car sped on past the barns and close-cropped fields of Ontario's late autumn.

Bill had estimated the time just about right. They were enjoying steaks in front of the fireplace by eight. He'd grilled the steaks and she'd tossed the salad. The room was lit by the candles on the table and by the glow from the fire. They ate in silence.

Everything that needed to be said was said with their eyes and their hands. The dry red wine had a rich, full-bodied, taste and Carol soon started to experience a pleasant flush. The flickering candles cast a soft, warm, glow on Bill's face. She was glad that she was with him.

As she lay cradled in his arms later that evening, she reflected on how gentle he had been in his loving of her. How knowledgeably he had attended to every erogenous zone of her body. This is what it means, she thought, when they say "these twain shall become one flesh." This really is a fusion of two bodies. Two halves reaching out to become a larger whole. Their bodies had shuddered in unison like long grass trembling in the summer breeze. She felt totally immersed in him. In the feel of him. The warmth of him. The enjoyment of him.

She didn't think of Derek Parkington at all when she made love with Bill. His presence permeated her entire consciousness. She knew she was finally free of Derek. Free to share and enjoy all the pleasant possibilities that can exist between a man and a woman. She felt with Bill the peace of mind and body she had been seeking.

They lay together, listening to the crackling of the logs in the fire and the sounds of the night outside. Fire shadows stole back and forth across the ceiling.

"Getting cold?" he asked.

"A little."

He reached down and pulled the cover he had made with muskrat pelts up over their bodies. The treated underside of the skin was soft and gentle against her flesh. There was a slight, fatty, smell to the pelt and she found it quite pleasant.

Perhaps, she thought, she should feel strange lying alongside this Blackfoot man with the muskrat pelt cover pulled up over her naked body. But she didn't. Their time together was the sort of thing of which beautiful sonnets are made.

"I told Gordon this morning it's all over between us," she said. "I don't want anything more to do with him. I want him out of the house."

"You mean you just ordered him out of the house? That seems a bit arbitrary and unfair, considering the situation we're in tonight."

"Oh, no," she said in a tone indicating how very much she wanted him to understand. "It has nothing to do with tonight. Gordon's been sleeping with one of his students. He's quite open about it. I think there were others before her. Tonight has nothing to do with it. And yet, if I hadn't had coffee with you after the meeting last night and enjoyed being with you as much as I did, I wouldn't have had the strength to get it over and done with this morning. It was a pretty heavy scene. He said some ugly things before he left – hurtful things. I suppose the thing that hurt the most was that most of them are true. Anyway, when I was going through that scene with Gordon this morning, I was really glad that I was going to be with you tonight. I don't think I could've taken it – being alone tonight. Not after the things he said about me this morning."

"Do you want to talk about it?" he asked.

"Not really. But, the thing about the house – about asking him to leave. I was born in that house. The children were born there. It makes sense that he should be the one to leave. You do see that, don't you?"

"Not entirely. What about your children? Will they want him to leave?"

"He hardly ever sees them."

"That's not what I asked, Carol. "Will they want to have their father leave?"

"He should have thought about that before he started sleeping around. And it's not just the sleeping around part. It's all that stuff that came out in the newspapers and on television and the radio. I find so much of what he says to be totally repulsive. He's just plain bigoted. And I feel embarrassment. Not just as his wife, but as a human being. He's out of his tree. Sick. Obscene. I don't want to be associated with him. In any form whatsoever. Least of all as his wife. He has to go. Things have been allowed to degenerate too far."

"Maybe. But that still doesn't mean the children will want him to go. What about them? What about their needs? For a father? For a family unit?"

"You're not in any position to hand out advice on that score. What about your own situation? What about Albert? And Jean? And Ian Starlight? What about all that?"

"I don't see what my situation has to do with your decision to deprive your children of their father. I didn't say what I did was right. I didn't say I'd done the right thing. I didn't say concentrating on the academic side instead of getting into the business world like my wife thought I should've was the right thing. I didn't say that not being able to buy her the things she wanted was the right thing. I didn't say any of that was right. All I'm doing is asking you if this is the right decision for your children. My situation has nothing to do with it. So, what about it? Is asking Gordon to get out of the house the best thing for the children?"

"How can I possibly answer a question like that? You'd have to ask them that."

Suddenly, she noticed the sharp edge that had crept into both their voices. "Why are we going at each other like this? How can we occupy so beautiful a space one minute – a really beautiful space – and then go at each other like an old married couple?"

He flashed a warm smile at her. The twinkle was back in his eye. "Because I'm still dealing with the guilt from my marriage breakup and you're just starting to deal with yours. Just getting that first bitter taste of guilt feelings. That's why we're tearing at each other a bit."

He kissed her on the tip of her nose. "You scratch my scar tissue and I'll scratch yours. Let's go for a walk."

"A walk?"

"Yep. It'll clear our minds. Just look at that moon outside. A walk 'll do us both good."

It was a good idea. They got dressed, pulled on their warm outer clothing and slipped out into the cold fall air. They walked hand in hand along the path by the lake, thighs touching now and again. The good feeling they had for each other quickly flushed away the effects of their first falling out. By the time they headed back to the cabin, they were arm in arm and ready for love.

The lights were off when Gordon got to the house. He couldn't recall ever coming home without there being a light on in the window. Anne must have forgotten to leave the living room light on when they left for the farm.

He went through to his study and sat at his desk – looking at the paintings of Robert the Bruce at Bannockburn and the bloody Battle of Culloden Moor. Somehow, that night, it all seemed so far, far away. *What*, he wondered, *has any of that to do with my life today?*

He toyed with the brass letter opener his father had given him, the one with the Highland piper on the handle. He wondered why his father had given him all those things – the paintings – the letter opener – his tartan ties. He hadn't started wearing the ties until after his father was run down by the drunk driver and left them to him. It was more as a reminder of his father that he wore them. He enjoyed the feel of wearing something that had belonged to his dad – just like he was going to enjoy wearing that winter coat with the seal fur collar.

He wondered if it was because he was half Indian that his father had placed so much emphasis on his Scottish heritage. Was that why he'd taken him to all the Highland games, the Robbie Burns dinners and all that? Was that it? To give him an identity? A Western European, Scottish, identity?

He wondered if his father had had difficulty accepting the fact that he was half Indian. Was that why he hadn't been told about his natural mother and Big Thunder and the true story about his Uncle Bill? And yet, no, his father had never been against different kinds of people. In fact, he'd gotten quite annoyed with Professor Henderson on the night of the lecture. Father said Henderson was a racist bigot.

What about Henderson — and the others? What will they say when they find out I'm half Indian? Will they still want me on the Equal Opportunities Council? And Henry. And the others on the Meadowbrook executive. Will they still want me to represent them in the House of Commons? I somehow doubt it. Doubt it very much. They certainly don't want their white knight to be half Indian. "The chair recognizes the Honourable half-breed from Meadowbrook." *That would go over well. Real well.*

What does all this mean? Why couldn't Mother leave things as they were? Dad was right. No earthly good can possibly come from telling me all this stuff. Then again, maybe she was right. Now that me and — and my brother — are into the pipeline thing, it — oh shit! How can I be expected to accept him as my brother?

And then his thoughts turned to his Uncle Bill, his biological father. He was glad he hadn't abandoned him. Hadn't just walked away. *Like Mum says, he wanted to have us — me and Bill — living with him again after the war. He wanted us to be a family. What would that have been like? What would he have been like as a father? Mum says he cared about us, cared about us a lot. He'd probably have been a good father. And now he's so far away, over there in that lonely grave in Hong Kong. It's kind of sad in a way. He was awfully young to die. Too young.*

He didn't fault his mother for telling him he was adopted. Especially not after seeing him and his brother on the television together. She'd meant well enough. *But something like this is better kept in the family. There's no reason to tell outsiders about things like this. None at all.*

He made himself a cup of Ovaltine and took it with him to his bedroom on the third floor. It was a strange feeling, being alone in the house. The full moon shone through the leaves and cast ghostly patterns on the bedroom wall. The rustle of the leaves in the breeze filtered through the open window.

He would like to have had Ruth in bed with him. Not for any kinky sex, mind you, but just to hold her in his arms. To have physical contact with another human being. To share a warm, caring, space in the night. *Damn, but it would be nice to have someone to talk things over*

*with right now. To get an opinion from someone who cares about me. Wish
Dad was still alive.*

But there was no one he could turn to. Oh, there were people
he was familiar with – acquaintances from the university and a few
Conservatives. But there was no friend – never had been – he could
turn to and say, "Hey, I need you."

It would have been good to have had someone to call on right
then – someone to sound out about this being half Indian business.
To get another opinion. To, somehow, get a handle on things. Exercise
more control over what was happening to him. But he didn't have. He
decided he simply couldn't think about the situation any more that
night. He'd think about it all in the morning. His mind would be
clearer by then. He hoped.

The sun's early morning rays crept into the room and warmed
Gordon's eyelids. He opened his eyes slowly and looked out the
window at what promised to be a clear sunny late autumn day. He
stretched his body, bunched the pillows up under his head and recalled
his mother's words. "William is your brother, Son. You can't change
that. He is your brother."

And yet, as she had said, their lives were separate and apart. Bill
was an Indian. He'd been raised as an Indian. *That shouldn't have any
bearing on my life, my identity.*

"You are what you are," she said. "What you've become as an
individual. What you were raised to be. You are Gordon MacArthur.
My son."

That was something they could never take away from him.
Nothing could alter the fact that he was her son. That he'd been her
son for thirty-five years. His whole life. She was his mother and that's
all there was to it.

But what about that other mother of his? The one who died so he
could live. What was she to him? If she had lived, he would have been
raised out west on the Morgan ranch. Perhaps he would have become
a cowboy or owned his own little ranch somewhere in the foothills of

the Rockies. That would have been an altogether different life for him – more along the lines of life on his grandfather's hill farm in Scotland.

That's the way it would have been if his biological mother had lived. He would have been raised on the ranch, learned to ride the horses, even to break them and – Bill would have been there. They would have been raised together – as brothers.

Gordon had always wanted a brother – or a sister. Most of the people he knew had brothers or sisters. Apart from Carol, he was the only only child he'd ever known. Being an only child was different. He'd always felt incomplete when he'd arrive at a picnic or a baseball game and find the other kids had come with brothers or sisters. Some older, some younger. Showing up without a brother or sister was like running around on one leg.

He wondered what sort of brother Bill would have been. He seemed pretty even-tempered and there was no denying his intelligence. In fact, some of his comments, especially the ones about taking the fish, the buffalo and all of the other natural resources, had stuck in his mind.

There was a ring of truth to what Bill had said. The European attitude toward North America had been extractive, right from the start. It had been a taking away from rather than a giving to. North America had always been looked upon as a place from which you took. Like drawing money on someone else's bank account. The big difference was that, as Bill had said, the Europeans were drawing from an account they had never made a deposit in. They hadn't saved up the fish, the trees, the gold, the buffalo and the other resources they drew on. It was another person's bank account. *The Indians'? No, you couldn't say the fish or the trees or the gold or the oil were the Indians'. But, what about the buffalo and the beaver? Maybe. Maybe Bill has a point there. We did pretty well exterminate the buffalo and the beaver. That's true. But that was a long time ago. A long, long, time ago.*

We're certainly doing all we can today to make things up to those of them who survived the European occupation of their territory. By ramming a gas pipeline through their land? Well, I'm not quite so sure about that one now. And that isn't because of Sarah. She's still nothing to me. She's Bill's mother. She's the one who raised him. She's his responsibility. Of course, that wouldn't have been the case if our own – our own?

– mother had lived. If she had lived, we'd both have been raised on the Morgan ranch instead of Big Thunder and Toronto. And Bill would have been raised as a MacArthur instead of an Eagletail.

If that had happened, he'd never have braided his hair like a woman and worn those bear claws around his neck. It'd be easier to accept him as my brother if he didn't insist on dressing up like that. That way, I could relate to him as a human being instead of as a professional Indian. If we had been raised together, I might – and I'm only saying might – have enjoyed having him as my brother. But we weren't. What if we'd both been raised in Toronto? He'd probably be into the tartan ties and kilts instead of that braided hair and bear claws. Interesting prospect.

He climbed out of bed and went to the bathroom to have his morning shower. After the shower, he put on a pair of jeans and a sweater and went to the front porch to get the *Globe and Mail.*

There was a story and two pictures on the front page about the demonstration the students had conducted at City Hall over the lunch hour on Friday. One of the pictures showed the students holding a sit-in on Nathan Phillips Square. The caption said there were more than four hundred of them. The other picture showed cops shoving a female student into a paddy wagon.

This thing's really getting big, Gordon thought to himself. *These students really are making quite a fuss about that pipeline. Maybe that's a good thing. Maybe they'll be able to stop Saunders from running his pipeline through Bill's mother's barnyard. Maybe that's just as well. All this stuff about whites freezing in the dark was a lot of hype anyway. Lot of PR. Like Bill said, Saunders' "big discovery" is only a drop in the bucket in the overall scheme of things.*

There was a picture of Sarah on one of the inside pages feeding one of her young calves from a bucket of milk. She was kneeling beside the nervous creature. Her arm was around its neck in a protective embrace. The cutline said: GUARDS CALF FROM BULLDOZERS. Her hair was tucked under a black cowboy hat. She was a big woman – not fat – but big. She was wearing a denim jacket over a checkered work shirt. Her smouldering eyes pierced the page of the newspaper. Her weathered face was quite lined and the hard set of her mouth reminded him of his grandfather.

"So, you're my aunt," he said. "My biological mother's sister."

He felt a compulsion to talk to her – to ask her about Big Thunder, his Uncle Bill and his – his other mother. What answers would she give him? What was Big Thunder like? *Should I go out there? See where I spent the first month of my life?*

His mother called to make sure he was all right. He told her he was a bit confused but there was nothing for her to worry herself about. She was still quite upset and came down hard on herself for not doing a better job of telling him about the adoption.

"Hey, Mum, no. No. Don't come down hard on yourself like this. I can't think of anything you could have done differently under the circumstances. You did fine. Just fine. And – and it's like you said last night, I'm going to have to find the answers by myself. By the way, there was a picture of Bill's mother in the *Globe* this morning feeding one of her calves. She reminded me a bit of Grandfather MacArthur."

"It's strange you should say that, Gordon. I'd never realized it until now, but you're right. Your Aunt Sarah and your dad's father are a lot alike. They both have a – an uncanny presence about them. Neither one of them says all that much about anything, but you – you're so aware of their presence. More so than you are of the people who are monopolizing the conversation. The two of them, just by their silent presence, seem to dominate any room they're in. While your grandfather is gone now, he was an awful lot like Sarah. I think you'd have liked her. I was only out there for a week but I enjoyed being with her so very much. She's a much stronger person than I am, you know. Much stronger. And young William seems to have picked up many of her characteristics. He also has a – a quiet strength. A – a presence. I was quite impressed with what I saw of him on the television."

She was obviously quite taken with this new brother of his. Gordon felt a stirring sense of jealousy. *Maybe she likes him better than me. Maybe it's the braids and the bear claws. Damn. Why is everything happening so fast? The divorce thing. Finding out I'm a half-breed. My head's spinning. Got to slow things down a bit.*

"Would you mind if we don't go up to the farm until tomorrow?" he asked. "I'm still sorting all of this out in my head and I'm not quite ready to be with the children yet. This affects them, too, you know. It means that Charlie and Diane are one-quarter Indian. I was reading in the paper the other day that some Indians are claiming that one-quarter Indian blood is all you should need to qualify for government funding. They said everyone who's one-quarter Indian should be covered by the treaties. I don't agree with that. Not at all. Charlie and Diane aren't one-quarter Indian. They're three-quarters white. And it's only right that the white, predominant, part of them should have the priority – white, Western European, Canadians. Anyway, Mum, I'm not ready to deal with all that quite yet. How about if I pick you up around eight tomorrow morning and we'll have a nice breakfast together on the way up to the farm? Would you like that? Would that be all right?"

"Yes, Son. That would be splendid. I'd like that. In fact, while my foot's a bit better today, it will be even better tomorrow. I do wish I didn't have the gout."

"That's my good girl. And I'm sorry about your foot. I know how much it must hurt. All right then, I'll pick you up at eight tomorrow morning. And, Mum, don't worry. I'm going to be fine. Just fine."

He went through to the kitchen and poured himself another cup of coffee. He still had a bad taste in his mouth from the wine and the vodka, but his head was quite clear. He realized he shouldn't have drunk so much at his mother's apartment. He returned to the living room, picked up the copy of the *Globe* and settled back into the plush comfort of the chesterfield. He put his feet up on the coffee table and carried on with the enjoyment of his morning coffee and the newspaper.

He opened the paper up at the page with the picture of Sarah feeding milk to her calf. *Mum likes her. You could tell from the tone of her voice that she thinks a lot of her. Despite the fact she only met her once. When she went out there to bring me home. Mother's right. She shouldn't have her life disrupted by running that pipeline through her yard like that. It is an imposition. There's got to be some other way of resolving this pipeline business. This puts a different slant on things. I can't support them ramming a gas pipeline through my aunt's barnyard. And then there's those documents they've got showing the pipeline wasn't supposed to go through her barnyard in the first place. I'll have to give this whole thing a serious second thought. A lot of thought. Maybe I should talk it over with Bill.*

With Bill? What about him? And what about that Toronto Focus *interview we're supposed to do Tuesday night? How can we go ahead with that now that he's my – my – brother? We can't. It just won't work. I'll have to straighten all of this out before Tuesday. Maybe even discuss it with Bill. Yes. That's what I'm going to do. I'll phone him and ask him to have a coffee with me. I'll say I've got something important to discuss with him and the phone's not the best place to deal with it. It'll be better person to person. Eyeball to eyeball.*

He looked Bill's number up in the university staff directory and phoned him at his house. The answering service said he was away for the weekend. They asked if he wanted to leave a message. *No. No message. Damn.*

The phone rang. It was Dave Saunders' secretary saying he had to cancel the lunch meeting. He was really sorry about having cancelled two times in a row but he would call Gordon at the beginning of the week and arrange another time. *Probably still dealing with that mess their engineer created by talking to the reporter from the* Globe. *Probably just as well he cancelled our lunch. Especially now that I'm half Indian. Wouldn't know what to say to him about that. Wouldn't know what to say to anyone.*

He wandered through the house and lingered in the emptiness of its rooms. He missed Charlie and Diane. He didn't see all that much of them, but he did love them. *There's no way I won't have visiting rights. I'll still be part of their lives. Not the same as living with them, though. But we'll work it out. Other fathers have been in the same boat. We will find a way to make it work. I'll make sure of that.*

～

Bill was sleeping when Carol woke up. She felt her head rise and fall in unison with his chest. He was a big man. A strong, gentle, loving man.

She drew away from his body, lay on her back and looked out the window at the sun-dappled leaves of autumn fluttering down from the branches of the nearest tree. It was a beautiful place. And very private. They had parked the car at a curve in the road and walked about three hundred yards through the thick bush. The one-room cabin was in a clearing at the edge of a slight slope running down to the water. It was more accessible by boat than by car.

She slipped out of his bed, taking care not to waken him, pulled on her robe and went over to the window by the kitchen sink. Long grass rippled in the breeze in the cleared space between the cabin and the dock. It was about a quarter mile from the dock to the nearest island. Everything looked so still. So pure. She was glad that she was there. And then she felt Bill's strong arms circling around her. He kissed her on the nape of her neck and she brought his hands up from her belly and placed them on her breasts.

"'Morning," he said. "How are you?"

"I'm just fine," she said. "Just perfectly fine."

He turned her body to his and kissed her lips. She responded eagerly and pulled his head down tight.

"Shall I light a fire?" he asked as he eased out of their embrace.

"No. No," she said. "The sun feels so warm. We don't need a fire."

They ate their granola with honey and fresh fruit in sunlight and silence –thoroughly enjoying each other's presence. Bill smiled as he passed her the pot of freshly brewed tea. His hair fell down over his shoulders. He had taken it out of the braids before they made love. The red headband across his forehead kept it out of his eyes. When she reached across the table and ran her hand across his cheek, he bent his head and kissed the back of her hand. She found him to be so gentle, so tender.

They made love again – and again – until the sun started to cross over to the other side of the cabin and no longer caressed their bodies through the windowpanes.

"Show me that island," she said, as they got dressed. "The one across from your dock. Can we go there?"

"That's funny," he said. "I was just going to suggest a ride in the boat. I need gas and we'll need some food and things. We'll take a lunch and I'll show you around."

"Fantastic!" she exclaimed. And then she remembered. "But what about your book? I shouldn't be taking you away from your work. Maybe we'd better not."

"No problem," he assured her. "I'll write tonight – after dinner. As long as I get in two hours, I'll be okay. And then, after that," he said with a warm suggestive grin, "we'll just let nature take its course."

She smiled. "Are you sure two hours will be enough? Maybe you should write now."

"It's okay. I'll write better after spending more time with you. You do good things to my head."

She was glad she stimulated him. They would have a couple of hours out in the boat and then, maybe, they'd make love again before dinner.

As Gordon washed his breakfast dishes, the movie projector of his mind threw the image of Sarah back up on the screen. His thoughts returned to Big Thunder and his newly-found brother. With the *Toronto Focus* interview coming up so soon, he thought, they were going to have to straighten out this business about being brothers. They were also going to have to decide what they were going to tell people about it – if anything. *We certainly can't go on like this. Especially not on live television.*

He wondered if Bill's answering service had a number where he could be reached. He decided to find out. The woman at the answering service told him there was no phone at the cottage, but urgent messages could be left at a local marina. When he dialled the number, the woman who answered said she could get a message to Bill if it was an emergency. Gordon told her it wasn't but he'd appreciate it if she'd tell him how to get to her place. She did and he thanked her for her trouble.

He looked out the kitchen window again. It was a gorgeous autumn day. A drive up to Lake Muskoka might be just the thing he needed to clear his mind. *It'll be good to talk to Bill. To see him face to face and find out what he knows about Big Thunder and what happened out there. Maybe his mum and dad told him all about it. He might know a lot more about it than I do. We'll see.*

He phoned his mother to let her know he was going to see Bill and tell him that they were brothers. "Are you sure that's the best thing to do?" she asked. "It's all so new to you, Gordon. Maybe you should think about it some more before telling William – before telling your brother."

"You're right about it all being new, Mum. But we're going to be on that TV show again Tuesday night and, under those circumstances, I think, the sooner Bill knows the better."

"Perhaps you're right there, Gordon. But do be careful how you put it to him. It's going to come as a bit of a shock."

"I will, Mum. I'm still in shock myself."

"Would you like me to come with you, for moral support?"

"No, thanks. I think it best that I handle this myself."

"All right, my son. Drop by to see me when you get back."

"I'll do that, Mum. Love you. Goodbye."

As he drove north towards Bill's cabin, Gordon reflected on the topsy turvy events of the last two days. Thursday night he was nominated as the Conservative candidate for Meadowbrook and was going to be the voice of white Canada in the House of Commons. Friday night, his mother told him he was half Indian. And now here he was on a bright sunny fall day on his way up to tell Bill Eagletail they were brothers.

When he arrived at the marina, which also served as a garage and grocery store, the woman told him he'd missed Bill by about an hour. "He was in for gas and groceries," she said, pointing to the Shell pump at the dock. "They left about an hour ago."

When she brought him his coffee, he asked her how to get to the cabin. She gave him the directions and told him to watch out for Bill's red '63 Buick which would be parked at a curve on the dirt road near the lake.

"Park beside it and you'll see a path running off into the bush on your right. Follow that for about three hundred yards and you'll find the clearing. I've only been there a few times myself. Mr. Ericson, who rented the cabin to Dr. Eagletail, usually comes over in the boat to get things. Anyway, you should be able to find it."

Gordon thanked her for the directions and finished his coffee. The mixed aroma of motor oil and rubber tires from the service bay tickled his nostrils. He paid for the coffee and slipped a quarter under the saucer. Then he got a handful of jelly beans from the candy machine with the chrome beaver on the front and went outside.

The mid-afternoon sun was quite strong and he enjoyed the feel of it on his face and on his arms. No wonder men have always worshipped the sun, he thought. There would be no life without it. Must have been a traumatic shock for the earth's first inhabitants when it went down for the first time. They must have figured they were all done for. And then, when it rose again at dawn the next day, they must have been willing to sacrifice anything, even the life of another human being, to prevent it from going away from them again. Maybe that's why the sun plays so large a part in the spiritual life of the Indians. Especially in Central America. Nothing could live without it.

He held his face up to the sky and let the breeze massage it with the sun's rays. It felt good. The light from the sun created an orange glow under his eyelids. He got into the car and drove toward Bill's cabin.

It was an old Buick. He couldn't tell if it was a '63 or not because he didn't know any more about cars than he did about boats or anything else mechanical. He parked behind it, locked his Pontiac and looked around for the path. It wasn't much of a path. You'd never find it in the dark.

The air was filled with the scent of pinecones and decaying under-brush. Birds punctuated the haunting silence with their shrill calls. He spotted a rabbit scurrying for cover and wondered if the hole at the bottom of one of the trees was home to a squirrel or a fox. It seemed a bit large for squirrels. By the time he got to Bill's clearing, the sounds and smells of the bush had lulled his mind into a more peaceful state than he had experienced in ages. It was like being at his grandfather's farm again.

Gordon knocked on the cabin door and waited for Bill to open it. There was no answer. He knocked again. Still no answer. *Perhaps they aren't back from the marina yet.*

He walked to the side of the cabin and looked down toward the dock. There was no boat there. Bill must have gone somewhere else after leaving the marina. *He'll probably be back soon.* He went back to the door and tried turning the knob. It was unlocked. He would wait inside.

The muskrat pelt cover was pulled back on the big bed in the middle of the room. A half-empty bottle of wine was on the bedside table. There were two glasses. *That's right. The woman at the marina said "they" had left about an hour before I got there. Probably Bill's wife. I wonder if she's Indian, too?*

There was a framed picture on the mantel over the fireplace. It was of a young boy, just about the same age as Charlie. He was dressed in a hockey outfit and skates. His stick was poised to score. *Must be Bill's son. My – my nephew?*

He looked more closely at the boy's face and searched for the MacArthur in him. He didn't find it. The boy had a look of his own. He didn't look at all like Bill. His face was rounder, fuller. Gordon looked around for a picture of Bill's wife, as if to find the answer to the boy's decidedly un-MacArthur appearance. But there was no picture of the mother. *Still, the youngster is quite good looking.*

Gordon had to go to the bathroom. As he sat on the toilet, he noticed that the terry cloth bathrobe hanging on the peg by the shower stall was the same colour as Carol's. The thought that it might be hers didn't so much as cross his mind. After flushing Bill's toilet, he opened the window so the stink of his shit would leave the room.

He sat in one of the big, stuffed, chairs by the fireplace and looked around for an ashtray. There was none to be found. He lit his cigarette anyway and flicked the ashes over the hearth. It was then that he realized that he had absolutely no idea what he was going to say to Bill. *How about, "Hi, I'm your little brother"? Or what about, "Excuse me, but I believe that you are my brother"? Or, maybe, "I understand that we have a mother in common." What am I going to say? What is Bill going to say?*

His throat felt tight and dry and, for a moment, he questioned whether he should have come at all. *What if Bill refuses to believe me? What if he doesn't want me for a brother? What if I don't want an Indian for a brother? There's so many what-ifs. Too many.*

CHAPTER
- 25 -

Gordon heard the sound of the outboard motor as the boat approached the dock. He went to the open kitchen window and looked down towards the water. It was quite a small boat. The woman was sitting with her back to the bow and he couldn't get a good look at her as the boat pulled alongside the dock.

When the boat stopped, Bill lifted some bags of groceries out onto the dock. Then he got out of the boat and reached down to help her out. She took his hand and stepped onto the dock with her back toward Gordon. She had her arms up around Bill's neck now and she was pulling his mouth down on hers. They embraced in the sunshine at the end of the dock.

Must be love, Gordon mused, as he took in the view from the kitchen window. *Maybe it'd be better for me to wait outside. After all, I hardly know them. There's no telling how they'll react if they find me sitting beside their fireplace.*

He went outside and sat on the lawn chair under the big cedar tree beside the hedge that blocked the view of the dock. He could hear the joyful sound of their laughter as they made their way up from the dock. They came around the corner of the hedge, arms filled with groceries – and stopped dead in their tracks when they saw Gordon sitting under the big cedar. He stared up in disbelief. He wanted to ask Carol what in the world she was doing there. But the words wouldn't come out of his mouth. He was struck dumb. Like a lamb before its shearers.

Carol wasn't. "What the hell are you doing here?" she demanded. "Did you follow me?"

He didn't know what to say to her. And Bill, obviously preferring to let them work it out between them, leaned against the side of the cabin and waited to see what would happen next.

"I asked you what you're doing here," Carol repeated. "Whatever would you come here for?"

"I – I came to see Bill," he started, in a faltering voice. "I – I – I had something to say to him. I had – I had no idea you'd be here – like – like this. I thought you had probably gone to Beaverton to spend the weekend with Jane Potts."

Bill was relieved to hear it wasn't a case of hot pursuit by a jealous husband. He decided to try and ease the tension. "Well, look," he said. "Let's not stand out here like orphans. Let's go inside and have some tea."

His suggestion did, to a certain extent, ease the tension that held them all in its grasp. And yet Carol didn't quite believe it was Bill Gordon had come to see. *But, if he wants to play it that way, that's fine with me.*

Gordon was still numbed by the sight of them together. It was all so totally unexpected – and inconceivable. He didn't know what to do or how to react. The whole thing intimidated him. *How can she be here with – with him? They slept together? Under that fur cover? Is he the first? Have there been others? Like, in Bermuda, was she with someone there? Was that why she kicked me out of her bed? Shit. I can't believe she actually slept here. Under that fur skin.*

They went inside and Bill put the kettle on for their tea. Carol put the groceries away.

"Well," Bill said, as he lit the fire. "What was on your mind? What was important enough for you to drive all the way up here?"

Gordon didn't know where to begin. *This was a bad idea. I should have stayed in Toronto. Or gone to the farm with Charlie and Diane. This is not where I want to be right now.*

Carol felt extremely uncomfortable about Gordon being in the same room where she'd made love with Bill that very morning. The bed was unmade and the two wine glasses were still on the bedside table. Looking so very much like "Exhibit A" in a second-rate divorce proceeding. "If this really is between the two of you, I think I'll take a walk," she said.

"It is," Gordon said hastily. "It is between us. It's got nothing to do with you. Nothing at all. Take your walk. This is just between us."

As soon as she left the cabin, he felt altogether better. Her presence had been overwhelming. Suffocating.

"About me and Carol," Bill started.

"I don't want to talk about that," Gordon said, strength returning to his voice. "What I have to say is altogether more important than that sort of thing."

Bill didn't like Gordon's reference to "that sort of thing", but he let it pass.

Gordon decided to get right to the point of his visit. "Let me tell you what I have to say – the way my mother told me about it last night. You'll see that it's quite important. Important in regard to Big Thunder and – and to you."

Bill was surprised by Gordon's reference to Big Thunder – and to him. It was obvious from the sincere look in Gordon's eyes that he really did feel it was important enough to drive all the way up from Toronto. And, considering the situation Gordon had found him in with Carol, it might be better to let him talk for a while – to get whatever it was that brought him up there off his chest.

Gordon told the story, pretty well the way his mother had told it to him the night before. "I'm serious, Bill. You are my brother. It's strange, I know. But it's also true. I was called Gordon because my Uncle Bill cared an awful lot for my grandfather on my biological mother's side of the family. What's your grandfather's name?"

"Gordon," Bill replied with some hesitation. "Gordon Dodging-horse."

"Right. And your grandmother's name is Vera and they lived about a quarter of a mile from the house where you were raised. My mum met them when she went out to Big Thunder to bring me home. She also says you have a younger brother with a bad case of asthma. If it hadn't been for the *Toronto Focus* interview last week, we'd never have known about any of this. But, when my mum saw us both on TV – and heard us talking about Big Thunder and – about Sarah – about your mother – she figured she just had to tell me. Tell me the true story about my Uncle Bill, about Big Thunder and – and about you. It's all true, Bill. Every word of it."

Bill reflected on what Gordon had been saying. *Can all of this be true? Can this white power Conservative actually be my brother? My God!, I can't believe it.* And yet he had an intuitive feeling that what Gordon was telling him was the truth. "Your Uncle Bill, tell me again what happened to him?"

"He stayed on at the ranch for a while and then he joined the army, the Winnipeg Grenadiers. My mum says he was killed fighting the Japanese at Hong Kong. He was only thirty. The army buried him over there. Now, my mum did say that he wanted to have us living with him. He was looking forward to getting a job in Calgary after the war and then he could have us living with him again. So, he didn't just abandon us, didn't just walk away. He was coming back. We were going to be with him. But, like my mum says, the war changed everything. For everyone."

"My mom did tell me she had a sister," Bill said, like a detective piecing disparate clues together. "A sister named Helen. Mom said she'd worked as a cook on a ranch up north of Cochrane. But she never said anything about her being married. Just that she'd died young one spring and they'd buried her at Big Thunder. Down at the Methodist church. That's all she ever told me about her."

"Maybe, like with my mum and dad ... he's dead now ... got killed by a drunk driver three years ago ... she didn't see any purpose in telling you any of this. With them both being dead like that, my dad said, it was better to leave things alone."

"Perhaps," Bill agreed. "Perhaps, if this is true, your dad was right. It probably was better that way. But I can see how, with us being on TV together like that and with the pipeline going through Big Thunder, I can see how your mom would think it was better to tell you about it. Things were coming to a head. And I think – I think if my mom had known it was you saying all those things about the pipeline and why it should go through her yard, and that we'd been on TV together and all that, I think she'd probably have told me herself. I think, under the circumstances, your mom did the right thing. But my God, this is weird."

"Yep," Gordon said. "Weird is the word for it. This time yesterday, I didn't know a thing about it. And I don't think any of it has really sunk in yet. It all sounds more like something that's happening to someone in a movie rather than something that's actually happening to me. I don't think the reality of it all has sunk in yet. It all seems so unreal. So – so far away. Like it was all happening in another world."

Gordon looked around the room. His eyes rested on the two wine glasses on the bedside table. "Weird is the word for it." He still couldn't believe that Carol had actually slept there. *Tells me she wants me out of the house ASAP and then she's in his bed – that bed over there – the very same night. What a deceitful hypocritical bitch. Kicks me out and then hops into bed with him. All in one day. What if she'd known he was my brother? Probably wouldn't have made any difference. We're all washed up as a couple anyway. She's been pretty clear about that over the last couple of weeks. It was over. Finished.*

Bill looked at the glasses, a bit guiltily, and at the bed where he'd made love to Carol. "If I'd only known," he started. "If I'd only ..."

"Don't," Gordon said. "You don't have to say anything. I'd hoped this thing would work out between me and Carol, but – I guess, it's over. Seeing the two of you down by the dock – hearing the sound of your laughter – she just isn't that way with me. It's over. If I didn't realize the truth of that on the way up here, I do now. You don't have to say anything."

"Last night was the first time," Bill said, as if he had to set the record straight. "It wasn't until after you'd agreed you were going to split up."

"We didn't actually agree. That was all Carol's idea. Besides, all of that seems so terribly unimportant right now. Carol made the right decision about us. It is over. Finished. Fini." He pointed to the picture on the mantelpiece. "Is that your son?"

"Yes. That's Albert. He's eight. He's all I've got. I wanted another son, or a daughter, but my wife said no. We're separated. Getting a divorce."

"Is your boy with you in Toronto?"

"No. He's at Big Thunder with my mother. Been living there for about three years now. I'm trying to work out a way for us to be together – all the time."

"I can imagine how that must feel," Gordon said. "Living a couple of thousand miles apart like that."

"Yeah, just like you and me 've been living at opposite ends of the country despite us being brothers."

They were both very unsettled by the adoption thing. It all seemed so surreal. Like it was happening, and yet, not happening. And then there was the Carol factor. The fact that she had slept with Bill in that unmade bed the night before and they'd probably be back there again in a matter of hours.

The door opened and Carol came back into the cabin. She had decided they'd had enough time to talk and it was now time for Gordon to get the hell out of there and let her and Bill get on with their weekend together. "Have you two finished your talk?" she asked, with a cold edge to her voice. "Have you finished?"

"We've only just got started," Bill said, a bit surprised by the coldness in her tone.

"Well, I hope you're not going to be much longer," she said, as she poured herself a cup of tea. "This isn't what I came up here for."

Again, Bill was puzzled by her tone and by her almost belligerent attitude. *She's probably feeling awkward about this whole thing and that's why she's going on the offensive rather than having to explain to Gordon what she's doing here. Then again, maybe this is another, not very pleasant, side of her.*

She sat down at the table and stared, somewhat challengingly, at the two of them as she tasted the tea. "Well," she asked, "are you going to get on with it?"

"Hey, hold on," Bill said, gently. "What's gotten into you? There's no reason for you to behave like this. Just be patient."

"Do you want me to go out again? Is that it?" she asked. "Am I supposed to go for another walk in the woods while you two talk about me?"

So that was it. "Carol," Bill said. "We aren't talking about you. This has nothing – nothing at all – to do with you. It's just something between the two of us."

She felt shut out. She resented the idea of the two of them having a conversation she couldn't be part of. "Well, if I'm intruding," she started. "I can ..."

"Carol," Bill said, "just settle yourself down. Please. You're not intruding. It's just that – that what we're talking about is – is personal. Just between the two of us."

"And what was that?" she demanded, pointing to the unmade bed. "What was that if it wasn't personal?"

"It's just not the same sort of thing," Bill said, wishing she hadn't drawn attention to the bed. "What we're talking about is a different kind of personal. It's not something we can discuss with anyone else."

"What do you mean by 'anyone else'?" Carol asked. "What 'm I supposed to be? A United Nations' observer or something?"

Gordon rather enjoyed seeing them going at one another like that. *Go ahead. Be my guest. Knock yourselves out.*

"No, it's nothing like that," Bill assured her.

"Then what on earth is it?" she demanded, obviously quite upset.

"We're not ready to discuss it with you," Bill replied, firmly. "There's nothing further to say right now."

She looked at him, then at the fireplace and then at Gordon. *What are they up to? What on earth is going on between them?*

"I don't understand this," she said. "We came up here to be together and now you're telling me I'm intruding on something personal – something between you and Gordon – like you were long-lost cousins or something. How 'm I supposed to react to all this? What's going on?"

"It's all quite complicated," Bill replied, in a gentler tone. "Even more complicated than it seems – with you and me being here the way we are and Gordon arriving on the scene like this. But, believe me, Carol, I don't want to shut you out. It's just that – that what Gordon has been telling me is something I can't share with you right now. I have to talk things over with Gordon some more before I can discuss this with you – or with anyone. It really is that personal."

Maybe it really doesn't have anything to do with me being here for the weekend. But what could they possibly be talking about that's more personal than that? "Would you like me to leave again?" she asked, in a warmer tone. "Would you rather have some more time alone?"

"I would," Bill said. "And do try to understand. I had no idea we'd be having this sort of discussion. Just let me have some more time with

Gordon to straighten things out – as much as they can be straightened out. I don't know if they can be."

"All right," she said. "I'll go for a walk. Or, could I use the boat? I'd like to go out by the island. Maybe catch a couple of fish."

"Sure," Bill said. "No problem. Don't be too long though. Gordon will be leaving soon."

She felt better when she heard Gordon wasn't going to be there when she got back. She found his presence very disturbing. *What must he be thinking? Especially after telling him I wanted him out of the house – away from the children. Finding me in Bill's bed like this – the very next day?*

"All right," she said. "I'll be back in less than an hour."

"That should be enough time," Bill said. "And be careful."

"I will." She didn't say goodbye to either one of them.

As Gordon heard the sound of the outboard motor exploding to life, he thought of their happier times together on the lake at her father's cottage. Carol always took charge of the launch. Gordon didn't know the first thing about boats.

Bill refilled their mugs. Then he settled back in his big armchair. "She's quite a woman," he said.

"Yeah," Gordon replied. "She is that."

"I'm sorry things haven't worked out for you," Bill continued. "I can imagine that she'd be quite a woman to live with."

"There was a time when things were working out pretty well. But that was a long time ago. Quite a long time ago." He sipped some of his tea. "And, yes, she was quite a woman to live with. What about you? Are you – are you serious about her?"

"I don't want to talk about that," Bill said, in a firm, big-brother, sort of tone. "That's not what we were talking about."

"Okay," Gordon said. "I suppose whatever happens between the two of you has nothing to do with me anyway. She wants a divorce. Be my guest."

He realized right away that he shouldn't have said that. But he was hurting, smarting. He had a need to lash out like he did with Carol Friday morning when she told him she wanted him out of the house.

"Don't talk like that," Bill chided. "You sound like an Eskimo offering his wife to someone for the night. If I'm anyone's guest, it'll be hers."

"You'd like her father's house," Gordon continued, unable to resist expressing some of the frustration he was feeling after finding they'd spent the night under the muskrat pelt cover. "It's in the right part of town."

"I don't need her father's house. Or to live in the right part of town," Bill replied with a noticeable edge to his voice.

"Still, you know, there are definite advantages to being Gran Winston's son-in-law. Although," Gordon said with a grin, "I somehow doubt braided hair and bear claws are her father's style. Maybe he wouldn't want an Indian for a son-in-law." *Probably won't want me either when he finds out my mother was a Blackfoot.*

That eased the tension somewhat. Bill smiled. "You mean he'd rather see me in a kilt? Is that it? If I want Carol, I'll have to dress up in a kilt and play the bagpipes?"

"I don't know about that. You could always dress half-and-half and let him have his pick."

"No. No half-and-half. It's got to be one thing or another. Indian is what I am. I don't want to change that. I can't change that."

"I feel the same way," Gordon said. "I thought about it a lot last night and again this morning. I want to stay Scottish. Being half Indian – or half Chinese, or half Pakistani – really doesn't appeal to me at all. I want to be all one thing. It's better that way."

"That's probably why your dad never told you about Big Thunder and that story about your Uncle Bill and my mom's sister. He knew you'd be better off being one thing or the other."

"He was right, wasn't he? Your mum and dad were right, too. There was no reason – especially with – with my Uncle Bill and her being dead and buried like that – there was no reason to say anything – to change things. What possible good could've come out of it?"

"None. None at all. And that's why, if things really happened the way your mother told you, you weren't told about what happened back there. It would've done no good. No good whatsoever."

They sat in silence and looked into the flames, as if the fire was a crystal ball.

"By the way," Gordon said. "I'd almost forgot. There was a picture of your mother in the *Globe* this morning. She was feeding milk to a little calf and the caption said 'Guards calf from bulldozers'. It was on one of the inside pages. The front page had a story and picture of the students holding a sit-in on Nathan Phillips Square over the lunch hour yesterday. The paper said there was more than four hundred of them."

"They've been a big help to our side," Bill said. "And they are a pretty determined bunch of students. Building up a lot of support for our position on the pipeline."

"I hope it works out. For you and your mother," Gordon said. "If I'd known what I know now, I'd have kept my nose out of it altogether."

"I believe that, Gordon. I really do."

"Anyway, I've said all I'm going to say about the pipeline issue. Saunders and his fat, five-roll, brother will have to fight that fight without me."

"Five roll?"

"Yeah. I had lunch with Jack Saunders' brother last week. Ate five rolls. One after the other. Real pig he was. Grease from the steak all around his mouth. And four Scotches to wash it all down."

"Sounds like a man who lives well," Bill said. "Steak, Scotch and five rolls."

"That's one way of putting it," Gordon said. He paused for a moment as if to gather his thoughts.

"What do we do now?" he asked. "About us being brothers. How're we going to handle the *Toronto Focus* thing on Tuesday? We really went at each other the last time and Fraser Deacon is going to be expecting more fireworks. That's why he wants us back on his show."

"I haven't a clue. I'd forgotten about the television interview. We'll have to work something out. Right now, though, that's the least of our problems."

The logs crackled. A bird called from the tree outside. The tap was dripping. Bill got up to turn it off. "Would you like a drink?" he asked, as he walked over to the kitchen counter.

"Yes, thanks. That would be nice."

"What will you have? Scotch?"

"Have you got vodka?"

"No. How about gin?"

"I'll settle for some of that wine."

Bill got the half bottle of wine from the bedside table and poured a glass for Gordon. He fixed himself a Scotch and water, filled a small wooden salad bowl with dry-roasted peanuts and returned to the fire. Gordon had been looking around the room again and his eyes fixed on the big forty-ounce bottles of J & B Scotch on the middle shelf of the cupboard.

"Do you always drink Scotch?" he asked, as Bill handed him the glass of wine.

"Nothing else has that same special taste for me."

"Maybe it's in your blood."

Bill laughed, a quiet gentle laugh. "Maybe. But how do you explain the vodka?"

"Might be a little Russian in me somewhere. If I had to be anything other than Scottish, it'd be Russian. I've always liked vodka. This wine's good, too." The thought that Carol had been drinking from that same bottle crossed his mind. *Can't believe she actually slept here last night. With my brother! My Blackfoot brother.*

"I suppose it's the pipeline business that brought all of this to a head," Bill said, as if he had been sorting things out in his mind. "Without that, and that stuff in the newspapers, and us being on TV, your mom would probably have left things the way they've always been."

"Probably," Gordon agreed. "If it could wait for the first thirty-five years of my life, it could probably have waited for the rest."

"It probably could have," Bill said. "My mom certainly never gave me so much as a hint of anything like this."

Gordon wasn't so sure he wanted to continue the conversation. Finding out that Bill was his brother was one thing. Finding that Carol had made out with him – on that very bed – was something else again. He decided he'd had enough for one day,

"There doesn't seem to be all that much more left to say right now," he said without even tasting the wine. "I think I'll just head back to Toronto and mull this stuff – all of it – over in my head. I must admit, nothing is at all what you could call clearly in focus. It's all quite blurred. Quite definitely blurred."

Bill felt pretty much the same way. It was really awkward finding out that Gordon was his brother on the very same day that he'd made love to Carol over there on the unmade bed. "Okay, then, let's leave it at that for just now. You're right about things being a bit blurred. I'm going to have to work a lot of things out myself. Discussing it further right now probably won't help either one of us. But I'm glad you decided to come up and tell me about what your mother had to say. I really am."

He got up from the chair, stood by the mantel, and took a look at the picture of Albert. "Would you like to have lunch with me on Monday?" he asked. "We can compare notes about being on *Toronto Focus* and on what we should do about – about us – about us being brothers."

"I'd like that," Gordon said. "I'm taking my mum to the farm tomorrow. The children will be there and I feel a real need to be with them right now. I really do."

"I know what you mean. I'd give anything to have Albert with me. To have him living in Toronto. I really miss him. But, he's settled in at the school out there and moving him now wouldn't be a good idea. So, about lunch on Monday, will the Sutton Place Hotel work for you? Say, around twelve thirty? We'll see if either one of us has come up with any brilliant ideas about what we should do from here on in. It's the understatement of the year to say that all of this was quite unexpected. Like you, I'm having difficulty believing it's actually happening. It's like watching an Italian movie without the subtitles."

"Closer to one would be better, if that's okay with you," Gordon said.

"Sure. One's fine."

"Okay," Gordon said. "I'll be there at one. Right on the nose."

"Good. Now, Carol will probably be back soon. I think you'd better leave. She seemed very unsettled by your being here."

"I understand. What about her? Are you going to tell her – about us?"

"I don't know. There's really no reason for anyone to know. Not yet, anyway. Not until we, between the two of us, decide what we should do and who we should tell about it. I probably won't say a word about it to Carol. I don't think you should either."

"I hadn't intended to," Gordon said, with a slight edge to his voice. Talking about Carol was getting under his skin. He was finding this part of the conversation a bit embarrassing, a bit demeaning. *My big brother's telling me to leave because my wife is coming home. Not my big brother's wife – but my wife. My Carol. God, this is a ridiculous situation to be in.*

Bill picked up on the vibes. "Hey, don't get so touchy. This is just as awkward for me as it is for you. I didn't plan things this way. Okay? Don't let this thing with Carol come between us. At least not until we've had a chance to straighten out our relationship. Give it time, Gordon. We can work things out. Okay?"

"Okay. You're right. I was getting a bit uptight. There's still some feeling there – about me and her."

"There always is. I've gone through this, too. My wife's living with a rich guy in Calgary. I know what you're feeling. Believe me. But, this thing between you and me is far more important than that. Think things through and we'll talk again over lunch on Monday. Come on, Gordon, I'll walk you to your car."

As she slipped the hook through a wriggling minnow so she could have a go at catching fresh fish for the supper she wanted to prepare for Bill, Carol hoped her hostility toward Gordon had not spilled over onto him and caused him to feel differently about her. If Gordon hadn't shown up like that, they would probably be making love at that very moment.

What did he come up here for anyway? How strange it was that Bill refused to let her in on what they were discussing. But then, she realized, it wasn't just their discussing something "personal", about which she had absolutely no knowledge, that disturbed her. She was even more disturbed by the things Bill said about her forcing Gordon to leave Charlie and Diane and how – how sluttish – she had felt being in Bill's cabin when Gordon showed up like that.

She wondered what Gordon must have thought. Especially after all she said to him about his relationship with that young woman he was sleeping with at the university. Telling him he should get her to wash his socks and underwear. And then there was the, what she now realized was, heartless way she kicked him out of her bed after Derek Parkington told her he wanted to go back to his wife and sons. She wondered what Gordon must have thought when she told him she could no longer stand the touch and smell of his body. An animal – that's what he said. She made him feel like an animal, like dirt, every time he wanted to touch her. Perhaps, she thought, he should have been told it was because of Derek that she reacted that way – because of the deadening effect Derek saying they didn't have what it took for a permanent relationship had on her mind and body.

She realized that Gordon was right when he said she dragged him down. Sold him short. She did carp at him a lot, undermine his confidence, sneer at his ideas, refuse to show understanding or acceptance of him. He didn't need to tell her all those things. She knew. But, she wondered, why? Why had she treated him so – so shabbily? Was it because they had to get married too young because of him getting her pregnant? *Perhaps. I did care for him – did have a crush on him – but that was altogether the wrong time. It would have been better if I hadn't had Charlie until after I'd gotten myself established at H and B. Maybe when I was thirty something.*

And yet, we were very happy together. And I really did love him. Things were going really well back then. And then I got pregnant with Diane and that spoiled everything. But then, over the last couple of years, he really did change. Took a turn for the worst. Started coming out with all that hateful stuff about the immigrants, the blacks and the Indians. He really doesn't like Indians very much. Almost foams at the mouth when he gets going on that pipeline thing. Yes, he really has become someone I would purposefully avoid at a cocktail party. His attitude really is repulsive. He has become, as that unnamed Conservative strategist said in the Toronto Star, *"a white power nut." Quite sick. And I don't want to be his wife.*

But it wasn't the fact that she no longer wanted to be Gordon's wife that Bill had questioned. What he had wanted to know was why that decision on her part should automatically result in Gordon being separated from Charlie and Diane. He'd asked her what she intended to do about their need for a father. And, he had asked, what about Gordon's need as a father to be with his children? She knew she didn't have the answers to those questions. All she did know was that she wanted Gordon out of the – *wait – wait – wait a minute. Why do I want him out of the house? Why did I tell him to go? Was it – was it because of Bill? Because I knew I'd be spending the weekend with him? Was that it? Did I force the issue with Gordon, tell him it was all over between us and I was going to divorce him, so I wouldn't feel so guilty about being in Bill's bed? Was that it?*

She had sensed she was going to get quite involved with Bill. Something about him drew her to him in an almost magnetic manner. She wanted to be with him. But, she wondered, what now? What must Bill be thinking of her now? She had been so – so cold – back there at the cabin with Gordon. Perhaps he was having second thoughts about her – wondering how she could possibly have been such an insensitive boor –*such a frigid bitch.*

A fish tugged tentatively on her line. She let it nibble some more. Then she eased the line with the lead sinker upward about a foot and the fish stayed with the minnow. She yanked the line sharply and reeled it in fast – the trembling pressure on the end letting her know the fish was hooked. It was a good-sized fish. She worked the hook out of its mouth, slipped the fish stringer through its gills and dropped it over the side of the boat. She put another minnow on her hook and let the line back down to about two feet above the lake bottom. She brought two more fish up in the next half-hour.

That should do it, she thought, as she put the last fish on the string. *That should make us a nice supper.* Her father had taught her how to fry fish in a special batter of flour and egg whites and she wanted to try it out on Bill. Gordon would be gone by the time she got back and, if Bill was having any doubts about her, she would have time to make things right between them again. She wanted to be with him. Not just for that night. Something about him, about that deep, seasoned, look in his eyes. The quiet strength of him. The assured, confident, tone of his voice – all of that – made her want to experience whatever was possible for them.

She hauled up the anchor and started back to the cabin. The sun was quite low in the sky. The water was a hard, metallic, grey-blue. Very much like the colour of Bill's eyes. *And Gordon's, too*, she suddenly realized. They were quite a bit alike as far as their physical appearance went. Bill had a touch of grey at the temples. You saw even more of the grey in his hair when it was out of the braids and flowing over his shoulders. It was, actually, quite streaked with grey. But then, Bill was older than Gordon. *Not much*, she thought, *but he does seem older. He's certainly wiser, deeper, more experienced and mature. What was that he said about his wife? About not saying he'd done the right thing by concentrating on his academic career instead of getting into the business world like she'd wanted him to? And not being able to buy her the things she wanted. He'd said he hadn't necessarily done the right thing. Does that mean he's had second thoughts about the way things worked out between him and his wife? And why's it this guy Ian Starlight that she's with instead of some white person? Do Indians prefer being with Indians?*

The people at Bill's meeting hadn't made any bones about the fact that they considered her to be an outsider. She felt different with them. Quite alienated. At least, until they opened up to her and told her they were glad she wanted to work with them. *Does Bill feel different with me? Would he prefer it if I was Indian? What was it he'd said about how he couldn't possibly think white? He said Indians have different brain processes. Different bodily chemistry. Different perceptions.*

"White is what you are," he said. "I can't think white any more than you can think Indian. We're different."

⌇

Bill was sitting by the fire, nursing his Scotch. She held up the three fish for his inspection. "Excellent," he said. "Christ couldn't have done better. But what about the loaves? No loaves? Just the three miraculous fish?"

For a moment, she wasn't sure what he was talking about. But then she remembered the story about Jesus Christ feeding five thousand people with five loaves of bread and two fish. He had twelve baskets of scraps left over. "It was two fish," she said with a smile. "Not three."

"Oh, well, that's the practical streak in me," he said, with a grin. "I figured he'd have had a better chance of feeding five thousand people with three fish than he would've had with two. But, if he did do it with two, then that's an even better miracle for you."

He kissed her on the cheek, put his arms around her and drew her close to him. She found his lips and they embraced.

"I'm sorry if I seemed edgy, bitchy, when Gordon was here," she said. "It's just that it was a pretty heavy scene for me."

"Not to worry," he said. "I think I understand how it must've been for you. I felt it myself."

They started to clean the fish at the sink. "Did you manage to work it out?" she asked. "Whatever you two were talking about?"

"We're going to talk about it again over lunch on Monday," he replied as he slid his knife into the soft belly of a plump fish.

"Can we talk about it?" she asked.

"I can't," he replied gently. "Not yet anyway."

She decided it would be better not to press the point. She believed him when he said it wasn't about her. But still, whatever could they have been talking about? She simply couldn't figure it out – any of it.

"We've still got tomorrow," he said. "Let's enjoy it. All of it."

"Okay," she said. "No more questions. Let's just enjoy. And you are going to enjoy my fish, even without the holy loaves."

"Gordon said there was a front page story in the *Globe* this morning about the sit-in the students staged at City Hall. Apparently, there was more than four hundred of them this time."

"That's great, Bill. Simply wonderful. I knew they'd come through for us."

"They're determined, those kids are. And they are making a big difference,"

"You're right there and you're also right about it being better that they're mostly white. Like you said, that does give the demonstration – and the message – a lot more credibility."

"Gordon said there was also a picture of my mom in the paper. Feeding one of her calves from a bucket of milk. The cutline said something like, quote, Guards calves from bulldozers. Pretty good, eh?"

"Great publicity. That will strike a chord with the white readers. Put the issue in human terms. Sounds good. Really good."

The evening didn't turn out to be quite as enjoyable as they had both hoped that it would. Gordon's presence lingered everywhere. Things between them weren't nearly as fresh and open as they had been when they first made love the night before. Or, when they embraced at the dock. Gordon's visit had affected them both and Carol felt Bill's refusal to tell her what he and Gordon had been talking about had compounded things – expanded the barrier that had developed between them.

"I just don't understand why you won't tell me what you two were talking about," she said as they ate the fresh apple pie Bill had picked up at the marina.

"Carol, please. I asked you to leave that alone. I'm not ready to talk about it with you. I've already made that perfectly clear. Please leave it alone."

She wanted to leave it alone. She really did. She wanted to have a long loving evening with him and put right any bad feeling her hostility toward Gordon that afternoon might have created between them. But she couldn't leave it alone. Sitting there, in the same room where Gordon and Bill had their talk, their "personal" talk, she couldn't help but wonder what it was they had been talking about. *If the conversation wasn't about me, then what could it possibly have been about? What could the two of them have to talk about? They're so totally different.*

"I've tried to leave it alone," she said. "I've tried. But I can't. I simply can't understand how you can reasonably expect me to sit here like this and not know what you and Gordon found so important that you have to see him again on Monday. I just don't understand what is going on."

"That makes three of us. Gordon and I don't understand it either."

"That's a big help," she said with a pronounced touch of sarcasm.

"My, but you can get bitchy at times," he said. "Like this afternoon. I couldn't believe the way you were acting. You were so hostile, so cold, toward Gordon. And I said to myself, 'Will she ever feel that way toward me?' I just didn't expect you could be so cold and collected. So rigid."

"Are you sure you don't mean frigid?" she asked.

"No," he said, with the smile returning to his lips and to his eyes. "There's nothing frigid about you, love. It's your head I was starting to worry about. How could you be so cold, so cruel, to someone you once loved?"

"I never really loved him. I've already told you we had to get married. It was, in every sense of the word, a marriage of inconvenience. I did not love him – at least not like being wildly in love with him."

"Did he love you?"

"He says he did."

"I think he still does."

"That's of no interest whatsoever to me. It's entirely irrelevant."

"That's what I mean. How can you talk about someone like that – about someone you've lived with for nine years – someone you had two children with? You're surely not suggesting that your daughter was conceived outside of love, too. Are you? Was Diane another accident?"

"I didn't plan on having Diane. The stupid diaphragm must have dislodged or something. Charlie would soon be starting Grade One and I was building my career in law. Getting pregnant with Diane derailed it all."

"I can't believe you," he said. "I don't want to believe you. How can you speak of your children as accidents? How – how can you?"

"Oh, come off it, Bill. Don't be so melodramatic. It's a fact that Charlie and Diane both happened by accident. I can't change that fact. But that doesn't mean I don't love them – that I don't want them now. I accept them. Both of them."

"You 'accept' them? You accept your children? The fruit of your womb?"

"Now you are getting all mushy. Is wanting to do something with your education – with your life – other than raising children – all that bad? Is that what you're saying?"

Her words brought back memories of Jean saying almost the same thing not all that long a time ago.

"Funny," he said. "That sort of sounds like what my wife used to say. She wanted me to 'make something' of myself. And she used to ask me if using my education to get us a better standard of living was a prostitution of my talent and my ideals. When I'd say nine-ty-nine point nine per cent of Indian people didn't live as well as we did, she'd say ninety-nine point nine per cent of Indian people don't have degrees from Berkeley. She didn't marry ninety-nine point nine per cent of Indian people. And then she'd ask when I was going to get off my ass and make us some real money. Money's what drove her and money's something that never interested me all that much. She's better off with Ian Starlight. He'll buy his way into that hard little heart of hers."

"Was it better with her? Better than being here with me?"

"It was different with her."

She recalled what he had said about how different Indian people were from white people – about how he couldn't possibly think or feel like a white person. "Would it be better for you if I was Indian, too?" she asked, wondering if she should be putting that kind of question to him in the first place.

"That was not the kind of difference I was referring to," he said. "What I meant was, I've been with her, made love to her, a lot longer than I have with you. That's the kind of difference I mean."

"So, it's not that I'm white that makes the difference," she said. "That's not what you meant."

"No, love. It's not your whiteness that makes the difference. I would still want to be with you if you were yellow, black or blue."

"How about green?" she asked, teasingly.

"Outer space people don't turn me on," he said. "I've never made out with a chick from Mars."

He was glad the lightness had returned to their voices. He didn't want Carol to experience anything like the wrenching sense of rejection he had felt with Sally Hurst.

"That's good," she said. "Although I would happily be green or red or blue for you. I think that's probably why I've been so on edge. There's nothing at all casual about what I feel for you. Gordon's showing up like that simply blew my mind."

"Was it guilt you felt?"

"Partly. But I think I felt more interrupted than I did guilty. We created such a beautiful space around us and – and his coming up here like that shattered it all."

"We can pick up the pieces," he said. "We can put it all back together again – if we want to."

"Do you want to?" she asked. "Do you really want to?"

"I want to," he said, reaching across the table and taking her hand in his, like he had at the table in the Davidson Lounge. "I want to, Carol."

She placed her other hand over his and looked deep into his grey-blue eyes. "Don't let me make gulfs between us," she said. "I know I can be bitchy, cold, carping, mocking, sarcastic. I know I can be all those things. But I don't want to be that way with you. Don't let me, Bill."

"I can't control that, love. You have to take responsibility for your own moods. Don't ask me to accept that responsibility. I don't want a puppet on a string."

"You're right. I don't know why I even suggested it. Actually, I'm a bit confused by everything that has happened – happened in so short a space of time. I didn't even know you two weeks ago. It all gets a bit unreal at times. A bit too much to handle."

"We can handle it," he said. He paused for a moment, reflecting on their situation. "I suppose," he started, not at all sure he should be opening this line of conversation, "that what happened between me and Gordon this afternoon makes things even more confusing and difficult for you."

"That's as good a word as any for it," she said, with a smile. "I must say I've never been in a situation like this before – where I'm shut out from a conversation my husband is having with the man I'm spending the weekend with."

"Have there been other weekends?" he asked.

"This is the only weekend I've had like this," she replied somewhat disingenuously.

"I'm glad," he said, although not altogether sure she had been completely honest in answering his question. Something about the tone of her voice told him she was holding something back. Was she saying there had been other weekends – other men – but not like this one? Or was she saying this was her first weekend with another man? He wasn't sure. She certainly made love as if she had been with other men besides Gordon. She knew exactly how to use her mouth and tongue to drive a man delirious.

"Will you be able to tell me about what happened with Gordon?" she asked. "Later, when you feel the time is right?"

"Probably."

"But you don't think the time is right yet?"

There she goes again. She's incapable of leaving things alone – of letting me tell her in my own good time. But then, as she said earlier, it did seem a bit unreasonable to expect her to be there, in the same room, and not know what happened between him and Gordon. Perhaps he should tell her. Maybe she would have some good suggestions about how he should deal with it all. But, then again, why tell her? Especially when he and Gordon might decide not to tell a living soul – to keep it between them – let it remain the secret it had been all of their lives.

"I don't think the time is right yet," he replied softly.

"Let me know when it is," she said, as she pulled her hand away from his.

He could feel her withdrawal. She was pulling away from him – away from the beautiful space they had created together. He wished she hadn't done that. But he could understand why she felt that way.

"Want to go for a walk?" he asked.

"No thanks," she said, as she started to clear the dishes from the table. "I think I'll just take care of these and then I want to read for a while."

"Okay," he said, as he helped her clear the table. "Perhaps you'll feel like a walk later."

"Perhaps," she said, convinced that she wouldn't. She simply couldn't understand his refusal to tell her what he and Gordon had been talking about. She felt isolated, alienated.

CHAPTER
- 26 -

It was after seven when Gordon got back to the city. As he hadn't had supper, he dropped by his mother's apartment for one of her roast beef sandwiches. She had eaten earlier and was reading her Bible when he got to her place.

He poured a cup of fresh tea for her and fixed a vodka and orange for himself. She closed the Bible on her lap as he handed her the tea and settled himself beside her on the floppy sofa.

"Well?" she asked, expectantly – asking the question that had been on her mind ever since he told her he was going to see Bill. "What happened between you and William?"

He told her about his talk with Bill and about their decision to meet for lunch on Monday. He didn't tell her Carol was at the cabin.

"Did he know?" Martha asked. "Did he know about your Uncle Bill and your birth mother?"

"No. He didn't have so much as a clue. No one told him anything. It was just as much of a shock for him as it was for me."

Martha thought about the letter she got from Sarah after Bill was killed. *So, they didn't tell him. Felt the same way about it as Tom did. Saw no good reason to let him know he had a brother.*

"How did he take it then? Is he all right with it."

"I wouldn't say either one of us is 'all right with it', Mum. Neither one of us relishes the prospect of being identified as a half-breed. We've sort of gotten used to being who and what we are. To change now, to have my friends and my associates and my neighbors and – and the children – thinking of me as being something other than what

I am – than what I've always been – would be quite an adjustment. I don't know what's going to happen – what we're going to do. That's why we're having lunch on Monday. To decide on the best way to handle this thing."

"I understand," she said. "Perhaps I should have left well enough alone. Not meddled in your lives like this."

"No. No. No, Mum. Don't say things like that. We both feel, Bill and I, that you did the right thing. The way the Big Thunder situation was developing, it would probably have come out anyway. Bill said, if it had been his mum who was in your shoes, she'd have done exactly the same thing."

He paused and sipped his drink. "That's not the problem – not the problem at all. The problem is what do we do now? We're supposed to be on *Toronto Focus* again Tuesday night – talking about Big Thunder and about the special studies programs and all that – and I haven't the foggiest notion about how we should handle this thing. Not the foggiest. Fraser Deacon says two hundred thousand people watch his show. Am I going to tell two hundred thousand people I'm half Indian? Not without giving it an awful lot more thought, I'm not. Not without coming up with a pretty compelling reason for why I should. But, if we don't tell them, then what do we do? We can't just, not now anyway, live in the same city and teach at the same university every day and not so much as speak to one another. And then there's all this stuff about the Equal Opportunities Council and Bill telling everyone who'll listen that I'm a neanderthal – a throwback to the nineteenth century. That's what he called me. What are we going to do about that?"

"I don't know, Gordon. I honestly don't know," she said as she stirred her tea. "I suppose, if your father were here tonight, he'd say, 'Martha, my darling girl, that's why I said we shouldn't tell the boy. That's why I said no earthly good would be served by putting all this stuff out of the past into his head.' Perhaps your dad was right, Gordon. Perhaps I should have left well enough alone."

"No, Mum. You did the right thing. Don't worry about that. Just help me know what to do now. It's to the future we've got to look – not to the past. We've got to think about now. What am I going to tell those people who want me to represent Meadowbrook in the House of Commons? What are they going to say when they find out?"

"I don't think being half Indian is something you should be ashamed of, Gordon. And William shouldn't be at all ashamed of being half Scottish. That's what you are. You can't change that. And there's no reason to change it. That's just the way things are. It's nothing for you to be ashamed of."

"But I'm not talking about whether or not I should be ashamed of it, proud of it or monumentally indifferent towards it. What I'm asking you is should I, or shouldn't I, tell two hundred thousand people about it on *Toronto Focus* Tuesday night? That's the question – the question for which I have no answer. And, if we don't tell them we're brothers, do we go on with the charade of Bill being the champion of the Indian underdog and me being the goose-stepping voice of white Canada? The whole thing's insane. Completely, weirdly, curiously insane. And that's only question Number One."

"Number One? What is question Number Two?" she asked with raised eyebrows.

"Number Two is what are people going to say if they do find out that we're brothers? That we're both only half of what we've always claimed to be. Only half Scottish. Only half Indian. How're they going to react to that? That's question Number Two. I've been quoted in the newspapers as making some pretty sweeping statements about immigrants and all that. You said yourself that some of my statements were – were 'a wee bit uncharitable, a wee bitty intolerant'. What are they going to say when they find out I'm not even white? Christ – I'm sorry Mother. I didn't mean to swear."

"That's all right, Son. I understand. I understand, but I don't comprehend. I listen to what you're saying – hear your questions – but I don't have any answers. It's as I said last night, Gordon, I don't have the words to give you. You're going to have to find those answers by yourself or – or with William – with your brother. Perhaps you'll be able to find those answers between the two of you. I do hope so, my son, because I honestly don't know what to say to you. I really don't. Your father would probably know what to tell you. He probably would. But I don't. I honestly don't. The Lord only knows I wish that I did know. He truly does know that."

"Well, maybe we can work it out – Bill and me. I certainly hope so. But don't you worry about it. We can handle it. Things will work out, Mum. You'll see. Don't worry yourself about it. And yet – to be perfectly honest with you – I haven't the slightest idea what Bill's going to want to do. We didn't talk about it all that much this afternoon. It was sort of awkward. To say the least. So, I don't know what he's going to want to do. Anyway, what about tomorrow? Are you still coming to the farm with me?"

"Of course, Gordon. Of course, I'm coming with you. You know how much I want to be with you and the children."

"Good. That's my good girl. I'll pick you up at eight and we can have breakfast together on the way up to the farm."

"We can have breakfast here, Son."

"No. That would mean you'd have to get up earlier. Just you relax and we'll eat on the way up. We'll go to the Driftwood. You'll like that. I can smell their hickory- smoked bacon already."

"All right, Gordon. That sounds just lovely."

"Fine. That's settled. Now I'd better phone Anne and let her know we're coming. I'll use the phone in the bedroom. Okay?"

"Of course, Gordon. Of course. Tell the children I was asking for them. Give them all my love."

He went into the bedroom and phoned Anne at the farm. She said there would be no problem at all having them come up. There was plenty for two more. He asked if the children were nearby.

"Yes. They're both here. We're just finishing a late supper," Anne replied.

"Would you put Diane on the line, please? I'd like to talk to her."

He could hear Anne telling Diane it was her father who was on the phone. As he waited for Diane to come on the line, he looked fondly at the picture beside his mother's bed of him and his dad standing beside the Llama pen at the Riverdale Zoo. He missed his dad. Missed him very much.

"Hi, Daddy," Diane said. "Are you coming to see us?"

"Yes, darling. Daddy and Grandma will be up to see you tomorrow. We'll be there before lunch."

"That's good," Diane said. "Anne bought some apple pie and ice cream. You can have some, too, Daddy. There's lots for everybody."

"Are you having a good time, darling?"

"Yes. I'm having lots of fun. Everybody's having lots of fun. But, Daddy, my bike's broke. Will you fix it for me when you come up? My wheel's all bent."

"How did your wheel get bent, darling?"

"I fell off."

"Did you hurt yourself?"

"No. But the rock bent my wheel. Real bad. Will you fix it for me, Daddy?"

"Of course, my good girl. Of course, I'll fix it for you. Are you sure you weren't hurt?"

"Sure I'm sure. I don't hurt easy, Daddy. I'm almost five now. I don't even say ouch anymore."

"That's a girl. Now go and finish your supper and let me speak to your brother. I'll see you tomorrow morning."

Diane called Charlie to the phone and he picked up the receiver. "Hi, Dad."

"Hi, Charlie. How's it going?"

"All right, I guess. Are you coming up?"

"Yes. I'll be up before lunch time tomorrow. Grandma's coming with me. We'll have a nice time together."

Charlie had noticed how cold his mom and dad were toward one another. He'd wanted to ask them why they were sleeping in different beds, but didn't feel it was his place to do so. If they felt he should know the reason why, he figured, they'd tell him when they were good and ready. Sometimes, being around them both was like walking on eggs. They were so uptight all the time. He could feel that something was wrong.

"What about Mom? Isn't she coming?" he asked.

"No, Son. Didn't she tell you about – about where she was going?"

"Oh, yeah. She said she was going up to Mr. and Mrs. Potts' place again. I forgot about that. So, it's just you and Grandma, then?"

"Just? Isn't that enough?" he asked, in a kidding tone.

"Sure. Sure," Charlie said, anxious not to have given the wrong impression. "I didn't mean it like that. Okay, then. You'll be here tomorrow?"

"Yes. You're in a hurry to get back to your supper. Right?"

"Sort of. We're having cheeseburgers."

"Okay, Charlie. Get back to them while they're still hot. I'll see you tomorrow morning."

"Okay, Dad. See you."

"See you. I love you, Son."

Later that evening, Bill sat at his desk trying to work on his book. But the words wouldn't come. There was too much on his mind at that particular moment to permit any concentrated focus on the Canadian government's record of broken promises with regard to the treaties they had signed with the Indians.

Carol was reading by the fire. They hadn't talked since supper. The frigid silence was disconcerting. Only that very morning, they'd made love like teenagers – tickling and giggling and enjoying themselves to the full. But now, here they sat like a middle-aged couple serving time in a desert of a marriage. Perhaps he should clear the air between them. Tell her what happened between him and Gordon. Let her be part of the solution to the problem. But no, she was holding herself back from him – refusing to walk with him or talk to him until he told her about his conversation with Gordon. She was holding hostage the beautiful space they had developed together and the ransom he was being asked to pay was the details of his conversation with Gordon. It seemed to be an open and shut case of emotional blackmail. *But, then again, maybe I'm reading her wrong.*

He went over to the kitchen counter and poured himself a cup of tea. "Would you like some tea?" he asked.

"Please. That would be lovely."

She seemed to be in a better mood. Perhaps she was feeling the strain just as much as he was. Perhaps he had misjudged her. As he placed the mug of tea on the table beside her, he let his hand brush across her hair.

"How's the book coming?" she asked, as she kissed the back of his hand.

"Not very well. I can't seem to get into it."

"Same here. I haven't read four pages in the past hour. My head's just not into it."

"What do you say we take that walk?" he asked.

"I'd say that'd be just fine," she replied. "I'd like that."

They left the full mugs of hot tea on the table and pulled on their windbreakers in preparation for the cold air outside. It was as cold as they had expected, but their bodies soon warmed up from the walking. The full moon shimmered on the surface of the water as they sat at the end of the dock after their walk and looked out at the black silhouettes of the islands. Two loons cried far out in the lake.

"I'm sorry things got like that between us," Bill said. "That silence was unbearable."

"I felt the same way," she said, slipping her hand into his. "I kept wondering what you must have thought of me for pushing you away like that, but I was afraid to ask or to apologize. I did want to."

They sat silently, listening to the sound of the water lapping against the dock, feeling the warm space developing around them again. Bill struggled with whether or not he should tell her about him and Gordon. He had told Gordon they should keep things to themselves for now. And yet, it was obvious that Carol was very upset about not knowing what they'd been talking about. If she hadn't been there that afternoon she wouldn't have known there was anything to know about. But, she was there. She did know that they'd been talking about something "personal". *It's bound to come out sooner or later. Might as well be now. She's clearly desperate to know what we were talking about.*

"About this afternoon," he said. "About the talk I had with Gordon and why I'm going to have lunch with him on Monday." He paused for a moment, searching for the right words. And then he decided he might as well come straight out with it. "Gordon told me this afternoon that he's my – my brother."

Carol was so startled she almost fell off the dock and into the water. "He's what?" she whispered, in a totally-winded voice.

"We're brothers. That's what he came up to tell me about. He only found out about it himself last night. His mother told him."

"I can't believe this. You must be joking."

"No, love. It's no joke. It's anything but that."

He told her the story about Big Thunder and what happened out there, exactly the way Gordon told it to him that afternoon. His voice sounded to her like something coming out of a dream – or a night-mare. She couldn't believe her ears.

"That's simply incredible," she said, when he finished. "I've never heard anything quite like it."

"Neither have I," he said with a soft smile. "I couldn't have done better if I'd made it all up myself. But it seems to be true. Gordon knows enough about Big Thunder and about my mother – and about her sister – for me to know it probably is true. All of it. He even knows that Hughie, my younger brother, has asthma."

They sat in the silence, looking out at the moon-swathed water and the black shadows of the islands.

"What are you going to do now?" she asked.

"I don't know. We're supposed to be on *Toronto Focus* again Tuesday night. I really don't know what we should do. What would you do?"

"Oh, please. Don't ask me that," she said. "I can't possibly tell you what to do."

"I'm serious. You are – well, sort of – you are one step removed from all this. Maybe you can have a better perspective on this than Gordon and me – a more objective opinion. What would you do if you were in my place?"

She wished now that she had left well enough alone – not pushed him into telling her about his talk with Gordon. *How can I possibly be expected to know what he should do?* "I can't," she said. "I can't possibly tell you what to do. I couldn't imagine being in your situation."

"Neither could I this morning," he said softly. "But I'm in it now and I'm trying to find a way to deal with it. What would you do?"

"Well," she started, "I can't imagine how you could live this long and not hear about this before. Your family must have known. Didn't they ever so much as hint at it? How could they possibly not let you know?"

"Mom and Dad would have known, of course. And my grand-mother and granddad. My aunt down at Standoff would have known. But I don't think my brother or sister could have. I'm the eldest. The way Gordon tells it, I must have been around two when I went to live at Big Thunder. That means Hughie, my brother, was only a few months old when I got there. And Janet is six years younger than me.

There's no way they could have known. As far as they knew, I'd always been there."

"But, Gordon's a MacArthur. How can you be an Eagletail? Why aren't you a MacArthur?"

"I guess my parents must have adopted me after my birth father died over there in Hong Kong. That's probably it. They must have adopted me and registered me as an Eagletail. Like when someone comes to live with us, even if they're from another tribe, they're adopted into the whole community. Once you're there, you're accepted as one of us – as part of the Big Thunder community. That's probably why nothing was ever said. They accepted me for what I was – Richard and Sarah Eagletail's oldest boy."

"That's probably it," she agreed. "They just accepted you as one of them."

"Yes, that's probably it," he said reflectively. "You know, quite a few of my friends, some of them in leadership positions in the Indian movement, are part something else. Part French, or part Irish, or Scottish, or something like that. They all refer to themselves as Indian. They all identify with their Indian side. Because Indian is what they are – in their thinking and in their living. It doesn't matter who their grandfathers are or who their great-grandfathers were. It's who they are that counts. And Indian is what they are. It's what I am, too. I have no interest at all in being half Scottish or half Irish or half anything else. I want to stay what I am."

"But there is a difference," she said. "A big difference between you and those other Indian people you're talking about."

"What difference?" he asked.

"They don't have a brother on television trying to keep the world safe for white people. They don't have someone in their own family saying he wants to represent the white, Western European, majority in the House of Commons. They don't have Gordon. Gordon is the difference. If it wasn't for Gordon, you wouldn't have as big a problem. It's Gordon who makes the difference."

"You're right," he said, as if something was slowly dawning on him. "Gordon is the difference – the problem. It's like being Hitler's Jewish half-brother. Everything he stands for threatens my existence as a human being."

"What's your gut feeling about what you should do now?"

"Sort of mixed. I don't want to be identified as being half Scottish, at least not at this late stage of my life. At the same time, I don't want to be in the position where – where I can't relate to Gordon as a human being. I'm still caught up with the fascination of what he told me this afternoon. About his dad and his Uncle Bill. How they came over here on the boat from Scotland and then got separated after his dad decided to go into the real estate business in Toronto. Then there was the way his Uncle Bill and my mother's sister met and got married and had – had us."

He stopped for a minute, looking out at the shadows of the islands and thinking about the things Gordon told him that afternoon. "And then there was him being raised in Toronto by his mom and dad and my mom and dad raising me at Big Thunder. And then, and this is the part that just blows my mind, for us to be teaching at the same university and not knowing we're brothers and then to be on *Toronto Focus* together – him talking on behalf of white people and me representing the Indian point of view. It's – it's – all so strange. So unreal."

He put his arms around her and gave her a hug and a kiss. "It's getting cold. Let's get back to the fire."

They walked together, arm in arm, feeling like they had when they were bringing the groceries up from the dock that afternoon. Halfway back to the cabin, with the moon floodlighting their bodies, he stopped and turned her around so she was facing him.

"Whatever happens between me and Gordon," he said, looking down at her with his hands on her shoulders, "whatever we decide to do, I don't want it to come between you and me. I want you to be with me, Carol. I need you with me."

"That's what I want, too, Bill. I want to be with you."

They kissed – a long, slow, deep kiss. Then they went inside and sat by the fire.

CHAPTER
- 27 -

Gordon lay in the bed in his third-floor bedroom very early Sunday morning staring out the window at the upper branches of the big maples. It had rained overnight and was still pouring buckets outside. He had intended to burn the leaves on Saturday morning but the trip to Bill's cabin had taken up all of his time. The weather man on CFTO predicted it would be sunny and clear on Monday. The leaves would be completely dry by Tuesday and he could clear them out then.

Why should I? Why should I give a damn about the leaves in a garden from which I'm being banished? Let Carol worry about the leaves. They're no concern of mine now. She can get her precious Bill to burn them.

He considered the possibility that Bill was making love to Carol at that very moment, on top of the muskrat cover on his bed. If it hadn't been for the *Toronto Focus* interview, she would never have met him. *How could they become so involved with one another? So quickly? Does that mean there really is such a thing as love at first sight? What about that? What if they do get more deeply involved? If Bill does move into the house? He'll probably take down the paintings of Robert the Bruce and replace them with a portrait of Sitting Bull or Red Cloud or another one of his ancestors. But, then again, he couldn't do that because, by that time, the paintings and my personal effects will no longer be here. Where will they be?* He'd forgotten about that problem for the moment – about the fact that Carol wanted him out of the house ASAP. *Where am I going to go?*

453

He could move in with his mother for a while but she only had the one bedroom. It would, he thought, be too much of an imposition on her – just like, as she had said, Jack Saunders' pipeline was going to be too much of an imposition on Bill's mother. He didn't want to impose on the little bit of space his mother had left to live in.

That would be weird, if it turned out that Bill moved into their home. Carol seemed quite taken with him and he had said he thought she'd be quite a woman to live with. *Maybe she'll let him deck her bedroom out with eagle feathers and bear claws and all the other trappings of his heritage. It certainly isn't my heritage. I could no more identify with his heritage than I could with Mao Tse-tung's.*

Mind you, I don't feel any hostility toward Indian people. But, as a culture, theirs simply isn't in the same league as the white, Western European, civilization. Compared to being white, being half Indian offers no advantage to me – no advantage whatsoever. The Indians have their eyes riveted on a past with no future. Speaking about the future, what about my future? Why am I, like a gypsy, having to determine where I should move to with all my earthly belongings? Why am I the one being asked to move?

Carol had been born in the house but he was the one who had been paying the taxes and the utilities since she left Haldimand and Brock. Besides, the title of the house was made out in both of their names. They were joint owners.

She can't make me move, he suddenly realized, *the house is half mine. I have rights. Property rights. No one can force me out of here. The nerve of her, demanding that I should move out of the house – and knowing full well she'd be in his bed that very night. What a nerve. What a colossal nerve. Expecting me to pack up my things and move out while she was – she was intent on having an adulterous affair with – with my brother. Well, if she enjoys being with him that much, she can damn well go and live with him. I'm not going to roll over and make way for him. In fact, if I wanted to, if I was that sort of person, I could divorce her on the grounds of adultery. That woman at the marina had seen them together. Probably laughing, hugging and kissing. I could subpoena her as a witness against them. Why should I be the one to do all the adjusting? Ruth? You really can't factor her into the equation. If I'd been getting what I needed on that score from Carol there wouldn't have been a Ruth.*

There was a fairly stiff breeze and it made the maples sway a bit. He thought about how high up in the sky the topmost branches were in relation to the ground and wondered what it is that holds a tree up. *It's incredible how they can stand so straight and tall*, he thought. *And, with the way their heavy branches spread out like that at the top, you'd expect them to fall over at any moment. It's the roots that hold them up. The roots give them the strength to withstand the onslaught of the wind. Without the roots, they'd never last – never get up into the sky in the first place.*

His roots were white, Western European, Scottish. Wherever in the world you found them, he thought, the Scots possessed a special quality that set them apart from all other people on God's green earth. Because they had spent centuries scratching a meagre living from the rocky terrain of their tight little country, the Scots were remarkably frugal and resourceful. They were also fiercely individualistic and yet, at times, surprisingly tribal. And then there was their kilts and their bagpipes and their very special manner of speaking. Even Gordon's father, despite having left Scotland while still in his early twenties to find a new life in Canada, spoke with a thick, rich, Scottish brogue and rolled his Rs right up until the day he was killed.

This sense of rooting, this sense of identification with the land and the people of Scotland, kept Gordon walking straight and tall. Without his roots, he'd fall flat on his ass the first time a strong wind came up. He couldn't survive without his roots.

Looking at things from that point of view, what concrete difference should my being half Indian have on the way I live my life? What, exactly, should I start doing differently because of the fact that my mother was Indian? A full-blooded Blackfoot. How can I, at the age of thirty-five, start to experience something that has been there all along but of which I've had absolutely no knowledge and which has had, as a result, absolutely no influence on the way I've lived my life – on my living, breathing, thinking or achieving? Is my life going to be, or need my life be, inalterably different because of what happened at Big Thunder more than thirty-five years ago? Something over which I had absolutely no control. Well? Is it?

As he got into the car to pick his mum up, he realized he was no closer to the answer to any of those questions than he had been the night before. He hoped Bill was having better luck. He picked his mother up at her apartment at eight and they were having bacon and eggs at the Driftwood by 8:45 a.m. They had exchanged small talk in the car and didn't get into any serious discussion until after their breakfast was served.

"So," Martha asked, "How are you feeling about having lunch with William tomorrow? How does he appear to be dealing with things – about the adoption and all that?"

"He seems okay with it. Mind you, it's a lot easier for him than it is for me. Finding out that he's half white is a plus for him. There's no plus for me in being half Indian."

"What do you mean by that, Son?"

"Well, let's think about it. The Scots invented the steam engine, the postage stamp, hypnosis, the telephone, the first steamboat. That's all part of Bill's heritage now. He can identify with all those Scottish inventors. Scots who made a positive difference in the world. You can't say that's not a plus, Mum. That's something he didn't have this time last week."

"Yes, I suppose you could look at it like that, Gordon. You could look at it that way. But, Son, I don't see anything wrong with that. Nothing at all."

"What's wrong with that is there's nothing in it for me. He gets to claim Watts and Alexander Bell and all the other famous Scots as part of his heritage. But, what do I get out of it? Sitting Bull and Geronimo? Being half Indian means I'm part of a long line of savages."

"Now, Gordon," she said crossly. "That's not an appropriate word to use. They are not savages."

"Sure they are, just like the Picts were when the Romans conquered Britain. They moved about in tribes, ran around in animal skins, painted their faces blue and chopped people's heads off – just like the Indians did. And they were savages, Mum, in every sense of the word. There's nothing wrong in saying that. That's what our ancestors were. Savages. That's why the Romans built that wall from coast to coast across Britain to make sure they stayed on their side of it. The Romans didn't want to have anything to do with them. And I can understand why."

"Yes, I know that. I know all about that, Gordon, but that was a long time ago, more than eighteen hundred years ago. I don't see what that has to do with things today. I don't see it at all."

"What it has to do with today is this. The Picts went on to become civilized. To become Scots. To invent steam engines, and telephones, and postage stamps and all those other things. But, the Indians, they stayed frozen in time. They were just the same when the white people arrived as they were back in the days of the Picts. Frozen in time. Hunters and gatherers clothed in the skins of animals, that's what they were. They didn't progress. Improve their situation. Keep up with the rest of the world. Like I said, Mum, they stayed frozen in time."

"Oh, I don't think you can say that, Gordon. That's not at all fair."

"Sure it is. They're really not all that different today, out there on their reserves, than they were when we first got here. Meanwhile, we have built a nation. We cleared the trees out by the roots and made the land come alive with wheat and with corn.

"We rerouted the rivers and built the dams to make hydro power. Built the cities, the schools, the churches, the Parliament Buildings and all of the other infrastructure you need for a modern nation. We've got Air Canada and Canadian Pacific Air Lines criss-crossing the skies and connecting us to Europe and Asia. The CNR and the CPR trains running on steel rails from coast to coast. The ships carrying wheat and iron ore up and down the Great Lakes. And we've got a fine army, navy and air force protecting everything that we have built.

"We have transformed a vast wilderness area that was once populated by scattered tribes of warring savages into a modern nation. We have built a new society and the values upon which that society was built are British. The Indians contributed nothing to that. Not a damned thing."

"I still don't see what you're driving at. That may be true. But, what has that got to do with you being half Indian?"

"It means that one half of me is no damned good for anything. I don't gain a damned thing, not a single thing, by being half Indian. Nothing. Zip. Nyet."

Martha wasn't sure what to do next. It was obvious that he was not nearly as open to being half Indian as he had appeared to be when he got back from his visit with Bill. "Maybe we should just finish our breakfast, Son, and drive on up to the farm. It's going to be good for you to be with Charlie and Diane. I see that you've got your bike with you. You can all go for a nice ride together."

"That's another problem," he said. "What am I going to tell Charlie and Diane about this? It affects them, too, you know. They're now one-quarter Indian. How are they going to react to that?"

"I'm sure they won't give it a second thought, Gordon. Not a second thought. Not in this day and age, my son. They'll just accept it and get on with their lives. I'm sure of that. And, like you said, they're only one-quarter Indian."

"Well, I'm not so sure. I'm not so sure about a lot of things. Take Meadowbrook. What are they going to say when they find out I'm half Indian? If they find out. I haven't decided on that one yet."

"I think I can understand that, Son. You did go on quite a bit about that white pride thing. They probably will want one of their own to represent them in Ottawa. Yes, I can understand that. That will make a difference as far as they're concerned."

"It's going to make a difference as far as a lot of people are concerned. It's not going to take long before my colleagues on the Equal Opportunities Council will be strongly suggesting that I should step down. Mind you, if they don't find out, things can go along pretty much the same as they were this time last week. They don't have to find out."

"I truly do wish I could answer these questions for you, Son. But I really don't know what to say. I honestly don't. By the way, I've got something for you. I've got something I think you would like to have."

She reached into her handbag and brought out the small framed picture of Tom and Bill that had been taken outside the farmhouse just before they left for Canada.

"That's your father on the right," she said. "He was only twenty at the time. And that's your Uncle Bill beside him with his arm around your dad. He was two years older. It's a bit faded, Son, but I thought you might want to have it. It's the only picture I have of your Uncle Bill."

"Thanks, Mum. I really appreciate this. I really do."

As he looked at the picture, his thoughts turned back to his visit to his grandfather's farm in Scotland and the good things they had done together that summer. "I'll put it on the wall in my study. Thanks, Mum. This is really worth having."

"You're more than welcome, Gordon. I thought you would want to have it. I've got lots of pictures of your dad."

"Thanks, Mum. Now, I don't think we should say anything to Charlie and Diane about all this yet. I'm not quite ready for that and I think, maybe, it would be better for Carol to be with me when I do tell them. We should both be there."

"Alright, Gordon. I won't say a word about it. Not a peep."

It was raining when Carol woke up on Sunday morning. She could hear the rain falling on the tin roof of the cabin. She could also hear the sound of bacon and eggs frying in the kitchen. The hickory-smoked flavor of the bacon pleased her sense of smell. Bill was making their breakfast. She could hear the sound of bacon fat spitting.

She lay still on the bed, with the muskrat pelt cover pulled up to her chin. She felt so warm and snug under it. She reached over to the spot where Bill had lain beside her, resting her right hand on the sheet where he had been, and ran the fingers of her other hand across her clitoris. Gently stroking herself, she thought about the beautiful time they had during their second night together. The business with Gordon had been set to one side and they'd simply relaxed and enjoyed each other in a beautiful, dream-like manner.

"Hi," she called over to him. "That smells good."

"'Morning," he replied. "You look beautiful."

"First thing in the morning?"

"Any time. You are the most beautiful woman I have ever met."

The thought of her first meeting with Derek Parkington flashed across her mind. The words were exactly the same. Surely it wasn't a line they both picked up in the *Playboy Advisor* column? It couldn't be. Bill was too honest to say things he didn't mean. He wouldn't deceive her. *Would he?*

"Thanks," she said. "You're a bit of a gorgeous hunk yourself."

"You like home fries?" he asked.

"Sure."

"Good, we've got some potatoes left over from last night. Not twelve baskets of them, mind you, but enough for breakfast."

She was amused by his reference to the wonders Christ performed with the holy loaves and the fish and how he had twelve baskets left over, despite having fed five thousand people. She pulled on her terry cloth robe and went to the bathroom.

It was nice being with Bill like this. They seemed to be on exactly the same wavelength. In fact, she thought, it was good they had some awkward – even bitchy – moments. That gave a deeper sense of reality to their relationship. She wasn't doing any starry eyed number. She truly did enjoy the man and wanted very much to be with him.

She went out to the kitchen and set the table for their breakfast. Bill had built a good fire and the inside of the cabin was warm and dry.

"What a day," she sighed, looking out the window at the rain and the storm clouds.

"It's a beautiful, gorgeous, absolutely fantastic day," he whispered, as he put his arms around her and drew her to him. "It's a marvellous day."

They held each other close, rubbed their bodies gently against each other and kissed. He undid their robes and pulled them open so their naked bodies could touch.

"You feel so beautiful," he said, as he kissed her breasts. "You are so beautiful. So very, very, beautiful."

"Let's have breakfast," she said, nibbling his earlobe. "I simply haven't the energy to go another round on the sheets."

He laughed. "You do have an odd way of expressing certain things," he said. "It's been years since I've heard anyone talk about hitting the sheets."

"I must have picked it up in a book somewhere," she said with a smile. "Does that sort of expression bother you?"

"Nothing about you bothers me," he replied. "Absolutely nothing at all."

He buttered the toast and scooped the eggs, the bacon and the home fries, onto their plates. They ate quietly, holding each other's hand. A few minutes later, Carol sensed the atmosphere was starting to change. There was an edge there. An unresolved edge.

"What have you decided to do about Gordon?" she asked.

"I don't know. I really don't. That was a fascinating story he told me yesterday but I really don't see how what happened back then changes who and what I am today. I am Indian. I'm Indian in my way of think-ing, in my way of living. In my heart and soul, I am a North American Indian man. The great-grandson of a Blackfoot chief. That's the way I was raised to be. Just like Gordon was raised to be Scottish and right-fully proud of being Scottish. We're both what we were raised to be."

"Yes, but, that doesn't change the fact that you are brothers. How are you going to deal with that?"

"I don't know. Maybe Gordon will have some ideas about that when we have lunch tomorrow. Quite frankly, I wish none of this had happened. Things were just fine the way they were."

"Does 'none of this' include me?"

"Of course not. You're the only good thing that happened this week. The only good thing that has happened to me for a long, long, time. That's not what I meant. Apart from you, I'd like everything to have stayed the way it was before Gordon and I went on *Toronto Focus*."

"That's another problem," Carol said. "What are you going to do about *Toronto Focus*? How are you going to deal with things on the show?"

"I'm not going to do the show. I'll cancel it tomorrow. There's no way, especially with the way I'm feeling about things right now, that I'm going to tell almost a quarter million people that I'm half white. No way. That will have to wait for another time. Probably another long time."

"I can understand that. Things are changing on an almost daily basis. I can see why you wouldn't want to deal with it on live TV. I can understand that."

"Maybe Gordon will feel differently about it but I'm definitely not going to go public with this – at least not until I've had an opportunity to tell my mom and Albert about it."

"And what about your mother? How are you going to deal with her?"

"That depends, to a certain extent, on what Gordon has to say when we have lunch tomorrow. This is about his life too. But I am going to phone her. Right after I have lunch with Gordon."

"That's a good idea," she said. "I'm sure it will be an interesting conversation."

"Yes it will," Bill said. "My mom's going to be surprised. Real surprised."

He paused for a minute, reflecting on this business of finding out, only the day before, that his birth father was Scottish. This was a development he had not been expecting. "You know, this means that Albert is more Indian than I am. Jean is full-blooded and that makes Albert three-quarters Indian and I'm only half. Only half Blackfoot. Only half of what I've always believed myself to be. That does make a difference. A big difference."

She could see he was struggling with the issue. The initial shock was wearing off and now the reality of it all was starting to sink in. "I don't see it as being such a bad thing, Bill. I mean, my grandmother on my mother's side was French, from the Gaspe. She married a Scottish blacksmith who came here from Glasgow. We've all got a little something else in us from someplace or other."

"It's not so much the fact that I'm half white that bothers me. It's just that I would have preferred not to have been told at this late stage of my life. If I'd known about it when I was growing up, that would have been different, a lot different. But, not being told about it until I'm thirty-seven, that's something else again. Under the circumstances, I would have preferred not to have known. If, as they say, ignorance is bliss, I would have preferred to have remained in the blissful state of not knowing a thing about it."

"I can understand that but, and I don't mean to be harsh, you do know about it now. That state of blissful ignorance has come to a crashing end. And now you know. You are half white. The question is, now that you know, what do you intend to do about it, about that irreversible fact of your life?"

"It's something I'm just going to have to live with, I guess. I am half white."

"Half Scottish, actually."

"Yeah, that's right. If I'm going to be half something white, it might as well be Scottish."

"You realize, of course, that means you could be a distant relative of Sir John A. Macdonald and he was, after all, the one who first sent the Indian children to the residential schools."

"Yeah, I know that. I know all about him, about Canada's first Prime Minister. He said he was born British and he was going to die British. Just like I was born Blackfoot and, despite this latest development, I am going to die Blackfoot. I owe it to all of those who have gone before me, to my forefathers, to remain a Blackfoot until the day I die …"

"But, Bill …"

"No, please, please, Carol, hear me out. We're not at all like the Canadians, like the people who came here from somewhere else to build a new life. We didn't come here like them. We've always been here. And, today, Carol, there are a lot fewer of us than there used to be. We are, in fact, a dying race. If I stop being a Blackfoot and start identifying myself as a Canadian, there will be one less of us. One less Blackfoot. And, if more of us decide to become Canadian, pretty soon there will be none of us left. No more Blackfoot. End of the line. So, that's why I have to remain true to who I am, a Blackfoot. I have a duty to keep the race alive. And that's why I just simply cannot become a Canadian."

"I hear what you're saying, but there's one thing wrong with that," Carol said. "One major flaw in your argument."

"And what might that be, my fair lady?"

"You're half white. You're no more Blackfoot than Gordon is. You're only half Blackfoot."

"Hmm," he mused. "You might have a point there."

"Half white is what you are. You might as well accept it and start getting used to it."

"You're probably right. Anyway, there's not much point in us talking about this any further right now. We'll have to wait and see what Gordon has to say tomorrow." He took a sip of his tea. "I was thinking we should head back to the city around four. That will get us back to Toronto around seven. Will that be okay with you?"

"Sounds fine to me. Charlie and Diane will probably be back from the farm by then and I'll be able to spend some time with them before they go to bed."

"Good. That's settled. How about fish for lunch? The rain's easing off a bit and they should be biting good off the island right about now."

"I'd like that," she said. "I really would. And, Bill, thanks. Thanks for – for being."

"Thanks to you, too," he said as he kissed her on the nose.

They dressed, got into their rain jackets, and headed down to the dock. Pretty soon, they were catching fish on the windward side of the island. They didn't talk much. Just enjoyed each other's presence and the feel of the wind on their faces.

"Well," Carol said, as she slipped the stringer through the gills of her second fish and dropped it beside the boat, "I guess this wonderful weekend of ours is coming to an end."

"Looks that way," Bill said as he put a fresh minnow on his hook. "But it's not the end, Carol. This is just the end of the beginning."

"I like that," she said. "I really enjoy being with you like this. This has been a wonderful weekend. A truly, truly, wonderful weekend."

"It has been that," he said.

"Charlie and Diane would have enjoyed it up here. I've missed them."

"By the way, and I don't mean to intrude, but what about the farm? How can you and Gordon afford a farm without you working? Neither one of us makes all that much at the university."

"Oh, it's not ours," she said, "and, no, you're not intruding. It's Dad's farm. He stopped going there after my mom died. He just couldn't bear the thought of being there without her. So, we've been using the farm for about a year now. Dad still has the cottage on Lake Simcoe, just down the road from the Briars Golf Club at Jackson's Point. He gets up there for a couple of rounds of golf now and then but, most of the time, he's on the road."

"Your dad travels a lot?"

"Yes, he's got properties from Nova Scotia to Vancouver Island. Mostly hotels."

"Oh, I didn't know that. So, I guess, your dad's quite well off."

"His company is worth about $400 million and he owns fifty-five per cent of the stock outright. He's expanding all the time. Right now, he's out in Calgary buying up some properties and, last year, he bought the Windsor Arms Hotel in Toronto. He's renovating it and converting it to a Winston Inn. It will probably open again under his name in time for the Christmas season."

$400 million? Bill thought. *That's the kind of sugar daddy Jean would drop her pants in a flash for. Makes Starlight look like a pauper.*

"I've been to the Windsor Arms," Bill said, never having imagined that he'd be fishing on Lake Muskoka with the daughter of someone who actually owned it. "They've got a really nice courtyard café. I've been there for lunch, quite a few times. It's quite close to the university. I usually walk there."

"I've been there a couple of times myself," Carol said. "And, yes, the Courtyard Café is a delightful place to have lunch."

She thought back to her afternoons at the Windsor Arms with Derek Parkington, back when she still thought theirs was going to be a permanent relationship. Sitting in the boat with Bill that afternoon, she was glad the affair with Derek hadn't worked out. If she'd known Bill back then, she wouldn't have become involved with Derek in the first place. Things had worked out just fine. She was with the man she wanted to be with. There was no doubt in her mind about that. Her thoughts turned to the things Bill had said about her relationship with Charlie and Diane and why asking Gordon to leave probably wouldn't be in their best interest.

"I've been thinking about some of the things you said. About forcing Gordon to leave the children. It all seemed so clear Friday morning. He was going to move out of the house and it was all going to be over – as simple as that. But now, after him seeing me here like this – with you – things are no longer quite so simple. I'm going to have to work all that out and I'm getting a different perspective on things from being in this quiet, beautiful, place with you."

"And I've enjoyed having you with me, Carol. I really have."

As they put their fishing gear away and got ready to head back to the cabin, Carol reached across the boat and placed her hand on Bill's. "Whatever you decide to do about you and Gordon, I'll understand. Whatever you decide won't change what I feel for you. And I do feel for you – deeply. I really do."

He took her hands in his. "I feel the same way about you. I couldn't ask for anything more."

Yes you could, she thought, *you could do a lot better.* Her thoughts turned again to what Bill had said about her "accepting" the children and how upset they would be if she forced Gordon to leave the house.

They might not forgive me for that, especially since I'm the one that wants to end the marriage. This is my initiative. Not Gordon's. Nor, for that matter, the children's. I'm the one who wants to change things. Change them dramatically.

She held her hand over the side of the boat and slipped it into the water. "I'm not going to ask Gordon to leave the children," she said. "That would be unfair. It's not him that should be leaving. It's me. I've known that for a long time now. I'm going to leave him."

"But," Bill said, "what about him being an MP and going to Ottawa?"

"I'd forgotten about that. Damn, that does complicate things a bit."

She thought about that problem for a moment. "Well, yes, that does complicate things but we'll just have to work something out. It's him that I'm leaving, not the children. But we can't both live in that house. I'll have to find some way of dealing with that."

"You'll probably find a way," Bill said. "It's probably going to be a joint custody arrangement and I'm sure you'll come up with an answer, sooner or later."

They were both silent for a couple of minutes and then Carol said: "I've thought about the children a lot, about how Gordon and me splitting up is going to affect them. It's going to be hard on them, and on me."

"It will be a shock for them. Always is."

"We'll have to take things slow, one day at a time. And, yes, it is going to be a shock, especially finding out at the same time that they're part Indian. That's going to come as quite a surprise."

"Maybe, and I'm only suggesting this," Bill said, "it would be better to tell them one thing at a time. Deal with the fact that Gordon is half Indian and then, when you feel the time is right, tell them you're leaving. I really do think, Carol, that springing both of those things on them at the same time is going to be a bit too much for them to handle. There's no point in making things harder for them than it needs to be. Maybe, keeping the two things separate is the best way to go, for now anyway."

"I think you're right. Absolutely right. Gordon probably won't have said anything about it to them and it might, as you say, be better to tell them only one thing at a time. I'll talk to Gordon about it when I get home. It is over between us. The only thing that matters now is to make it as less stressful as possible for Charlie and Diane.

"Things are over. There's nothing left between us. I just simply have to get out of that house. Some of the things that happened over the last couple of years should not have happened. But they did. And I regret that they happened. But that's all over now. I know now what I want to do. I want to practise law again. And I've got so much catching up to do. Four years have passed me by. But, I'll make it. They l hear from this Winston. I will make my mark. And – and – I think that I will be better able to do that if I'm removed from that situation – away from that house. I'm going to leave Gordon and – and the children. I do love them, Bill. Believe me I do. But I'm – I'm suffocating in that environment. I must get out. I must become what I was meant to be. I must practise law."

Carol sat on the floor between their seats with her back toward him and rested her head on his knee. She closed her eyes as the spray splashed her face and Bill stroked her forehead with his strong wet fingers. She felt good being with him.

When they got back to the cabin, Bill cleaned the fish and started to fillet them. Carol made them a fresh garden salad. They ate their lunch in silence, holding hands and drinking white wine. And then they sat by the fire and watched the embers slowly dying out and turning ash white.

As Gordon pulled up to the farmhouse, Diane ran out to meet him. "Hi, Daddy," she said as he caught her up in his arms and gave her big kisses on both cheeks. "I missed you. Really did."

"I'm here now, darling, and we're going to have a great day."

"There isn't much day left," she said, a bit despondently. "I'd hoped you and Grandma would have been up here yesterday."

"I'm sorry, darling. I really am, but something came up that I really had to attend to. But I'm here now and we are going to have a great time together. Where's Charlie?"

"He's down at the barn fixing my bike. Jason and his sister were over earlier but they've gone back to their place for lunch. So, it's just us."

Diane gave her grandmother a big hug and they went into the house to see Anne.

"I've been expecting you," Anne said. "Lunch will be ready around one-thirty. I thought I should allow a little extra time in case you and your mom got delayed. Is that okay?"

"Just perfect, thanks, Anne," Gordon said. "And thanks for looking after Charlie and Diane. It's been a crazy weekend."

Martha went to the kitchen to help prepare lunch and Gordon and Diane headed down to the barn to take a look at her bike. Charlie had placed the wheel on an old anvil and was banging away at it with a big hammer.

"Hi, Dad," he said as he took another swing at the bent wheel. "I'm not so sure this is going to work."

"Neither am I," Gordon said as he reached down and gave his son a hug and a kiss. "Looks pretty banged up to me."

It was clear Charlie's well-intended hammering had made matters worse but Gordon decided to let it pass. "I don't think that's going to work, Son. We'll get Diane a new wheel when we get back to Toronto."

"I think maybe you're right," Charlie said. "That was my best shot."

"Well, we'll have lunch and then we'll all go for a nice ride. The rain's just about over now so we should be okay. I brought my bike along and we can put a pad on the rear carrier for Diane. How's that sound?"

"That sounds great," Charlie said. "Should I put Diane's bike in the trunk of your car?"

"Yes, Son, thanks. That would be a good idea. Take the training wheels off first. We'll take the front wheel, too. The tire still looks okay."

They went up to the Pontiac, removed Gordon's Raleigh roadster from the rack and put Diane's little bike in the trunk. Then they went to the farmhouse to have their lunch.

As Martha exchanged small talk with Anne, Gordon's thoughts turned to Carol. She probably was right. Things *were* over for them, had been for quite some time. *We did have some good times. A long time ago, but we did have them. Maybe, if we hadn't had to get married, things would have worked out differently. I should have pulled out like I promised. Another mistake, Gordon. You've made more than your fair share, my boy. Well, that's all kind of academic now. There is no us. But there's still Charlie and Diane. I still have them and I'm glad they're part of my life. Always have been, always will be.*

"How about that ride?" Gordon asked as they finished their lunch. "Are you guys ready for a nice ride with your dad?"

"We sure are," Charlie said with enthusiasm. "I'm ready to go."

"How about you, Diane? Are you ready for a ride?

"Yes, Daddy, I really am and I'm going to be fine on the back of your bike. I'm not scared at all."

"I'll help Anne clear things up here," Martha said. "When were you thinking of heading back to Toronto, Gordon?"

"Well, it's two-thirty now," Gordon said as he looked at his watch. "Let's leave around six. We can get something to eat at the McDonald's on the 401 near Bowmanville. How's that with you, Anne? Will that work for you?"

"Of course it will," Anne replied. "We'll have everything packed up and ready to go by five thirty. You enjoy your ride with the children. We'll be just fine. Perfectly fine."

Gordon got a foam pad for Diane from the workshop in the barn and tied it to the rear carrier on his Raleigh. He hadn't been on the bike for more than a year and he was looking forward to a good ride with the children.

CHAPTER
- 28 -

Carol was sitting on the sofa in the living room when Gordon and the children got back from the farm. She immediately got up, opened her arms wide, and Charlie and Diane ran towards her.

"And how are my darlings?" she asked as she hugged and kissed them both.

"We're fine, Mommy," Charlie said. "But we missed you. We really, really, missed you."

"Me, too," Diane said. "We missed you really awful."

"And I missed you guys. But I'm here now. I'm here now, my darlings."

Gordon helped Anne bring the things in from the car. He'd dropped his mother off at her apartment.

"Will you be needing me in the morning to give the children their breakfast?" Anne asked.

"No thanks, Anne," Carol said. "We're going to have a nice family breakfast together. But, thanks just the same. I would appreciate it if you could come after breakfast on Tuesday, though. I'm going to be out for most of the day. There's quite a bit of cleaning that needs to be done. It might be as well for you to plan on being here on Wednesday, too, if you can manage that."

"Sure, no problem," Anne replied. "Tuesday is fine. I can handle Wednesday, too, if you want."

Carol wrote a cheque from her trust fund to cover Anne's salary for the week and the money she had spent for the things they had taken to the farm and then Anne left.

"How are the children?" Carol asked Gordon. "Are they hungry? Should I get them something?"

"No, we had a good lunch and then we had a bite to eat at McDonald's on the way back. They'll be fine."

"You know how I feel about the children eating at McDonald's," she said reprimandingly. "I do wish you had found somewhere more appropriate than that."

"Carol, I've only been home for ten minutes. Let's not start going at each other again."

"You're right. I'm sorry. Let's get them off to their rooms and then I'd like to have a talk with you – a positive talk."

"That's fine with me," he said. "I'm sure we'll find a lot to talk about."

Diane was quite tired and it was pretty obvious she would be asleep in no time at all. Charlie said he wasn't at all tired and wanted to read in his room for a while.

"I'll take them up," Gordon said, "and then we'll have that talk you mentioned."

He got them both upstairs and into their rooms. Diane was ready for sleep but Charlie sat up in his bed so he could read. When Gordon got back down to the living room, Carol was sitting in one of the armchairs by the fire.

"You want a drink?" he asked.

"That would be nice, thanks, Gordon."

He fixed their drinks, Scotch and soda for her and vodka and orange for himself and handed her the Scotch on his way to the other armchair.

"So, how was your weekend?" he asked.

"It was fine, quite enjoyable, but I'd rather not talk about that. I think it best that we talk about where we go from here rather than revisiting what either one of us did, or did not, do over the weekend. Or, in the past."

Carol didn't want to get into a discussion about being at Bill's cabin. Neither did Gordon. *There's really not all that much left to say,* he thought. *We're done like toast.*

"Okay, I can go along with that," he said. "Has anything changed or are things still the same as they were Friday morning?"

"There is one big change. Bill told me the story about you two being brothers."

"He did? He had no business telling you that. We'd agreed we weren't going to tell anyone until after we talked about it some more and decided what was the best thing to do."

Why would he do that? Tell Carol without letting me know he was going to? But, then again, maybe he had his reasons. Maybe things were a bit edgy between them, because of that talk we had when she was out on the boat, and the time felt right. What's done is done, I guess. Can't change that now.

"Well, he did tell me. I guess I kind of pushed him into it. I just couldn't bear sitting there not knowing what you two had been talking about. So, in fairness to him, it took a lot of prodding on my part."

"I guess it was all bound to come out anyway. Still, I'd like to have told you about it myself."

"That must've come as quite a shock for you. Finding out you're brothers. It certainly hit Bill hard. How are you dealing with it? Are you okay?"

"As okay as can be expected under the circumstances. It's certainly not something I wanted to know. Especially not at this stage of my life. All hell will break loose when people find out I'm half Indian. My whole life's going to change. Not for the better, I'll tell you."

"Well, if there's anything I can do – anything at all – just let me know. I just can't imagine what this must be like for you."

"Thank you, Carol. I really do appreciate that."

"I mean it, Gordon. Anything I can do, just let me know."

"Thanks. Is that what you wanted to have the 'positive talk' about?"

"Not really. There's another change I wanted to talk to you about. A major change." She paused and took a sip of her Scotch. "I'll be leaving the house by the end of next month."

"But I thought you wanted me to be the one to go," he said with a look of total surprise.

"I did but, now, I think it best that I be the one to leave. I need a fresh start. I expect that I'll be going back to Haldimand and Brock. I've set up an appointment with Jonathan Hollinger for Tuesday. I think I stand a pretty good chance of getting back with them. And then, I'll just take it from there."

"That sounds okay. They're a good big firm and I'm sure they'll be happy to have you back. You were doing rather well there. I have no doubt that you'll quickly work your way back up the ladder with them. That part sounds okay."

"Which part doesn't?"

"I don't understand."

"You said 'that part sounds okay'. Which part doesn't sound okay?"

"Well, the part about you moving out at the end of next month. It's going to hit Charlie and Diane pretty hard. I'm not at all sure you've given enough thought to that part of it."

"You're right. I haven't. All I do know is that I want their lives to be disrupted as little as possible. Although, if you get elected and spend most of your time in Ottawa, that will complicate things even further. We'll have to work something out."

"Well, I don't think that's going to happen – not when they find out I'm half Indian."

"You're probably right about that. And, yes, that would make things a little less complicated. Either way, as I'm the one who's leaving, I want to tell the children that myself, in my own way. I do want them to understand. I don't want them to hate me for this. If I could think of any other way, any other way besides leaving them, I'd take it. But there isn't any. If this was back before we had Charlie and Diane, things would be different. Right now, though, I want to get back to practising law and the way I want to practise it, it's going to be a consuming, all-out, full-time career. I've got a lot of catching up to do. Four years' worth. The pressure on me is going to be quite enormous."

"I understand. Law is what you've always wanted to do."

"It is and I think I'll have a better chance of catching up if our life together is officially ended. We'll need a full-time housekeeper for you and the children. I'll pay half of that cost and half of all other costs related to Charlie and Diane."

"You don't need to do that."

"I do. That's the way I want it to be."

She looked at him, almost contritely. 'I'm sorry for the shabby way I've sometimes treated you in the last couple of years. You deserved better than that. Just about everything you said about me Friday morning was true. We just couldn't go on like that."

"Yeah, I guess things were coming to a head."

"They were, Gordon. And now we've got a great many things to discuss about the children and their future, especially with this new thing about you and Bill being brothers. I'd rather we concentrated on Charlie and Diane and on what happens next rather than getting bogged down in recriminations about rights or wrongs in the past, or present. I hope you see it that way, too."

"I do. They will always come first."

"Let's do all we can to make this as easy as possible on them. They'll need all of the support and understanding both of us can give them. And yet, you know, when you come right down to it, our life together wasn't all bad. We've had some good times. A lot of good times. Before Diane. But, right now, I think we both deserve more than either one of us can provide. Our marriage is over. We both know that. We simply can't go on like this, sleeping in separate rooms, nagging away at each other in front of the children. It's over, Gordon. You know it and so do I."

He couldn't help but wonder if it was because of her weekend with Bill that she had suddenly decided that she should be the one who was going to leave. *Is it because she has fallen hopelessly in love with him and wants to move in with him ASAP? Are they going to become a permanent item?* "Yes, I understand that, but, I get the feeling you will be moving in with Bill. Right?"

"No. I won't be moving in with Bill. I need time to be on my own – alone – and space to breathe while I get back to being a lawyer. I'll probably find an apartment somewhere with enough room for the children to visit on the weekends and on holidays."

"Oh, I thought you two were an item."

"Right now, the most important thing for me is to get re-established as a lawyer and to make sure that, in the process, Charlie and Diane are okay with the transition. We'll have to be careful how we handle all that. It's going to be pretty upsetting for them. Regardless of which one of us it is that actually leaves. Pretty disturbing. Bill suggested we should put some space between telling the children that you're half Indian and the part about me leaving the house."

"That sounds like a good idea," he said. "We could certainly use some good ideas. Everything is changing, something every day." He paused for a moment. "I expect that I will have to give up the Meadowbrook nomination. That's not something I'm looking forward to."

"I understand how you feel about it, Gordon. How much you were looking forward to being an MP. But, I just don't see that happening for you now. Not when they find out your birth mother was a Blackfoot Indian. It's just not in the cards. Not in Meadowbrook."

"Guess not," he said rather despondently. "So, what do you think? Should we tell Charlie and Diane about me and about my Uncle Bill and all that?"

"I don't see why not. It's nothing to be ashamed of."

"That doesn't mean they'll be okay with you moving out."

"Probably not. I'm going to have to be very careful with that one."

"Well, like Bill says, they don't have to hear both things at the same time. Why don't we tell them about me first and then, when you feel the time is right, you can tell them about the other thing."

"You've got a point there. They'll be alone with us at breakfast. That would be a good time for you to tell them."

"Okay, that's what I'll do. Let's hope they take it okay."

"Let's hope that they do, Gordon. Let's hope they are going to be okay with this. Now, I am going to turn in. I'll get breakfast ready in the morning and then we can tell the children about you and what happened out at that ranch."

"Yeah, that sounds fine," he said. "Sleep well. I'll see you in the morning. And, Carol, I really do wish you all the very best. I know how unhappy you've been and you deserve something better. We both do."

"We do, Gordon, and I truly do hope that you find happiness, too. Life is too short to live without it."

She walked over, cupped his head in her hands and gave him an affectionate kiss on the forehead, and then she went upstairs to her room.

That was nice, Gordon thought. *She really does still care. But, when you think it all through, it really is good that she's leaving. We couldn't go on any longer like this. Separate bedrooms, separate lives, separate ways of looking at life. It was bound to end sooner than later. There really is nothing left. Still, it's going to be hard on Charlie and Diane. It's going to be a lot easier for them to accept the fact that I'm half Indian than it'll be to see their mother actually packing her bags and leaving them. That is going to be quite a scene. But, it doesn't have to be. If we tell them about it the right way, prepare them for it, they might be okay. Families split up every day of the week. With all of our love and support, they should be able to adjust to it reasonably well. We'll just have to make sure that they do. Make it as easy on them as we possibly can.*

Gordon was having his coffee at the breakfast table when Charlie and Diane came into the room. Their bran flakes were on the table and Carol was making pancakes. Diane gave him a hug and a kiss and then she hugged her mom from behind before taking her place at the table.

"Hi, Dad," Charlie said, as he sat down. "Hi, Mom. The pancakes smell real good."

"Hi, Charlie. They won't be long."

Gordon decided to get right to it. "There's something I want to tell you both. Something I only just learned about a couple of days ago."

"Something bad?" Charlie asked.

"No, not bad. But, something real important. Something that affects all of us."

Charlie reached for the orange juice and waited for what his father was about to say. Diane kept on eating her cereal.

"Remember how I told you about Grandfather MacArthur coming over from Scotland a long time ago and him and his brother going to work on a ranch out in Alberta?"

"Yeah," Charlie said. "Out near Calgary."

"That's right, near Calgary. Well, after a couple of years, Grandfather moved to Toronto and started selling real estate. His brother, my Uncle Bill, stayed out there and fell in love with an Indian lady who was the cook at the ranch. She was a Blackfoot. A full-blooded Indian. They got married and, on the night that their second son was born, things got pretty complicated and she died. Right that night, she died. Bled to death."

He paused for a moment and took another sip of his coffee. "That second son was me. So, my Uncle Bill was actually my real father."

Charlie was quite taken aback. "You mean Grandfather's not your dad?" he asked incredulously.

"No, no, Son. Grandfather is my dad. There's no doubt about that. No doubt at all. He and Grandma are the ones that raised me, right from the time I was born."

"How can that be?" Charlie asked. "With you being born out there in Alberta and Grandfather and Grandma living here?"

"Well, it is a bit complicated. You see my, what you call, biological mother was the cook at the ranch and, when they got married, my Uncle Bill moved into the cookhouse with her. But, when she died, the rancher hired another cook and that meant my Uncle Bill had to move back into the bunkhouse. He couldn't look after me and my brother there. We couldn't sleep in the bunkhouse with the other men – there was eight of them – and there would be no one to look after us and feed us during the day when he was out working in the fields."

It was time for another sip of coffee. "Anyway, to make a long story short, when Grandfather and Grandma heard about it, they offered to have one of the sons, me, come and live with them in Toronto. And that's how it happened."

"And what about your Uncle Bill?" Charlie asked. "What happened to him?"

"He was killed in the war over in Hong Kong. I wasn't even three when he died."

"And the other one?" Charlie asked. "The one that was your brother? What happened to him?"

"He was raised at the Big Thunder Indian reserve just outside of Calgary. He was raised as an Indian."

"Is he still out there?"

"Actually, no, Charlie. He's not out there anymore."

Carol stopped eating her pancakes and waited to hear what was coming next.

"So where is he? He's our uncle, right? Where did he go to if he's not still out there?"

"Well, Son. He's actually here in Toronto, teaching at the university. I didn't know anything about him until three days ago, when Grandma told me all about it. I didn't even know before that that I was adopted. So, this is all news to me. News that isn't even a week old yet.

But, yes, he's here and he's teaching at the university. Actually, he's the Director of the North American Indian Studies program."

"When do we get to meet him?" Charlie asked.

"Yes," Diane said. "When can we see our uncle? We've never had an uncle before, Daddy. Can we meet him, please? Please, can we meet him?"

Gordon was not at all sure what he should do next. He looked over at Carol and she just shrugged her shoulders. It was his call.

"Sure, you can meet him. You can meet your uncle. I'm having lunch with him today and I'll ask him if he'd like to come over and have dinner with us sometime. How about that, Carol, will that be okay with you?"

If looks could kill, Gordon would be dead on the spot. *Sonofabitch,* Carol muttered under her breath. *Why'd he have to go and do something stupid like that? He's just trying to complicate things for me and Bill.* "Of course that will be perfectly fine, Gordon. I'd like to meet him, too. I'm sure he'll turn out to be a rather interesting character. Why don't you invite him over for dinner sometime soon? We'll have a nice family dinner with you and your brother."

"How about this Thursday?"

"If he's clear, that's fine with me."

"Does he have any children?" Charlie asked.

"Yes, he has a son."

"So, that means he's our cousin, right? And he's here in Toronto, too, right?"

"Yes, Charlie, he is your cousin. His name is Albert and he's just about the same age as you. But your uncle is separated from his wife and his son lives on an Indian reservation near Calgary."

Charlie thought for a moment. "So, that makes you half Indian. Right?"

"Yes, Son, I am half Indian."

"So, I'm part Indian, too? Me and Diane are part Indian?"

"Yes, Charlie, you're both part Indian."

"We're part Indian?" Diane exclaimed, almost spilling her orange juice. "Which part of me is Indian, Daddy, the top half or the bottom half?"

"All of you is part Indian," Gordon replied.

Diane wasn't quite sure what to make of that. She'd seen Indians in the movies on TV attacking white settlers and burning their wagons. They were half naked and their faces were covered with paint and they kept yelling all the time. *Whoop. Whoop. Whoop. Whoop.*

Carol decided it was time to intervene. "So, how do you guys feel about your Dad being half Indian? Are you okay with it?"

"Don't know," Charlie said. "It's all pretty new. I don't know. How come we're only hearing about this now? Why didn't we know before?"

"Well, your Dad only found out about it himself Friday night when Grandma told him about it."

"And she never told him before? Not even once when he was growing up?"

"Not once, Charlie," Gordon said. "This is all news to me, too."

"Maybe she had a reason," Charlie said. "Maybe Grandma thought it would be better you didn't know you're half Indian."

"I don't think that was it," Gordon said. "I think Grandma had other reasons. But, that aside, how do you feel about it?"

"It's no big deal, I guess. Frank Fontaine's grandfather's an Ojibway. He lives on a reserve up on Manitoulin Island. Frank goes up there every summer and his grandfather takes him trapping beavers and all sorts of stuff like that. He really likes it up there."

"Who's Frank Fontaine?" Gordon asked.

"One of my friends at school, probably my best friend."

"And where does Frank live, Charlie."

"Just a couple of blocks away from the school, at an apartment building on Sandringham."

"So, that would mean your friend's father is part Indian."

"He's all Indian. All Ojibway. Frank's mom's Ukrainian. I like hanging out with Frank."

Well, this is interesting. I'm all worried about how Charlie's going to react to the fact that I'm half Indian and he's hanging out with some kid whose father is Indian and whose grandfather takes him trapping beavers at a reserve up on Manitoulin Island.

"So, your friend's father is Indian. An Ojibway. How did you react to that, Charlie?"

"What do you mean how did I react?" Charlie asked with a puzzled look on his face.

"Like when you found out your friend's father was an Indian. How did you react to that?"

"No big deal. Henry Lee's Chinese and he hangs out with us. He lives in the same building as Frank. It's no big deal, Dad. Willie Roach is Black and I play pinball with him after school. He's one of us. No big deal."

"Better get your Equal Opportunities Council working on that, Gordon," Carol said with a chuckle. "There goes the neighborhood."

She decided it was time to bring the conversation to an end for now. Things were getting altogether too complicated – Bill being invited to dinner and now Charlie and Diane wrestling with the question about being part Indian.

"Okay, children, it's time for school," she said. "Let's get going. We'll finish this talk tonight, over dinner."

They both gave Gordon a hug and a kiss as they picked up their school bags and jackets and headed out the door to Carol's car.

"I'm not sure how well that went," Gordon said as Carol pulled on her overcoat. "Charlie seems okay with it, especially with his friend being half Ojibway. But neither one of them seems particularly positive about it all."

"It will take time," Carol said. "That's quite a lot for them to absorb at one sitting. And, speaking about the children, that part about having Bill over to dinner was a pretty low blow. I expected a lot better of you, Gordon. A lot better."

"No low blow intended. He is going to be part of their lives and this strikes me as a pretty natural way to start things off. He is their uncle. I did it in good faith, Carol. I really do think this is the best way to go about it."

"Maybe. But you should have discussed it with me first. After all, it does affect my life, too."

"Just like you discussed things with me before you went off to spend the weekend with him? Telling me you wanted me out of the house 'as quickly as possible' and knowing full well you were going to be making out with him at his cabin that very night?"

So that's it. He's still angry with me for telling him I wanted him out of the house. Mr. Magnanimous, he ain't.

"Well, Gordon, it would appear that inviting Bill over to dinner wasn't so gracious a gesture on your part after all. You're quite a piece of work, Gordon. Quite a piece of work." With that, she left the house and drove Charlie and Diane to school, Diane to Montessori and Charlie to Brookdale Elementary.

As Gordon walked to his car, he noticed the *Globe and Mail* lying on the porch step. In getting his head ready to tell the children about the adoption thing, he'd forgotten to pick up the paper.

There was a story about Gran Winston on the front page.

Conservative land deal 'stinks'
Liberals call for public inquiry

Gordon went back into the kitchen to read the rest of the article.

OTTAWA – A special deal between the Conservative government and a prominent party supporter will cost Canadian taxpayers "several million dollars", Liberal candidate John Hudson charged last night.

Hudson, Liberal candidate for Calgary South, told *The Globe and Mail* in an exclusive interview that he has documents showing that Winston Holdings Limited acted on "inside" government information when it purchased 1,000 acres of land just outside of Calgary under the name of an unidentified numbered company.

Hudson said the Liberal party's research staff can prove that:

- The numbered company that purchased the property is a wholly-owned subsidiary of Winston Holdings Limited.
- Winston Holdings is the only developer the Department of Public Works talked to before signing a 99-year lease agreement for four office towers to accommodate federal employees who are being transferred from Ottawa to Calgary.

- The four office towers will be the centrepiece of a commercial/residential project Winston Holdings plans to develop on its 1,000-acre property.
- It is because of the federal government's deal with Winston Holdings that the Saunders Energy Corporation is trying to force a gas pipeline through the Big Thunder Indian reserve which lies on the border of the proposed development.

"This deal stinks," Hudson said. "The Canadian public is being taken for a costly ride. The only way to clear the air on this thing is to bring it before Parliament."

As Parliament is not sitting this week, the earliest Opposition Leader Harold Davidson will be able to raise the issue during Question Period will be next Monday.

Granville Winston, Chairman of the Board and Chief Executive Officer of Winston Holdings Limited, is a long-time financial supporter of the Conservative Party of Canada. His company is believed to have contributed hundreds of thousands of dollars to the party.

"Granville Winston is privy to a considerable amount of information about what goes on inside this government, mostly behind closed doors," Hudson said. "It is obvious to me that, in this case, he is profiteering on that inside information."

A highly-placed source told *The Globe* that the Prime Minister's Office had no knowledge about the multi-million dollar deal between Winston Holdings and the federal department of public works.

"Prime Minister Walter Floyd had absolutely no knowledge about the deal for the office towers," the source said. "He was not involved in any way."

Liberal candidate Hudson said he expected that much of the information about the government's "unconscionable" deal with Winston Holdings will come out when the Energy Resources Conservation Board of Alberta hearings on the Saunders gas pipeline resume on Tuesday morning.

Meanwhile, he said, his party will push to have the matter brought before the Public Works Committee so the Conservative government's role can be subjected to "a thorough investigation."

Good God, Gordon thought, as he put the paper down, *what on earth has Gran been up to out there? This is pretty serious stuff. Looks like he's skating on pretty thin ice. All hell will break loose now.*

The phone rang. It was Henry Bracken. "Have you read the *Globe*, Gordon? The story about Gran and a land deal out in Calgary?"

"Yes, Henry. I just finished reading it."

"I had no knowledge of this – none of this – whatsoever. And, it would appear that the Prime Minister didn't know about it either."

"How could he not know?"

"Public Works is Harold Barton's department and he has a pretty free hand to run things in whatever way he sees fit. However, this office tower thing is way over the line. It should not have happened – at least, not the way that it appears to have happened. It should have gone to tender. Now, I believe them when they say the Prime Minister didn't know anything about the deal for the office towers. This would appear to be something that was cooked up on the sly by Barton and Gran.

"As you know, Gran was co-chair of Barton's leadership campaign and they came close. Remember? The Prime Minister only won by eighty eight votes on the final ballot. If Pat McGee hadn't insisted on leaving his name on that last ballot, Barton might very well have won. Probably would have. It was that close. Barton's people have never accepted that loss. Nor have they given up on their dream of having him become Prime Minister.

"So, getting back to the office towers, if this story turns out to be true, I doubt very much that Barton will be Minister of Public Works this time next week. You saw how quickly the Prime Minister dealt with Hal Davies when he got that Indian girl pregnant and how he was ready to block you from getting the nomination. He's hard as steel when it comes to this sort of thing. And then, with Barton out of his hair, the Prime Minister can plan his retirement without Barton's people putting pressure on him to leave before he's good and ready."

"It's quite a mess, isn't it?"

"Yes, it is, Gordon. But I doubt very much that it will create any problems for Meadowbrook or for your candidacy. This deal was cooked up by Barton and your father-in-law. It has nothing to do with us. Absolutely nothing at all."

Gordon toyed with the idea of telling Bracken about the adoption thing. *It's going to come out anyway, probably sooner than later. Maybe I should just get it over and done with. But, no, I really should talk to Bill first. I'll see what he has to say about it at lunch. Maybe he doesn't want anyone to know. Anyone outside the family that is.*

"Now, Gordon, I have a meeting to attend. We'll monitor this situation and see where it goes from here. Can you join me for lunch tomorrow? Say, around twelve thirty? I've got a few things I want to discuss with you about the election. You're going to need a campaign manager and we really must get that office Dave Saunders offered us up and running as quickly as possible."

"Sure, Henry. I can be there."

"Good boy. Join me at the Commonwealth Club at twelve thirty."

"Fine, Henry. I'll be there."

Gordon poured himself another coffee and read the story over again. *This is serious. How could Gran get himself into a mess like this? Maybe Henry's right. Maybe this won't have any impact on Meadowbrook. But, then again, it might. Everything's so interconnected in politics. It's bound to have some effect. Bill's certainly going to have something to say about Gran's deal for the office towers. This is good for his side of things. How's he going to react when he finds out it's Carol's father who's behind all this? What a mess.*

Bill was sitting at one of the tables beside the window in the dining room of the Sutton Place Hotel. His hair wasn't braided. It fell over his shoulders with a red headband keeping it out of his eyes. He did have the bear claws around his neck. They shook hands as Gordon sat down and beckoned for the waitress.

"How are you?" Bill asked.

"Fine. And you?"

"I'm okay. However, I got a call from Carol this morning and she was quite upset. Apparently, you told the children about us being brothers and then you said you were going to invite me over for dinner sometime."

"Yeah, why not? You are their uncle, part of our family now. They want to meet you because they've never had an uncle before – neither me nor Carol have brothers or sisters."

"Don't pin it on the children, Gordon. You didn't do it for them. You know full well you did that in order to create problems for me and Carol."

"Well, in hindsight, maybe there was a little bit of that but, quite honestly, it did seem like the right thing to do at the time

"That may be so, but you had no business doing that without discussing it with Carol and me first. Things are complicated enough as it is without us all getting together for a family dinner."

"Is that how you feel about it?" Gordon asked as he ordered a vodka and orange.

"It was when Carol first told me about it. I was really angry with you. But, now, now that I've had some time to think about it, I think it's going to turn out to be a good move after all."

"Why do you think that?"

"I went through the separation thing with my wife and it was really hard on Albert. He was really confused and hurt by the whole thing. It's up to you and Carol to make sure Charlie and Diane don't go through the same sort of ordeal. You've got to make it as easy on them as possible. Having them get to know me as their Uncle Bill might make it easier on them when Carol moves out. Give them another shoulder to cry on."

Gordon looked over at the next table and saw a woman in a brown suede pantsuit reading the *Globe and Mail*. He'd forgotten to mention the article they ran on Gran Winston and the office towers.

"That was quite a piece the *Globe* had this morning about Carol's father and that land deal he's involved in out in Calgary," he said.

"I knew about the numbered company being based in Toronto but I didn't know it was a subsidiary of her father's company. That was news to me."

"Well, it's certainly not going to hurt your case," Gordon said. "Bad news for Gran, but good news for you."

"Good news, but messy news. Didn't know it was Carol's father behind it all but I did know there was something really rotten going on. There usually is with white people."

"Not so fast," Gordon said. "You're half white. Remember?"

"Let's just call that my dark side," Bill said with a chuckle. "That probably accounts for all the really bad things I've done in my life."

"Anyway, that's a real mess her father's gotten himself into out there", Gordon said. Pretty bad. It's got nothing to do with me. Absolutely nothing. That's for him to sort out – if he can. I doubt very much that Carol knew anything about what he was up to out there. She didn't say a word about it to me."

"Me neither," Bill said. "I'd be really surprised if she did know. Certainly can't see her approving conduct like that. Anyway, we're definitely going to make good use of this new development at the Energy Board hearing."

Gordon paused for a minute. "What about *Toronto Focus*? How do you think we should handle that tomorrow night?"

"We shouldn't go on the show. It's too soon. Way too soon. If it's okay with you, I'm going to call Fraser Deacon this afternoon and say we can't make it."

"No skin off my back. It's not something I was looking forward to – not with it being live and a quarter million people watching."

"Okay, then. I'll cancel and say we'll get back to him some other time."

"Sounds good to me. But, you know, that's the least of our worries. I've still got to deal with the Meadowbrook thing and the Equal Opportunities Council. I'll probably have to resign from both – if we decide to be open about this adoption thing."

"Can't see how we can keep it hidden. Especially not with Carol and your kids knowing about it. I'll be calling my mom about it after our lunch. It's bound to come out some time or other."

"You're probably right about that. The only question is whether it leaks out somewhere or whether we control how it comes out."

"Not sure what you mean by that?"

"Well, with all this media focus on Big Thunder, hundreds of students out demonstrating, stories in the paper about Carol's father owning the property next door and all that, some reporter might start snooping around out there and stumble upon the fact that you had another brother. Someone who might have known our birth mother before she died might let something slip."

"Hadn't thought about that. They do have a way of digging out things people would rather keep private. You're right. One of the elders just might say something when being questioned hard by some nosy reporter. Wouldn't be hard to put two and two together. Some of the elders are bound to know I wasn't born there. Didn't get there until after my mom's sister died. I'll ask my mom about it when I call her after our lunch. She'll know who might, or might not, let something like that slip. Of course, I won't be asking her anything like that until after I tell her I know about her sister. About us being brothers. Being adopted. That's going to be quite a conversation."

"Let me know what she says. Even if there's no risk of it coming out at that end, I'm still leaning toward controlling the message at this end. Like they say, 'he who controls the ball controls the game'."

"Okay, I'll give you a call after I talk to my mom."

Gordon's thoughts turned to Carol. If she wasn't going to move out until the end of next month, he figured, she would probably be spending a lot of time with Bill before the move. *Maybe she'll go back to his cabin with him. Back under the muskrat fur.*

"Is Carol going with you? To the cabin this weekend?"

"No. Not with Charlie and Diane finding out they're part Indian. It's going to be quite an adjustment for them and she wants to spend as much time with them as she can before she gets a place of her own."

"I think that's a good idea. They seemed okay with it but you never know. It's all so new for them – and for me."

"And for us. This is a new thing for me, too."

"You're right about that."

"About having dinner with you and the children, Carol says you were aiming for Thursday night."

"Yes, if you can make it."

"I can make it"

"Good. I'll look forward to it."

"All right, Gordon, we'll play it by ear. However, I do want you to understand one thing. And about this I'm absolutely certain. No matter what happened at the ranch or at Big Thunder, I am Blackfoot and that's the way I'm going to stay. The great-grandson of a Blackfoot chief."

Gordon was silent for a moment, reflecting on how different Bill looked without his hair in braids. "Actually, you're not," he said. "Your birth mother, our birth mother, wasn't descended from a Blackfoot chief. It's your adoptive father, our birth mother's brother-in-law, who had a grandfather who was a Blackfoot chief. Your birth father, our birth father, is actually descended from a long line of Scottish farmers – dirt-poor hill farmers. So, with all due respect, you can wear your hair in braids and hang the bear claws around your neck all you want but that does not, does not, make you the great-grandson of a Blackfoot chief. Our great-grandfather was Scottish. And that means, dear brother of mine, that you're no more Blackfoot than I am. What do you think of that?"

"What are you, some sort of master logician?" Bill asked good-naturedly. "Yeah, I guess, if you take a logician's approach to our family tree, you're right. I am no more Blackfoot than you are, at least not from a genetic sense. And, yes, when you look at it that way, I am not the great-grandson – great-great-grandson, actually – of a Blackfoot chief. I somehow doubt that I should be thanking you for pointing that out. I kind of preferred things the way they were this time last week, before we were told about being adopted and only half Indian, half white. Anyway, you are right. Neither one of us is descended from a Blackfoot chief. But you've got to admit, Gordon, being a Blackfoot chief trumps being a Scottish hill farmer."

"Maybe, but let's not get too hung up on our ancestry, real or imagined. We are what we are today and we'll just have to make the best of it."

Gordon picked up a copy of the *Toronto Star* on his way to the parking lot across the street from the hotel and tucked it under his arm. He didn't look at it until he got back to his office.

There was a story about him on the front page.

Conservative money man 'bought' Meadowbrook
By Harold Stewart

OTTAWA – A well-placed inside source confirmed last night that a wealthy land developer with Conservative connections "bought" the Meadowbrook Conservative nomination last week.

The source said developer Granville Winston, a well-known financial supporter ot the Conservative Party of Canada, contributed $25,000 to the Meadowbrook election campaign fund – on the condition that his son-in-law be given a "no-contest" nomination.

Winston's son-in-law, University of Toronto political science professor Gordon MacArthur, was acclaimed as the Conservative candidate for Meadowbrook last Thursday night. No other candidate was nominated.

MacArthur, 35, has been dubbed the "white power Conservative" because of allegedly racist comments he has made about minority group people.

Liberal candidate John Hudson charged in Calgary last night that Winston Holdings Limited has a "sweetheart deal" with the federal government in connection with a commercial/residential development that is being planned on the border of the Big Thunder Indian reserve.

Winston Holdings was the only company to bid on four office towers that will be built in the new development to house government employees who are being relocated from Ottawa to Calgary.

A source in the office of Prime Minister Walter Floyd told *The Star* that Winston "put pressure" on key Conservative party officials to make sure his son-in-law got the uncontested nomination.

Winston was not available for comment at press time.

MacArthur has been quoted in news reports as saying that white women and children will "freeze in the dark" if a gas pipeline proposed by the Saunders Energy Corporation is not allowed to go through the Big Thunder Indian reserve which borders on Winston's property.

Hudson, Liberal candidate for Calgary South, says the only reason the pipeline is being forced through the Indians' land is because it would depreciate the value of Winston's property.

"They don't want that pipeline going through the new project Winston is developing. That's the only reason that it's going through the Indians' land," Hudson told *The Star* in an exclusive interview.

The inside source in the PMO told *The Star* that comments MacArthur has made in support of the pipeline proposal indicate that "he is part and parcel of the whole sordid mess."

The matter is expected to be raised in Parliament early next week.

This is getting ridiculous. How in the world could they have concocted something as ludicrous as this? Maybe what they're saying about Gran is true but I – I certainly didn't know anything about this land deal. Nothing. Not a clue.

Maybe it is true, he thought. Maybe that is why Gran helped him get the nomination. Helped him? Might as well admit it – Gran did buy it for him. How in the world had he gotten himself into this situation? And then he remembered how interesting it had all sounded when Gran first suggested that he fill the vacancy created by Hal Davies' unexpected announcement that he would not be running in the next election. Gran's suggestion about running for office had seemed so intriguing. He was going to be able to fulfill his long-standing ambition of becoming a Member of Parliament. Hon. Gordon MacArthur, P.C., M.P.

Was that why Gran had made the offer in the first place? Because he saw in Gordon an easily-manipulated individual who would look out for his interests in Ottawa and – as he had said on the phone – advise him of matters that could have an adverse, or a beneficial, influence on the earnings of Winston Holdings Limited?

Looking at it from that point of view, Gran probably did see buying the nomination as just another aspect of doing business – of protecting his investments. And, if he hadn't spent a lifetime protecting his investments – making sure, like he said on the phone, that the right people in Ottawa had a sympathetic attitude toward his business interests – his wouldn't have become one of the largest real estate development companies in North America. That's why he was able to write a cheque for $25,000 for the Meadowbrook campaign. That's why he would be writing the $250,000 cheque the national campaign committee was expecting him to come through with. To protect his investments.

And yet, thinking back on it, Gran had been quite open about the arrangement. He said he needed someone in Ottawa with a sympathetic attitude toward his business interests. That, clearly, was why he wanted Gordon to get the nomination. That's what it all boiled down to. Taking care of business.

What a mess he'd gotten himself into. Carol was ending their marriage. Bear Claws Bill had turned out to be his long-lost brother. And now, the business about Gran and his Calgary land deal was escalating. *Surely to God they won't expect me to go to Ottawa to testify before the Public Works Committee.*

The phone rang. It was Henry Bracken. He asked Gordon if he had seen the story in the *Toronto Star*. "Yes, Henry. I just finished reading it."

"This is serious stuff, Gordon. Damned serious. I had never expected that Gran would get us involved in something like this. I didn't have the slightest knowledge of this development project of his. Or, of the untendered deal for the office towers."

"Neither did I, Henry. It's all news to me."

"Well, the office towers are one thing but, this thing about Gran buying you the nomination, is something else again. This could kill us."

There was silence for a moment and then Bracken continued. "Damn. I just know that it's Don Mitchell who's feeding them all this information. It has to be him. He has to be their so-called source in the Prime Minister's Office. Doesn't he realize this isn't the way things are done? All of this should have been taken care of quietly – among ourselves – without bringing the media into it. Mitchell knows this isn't the way we deal with these things."

"Maybe Mitchell doesn't like the way we deal with 'these things'," Gordon said. "And I don't like the way Gran has been using me. I don't like picking up a paper and reading about me being bought-off as part and parcel of his Calgary land deal. I don't like it at all. Not one bit. And you know, Henry. You know that's the only reason he put up the money for the nomination in the first place. How could you go along with something like that? I trusted you."

"Believe me, Gordon, I didn't know a thing about what Gran was up to in Calgary. I had no idea. But I did – and believe me I did – I did want you to have the nomination. I have always liked you, Gordon. You've always been one of my favorite young Conservatives. And the fine work that you're doing with the Equal Opportunities Council gave me even more reason to support you for the nomination. I would have supported you without Gran's contribution. I believe in what you're doing, Gordon. I would have supported you anyway."

He certainly sounded sincere about it all. "Thanks, Henry. I believe you would have. Thanks for saying that. But it's all sort of academic now. Isn't it?"

"Maybe so, Gordon. Maybe so. Gran certainly has played fast and loose with us all in this matter. He should have told us what he was up to out there. He shouldn't have gotten us so involved in so – shabby is the only word for it – in so shabby an affair. I expected better from him. Much better. I've tried phoning him but he's out looking at some properties in the foothills around Calgary and can't be reached. He isn't expected back at the hotel until later this afternoon."

Bracken was silent again, and then he said: "This matter is going to do us a lot of harm. It could cost us the election."

"In Meadowbrook?"

"Right across the country if it isn't handled properly. Things like this can be sensationalized out of all proportion by the media and do irreparable harm. Damn Mitchell anyway. I simply can't understand why he would have leaked something like this to the media. I really can't. But he did. And we can't just walk away from it. The problem won't go away. We've got to deal with it. It has to be resolved."

Another silence, and then: "Damn Mitchell. And damn Gran, too. This is a dreadful business."

"Politics?"

"No. No. This business about the situation Gran has gotten himself – and the party – into out in Calgary."

"From what I've seen lately, it's hard to know where you draw the line," Gordon said. "Gran and Edwards and Saunders and all those other people are into so many deals together. It's hard to know which is politics and which is business."

"I regret having to say this but that does appear to be the way things often are. But you must bear in mind, Gordon, that they are all – all of them – very busy men. They couldn't devote the time they do to political affairs if they weren't able to look after their business interests in the process. And, this Calgary situation to the contrary, the public is better off having men like Gran Winston and Harland Edwards involved with both politics and business. What they do is, usually, in the best public interest. Among them and their associates, they create a tremendous number of jobs and pay a great deal of corporate and personal income tax.

"Without them, the country wouldn't be what it is today. I know that the Conservative Party simply couldn't function without their support. And, without the party, we wouldn't be able to win elections and form governments. You can't expect men of the calibre of Gran and Harland, or Jack Saunders for that matter, to put the time that they do into politics if they aren't provided with some mechanism for satisfying the self-interest of themselves and the corporations they represent. Things do, at times, and this Calgary deal is a perfect example of that, get out of hand. But, all in all, the overall public interest is served in the longer term."

"But, Henry, what do you do when, as with this deal of Gran's, things get out of hand?"

"We get them back in hand as quickly as possible so we can move forward with our objective."

"What is the objective, Henry?"

"The acquisition, retention and exercise of power. If you haven't got it, you can't exercise it. That's why we must stay in power."

"I see. It gets clearer by the minute."

"Right now, what we have to do is nip this thing in the bud. Get out of the line of fire. Can you come over to my office? We need to deal with this as expeditiously as possible."

"Sure, Henry. I can come over. I don't have any classes this afternoon so I'll have no trouble getting away. I'll be with you within the hour."

As Gordon drove towards Henry's office, he thought again about the prospect of some reporter snooping around Big Thunder and finding out about him and Bill being brothers. *Mum said Bill was born at the Morgan ranch and didn't move to Big Thunder until he was about two. There's bound to be people out there who know he wasn't born there. That his mum – our birth mum – died at the ranch and was buried at Big Thunder. If a snoopy reporter stumbles on that, he'll do some more digging around and find the real story. And then it'll wind up on the front page of the* Globe *or the* Toronto Star. *It's probably only a matter of time.*

When he arrived at Henry's office on the top floor of the main Bracken Department Store building, his secretary led him to the corner suite.

Bracken got right to it. "What Gran has gotten himself and the party into by putting together that deal about the office towers is one thing. But, this business coming out of the Prime Minister's office about Meadowbrook being 'bought' is another matter altogether. And I have absolutely no doubt that Mitchell is at the centre of it all. He does not want you to be the candidate for Meadowbrook."

"I don't understand," Gordon said. "The nomination meeting is over. I am the candidate. There's nothing Mitchell or anyone else can do about it."

"It's not entirely about you, Gordon. It's about your father-in-law and that questionable deal he wangled for the office towers. The point that you're missing, and I can understand perfectly well why that is so, is that this story about the nomination wouldn't even be in the paper if it wasn't for the fuss the Liberals are raising about the sweetheart deal for the office towers. Without the one, there wouldn't be the other. Gran is news because of the deal for the office towers. If the media didn't have their sights trained on him because of that, they would have ignored this stuff about you and the nomination altogether.

"If it wasn't for the fact that you are Gran's son-in-law, there would be no mention of Meadowbrook. None whatsoever. What this latest story is about is an attempt by the PMO to get the Prime Minister out of the line of fire. They've been looking around for a place to shovel hot coals, Gordon, to get the heat out of their kitchen.

"That's why someone up there has found out about, and leaked, our arrangement with Gran concerning the nomination. No one in Meadowbrook would have provided that sort of information to the newspapers. There is no reason at all why Meadowbrook should be caught up in this messy business. No reason at all."

And, Gordon said to himself, *there's no reason for me to stay caught up in it either. There's no denying Gran bought me the nomination. Everyone on the Meadowbrook executive knows about it. It's not going to go away. I'm tainted meat. And then there's the adoption thing. My goose is cooked either way. Might as well get it over and done with before I find myself reading about what someone at Big Thunder says about my birth mother on the front page of the* Globe. *This might be my only chance to exercise some control over the message. Control the ball. Henry has always been so supportive. He'll understand. He'll know how best to deal with it.*

"Actually, Henry, there's something I want to share with you. Something very personal."

"Oh," Henry said as he took a couple of puffs on his cigar, "and what might that be?"

"I'm half Indian."

"You're what?" Bracken exclaimed, almost choking on his cigar. "Half Indian?"

"Yes. That's what I am. Half Indian."

"You can't be serious. How on earth can that be?"

Gordon told him the story, pretty much the way his mother had laid it out for him on Friday night.

"Good God!" Bracken exclaimed. "I certainly hadn`t expected anything like this. This is incredible, Gordon. Quite incredible. I don`t know what to say."

"Neither did I when I first learned about it. And, even now, it still seems pretty incredible. But it is true. There's no getting away from it. It's true. Every word of it. I am half Indian.

"But – but why now? Why would your mother wait until now to tell you something like this?"

"Remember that Dr. Bill Eagletail who was on *Toronto Focus* with me? The guy with the braided hair and the bear claws?"

"Yes. Yes, I remember him well. Quite articulate for an Indian. Yes I remember him."

"He's my brother. It turns out we were both born on a ranch out in Alberta. He was raised at the Big Thunder Indian reserve, raised as a Blackfoot. When my mum saw him on TV and heard it was his mother's land Jack Saunders' pipeline is going through, she decided it was time to tell me about my birth parents, and the fact that Eagletail's my brother."

"My goodness, Gordon, this does put a different light on things. A different light indeed. If the newspapers get hold of this, they will crucify you. I've seen it before – seen them get hold of some personal matter about someone in public life – and hound the man until he is nearly out of his mind. They are merciless in their pursuit of anything that they consider to be in the public interest. In the public's right to know."

Cigar smoke swirled around Bracken's head as he took another couple of puffs. "The media would have a field day with this piece of information. Your being half Indian would be the main focus of their attention. They would set aside everything else about you and zero in on the unusual circumstances of your birth. They would never accept you as being our legitimate representative. They would start their stories off with something like: 'MacArthur's supporters do not feel that the fact that he is half Indian will hurt his chances of winning the election.' By the time they repeated that several times, the fact that you're half Indian would have become an issue – an issue that it would not have become if they had left well enough alone. And that would undermine your ability to represent Meadowbrook in the House of Commons."

Bracken paused. "Let me think for a moment. This is certainly not something I had expected to be dealing with – especially not on top of this other stuff about your father-in-law buying you the nomination."

He puffed on his cigar and thought things through. *This is quite a development. I would never have imagined, not for one moment, that he was a half-breed. Certainly doesn't look like one. But, he is and that means he's no damned good to us now. Not one bit. We can't possibly have someone like that – a person of mixed race – representing Meadowbrook in the House of Commons. He will have to be replaced. At the earliest possible opportunity. The sooner the better.*

He had a dozen phone messages on his desk from reporters who wanted to talk to him about the story in the *Toronto Star*. They would be asking some pretty pointed questions. *If Gran bought the nomination, then that means I must have sold it. I'm as involved in this as he is. And I don't see any way out of it. We did have a deal. Everyone on the executive knows about it. And yet, the fact that Winston is putting up the $25,000, when you come right down to it, is neither here nor there. That can be handled. It's not really all that different than the $15,000 he contributed toward Hal Davies' 1970 campaign. However, when the $25,000 is tied in with the statements Gordon has been making in the newspapers about Jack Saunders' pipeline, that puts an altogether different slant on things. It does appear, on the surface at least, that the two are tied together. The $25,000 for the nomination and Gordon's public support of the pipeline proposal.*

He moved over to his liquor cabinet and poured himself a Scotch and soda. "Would you like a drink, Gordon?"

"Thanks, Henry, I could use a drink about now. Vodka and orange if you've got it."

Bracken handed Gordon the drink and then sat at his desk and reread the article in the *Toronto Star* about Winston buying the nomination. "Who knows about it?" he asked. "About you being half Indian."

"My mum, Carol and the kids and Bill Eagletail. As I understand it, he's going to tell his mum and his son. And now you."

"Does your father-in-law know?"

"No, and I'm in no hurry to tell him."

Bracken lit another cigar. "So, I suppose, it's only a matter of time before others will know. People from outside your family."

"Guess so. It's all going to come out in the wash, as they say."

As it is going to come out eventually, Bracken thought, it might be as well to get it over and done with now. *Our white-pride candidate being half Indian will make quite a splash in the newspapers. Quite a splash indeed. And, depending on how we spin it, it could overshadow the stuff about Winston buying him the nomination and get the riding association out of the line of fire. All of the media attention will be focused on him and his Indian brother. The more there is about them, the less there will be about Winston buying him the nomination. All things considered, this would, in the longer term, be the least damaging course of action for the party. It is going to be a bit messy, though.*

"Gordon, I am going to need your resignation. Right now. Today."

"You want me to resign? Right now?" Gordon asked in stunned amazement. This was not at all what he had expected.

"Yes, I'm afraid that is the only way it can be."

Gordon was quite startled. He hadn't expected that Bracken would act that fast. Demand his resignation on the spot.

"But, why does it have to be today? Right now?"

"Because I've got a stack of messages from reporters to return and I need to nip this thing in the bud. Right now. I need a letter of resignation from you setting out the circumstances of your birth and acknowledging how that takes you out of the running as far as being a legitimate representative for Meadowbrook."

"Because I'm half Indian?"

"Yes, Gordon, because you're half Indian. People just wouldn't understand how we could possibly have you as our candidate. Being half Indian changes everything. You presented yourself at the nomination meeting as being white. As one of us. No one had any suspicion that you might be half Indian."

"But I'm half Scottish, too. Only half of me is Indian. I've been raised Scottish. That's what I`ve been all my life."

"Maybe so. That might well be so. But it's the Indian half of you that will get the media's attention. They'll see you as half Indian. Not half Scottish. Their emphasis will always be on the Indian side of you."

He's serious. He really does want me to resign just because I'm half Indian. Today. Right now. Fini. Got to buy some time. "I can't do that, Henry. This is all too personal to simply write a letter right now saying I'm resigning because of the fact I`m half Indian. I mean, I'm not the only one involved here. Bill Eagletail's involved, too. I can't just let you release a letter to the media saying we're brothers and that I'm resigning because I'm half Indian. I have to discuss it with him first."

"You might have a point there. I had forgotten about him. But that does not change the fact that I need your letter of resignation today. Talk to him about it and then get back to me – with the letter of resignation. It has to be today, Gordon. I can't put off returning these calls indefinitely. The reporters are all over me."

"Well, all right, I'll talk to my brother and get back to you. Mind you, he might not want to go public with this. Especially since he wants to talk to his son about it one on one. He's only eight."

"Perhaps it will not prove necessary to mention your brother. If he's not comfortable with it, the letter could just mention your part in the whole affair. You could leave him out of it altogether."

"That might be so, Henry, but I'm not going to commit to anything until after I have a chance to talk this over with him. I'll try and get back to you before eight. I'll move things along as quickly as I can."

"I suggest that you get back to me before seven, Gordon. Even at that, it will be a bit late for the *Globe*. Their Tom Ferguson has left three messages. I need to hear from you before seven."

"I will, Henry. I will get back to you before then. If I could use your phone, I'll set up a meeting with Bill Eagletail right now."

"By all means, Gordon. I'll let you have some privacy."

With that, Bracken picked up a file from his desk and left the room. Gordon placed a call to Bill.

As soon as Gordon left his office, Bracken poured himself another Scotch, sat down at his desk and lit a cigar. He puffed on his cigar and contemplated the best course of action, the best way of getting Meadowbrook, and the Conservative Party, out of the line of fire.

Maybe this story about Winston buying him the nomination is a bit of a godsend after all. If it hadn't been for that, this half-Indian business wouldn't have come to a head and we might not have learned about MacArthur's unfortunate Indian bloodline until the middle of the election. That would be disastrous. We couldn't possibly hold Meadowbrook under those circumstances. This way, we know soon enough to take appropriate action.

Bracken asked his secretary to put him through to the manager of the New Caledonia Hotel in Calgary. He told the manager that he was a close associate of Granville Winston's and needed to talk to him about an urgent matter.

"I understand that Mr. Winston is out looking at some properties in the foothills and is not expected back at your hotel until later this afternoon. It is imperative that I speak to him on the telephone the very moment he gets back. Can you take care of that for us? I know that Mr. Winston would be most appreciative of anything that you can do."

The manager said Winston was using the hotel's station wagon and he would try and contact him.

"I can get through to him on the radio phone – as long as he isn't behind some mountain. We should be able to get through to him, Mr. Bracken. Shall I try that, sir?"

"Please. Please do, Mr. – I didn't catch your name."

"Ainsworth, sir. Harold Ainsworth," the hotel manager said, rather proudly. "Harold Ainsworth, sir. Mr. Winston will know my name."

"I am sure that he will, Mr. Ainsworth. And I know how appreciative he is going to be. Now, Mr. Ainsworth, please get through to Mr. Winston as quickly as you possibly can."

Bracken gave him the number for the direct line to his phone. He asked the hotel manager to make sure Winston didn't return any calls before speaking to him first. Then he lit another cigar, leaned back in his chair, and sent smoke signals spiraling to the ceiling.

Winston's call came through shortly after four-thirty. He was calling from a phone booth at a service station in the foothills northwest of Calgary. "What's the problem, Henry?" Winston asked.

"I'm calling about a story in the afternoon edition of the *Toronto Star* that quotes someone in the Prime Minister's Office as saying that you quote bought Gordon the Meadowbrook nomination. The *Star* quotes someone in the Prime Minister's Office as saying that you contributed $25,000 to our election campaign fund on the condition that Gordon was to get the nomination without any competition."

"I'll be damned," Winston exclaimed. "Who would put them up to something like that?"

"My bet is on Don Mitchell," Bracken replied. "He was the anonymous source the *Star* was talking to before the nomination meeting last Thursday – when he made the crack about Gordon being a white power nut and out of his tree. He probably is their source. He'd do anything to keep Gordon from running under the Conservative banner. But that is not what I am interested in at this moment, Gran, not at all. I want to straighten out this matter about you having 'bought' the nomination. I want you to know that I will not accept your contribution."

"Won't accept it? What are you talking about, Henry?" Winston asked in a perplexed tone.

"Your offer of $25,000 in connection with Gordon getting the nomination is not acceptable to me. I will not, on behalf of the Meadowbrook Conservative Association, accept your offer."

"What do you mean not acceptable? You've already accepted it, for God's sake."

"I have? I have received a cheque from you in the amount of $25,000?"

"Of course you haven't got the cheque yet. You would have had it on the night of the nomination meeting but I got held up here. I won't be back in Toronto until Friday. You know that you haven't actually received the cheque yet."

"Then, as far as I am concerned, if there was no payment, there was no acceptance. Your offer was unacceptable."

"For God's sake, Henry, don't play games with me. You know that you accepted my offer. We had a deal. Gordon got the nomination, didn't he?"

"Gordon would have won the nomination without your money, Gran. He didn't need to have you buy the nomination for him."

"Oh, wait a minute. Wait a minute," Winston said, mulling things over in his head. "I think I get the picture. It's all coming together. Yes. I've got it now. It's all because of this stuff in the newspapers. Isn't it? Even if we did have a deal, the deal's off because of this stuff in the newspapers. Isn't that it, Henry. We can't close our deal because of this stuff in the newspapers. Right?"

"The reports in the newspapers about your untendered deal for the office towers are quite disturbing. The Liberals are going to push this one all the way. They smell blood and they're going to get their pint. But that's your concern. That has nothing to do with Meadowbrook. Nothing whatsoever. What does concern Meadowbrook is the allegation that you bought the nomination. The purpose of this call is to inform you that your offer is unacceptable. I will not accept your contribution."

Winston was silent for a moment, reviewing in his head what Bracken had been saying. He knew Bracken had him at a disadvantage. The deal for the government offices was going to look pretty bad when all of the details were wormed out at the Energy Board hearings and at the Public Works Committee. If he didn't handle things right, heads were going to roll – including his own. He could tell from Bracken's tone that he took a pretty dim view of the deal and felt that he had created a messy problem for the party. But he could handle that. He'd find a way. Meanwhile, he didn't want to lose Bracken's support altogether. He might prove useful to him later on. As for Gordon and the nomination, if Bracken was going to let Gordon keep the nomination without the $25,000, that meant he was getting an Ottawa contact he could rely on without having to pay a nickel for it. He couldn't have asked for a better deal than that.

"All right, Henry. I'll go along with that. If that's the way you want to play it. There will be no contribution. Gordon is the candidate and there will be no contribution. I will go along with that. Is that the way that you want to deal with it?"

"Yes, Gran, that is the way that we are going to deal with it."

"Fine. I read you, loud and clear. Gordon will be the candidate. Is he there? I'd like to talk to him."

"No, Gordon's not here."

"But he will be the candidate, right?"

"Gordon is the candidate," Bracken replied. He saw no point in telling Winston he had asked Gordon to resign because he was half Indian. All of that would come out later. The main thing right now was to deal with the story about Winston buying him the nomination.

"I called you, Gran, so that you would know how to deal with questions resulting from the story in the *Toronto Star*. As there was no $25,000 contribution – no deal – Meadowbrook was not bought. The report from the unnamed source in the Prime Minister's Office is false. If any of the reporters get through to you, I suggest that you tell them that the allegation is false. That is all that you need to say about the matter. Is that clear, Gran?"

"But other people knew. Your executive knew. They even discussed it."

"We will not deny, if it does come to that, that there were discussions, Gran. The key point however is that nothing came of those discussions. He got the nomination and you did not pay one red cent. That, and that alone, is all that matters. Also, and I believe this will work to our advantage, it would be helpful if you could have your office provide a copy of the cheque you wrote for Hal Davies' 1970 campaign. It was for $15,000 as I recall. That establishes a precedent. Shows that there is nothing untoward about you paying a substantial amount of the cost of the Meadowbrook election campaign. What is untoward is the connection that has been made in today's *Toronto Star* between your contribution and the comments Gordon has been making in support of running that pipeline through the Indian reserve. Keeping it off your land. It does, in my mind, smack of collusion. Makes it look like there was some agreement between you and Gordon. A *quid pro quo.* However, that is for you to deal with. It has nothing to do with Meadowbrook."

"Okay," Henry, "I get your point. You don't have to rub it in. And, yes, that is for me to deal with – along with all the other questions I will have to address regarding the deal for the office towers. I understand."

"Good, Gran. I'm glad that we see eye to eye. Just deal with any questions about the $25,000 the way I suggested. Deny it. Deny it forcefully. As no money changed hands, they can't prove a damned thing."

CHAPTER
- 30 -

Bill was waiting for Gordon at a table by the window in the restaurant at the Sutton Place Hotel. He'd been working on some papers in his office when Gordon called and said he needed to meet with him on an urgent basis. Gordon didn't give any details. Just said they had to talk ASAP.

"So, what's the emergency?" Bill asked as Gordon ordered a coffee. "Something to do with that story in the *Toronto Star*? Pretty messy stuff – him buying you the nomination like that. I wouldn't want to have something like that on my record."

"It's not the way it looks," Gordon said. "I'd have gotten the nomination even without the $25,000 contribution which, by the way, goes toward the cost of the election campaign. I don't get a nickel of it."

"Maybe so. Politics is bad enough as it is without making it worse," Bill said.

It was only then that Gordon fully understood the seriousness of the business about his father-in-law buying him the nomination. He hadn't given it all that much thought when Gran and Henry first made the deal. He had just rather naively considered it to be part and parcel of the political process. But that wasn't the way the media looked at it. And it obviously wasn't the way Bill looked at it either. To Bill and the others, it seemed to be as serious an offence as accepting a bribe. *This is not the time to get into that can of worms.*

"Anyway, that's not the reason I needed to see you. Henry Bracken, the president of the Conservative riding association, called me after the story came out and asked me to come to his office. I told him about me being born out at the Morgan ranch and he wants me to resign as the candidate for Meadowbrook. He wants my letter of resignation tonight."

"Why would you tell him about that? Where's the benefit in that?"

"Because, it's all going to come out somewhere down the line and I thought this was as good a time as any to get it over and done with. This stuff about Carol's father buying me the nomination is pretty serious. Serious enough that I'd probably have had to resign anyway. So, I did it. Got it over and done with."

"Does that mean you told him about me, too?"

"Yeah, because, if it wasn't for being on *Toronto Focus* with you, I'd never have known about it in the first place."

"You should have talked to me first, Gordon. You had no business telling anyone about me without giving me a heads up."

"Just like you consulted me before telling Carol we're brothers? It's not from me she first heard that. She learned about that from you."

"Touche," Bill said with a smile returning to his lips.

"Anyway, that's no longer the point. It was all going to come out at some stage anyway and I thought, under the circumstances, the time had come to tell Henry Bracken. Mind you, I didn't think he'd make me resign on the spot. He's always been very friendly toward me. Very supportive. But, he's pretty definite about it. Wants me to get back to him before seven o'clock tonight."

"That's pushing it," Bill said. "That's less than two hours from now."

"I know, but, he's got a pile of messages from reporters wanting to ask him about the story in the *Star* about Carol's father buying me the nomination and he can only keep them at bay for so long. That's why he said seven."

"Well, that's not going to happen. Two hours is not nearly enough time. He's going to have to make them wait."

"I'm with you on that. Things are happening too fast, way too fast. And I think I know what he's up to. He wants to shift the focus away from the story about Carol's father buying me the nomination and put it on me resigning because I'm half Indian. That's what the headline's going to be: 'White power candidate half Indian.' The media's going to have a ball with this."

"You're probably right. Smart move on his part. That said, there's no way we're going to settle this tonight. I just can't go public with this, or have anyone else go public with it, until I'm able to sit down with my mom and Albert. Albert does need to hear everything, directly from me."

"I'm with you on that. There's no way I would have told Charlie or Diane about something this personal over the phone. It does have to be done in person."

"Actually, I phoned my mom right after our lunch today. I'd meant to call her sooner but thought it would be best to wait until after we had our talk. She's pretty upset. She went on and on about how they should have told me about it but, almost word for word the way your mom put it to you, they felt that, with both our birth parents dead and buried like that, it was best to leave well enough alone and not talk about it. Like you did with your mom, I told her not to come down so hard on herself and that I still loved her and no one could ever take her place. She's my mom and that's all there is to it."

"Yeah, it's hard on them, too. I can understand how our mothers must feel. It's going to take some time for all of us to adjust to this new reality."

"You've got that right."

"Did you ask her about the chances of some reporter finding out we're brothers?"

"Yes, and you're right. Most of the older people who knew my mom and her sister know about me. That I wasn't born there. As far as they were concerned, it was no big deal. Just accepted me as being her son. But, if someone did start poking around, it wouldn't be too hard to find out about us."

"I'd as much as suspected that. It's probably all going to come out sooner than later."

"Probably, especially with all the media attention about the pipeline. Anyway, I phoned my mom again right after I read the story in the *Star* about Carol's dad buying you the nomination. There's a reporter from the *Calgary Herald* who wants to interview her tomorrow – not about the selling of the nomination – he wouldn't have known about that yet. But about the pipeline proposal. She put it off but you can't do that forever. The reporters are like wolves. When they smell blood, nothing can stop them. Anyway, she wants me to be there when the reporter interviews her and, beside that, I really do need to tell Albert about the adoption thing. So, I'm going out there. I've booked a flight for eight tomorrow morning. I really want to be with my mom and my son right now and I have a real need to be at Big Thunder, to spend some time there. I need to re-establish my connection with the land and – and – with my people. I am a Blackfoot, Gordon, and that's the way I want to stay."

"Just like I want to stay Scottish. That's who I am. And that's the way I'm going to stay – despite what happened out there at the Morgan ranch."

"Yes, Gordon, we're both going to stay who we are – who we were raised to be. Meanwhile, I want you to stall Henry Bracken. Don't let him say anything about us until after you hear back from me. Okay? I'll talk to my mom and Albert and then I'll get it straightened out and get back to you probably sometime around supper your time tomorrow night. Meanwhile, Bracken's just going to have to keep his mouth shut about us."

"He won't like that."

"Screw him. This is our lives we're talking about. Ours and our families'. He's just going to have to keep a lid on things until after I get back to you."

"I'm with you there but, in fairness to him, that's about twenty-four hours from now. That's a long time to put the media on hold."

"If he's as smart as you say he is, he'll find a way. This is the best I can do. I'll try and have it all wrapped up by this time tomorrow. That's my best offer, Gordon. Take it or leave it."

"I'll take it and, I'm pretty sure, Henry will find a way to put things on hold until tomorrow night. He's a shrewd old bird. Still, that doesn't change things. I'm still going to have to resign. You should have seen the look on his face when I told him I was half Indian. He actually turned pale. All the colour left it. You could see in his eyes that that's it as far as he's concerned. There's no way they'd accept me as their representative in the House of Commons."

"You're right about that – absolutely right. I'm pretty certain it will be the same thing for the Equal Opportunities Council, too. I've heard

Don Henderson's Rule Britannia spiel more than once. He'll turn his back on you faster than you can spit."

Yep. There goes me down the drain. Gurgle, gurgle, gurgle. Bye bye, Gordie. Ain't life grand? "Maybe, with this pressure Henry's under from the reporters, I could give him a letter of resignation dealing with my part in this —not mention you. That way, he could get back to them tonight like he wants to – around seven."

"That wouldn't work. The first thing the reporters will ask is 'Why now?' Why'd your mother wait all these years – thirty-five years – and all of a sudden decide to tell you now? When they ask that, you'll have to tell them about being on *Toronto Focus* and about me. No, Gordon, we've got to do this clean. We're both going to have to come out at the same time. Let's see how things stand tomorrow night."

"Alright. That's how we'll do it. I'll tell Henry you're flying out to Calgary tomorrow morning and we can't do anything until after you've had a chance to talk to Albert – one on one."

"Okay. Now, I've got to go. I've made arrangements for someone to take charge while I'm away. I'll probably stay out there for a few days – and I've still got to pack."

"Alright. I'll call Henry right now from the phone in the lobby. I'll call you later and let you know what he has to say."

〜

When Gordon got through to Bracken he told him about his meeting with Bill and that they would appreciate it very much if he could stall things until Tuesday night.

"I'm afraid it's a bit late for that," Bracken said. "Tom Ferguson from the *Globe* came to my office just after you left, parked himself in the reception area and insisted on seeing me. Now the *Globe* has been very favorable in its coverage of my rezoning application for the new store I want to build out in Scarborough and, quite frankly, I really do need to keep them on side. So, I granted him a brief interview. He was on a very tight deadline and there was no way I could put him off."

Damn, Gordon muttered. *Probably told the reporter all about me and Bill.* "And what did you say to him, Henry? Did you tell him about me being half Indian?"

"Of course not. I would never do anything like that. That is something for you, and you alone, to deal with. What I did do was tell him that the story about your father-in-law buying you the nomination was false. Absolutely false. Not one penny changed hands."

"But you did have a deal, Henry. Everyone on the executive knew about it."

"That's true. However, I told him that, while there was one discussion, no deal was made. No money changed hands. I also brought it to his attention that your father-in-law paid a substantial amount of the costs of Hal Davies' 1970 campaign. So, there is a precedent. What is different this time is the unfortunate connection that has been made between your father-in-law's contribution to the upcoming campaign and your comments in the newspapers supporting the gas pipeline they want to put through that Indian reservation. I told him I knew nothing – absolutely nothing – about that and that he would have to address any questions along that line to your father-in-law."

"I see. So, you said nothing about me being half Indian?"

"Not in those exact words. However, I did say that I had been given to understand that you would be resigning as our candidate for personal reasons. Not for anything to do with the questions that have been raised about your father-in-law's contribution to the election campaign."

Sonofabitch, Gordon muttered, *he really is cutting me loose.* "Why would you do that, Henry? Why would you say I was going to resign?"

"Because you are going to resign. There is no other way. I need your resignation and I need it tonight. I want this issue off my plate. Tonight."

Damn. He's really pushing hard. Can't wait to be rid of me. "But couldn't it have waited until tomorrow night? Until my brother had an opportunity to tell his son face to face. What's the big rush?"

"The big rush is that the election could be called any day now and I'm going to have to find an appropriate candidate to take your place. I'll have to call another nomination meeting and have someone in place to start campaigning as quickly as possible. That's the 'big rush'. I'm running out of time. Your resignation has to be effective immediately."

"So, my being half Indian really does make that much difference?"

"It makes all the difference in the world. We couldn't possibly have you representing us in the House of Commons. The whole situation has changed. Irreversibly."

Gordon decided there was no point in pursuing that line of discussion. Bracken's mind was made up, and closed. "So, did you tell the reporter from the *Globe* that I would be resigning right away?"

"Yes. I told him that I expected I would be receiving your letter of resignation early this evening. Mind you, now, I did not give him so much as a hint of the fact that you are half Indian. I just said it was something personal, extremely personal, that had come up in the last couple of days and that you would be laying it all out in your letter of resignation. I did not make so much as one comment about that other matter."

Thanks a million, Henry. That's mighty generous of you. Stick me in the pot and let someone else light the fire. "So, is he going to call you later on to see if you've received my letter of resignation."

"Actually, no. As I told you, Ferguson is on a very tight deadline. It is my understanding that he was going to phone you at your office and ask you why you were going to resign."

"Thanks a lot, Henry. That's real generous of you. You really are determined to hang me out to dry."

"There's no reason to talk to me in that tone of voice, Gordon. This isn't something of my doing. If your mother had told you about this at the appropriate time, we wouldn't be in this unfortunate situation."

"Leave my mother out of it, Henry. She had her reasons for not telling me about this before."

"That might very well be so. But it's neither here nor there. I have to play the hand that I've been given and I'm dealing with it in a manner that I believe to be in the best interest of Meadowbrook and of the Conservative Party. And now, I must go. I have a meeting that starts in about ten minutes and I can't discuss this further with you at this time. I'll leave it to you to deal with Ferguson and the other reporters in whatever way you see fit."

"The other reporters? What other reporters?"

"As things went over so well with Ferguson, I decided to deal with the other reporters while I was at it. So, I returned all of their calls. I had already called your father-in-law and he knows what to say when they call him. Plausible deniability. That's the way we are playing it. Deny. Deny. The nomination matter is now dealt with. The only item outstanding is your letter of resignation."

"You son of a bitch. You're hanging me out to dry."

"That is your interpretation. Now, I must go. Goodbye." With that, he placed the phone on the receiver, lit another cigar and complimented himself on a job well done.

Gordon called his office right away. The receptionist was just leaving for the day and, yes, there were several messages for him. One of them, marked "urgent" was from Tom Ferguson of the *Globe and Mail.* He said he really needed to talk to Gordon before seven o'clock. The others were from the *Toronto Star,* CFTO, the CBC, *Toronto Sun* and a couple of radio stations. And, Carol had called – had actually called a couple of times that afternoon – and wanted him to know she had taken the children to the swimming pool and they wouldn't be home until around seven.

Gordon asked the receptionist to leave the messages on his desk and said he would return the calls when he got there. Then he went to the bar and ordered a vodka and orange. He looked at the clock on the wall. It was just after six.

Well, no one knows I'm here. Can't do much damage sitting here having a quiet drink. I need some time to get my head straight. Damn Henry. He's really put me in a corner. This changes everything.

He finished his drink, went back to the lobby and phoned Bill at his house. When he got Bill on the line, he told him about his phone conversation with Bracken and about the stack of messages that were waiting for him at his office.

"Sonofabitch," Bill said. "He really knows how to change the channel. The whole focus is going to be on you and me now. The stuff about your father-in-law buying you the nomination is old news. This gives the reporters a juicy new bone to chew on. Sonofabitch."

"He is that," Gordon said, "but that doesn't change the reality of it all. What should I do?"

"Let me think. Let me see if I can figure out our best move."

Bill was silent for a moment, sorting things out in his head. "Well, the key thing right now is that reporter from the *Globe*. If you talk to him tonight, like he wants you to, there'll be a story about what you said in the paper tomorrow morning. Canadian Press will probably pick it up and it will be in the *Calgary Herald* tomorrow afternoon. Same thing goes for the TV and radio reporters. In fact, they'll have something on it right after you talk to them. And we don't want that. We need more time."

"You mean I should just ignore them? Not call them back?"

"Why not? Screw them. They're only interested in selling newspapers. Selling cars, cigarettes and beer. We don't have to go by their schedule. Screw them."

"But, what about Henry. If Ferguson doesn't hear from me by seven, like he said in the message he left, he'll be calling Henry and asking if he got my letter of resignation."

"Then that will be Bracken's problem. Let him deal with the *Globe*. If he doesn't have a letter of resignation from you, there's not much he can say about it."

"I don't know about that. He'll probably tell him anyway."

"Not necessarily. From what you told me, the reporter from the *Globe* reacted quite positively to the spin Bracken put on the part about Carol's father buying you the nomination. That cools that part down. Considerably. No, I think that, with that out of the way and the reporters knowing that you are going to resign, Bracken will be inclined to let things take their course. As far as he's concerned, he's in the clear. The nomination thing has been dealt with and you're going to resign. He's probably happier than a pig in shit."

"So, I ignore the reporters?"

"For tonight anyway. I'll see if I can switch to the eight-thirty flight tonight. That would get me there around eleven Calgary time and I can have everything wrapped up by noon tomorrow. Mom, Albert, the whole thing. I'll ask my brother to pick me up at the airport. Yes, that's the best way to deal with it."

"Okay. I'll just go straight home. That way, I won't get the messages at the office until tomorrow morning. And I won't take any calls at home. Carol can tell them I'm out at a meeting and can't be reached."

"Sounds good, Gordon. That will buy us time. Give me the number you're calling from and I'll call Air Canada and see if they can get me on the eight-thirty flight. I'll get right back to you."

Gordon gave him the number for the pay phone and waited to hear back.

"It's all set," Bill said when he called back. "I'm on the eight-thirty. It's tight but I'll make it if I leave right now. Hughie will pick me up at the airport."

"Okay, then I'll just stay here and have another drink. I'm in no hurry to do anything. No hurry at all."

Gordon went back to the bar and ordered another vodka and orange. As he sat there sipping his drink, he looked up at the big mirror behind the bar and thought he recognized someone sitting alone at one of the tables. It looked an awful lot like Hal Davies, the Meadowbrook MP the Prime Minister asked to get out of politics after he got the daughter of the president of the United Indians of Canada Association pregnant. He'd known Davies for quite some time and they had always been on good terms. Gordon was the canvass captain for Davies' last two election campaigns.

He turned around for a closer look. It was Hal Davies. He picked up his drink and walked over to the table. "Well, hello, Hal," he said. "May I join you?"

"Of course, Gordon, of course. Please sit down. Actually, I had been meaning to call you."

"You were? About what?" Gordon asked as he settled into the cushioned chair.

"About the statements you've been making in the newspapers about the pipeline Jack Saunders wants to run through the Big Thunder Indian reserve. I thought that ..."

"Hold on, Hal. Hold on. All of that has changed. Changed like you wouldn't believe."

He paused for a moment and wondered if he should tell Davies about Bracken wanting him to resign. Perhaps, he thought, as Davies had gotten that Indian girl pregnant, he'd be a lot more understanding about things than Bracken had been. And, Davies was known to be a strong supporter of the Indians, especially when it came to their unsettled land claims. He decided that he would confide in Davies. *What the hell, I've already told Henry.*

Gordon told him the story about his Uncle Bill and Big Thunder and the fact that Bill Eagletail was his brother. He also told him about Henry Bracken's negative reaction to the whole affair and that he wanted him to resign as the candidate for Meadowbrook.

"He wants my letter of resignation tonight. Can't wait to be rid of me."

"That doesn't surprise me," Davies said. "Henry has no tolerance whatsoever for anyone who doesn't salute the Union Jack morning, noon and night. He is, actually, a full-blown bigot. If his customers knew how he felt about immigrant people, there would be a helluva lot fewer of them buying stuff at his stores. I once heard him, in private, referring to them as the 'Off-the-boat people'. That said, I can understand why he would want you to resign. Your being half Indian would not go over well in Meadowbrook. They will want someone of their own kind representing their interests in Ottawa. I know those people, Gordon. I've been their MP for seven years."

"And you were a good MP, Hal. One of the best. I heard about the way the Prime Minister forced you to step aside over the incident with that young Indian girl. I'm sorry things worked out that way."

"Don't be, Gordon. There's nothing to be sorry about. And, it was no 'incident'. We're getting married next July – right after Josephine graduates. My divorce will be final by then."

"You are? Well, congratulations. I wish you both all the very best."

"Thanks, Gordon. Yes, things did work out rather well. Her father's okay with things now. It was her being pregnant that set him off on the warpath. But he's okay with me now. We get along very well together. In fact, I'm doing quite a bit of legal work for the United Indians of Canada Association and, after we get married, I'll be moving my law practice to Calgary. I've got a lot of work lined up out there. Now, back to your situation. I don't see any option open to you other than to resign. Henry's right on that score. You just simply can't represent Meadowbrook now. I'm not saying that's fair, or just, but that is the reality of the situation."

"You're probably right. I've sort of accepted that. What I didn't tell you, though, was that Henry has already told Tom Ferguson from the

Globe that I'm resigning 'for personal reasons' and that he's expecting my letter of resignation tonight. He told some other reporters as well."

"Sonofabitch," Davies exclaimed. "He's playing hardball with you. Anything to get the focus off your father-in-law buying you the nomination and onto the fact that you're half Indian. Sonofabitch."

"That's what my brother said when I told him what Henry was up to. 'Sonofabitch'. In fact, I called him that myself just before he hung up on me."

"Still, I can understand Henry's position. The party has always come first with him. He'll do whatever it takes to protect the party and Meadowbrook. That's the way politics works."

"I've seen all too well how politics works lately."

"That's why they call it a blood sport, Gordon. That's what it is. How is your brother taking all this? Bill Eagletail?"

"Actually, he's catching an eight-thirty flight to Calgary tonight so he can tell his son – who's only eight – about all this before it hits the papers out there. I'm not going to say anything to the reporters until I hear back from him."

"That's a wise decision, Gordon. They're going to make a big deal out of the fact that you're half Indian. Especially after all you've been saying about 'renegade Indians' threatening our gas supplies. That's why I was going to call you. You had it all wrong."

"Probably, but that's all academic now. What I've got to do now is figure out how best to put this to the reporters when I do get around to returning their calls."

"Don't rush into that. They have their agenda and you should have yours. You don't have to march to their drum. Don't do anything until you're absolutely sure that whatever you decide on is the best course of action. The best option to exercise. And now, Gordon, I have to be off. I'm meeting someone at seven fifteen and I really must take my leave. Good luck and let me know how things work out. If there is ever anything I can do for you, anything at all, don't hesitate to call. Here's my card. Trying me at my law office first is the best bet."

"Thanks, Hal. I'll keep that in mind," Gordon said as they shook hands.

Gordon stayed at the table and ordered a roast beef sandwich and another vodka and orange. He was in no hurry to get home. He'd give Carol a call and see if any reporters had been trying to reach him.

"Where have you been?" Carol asked when he called her. "I've been calling all afternoon. I read the story in the *Globe* about Dad owning the property that's blocking Saunders from running his pipeline down the side of Big Thunder and then I read that story in the *Star* about Dad buying you the nomination. I knew about the deal for the nomination but I had no idea – not the slightest – that Dad's company owned that property adjacent to Big Thunder.

"He's never breathed so much as one word about it to me. Not a word. I tried calling him at the hotel in Calgary but they say he can't be reached until later tonight. And, I've been trying to reach you. Your receptionist said you had gone out but she didn't know where."

"I had a meeting with Henry. He called me right after he read the article in the *Star*. Then I met with Bill."

"This is serious, Gordon. The Liberals and the media are going to crucify Dad – and you – about the deal for the nomination and I'm certainly going to give him a piece of my mind about forcing Saunders to run his pipeline through Big Thunder."

"It does look bad," Gordon said. "Pretty awful."

"What about you? What's the situation?"

"It's a bit complicated. It's better that we talk about it when I get home. I'm just having a bite to eat right now and I'll be home as soon as I can."

"Well, alright, but that was quite a story in the *Star*. Whatever are you going to do about it?"

"You're right, but that's all academic now. Henry asked me to resign."

"What on earth for?"

"I told him I'm half Indian and he said that changes everything."

"Why on earth would you tell him something as personal as that?"

"Because I am and I don't see any point in trying to keep it secret. It will all come out anyway. Everything's kind of going to shit."

He gave Carol an outline of what had happened between him and Bracken and, also, about the discussion he had with Bill.

"Bill's flying out to Calgary tonight so Albert will hear this directly from him. He doesn't want to do it over the phone."

"That's good. Albert will need to have Bill with him."

"Yes he will. Anyway, let's leave it at that for now. I'm still sorting things out in my head and we'll talk some more when I get home. Were there any calls for me?"

"No. Mind you we only got home about ten minutes ago."

"Well, if anyone does call, anyone from the newspapers or the radio and TV stations, tell them I'm at a meeting and can't be reached. Henry told Tom Ferguson from the *Globe* that I'd be resigning tonight 'for personal reasons'. Ferguson's already left an 'urgent' message at the office. I don't want to talk to any of the reporters until after I hear back from Bill. Until after he's had a chance to talk to Albert."

"That's good, Gordon. That's good, waiting until after you hear back from Bill about how Albert is taking it all. All right then, I'll tell any reporters who call that you're at a meeting and can't be reached. I'll also tell Charlie and Diane not to answer the phone. So, I'll see you later?"

"Yes, I'll be there."

Gordon decided to take a drive through the west end of Toronto on his way home. He wasn't in any hurry. He drove south on Bay and turned west on Dundas. The House of Chan Restaurant was on his right and the Peking Tavern on his left. The sight of the restaurants and stores in Chinatown reminded him of the smell of the Chinese hand laundry his mother had used from time to time. She'd send him off with the yellow ticket with the black Chinese letters on it and, as soon as he walked in the door, his nostrils were greeted with the smell of the steam, starch and laundry detergent.

He had often noticed, while walking through Chinatown, that there was about a third more men than there was women. That was because, his father had told him, the Canadian government had, after about sixty-five hundred Chinese labourers helped build the Canadian Pacific Railway, passed the *Chinese Immigration Act of 1885* barring Chinese women from getting into the country to be with their husbands. The *Act* imposed a "head tax" of $50 on every Chinese person entering Canada and made family reunification next to impossible. His dad told him that that was because it was widely believed at that time that the Chinese bred like rabbits.

How awful it would be, he thought, if he were to move to Australia and find that he couldn't send for Charlie or Diane to come and live with him. That was one of the advantages of being white. The Australians would never dream of doing that to a white person or his family. Gordon was one of their own kind. At least half of him was. *What if I moved to Australia and they found out that I'm half Indian? Would that make a difference? It probably would.*

He turned north at Bathurst and then west on College through the shops and stores of Little Italy. Lombardi's Supermarket. Giovanna's Pizzeria. Sicilian Ice Cream Store. Foglia Meats. When he got to Roncesvalles, he turned south towards the Queensway. Polish shops like Sir Cazimir's Bakery. Polska Butcher. Kowalski's Fine Furniture.

As he turned west on the Queensway and headed home, he reflected on the fact that there wasn't a single MacGregor's Meats on the entire route. Nowhere to buy black puddings, tripe or Scotch pies. He wondered where all the Scottish butchers of his youth had gone.

Carol was sitting in the chair beside the fireplace reading *Zorba the Greek*. She reached for her drink and thought about Bill as she watched the flames chip away at the logs. He had called from the airport to tell her he was flying to Calgary and would probably be away for a few days. She told him Gordon had filled her in on their discussion and the reason for the sudden trip.

"This is something I have to do," Bill said. "With this latest stuff in the papers about your father buying Gordon the nomination things are coming to a head. God knows where that's going to take us. So, I need to go out there and talk to my mom and Albert about the adoption thing. I need to prepare him for whatever comes next."

"I think that's a good idea, Bill. I only wish I could have seen you before you left."

"Me, too. I was originally going tomorrow morning and I was going to ask you if you could have a coffee with me tonight. But then

Bracken told the reporters Gordon was going to resign tonight and I had to move things up. But I will call you tomorrow. Let you know how things are going."

"I'll be waiting and, Bill, I really do hope things work out for you and Albert. I know how much you care for him and how important it is for you to be with him right now. He's lucky to have you."

"Thanks, Carol, I really appreciate that. I really do."

"About that article in the *Globe* this morning – about my dad owning the property next to your community. I want you to know that I had absolutely no idea that Dad owned that property. He never breathed so much as a word about it to me."

"I was quite sure that you didn't. The property only changed hands a few months ago. And, with it being held in trust by the lawyers, he probably didn't want anyone to know about it. That's a pretty high-stakes business your father is involved in. I imagine he keeps a lot of things close to the chest."

"He does. Anyway, I'm going to talk to him about forcing Saunders to run his pipeline through your land. I'm certainly going to talk to him about it as soon as he gets back to Toronto."

"That'd be good, Carol. I'd really appreciate – oops, got to go. They're calling my flight. I'll call you tomorrow." And then he was gone.

When Gordon got home, he went straight to the kitchen and poured himself a vodka and orange. "Want a drink?" he asked.

"Got one, thanks. But I could do with a top up."

"So," Gordon said as he poured her some more Scotch, "were there any calls?"

"That Tom Ferguson from the *Globe* called about half an hour after I got home. I told him you were at a meeting and couldn't be reached. He asked me about the letter of resignation and I told him I hadn't the slightest idea what he was talking about."

"That was a good way to handle it. Anyone else? Any other reporters?"

"No. Ferguson was the only one. By the way, he wants you to call him at his office after ten tomorrow morning. He said he has some questions he wants to ask you."

"He'll have a long wait in Hell for that," Gordon said. "I'm in no hurry to talk to any of them, at least not until after I hear from Bill."

"Bill called me from the airport," Carol said. "He's on his way now."

"What did he say?"

"Not much. Pretty much what you'd already told me."

"Where's Charlie and Diane?"

"They're watching TV. I'll be getting them ready for bed soon."

"Have you said anything more to them about me being half Indian?"

"No, I think we should both be present when we discuss it further. They didn't say a thing about it when we were at the swimming pool. I don't think it's going to be that much of a problem for them."

The phone rang. "Shall I get it?" Carol asked.

"Sure. Just don't tell anyone I'm here."

"Oh, hello, Dad. Hold on for just a minute," Carol said as she placed her hand over the receiver.

"It's Gran" she whispered.

Gordon shook his head and placed his finger over his lips. She got the message.

"Sorry about that, Dad. I had a pot on the stove."

"Is Gordon there? I need to speak to him."

"He's at a meeting and I don't expect him home until quite late. Shall I have him call you?"

"Yes. Please do. I need to talk to him about this stuff in the *Toronto Star* suggesting that I bought Gordon the nomination."

"Suggesting, Dad? You did buy it for him."

"That may be so but Bracken and I are going to deny it. Outright deny it. Not a penny has changed hands."

"Well, that's between you and Henry. I'm sure you'll be able to deal with it."

Carol had suspected for some time that her father was using Gordon – buying him the nomination so he would be able to make use of him when he got to Ottawa. While she took a pretty dim view of it, she decided not to say anything. Gordon wouldn't be the first person her father had used to further his business interests. That's how he worked. Always had worked.

"I expect you'll have more difficulty with the item in the *Globe* about the deal for the office towers," she said. "That's quite a lot to have on your plate at one time."

She wanted to tell him how disappointed she was to find out that it was because of him that Saunders was trying to ram his pipeline through Bill's land. But then, that could lead to him asking her why she was so interested in the issue and then she might be inclined to let him know she'd be fighting the pipeline alongside Bill. *That really would complicate things. Better to wait until he gets home and have it out with him face-to-face.*

"I'll handle it. It's not unmanageable. Anyway, I've got to go now. I have a meeting with Jack Saunders in about ten minutes and I really must go. Please have Gordon call me the minute he steps in the door."

"I'll tell him, Dad. And good luck with those problems you're dealing with. I know you'll make it all go away. You always do."

"What did he say?" Gordon asked after Carol put the phone down.

"He says they're going to deny that he bought you the nomination. No money changed hands so, as far as Dad and Henry are concerned, no one can prove a damned thing."

"It'll probably work. The whole focus now is going to shift to my being half Indian. Bill said Henry is probably happier than a pig in shit."

"I've no doubt that he is," Carol said. "Henry's as shrewd as they come."

Charlie and Diane came into the kitchen to get some more potato chips. The program they had been watching had just ended. "Hi, Dad," Charlie called through to the living room. "Didn't know you were home."

"Hi, Daddy," Diane said. "Me neither."

Gordon decided this was as good a time as any to tell them he was no longer going to be a Member of Parliament. "Come through here for a couple of minutes," he said. "I've got something I want to tell you both – something important."

"Two 'important' things in one day," Charlie remarked as he sat down on the couch. "This is probably going to be a day to remember."

"It is," Gordon said as they sat down at the table. "It is going to be a day we will all remember."

He told them about the meetings he had with Bill and Bracken that afternoon and that Bracken had asked him to resign. "So, it looks like I'm not going to be a Member of Parliament after all."

"Because you're half Indian?" Charlie asked.

"Yes, Son. Because I'm half Indian. Most of the people in Meadowbrook are white and they wouldn't want someone who is half Indian representing them in Ottawa."

"Why not?" Diane asked. "We're part Indian, too. Why wouldn't they want you?"

"They just wouldn't," Charlie said. "Frank told me how some people in the apartment building act toward him and his dad. They're the only Indians there. Some people don't like Indians. They don't like the Chinese either. Henry Lee lives in the same building as Frank."

"But Daddy is only half Indian," Diane said.

"Doesn't matter," Charlie said. "That's the way they are. That's bad news for you, Dad, but it's good news for us. I didn't like the idea of you being in Ottawa most of the time. I like it better when you're here."

"Me, too," Diane said. "I doesn't like you being in Ottawa neither. No way, Jose. You belong here with us. And you, too, Mommy. You guys belong with us. Ever and ever."

Carol hadn't expected that. Leaving the children was going to be a lot harder than she had thought. Things weren't nearly as clear as she had expected them to be. Too many "what ifs?" She decided she'd call Ben Horowitz first thing in the morning and, depending on his availability, put the meeting about the divorce over until later in the week. "Of course you'll always have us. Forever and ever," she said reassuringly. "We're always going to be a part of your lives."

"That's good," Diane said. "That's the way it's supposed to be, Mommy."

Charlie said he wanted to go to his room and finish a book he was reading. Diane was pretty tired from swimming and wanted to go to bed.

"I'll take them up," Carol said.

"Okay," Gordon said. "I've got some essays to mark and then I think I'll turn in myself. I didn't sleep much last night."

"Then I'll see you in the morning," Carol said. "I'm going to my room after I put them to bed."

She picked up *Zorba the Greek* and took the children to their rooms.

Bill's brother was waiting for him at the luggage carousel. They gave each other a warm hug and headed out to the yellow and blue pickup truck from the garage in Okotoks where Hughie worked as a mechanic.

"So, what brings you out here all of a sudden?" Hughie asked as he pressed down on the clutch pedal and put the truck into gear. "What's up?"

"Did Mom say anything to you? About why I'm here?"

"Not really. She said something about wanting to have you with her when she has to deal with the reporters. They've really been pestering her over the last couple of days. But that's about it. Except, she wants me to take you straight to Janet's place. She's not been feeling too well the last couple of days. Couple of dizzy spells. Albert's with Janet. She's going to leave the lights on and wake you in time to have breakfast with Albert before he leaves for school. Mom's going to join you in the morning if she's feeling up to it. But, other than that, that's all she said. So, what's up?"

Bill told him the story about his birth parents and being with Gordon on *Toronto Focus*.

"Holy crap!" Hughie exclaimed. "That's some story. Pretty incredible if you ask me. Crap! I can't believe it."

"I didn't want to believe it either. But it is true. Mom told me when I phoned her this afternoon. It is true. He even knew you had asthma when you were a kid."

"You're kidding? He knew about that? Well, if Mom says it's true, then it probably is. What you going to do about it?"

"First thing, I've got to tell Albert all about it. Tell him myself. That's why I'm here now. I'm pretty sure all of this is going to come out in the Toronto papers over the next couple of days and I want to prepare Albert for when it hits the *Calgary Herald*."

"Can't see that it's such a big deal," Hughie said. "Most of the Indian leaders I know are half white. Metis or half Scottish or Irish or something like that. I wouldn't get all worked up about it if I was you. Roll with it. It's no big deal."

"Maybe not. But, I want Albert to hear about it directly from me. I need to be the one who tells him about it."

They drove on in silence for about a mile and then Hughie lit another cigarette. "I guess you haven't heard about Jean. She's back at Big Thunder. Came back last week."

"She is? No I didn't hear about it. How did that happen?"

"She caught Starlight screwing some white woman. His secretary I think it was. Came home early one afternoon and found him in bed with her. From what I hear, it wasn't the first time Starlight cheated on her. Anyway, as far as I can tell, it's all over between them."

"Good. She had that coming to her. Should never have walked out on Albert like that."

"She's staying with Starlight's sister until she gets a place of her own."

"That won't be for long. She'll find some other rich guy who'll buy his way into her ice-cold heart."

CHAPTER
- 31 -

Carol was sitting at the kitchen table reading that morning's *Globe and Mail*. "There's a story here I think you should read," she said as she handed Gordon the paper with her finger pointing to an article in the lower left corner.

He took the paper and cast his eyes on the story.

Conservatives look for new candidate
By Tom Ferguson

The Meadowbrook Conservative Association is calling "an emergency" nomination meeting to replace "white power" candidate Gordon MacArthur. No date has been set.

Riding president Henry Bracken told *The Globe* in an exclusive interview last night that MacArthur, a professor of political science at the University of Toronto, has resigned "for personal reasons."

Bracken, who is Chairman and Chief Executive Officer of Bracken Department Stores, said he was not at liberty to discuss what MacArthur's "personal reasons" were.

"It's something that came up in the last couple of days," Bracken said. "MacArthur decided that, under the circumstances, he had no option but to resign. I agreed with that assessment."

Bracken said he was expecting MacArthur's letter of resignation last night. As of press time, no letter had been received.

"We are moving forward with an emergency nomination meeting," Bracken said. "MacArthur's letter is a mere formality."

Reached at their home last night, MacArthur's wife said he was at a meeting and could not be reached. Calls placed to MacArthur's office at the university yesterday afternoon were not returned.

"I don't know anything about any letter of resignation," Carol MacArthur said. "Gordon certainly didn't give me any indication that he was going to resign."

Bracken said there was no connection between MacArthur's sudden resignation and reports that his father-in-law, Granville Winston, CEO of Winston Holdings Limited, had "bought" him the nomination.

"That report is false. Absolutely false," Bracken said. "We did not receive so much as one red cent."

A report in another newspaper claimed yesterday that Winston had paid $25,000 toward the cost of the Meadowbrook election campaign on the condition that his son-in-law get an uncontested nomination.

"There's no truth to that. No truth at all," Bracken said.

MacArthur was acclaimed as the Conservative candidate for Meadowbrook last Thursday night. No other name was put forward.

Winston is believed to be on business in Calgary. Calls to the hotel he is staying at were not returned.

MacArthur has been dubbed the "white power Conservative" because of allegedly racist comments he has made about minority group people.

He is the driving force behind the recently-formed Equal Opportunities Council – a group of university professors fighting for "equal rights" for white students.

Bracken said he has called a meeting of his riding executive to set a date for the "emergency" nomination meeting.

"We will have an appropriate candidate in place as quickly as possible," Bracken said. "With the election expected to be called any day now, we have to move forward with the utmost dispatch."

"My God!" Gordon exclaimed. "Henry really is playing hardball. Why'd he go and do a thing like that without telling me?"

"Henry's only interest is in doing what's best for the party and for Meadowbrook," Carol said. "He's shoving you as far away from them as he can. Doing a pretty good job of it too, I must say."

"Well, any letter of resignation is sort of academic now. Isn't it? As far as Henry's concerned my candidacy's as good as dead and buried."

"Afraid so, Gordon. He's already got you in the coffin. There's not much point in giving him a letter. It is, as you just said, kind of academic now."

Gordon thought things through for a minute. "Maybe, with this story in the *Globe* saying Henry's already looking for another candidate, there's not much point in returning any of those calls from the reporters. Maybe, with this out in the open now, they'll leave me alone."

"Don't count on it Gordon. Remember what you said to me before you stomped out of here Friday morning? 'I'm on the front page of *The Globe*. I'm a reality. Living history. Screw you, you goddamned virgin.'"

"You remember that?" Gordon said rather sheepishly.

"Yes, Gordon, I remember vividly every word you said that morning. While much of what you said was true, you could have found a better way of expressing it. Still, let's not get back into that. What I'm saying is that you are front-page news. 'Living history' as you put it. That's why you're back on the front page of the *Globe* this morning. They're not going to leave you alone."

"Guess not. Still, I'm not going to return any of their calls until after I hear from Bill. This concerns him, too."

"Yes, it does and I really appreciate the fact that you're thinking about what's in his best interest as well."

"Well, there are two of us involved. He's come up with some good ideas about how we should deal with this mess. I'm glad I'm not going through it alone."

"You're not alone. Gordon. You've got me and the children. We'll see to it that you get through this in one piece. We're all in this together."

"Thanks, Carol. I really do appreciate how supportive you've been throughout this whole thing. It's meant a lot to me. And, I really am sorry for the way I spoke to you Friday morning. I shouldn't have lashed out like that. I am sorry."

"We've both said and done more than enough to be sorry about. Let's not get back into that. Let's concentrate on what's the best course for you right now."

"You're right. Still, there's not much to do until I hear back from Bill. They're two hours behind. He should be getting up any time now."

Charlie and Diane came in for breakfast, sat down at the table and started in on their bran flakes.

"And how are you guys?" Gordon asked. "Sleep okay?"

They'd both had a good night's sleep.

"Daddy," Diane said as she reached for the milk, "which part of me did you say is Indian? The top part or the bottom part?"

"Just one quarter. You're only one-quarter Indian."

"That's all?" she said.

"Dad's right," Charlie said. "We're only a quarter Indian. Hawkeye was born white but he became as much an Indian as any of the Mohicans."

"Who's Hawkeye?" Diane asked. "I don't know nobody called Hawkeye."

"He's the main guy in the book I'm reading. It's called *The Last of the Mohicans.* Hawkeye was raised by the Indians and then he rescues these two white sisters after they're kidnapped by the Hurons."

"Did they hurt them?" Diane asked.

"Just a little bit but Hawkeye got them back to their parents safe and sound."

"That's good," Diane said. "So, they all lived happy ever after, right?"

"Yes," Carol said as she put the pancakes on the table. "Everybody lived happily ever after. I've made a fresh pot of coffee, Gordon, do you want some?"

"Yes, please. That would be lovely."

He turned to Charlie. "Why would the school have you reading a book like that? I wouldn't expect you to be reading something like *The Last of the Mohicans* for another couple of years yet."

"Oh, it's not from the school, Dad. I got it from Frank Fontaine. My best friend I told you about. The one whose Granddad lives on the reserve up on Manitoulin Island?"

"Oh, yes. I remember. The boy who lives in the apartment building near your school. So, you like the book? I haven't read it myself but I have heard about it."

"Yeah. There's lots of action in it. The Mohicans adopted Hawkeye when he was real young and, when he grew up, he rescued two white sisters who'd been captured when the Hurons and the French wiped out British troops and settlers during a massacre. Back when they were having something called the French and Indian wars. It's a really good book."

"I read it," Carol said. "It's pretty ponderous and gets a bit bogged down at times but it does paint a very positive picture of the Indians. They had a movie retrospective at the Bloor Cinema a couple of years ago and I saw Randolph Scott playing Hawkeye in a 1936 adaptation. It was a great movie and that's why I bought the book. Believe me, Gordon, the book is hard reading. The movie's a lot better."

"Yeah, some parts are a bit hard to read. A bit thick," Charlie said. "But I really like the story."

"Maybe the movie will be playing again some time and I'll take you to see it," Gordon said.

"You're on, Dad. I'd like that."

"Me, too," Diane said. "Don't forget me. I'm Indian, too."

"Yes, you'll see it, too," Carol said. "We'll all see it together – as a family."

They finished their breakfast and Carol got the children ready for school.

"I'll be out for most of the day," she said. "Anne should be here any time now. She's got a fair bit of cleaning to do. As for me, I'm having lunch with Jonathan Hollinger. From what he said on the phone last week, I'm pretty sure I'll be back at Haldimand and Brock in no time at all."

"That's good, they're a very good firm and I'm sure you'll do well there. Do they still handle all of your father's business?"

"Yes, but that's not why they're thinking of taking me back. Jonathan made it perfectly clear that he thinks a lot of me and they would consider taking me back with or without my father's account."

"I didn't mean to imply anything like that. Sorry if I gave the wrong impression. I was just wondering if Gran was still a client of theirs."

"No offence taken. I know you didn't mean it that way. Yes, he's still one of their major clients. What about you? What are you going to do?"

"I'm going to hide out here. If I go to the university, Henderson and the others will be all over me about the story in the *Globe.* They'll be pressing me on the 'personal reasons'. I don't have any classes today so I'll stay here, at least until I hear from Bill. I'll ask Anne to screen any calls that come in. I'm not going to say a word to anyone until Bill gives me the green light."

"Good idea, Gordon. Now, I'm off. Have a good day. We'll talk again at supper."

With that, she headed out the door with Charlie and Diane.

Albert's face lit up when Bill walked into the kitchen. "Hey, Dad," he said excitedly as he moved toward his father. "Aunt Janet said she had a surprise for me but I didn't expect it would be you."

Bill gave him a big, long, hug and kissed him on both cheeks. "And how's my boy? How're you doing?"

"I'm fine, Dad. Just great, especially now that you're here. Why didn't you tell me you were coming?"

"Didn't know I was until yesterday," Bill said. "I'll fill you in later."

He gave them all a hug – his mom, sister, Hughie, Janet's husband Alf and their two young children – his nieces. Sandra was a year younger than Albert and Debra was four. Bill sat down at the table between his mom and Albert.

"You're looking good," Sarah said. "Been working out?"

"No, Mom. But I walk a lot. It does good things to my head. I hear you haven't been feeling too well."

"Been getting dizzy spells. Find I have to lie down a lot. But I'm okay today."

"When did you last see a doctor?"

"Had a check-up a couple of years ago."

"Mom, that's not good enough. We'll go to the health centre tomorrow and get them to have a look at you. Could be high blood pressure or something like that. I'd feel a lot better if someone had a look at you. We should get your blood tested."

"Okay, I'm not going to argue with someone who has a PhD," she chuckled. "We'll go tomorrow."

They exchanged chit chat as they ate their bacon and eggs and drank strong, dark, coffee. When it looked like they had all just about finished, Bill decided that, since they were all family, he might as well tell them the story about him being adopted and half white. It would probably be better, he thought, for Albert to hear it with people who loved him hearing it at the same time.

"I've got something to share with you all," he said. "Something Mom has known about for a long, long, time but never got around to telling me."

"I had my reasons," Sarah said, a bit defensively.

"I know you did, Mom, and I'm glad you and Dad decided to handle things the way you did. I've no complaints about that. Not a single one." He reached over and gave her hand a gentle squeeze.

It was clear that the curiosity of everyone in the room was now on full alert so he went ahead and told them the story, almost word for word the way Gordon had told it to him only three days before.

"He told me last night," Hughie said rather proudly when Bill had finished, "on our way home from the airport. I'm still having trouble believing it's all true."

"It is true, Hughie," Sarah said. "Every last word of it. Just the way William told it."

Bill reached over and put his arm around Albert's shoulders. "So, my son, what do you think about all that?"

"It's hard to say," Albert said. "I hadn't expected anything like that. I don't know."

Sarah reached in front of Bill and took Albert's hand in hers. "It's really nothing for you to be all that concerned about, Albert. My sister loved your dad's birth father very, very, much. It was lovely to see them together. How much they loved one another. But then, fate intervened, as it has a habit of doing at times, and we lost Helen, my sister, just like your dad just said we did. And then, as your dad just said, his birth father got killed by the Japanese over there in Hong Kong. So then, they were both gone. Your dad has lived with us since he was just about two and his brother was raised way out there in Toronto.

"None of us expected that they'd ever meet. Not with them being two thousand miles apart like that. But then, like your dad just said, they did meet and now they know they're brothers. And that's why your dad's here now. To make sure you hear all this from his own lips. Like, maybe, he should have heard it from mine – at the right time."

"No, Mom," Bill said. "You didn't do anything wrong. Under the circumstances, with them both being dead like that, there wasn't anything else you could do."

"I'm not so sure about that, Son, but it's all water flowing under the big bridge now. We can't change what's past. It's about tomorrow and the future we've got to look."

"Let me get another pot of coffee," Janet said. "I think we could all use a cup about now."

"Scotch would be more like it," Hughie said jokingly.

"Not at this hour," Sarah said rather firmly.

"That's another weird thing," Bill said. "I really like Scotch. Always have. But my brother, Gordon, drinks vodka all the time. He says it's probably because I've got Scotch in my blood. When I asked him about the vodka, he said maybe there's a little bit of Russian in him."

That lightened things up a bit. They had all found Bill's story very unsettling.

"What happens now," Janet's husband asked.

"Well, Alf, that's one of the reasons I'm here – here on such short notice. My brother, Gordon, was going to be the Conservative candidate for a lily-white riding in Toronto but now, now that he told the riding president he's half Indian, he's been asked to resign. They don't want someone who's half Indian representing them in the House of Commons. It'll probably be in the Toronto papers and that means it's only a matter of time before it's in the *Calgary Herald.*"

"The reporters have been calling me just about every day about the pipeline thing," Sarah said. "I asked William to come out here and help me deal with them. He wasn't supposed to be arriving until today. But then, that president he mentioned demanded his brother's resignation yesterday afternoon and that kinda speeded things up a bit."

"I see," Alf said. "You're probably right. It's only a matter of time before they'll be banging on the door. Somebody told me there was a professor at the University of Toronto raising a big fuss about Saunders' pipeline. Saying that white women and children would freeze in the dark next winter if the pipeline didn't go through our land. Is this brother of yours connected with him? The white guy who's been stirring up all the trouble?"

"That is him," Bill said with a smile. "One and the same. Gordon MacArthur, champion of the white underdog. But, seriously, yes, that's him. That's Gordon. Mind you, he's changed his mind about a lot of things, including the pipeline. Especially now that he knows he's half Indian."

"No crap," Hughie said. "That was him? I heard about it, too. That makes it even more weird."

"Watch your mouth, Hughie," Sarah snapped. "This isn't a locker room."

"Sorry, Mom. I'll keep a zip on it."

"I suppose he has family," Janet said. "Are they with him in Toronto?"

"He says his dad died about three years ago," Bill said. "Got killed by a drunk driver as he crossed the road on a green light. His mom's still alive."

"Just like Granddad Eagletail," Janet said. "The guy who hit them with the truck was drunk at the time."

"Yes, he was," Sarah said. "There's all too many folks drinking and driving. What about a wife? Does this new brother of yours have a wife and family?"

"Yeah, he's married. Got a wife and two kids. The boy's about Albert's age and his daughter is – is about four, I think. Haven't met them yet but I've been invited to have dinner with them when I get back to Toronto."

"So you're their uncle. That's weird," Hughie said. "I'm their uncle, too. Weird, eh?"

Bill thought they would consider it even weirder still if he told them he'd spent the weekend with Carol up at the cabin. *That would really catch their interest. But this is most definitely not the time for that.* "So, that's the situation," he said. "I wanted to come out here so you would hear it from me – especially you, Albert – before there was anything about it in the *Herald* or on the TV or radio."

"I'm glad that you did," Janet said. "Especially for Albert, like you said. Maybe it would be better if Albert skipped school today and spent some time with you. What do you think about that, Albert? Would you like to spend the day with your dad?"

"Are you kidding?" Albert said. "Me skip school and spend the day with my dad? You bet it's okay. That's a double bonus. No school and a whole day with my dad."

"How come him and not us?" Sandra asked. "We'd like to spend time with Uncle Bill, too."

"I'm sure you would but this is a special day for Albert and your uncle. They need to spend some quality time together. A ride would do them both good."

"Are you sure about that, Janet?" Bill asked. "Are you sure that'd be okay?"

"It would. Albert's way ahead of most of the other kids in his class. It'll be fine. I'll call the school right now and tell them you're only here for a couple of days and want to spend some time with Albert. I'll tell them he'll be back in school tomorrow. You can take him for a ride if you want. Albert gets on real well with the Pinto and you can have Alf's Mustang. It's settled down a lot since he first broke it. You should be able to handle him."

"William's a good rider," Sarah said with a note of pride in her voice. "His dad taught him real well. He'll have no trouble at all handling that horse."

"Okay," Bill said. "I think it's a great idea. But, right now, though, I'd better call Gordon in Toronto and tell him it's okay to speak to the reporters. I'm going to convince him not to say anything about me at this stage. Just give his own reasons for stepping down as the candidate."

"Why would you do that?" Hughie asked. "What's there to be ashamed of? So, you're half Scottish? So what? Who gives a damn one way or the other?"

"I'm with Hughie on that one," Alf said. "My grandfather's Ukrainian. Never bothered me. Never cared two hoots about it."

"Fred Manywounds' granddad is Irish," Janet said. "Used to trap martens on Thunder Mountain. Doesn't do any trapping now but he is Irish."

"What about you, Mom?" Bill asked. "What do you think I should do?"

"I agree with Hughie and the others," Sarah said. "This is going to be a lot harder on Gordon than it is on you. Being half white goes over a lot better than being half Indian. At least that's the way I've always heard it. People are more tolerant of Indians who have Scottish, French or Irish fathers than they are when things are the other way around. Like, when it's a white person with an Indian mother. That's what I've always known."

"And you, Albert? What do you think, my son?"

"It's up to you, Dad. Do what you think's best. I'm fine either way, especially if our day together includes a ride on the Pinto."

Bill thought for a moment. "Okay, that's the way it will be. I'll tell Gordon to tell them the whole story. The whole shebang. And you're right, Alf, there is nothing to be ashamed of. Your grandfather was Ukrainian and mine was a dirt-poor Scottish hill farmer. A hundred years from now it's not going to make any difference one way or the other. Okay, can I use the phone in the bedroom, Janet? I'll call Gordon right now."

"Of course you can. I'll just clear up these dishes. And, Bill, I'm glad you're here. I've missed having you around."

"I've missed you, too, Sis. It is good to be home again."

Bill's call came in around 11:45 a.m. Toronto time. Anne almost missed it because she had the vacuum on in the living room. Bill gave Gordon an overview of how things had gone with Albert and the family and said it was okay with him for Gordon to get back to the reporters.

Gordon told him about the item in the *Globe* that morning and that it was clear that Bracken was hanging him out to dry.

"If it's in the *Globe*, it will most likely be in the *Herald* this afternoon or tomorrow," Bill said. "It's a good thing I came out here."

Gordon told him about the reporters who had called.

"I'm not sure I want to call them back, one by one," he said. "There were three more calls this morning. Our housekeeper took the messages and said I couldn't be reached. It might be better for me to put out a statement and say I won't be taking any questions. I really don't want to go into any detail with them. It's none of their damned business."

"I don't know what to advise," Bill said. "I've never dealt with anything quite like this."

"Me neither," Gordon said with a chuckle. "It's as new to me as it is to you."

"I can understand why you wouldn't want to deal with them one by one," Bill said. "They can get quite intrusive with their questions. But, then again, I really don't know."

"Hal Davies, my current MP, would know," Gordon said. "He's had a lot of experience dealing with the press as an MP. I bumped into him in the bar at the Sutton Place Hotel last night and he gave me his card and said to let him know if I ever needed any help. Hal's a lawyer."

"I know that," Bill said. "I've met him a couple of times on some work he's doing for the United Indians of Canada Association. Yes, he would have a better idea of how to handle the media end of it."

"He didn't say anything to me about having met you."

"Probably didn't think it was appropriate at the time. Anyway, give him a call."

"I'll do that – right now," Gordon said, "and I'll let you know what he says."

"You're not going to be able to reach me until later this afternoon, Calgary time. I'm taking Albert for a ride. My sister will pack us a lunch and we'll probably be out for four or five hours. I have every confidence that you and Davies will quickly settle on the best course of action. As for me, I'm going riding with my son. Being with him right now is more important to me than any of this other stuff. And, for what it's worth, I prefer just issuing a statement. You can tell them, very briefly, about me if you want and emphasize that neither one of us will be taking any questions from the reporters."

"Okay, that's how we'll handle it. Sounds like you're having quite a good time out there."

"I'm home, Gordon. This is where I belong. Home with Albert and my mom."

When Gordon phoned Hal Davies at his law office, he brought him up to speed on the latest developments. "The big question is, do I deal with the reporters one by one or just issue a statement and say I won't be taking any questions?"

"On the face of it, I'd lean toward the statement," Davies said. "But, it would have to be very carefully worded. You don't want to get off on the wrong foot."

"I'm already off on the wrong foot if you ask me. But, you're right. I don't want to do anything that would make matters worse than they already are."

Davies paused for a moment. "Gordon, I'm going to help you get through this. Quite frankly, while I have some sympathy for Henry's position on this matter, on the question of the impact your being half Indian would have on the election, I really don't like the way he's going about it. Especially not with the way he put things in that story in the *Globe* this morning. He really is, as I said last night, playing hardball with you. You deserve better than that. I suggest that you come over to my office and we will draft the statement together. My office has the fax numbers for all the newspapers, radio and TV stations and all that, and we can handle getting it out for you."

"That would be great, Hal. Are you sure you're okay with that?"

"Absolutely sure, Gordon. You're in a tough spot – tougher than it needs to be. I'll be more than happy to help you get through this. Can you come over in about an hour? I'm tied up right now but I should be clear by around one. I'm on the ninth floor of 330 Bay Street, right at Bay and Adelaide."

"Great, Hal. I'll be there. And thanks. Thanks a million."

"You're more than welcome, Gordon." He paused. "You understand, of course, that if Josephine, the girl I'm going to marry, hadn't had the miscarriage, our child would have been half Indian. Just like you. So, I have a personal interest in seeing that you get through all this in as unscathed a manner as possible. I'll see you at one."

"Hadn't thought about your children. That goes for Charlie and Diane, too. They're now one-quarter Indian. I'll be there."

Carol sat across from Jonathan Hollinger at the Haldimand and Brock conference table and munched on the smoked salmon on rye he had ordered for their lunch along with the lobster bisque. The conference room was on the southwest corner of the thirtieth floor of the Royal Trust Tower. As she reached for the Perrier, Carol looked down the long boat-shaped oak table surrounded by about thirty blue Italian leather executive chairs. She then looked south and took in the view of the Toronto Islands and the plane taking off from the island airport. *This is it. This is where I'm supposed to be. Back where I belong.* She settled into the plush comfort of the chair, took another glance out the window at the Toronto Islands, with Lake Ontario stretching out beyond, and focused her attention on Hollinger.

"So, you're ready to get back in the game," Hollinger said as he poured the coffee into the Royal Albert fine bone china cup. "That's good. And you are good Carol. I always knew that you'd make a good lawyer. We've missed having you with us."

"It was really tough missing out on the Gotham Gold Corp. case," Carol said. "I put a lot of work into that."

"You did and, because of the foundation you laid, we should have won the case – with costs."

"I know. Read about H and B losing it in the newspapers. Anyway, I had some difficulty after I had Diane but I feel the time is right to, as you put it, get back in the game. I am ready."

"When can you start?" Hollinger asked.

"I'll have to make some arrangements about the children and other things. How about first thing Monday morning?"

"That will be perfectly fine. Next Monday it is."

At that point, Hollinger slid a thick blue briefing book across the table. "This is a case we're handling for the Toronto Children's Hospital. It's pretty complex. Quite challenging. Jack Stinson is heading up the team. He's an absolutely first-rate lawyer. Superb. You'll enjoy working with him."

"I'll put forward my best effort," Carol said. "I'm sure that I can make a positive contribution."

"I've no doubt about that," Hollinger said. "You're going to do well being back here again. Now, I have to go. I have to be back in court. Sorry for the rush but I ran into some unexpected complications this morning. Please relax and finish your coffee. When you get here Monday morning, ask for Julia Hamilton, our new office manager. She'll have some papers for you to sign and then she'll assign you an office. Always remember, Carol, you are a great lawyer. One of the best."

He's right, Carol said after saying goodbye to Hollinger, *I am one of the best. Got what it takes to be a damned good lawyer.*

She took another look down the long conference table and imagined it surrounded by top-ten lawyers listening to her outline the strategy for a complex, multi-million dollar court case. Then she looked out the window at another plane taking off from the island airport. *Up up and away. Up there where I belong. Up there where eagles fly.*

Gordon got to Hal Davies' office just before one o'clock.

"I'm glad you called," Davies said. "I was thinking about our talk at the Sutton Place Hotel after I got home from my meeting last night. What's happening to you could very well happen to one of my children twenty years from now if things don't change. The Henry Brackens of this world are just going to have to move over and give others a chance. The lily-white world they grew up in has gone the way of the horse and buggy. We are, in every sense of the word, a multicultural society.

People from all over the world have settled here in search of a new life. Just like your dad and your Uncle Bill.

"They came across the ocean from Scotland because they wanted a new life in a new land. And they found it. They found it here in Canada. You're part of that new life that they found. You're part of that new generation of people. A new breed of people on the face of the earth. The people they call Canadians. That's what we are, Gordon, Canadians. Bracken and all the other diehard dinosaurs are just going to have to adjust to that new reality."

"You're right about your children. If things don't change, they could very well experience what I'm going through twenty years from now. Just like it could happen to Charlie and Diane. You're right about that, Hal."

"You bet I am. If this happened to a mid-level executive at Bracken Department Stores, Bracken would be open to a pretty expensive suit for wrongful dismissal. His decision is based, one hundred per cent, on the newly-discovered fact that you're half Indian. And that, Gordon, is outright discrimination. Race-based discrimination."

"Maybe I should sue him," Gordon said with a chuckle.

"If you were an employee at one of his stores, you could. But, you're not. Now, let's get down to the business at hand. The main thing right now is to get you out of the media's line of fire with as little damage as possible. I've thought it through and a simple statement is the best way to go. Let's put something together that will be acceptable to you and your brother and get it out to the newspapers within the next hour."

"You don't have to worry about Bill. He's out riding with his son. As far as he's concerned, the most important thing right now is to be with his son and he said he'll be fine with whatever we decide."

"Good for him. That's exactly what I'd do if I was in his shoes. Being back at Big Thunder for a few days will do him the world of good."

They worked on three drafts of the statement and then settled on the one Davies thought was the best. Davies had decided that it would complicate matters if they were to make any mention of Bill in the statement. It would create a distraction, he said and there was no valid reason to go into that at this stage.

"That should take care of it rather well," Davies said after he read the statement over again. "I'd like to be there when the reporters ask Bracken to explain why he demanded your immediate resignation."

"Me, too," Gordon said. "And I think you're right about leaving my brother out of it. I'm the main focus of attention right now – they don't have a clue about Bill being my brother. This will give him more time to deal with it in his own way."

"That is the wiser course, Gordon. Bringing your brother into it at this early stage would make matters even worse. It would cause even more controversy. Let him know this is the way we decided to deal with the matter – read the statement to him if you want – and tell him to take it from there in any manner that he sees fit. It's his life. Let it be his call."

"Okay, and thanks, Hal. I couldn't have dealt with this without your understanding of politics and the press. I really like switching the focus to Henry like that. He's going to be really pissed with me."

"Let him be. Two can play hardball. Putting the ball back in his court is a smart move. It will be interesting to see how his customers react when this comes out in the newspapers. It's time the public saw Henry for the WASP bigot that he is. And now, Gordon, I have to be off. I've got a meeting at three and it's up in Woodbridge. I've got to get going. My secretary will type this up and get it out to the media. We're just going to send it to the newspapers, the *Globe,* the *Star* and the *Sun.*"

"Why's that? Why not to the radio stations and the TV?"

"For one thing, they'll call you right away. Probably have something on the air within a matter of hours. That's too soon. We need more time. When the *Globe* and the *Sun* hit the streets tomorrow morning, the radio and TV reporters will get the story from there. Right now, we'll just send this to the newspapers. We'll get better, coverage there than the ninety seconds we'd get with a radio report."

"I see. Learning something all the time."

"The fax will have my firm's name and fax number at the top of the page. Doesn't hurt to let them know that you've got a lawyer working with you on this."

"Thanks, Hal. I appreciate all that you've done. I was thinking about going to the university but I think I'll just go for a drive and clear my head. I'll tell the receptionist I won't be there."

"Good idea. If you went to the university, they'd be all over you like a bear on honey. Tomorrow morning is soon enough. If, for whatever reason or other, some reporter does get through to you, just confirm what is in the statement and be quite emphatic about the fact that you have nothing further to say about this matter. Not one word. Meanwhile, you can call your brother from here if you want. Just dial eight to get the long-distance line."

When Gordon dialled the number Bill had given him, his sister answered the phone. She said Bill had filled them all in about the situation at breakfast and he had taken Albert for a ride.

"I'll bet he takes him up the mountain," Janet said. "Bill loved going there with my dad." She paused for a moment. "So, I guess we're sort of related, you being Bill's brother and all that."

"Looks that way," Gordon said. He really wasn't inclined to get into a conversation with her. *It's a bit early for us to get all lovey-dovey and into the* All in the Family *thing.*

"We're all real proud with the way things turned out for Bill – going to Berkeley and being a professor and all that," Janet said. "Real proud."

"And you have every right to be. Now, when you see him, please tell him that we decided on a statement, as he had suggested, and it's going out to the newspapers right now. Tell him we decided not to say a word about him because that's something he should do himself whenever he feels the time is right. So, he should not be expecting any calls from the newspapers about this. They're not going to bother him."

"I will," Janet said, "but you should know he feels okay about letting people know he's half white. We all do. It was discussed at length at breakfast and everyone feels fine with it – my mom, Hughie, my brother, and, I guess most important of all, Albert. No one sees any problem with it. In fact, my mom says it's probably going to be easier on Bill than it's going to be on you. People are more accepting of Indians whose fathers are white than they are of white people whose mothers are Indian. At least, that's the way Mom put it to us this morning."

"Your mum's probably right about that," Gordon said. "I don't see Bill having to resign from anything because of the fact our dad was Scottish. But, me, I've already had to resign as the candidate for Meadowbrook and I'll probably have to resign as the chairman of a group I started up at the university. Yes, it is going to have more of an impact on me. Anyway, Janet, it was good talking to you and I really would appreciate it if you would pass my message on to Bill and have him call me at home. I should be there around five or six Toronto time."

"Good talking to you, too, Gordon. I'll have Bill call you as soon as he gets home."

Bill and Albert were on the right-of-way about halfway up Thunder Mountain eating the lunch Janet packed for them. The horses were tethered in the shade of the trees at the side.

"That's quite a horse," Bill said pointing to the black Mustang. "But he knows who's boss now."

The Mustang was quite high strung and had tried, unsuccessfully, to buck Bill off three or four times during the first ten minutes of their ride.

"You should have seen him when Uncle Alf brought him home for the first time," Albert said. "No one had been on him before. Took a lot to break him but he's okay now. You did good, Dad. For a minute there, I thought he was going to throw you."

"He gave it his best shot," Bill said, "but we've reached an understanding, me and that horse have."

They sat silently by the campfire looking east over the prairie stretching out toward Calgary. Things looked pretty much the same as they had when Bill's dad took him hunting whitetail deer back when he was fourteen. Except, now, Calgary had spread out a lot more, the Husky Tower dominated the skyline and there was a lot more traffic toing and froing on the Trans-Canada Highway. And, down on the left, he could see three of Saunders' gas wells.

He wondered if the dizzy spells his mom had been getting lately had anything to do with leaks from those wells. *Got to find out if that sour gas is causing those dizzy spells Mom's been getting. That's really dangerous stuff. Hydrogen sulphide. Poisonous as you can get. Should also check with Hughie when he gets home from work and see if his asthma's any worse lately. They should both have their blood checked. No telling what might happen with that sort of stuff in the air.*

He took another look at the steel skeleton of the processing plant Saunders was building and put another branch on the fire. Then he put his arm around Albert's shoulders and gave him a hug.

"All of this territory used to belong to the Blackfoot," Bill said, pointing his finger from north to south, just as his dad had done twenty-five years earlier. "It was all ours."

He told Albert the story about the Blackfoot and the white settlers, much the same way his dad had told it to him. "There's a lot more of them now, an awful lot more, and a lot less of us," he said. "But, we've still got Big Thunder. This is still our land."

"And I like it here, Dad. I really do. It would be great if you were here, too. I really miss you."

"I miss you, too, Son. More than you can imagine. It really tears my heart out for us to be so far away from one another. It really does."

"When will I be going back to live with you in Toronto?"

Bill poured them both some more tea from the pot on the rock at the side of the campfire. "Would you like that?"

"Living with you again, yes. Toronto, I'm not so sure. I really like it out here. It's a lot different than the city."

"You're right about that, my son. I feel I belong here. Like, this is home. I never felt the same about Toronto as I do about Big Thunder."

"Me, too. I belong here, too."

Bill told him about the offer he had received from the University of Calgary.

"Are you taking it?" Albert asked.

"Actually, yes. I've been thinking about it a lot lately and now, being back here at Big Thunder, it looks more attractive by the minute."

"We could stay here. Right? Stay here with Grandma and Aunt Janet. Not go back to Toronto."

"On the weekends anyway. If I do take the job, we'd probably get a place in Calgary and spend the weekends here. We could stay at Grandma's house."

"Great! And we could ride all we wanted to. Uncle Alf would let us ride his horses. I just know he would."

"He wouldn't have to. We'll have our own horses. Would you like a Pinto?"

"I'd rather have a Mustang like Big Black over there. Pintos are for kids."

"Oh, I wouldn't say that, Albert. Back in the old days, most of the Blackfoot war chiefs rode Pintos. But, that doesn't change the fact that you're not ready for a Mustang yet. I'll get you a nice Appaloosa like my dad used to ride."

Albert really liked being with his dad. He had missed him, terribly, and the last few hours had been among the happiest of his young life. And now, with the prospect of his dad getting that job at the University of Calgary and them living there and being at Big Thunder together on the weekends, everything was looking better by the minute.

Bill took another sip of tea. "I think I am going to take that job."

Albert gave him a big hug. "That's great, Dad. I don't want to go back to Toronto. I want to be here with you at Big Thunder."

"Then that settles it. You are going to school in Calgary next year and you are going to ride here on the weekends. We're staying here. Staying at Big Thunder."

"So now it's a three-bonus day for me. No school, a ride with you up the mountain, and now we're staying at Big Thunder. I've hit the jackpot. Thanks, Dad. This really is what I want."

"Me, too. Now, let's head back. I've got a few things I want to do this afternoon. Like set up an appointment with the Chairman of the Sociology Department at the University of Calgary for Thursday, if he's available."

"Sounds good, Dad. You'll get no argument from me." *This is great! Couldn't have asked for more. Me and Dad together again at Big Thunder. With horses of our own. An Appaloosa for now and a Mustang when I get older.*

Janet and Sarah were sitting at the kitchen table having a coffee when Bill and Albert got back.

"How was it?" Janet asked. "Did you go up Thunder Mountain?"

"Yes," Bill said. "After that Mustang settled down a bit. He's quite a horse to handle."

"You're the only one to ride him besides Alf," Janet said. "But we were pretty sure you'd be able to handle him. And how was it for you, Albert?"

"Great. I hit the jackpot. No school, a ride with my Dad, and now we're going to stay at Big Thunder."

"You are?" Sarah asked Bill with a note of surprise. "And what may I ask brought that on?"

"Being here, Mom," Bill said as Janet poured him a cup of coffee. "That's what brought it on. This is my place. I belong here at Big Thunder. With you, and Albert, and you, too, Janet. Big Thunder is my home."

"Well, that's a welcome development," Sarah said. "That really is good news."

"Yes," Albert said, "and Dad's got a new job at the University of Calgary. We're going to get a place in Calgary and spend the weekends at your place, Grandma, if that's okay with you."

"Of course it's okay with me," Sarah said. "You're more than welcome. Anytime. But, William, what's this about the University of Calgary?"

He told them about the offer to replicate the North American Indian Studies program and that he was going to call that afternoon and try to set up an appointment for Thursday.

"That would be wonderful, Son," Sarah said. "I'd so like to have you living here again. Back at Big Thunder where you belong."

"Won't be Big Thunder, Mom. Probably get a house for me and Albert in Calgary. But we will be with you on the weekends and the holidays."

"Sounds fine to me. I'll settle for the weekends and the holidays. Just don't like the idea of you being all the way out there in Toronto. So far away."

"Being back here would be good," Janet said. "We really miss having you around, Bill. And it will be great having you here, even if it's only on the weekends. You and Albert can use the horses any time. Alf won't mind."

"We'll have our own," Albert said enthusiastically. "Dad's getting me an Appaloosa, just like Granddad used to ride."

"There's lots of room in my stable," Sarah said. "Lots of room. Haven't had any horses in there since your dad died."

Bill asked Janet if he could use the phone in the bedroom to set up an appointment with Dr. Harold Chamberlain at the University of Calgary.

"Sure, no problem. After you're done, would you mind going down to the feed mill and getting us some molasses for the bulls? Alf's out fixing some fences and he probably won't be back until after they close."

"No problem, Sis. I'll just get this out of the way first."

"Can I come to the mill with you?" Albert asked.

"Absolutely," Bill said. "You're always going to be with me."

"Nice to hear that," Sarah said. "You two belong together. While you're down there, would you mind picking up some flour for me at the store? I'm just about out."

"Sure, Mom. No problem. Anything else you need."

"You might get some of that hickory-smoked bacon you enjoy so much. I'd like to have you over for breakfast tomorrow morning. We need to talk some more, you and me do."

"Okay, Mom. I'll take care of it."

"Oh, I almost forgot," Janet said. "Your brother in Toronto called. He said they're going ahead with the statement for the newspapers but they won't be saying a word about you. He said you should be the one to say anything about being half white whenever you feel the time is right. And he'd like you to give him a call at his house some time after five his time."

"I'd forgotten all about that, believe it or not. I just got so caught up in the good feeling of being back here that I haven't given one thought to it since breakfast." Bill looked at his watch. "It's after five their time right now. I'll give Gordon a call after I set up the meeting for Thursday."

"You seem to like this new brother of yours," Sarah said with a quiet smile.

"He's not as bad as he appears in the newspapers or talking on radio or TV. Talking to him like I did over the last couple of days gave me a better understanding of how his head works. Why he is the way he is."

"Maybe you should ask him out for a visit," Sarah suggested. "Let him see where he spent the first couple of months of his life. Maybe even take him up to the Morgan ranch and show him where you spent the first two years of your life. Mr. Morgan's passed away now but I'm sure David wouldn't mind."

"David wouldn't mind at all," Janet piped in. "Alf and him have been friends all their lives. He'd be happy to see you and your brother."

"I'll think about it," Bill said. "Gordon might not want to come all the way out here. But, then again, this is where his life's circle started. He might like the idea. I'll get together with him when I'm back in Toronto and see what he thinks about it. Like you said, Mom, we are brothers. I suspect we're going to find a lot of things to talk about. Lot of things."

"That's good, Son. He's more than welcome here. I really liked Bill, his dad. Seeing the way he was with my sister really made me feel good. They were so much in love. I'd like to meet this new brother of yours – this nephew of mine."

Gordon wasn't at home when Bill called just after five that after-noon. He'd taken a drive up the Airport Road to Highway 89, crossed over to Alliston and had a late lunch of fish and chips. He'd taken Highway 27 back to the city. Driving past the fields and barns and through the small villages was good for his head. He needed to be in a different space that afternoon. When he got closer to the city, around five o'clock, he stopped at a pay phone and placed a call to Hal Davies' office.

"The statement's out. Went out to the papers before three," Davies said. "Barry Jones from the *Toronto Star* called my office around three-thirty. I was still in a meeting in Woodbridge but I called him from there when my secretary passed on his message. Barry and I go back a long way and he's always been very good to me in the way he covers stories I'm involved with. Barry's pretty liberal in his way of thinking and he took a pretty dim view of Henry throwing you under the bus like that. He's going to call Henry and press him about why he acted so quickly, and harshly.

"It's too late for anything to be in the *Star* this afternoon but they will have a good story about it tomorrow. Barry won't be quoting me but I gave him a pretty good perspective on things off the record. From the way he sounded on the phone, I think you're going to be quite pleased with the story. But I still don't want you to say anything, not even to Barry Jones, beyond what you've already said in the statement. There is absolutely no reason for you to go beyond that.

"One other thing, there was another big student demonstration today. City-TV says there was about five hundred of them this time. Held up traffic for about an hour at Queen and Bay. It's just great to see how those young white students are responding to the Big Thunder issue. Most of the leaders are from your brother's special studies course on the North American Indians. They're doing a great job. Now, Gordon, I've got to go. I'm off to another meeting. We'll talk tomorrow morning."

Gordon thanked Davies for all that he had done for him and then got back in the car, feeling a lot better than he had for quite some time. *Looks like Jones from the* Toronto Star *is going to put Henry on the spot. And he should. Like Hal said, if I worked for Henry at one of his department stores, I could probably sue him for wrongful dismissal. Sonofabitch. Let's hope he gets a good dose of what's coming to him. Still, that doesn't change the fact that I'm dead in the water as far as Meadowbrook goes. There's no way I'm going to be an MP now. Let alone get appointed to the cabinet.*

Carol was getting supper ready when Gordon got home, just a little after six. Charlie and Diane were watching TV in the family room.

"There was a message from Bill," Carol said. "Anne took it while you were out. She also took three other messages. One of them was from Ross Palmer."

"I went for a drive," he said. "Up the Airport Road and over to Cookstown. It's a great drive, especially going up and down those roller- coaster hills north of Caledon. Did you call Bill?"

"No. With all that's going on, and the way it keeps changing by the minute, I thought it would be better for you to call him yourself."

He filled her in on his meeting with Hal Davies that afternoon and the conversation he'd had with Davies from the pay phone.

"I like that," Carol said. "The *Star* is a very liberal paper and you can spell that with a capital L. They've always endorsed the Liberals in every election I can remember. I've no doubt they're going to take a rather negative view of the discriminatory way Henry is dealing with you. Wouldn't surprise me if they write a lead editorial wrapping him over the knuckles. And, he deserves it. It's a good thing you got together with Hal Davies on this. He knows how to deal with these things."

"He sure does," Gordon said. "He's been a real help. Anyway, I'm going to call Bill from my study and see what he has to say."

"Say hello for me," Carol said. "I'll get supper ready. Pork chops okay with you?"

"Sounds good. Got any of that Italian bread?"

"Yes we do. I picked some up on my way home."

"That's right. You were out. I forgot about that. How did it go with Hollinger?"

"I start first thing Monday morning."

"Good for you. Congratulations! That's going to be a really good move," he said. "You're going to enjoy being back practising law. It will be a good change for you."

"I think so, too, Gordon. We could all use a positive change right about now. So, give Bill a call."

When Gordon got Bill on the line, he filled him in on the events of that afternoon and told him he was expecting a reasonably good story in the *Toronto Star*. "And how's it going with you?" he then asked.

"Couldn't be better. It's great being back here – back where I belong. I spoke to the Chairman of Sociology at the University of Calgary this afternoon and told him I'm going to accept the position he offered. We're going to finalize things over lunch on Thursday. I'll be starting here in the second week of January."

"Things really are coming together for you. What have you decided to do about the half white thing? About being adopted and all that."

"Nothing that I don't have to. I really appreciate the fact that you kept me out of the statement you sent to the media. But, to be perfectly honest with you, I'm in no hurry to deal with that. If it comes out some day, fine. But, until then, I'm not going to give it much thought. I'm a Blackfoot and I'm back at Big Thunder. The universe is unfolding as it should."

"Okay, but don't run away from it. You are half white, half Scottish, and there's nothing you can do to change that fact. You're no more Blackfoot than I am, Bill. Just half of you is."

"I know. Like you keep reminding me, I'm descended from a long line of dirt-poor Scottish hill farmers. But, that doesn't change who I am now – who I was raised to be. Anyway, I'm in no hurry to make it public. My family knows and they're okay with it. Albert thinks it's perfectly fine, especially now that we're going to be living together again. I'm just going to leave things as they are for now."

"That's your call. I'm certainly not going to say anything about you to anyone. You have my word on that. Mind you, Henry Bracken knows but there's not much we can do about that now. I don't expect him to say anything about it. He's going to have more than enough on his plate when the *Toronto Star* takes him to task for dumping me the way he did."

"Thanks, Gordon. I hope they string him up by the balls. Is Carol there?"

"She is and she said to say hello. She's got some pork chops in the pan right now and it might be better to call her later tonight."

"Okay, I'll do that. Tell her I'll call around ten your time. I'm going out for a while right now."

"Okay, Bill. Now I'm off to have my supper. We'll talk again tomorrow and I'll let you know how the *Star* plays the story about me being forced out of Meadowbrook because I'm half Indian."

"I'll look forward to your call, Gordon. And I'll call Carol around ten your time tonight."

Gordon started to make the salad as Carol checked on the pork chops. "Bill said he's going out for a while but he'll call you around ten our time."

"Thanks, Gordon. What did he have to say?"

"Things are going well. He's glad he went out there. I think he really likes it at Big Thunder. That is where he grew up. He's glad we didn't say anything about him in the media statement. He's in no hurry to make that public. I think that was a good move on Hal's part."

This is weird, he thought, *why'm I passing on messages from her new lover? Having an Indian for a brother is one thing. Having him sleeping with Carol is an entirely different matter. Be glad when he moves back to Calgary. Let him tell her he's taking the job out there.*

"Yes, that was good. Chops are just about ready. Please ask the children to get their hands washed for supper."

The chops were good. "Nice and juicy, Carol. You always do a good job with them."

"Yes, Mom. These chops are great," Charlie said. "I like the bread, too."

"Me, too," Diane said. "It's nice and crunchy. I like Italian bread."

"What's happening now, Dad?" Charlie asked. "About not being an MP?"

"Nothing has really changed," Gordon said. "There'll be a story in the *Toronto Star* tomorrow afternoon and I expect the *Globe* will have something first thing tomorrow morning. There'll probably be a story in the *Sun* as well. From what I've been told, the story in the *Star* will be pretty positive but I don't know what to expect from the *Globe,* the *Sun* or the radio and TV stations. Other than that, there's no real change."

"What about your brother?" Charlie asked. "Is he OK?"

"He's out with his son at the Indian reserve. He called just a little while ago and, from what I understand, everything's going as well as can be expected under the circumstances."

"He's still having dinner with us. Right?" Charlie asked.

"Not this week, Son. He's got a few things to take care of out there right now. But, we will have him over for supper sometime after he gets back to Toronto."

Carol decided to change the subject. "I have some good news to share with you guys. I got a job today and I start next Monday. I'll be back at Haldimand and Brock. They're one of the biggest law firms in Toronto and they handle all of Grandfather Winston's legal work."

"What about us?" Diane asked. "Who's going to look after us?"

"Anne's going to be staying here full-time for the next few months. At least until I get settled in at the firm. She'll be living with us and she'll take good care of you. She'll get you off to school in the morning and look after you until your dad and I get home at night."

"I like Anne," Diane said. "She's real nice and she cooks good stuff."

"You mean you don't like my pork chops?" Carol teased.

"No. No. They're real good. Real juicy. Just like Daddy says they are. But I do like Anne's cooking. We had cranberries sauce."

"Cranberry," Carol said.

"Okay, Mommy. Cranberry sauce."

"Will Anne be using Dad's room up on the third floor?" Charlie asked.

"No, Charlie," Carol said. "We'll fix a place up for her in the basement. At least for now anyway. We'll see how things work out."

"I don't like you guys not sleeping together," Charlie said. "It doesn't look right. Frank's dad sleeps with his mom and so does Henry's. All the dads I know sleep with their wives."

This was the first time Charlie had said anything at all about their separate sleeping arrangements. They had never even thought about explaining it to him, or to Diane.

"Well, we're not going to get into that discussion tonight, Charlie," Carol said. "We'll see how things work out."

"Well, I hope you do work it out," Charlie said rather emphatically. "I don't like it this way."

"Me neither," Diane piped in. "All the mommies and daddies on the TV sleep together. All the time. That's the way it's supposed to be. Right, Charlie?"

"Right. That is the way it's supposed to be."

"Let's leave it at that," Gordon said. "You're right. Your mum and I should have told you why we weren't sleeping together – like the mummies and daddies on TV. We'll talk about it, your mum and I, and then we'll talk about it with you."

"Not just with Charlie," Diane said. "It's got to be me, too."

"It will be you, too," Carol said, as she reached over and gave Diane a hug. "Your dad and I will have that talk he just mentioned and then we'll have a talk with both of you."

That's going to be an interesting talk, Gordon thought, *she seems a lot different over the last few days. Ever since she found out I was half Indian. Be interesting to hear what she has to say.* "Okay, I've got some student essays to mark and that's going to take me a couple of hours," he said. "Let's clean up these dishes and then we'll all do whatever it is we have to do tonight. I'm sure you both have homework."

"Charlie does, but I don't," Diane said. "I'm too young for that stuff."

"Not for long, you won't be," Carol said. "You'll be doing homework soon enough."

"Ugh. I don't like that," Diane said. "No way, Jose."

They washed the dishes and then Gordon went to his study to mark the student essays. Charlie and Diane went to their rooms and Carol sat down at the kitchen table and started reading the briefing book on the case she was going to be working on for the Toronto Children's Hospital.

When he was halfway through the fourth essay, Gordon set the papers aside, took another sip of his vodka and sat back in his chair looking at the paintings and plaques on the wall. He looked first at the Royal Herald of Scotland, more commonly known to Scottish soccer fans as the Lion Rampant. That's the one the Queen runs up the flag pole whenever she's at Holyrood Palace to show that she's the Queen of Scotland.

He sipped his drink and looked up at the painting of King Robert the Bruce on his Highland pony. "So," he said to King Robert. "It turns out we don't have as much in common as we first thought we had. You're only part of my heritage. Part of one half of it."

He ran his eyes briefly over the paintings of Dunstaffnage Castle and the bloody Battle of Culloden Moor. Then he looked at the framed picture of his father and his Uncle Bill he had placed next to the plaque with the crest and tartan of the MacArthur Clan. He took another sip of his vodka and looked at them again.

So, in a way, you're both my father. If it hadn't been for the one, I wouldn't have had the other. Dad wouldn't have been my dad if you hadn't fathered me in the first place. I wish I'd had a chance to get to know you, Uncle Bill. From what Mum says, you were quite an alright sort of guy. Yes, I would like *to have known you.*

As Gordon looked at the plaque with the badge of the 48th Highlanders of Canada, just next to the MacArthur Clan crest, he thought back to the time, twenty-two years earlier, when his dad took him to the 48th Highlanders' Regimental Memorial at the top of Queen's Park. He remembered, again, looking up at the big stone monument with the main battles from the Second World War engraved on the south side. He wondered what it must have been like for his dad and the other men in the boats on that rough sea before they landed on the beach in Sicily and fought their way north.

From the sounds of it, Ortona was the worst battle of them all. His dad said the German paratroopers were "tough as nails" and all too many young Canadian soldiers were killed in that war. He remembered his father's exact words. "War's an awful thing, Son. I hope God spares you from ever having to go through anything like what it was like for me over there in Italy."

Well, God did. My generation has never had to fight, never had to go to war. If there is a god, he has my most grateful appreciation on that score.

And then there was Holland, where his dad lost his left eye. He remembered his dad making a joke of it and saying "things have never looked the same." He was glad his dad made it back from the war, relatively safe and sound, and that he got to know him better and take all those long walks with him. He missed his dad, missed him a lot.

There were several calls that evening, mostly from reporters. Gran Winston called around eight and Carol chatted with him for a few minutes. When she told him she was going back to Haldimand and Brock on Monday, he said that was a great idea.

"Things are going to come together for you now, Carol. I've always believed in you. You'll make a great lawyer."

"Thanks, Dad. Your support has always meant a great deal to me. I take it you want to talk to Gordon." She didn't want to get into a discussion with her dad right then. She was still quite angry with him for forcing Saunders to run his pipeline through Big Thunder.

"I do. Is he there?"

"Not right now, Dad. I don't expect him back until around midnight. But I will tell him you called."

Gordon had said he didn't want to get into a conversation with Gran right yet. He was still angry and disappointed with him. "He really was using me," he said. "Treating me like I was an appendage of his business empire. When I do talk to your father, I want it to be face to face. I've got more than a few things I want to say to him."

"Me too," Carol said. "Dad's going to get a piece of my mind about forcing Saunders to go through the Indians' land. If they ran the pipeline underground through his property his buyers would never even see it. I'm going to work on him on that one."

Carol told the reporters who called that Gordon was out for the evening and wasn't expected home until around midnight. She said she would give him their message "the minute he walks in the door."

The phone rang just before ten o'clock. It was Bill. "How are you?" he asked. "How're things down there in the east?"

"Pretty good," she said. "And you? How are things out there in the west?"

"Things are going well, really well. I had a great ride with Albert today. It's good to be home. He seems fine with the adoption thing. Doesn't seem to bother him that I'm half white. Could be half green as far as he's concerned as long as we're going to be together."

"I'm glad you were able to spend some time with him. He needs you in his life."

"I had a good chat on the phone with the Chairman of Sociology at the University of Calgary today. I've accepted his offer to teach here. He wants me on site by early January. I'll spend Christmas at Big Thunder and probably stay there until I line up a place for me and Albert near the university. He'll be able to transfer to a school in Calgary. We'll spend the weekends at Big Thunder."

"Well, congratulations. Good for you. I had a feeling you were heading in that direction."

"I feel a real need to be at Big Thunder and re-establish a connection with the land and … and … with my people. I am a Blackfoot, Carol, and that's the way I want to remain. I just can't see staying on in Toronto, especially not with Albert out here and me missing him so much. I want to be with him … and … I need to be with him. He doesn't want to live in Toronto again. As for me … I just … especially with this being half white thing and all the rest of it … feel a need to be here. Where I was born. Where my journey started out. It's been a good journey, Carol, but it's time to get back to the source. Complete the circle."

"I can understand that. I understand why you would want to be out there. Gordon told me he spoke to you about the story the *Globe and Mail* ran about Henry telling him he could no longer be the candidate for Meadowbrook and how he and Hal Davies are dealing with it."

"Yes, he did, and I have every confidence in their ability to handle it. Hal Davies is one smart lawyer. I've worked with him on a couple of cases and have always been impressed with his ability to put things in context, work the angles."

"That doesn't change the fact that it's game over for Gordon as far as being the candidate for Meadowbrook. That chapter is closed. Slammed shut. And I have no doubt the Equal Opportunities Council will feel the same way. They won't want the son of a Blackfoot woman fronting their organization. Especially not Don Henderson."

"I know all about Henderson," Bill said. "I've heard that stuff he spouts ad nauseam. He's a real racist sonofabitch."

"He is that. There's no way now he'll accept having Gordon on the Equal Opportunities Council."

"I'm a bit worried about my mom. She's been having dizzy spells lately. Says she gets tired more than she used to. I hope to God it isn't because of hydrogen sulphide leaking from Saunders' gas wells."

"That is dangerous stuff. You should get her to a doctor ASAP."

"I'm doing that tomorrow and I'm also going to have Hughie get his blood tested. With his asthma, he's more vulnerable than most people to that poison gas."

"That's an angle we should work into the Energy Board hearings. If Saunders wins the case … and I don't expect that he will … but, if he does, we've got to make sure every step possible is taken to safeguard the health of the people at Big Thunder. That's really dangerous stuff."

"Yes, it is. We'll gather some more information when I get back and I'll be bringing you stuff from my Dad's files."

"Good. We'll get working on that as soon as you get back. And now, Dr. William Eagletail, I have something I want to tell you."

"You do? And what might that be?"

"I had a rather good lunch today. A very good lunch."

"You did? Tell me?"

"I met with the managing partner of Haldimand and Brock and they want me back. Start first thing Monday morning."

"Good for you. That's just simply great. So, we're both getting back on track. Me out here in the wild west and you in the office canyons of downtown Toronto."

"Looks that way and I feel just great. Haven't felt this good since before I had Diane."

"Well, I think this news is just wonderful. You'll quickly pick up where you left off. You've got what it takes to make the top-ten list."

"Thanks for that. You're a top-ten yourself. Call me as soon as you're back in town."

"I most certainly will. You can bet your life I'm going to call. Can't wait to see you."

"Good. I'll be here."

Carol went back to the kitchen table and continued reading the Toronto Children's Hospital briefing book. She decided not to tell Gordon about her conversation with Bill. Gordon decided not to ask.

She turned her thoughts to Gordon and the children. *Now what? Do I get an apartment or stay here with Gordon and the children? It's clear Charlie and Diane don't want me to leave. "Ever and ever." That's the way Diane put it. "You guys belong with us. Ever and ever."*

Maybe I should stay at the house at least until I get established again at Haldimand and Brock. Gordon would probably be okay with that. I believe him when he says there's nothing, or nearly nothing, to his affair with that young student. Let's face it, we've both been unfaithful. There's still the white power stuff but, maybe, now that he's half Indian, he'll probably have a different view on immigrant people and the extra special role he believes white people have played in the world. That phase really was sick.

If we do separate, that's going to mean Charlie and Diane trekking back and forth between our separate places. That would be pretty disruptive for them. They need stability in their young lives. Maybe, just maybe, it would be better to stay here. At least for now. Charlie and Diane seem to be okay with him being a half-breed. That's a harsh word. But, in the minds of most people, that is what he is. Bill too for that matter. What's going to happen between me and Bill? Are we going to continue seeing each other when he gets back? Is there any point in that when we're going to be living two thousand miles apart when he starts teaching in Calgary? Lots of questions. Precious few answers. Got to think straight. Sleep on it.

Decide what's the best thing to do in the morning. Maybe Ben Horowitz will have some good ideas when I see him Thursday afternoon.

The phone rang. It was Hal Davies and he wanted to speak to Gordon. Carol called through to Gordon and told him Davies was on the phone. Gordon said he would take the call on the phone in his study.

"I've just picked up the bulldog edition of the *Globe and Mail,*" Davies said. "Got it from the old Polish guy at the corner of Spadina and Bloor. There's a story about you on the front page."

"I thought the *Globe* didn't come out until first thing in the morning," Gordon said.

"That's the edition that's delivered to the newspaper boxes and your front door," Davies said. "The bulldog hits the streets around ten. Here's what the headline says. Quote: Tory candidate dropped because he's half Indian. End of quote. That is what it says."

"It says that? Good God! What else does it say?"

"I'll read it to you. It isn't that long. But it is on the front page. And it's not too bad. Anyway, here's what it says. Quote: University of Toronto professor Gordon MacArthur claims he was dropped as the Conservative candidate for the Toronto riding of Meadowbrook on Monday because he is half Indian.

"In a statement that was released to the media yesterday afternoon, MacArthur claims that Henry Bracken, the president of the Meadowbrook Conservative Association, told him Monday afternoon that the fact that he is half Indian prevents him from being the Conservative candidate in Meadowbrook.

"He quoted Bracken, who is also the Chief Executive Officer of Bracken Department Stores, as saying: That takes you out of the running as far as being a legitimate representative for Meadowbrook. We couldn't possibly have you representing us in the House of Commons."

"Henry won't like that," Gordon interjected. "That will put him on the spot."

"It will, with some people," Davies replied. "But, unfortunately, some of the hard-core Conservatives in Meadowbrook will applaud him for what he did, and the harsh manner in which he did it. Let me read on. Quote: MacArthur says in his statement that he only found out that he was adopted — and that his mother was a Blackfoot Indian from the Big Thunder Indian Reserve near Calgary — after he was acclaimed as the candidate for Meadowbrook at a nomination meeting last Thursday night. He said that, when he told Bracken about it, Bracken demanded his immediate resignation.

"Bracken could not be reached for comment at press time. His secretary told a reporter from the *Globe and Mail* that he was in a meeting and could not be disturbed.

"MacArthur said in his statement that, despite the fact that he did not provide Bracken with a letter of resignation, Bracken told a reporter from the *Globe and Mail* that he had resigned and that Bracken hoped to have another candidate in place as soon as possible.

"Quote: It's clear, MacArthur said in his statement, that Mr. Bracken no longer finds me acceptable as a candidate. His mind was most definitely made up, and closed.

"MacArthur said in his statement that his birth father was Scottish and both his birth parents died before he was three. He was raised by his dead father's brother in Toronto.

"MacArthur has been dubbed 'the white power Conservative' because of racist statements he has made about immigrant groups."

"I figured they'd drag that up," Gordon said. "That's how they sell papers."

"Gordon," Davies said rather crossly, "stop interrupting and let me finish reading the story."

"Okay. Sorry."

"Quote: He said in the statement that his comments 'were insensitive and completely unacceptable. I regret having made them and apologize sincerely to anyone who took offence.'

"MacArthur said he has also changed his mind about widely-publicized statements he has made in support of a gas pipeline the Saunders Energy Corporation wants to run through the Big Thunder Indian reserve southwest of Calgary.

"My birth mother was born on that land, MacArthur said in his statement. Jack Saunders should find somewhere else to run his pipeline.

"MacArthur said that, due to the personal nature of these most recent developments, he will not be taking any questions from reporters.

"As far as I am concerned, this chapter of my life is closed. I have nothing further to say, he said in his statement.

"The statement was issued from the law office of Hal Davies, the current Member of Parliament for Meadowbrook who announced recently that he would not be running again in the election which is expected to be called in a matter of weeks. End of quote. That's it, Gordon. That's what the story said."

"That wasn't too bad. I'd expected it would be a lot worse. What do you think, Hal."

"Considering that it was the *Globe* and not the *Star* that published it, I'd say it's rather good. The *Globe* is very close to the Prime Minister and I had expected that they would come down quite hard on the fact that you're half Indian. The *Star*, as we will see when it comes out tomorrow afternoon, will be very sympathetic toward your situation. And that is to be expected. I hadn't expected something this balanced from the *Globe*. It could be, and I somehow think that it is the case, that someone from the PMO spoke to them on background and they are not too pleased with the way Henry is handling this.

"That could also explain why Henry had nothing to say to them. He's on very close terms with the publisher of the *Globe* and they report very favourably on just about anything he's involved with. I get the feeling, and this is only a feeling, Gordon, that the PMO is hanging Henry out to dry. Distancing themselves from the discriminatory position that he has adopted. Time will tell. And now, Gordon, I have had a long day and I'm going to enjoy a nice hot toddy before I turn in for the night. We'll talk again in the morning."

"Okay, Hal, and thanks again. The way you drafted the statement really worked to our advantage. The *Globe* followed it, almost word for word. You really know how to work the media."

"Thanks, Gordon, and you're most definitely welcome. I want some changes made before the children I'm going to have with Josephine arrive in this world and this case of yours is as good a one as any to get started on. We're going to get you through this. It's important that we use your case to teach the Henry Brackens of this world a lesson they should have learned a long time ago. Britannia no longer rules the waves. It's Uncle Sam who does that now. This world of ours has changed and Bracken and his friends at the Commonwealth Club are just going to have to adjust to that new reality. Goodnight, Gordon, I really must take my leave now."

"Goodnight, Hal. And thanks for being such a good friend."

Gordon went through to the kitchen and told Carol about the article in the *Globe and Mail*.

"That sounds good. Looks like things are going to turn out pretty much the way Hal said they would. You're lucky to have him helping you with this. He is very, very, good."

"He is that and the story in the *Globe* is a nice note to end the day on. We'll see what the *Toronto Star* has to say about me tomorrow afternoon. Hal thinks that story will be even better. I'm turning in now. What about you?"

"I think I'll spend another half hour on this report. It's fascinating stuff."

"What is it?"

"Actually, it's about a case I'm going to be working on and I'm not at liberty to discuss it outside the office. Client confidentiality and all that. You do understand?" she said with the look on her face emphasizing that she really did hope he understood that it was nothing personal.

"Sure, I understand. Okay then, I'm going to bed. I'll check in on Charlie and Diane on my way up to my room."

"Good, Gordon. I'll see you at breakfast."

The toadstool lamp was on in Diane's room and she was fast asleep with her arm around her teddy bear. *She looks so beautiful. So peaceful. Carol probably looked a lot like that when she was going on five. Sleeping in this very same room.* He pulled the blanket up to Diane's chin, kissed her on the forehead, turned off the light and went across the hall to Charlie's room.

It looked as if Charlie had fallen asleep after finishing *The Last of the Mohicans*. He was still in his jeans and the book was lying closed beside his pillow. *So, he likes Hawkeye. And the Mohicans. He's probably going to be okay with me being half Indian. That doesn't mean I'm going to be. I still can't believe this is happening.* He covered Charlie up and turned off the light.

As Gordon lay on the bed in his room on the third floor, he wondered what was going to happen next. He wasn't in control of anything. Things kept changing all the time. While he took some satisfaction from the fact that the story in the *Globe* made Henry Bracken look pretty shabby ... *that doesn't change the fact that, like Hal Davies said, a lot of the Meadowbrook Conservatives will applaud him for tossing me under the bus. They'll probably think he did exactly the right thing. So will Henderson and the others on the Equal Opportunities Council. And Dave Saunders. No more five-roll lunches with that big-time powerbroker. No Honourable Gordon MacArthur, P.C., M.P. Speeches in the House of Commons. Criss-crossing the country in government jets and being whisked around Ottawa in a shiny black limo. None of that. And now everybody's going to know about me. That I'm a half-breed. The* Globe *will be on the doorsteps first thing tomorrow morning and, like Hal says, the radio and TV reporters will pick the story up and run with it.* "White power candidate a half-breed." *That's what they'll say. That's what everyone will say. I'm done like toast.*

He turned the light off, bunched the pillow up under his head, and tried to go to sleep. *One day at a time. That's what Dad always said. I'll just have to take it one day at a time.*

ABOUT THE AUTHOR

Scottish-born Toronto author Robert MacBain has spent more than 60 years in journalism, politics and public relations.

MacBain is a former senior reporter at the *Toronto Star* and *Globe and Mail* and news director of Canada's second-largest radio station.

He was director of communications for the 1974 national Liberal campaign, speech writer for Economic Development Minister Donald Johnston in the 1984 Liberal leadership campaign and speech writer for David Peterson in the game-changing 1985 Ontario campaign.

MacBain spent 28 years providing public relations counsel and service to the Chief Executive Officers of major corporations, financial institutions, government departments, hospitals, social service agencies and trade and professional associations.

He is the author of two non-fiction books on Indigenous issues, *Their Home and Native Land* and *Lonely Death of an Ojibway Boy*.

Still living a full and active life at 87, MacBain lives in the Upper Beach area of Toronto with his wife of 41 years, former International Cooperation Minister Maria Minna.

www.ingramcontent.com/pod-product-compliance
Lightning Source LLC
Chambersburg PA
CBHW031043110726
47900CB00003B/793